I0587276

Breaking Away

Mabel G. Ebner

PUBLISHED BY FIDELI PUBLISHING, INC.

ISBN: 978-1-60414-955-5

Dedication

I would like to dedicate this book to my aunt and uncle, Edgar Paul and Juanita Stoumbaugh They have always been the best aunt and uncle a person could ever be blessed to have. Aunt Needer, as I lovingly call her, has been the most loving and generous person one could know. I told Aunt Needer: "Since Uncle Dutch has a nick-name, you have to have one too. We called her Needer because when you need her, you need her. Uncle Dutch, as we loving called him, is someone whom I have always looked up to and admired for his love, goodness and kind generosity. They're a great example for me to emulate.

Acknowledgements

I would like to thank, Janice Lyon for taking the time to proof this novel for me. She has not only been there all through my novels, encouraging and supported me along the way, but she also has a generous, kind heart as well. I want all to know that I'm truly grateful for all she does for me.

At this time, I would especially like to thank my cousin, Pauline Perkins for the wonderful love and support she gives me in my writing endeavors, as well as in many other ways. I want to thank her for taking the time out of her busy schedule to proof read this novel as well.

List of Characters

Gerald Stillman, Doctor in Cardston

Joseph, Shirleen's Angel

Lance Ramey, Ranch Manager

Robin Weaver, Nurse in Children's Ward

Fred Holmes, New York police officer

Frank Kessler, Police Officer in New York

Carol, Gregory Jones' Secretary

Walt, Employee in Jones' Office

Millicent, Judge Harris' Secretary

Harvey Metcalf, drove a U-Haul for Graham

William Barnes, drove a U-Haul for Graham

Mr. Hubbard, Ohio bank manager

Nathan White (Nate), hit man for Murdock

Thomas Wilson, Body Guard and Hit Man

Vincent Crowley (Vinnie), Body Guard and Hit Man

Paul Thompson, Limo Driver

Charles Abram, Police Captain

Leonard Montello, Police Officer

Dr. Stone, Hazel's Doctor

Mr. Holmes, Hazel's Banker

Kathy Neilson, Murdock's Housekeeper

Myrtle Lawson, Murdock's Cook

Frederick Walker, Vice President of Gerber's

Jared Maxwell, Manager of J.C. Company

Adam Kendall, Manager of Wal-Mart

Stella Holbrook, Works at Employment Center

Harriet Beal, Nurse's Aide

Susan Thompson, Nurse's Aide

Louise Rogers, Brook's Housekeeper

Dawna Twitchell, Theodore's Housekeeper

Melvin Dixon, Police Sergeant in Spokane

Richard Harris (Sergeant), Dixon's Partner

Author Quigley Annabelle Croft's Brother), Murderer

Annabelle Croft, Quigley's Sister

Mark Holmquist, Mountie

David Black, Mountie

Adam Morgan, Bunkhouse Cook

Robert Rhodes, Police Officer

Julia Robinson, Nurse at Hospital

Clara Reese, Psychiatrist

Josh Hamlin, Police Officer

Jethro Sparks, Police Officer

Todd Hobart, Leading Angel of Death

Tucker O'Malley, 2nd Angel of Death

Nelson Richards, 3rd Angel of Death

Howard Bates, Reverend of Lutheran Church

Chapter 1

Ruth Murdock turned toward the sound of someone entering the room. Her expression became concerned when she saw her daughter Leslie's angry expression. Worried, Ruth called out to her, "Leslie?"

Leslie paused a moment then rushed out of the room.

Worried, Ruth followed her to the room she'd been assigned in their host's house. She caught the door just as Leslie started to slam it shut. Following her daughter inside, she gently closed the door. "Let's not attract any more attention. Okay? That way we can talk in private."

Leslie, who had just turned sixteen, whirled around to snap, "I don't give a hang if anyone hears me or not! I'm so angry I could scream!"

"Let's go sit down so we can talk." As she spoke, she led her daughter over to the bed then gently pushed her down. When Leslie was seated, Ruth sat down beside her and asked, "Why are you so angry?"

When Leslie remained silent, Ruth didn't push her. As she waited for her to speak, she wondered if it could have anything to do with Jethro Borden, the son of the people they'd been spending the summer with. When she thought about the Bordens, she felt a little angry herself.

Ruth was married to Bruce Murdock, a wealthy lawyer. Knowing him as she did, she knew he got to where he was by illegal means. He didn't care who he hurt while getting to the top of the social ladder. Ruth hated her husband with everything in her. She wouldn't be married to him if her father hadn't forced her into it.

Even after all of these years, Ruth never knew what hold Bruce had on her father, but whatever it was, she knew it wasn't good. Glancing into the mirror over the dresser beside the bed, she absently adjusted a stray strand of hair. Bruce demanded perfection at all times. Heaven knew she had suffered his verbal abuse often enough when she'd been cleaning and he'd come home early. He'd immediately hired a maid, as well as a handy man to take care of the house and yard. He told her that her job was looking beautiful.

Ruth was indeed beautiful. Her chestnut hair was fashioned in the style of the times. Her heart-shaped face was flawless. The makeup she wore had been perfectly applied. Thick eyelashes brought out the depth of her hazel eyes, while a ruby lip color defined the shape of her delicate mouth. She was short, standing at about 5' 2". She was well proportioned and nicely filled out the light green pantsuit she was wearing. The matching high-heeled shoes added to her polished look.

Sighing, she looked at her daughter's angry face. Leslie had the same blond hair as her father, only with a softer sheen. She wore it in a ponytail, like all the girls her age were doing. There were a few bangs hiding her high forehead. Leslie was also short, yet thin. Ruth had often worried about her weight, but she guessed it was because her daughter was so active. Her face was a younger carbon copy of her mother's.

Leslie sat wringing her hands in agitation. Ruth could see the anger was mixed with fear. This really caused her great concern. "Please, honey, tell me what has you so upset. I won't get mad or cause a scene. I just want to help."

"It's that rotten Jethro Borden."

Jethro Borden was the only son of Matilda and Henry Borden, their hosts. They were to stay with them for a month so Bruce and Henry could golf and catch up on business. Ruth disliked Matilda, who had a nasty disposition and meddlesome matchmaking of their children. Ruth suspected Leslie disliked Jethro as much as she did Matilda.

"Tell me what happened with Jethro, Leslie."

"He tried to rape me," she sobbed throwing herself at her mother.

Ruth hugged her, and swallowing past the lump of fear in her throat, asked softly, "Did he succeed?"

"No, I kneed him right where he lived, then ran as fast as I could."

A smile tugged at Ruth's mouth, and she replied, "Good deal."

"You aren't angry with me for spoiling things?"

"Not on your life. I'm proud of you for fighting back. If your father doesn't like it then that's just too bad."

"Oh, Mom, you're the best!"

"Leslie, do you want to go home?"

"Yes, please. If I stay here, I'm liable to kill that pompous snake in the grass."

"Fine. Leave it to me to think up an excuse to get us out of here."

Straightening up, Leslie mopped at her face in an attempt to dry her tears. "Thank you for understanding, Mom."

"Did you think I'd side with your dad over something like this?"

Leslie hesitated for a moment then nodded, "Yes, I thought you'd be afraid of Dad's reactions to what I did."

"Well, honey, you come first, so what you feel is important to me." Leslie hugged her in gratitude. "It's almost time for you to go back to school," continued Ruth.

"How do you feel about the two of us going shopping for school clothes? That will get us out of here and give us time to figure out what else we can do."

"I'd like that, Mom."

"Then freshen up while I go talk to your father." Kissing Leslie's cheek, Ruth went in search of her husband. She found him sitting by the pool drinking an alcoholic beverage. He glanced up at her then promptly looked away.

She hesitated a moment as she looked down at this man she despised so vehemently. Bruce Murdock's pudgy frame was slumped into the lounge chair. His once golden hair was turning gray and he was balding at the top of his head. His face, always wearing a sneer, was ugly to gaze upon. His blue eyes were hard. She suspected he was mixed up with the mafia, but she could never prove it. The thought of it scared her so badly that she'd dismissed it from her mind as quickly as it entered. Shivering as if she were cold, she said, "I need to talk to you, Bruce."

"Okay, but make it fast. Henry and I are going golfing this afternoon."

"I'm going to take Leslie back home, then the two of us are going to go shopping for school clothes."

"She's not going back to school," Bruce said, without looking at her.

"Why not? She'll graduate this year."

"Because she's going to marry Jethro. I've given my consent to Henry. Jethro has graduated from law school and passed the bar."

"But she doesn't love him!" Ruth was furious, but wisely hid it.

"That doesn't matter. She'll learn to live with her circumstances. A woman should be taken care of, not pampered or loved."

"Then if that's the case, I'll take her to New York to get her wedding dress and her trousseau."

"I thought you'd see it my way."

"Of course. What else could I do? Isn't that how it's been for us all these years?"

"Yes ... and it will stay that way too!"

"Well, I'd better get ready. I'll need your credit card to pay for everything. Is there a on what I can spend?"

Removing his wallet from his pocket, he took out the card. "No, just get what you think is best. When I get through here in a couple of weeks, we'll make plans for the wedding."

Taking the card, Ruth stood to leave. "Fine. I'll see you in two weeks."

Grabbing her hand, he scowled up at her. "Remember, if you try anything funny, I'll make you suffer. I'll take Leslie from you. She *will* marry Jethro and you'll *never* be allowed to see her again."

Jerking her hand free she replied, "I'm not about to forget."

"Good." Waving her away, he added, "I've got to get ready to go golfing."

Seeing she was dismissed, she slowly walked back into the house. Matilda, who was wearing a pleased look on her face, met her. Matilda was a heavyset woman who was always over dressed — today it was in too tight a pantsuit. Her gray hair was falling out of its fancy up-do, and her wide mouth was painted with an extremely bright red lipstick. Her brown eyes were shinning with excitement.

"Isn't it wonderful?" She began excitedly rubbing her hands together. "Our children are getting married. We'll be family!"

Ruth smiled sweetly. "It looks that way."

"You don't seem too enthused about it."

"I am; I just have a lot to do to get ready for the big day. Excuse me while I go tell my daughter the good news. She'll no doubt be as excited about it as I am."

"Then, by all means, don't let me stop you."

"We'll be leaving this evening to go shopping in New York. When we get back, I'll get in touch with you to help with the planning."

Clapping her hands excitedly, Matilda exclaimed. "Oh, won't that be grand?" Moving aside to let Ruth pass, she added, "I'll be looking forward to your call."

Over my dead body, she told herself. Smiling sweetly, she walked calmly up stairs. She knocked on her daughter's door and went inside.

Leslie rushed over to her mother. "Well, are we getting out of here?"

"Yes, but I have to talk to you first."

Seeing the strange look on her mother's face, she backed away from her to sit on the bed. "What's wrong, Mother?"

"Let me collect my thoughts first, then I'll tell you what needs to be done. Something awful is about to happen unless we can think fast." A moment later she began to speak. "Just act like nothing is wrong when I tell you what your father's cooking up. He's made an agreement with Henry for you to marry Jethro."

Leslie clutched her chest as she stared at her mother in distress. "No, that can't happen. I hate that jerk!"

"I know you do and I promise you won't have to marry him."

Leslie relaxed a little then asked, "I won't?"

"You won't!"

Leslie sighed audibly. "How can you stop it?"

"First of all, I want you to go along with the plan. You've got to act like this is all right with you—"

"How can I do that?"

"You've got to put on the performance of a lifetime. If you throw a fit, your father will never let us leave. Is that what you want?" Leslie shook her head no. "Then just take it in stride. I'm not saying to get excited. That would never do after you attacked Jethro. Just accept it like you're doing it to please your father and his friend."

Leslie sighed, "Okay. I think I can do that."

"Good, because our leaving depends on how convincing you can be. After we've gotten away, there are some things I need to tell you. I can't do it here, because I don't know if the walls have ears. I need you to help me pull this off so we can leave without a scene. Do you think you can do it?'

Leslie grew thoughtful then nodded affirmatively, "Yes."

"Good. Get packed and meet me in my room. Don't say anything, in case your father is there. Just tell him you're sorry you hurt Jethro and you'll obey him in his decision because you know he only has your best interest at heart."

"Okay."

"Get a move on so we can get out of here as soon as possible." Ruth kissed Leslie's cheek then added, "I promise you'll never have to marry that low down skunk!"

"I trust you to know what to do, Mom. Whatever you decide, I'll support it."

"Thank you. Now hurry," she said and left the room.

When she got to the room she shared with her husband, she got down her suitcases, and crossed over to open the closet. She hurriedly removed her clothes from the hangers then tossed them on the bed. When the closet was empty, she opened the suitcases. Working as quickly as possible, she packed everything neatly. She'd just finished when there was a knock at the door. She called, "Come in."

As Leslie entered, Ruth said, "I'm almost done. I only have to close these cases then check to make sure I didn't miss anything," she told her daughter. A few minutes later they had everything packed into the car.

Just before leaving, as they were thanking their hosts, Jethro returned to the house. It was plain he wasn't feeling well.

"Oh, what's is wrong, son?" asked Matilda, as she rushed forward.

"Nothing, just the heat."

"Have you heard the great news? Your father has arranged for you to marry Leslie. The wedding will be on as soon as it can be arranged."

"Really?" asked Jethro. "And when is this event supposed to take place?"

"As soon as they get back from buying the wedding dress and trousseau."

"Well, how about that?" The look he gave Leslie was scathing, but he remained silent. Quickly masking his feelings, he turned back to address his mother. "I need to go rest up before dinner. I'll be down at eight."

"Well, you'd better give your fiancé a kiss good-bye first."

Jethro turned to kiss Leslie. As he hugged her to him, he whispered in her ear, "When we're married you'll be so sorry for what you did to me. I'll make sure of it."

Smiling sweetly, Leslie stepped back, and replied, "Good-bye for now, darling. I'll see you soon." Not waiting for a reply she turned to walk toward the car. She never saw the scathing look he gave her retreating back, but Ruth did.

Hugging Matilda, she said, "When we get back, I'll call you to come and help plan for the wedding."

"I'll be ready."

Walking to the car, Ruth got into the driver's side. With head bowed, she reminded Leslie, "Smile sweetly, then we'll be on our way. Don't forget to wave."

"All right," replied Leslie, doing as she was told. After putting on the show, she faced forward without once looking back.

Soon Ruth had the car running and shifted into drive. She waved goodbye with a smile and slowly started to drive out of the driveway. "When we get back to town, we'll stop at a café for something to eat and I'll talk to you about everything then. Meanwhile, I suggest we silently pray that we can get away from here safely."

She had no more than gotten the words out of her mouth, when Bruce and Henry pulled in the driveway. Ruth put on the brakes and shifted into park. Bruce got out of his car and came over as Ruth rolled the window down. "We're on our way now."

"What's the hurry?" asked Bruce lightly.

"I thought you wanted us to hurry," replied Ruth.

"Well, I guess it's best to get things over with." Looking at Leslie, he asked, "Well, how do you like the big news, Kitten?"

"I don't love him, Daddy."

"Who said you had to love him? He has loads of money, or will have. Besides he has a rich father who'll see you both have everything you want. Love doesn't matter. *Money* does. Besides, you'll adjust to the situation in time."

Sighing deeply, Leslie smiled sweetly then replied, "You always know what's best for me, Daddy, so I'll do what you want."

Bruce smiled broadly then said, "That's Daddy's girl. Well, hurry off so you can get back soon." Stepping back he watched as Ruth shifted into drive.

Smiling sweetly up at him, Ruth let the car ease forward. It wasn't until they were headed to town that she realized she was holding her breath. Letting it out, she settled into the thirty-minute drive. Leslie remained silent beside her.

When they reached the outskirts of town, Ruth headed to the only café and found a parking spot. When she parked the car, she said, "Listen, honey, we need to talk out here for a while so we have some privacy."

"I'm listening."

"Seventeen years ago, I was invited to a party with a bunch of socialites. I didn't want to go, but my father insisted. Mother tried to intervene, but it was no use. When Dad made up his mind about something there was no changing it. When I got there, I was immediately snubbed. A few minutes later, your father walked in with a real beauty on his arm. I didn't like him on sight. I felt the same way about him that you do Jethro.

"Anyway, an hour into the party, people began getting drunk. I've never liked to drink, although your father has often tried to get me to do so. Something happened to the girl who came with Bruce. One minute she was there and the next she wasn't.

Bruce came over to stand near me. I tried to be polite, but it was hard. The more I tried to get away from him, the more of a pest he became. Finally, I'd had enough. I excused myself to call a taxi. As I got into that taxi, I was so relieved to be out of there and I hoped I would never see him again.

However, that wasn't to be the case. Daddy tried to get us together, but I refused. Then one night he informed me I was going to marry Bruce Murdock. When I refused, he hit me and told me I would do as I was told. Mother tried to intervene, but he told her to shut up. When she didn't, he hit her so hard it knocked her out.

I was outraged, and I hit him as hard as I could. He grabbed my arm in a tight grip, and peered into my face while hissing through clenched teeth, "You can hit me all you want, but it won't change a thing. If you want to see your mother again, you'd better do as you're told. Otherwise I'll see that Bruce takes you as far away as he can and you'll *never* see her.'"

"Oh, Mom." Leslie touched her mother's hand. "I can see why you obeyed him, but how did you ever stand it all of these years?"

"I escaped into another world whenever he touched me in an intimate way. The day I learned I was pregnant with you, I started to live again. While I was carrying you, he left me alone. After you were born, I tried to run away. He told me that if I ever tried that again he would take you away from me. He'd take you so far away I'd never find you. That scared me so badly that I never tried again. There were times when I thought about it, though. I loved you more than life itself, so there was no way I would actually do it. That is until now."

"What are you trying to say, Mom?" Leslie looked at her mother hopefully.

"About two years ago, Momma told me Daddy had told her father they had consensual sex … and Momma was pregnant. He told her father he felt it was his duty to marry her. When her father called her on it, Mother vehemently denied it. However, her father didn't believe her. Before Mother could protest any further, she found herself married to a man she hated." Ruth smiled, "Grandma got in the last lick though."

"She did?" asked Leslie. "What did she do?"

"She took Mother to a doctor to have him insert an IUD. This device blocks pregnancy and lasts for five years. When she didn't show, Daddy told Grandpa that Mother had miscarried. They tried for two more years to get Mother pregnant.

"Frustrated, Daddy decided to have himself tested to see if he could father a child. Finding he could, he demanded Mother get tested. Mother went to the doctor who had inserted the IUD and explained the problem. She confided to her doctor what had happened then begged him to inseminate her with someone else's sperm. She felt it was better to have any other man's child but my father's."

"Did he do it?" asked Leslie?

"Yes, he did. I don't know who my real father is and frankly I don't care to know."

"When you learned what Grandma had done, were you angry with her?"

"To be completely honest, no, I wasn't. I had learned to hate the man I called Daddy. When I learned what Mother had done, I was so relieved that I didn't have his genes, you just don't know. She told me she had another surprise, but she couldn't tell me until she knew I was safe. I admit I've been curious, but I know when the time is right, she'll tell me."

"How do you think Grandma will feel about us running away?"

"If I know my mother, which I think I do, she'll want to go with us. I don't think she wants to be married to Gordon Spielberg, either."

"What if we gave her a call before we go in to eat."

Ruth thought about it for a moment then began to smile. "I think that's a really good idea. If Gordon's there, we'll ask her to meet us somewhere. I suspect those walls have eyes and ears, too."

She got out her cell phone and dialed her mother's number. As she waited she tapped her fingers nervously on the steering wheel. The phone rang a couple of times before Rose, her mother's maid, picked up the phone. "Spielberg's residence. How may I help you?"

"Hello, Rose. Is my mother there?"

"Yes, ma'am, she is."

"May I speak to her, please?"

"One moment, please." Rose put the phone down and Ruth heard receding footsteps.

A moment later there were more footsteps and the phone was picked up. "Hello, Ruth. How are you enjoying your vacation?"

"Before I answer, is Gordon home?"

"Yes, but he's about to go golfing with some of his buddies. Did you want to speak to him?"

Ruth hesitated for a moment then replied, "Yes, he might as well know our news. After I've spoken to him, I was wondering if you'd go out to your car on the pretext of looking for something for me. I'll talk to you then about what's on my mind."

"Okay. Let me get your father." Again Ruth heard the phone clank onto the desk. Suddenly she heard Gordon ask. "Who's on the phone?"

"Ruth wants to speak to you."

"Oh," was the reply. Suddenly Ruth heard her father's booming voice say, "Hello, Ruth. How are you enjoying your vacation?"

"Fine," replied Ruth. "I have some news. Leslie is marrying Jethro Borden."

"You don't say. When?"

"As soon as it can be arranged. We're going to New York to get her wedding dress, as well as put together a trousseau. We were wondering if Mother could go with us to help us get it all done quickly."

"I don't know. How does Bruce feel about this arrangement?"

"It was his idea to have her marry Jethro. He gave me his credit card and told me to spare no expense. We could use Mother's help. Would you mind if she went with us?"

"How long do you plan to be gone?"

"Three days to a week. There's a lot to do. It will also give Leslie time to be with her grandmother before she's married."

"Well, I don't see why she can't go. When are you leaving?"

"As soon as we can get ready. It will probably be a couple of hours before we can get everything together."

"I'll see that she's ready."

"Thank you, Daddy. I'll see you when we get home."

"Until then." There was a sudden click, denoting the conversation was over.

Turning to face Leslie, Ruth said, "I'm sorry I had to bring up this terrible problem, but it was the only way to get his permission."

"I know." Leslie shuddered and added, "I know it isn't going to happen, but it's still hard to hear it out loud."

"I know, honey."

Suddenly the cell phone began to ring. Relieved to see it was her mother calling, Ruth answered it. "Hello, Mother."

"Hello, dear. Gordon told me Leslie's getting married. Is she happy about this?"

"Before I answer you, I have a question. Do you want to stay married to Gordon?"

"No, only I can't see a way out. Why do you ask?"

"We're not sticking around to see Leslie go through what we did. If you want to go with us, we want you to come."

"Oh, Saints be praised. You bet your sweet Aunt Petunia I do. What do I need to do?"

"Have Rose pack what you want to take. Make an excuse to get her out of the room, then quickly pack what you want most."

"There isn't anything important except the picture albums. I don't need them, as I can get more pictures of the two of you. If I were to take anything, it would draw attention to the fact that we ran away." She grew silent a moment then added, "No, I'll pack as if I we're going to return."

"That's a good point. We were going to take those things that were most valuable to us, but we won't now. We're about ten minutes away. We want to get something to eat before we head out. When you get packed, go to our house. We'll meet you there."

"Why don't you just come on home? Since there's no one at your place, I'll stop and pick up a pizza, along with something to drink. When you get there, we'll eat and then be on our way."

"That sounds good. While we wait, I'll water the plants one last time. It will be a long time before they get watered again. Hazel hates plants, so she refuses to water them. They're the one thing I wanted to take, but I won't."

"I know how much you love your plants, but it just can't be helped. I have to run a few errands before I go to your place, so I'd best get crackin'."

"We're both thirsty, so we'll stop at McDonalds and get something to take with us. We'll see you as soon as we can. I love you, Mother."

"I love you too, sweetheart."

Putting the cell phone back into her purse, Ruth looked up to smile at her anxious daughter. "She's going to come with us."

"Oh, wonderful!"

"Let's go to McDonald's for something to drink then hurry home. Mother said she would have something for us to eat before we get under way."

Leslie settled back as she replied, "That suits me just fine. I can't wait to see Grandma again."

"Me either." Ruth grew silent a moment then said, "I sure hope we can pull this off with out a hitch."

"Are you worried we won't get away?" Leslie looked at her anxiously.

"A little bit," replied Ruth. "I just hope Mother can get all that she had to do completed before we get there."

"Me, too."

Soon they had driven up to McDonald's where they ordered soft drinks. They decided to stop at the Wal-Mart just out of town to pick up a few things to take with them. Not long after that, they were on their way home.

It was about dusk when they arrived. Seeing a strange car in the drive, Ruth went up the road a little way, then phoned her mother, Sarah. When her mother answered, Ruth said, "Don't come to the house, Mother. There's a strange car in the driveway."

Sarah chucked lightly. "It's all right. That's my new car. I'll explain when you get inside. I have dinner ready, so the sooner we eat the sooner we can get on the road."

"Oh, what a relief!"

Ruth turned the car around and pulled up to the house. Sarah greeted them warmly as they went inside. Hugs were passed around before they went to the dinning room to eat.

As they ate, Sarah said, "Do you remember when I told you Gordon wasn't your biological father?"

"Yes," replied Ruth, wondering what her mother was leading up to.

"Do you also remember I told you when it was safe I had a surprise for you?"

"Yes, I remember. I must admit I was curious, but I knew you'd tell me when you could."

"Well, today I feel it's safe to tell you both. When Momma found out she was dying of cancer, she came to see me. Gordon was off on business at the time. Momma wanted me to go to Citizen's Bank so she could show me something. I was curious but I didn't ask what it was.

"When we got to the bank, Momma took me over to the bank manager and then dropped the biggest bomb on me ever. When Momma's father died, a month before Momma learned she had cancer, she learned he'd left her well off. Then a about a year before her mother died, she received a large inheritance from a distant relative. My mother told me she'd put it in a special account for me so Gordon couldn't find it."

"How much was in the account, Grandma?" Leslie asked, watching her grandmother anxiously.

"Three million dollars."

"Say that again," ordered Ruth in amazement.

"Three million dollars. There's a million dollars for each of us."

"How do you plan to keep this money secret, Mother?"

"I think the three of us should change our names. I'll take the name my mother put on the account — Shirleen Webb."

Leslie, catching on to the reason for the change of names, replied, "I've always liked the name Meagan. So my new name is Meagan Webb." Ruth just stared at both of them in an attempt to take it all in. "Mom, I think you should be called Juliana Webb. There's no way Dad or Grandpa will guess these names."

"Okay, I'm Juliana," declared Ruth.

"I bought several bottles of hair dye to help disguise us," continued Sarah. "My hair is gray, so I'll become a brunette."

"I've always wanted to be a spicy redhead," Ruth said with a saucy look.

"I don't like this blond hair, so I'll go black," declared Leslie.

"When we get to the motel for the night, we'll dye our hair. Then, we can throw the bottles out the window somewhere on the way," continued Sarah/Shirleen.

"Mom, Grandma, there's something else we need to do to make this transition complete." The others, looking at her questioningly, waited for her to continue. "We've lived the life of luxury all our lives. We need to downsize. No more expensive clothes or jewelry. We'll shop at thrift stores or places like Wal-Mart. They'll expect to see us decked out like we've always been."

"That's true," said Ruth thoughtfully. "That's good thinking, honey."

"I agree," said Sarah. "Are we all in agreement on this?" When the younger women nodded, Sarah sighed audibly. "We also can't take anything with us that would make Gordon or Bruce suspect we've run away. Take the clothes you have right now, then we'll buy others on the way."

"Grandma's right, Mom. We can't take the chance. We need all the leeway we can get. They won't suspect us. They'll just think we're going to be home in a few days. By the time they realize something's wrong, we should be long gone."

"We'll load your stuff into the new van outside, then we'll find a place to push the car over a large embankment. The new van will be our transportation."

"What did you do with your old car, Mother?"

"I had my gardener take it out of town, pour gasoline all over it and set it on fire."

"Are you sure you can trust Stanley, Mother?"

"Yes, I most definitely can. He hates Gordon almost as much as I do. He told me once if I ever needed him, I only had to ask. When I told him I was leaving, he said he was going to leave, too. He'd only stuck around to help me.

"I drove him out to Dead Man's Bluff. You know, where all the people run off of the road. That drop off is so deep no one can get to the wrecks. So what's one more added to the pile? I moved the van a good distance away, then watched as he doused the car inside and out with gasoline. When he was finished, he pushed the car to the edge. As it started over, he struck a match and tossed it on the car. It caught quickly as it went over the edge. It exploded when it hit the bottom and we watched until it had completely burned up. We wanted to make sure nothing else caught fire. When it burned itself out, we came back to town and I took Stanley to the bus station and saw him off." Shrugging nonchalantly, she continued, "Then I came here."

"What if a car had come by?"

"We never thought of that. The road isn't heavily traveled."

Sighing, Ruth said, "That's a good thing."

"That was genius, Grandma," said Leslie proudly.

"Thank you, love." Sarah patted her hand affectionately. Finishing the last of her pizza, she continued, "As soon as we've finished eating, we'll clean up the kitchen and take the garbage out to the dumpster."

They fell silent for a few minutes, then Ruth asked, "Momma, since we're going to have to drive a long way to ensure we're safe, I think we should take turns driving. That way we won't get so tired we become careless."

"You're right," agreed Sarah. "The last thing we want to do is to get careless. That will get us caught quickly." She paused a moment then continued, "While I was getting things ready, I got an atlas. Perhaps we should think about where we want to go."

Growing excited, Ruth asked, "Do you have it with you?"

"Yes." Putting down the rest of her uneaten piece of pizza, Ruth wiped her hands and rose. "If you give me the keys to the van, I'll go get it"

Setting down her drink, Sarah wiped her mouth then went to get the keys, which she handed to Ruth. "The atlas is in the front seat."

"I'll be right back." Without waiting for a reply, Ruth hurried out to the van. When she returned, they opened the atlas to the map of the United States. "We could go down to Mexico," mused Ruth.

Leslie opted for going to California. "That's such a big state, we could get lost in Los Angeles, Sacramento, or even San Francisco."

Pointing to Florida, Sarah asked, "What about Florida?"

Leslie looked first at Ruth then over to Sarah as she asked, "Why don't we just get in the van and start driving. We can decide where to go when we feel safer."

"That's a good idea," replied Sarah. "Let's head toward Ohio. When we get to the border we'll find a place to pull off and decide then."

"I agree with you both," replied Ruth. "The most important thing right now is to get out of here before we're stopped."

"Then that's exactly what we'll do," declared Sarah. "Right now, let's finish up so we can get ready to leave."

Nothing more was said as they finished eating. When the kitchen was put to rights, Leslie gathered up the garbage bag to take it out to the dumpster out back. Ruth helped Sarah organize the items from the car into the back of the van. When she was satisfied the car was empty, she turned to her mother. "Where will we get rid of this car, Mother?"

"The same place. It's near the town limits. When it's gone to the bottom, we'll start on our new lives."

"I'll follow you, so the van can shield us from passing cars."

Leslie, followed her mother out of the house and went to join her grandmother in the van, while Ruth locked up the house. Sarah, backed the car out of the driveway and pulled forward to wait for Ruth. Slipping the keys into her handbag, Ruth went to get into her car. When Ruth pulled out of the driveway, Sarah started forward.

Dead Man's Bluff was close by, so they soon arrived. They turned around at a turn out, and Ruth was relieved to see there were no cars coming from either direction. After getting as close to the edge as possible, Ruth left the car idling with the hand-brake on. She took Bruce's credit card out of her handbag and slipped it into the glove compartment, picked up her handbag and got out of the car.

When she was satisfied no one was coming, she released the hand brake. In slow motion, the car crept closer to the edge. Suddenly, it plunged over the embankment, careening to the bottom. Near the bottom, the car exploded and burst into flames. They watched until it had burnt out. Satisfied nothing else had caught fire and they hadn't been seen, Ruth and Leslie sighed in relief.

They all got back into the van and started back toward town. Once they were through town, they turned north and drove away. Only then did they start to relax a little, though none of them truly felt safe. The three of them knew that once the men knew they'd run away, they would stop at nothing to find them.

Chapter 2

Sarah Spielberg, now Shirleen Webb, drove the van for a couple of hours before finding a motel for the night. When they were settled into the room, they each took turns dying their hair. When they had the job done, the changes were impressive.

Shirleen no longer had gray hair. Her brown tresses made her look at least twenty years younger. She was a little taller than her daughter, yet was just as well proportioned. Although her face was starting to show some wrinkles, her skin was flawless. Well-defined cheekbones complimented her stubby chin, and hazel eyes added to her beauty. As she stood there, hair streaming down her back, she didn't even look like her younger self — this new look was softer. The color changed her completely.

Meagan Webb, alias Leslie Murdock, blinked her eyes as she gazed in awe at her grandmother. "Wow, Grandma. You look so much younger!"

Beaming Shirleen said, "Thank you, precious."

Gazing at her granddaughter, who on the other hand looked much older with her jet-black hair. The color made her blue eyes stand out and complemented her pale complexion. "Wow," said Shirleen. "You not only look stunning, but you look at least ten years older."

"Thank you, Grandma," grinned Meagan. "Hopefully this look will help to camouflage me better."

"It sure it does. What do you think, R- I mean Juliana?"

"I would never have recognized you, honey. It's hard to get used to seeing you this way, but I know it's necessary." She paused a moment then added, "Grandma's right. You're absolutely stunning!"

Meagan beamed, as she replied, "Thank you Momma. That means a lot to me."

Meagan's mother looked at her strangely then asked, "What happened to calling me Mom? I thought calling me Momma was for little kids."

"I've called you Mom for a long time, so I decided to start calling you Momma, so it won't tip Daddy off. I think I like it, too."

"You're right about your father. That was really great thinking."

Meagan beamed but remained silent.

Shirleen and Meagan looked at Juliana, alias Ruth Murdock, who was absolutely gorgeous with red hair — her hazel eyes seemed to come alive and her complexion had a rosy glow, which made her appear healthier.

Shirleen was first to break the silence. "I've always thought you were beautiful, but with that hair color you're absolutely gorgeous!"

"I agree with Grandma, Momma. You're even more beautiful than before."

Juliana wiggled her hips as she wrinkled her nose. "Thanks, Sugar. I quite like the effect myself."

Seeing her brazen antics, the other two laughed, breaking the tension they'd felt all evening. They joked around some more as they relaxed.

Suddenly, Shirleen said, "I just had a thought. I want the two of you to think about this, too."

"What's that, Grandma?" asked Meagan as she plopped onto the bed.

"We've all dyed our hair, so we might just as well go all the way and cut it too. That should help to complete our transformations."

Meagan turned to her mother excitedly. "Oh, Momma, Grandma's right. They'd never believe we'd cut our hair." When Juliana remained silent, Meagan hurried on, "Don't you see. We've always worn our hair long and in the same style."

"You're right, honey," agreed Juliana. "I just never thought of doing something so drastic. The more I think about it, the more I like the idea of getting rid of this heavy mess. I've wanted to cut it off for years, but every time I tried, your father would threaten to cut it to my scalp then force me to wear one of those hot wigs. Knowing I can make my own decisions now makes me feel a little giddy!" She paused to run her fingers through her hair, and giggled like a teenager. "Oh, I'm going to cut it real short!"

Shirleen, smiling her approval, said, "After we have breakfast, we'll travel until around noon. We'll have lunch, and then go to a beauty salon and get new hairdos."

"I'm game," said Meagan

All of a sudden Juliana laughed. "I'm more than up for it. I can hardly wait to see how different I'll look."

"That's settled," declared Shirleen. "Before we go to bed, I have something else to show you."

The other two gathered around Shirleen as she pulled out a huge bag and lugged onto the bed. Opening the zipper, she lifted the lid so they could see what was inside.

"Oh, Momma," was all Juliana could say.

"Grandma! What are you doing with so much money?"

"I withdrew one million dollars so we didn't have to mess with the bank until we decide where we're going to settle down. There may be emergencies along the way and we'll have plenty of cash to cover them."

"That may be true, but how will you keep it safe?" asked Juliana.

"We'll bury this under everything we have. If we run into an emergency, we'll deal with the problem then."

"Listen, Momma, why don't you put some of it in your purse, say one to two thousand at a time. If we have problems that cost us more than that, then we'll consider what to do them."

"How would the two of you feel about taking another two or three thousand dollars with you?"

Juliana sighed, "Carrying that much money around scares the heck out of me, but at least you won't be the only one in danger."

"Good! I'll count out three thousand dollars for you right now. Do you have something to put it in?"

"Only my makeup bag. I could get a small pouch at a store tomorrow then when we get to our next motel room, we can count out the money."

"I'll get one too so I can do the same thing," replied Meagan.

Shirleen looked over at Meagan. "Would you carry some of it in a handbag, too?"

Meagan looked at Juliana to see what she thought. "What do you think, Momma?"

"We'll get you a pouch, along with a larger purse." She ran her hand through her hair then continued, "At least you won't be the only one carrying a lot of money, Momma."

"Thank you dear. I don't like to think of the two you caught in the middle of this, but we may need the money, so it's better to do this than try to get money from a bank whenever we need it. That could raise a lot of suspicion."

"I know." Sighing, Juliana added. "We're going to need clothes, food, and necessities. I suggest we only carry $500 in our wallets. That reminds me, we need to get you a new wallet too, Les …" Growing frustrated, Juliana exclaimed, "Oh, shoot! I mean Meagan." She mopped her face with her hand. "Boy this name business may be the death of me before I get the hang of it."

Meagan rose to comfort her mother. "Don't worry. You'll get used to calling me Meagan before long. To be honest, if I didn't call you Momma, I would've slipped up many times."

Juliana hugged her close and kissed her cheek. "Thanks, honey," she replied. "Confessing this makes me feel a little better. If I forget, just hit me as a reminder that I slipped up."

"When I see you're about to call me Leslie, I'll cough to drown it out."

"Good idea. Maybe we could all do that."

Shirleen chuckled. "We'll all sound like we've got bad colds."

"You too, Momma?"

Shirleen nodded affirmatively then said, "Me, too!"

"Then," said Juliana, "I suggest we don't forget. That might just draw unwanted attention too."

"Momma's right, Grandma."

"She sure is." Shirleen closed the lid on the suitcase, and then zipped it shut. Putting it beside the other luggage, she rose to address her family. "Well, we won't worry anymore about this tonight."

"I think it would also be a good time to dump our cell phones," added Juliana.

"Now's as good a time as any," replied Shirleen.

Looking from her grandmother then back to her mother, Meagan asked, "What will we do for phones?"

"We'll change services," replied Shirleen. "We'll just get new chips. For now, let's just turn them off."

"Okay."

Each of them turned their phones off and put them away. Not long after that, they turned out the lights and went to bed.

They were on the road long before daylight the next morning. They had shoved the bag of money to the bottom of the pile of bags. No one spoke of it, but it was never far from anyone's mind. They stopped for gas at daylight, and then went in search of a place to have breakfast.

They found a little out of the way spot, parked the van and went inside. There were only a couple of other patrons inside, so finding a secluded booth was easy. Soon, a waitress dropped off menus, and then left to give them time to decide what they wanted.

She returned with a tray filled with water glasses, which she placed before them. Taking out her pad she waited to take their orders. Once they had placed their orders, they sat back to wait for their meals. They sat in companionable silence, lost in private thoughts.

A few minutes later the waitress returned with their meals. It didn't take long to make short work of the food. Just as they were finishing up, the waitress brought them their bill. Shirleen took the money for the bill out of her purse, being sure to add a good tip. After a quick restroom break, they were ready to hit the road again, this time with Juliana doing the driving.

They reached Buffalo before noon, so they decided to find a thrift store. It didn't take them long to find one, and it was busy. Signing audibly, Shirleen said, "Good, we can get lost in the crowd while we shop. We should probably stick close to each other, in case something happens."

"That's a good idea, Momma. Let me get this huge thing parked." They went inside, grabbed a cart, and headed to the many racks of clothes. Soon they'd found a good number of things to buy. They even found some jewelry to go with what they'd picked out.

Next, they saw some purses hanging from a rack. There was a huge purse that would work for Meagan, so they added it to the cart and moved on to look at wallets. None of them were in good condition, so they decided to check out.

They loaded their purchases into the van and hit the road again, looking for a good restaurant for lunch. All of them could hardly wait to finish eating so they could find a salon and get their hair cut. They fond a salon nearby and the chopping commenced.

Happy with their new styles, they got back on the road and drove for several hours before changing drivers. It was nearing eight o'clock, so they stopped at a Burger King for something to eat. They were all so tired they decided to stop soon.

Before finding a motel, they stopped at a drug store and bought makeup, makeup bags, three pouches for the money, and a wallet for Meagan. They also stopped at another Wal-Mart to buy three sets of luggage, and more clothes. While they were shopping, Shirleen said, "Since the clothes we bought at the thrift store have to be washed before we wear them, let's get two or three sets of pillowcases to put them in so we can go to the Laundromat."

"That's a good idea, Momma. We don't want to leave them in the thrift store bags." They headed to the bedding section and added three sets of pillowcases to their cart.

Since they were close to the jewelry section, they also decided to get some more cheap jewelry to go with their new clothes.

Soon they were on their way to find a motel for the night. Shirleen said, "Let's pack up the clothes from our old lives and leave them at a thrift store tomorrow. We have enough new stuff to work with for a while, don't you think?"

Nodding in agreement, Juliana replied, "More than enough as far as I'm concerned. If we decide we need something else along the way, we can just stop and buy it."

Shirleen continued, "One other thing we need to do tomorrow is find a shoe store and get some cheaper shoes. These we have just scream expensive."

"You're right," said Juliana, "but these are so comfortable I hate to part with them."

"I think we all feel that way, Momma, but Grandma's right. We can't wear thrift store clothes and designer shoes."

Juliana sighed. "You're both right. I'll get some cheap shoes and give away my favorites."

"Good girl," said Shirleen. "We're doing really well so far. Let's not take a chance on getting caught for something as trivial as the wrong pair of shoes."

"I agree, Momma."

Not long after that they found a fast food restaurant and stopped to have something to eat. "I'm going to take mine to the motel so I can eat in peace," said Shirleen.

"I think that's a great idea, Grandma."

"I agree with both of you," Juliana said.

Just then they saw a motel with a vacancy sign. Shirleen glanced over to Juliana then back to Meagan. "This motel looks inviting. Is this place all right with you?"

"I'm so bone weary," sighed Julian, "that anything looks really good right now."

"I feel the same as Momma."

"Good, I was hoping you'd both agree. I could sleep for a week."

"Me, too!" chorused the others.

"Meagan, would you go with me to register?" Turning to Juliana she said, "We'll leave you to hold down the fort until we get back. We'll lock you in for protection."

"I'll gladly wait out here," said Juliana. Sighing, she settled deeper into her seat as they locked her in. When they went inside, Juliana sat pondering their situation. *Well,* she thought, *we've made it through one day. I can't wait 'til we're out of New York.* "Oh Lord," she prayed aloud, "please help us to get away without them ever finding us. I don't know what I would do without my mother and daughter. Could you please protect us from our spouses and any unseen danger lurking ahead? If only—"

She stopped mid-prayer as her mother and daughter returned to direct them to the room they would be staying in for the night. It didn't take them long to get unloaded and into their room. After locking the door, they washed up and ate their meal. After they'd thrown their trash away and straightened up their room, they all took turns taking a bath so they could rest easier.

When they were all assembled in the bedroom, Shirleen brought up the subject of the money. "Now that we all have pouches and wallets, let's take care of the money distribution. That way we won't have to do it in the morning."

They got everything out and Megan asked, "Grandma, how did you ever get out of the bank without being hit over the head for all this money?"

"When I told the bank manager my plans, he tried to talk me out of getting it all at once. I told him it was imperative I take the full sum, so he asked me if I had a big enough suitcase to haul it in. I'd bought a huge bag for just that purpose, so he told me to bring it to the back of the bank and he'd fill it and help me get it to my van."

"Where was Stanley at this time?" asked Juliana.

"I'd already taken him to the bus station. Anyway, the manager was waiting for me when I got to the back door. He even helped carry it to the van."

"I could barely lift it when we unloaded the luggage that first time!" Juliana said. "Now I know why it nearly gave me a hernia."

"I'm sorry, dear, but I didn't feel it was safe to let you know what was in it at that point."

"I think I would've had a heart attack had I known beforehand."

"Well, let's get this divided up so we can go to bed. I think we should drive for another day before we get rid of our clothes. We need to find a Laundromat and wash the thrift store stuff first, anyway. I just want to be far enough away that the clothes won't be connected to us."

It didn't take them long to put three thousand dollars into each of their pouches and wallets. When the money was taken care of and the huge bag closed, Shirleen said, "From now on, you'll have enough money in your wallets that you can pay for things yourselves. It doesn't look good when I'm the one always paying for everything. That draws attention to me."

"I don't mind paying for what I buy, but I hate using your money, Momma. Somehow it just doesn't feel right."

"Why not? This money would've been yours if I'd died. You're just using it while I'm around to see you do it."

Juliana leaned down to kiss her mother's cheek. "I hadn't thought of it that way."

"Well, it's true. I'm having fun watching you buy things."

"Thank you so much."

"Grandma," Meagan said, "I've always thought you were too generous for your own good. Now I know you are." Tears glistened in her eyes as she gazed at her grandmother. "When we get through this mess, I plan to make things right with you." She held up her hand when Shirleen started to speak. "No use arguing with me, because you won't win." Grinning she added, "So just say thank you and kiss me."

Shirleen laughed at Meagan, then complied. "Thank you." She then kissed her cheek. "I have the most wonderful daughter and granddaughter in the whole world."

"Isn't that the truth," teased Meagan.

That set them off on a laughing fit. Finally, they put their thrift store clothes into the new pillowcases then went to bed for some much needed rest.

Juliana and Shirleen woke with a start. Something was terribly wrong. Then Meagan screamed at the top of her lungs. Juliana, who was sleeping beside her, reached over to gently call her name, but she just kept screaming. "Leslie, wake up, honey. You're having a bad dream."

Megan woke with a start to see her mother hovering over her. She reached up to pull her close. She was shaking so hard Juliana worried she wouldn't be able to calm her down.

Shirleen came around the bed to sit next to her. "Meagan, honey, you're safe now."

Meagan released Juliana only to grab her grandmother. "Oh, Grandma ... it was so horrible."

Shirleen held her tight while talking soothingly to her. "Tell us all about it and we'll try to help you sort it out."

Meagan released her grandmother and put her face in her hands until she was calmer.

Juliana asked her, "What was the dream about?"

"I dreamed Daddy got suspicious when we didn't call him."

"Oh, I forgot all about calling him!"

"So did I," admitted Shirleen, looking aghast. "I was so busy getting us away I forgot that simple little detail."

Juliana turned back to Meagan. "What else?"

Meagan shuddered then plunged in. "I dreamed he found us. He killed you and Grandma, and then I was forced to marry Jethro. My life was a living hell. He beat me unmercifully for kneeing him. And that's not all," she paused to look at them with concern. "I dreamed Daddy, Grandpa and Henry are all part of the Mafia."

"I've suspected that very thing," declared Juliana.

"You have?" Meagan looked at her mother incredulously.

"Yes. There's just too much evidence that says they're up to their necks in that nasty business."

"I know for sure Gordon is."

"How do you know that, Momma?" Juliana asked her mother suspiciously.

"I overheard him talking to a man who'd come to give him some information. It seems that an acquaintance they knew was turning state's evidence. Gordon told the man to put a hit out on him, and then report to him when it was finished."

"Oh no!" Juliana had turned deathly pale. "Did he kill the man?"

"Yes. The guy came back to report it was done. That was two days before we left."

"Grandma, Momma, We've got to get out of here as soon as we can get ready. I don't know if they're onto us or not, but I think that dream was a warning."

"I do, too," replied Juliana.

Shirleen looked at her alarm clock; it is nearly three a.m. "Let's get dressed, load the van then get out of here. We'll drive until nine o'clock, stop long enough to get something to eat and get right back on the road after we buy some food to take with us so we can eat in the van from now on. We can take turns driving so we can go all day and through the night without stopping again."

"That sounds like a plan, Mother." She hugged Meagan close and then they hurriedly got dressed and loaded the van. As they checked out the room to make sure there was nothing left behind, Meagan said, "From now on, we need to pray for safety and good traveling."

"I should've thought of that, too," replied Shirleen. "Let's close the door and do that right now."

A few minutes later they piled into the van and Shirleen took the first shift driving. By nine o'clock they'd gone many miles, so they decided to stop for breakfast and grocery shopping. After that, Meagan took over the driving, and they stopped only once for a bathroom break at a rest stop.

Three hours later, Meagan pulled into another rest stop. "I have to go bad," declared Meagan.

Juliana, who had been napping, stretched and said, "Let's have a light snack while we're here."

"That's a good idea. I'm thirsty, too," replied Shirleen.

While Megan took care of her bathroom needs, the others made sandwiches with chips, cookies and Coke to complete their meal. They wolfed down their food, and then Shirleen took her turn driving.

They didn't stop again until ten o'clock that night. They made a pit stop and had another meal from their grocery stash. As soon as they finished, Juliana took the wheel and they were back on the road again.

Four hours later, at 2 a.m., they were out of New York State. Juliana didn't know where to go from there, so she pulled into an all night truck stop to confer with her mother. "Momma, we've just crossed over into Pennsylvania."

Shirleen groggily sat up and asked, "We have?" She rubbed her eyes, trying to wake up. "Let me get the atlas and we'll figure out where to go next." She went to the back of the van, found the atlas and came back to her seat. Juliana turned on the overhead light so they could see. Shirleen turned to Juliana and Meagan and asked, "Where should we go?"

Meagan was the first to speak. "I feel like as long as we're in the New York / Pennsylvania / Ohio area, there's a greater chance that we'll get caught."

"Meagan's right," Juliana said. "They won't stop until they've found us."

"That's true, they won't," admitted Shirleen. "What should we do?"

Meagan sat silently pondering the situation. Finally, she looked up and said, "The first thing I suggest is we pray for guidance about where to go. It might mean more days on the road, but I think the answer we get will be the correct one."

"That's fine with me," replied Juliana. "The farther away we get the better it suits me."

"The same goes for me," Shirleen said, then hesitated. "What if we go to Canada or Alaska? I know it's cold during the winter months, but at least we'd be safe until spring. By then, we could decide what to do next."

"We don't have any winter clothes," protested Juliana.

"Then when we get to Canada or Alaska we'll have to purchase some, won't we?"

"Why are you dragging your feet, Momma? Meagan studied her mother closely.

"I'm not dragging my feet, honey. I'm just trying to make sure we don't get up into that cold country and get into worse trouble than we're already in. That's all."

"You have a good point," replied Shirleen softly. "I think we should discuss it a little more before we do anything so drastic. We might find we've jumped from the frying pan into the fire."

"Oh, I see." It was evident Meagan didn't, but no one corrected her. They were both to busy trying to figure out where to go.

Finally, Shirleen looked up from the map and said, "I think your suggestion to pray about it is a good one. After we've prayed, we'll discuss it again."

"Thank you for understanding my feelings," sighed Meagan. "I just want us to be safe, that's all."

"I know you do. So do I."

"I'm sorry I thought you were dragging your feet, Momma," apologized Meagan. "I'm just scared."

"I know you are, sweetheart. So am I. I want us to be as far away from those evil men as we can get. I just don't want us to get into trouble by heading someplace where we're trapped."

"Oh, I hadn't thought about that." Meagan grew thoughtful then added, "I trust you and Grandma completely. I won't say anything else, and I'll give you some space to think everything out."

"Thank you for your vote of confidence. Just remember this …you're just as deep in the mud as we are. Your thoughts and feelings matter just as much as ours."

"Thank you. That means a lot."

"Do you want to offer the prayer this time, Meagan?"

"Yes." When their heads were bowed Meagan began. "Dear Lord, we're in a terrible predicament. If we go back, Momma and Grandma will probably be killed and I'll be forced to marry Jethro Borden. I know you don't want that to happen. The other problem we have is where to go so that we're safe. Should we go to Canada or Alaska, or even some place different all together. Please touch our hearts to know where we'll be the safest. Thank you for protecting us thus far …"

When she had finished with the prayer, they all sat silently lost in thought.

A few minutes later, Meagan said, "I opt for going to the deepest part of Canada."

Shirleen looked at Juliana who nodded in agreement. "I agree."

Sighing deeply in relief, Shirleen replied, "I had the same feeling. Where should we go exactly though?"

They studied the map and Shirleen asked, "How about some place near Alberta or Calgary?"

"Let's ask the Lord what he thinks," volunteered Meagan.

"We all came up with the same answer before," declared Juliana, "so perhaps we'll be in agreement again. First of all, let's ask about Cardston in Alberta."

When all of them agreed, Meagan again led the prayer, and then they waited for inspiration. Suddenly, Meagan said, "I feel the answer is yes."

"I have the same feeling," Juliana said. "What about you, Mother?"

"Let me take a walk and think about it, then I'll give you an answer when I return." Not waiting for a reply, Shirleen got out of the van.

Soon she had walked off into the darkness. She was gone so long the women got nervous and kept peering into the darkness looking for her. About forty-five minutes later they saw her emerge into the light of the truck stop. Getting into the van she turned to smile at her family. "Cardston, Alberta is indeed the place."

"We were so worried about you, Grandma."

"I didn't mean to worry you, I was just torn between Cardston and Calgary. I found a spot near a large boulder and sat there so I could pray and then listen. When nothing happened, I repeated the process until I saw a man coming toward me. I was about to run when he told me not to be afraid." She sighed at the memory. "He said, 'Sarah, you know Cardston is better than Calgary, so why do you hesitate?'"

"You saw a strange man who knew your name?" asked Meagan

Shirleen nodded then continued, "I told him how scared I was that we'd get caught. He told me I should trust the two of you. His exact words were, 'Just be prayerful and then listen to your intuition. It will guide you.'"

"What did you say, Grandma?"

"I thanked him and then promised I would not only do what he said, but I would also listen to the two of you and try not to be a know it all."

"You're hardly being a know it all, Momma. You're just trying to keep us safe. We always need your input."

"Thank you, but I fear I took things into my own hands. I'll try to consider your feelings from now on."

Juliana looked at both of them and asked, "Then we agree we should go to Cardston?" They both agreed, so she asked, "Which road should we take?"

Shirleen consulted the atlas then told Juliana how to get to the interstate.

By mid morning they had reached a small place several hundred miles from Erie, where they stopped for breakfast. Once back in the van they assessed their mobile food supply. There wasn't much left, so they decided to go grocery shopping before hitting the road. They found a small store where they stocked up on soft drinks and sandwich ingredients. They also saw some small coolers and decided to get those as well. With them, they could add some more interesting meats and condiments to the selection without worrying they'd spoil. They topped their cart off with some packaged cookies, crackers and chips.

Once they had everything, they joined the long line at the cash register. As they waited in line, Meagan started looking at the different magazines in the rack for something to read during the long drive.

Suddenly, two young, rough looking men entered the store and looked around. Meagan knew they were up to something, so alerted Shirleen and Juliana. "They're up to something."

Looking in the direction Meagan was indicating, her mother and grandmother were suddenly on the alert. There were still three more customers in front of them in line. "I don't like this one little bit," whispered Juliana.

Finally it was their turn to check out. Just as they were paying, Shirleen saw one of the young men had a gun. As she accepted her change from the cashier, Shirleen warned the cashier, "Come with us. That guy over there has a gun."

Not needing to be told twice, the cashier grabbed the rest of their items and calmly followed them to their car. When they got there, Shirleen dug her cell phone out of her purse and called 911. When the dispatcher answered, Shirleen said, "There are two young men in the store at 9th and Main. I think they're going to rob it. One of them has a gun."

"Is the cashier still in the store?" asked the dispatcher.

"No, we warned her and she's standing outside with us."

"Don't go back into the store. The police are on their way."

"How far away are they?"

"Two blocks."

Just then a cruiser pulled into the parking lot, and one of the policemen motioned for them to leave. The four of them got into the van and drove up a block. When they got out of the van to wait with the cashier, they heard gunshots. As quickly as the ruckus started, it was over and two policemen came out of the store with the young men in handcuffs.

Since the danger was over, they took the cashier back to the store. As they got out of the van, the woman said, "This is the third robbery in as many months. I'm quitting. Enough is enough!"

Two policemen approached them and asked, "Who reported this incident?"

"I did," replied Shirleen.

"Well, you saved this woman's life. Good work."

"Thank you," stated Shirleen in relief.

The other policeman stepped forward and asked, "What made you suspicious?"

Meagan stepped forward to say, "Something about them didn't sit well with me. I can't say for sure what it was, but I didn't like how I felt when they came in the store. Then, when I saw one of them had a gun, I knew we had to get out of there."

"Good thing you were so observant, young lady. Things could've ended in a much worse way. Good job."

While they were talking to the police, the cashier called her boss to tell him she was locking up until he found someone else to do her job. The others heard her say, "I'm quitin' this very minute!"

As everyone filed out of the store, the cashier locked the doors and turned to the girls and hugged each in turn. "Thank you for saving my life."

"You're more than welcome, dear," replied Shirleen. "Good luck in your new job, whatever it is."

"Thank you."

After the cashier left, the women piled into the van and they were soon back on the interstate. No one spoke of the incident for a long time then only to thank the Lord for his protection.

Chapter 3

By late afternoon, they were all so tired they decided they couldn't go much further. They found a Laundromat and decided to do some laundry. When that was done, they stopped at a Burger King drive thru for dinner, then started looking for a place to stay. They quickly found a small motel, got a room and quickly got their things out of the van.

After eating, they put their new clothes into their new suitcases and put them back into the van. Their old clothes and suitcases were now ready to find new homes. They quickly got ready for bed and gratefully fell into bed.

The next morning, they slept in a little later, then packed up their things and went in search of breakfast. On the way out of town, they stopped at Wal-Mart and got several pairs of inexpensive shoes to go with their new outfits. When they got to the van, they switched the shoes they were wearing with the new ones, and put their old shoes in with their old clothes.

Next, they drove around until they found a thrift store where they could leave their suitcases full of clothes from their old lives. While they were there, they shopped a bit before hitting the road again. Shirleen offered to drive for the first half of the day, so Juliana got into the passengers side of the van, while Meagan got in the back.

They traveled until noon, then stopped for lunch and Meagan took over the next driving shift. They didn't stop again unless they needed to make a pit stop until dusk. They ate a quick meal, then opted to continue driving for at least two or three more hour, so Juliana took her turn at the wheel.

Eventually, they found a motel and settled in for the night. They were travel weary and fell asleep instantly. Suddenly there was a disturbance just outside their door. Shirleen, whose bed was closest, rose to peek outside. Her heart nearly failed her when she recognized her husband nosing around. Silently, she motioned for the others to be quiet. Getting out her cell phone, she slipped into the bathroom where she phoned the police. "Hello, someone is trying to get inside our motel room."

"What motel are you in, ma'am?" Shirleen gave him the information. "We're on our way."

Not giving him a chance to ask any questions, Shirleen ended the call. She then picked up a chair and slipped it under the doorknob. Walking over to the bed Meagan and Juliana were sharing she whispered, "It's Gordon. I called the police to report a prowler outside of our room."

"Oh my," whispered Juliana. "How did he find us?"

"I don't know."

Meagan began to sob quietly. "Don't let him in, Grandma."

"Be quiet, honey. We'll be fine." Each of them began silently praying for the Lord to help them.

Suddenly, the doorknob rattled. Meagan turned to burry her face in her mother's shoulder. When the door wouldn't open, the person began to bang on the door. "Sarah, I know you're in there. You better open this door!"

No one moved. "I mean it! Open this door or I'll break it down!" Still no one moved.

All at once they heard a voice yell, "Raise your hands and turn around slowly."

"Don't shoot officer. My wife is inside. We're having a domestic squabble."

"I don't care if you're having a love fest. Walk over here slowly — don't make any sudden moves."

"Sarah, open this door. Please, tell him who I am."

Again no one moved inside the motel room.

"That's it! You're under arrest."

"You don't understand officer, my wife's inside that room."

"I don't care if your mother's in there. You're under arrest."

Shirleen slipped off of the bed and peeked through a crack in the curtain. Relief flooded over her when she saw Gordon handcuffed and led to the police car. When he was inside, the officer returned to knock on the door. Shirleen opened the door a crack to ask, "Yes, officer. How may I help you?"

"Is this gentleman your husband?"

"I have never seen him before in my life, sir."

"Thank you. We'll take him in for questioning. Have a good night, ma'am. I'm sorry for the inconvenience."

"Thank you, officer." She watched the officer stride off, then closed the door and locked it.

"Now what do we do, Mother?" Juliana asked.

"We get dressed, packed, get in the van and get the heck out of here!"

No one had to be told twice. The three of them seemed to fly around the room as they prepared to leave. Once the van was loaded, Juliana closed and locked the door, while Meagan ran the key back to the office.

Meanwhile, Shirleen got the van going and when they were all inside, she quickly drove away from the motel and out to the interstate. Everyone was still so frightened that no one spoke for a while. Sighing audibly Juliana asked, "How do you think he found us, Momma?"

"I have no idea. Surely he hasn't been following us."

"He must've been. How else did he catch up to us so fast?"

"My dream was real," sobbed Meagan.

"We're still free for now. However, we've got to ditch this van; he knows what we're driving now.

"What are you cooking up in that wonderful mind of yours, dearest Mother?"

"We've got to have new transportation and we need to be able to be out in public without getting caught again."

"That's a given, but what do you think we should do?"

"Let me mull it over for a little while, then we can discuss it."

"I hope you come up with something fast."

Shirleen grinned as she replied, "Me, too."

Several miles later they reached the Ohio turnpike. At the next rest stop, they turned in so they could stretch their legs and relieve some of the stress they were all feeling. Eventually, Shirleen looked at Juliana and Meagan and said, "I think I know how we got caught so easily. I think the dealer at the car lot knew Gordon. Otherwise, there's no way he could've found us so easily."

"That must be what happened," declared Juliana.

"As I was praying then listening to my thoughts, I got the feeling we need to keep the van for at least the rest of the day. I believe we'll be led to the person we need to see to help us fix this problem. All we have to do is listen to our inner voices."

Juliana watched her mother for a moment then asked, "What are you thinking, Momma?"

"They think we'll get rid of this van and then get another car. What if we got a motorhome instead? We'd have everything we needed and wouldn't have to keep finding motels. We'd be safer in the motorhome parks, because someone with a motorhome wouldn't be suspicious. I think you can even get them with a washer and dryer, so that would eliminate one of the things we'd have to do in public."

"I saw an ad for a motorhome that has everything, even storage units along the sides, Juliana said. "We could store groceries and other consumables so we didn't have to shop so often."

"Oh, wonderful. We're almost to Cleveland. Let's look for a dealer and see what we can find."

"Fine, but there's just one problem. How are we going to pay for it? We can't walk in off of the street and pay cash for something that expensive."

"No, but we can shop for one then go get a cashiers check."

"How are you going to explain why you have a hundred thousand dollars in your handbag?"

"We can each have some cash. We'll tell them we withdrew it out from our bank but decided having that much cash was scary, so we want a cashier's check."

"It might work." Growing thoughtful for a while, Juliana added, "At least it's a good try."

"How do you feel about the idea, Meagan?"

"I don't know. I'm still so scared I can't think straight. I'll leave it in your capable hands."

"Well, I think we should pray we find an honest bank teller," continued Juliana. "We don't need someone who's part of the Mafia or who will accept a bribe for information."

Late that afternoon, they got to Cleveland and started looking for a motorhome dealership. They found a Charleston dealer about five blocks in from the interstate.

A friendly older gentleman came up to help them as soon as they got out of the van. "How can I be of service to you?"

Shirleen looked at Juliana who nodded for her to do the talking. "We'd like to look at one of your Charleston motorhomes."

"Right this way." He took them to a huge model, and helped them inside. They took their time, going over every part of the coach. Satisfied this was indeed what they needed, they decided to talk price. He told them how much it would cost for the coach, the taxes, and all other fees.

Smiling sweetly, Shirleen asked, "Could we have a few minutes to discuss this privately?"

"Of course. Take all the time you need. When you're finished, come to the office and we can discuss your decision."

"Thank you so much."

Nodding politely, he left them alone.

When he'd entered the office, they began their discussion. "I like this motorhome, Grandma. I think we can be safer in it."

"I agree with Meagan," replied Juliana. "Now that we've seen it and agree we like it, how are we going to get the money from the suitcase to take it to the bank?"

"We'll get a motel for tonight and first thing in the morning we'll go to the bank for a cashier's check."

"Do you think it's safe to get another motel room after last night?"

"No, but we have no choice," replied Shirleen.

"You're right. All we can do is pray we aren't found."

With that settled, they went to speak to the dealer. They found him behind his desk working on a stack of papers. "We really like it, but we've decided to sleep on it tonight then if we still feel the same way in the morning we'll be back to buy it," said Shirleen.

"Okay, thank you for coming in."

They found a good motel and settled in for the evening. After eating the meal made from their stash in the coolers, they got ready for bed. When they were all in their PJs, Shirleen got out the suitcase of money. With Juliana's help, they counted out the money until they had the total the dealer had given them. They put it into separate bags, set it aside, and went to bed early.

The next morning, after saying their morning prayers, they loaded the van and went to breakfast while they waited for the banks to open. They constantly kept looking over their shoulders, worried they'd be found.

Finally, the banks were open, so they decided to go to a little out of the way establishment to take care of business. When they went inside, they were the only ones there. They asked to speak to the bank manager, and were taken to his desk. "These people need to speak to you, Mr. Hubbard," the receptionist said.

"Won't you please be seated?"

"Thank you," replied Shirleen. Taking out the paper the dealer had given her with the total written on it, she said, "I need a cashier's check for this amount. I have the cash with me."

"What?" The manager asked, startled. "Do you mean to tell me you have this much money on your person?"

"Yes, sir, I do."

"Good grief! I'm surprised someone hasn't tried to rob you."

"I've been careful, sir." She looked at him intently then asked, "Can you help me get a cashier's check?"

"Yes, ma'am, I can."

With that, the women took the cash from their bags and put it on the desk. He patiently counted it and then went to have a teller make out the check. When it was ready, he brought it back and asked, "Who wants it?"

Juliana motioned for Shirleen to take it. "You take it, Momma."

"Okay." Shirleen took the check, and tucked it in her handbag. "Sir, I'd like to ask that you tell no one about this transaction. If you do, our lives could be in danger. We have it on good authority there are people following us who want to see us dead."

The bank manager gasped. "Are you sure about this, ma'am?"

"Yes, sir. I'm sure. They found us last night, but we were rescued by the police."

"You have my word; no one will ever know you were here. I'll let my employees know this as well."

"Thank you. We truly appreciate it."

As they roses to leave, the manager added, "Please be safe." He grinned broadly as he added, "Please don't carry so much cash around with you in the future. That will certainly make your lives safer."

"Thank you for the sound advice. Have a good day."

"Good day to you too, ladies."

He watched them leave then mopped his face with his handkerchief before going back to speak to the tellers. "None of you saw those three women enter this bank. If you say a word, you'll be fired and that's a promise."

Once they were back in the van they drove to the motorhome dealership, and the same man came out to greet them. "Good morning, ladies. Have you come to look at the motorhome again?"

"Yes, sir, we have. In fact, we've decided to buy it."

"Excellent! Let's go to the office and get this taken care of." After the three ladies followed him inside, he said, "Please, take a seat while I write up the contract."

Soon, the paper work was taken care of and Shirleen took the cashier's check out of her wallet and handed it to him to complete the deal.

"We have a question for you. Do we have to get new license plates for the motorhome?"

"Yes, ma'am. You'll also have to register it. I can give you the title right now, though. Because you paid in full, I'm going to give you an extra spare tire."

"Can you tell me where the local BMV is?"

"Sure." He wrote down the directions then handed it to her. "It won't take long to get the license plates. When you get them, come back and I'll put them on for you."

"Thank you, that would be great."

"Here are two sets of keys," he said and handed them to Shirleen. "Enjoy your new motorhome."

"Thank you, we will. As soon as I get the plates I'll be back to get it."

"I'll gas it up for you while you're gone."

"Oh, thank you."

They drove straight to the BMV, took care of business, and then headed back to the dealership. Meagan watched the salesman put on the plates and chatted with him like they were old friends. "So, how did you get into this business?"

"I ran it for a friend for many years. He was killed in a terrible car accident, and then one day his lawyer contacted me and told me he'd left the business to me. That was a huge shock, especially since I was getting ready to quit because I didn't want to work for the new manager."

"That was really nice of your friend."

"Yes, it was. Where're you girls headed?"

"We just want to travel around a bit before school starts."

Rising, he looked her in the eyes. "Listen, honey, I know when people are on the run. Are you in some kind of trouble?" Meagan turned pale, but remained silent. "You can trust this old man to keep a secret."

"Grandma thought she could trust the man who sold her the van, but he told the people who are after us and we barely got away with our lives. I'm not about to tell you anything."

"All right, I understand." Wiping his hands on a grease rag, he walked back to where the other two women were waiting. "I have something to ask you ladies. Are you running from the law?"

Shirleen swallowed past the lump in her throat. Deciding honesty was the best policy, she replied, "No, we're not running from the law. Our husbands are part of the Mafia. If they catch up to us, they'll kill my daughter and me, and then force my granddaughter to marry a real heel."

"Oh, good grief. Your granddaughter told me you trusted the guy who sold you your van but he sold you out."

"Yes, apparently he blabbed everything to my husband, and he tracked us down night before last. I called the police and he was arrested, but that won't stop him for long."

"At least he's out of your hair for a little while."

"Do we need to worry about you, sir?"

"Come back into the office and I'll give you my copy of the contract. It will be like we never made a deal."

"But you have the cashier's check…"

"I'll deposit it immediately, and then destroy all the records. What do you plan to do with your van?"

"We haven't figured that out yet."

"Load your stuff into the motorhome and then follow me. I know of a road that runs next to a high cliff, we'll just have a little accident with your van."

He helped them load everything into the motorhome, then they removed the registration and insurance information from the van. They followed him a ways out of town to the aforementioned cliff. Shirleen, who had been driving the van, put the van in neutral, set the hand brake, rolled down the window, and then got out.

With everyone watching, she reached in the window and released the brake. They all got behind the van and gave it a push, then watched as it slowly rolled forward. They watched at it went over the edge and careened down the steep incline, bursting into flames when it crashed at the bottom.

Satisfied, they went back to the dealership to retrieve the new motorhome. The dealer shook each of their hands, and said, "Good luck, ladies. Your secret's safe with me." He hugged Meagan then told her, "Don't ever marry anyone you don't love."

"I won't if I can help it."

Turning to Shirleen he added, "Please stay safe. I wish you the best of luck."

"Thank you for all of your help. If Gordon Spielberg or Bruce Murdock come around, play dumb; it might be the only thing that saves your life."

"I'll definitely remember that. Thanks for the warning."

They climbed into the motorhome and waved as they drove away.

It took Shirleen a while to get used driving the big motorhome, but she eventually figured it out and relaxed a little. They drove until late that afternoon, then found a Wal-Mart just inside of a little town and stopped to buy all the things that would make their new home more comfortable, as well as all the groceries they would need for a while.

It took them three hours and several trips to the motorhome to unload the goodies. When they had everything all inside, it took all three of them another two hours to get everything put away. After that, they ate a light supper and headed back to the interstate.

They traveled until midnight before pulling into a rest stop, where they parked in the back so as not to attract attention. Satisfied they were relatively safe, they went to sleep fully dressed.

The next morning they prepared a light breakfast and got ready to hit the road again. This time, Juliana would be driving. "You have to get used to how big it is, but it's not that bad once you figure it out," Shirleen said.

They drove for six hours, then stopped at another rest stop to eat and switch drivers. It was time for Meagan to take her turn at the wheel.

"Oh," cried Meagan in surprise, "Driving this beast is certainly different than driving the van."

"Just stay in the right hand lane until you get the hang of it. You'll be just fine," encouraged Shirleen.

Several days later, they found themselves at the Kansas border and were glad to be leaving the flat, boring scenery behind. It was late afternoon, and the weather had been hot and humid all day. Suddenly, Meagan cried out. "A tornado to the right of us."

Shirleen, who was driving, looked quickly to the right and decided to try to outrun it. The storm was upon them in seconds, and all she could do was to pray and keep looking for a safe place to turn off. She saw the tornado pick up a barn and carry it toward them. The other cars came to a dead stop along the road, so Shirleen decided to do the same. She'd just got the vehicle stopped when the barn whizzed past them and broke into pieces.

Fear, such as she had never known, gripped her. She saw the tornado split into two different cells, wreaking havoc everywhere. Another building flew past then broke apart. They watched in horror as a house broke apart ahead of them. Suddenly, just as quickly as it came, the tornado was gone.

They were stuck where they had parked for the time being, because trees were down all over the road. Soon road crew came onto the scene, and three hours later they were on their way once more.

They definitely wanted to get as far away from the storms as possible, so they started through Nebraska and drove for three hours before stopping at a rest stop. They said a prayer of thanks for their safety, and decided to nap for a while.

When they woke four hours later, it was dark. They ate a light supper, said a prayer for continued safety and got back on the road. This time Juliana was at the wheel.

Late the next morning they found a place to pull over near a small stream. They studied the Atlas while enjoying the pretty scenery. They still had a ways to go before they reached Wyoming, and decided to take a side trip through Yellowstone Park. Shirleen made notes on how to get to the right road, then they got under way.

They stopped in the next small town to gas up and bought a paper to see what was happening in the news. Their pictures were plastered on the front page. As they read the accompanying article, they were filled with fear. There was a huge reward for any information on their whereabouts. After seeing this, they decided to save Yellowstone for another time. They had to get into Canada as quickly as possible, or they'd be doomed.

Shirleen continued to scan the paper. There was another headline that let her know they were in imminent grave danger — someone reported seeing them when they pulled over for the tornado in Kansas. They didn't look the same, but apparently they still looked enough like themselves to be noticed.

"What has you so troubled, Grandma?" asked Meagan.

Deciding Meagan deserved to know the truth, she showed her the newspaper article. A little cry escaped Meagan's lips, but she remained silent. "As you can see, we've got to get to Canada."

"Yes, I can see that."

"Buck up. With the Lord on our side, we have nothing to fear.

After saying their morning prayers they took off again. Eventually they came to an RV park and decided to stay the night there and leave early the next morning. It was the best night's sleep they'd had in days.

The next morning after breakfast, they got ready to go. Prayer was their anchor, so before they left they said a good one. Going to the dumpsite, they emptied out the sewage tank before continuing on.

They drove as fast as they could without drawing attention and were nearly out of Wyoming in no time. Most of the time they stopped only to fill up the gas tank or buy more food. As they drove though the outskirts of Idaho Falls, they decided to stop and see the falls. They pulled in the lane designated for buses and got out to sit on a bench overlooking the falls. The water was soothing to their frazzled senses. They took time to feed the ducks and geese that surrounded them begging for food. Suddenly, Shirleen looked up and saw someone staring at her. She quickly turned away and got Juliana's attention. "Don't look up, but we're being watched."

Juliana casually looked around. The man was still watching them. Juliana walked over to where Meagan was feeding the birds and pretended to look out over the water as she whispered, "Start toward the motorhome as casually as you can. Don't look back."

"Why, Momma?" Meagan whispered.

"We're being watched." When Meagan started to look back, Juliana whispered, "Don't look back, honey. Act natural."

As they started to walk calmly to where Shirleen was sitting, they saw the man walk away looking like he'd seen a ghost. He hurried over to get into his car. The police officer slowed down to watch him. He stopped the patrol car just behind the man's car and got out.

He cautiously approached the man on the driver's side. Suddenly, the man pulled out a gun and shot the officer. As he was knocked back by the impact, he managed to get his gun out of his holster and shot the man in the head.

Meagan looked away from the scene, but Juliana and Shirleen hurried over to see if they could help the downed officer. He was bleeding profusely, but he wasn't seriously wounded. The bullet had bounced off of his badge then grazed him.

"Call for help on my radio."

Shirleen did as she was told. After making the call, she went back to quiet the officer while they waited. Soon they could hear the wail of the ambulance coming. She wanted to leave, but something held her back. Looking around, Shirleen was surprised to see so many onlookers. Juliana and Meagan hovered close.

Soon the ambulance came into sight. "You're in good hands now, sir. I have to go."

"No! Please wait. I want to get your names."

"Sir, the mob's after us. If we tell you our names, our lives and yours will be in grave danger."

"Who's after you?"

"Our husbands. If they catch us, they'll kill us and force my granddaughter to marry a terrible man. We have to go so we can stay ahead of them."

"Tell me their names and I'll try to keep them off your trail."

"Gordon Spielberg, he's my husband, and Bruce Murdock, my son-in-law"

"I've heard of them. Go in peace and thanks for your help. I'll see what I can do to make their lives difficult."

"Thank you. Get well, soon."

Without waiting for a reply, they hurried over to the motorhome, got in and drove away. They passed a Wal-Mart on their way to the interstate and decided to stock up while they had the chance.

Shirleen pulled into the turn lane and parked at the end of Wal-Mart's parking lot. They shopped quickly, ate a light meal and then went back to get on the interstate. Once they were on their way, they didn't stop for hours until they came to a campground. After saying their nightly prayers, they went to bed, and immediately fell asleep.

Shirleen woke later to the sound of rain beating on the motorhome's roof. They were parked in a low spot and the campground was primitive. Fearing they might get stuck, she woke the others and told them to get dressed so they could leave."

Shirleen backed up and then shifted into gear and eased out of the campground. She drove until they got to a paved rest stop, where they parked for the rest of the night.

By morning the rain had stopped, so they ate a good breakfast and started off again. It was nearly the end of September, so they didn't have much time to get to Canada before the snows came. Knowing this, they pushed relentlessly on.

They finally arrived in Cardston on the third of October, and found a trailer park where they could rent a space while they looked for a house. They took two days to rest up then began house shopping. They called a realtor and he took them all over the place. Finally, five days after their arrival, they finally found a nice home a good distance out of town. Although the house was sound the furnace needed replaced. The realtor assured them there was time to get another furnace installed before winter set in.

There were fireplaces in all seven bedrooms, as well as the living room. It had a large dinning room, kitchen, and a large living room. The house was huge and beautiful.

They decided to put the rest of the money they were carrying in a bank as well as transfer the funds still in New York. They signed the contract for the house then spent the next two weeks waiting for it to close. While they waited, they bought furniture for every room and moved everything from the motorhome into the house.

Shirleen talked to the principle of the school who told her where to order books so Megan could be home schooled. This form of schooling was popular with several families in the outlying areas because the winters were so harsh here and often made it impossible to get to school from their remote location.

They decided to live in the motorhome until the new furnace was installed. Shirleen was antsy about being in the house before the snows came. When she woke up on Monday of the third week of October, she wondered if this would be the day the new furnace would finally be installed.

It was already 9 a.m. and she wondered what was keeping the furnace man. She decided to take a walk around the house and had just gotten around it the second time when she saw the installer's truck pulling up. Shirleen walked over to meet him, and asked, "Is today the day?"

"Yes ma'am."

"Good! Snow will be here before we know it and I don't want to get caught without heat."

"We should have it installed in a few hours. We have to remove the old furnace before we can install the new one."

"Wonderful! I can't wait!"

"I'm sorry it took so long to get out here, but the new furnace didn't get here until last night right before we closed. We only got it uncrated and loaded into the truck an hour ago."

"I see," replied Shirleen. "I didn't mean to be so snappy, but you can see why I'm concerned."

"I sure do, ma'am. To be honest with you, we were a little worried too. This furnace should've been here sooner, but we had to order it and have it shipped in." Smiling, he added, "I'd better quit talking and get to work or this will never be installed."

"I'll leave you to your job."

True to his word, the furnace was installed within a few hours. When the installer left, the women finally moved into their new home.

A few days later the schoolbooks arrived so they were able to start home schooling Meagan. The day after they returned from getting enough supplies to get them through the long winter, it began to snow. Watching the falling snow, Shirleen remarked, "I'm sure glad the snow held off until we got everything ready to last out the winter."

Chapter 4

When he tried to contact Ruth on her cell phone, Bruce Murdock was surprised she didn't answer. *She must be where she can't answer it. I'll call her back later,* he told himself. When he couldn't reach her for two days, he started to grow suspicious. Finally, on the third day, he knew without a doubt they'd all run away.

To say Bruce Murdock was angry would be a gross understatement. He was livid. *How dare she take Leslie and run away? I thought I'd made her understand I was serious about taking Leslie. Well, now I'm not only taking Leslie away, but I'm gonna kill Ruth in the process.* Murder wasn't new to him; he'd seen to it that many had met an early demise.

Calling Gordon Spielberg, he asked, "Have you heard from Sarah?"

"No, and that isn't like Sarah or Ruth," he replied. "Have you heard from them?"

"No, an if my suspicions are correct we won't."

"They made a break for it?"

"That's my best guess."

"Let me check into things here, and then I'll get back to you."

"What do you plan to do?" He hesitated a moment then added, "When I get a hold of Ruth, she'll be sorry."

"So will Sarah!" Bruce could tell Spielberg was just as furious as he was. Being the Godfather of their organization, Spielberg could get better results than he could. "I'll phone you if I hear anything. For now, just act like nothing's wrong."

"That's all well and good, but I'll only wait so long."

"Don't get your shorts in a twist until we see if something's happened to them or whether they're running."

"I'll give you 48 hours, then I'm sending out my men to start looking."

"Fair enough. Meanwhile, I'll get started. Talk to you later, Bruce."

"Later." Bruce hung up the phone then started pacing. He really wanted to oust Spielberg then take his place. He would give his father-in-law the 48 hours, and then he'd put his plan into effect. He had several men working for him who hated Gordon Spielberg and wanted him replaced. Everyone thought he had grown soft. They'd been plotting his overthrow for almost year.

He called his men and by the time he put his phone on the charger, things were in place. Smiling for the first time since learning about Ruth, he went down to speak to Henry.

Bruce was tall and pudgy. His gray eyes were hawk-like and his high cheekbones and pointed chin completed his decidedly ugly countenance. He was always neatly dressed with not a hair out of place. He was so arrogant that he even considered those he did business with to be beneath him, but he was a master at hiding these feelings.

Bruce disliked Gordon Spielberg the first time he met him, and was disgusted by how out of shape he was. His stomach hung over his belt and he breathed heavily with the slightest exertion, and his huge hands and fat rolls added to Bruce's disgust. Whenever he had to deal with Gordon Spielberg, he found it hard to hide how he felt about the man.

He found Henry Borden in his study, and paused to scrutinize him before getting his attention. Borden was a short, squat man with a medium build. He was not only well dressed, he was also in impeccable shape. His dark hair, blue eyes, perfectly shaped face and healthy complexion, completed a handsome package Bruce envied. Henry was everything in appearance he was not.

Suddenly, Henry looked up from the magazine he was reading, surprised to see Bruce Murdock staring at him. "I didn't see you standing there, Bruce. Have you been there long?"

Bruce smiled then answered, "No. I was just wondering if I should interrupt you or come back later."

"Don't be silly," he replied as he threw the magazine onto the coffee table. "I was trying to stay occupied until you came to tell me news about Ruth and Leslie."

"Well, it seems they're missing. We don't know yet if they've had an accident or just skipped out. Spielberg is checking into everything and will get back to me. All of their belongings were still at the house, so it's possible they just got carried away with their shopping and forgot to charge their phones, though there was a rumor they went over the embankment at Dead Man's Bluff."

"That is a deadly curve in the best of conditions. Maybe that's what happened."

"I don't know, because Spielberg's wife is missing too. She was supposed to go shopping with them."

"Well, they've only been gone for about three days. Surely you'll hear from them soon."

Feeling disgusted with Henry's naiveté, he replied, "Perhaps you're right. I guess I shouldn't borrow trouble until I have to."

Just then Matilda entered the room. "Dinner is ready, dear."

"Thank you, honey. We'll be right there." When Matilda left the room, Henry added, "I haven't told Matilda. She'd just fret and with her poor health that's something I just don't want her to do."

"Understandable," replied Bruce. Together, they went to the dining room to eat. Bruce held his own council, deciding to remain aloof until he heard from Spielberg, then he'd put his own plan into action.

Forty- eight hours later, Bruce's cell phone began to buzz. He saw it was Gordon Spielberg calling and answered. "What did you find out?"

"We tracked down my gardener, Stanley Harris, an hour ago. He told us he helped her ditch the car. He wouldn't say where, only he helped her."

"That means she bought another vehicle."

"That was my thought, so I pursued it. I found out she bought a van from a local dealer the same day they left. Hazel, your maid, said when she checked the house over there wasn't anything missing. Everything was as you had left it before going on vacation."

"Well," demanded Bruce impatiently, "did you find anything?"

"Yes. It took a while, but we found the dealership that sold her the van. It turns out he's one of your men. He figured they went north so we'd think they went to New York."

"Knowing Sarah, she'd think that."

"You're right about that," declared Spielberg.

"What happened to Stanley Harris?"

"He got a bullet in his brain and is resting comfortably in the Hudson River."

"Good place for him. Is there more?"

"Yes, there is. I spoke to your man, Nathan White, last night. He called to ask me why he'd seen Sarah, Ruth and Leslie in Buffalo. He told me they had all dyed their hair, but he still recognized them. I told him what was going on, and then asked him to follow them and let me know where they went. Three hours later, he called and told me he'd located them at a motel near the Ohio turnpike. I told him not to do anything until I got there. I'm flying out in half an hour. I'll let you know when I have them."

"Good. Kill Ruth, do what you want with Sarah, and then bring Leslie to me. When I'm done with her, there'll be a wedding. No punk kid is gonna ruin my plans."

"Fine, I'll let you know when it is done."

"I'll be waiting for your call."

After slipping the cell phone back into his pocket, Bruce sat contemplating his next move. *As soon as Sarah and Ruth are out of the way, I'll be able to control Leslie.* He continued thinking, plotting how he'd handle the situation.

◄ • ►

Anger washed through Gordon Spielberg as he rode toward the airport. *Sarah has crossed me for the last time!* When they were first married, she'd told him she hated him, and he'd beaten her into submission. When he was done, he told her to watch her tongue or he'd beat her again. After that, she'd done as she was told. Spielberg's father had been the Godfather of the organization then, and he'd turned it all over to him before his death.

Spielberg had proven he was more than capable of taking over. He'd done everything his father asked, as well as taking out a few men he thought needed it. He'd been ruthless from the time he was sixteen. He took special delight in torturing his victims before killing them. Now was no different.

As he boarded his private jet, he began plotting Sarah and Ruth's murders. He'd never really loved his daughter. She was supposed to be a boy — someone he could teach and turn over his empire to. Ruth hated violence of any kind, so she'd never been a part of his world. Now that she'd crossed him, she wouldn't be any part of this world.

It was 9 p.m., and with any luck it would all be over in a few hours. He fixed himself a drink and settled back into the plane seat to have a cigarette. Knowing he had to keep a clear head, he didn't make the second drink he wanted. He passed the time thinking about the best way to kill Sarah and Ruth. He knew he'd have to threaten Leslie with the same if she didn't come quietly.

He truly loved Leslie and knew it would be difficult to threaten her. *She needs to learn it's a man's world and a woman has to do as she's told or else face the consequences.*

The plane landed in the Erie Airport, and as he was ready to deplane, the Captain asked, "Will you need the use of the plane later, sir?"

"I don't know yet, Jones. Stay close so I can let you know at a moment's notice."

"Yes, sir."

Spielberg rented a car and took the time to add the silencer to his gun before pulling out of the lot. He was a little hungry, so he stopped at a café to have something to eat before heading to the address he'd been given. Spielberg watched as a tall, slender waitress walked toward him. Her red hair, piled on top of her head enhanced her green eyes. A smattering of freckles ran across her nose and delicate cheeks, adding to her beauty. The feature that attracted him the most was her full lips. The conscious way she swayed her hips as she walked turned Spielberg on. Swallowing to gain control, he ogled her.

Handing him a menu she asked, "What can I get ya?" Taking a pad from her pocket, she reached for the pencil behind her right ear and waited for him to speak.

"Let me look over the menu for a minute."

Smiling sweetly, she replied, "Sure thing, sugar. I'll take this gentleman's order, and then be right back."

"Thanks." As she moved over to the other table, Spielberg watched, lusting after her. He quickly looked at the menu just before she came back.

"I'll have the burger with a side order of fries." He watched her write the order down, then added. "I'd like coffee with that."

"Yes, sir. Will there be anything else?"

"What kind of pie do you have?"

"Pumpkin, pecan, banana cream, peach and strawberry rhubarb."

"I'll have a slice of pumpkin with whipped cream."

"Very good." Taking the menu she replied, "I'll bring your order out as soon as it's ready."

Nodding, Spielberg watched her walk away. She was soon forgotten as he went back to plotting the demise of his wife and daughter. He was still reveling in his plot when the waitress returned with his meal. Putting his murderous thoughts aside, Spielberg made short work of his meal.

He was nearly finished when the waitress brought him a slice of pumpkin pie heaped with a generous amount of whipped cream. Filling his coffee cup for the third time she asked, "Can I get you anything else?"

"Yes. Could I get a large black coffee to go?"

"Sure thing, sugar."

By the time she returned, Spielberg was finished with his pie. She set the coffee on the table and put his bill beside it. As she walked away, Spielberg picked it up, took out his wallet and left enough to cover the bill plus a hundred dollar tip. He went up to the register, paid his bill, and without a backward glance at the waitress, took his coffee and left.

Soon he was at the motel. He parked the car and noticed a man waiting in the shadows. As he stepped into the light, Spielberg recognized him. "You ready, Nate?"

"Sure am."

"What room are they in?"

"Eight. They've been asleep for a while so they don't suspect a thing."

Spielberg asked, "Is that the new van?"

"Yes, sir."

"I'll go in first. If things go south, you hightail it out of here."

"Got it," Nate replied, and slipped back into the shadows. He didn't have long to wait before things started happening. What Spielberg didn't know was he'd been hired by Bruce to take him out.

Nate watched as Spielberg bungled the operation. He was about to shoot him in the back, but the wail of police sirens stopped him. He slipped further into the shadows to see what was going to happen. He stayed until the scene had played out. When he saw Spielberg had been arrested, he decided to leave. After getting away, he went to a café and called Bruce Murdock.

"This'd better be good," Bruce snarled into the phone.

"It's Nathan White, boss."

"Do you have something to report?"

"Yes, and it isn't good."

"What happened?"

"The idiot botched the job. I was about to shoot him, but the police got in the way. He wouldn't shut his yap, and they arrested him."

Bruce let loose with a string of colorful curse words all aimed at Spielberg. "I was afraid of this. Well, can't be helped now. Get back to the motel and keep an eye on the trio. When Spielberg gets out tomorrow, be there to pick him up. Take him somewhere then do him."

"You got it."

"If the trio leaves, let me know so I can put a tail on them."

"Got it boss. I'll call you if things change."

"See that you do."

Bruce lit a cigarette after the call ended, and paced the circumference of his room. Having his plans botched wasn't something Murdock dealt well with. He always had to be in control. He crushed the cigarette in the ashtray a little more forcefully than necessary, then grabbed his cell phone and scrolled through his phone looking for a good hit man, then pushed call.

"Tom, I need you to meet me in New York as soon as you can. We have some business to take care of immediately."

Tom Wilson, who was one of Murdock's bodyguards and his best hit man, responded, "Let me get a shower and I'll be on my way. I'll pick up something to eat on the way. I work better on a full stomach."

"I don't care what you do, just get here as soon as possible. Bring Vincent Crowley with you."

"I'll get him on the horn as soon as we hang up."

Bruce ended the call and called his limo driver, who had remained in Syracuse.

"Paul, this is Bruce. I'm still here at Henry's house. I want you to gas up the limo and get here as fast as you can."

"Yes, sir."

"And don't tell anyone you're coming here."

"I won't, sir.

"Be here in two hours."

"I'm leaving right now."

That's the way I like it — when I say jump, you say how high, Bruce thought as he ended the call. Paul Thomas had been his personal driver for years, and he was loyal.

He went to Henry's room, and knocked.

Henry opened and asked, "Is something wrong, Bruce?"

"Yes. Meet me in your office."

"I'll be right down."

When Henry closed his bedroom door, Bruce went to put on his robe and slippers then headed downstairs. Henry was already waiting for him when he got there. Bruce closed the door and said, "I just got a call from Nathan White. He gave me some disturbing news."

Sitting forward in his chair, Henry asked anxiously, "What happened?"

"Spielberg blew the whole damn thing."

"How?"

Filling him in, Bruce said, "I don't know if I can get to them soon, but I'm sure gonna try. I'm meeting some men in New York, so as soon as I get ready I'm leaving."

"I'll leave you to your business."

Murdock had just gotten a shower when his cell phone rang again. Drying himself off as he entered his bedroom, he reached for the phone. Seeing it was Nate White, he quickly answered it. "What's up?

"By the time I got back to the motel, the women were gone. I drove all over trying to find them, but they seem to have dropped off of the face of the earth."

Bruce let out a string of curse words. Finally, when he got himself under control, he asked, "Can't *anyone* do *anything* right?"

"I'm sorry, sir. They must've left while we were talking on the phone."

"No doubt."

"Do you still want me to do Spielberg, or do you want me to try to find the women?"

"Do Spielberg, then I'll pick you up tonight. Stay hidden until I come for you."

"Will do. Sorry for losing them."

"Spielberg did that for us. I'll call you when I'm there," Bruce said and ended the call.

After getting dressed, he quickly packed a light bag. He'd just finished when Henry knocked on the door.

Henry came in and said, "I had the cook whip something up so you can eat before you go."

Bruce smiled, then said, "Thanks, man. I'm suddenly really hungry."

"When you're ready, come down and eat."

"I've nearly finished here. I'll bring my luggage down to set it near the door before going to eat."

"Fine, I'll leave you to it."

By the time he had finished breakfast, his driver had arrived. Not long after that, they were on their way to New York.

◀ • ▶

Nathan White feared he'd brought the wrath of Bruce Murdock down on his own head. When Bruce blamed Spielberg for everything, he relaxed. He found a budget motel room and slept for a few hours. When he woke, he had some breakfast and went to see what was happening with Spielberg.

When he got to the jail, Spielberg was being released. Nate met him outside. "I thought you'd appreciate seeing a friendly face."

"Yeah, I do." After getting into Nathan's car he asked, "Would you mind taking me someplace to eat. I'm starving."

"Sure." *This will be your last meal on earth, old man, you'd best enjoy it.*

After they ate, they got into Nathan car and headed out of town.

"Where are you going?" Spielberg asked suspiciously.

"I thought we'd drive around to see if we can find any sign of your family."

"Oh, that's a good idea," Spielberg said and visibly relaxed.

They rode around town for a while, then suddenly White turned down a road, headed in the opposite direction of the interstate. At Spielberg's questioning look, White replied, "I want to see if they came this way to try to throw us off." Spielberg seemed unconcerned after hearing this.

When they were a good distance out of town, White stopped the car. Getting out, he pretended to look around. Spielberg, growing curious, got out of the car to see what he was looking at.

When he walked up, Nate turned to face him and pointed a gun at his head.

"What do you think you're doing?" asked Spielberg.

"I've been hired to take you out."

"What?" Spielberg was dumbfounded. "If you do me, you'll start a blood bath the likes of which you've never seen."

"We'll just have to take that chance. At least you won't be around to botch anything else up."

"Who hired you? I have the right to know who ordered my death."

White stood there pondering the question. "If you must know, it was your son-in-law. Did you realize he hated you that much?"

"Bruce?"

"Yup!" Before Spielberg could reply, White shot him in the head, then in the heart after he was down. Satisfied he was dead, Nate pocketed the gun, went back to his car, turned around and drove back to town.

I'm glad I didn't check out of that motel; I can go get cleaned up. When he was finished with his shower, he put on clean clothes and stuffed the bloody clothes into a shopping bag, which he took out to the dumpster behind the café where he'd taken Spielberg for breakfast. After that, he went back to the motel to nap and kill some time before Murdock arrived.

◀ • ▶

Tom Wilson and Vincent Crowley met Murdock in New York.

"Let's get out of here and go find somewhere we can talk in private," Murdock said to the two men.

"We have a hotel room a few blocks away. We can talk there without being overheard," said Crowley.

"Good, let's go."

No one spoke until they were settled in the hotel room. Bruce regarded his men. Vincent, or Vinnie as his friends called him, was hard to the core, which made him a top hit man and bodyguard. Vincent's favorite sport was breaking all of his victim's fingers before he broke their necks. He was a good-looking Italian who was a big hit with the women, even though he was gay. Murdock ignored what he perceived as a flaw because Vinnie was good at his job.

When he turned his attention to Tom, he saw another huge, muscled man who was as ugly as Vincent was handsome. His close set eyes made him look like he wasn't all there most of the time, but those who knew him knew different. He was always neatly dressed, like he was trying to compensate for his lack of looks. Tom was also good at his job, though not quite as sadistic as Vinnie.

Tom made drinks for everyone except Paul, who excused himself and went outside to sit in the car.

"That's a good idea, Paul," said Murdock, "We may need to leave in a hurry." Lighting a cigarette, Murdock took a few drags and finished his drink before speaking again. "From now on, I want one of you with me at all times. I had Nathan White take out Spielberg this evening."

"Glad that's done," said Vincent in a matter of fact way.

"It was about time someone took him out," agreed Wilson. "He was an old softy. It took him ages to make a decision, too."

"Well," replied Murdock, "we're facing an even bigger problem now. Spielberg had a lot of faithful followers, and his death won't be taken lightly."

"That's a fact," agreed Vincent. "What do you think will happen, boss?"

"They'll know it was me when I announce I'm claiming leadership." Taking a few more thoughtful drags on his cigarette, he added. "There's going to be some retaliation … maybe even a war between our side and those loyal to Spielberg. What we have to do is strike first."

"There were a lot of men under Spielberg, boss. Do we have enough support to deal with them?"

"Not quite, but what we don't have in numbers we'll make up for in the surprise attack."

Both men digested this information, then Tom said, "I've never run from a fight. You can count me in."

"Thanks, Wilson. I knew I could count on you."

Vincent sat mulling things over, then looked up and grinned as he cracked his knuckles. "Bring on the fight, 'cause I'm a aching to crunch me some bones!" He cracked his knuckles again in readiness.

Murdock grinned. "Cool your jets, Vinnie. We aren't ready to crunch bones just yet. We still have a little time before we spring our surprise."

"How long do you think we got?" asked Tom.

"The way I see it, they won't know about Spielberg's death for a while. The police have to investigate it, and it will take a while before they release the information to the next of kin. Since his wife, my wife, and my daughter have disappeared, it will take a little longer than usual."

"But Boss, when Spielberg doesn't get in touch with one of his king pins, won't they get kind of suspicious?" asked Tom

Murdock thought that over, then nodded. "Yeah, they will. They know he went to Ohio to find his wife and daughter. They'll be suspicious. We'll make our move in a few days. They won't have enough time to do anything. First, I have to finish setting things into action."

"We'll sit back to wait for the signal to charge," said Vincent.

"Since most of Spielberg's men are here in New York I need the two of you close to me at all times," Murdock reiterated.

"We'll be there, boss," promised Wilson. "We don't want to be any other place than by your side."

"I appreciate that." Rising, he crushed out his cigarette. "I have to meet with some men here, then we'll decide on the best time for our little surprise."

The other two men stood, ready to accompany him. "We're ready when you are," declared Vincent.

"Let's get to it."

Several hours later, Murdock's men were ready to attack when he gave the signal. "We'll go in three days," stated Murdock. "We'll start out knocking them off one at a time. When we've thinned them out a little, we'll invite the rest to a big party. When they show up, we'll treat them to a little fire works, if you get my meaning."

Smiling, the men nodded. "We've got it," declared a huge muscular man.

"Then let's start thinning them out."

For the next two days, the police were busy trying to keep up with the murders all over the city. They knew they were mob related, but couldn't prove it.

Soon the numbers had been thinned, and many of Spielberg's men received invitations to the "party." The night of the big event, Murdock had everything in place for the fireworks. He hid in the kitchen with his two bodyguards, waiting for things to come together.

People started arriving, dressed in their finest. Some had dates with them, while others had brought their wives. When everyone was there, the waiters started serving. When the main course was nearly finished, the waiters delivered the dessert. People had only taken a few bites when Murdock's men opened up with their machine guns.

The restaurant's staff had fled prior to the shoot out and the guests dropped like flies. When the guns quieted, no one was left. The shooters walked around the room, finishing off anyone who was still alive. When it was all over, one hundred people lay dead.

The shooters gave Murdock the signal, and he and his men left. Murdock was secure in his takeover. His shooters came to his hotel after cleaning up and they all headed back to Syracuse. He told them, "We'll lay low for a while, and then I'll announce I'm in charge. When we get to Syracuse, I'll go back to work like nothing happened. I want the two of you to do another job for me," he said to his loyal bodyguards. "I'll fill you in when we get home."

They got back late the next morning. After a few hours of rest, Wilson and Crowley returned to Murdock's to find out what he wanted them to do. He took them to his office and said, "My wife, daughter and mother-in-law have skipped out. I want you to put feelers out and see if you can find them. We know they got as far as a small town in Ohio. Wilson, I want you to go there and see if you can find any leads. Stay on it until you find them. I want you to search southern Pennsylvania and Ohio first. When you find them, I want you to kill my wife and mother-in-law. Bring Leslie back here to me so I can show her what happens to people who cross me. When I'm done with her, she's going to marry Jethro Borden."

"When do you want me to leave?" asked Wilson.

"Tomorrow morning."

"If I can't find them in Pennsylvania or Ohio, where do you want me to go from there?"

"If you don't find them, then call me. I expect you to report in every day."

"Yes, boss."

"Crowley, I need you to stick to me like glue. With what went down in New York, we can't take any chances until I've declared my plans."

"You got it, boss."

"Starting tomorrow, I'm going to go back to work like nothing's going on. You keep your eyes peeled for anything out of the ordinary, do you hear me?"

"I hear you, sir."

"Good. Tom, get ready to leave in the morning. I expect a call when you get on the road."

"I'll call you first thing."

When the men left, Murdock sat back in his chair to have another cigarette. His maid, Hazel Lockwood would be returning in the morning, which was good. He didn't like going to restaurants — it was now too dangerous. *I'll have to be extra careful for the next few weeks.*

Chapter 5

Meagan "Leslie Murdock" Webb watched the falling snow with mixed feelings. Part of her was relieved because snow meant she was safe from her father, at least until spring. The other part of her knew they would be snowbound until then with no hope of going anywhere. Sighing, she resigned herself to the inevitable boredom and went to do something constructive.

Shirleen, alias Sarah Spielberg, knew just how her granddaughter felt. She loved to socialize, and she was a snow prisoner stuck in a foreign place.

Shirleen smiled when she thought of how happy her daughter Juliana was at the moment. She was tucked away in the extra bedroom they'd converted to an art studio. She loved to paint and probably wouldn't mind being snowbound for the winter.

Shirleen thought back on the many trips they'd made to town as they stocked up for the long winter months. *As least we decided to buy some things to keep us busy.*

Besides Juliana's painting supplies, they'd bought several charcoal sketchpads, Charcoal pencils, and a special spray to set them for Megan. Shirleen was impressed with Megan's talent. Shirleen loved to do all types of needlework, embroidery, crocheting, needlepoint, knitting, as well as tatting, so she got several skeins of yarn, embroidery thread, spools of crochet thread, needlepoint kits and many patterns and pre-stamped dresser scarves, pillowcases and pre-stamped blocks of the United States with the state birds and flowers.

Shirleen put aside the dresser scarf she was embroidering and got up to stoke the fire in the fireplace in the living room. She repeated the process in all of the bedrooms. When she was finished, it was 3:30 in the afternoon; time for tea.

She went to the kitchen and made tea for her and Juliana, and a cup of hot chocolate for Meagan. She also added a plate of some of the cookies she'd made the day before and set everything on a tray. She took it to the living room and put it on a table near the fire. Meagan, who was reading her history book because Juliana told her she would have a test for her in the morning, looked up to see what her grandmother was doing.

"Put your book down, dear. It's time for afternoon tea."

Slamming the book shut, Meagan tossed it to the side and went to get her mother. "It's time for tea, Momma. I don't know about you, but I'm famished."

Laughing, Juliana put her brush into a little jar of turpentine and went to wash her hands. Joining them she took the cup of tea her mother handed her, along with a couple of cookies on a napkin "It must be all this cold and show, lately I'm always hungry."

"Me too," replied Shirleen.

"Same here," giggled Meagan. "I can't seem to get full."

Juliana looked at her daughter intently before replying, "Whatever it is, it agrees with you. You look better than I've ever seen you look. There are roses in your cheeks, a glow in your eyes, along with a spring to your step."

Meagan smiled as she replied, "Thank you for the compliment, Momma. I've noticed the two of you have that same rosy glow."

"Flattery will get you everywhere," teased Shirleen.

"No, Grandma, it's true. Do you think we're like this because we finally got away from the evil men in our lives?"

Shirleen thought about that question for a while before saying, "I don't know. Maybe. I know I feel at peace here. I don't have to keep looking over my shoulder all the time."

Juliana set her empty teacup down, wiped her mouth with her napkin and said, "That's exactly how I've been feeling."

"Whatever it is," added Shirleen, "I like it. I like it a lot!"

Suddenly there was a knock at the door. Everyone froze in place. Shirleen finally got up the courage to go see who it was. She opened the door cautiously, and was surprised to see a Mounty standing there.

Shirleen's heart nearly failed her when she saw the handsome young man. He looked like he was just a little older than her Juliana. Shirleen couldn't help thinking he had the most beautiful blue eyes she'd ever seen, and his cheekbones seemed to have been chiseled out of stone. When he reached up to remove his hat, a mass of curly dark hair completed his good looks. As Shirleen looked at him, she thought, *He's got to be the most handsome man I've ever seen.*

Suddenly, Shirleen realized she'd been staring. Feeling her face turn red, she said, "Excuse me for staring, but I've never seen a Royal Mounted Policeman before."

"That is quite all right, ma'am. At least I didn't get attacked by a dog before I had the chance to state my business." Bowing slightly he added, "I'm Sergeant Timothy York. My full name is Timothy Titus Obadiah York." When he saw her stifle a smile, he grinned, "You don't have to hold back your laugh; I get that reaction every time I tell it.

Shirleen grinned in spite of herself. "I must admit to being a little surprised to hear that combination of names all attached to one person. That must've been a challenge for you growing up."

"That's not the half of it, ma'am. Tortured would be more accurate."

Moving aside to let him enter, she said, "Won't you please come in?"

"Thank you ma'am, I'd appreciate a chance to get warm."

As he entered, Shirleen saw his team of dogs. "No wonder I didn't hear a car drive up, you have a sled."

"I have a vehicle that's four wheel drive, and I use it a lot. However, during the winter months I like to use the sled. When I use the dogsled, I don't have to worry about being stuck in the snow."

"Smart thinking."

Meagan came up to see what was going on, and did a double take when she saw the handsome man standing in her house. Seeing the team of dogs, she asked, "Are your dogs friendly?"

"Yes, but they've been trained to attack a man if he is resisting arrest. If I tell them to mind their business, they stay calm."

Looking from the dogs then back to the officer, she asked, "Do you think I could pet them?"

"I don't see why not. Let me introduce you first."

They went outside and walked up to the dogs. He gave them a command, and they immediately relaxed. Turning back to Meagan he said, "Never reach for a dog, let the dog smell your hand first. Then slowly reach out to stroke them."

Meagan walked up to the dogs, who eyed her warily, but didn't move. She went up to the lead dog and let it sniff her hand. Suddenly it licked her fingers and Meagan giggled, then slowly reached out to stroke the dog's fur. "Oh," she cried, "their fur is so soft."

"Is this the first time you have ever petted a dog?"

"Yes, sir. I just never had a chance before."

"Well, love away, but be prepared to be mauled by the whole group." He had no more than said the words out when the entire team tried to get to her for their share of attention. Laughing, Meagan began petting them all. Tim stayed close, just in case.

Finally, Meagan stood and headed back to the house. "Thank you for letting me pet them. That was wonderful."

"You're more than welcome, Miss.

When they were all back in the house, Shirleen, pointed to a chair and said, "Please have a seat here by the fire. I'll get you a fresh cup of tea and some cookies."

Sinking gratefully into the chair, he sighed in contentment. "This is the first time I've had a chance to sit down all day. It feels really good." Holding his hands out to the fire, he fell silent.

Shirleen soon returned with an extra cup, as well as another plate filled with cookies. Taking a sip of tea he took a bite of a cookie then moaned in delight. "Wow! These are the best cookies I've ever tasted!"

"They're Grandmas secret recipe," proclaimed Meagan proudly.

"Too bad you won't share it. I'd love to make these."

Meagan looked at him in surprise as she exclaimed, "You can bake?"

"Sure." Seeing her look of amazement, he added, "Don't look so surprised. I came from a large family. I'm the second of eighteen children."

"No way!" Meagan said, surprised.

"Yes way. I have nine brothers and eight sisters. My mother thought us boys should know how to cook, wash and iron our clothes, as well as keep a clean house. The girls were taught how to milk a cow, slop the hogs, feed the chickens and a bunch of other outdoor tasks." He grinned, as he added, "They even had to chop the wood, then bring it in for the fireplaces. As Mother use to say, 'Knowing how to do every task will make things easier for you when you go out into the world. You won't have to depend on anyone for help.' She was a real stickler about that."

"Well," said Shirleen, "We all grew up being pampered. I had to go to culinary school to learn to cook. I was sent off to a boarding school for my education. We learned to care for a house there."

"I had a mother who taught me everything," Juliana said, beaming at her mother.

Shirleen looked disgusted with herself. "Oh good grief, this is the second time I've forgotten my manners. Please let me introduce my everyone. I'm Shirleen Webb, and this is my daughter, Juliana Webb, and my granddaughter, Meagan Webb."

Nodding, Tim replied, "Pleased to make your acquaintance." Setting his empty cup on the end table he turned to address them. "I learned you ladies bought this place a while back, so decided to come and meet you. Feel free to call on me whenever you need help."

"Well, as a matter of fact," said Shirleen, "we do need help. We need someone to cut wood for our fireplaces. The wood's nearly gone. We need to buy quite a bit more to get us through the winter. We also need a carpenter who can build a shelter over our motor home."

"As far as the wood goes, Jason Stewart has wood for sale out at his place. I'll see if he has any left." He paused to ponder her next problem then brightened. "Jeff Borton, a neighbor down the road, is an excellent carpenter. Jeff is as honest as the day is long. He'll treat you right. Want me to talk to him for you?"

"We don't want to take him away from doing for his family," Shirleen said with concern.

"Mr. Borton is a widower. His wife died of a heart attack about a year ago. He's been like a lost sheep. This would give him something to do."

"We can pay him; that's not a problem. We just need to know what he'll charge so we can pay him fairly."

"I know you will. The three of you seem like honest ladies."

"We want to be," declared Juliana.

"Well," replied Tim, "I'll get on it today. As soon as I have the answers, I'll let you know."

"Thank you, Sergeant."

"You're welcome." Looking longingly at the last cookie on the plate, he asked, "Do you mind if I take this last cookie? They're so incredibly delicious."

"Please, help yourself. While you're getting ready to go, I sack up a few more for you. When you come to give us the information you promised, I'll share the recipe with you. However, you must promise never to give it to anyone else."

"Scout's honor, ma'am."

"Then we'll see you again soon."

"You bet." Stuffing the rest of the cookie in his mouth he put on his heavy gloves. Tucking his hat under his arm, he prepared to leave.

Shirleen, who had disappeared into the kitchen, returned with a sack filled with cookies. "Here you go. These should last until you come again."

"Bless you, Mrs. Webb," replied Tim, reaching for the sack. Nodding slightly, he walked over to the door. "I'll be back, either tomorrow or the next day with the information."

They all watched from the window as he stepped onto the runners on the back of the sled then cracked the whip over the dog's heads. With a jerk, they were off.

Meagan went back to reading her history book and her mother went back to paint. After an hour, Shirleen put her work in her lap and stared into the fire. She didn't move until Meagan asked, "Grandma, are you all right?"

"What?" Shirleen came back to reality with a start. "Yes, I'm fine.."

Meagan smiled in relief. "I watched you for quite a while. You never even blinked — you just stared straight ahead."

"I'm sorry I worried you, sweetheart. To tell you the truth, I don't even know what I was thinking about. Now, that's sad isn't it?"

"No, it isn't. I find myself mesmerized by the flickering fire whenever I gaze into the fireplace. I don't even know what I'm thinking either."

"Thank you for making me feel better, dear."

Meagan smiled. "You're welcome, Grandma." She went back to reading her history book.

Looking at the clock over the mantle, Shirleen saw it was time to make dinner, so she put her project away and went to see what Juliana was working on before she got busy cooking. "Is it all right to see what you are doing, dear?"

"Sure. I'm just about done for the day," she said as she started cleaning her brushes.

Shirleen was speechless as she stared at the exact replica of Meagan. Finally finding her voice, she said, "Oh, this is wonderful. It's like looking at a carbon copy. You've captured every aspect."

"Thank you, Momma," replied Juliana, laying her brushes back on the table. "I have a few little finishing touches to do, and then it will be finished."

"Well, I can't wait until you show it to Meagan."

"I want to keep this hidden until Christmas. I have some other paintings I want to get done before then, too.

"That's only a month and a half away." Shirleen sighed. "We need to go to town for some Christmas decorations next week. While we're there, I plan to do some serious Christmas shopping.

"I'm so glad you insisted on getting that van with four wheel drive. We'll need it when we go anywhere this winter." Grinning she added, "If I know my mother, she'll get carried away and have that poor van filled 'til it groans getting up our steep mountain."

Pretending to grow stern, Shirleen snapped, "That'll be just about enough out of you, young lady. Why the very thought of such a thing. Would I do something like that?"

"Yes, my wonderful mother, you would."

Shrugging her shoulders nonchalantly Shirleen responded, "Well, it's fun to shop for those you love."

"I know," giggled Juliana. "I'm just as bad. Christmas has always been my favorite time of year. I think this year is my favorite because I'm free and. I get to share it with my two favorite people. So, let me tell you, mother mine, I plan to have the time of my life!"

Hugging her, Shirleen replied. "Me, too!" Suddenly she grew excited. "Why don't we plan out what we're going to do in town?"

"I think that would be fun. We can even decide our Christmas dinner menu, and if we want to get a real tree or a fake one, plus get all the ornaments and then shop 'til we drop."

"That sounds like a plan! I'll get supper started while you finish up here. Meagan is working hard on her schoolwork. She told me the other day it was more enjoyable doing her learning at home, because she has two good teachers."

"I've been a little surprised to see how hard she's studying. She had a hard time at school but she seems to be excelling here."

"With a father and grandfather like hers, is it any wonder she was having trouble at school?"

Juliana shook her head no. She hesitated a moment then added, "You know, Momma, I can't help but wish things were different. I wish Bruce and Gordon had never been born. They've been nothing but a headache since they were young boys."

"I've often thought that very thing, sweetheart. We were so blessed to get out of there when we did. I have a feeling things would've only gotten worse instead of better."

"I didn't want to alarm you, but I have had the same feeling. Something tells me neither one of us would've been alive much longer.

"I think you're right." Moving toward the door, Shirleen replied, "This isn't getting supper on the table, is it?"

"I'll hurry to clean this mess up, and then come in to help you."

"Thanks."

A couple of hours later, supper was over and everything was cleaned up. They settled down and made plans for their shopping trip.

Around midnight, Shirleen woke with a start. She lay there for a moment before she heard a blood-curdling scream of terror. Fearing it was Meagan, she rushed toward her room, but she met her in the hall. "What is wrong, Grandma?"

"I heard you scream, so came to find out what was wrong. Just then there was another scream. Suddenly, Juliana came tearing out of the bedroom, headed toward Meagan's room. Seeing the others standing there looking perplexed, she stopped.

All at once they heard a loud thud just outside. Shirleen plucked up her courage and went for a flashlight, then went to wood box by the fireplace and picked up a good-sized piece of wood. Cautiously she walked over to check the front door. Satisfied it was still locked, she went to check the garage.

Slowly opening the kitchen door, with the wood held high, she flashed the light around the area. She went down the steps, with the wood raised high, then walked around the car and looked inside. Nothing was amiss here, so she checked to see that the side door was locked. Flashing the light over to the large garage door, she could see the lock they had attached to it was still in place.

She went back into the house and switched the light off. She guardedly moved over to peer out the crack of the drapes covering the front window. Though she looked hard, she couldn't see anything outside because the snow was falling so hard she couldn't see far.

She could hear something, or someone walking around in the snow. The crunch of the snow under their feet wasn't loud. Fear they'd been found coursed through Shirleen's body. *Oh, why don't they just break the door down already?* she wondered.

The silence was heavy. The only sounds in the house were the ticking of the clock over the mantle and the snapping of the wood in the fireplace. Shirleen jumped when she heard another loud thud. Shirleen waited with baited breath for she knew not what, but nothing happened. She was about to move from the window when she heard something being dragged across the yard.

The minutes ticked away as she tried to see who was out there. Several more minutes passed without another sound, so she figured whatever was out there had gone. She put the wood back into the wood box and went to join the others, telling them, "The snow's coming down so hard that I can't see anything. I'm going to check the door in the kitchen to make sure it's locked, and then I'm going back to bed."

The front door was securely locked, so Shirleen rejoined her frightened family. Sighing, she replied, "Since we can't do anything tonight, let's all go back to bed and get some rest."

◄ • ►

The following morning the snow was still falling. Shirleen gazed out the kitchen window as she did the breakfast dishes. She knew the snow had erased any tracks that had been there.

Juliana was giving Meagan a test in history, so after the dishes were done, Shirleen checked to see how much bread they had left. When she did, she noticed they were almost out of cookies, so she decided to make another batch.

As she got out the tools to do the job, she wished she could just go to her recipe box. Unfortunately, that was back in Syracuse. Having picked up some recipe books in town, so she took one down and found recipe that sounded good.

Baking not only eased her mind, it was also something different to do. When the cookies were all baked, she still didn't want to work on her embroidery project, so she consulted the cookbook for something else fun to make. She decided on a chocolate pie and two cherry pies.

When the pies were done and the kitchen straightened up, Shirleen went to the woodshed out back to bring in an armload of wood. She was so thankful to find the snow had finally stopped. Putting the wood in the wood box, she went out for another load. When that job had been completed, she put a roast into the crockpot for supper.

By the time she was finished, it was her turn to tutor Meagan. Juliana had given her assignments in math, geometry and algebra. These were easy subjects for Juliana. She never got to peruse her desired goal of becoming a teacher because of Gordon and Bruce. Shirleen smiled, knowing Juliana was happiest when she was teaching her daughter the two subjects she loved.

Shirleen's forte was English, with some literature. Teaching Meagan was a joy, because she always tried so hard to excel at what she did. Shirleen also taught Meagan spelling and reading appreciation. The rest of their morning was taken up with these three subjects.

As they finished their tutoring session, Megan asked her mother why she hadn't taken some online college courses and realize her dream of becoming a teacher. She noted they'd have to get a computer for that to happen and let the subject drop.

That evening, Shirleen looked longingly at the piano. "I'm so glad the two of you talked me into buying this," confessed Shirleen. "Playing is a great way for me to relax." She entertained them with show tunes, Bach, Beethoven and a few other classical pieces before going to bed, and the others soon followed her. They'd all been going to bed early since the weather had turned cold.

Early the next morning, they heard a car coming up the road and froze. Theirs was the last house for miles. Would it be Tim, the friendly Mountie, or had someone found them? Juliana went to see who it was, and was relieved to see Tim step out of the driver's side of the truck. When an older gentleman got out of the passenger side, she almost panicked, but kept her cool.

When Tim saw Juliana, he smiled and said, "Hi, Juliana This is Mr. Borton. I thought I'd introduce you all." Hearing the name, Juliana relaxed visibly.

"Won't you please come on in out of this awful cold?" Juliana asked.

Once they were inside, Juliana closed the door and joined her family on the couch. Tim made the introductions, "Jeff this beautiful lady is Shirleen Webb. Next to her is her granddaughter, Meagan. And last, but not least, is the gorgeous Juliana."

"Pleased ta meet ya," Jeff said and grinned.

Shirleen took time to study him. He was a short, thin man with balding gray hair. He was wearing a sloppy pair of blue jeans and a thick green coat. Heavy boots completed his attire. Shirleen noticed he had huge beefsteak hands, scared from hard work. Jeff was still handsome, even though it was evident he was no longer a young man. She suddenly noticed that his soft, gentle blue eyes studied her, too.

"Why don't you tell him what you want him to do, and then we can talk about the wood?"

Shirleen told him they wanted a shelter for their motor home. "Let me walk outside to take a look so I can tell you what supplies I'll need and estimate a cost."

"I'll show you where it's parked, Mr. Borton," offered Juliana. "Just give me a minute to put on my coat and boots." Without giving him a chance to answer, she hurried off to get ready. Soon she returned. "I'm ready, sir."

"Oh, call me Jeff. This sir business is for the military."

Juliana grinned. "Okay, Jeff it is." When they were outside, Shirleen filled Tim in on the scary events of the night before. She ended with, "Of course, the snow covered up any tracks there might have been."

"Someone screamed like they were in mortal danger?"

"Yes, it was horrible," replied Shirleen.

"I don't think you need to worry. It was a cougar. When they yell, it sounds like a woman screaming. Do you have a rifle?"

"No."

"Well, the next time you go to town, you should get one along with plenty of ammunition." At Shirleen look of disgust he added. "You need protection from the cougars during the winter and hungry bears in the summer   they raid the trashcans every chance they get. They can be real pests."

"Oh, dear. Maybe moving here wasn't such a great idea," Shirleen said with a worried look.

"Nonsense! You just have to learn to shoot accurately and most of the time you're not trying to shoot the animal, you're just trying to scare them away." When Shirleen looked dubious, he continued. "I'll tell you what, you buy the rifle and I'll teach you how to use it."

"I'll definitely need lessons." She hesitated a moment before adding, "I've always hated guns."

"Using weapons for the wrong reasons is bad, but to protect oneself, or one's family — that's completely different."

"I suppose you're right. I'll just consider it a necessary evil needed to protect my family."

"When will you be going back to town?"

"Thursday. Why?"

"I'll meet you in town and help you pick out the best rifle and ammunition."

"Oh, that would be great," Shirleen said in relief. "Thank you so much."

"No problem." He was prevented from saying more when Juliana and Jeff came back inside.

"It won't be a problem building what you want for your motorhome. I have to go to town tomorrow, so I'll get the lumber and supplies and bring them over in the afternoon."

"How much will it be?" asked Shirleen.

"I don't know what the supplies will cost, but don't worry about it yet — I have enough to pay for everything. I'll bring you the invoice and you can pay me back then."

"That sounds like a plan."

"I talked to Jason Stewart yesterday," said Tim. "He still has about six cords of wood left, which should be enough to see you through the winter. He charges $100 a cord."

"Do I pay you or him?" asked Shirleen.

"He said you could pay him when he delivers it. He also said he'd be here before nine o'clock on the day he delivers it, but he needs to know where to put it."

"Have him put it a little ways from the woodshed," Jeff said. "I'll cut it up then stack it inside."

"If I pay you sixteen dollars and hour, will that work?"

"That's too generous. Twelve is fine."

"If I agree, then you have to eat your meals with us when you're working here."

Beaming, Jeff said, "That would be great. I miss my wife's cooking."

Laughing, Shirleen replied, "Better save you compliments until after you've tasted the food."

"If her cookies are any indication," bragged Tim, "you're in for a real treat."

Shirleen went over some other things with Jeff before he left, including snow removal.

"I have two snow blowers, so I'll bring the extra one here so I won't have to drag it back and forth."

"I could buy one," volunteered Shirleen.

"Mine will just sit in the shed, might as well bring it here so it gets used."

They finished their negotiations and Jeff said, "I'll be here with the supplies as soon as I can tomorrow afternoon. I'll start work on the construction at eight o'clock the following morning. This job should take about two or three days and then I'll start on all the other things you need done."

They rose to leave then Tim turned his attention to Meagan. "Miss Meagan, you'll be happy to know my dog, Molly, gave birth to nine healthy pups about three weeks ago. The father is pure Collie, and the mother is pure Husky. They should be some beautiful dogs. Would you be interested in one or two of them?"

"I'd love to have two of them, but I don't know if I can."

Shirleen thought about it for a moment then asked Juliana, "What do you think about having a couple of dogs?"

"I don't know. I'll have to think about it."

"They'll be weaned in five weeks, so you have time to think it over," said Tim.

"Good. I'll probably take that long," replied Shirleen.

"Meagan, I'll let you know when they're weaned. I guess we'll both see you tomorrow."

A while later, Shirleen played the piano again and this time Meagan sang along. When the last note faded away, Shirleen looked at her in surprise. "I had no idea you could sing that well, Meagan.

"I never let anyone hear me after the day Daddy caught me singing."

"You never told me about that," chided Juliana.

"I was singing "Danny Boy," and he stormed in, turned off the radio and yelled. 'Stop that caterwauling! You sound like a sick dog.'"

"Oh, blast that man," snapped Juliana angrily, "there's not one redeeming quality about him!"

Going through the sheet music she'd just bought, Shirleen found "Danny Boy" and asked Meagan to sing as she played it. Their rendition was so beautiful that they just sat there long after the last note died away.

Scooping Meagan close, Shirleen exclaimed, "Your voice is so sweet and pure; it sounds like you've taken voice lessons."

Meagan was rendered speechless.

Chapter 6

Shirleen woke with a start from a nightmare. Turning to look at the clock on her nightstand, she saw it was nearly 2 a.m. She tried to will herself back to sleep, but it was impossible. She got up and went to the bathroom to wash her face, then went to the kitchen to get a glass of water.

She sat down at the kitchen table and remembered thinking having well water wasn't a good thing, but their water was sweeter and purer than what she'd had in the city. There was a well house several feet away from the house, which housed the pump that brought the water. Feeling better, she went back to bed.

She'd just burrowed under the covers when she heard the snowplow go past. A few minutes later she heard its return. Not long after , she fell asleep. An hour later she sat upright in bed, awakened by yet another nightmare. *This is the third night I've had the same dream over and over. Why?* she wondered.

Laying back down, she replayed the scenes from the dream, but couldn't figure out why she was dreaming like this. Looking at the clock, she was frustrated to see she'd only been asleep for an hour. Turning onto her right side, she tried to think of something else, but it just didn't work.

Finally, she got out of bed and knelt in prayer. She asked the Lord to help her understand the dream. She also prayed for protection for her family and prayed she wouldn't have the dream again that night. Then, she got back into bed and fell asleep.

Just before daylight, she sat bolt upright, her heart pounding. This time, it was the same dream but there was more to it. Giving up hope of sleeping more, she went to take a shower. By the time she was dressed, dawn was breaking. The snow had stopped sometime in the night, which made her feel relieved.

Poking the hot coals, she added a couple of logs to the fire and then gathered her needlework and went over to sit by the fireplace. She didn't want to sit near the window because it made her feel vulnerable. She worked to finish the scarf she was working on. She was tying off the last stitch when she heard a vehicle drive up the road and stop.

Every time this happened, fear gripped her, making her weak in the knees. This time was no different. There was just enough daylight to see, and as she peeked out the window she saw a man removing something from the back of the truck. She couldn't see what it was because of her position. He walked in front of the truck and she could see he was wearing red pants. "It can't be Sergeant York," she whispered.

She watched the man turn off the truck's lights and then go back to whatever it was he'd taken out of the truck. As he jerked on a rope, Shirleen heard a strange sound. She thought it sounded like the snow blower they had in Syracuse. Continuing to watch, she saw him inch forward.

As he got closer, she was relieved to see it was Sergeant York.. He was clearing their driveway. *I thought Jeff Borton was going to do that.* She decided to see what was going on and opened the door.

Tim saw her and said, "I told Jeff I'd clear everything so he could get the truckload of lumber backed in without a problem."

Shirleen smiled in relief. "I see. I wondered what was going on."

"I'm also doing this so Jason Stewart can deliver your wood."

"Thank you. As deep as the show was, it probably would've been a problem."

"It sure would have."

When he started to go back to work, Shirleen stopped him by calling out, "Sergeant York? I have something else I'd like to talk to you about before Meagan gets up. Do you have a minute?"

"Sure. What's on your mind?"

After looking back into the house to make sure they were alone, she said, "It's about your puppies. Will they be weaned by Christmas?"

"Yes, about a week before. Why?"

"Would you mind picking out a male and a female for us? You'll know which will be best better than we will."

"Sure. When do you want me to bring them to you?"

"Would Christmas morning be all right?"

"Oh," he said and smiled. "They're Christmas presents."

"I think they'll be the perfect presents for Megan."

"I'll be sure to be here early enough so you can put them under the tree."

"One more thing?"

"Yes?" He watched her suspiciously.

"You'll think this is pretty dumb, but neither Juliana nor I have ever had a dog. We don't have a clue about what to feed them or how to train them. Could you give us some help with that?"

"Is that all?" Relieved he readily agreed to help. "My sister, Diane, is not only a veterinarian, but she's also a reputable dog trainer. I'll bring her by the day after Christmas and you can all learn together."

"Oh, that would be great. I feel silly for not knowing, though."

"Nonsense, if you haven't had a dog before there's no way you'd know what to do."

"Thank you so much. I'll let you get back to work."

"I'll get out of your hair as soon as I'm done. Have a good day, Mrs. Webb."

"Thank you, Sergeant. You, too."

She started to go back into the house, but he said, "Mrs. Webb, could you please call me Tim? There's no need to be so formal."

"Only if you'll call me Shirleen."

Removing a glove, he extended his hand to shake hers. As they clasped hands, he said, "It's a deal!" and went back to work.

A few minutes later Juliana and Meagan were awakened by the commotion.

"What's all the noise, Grandma," asked Meagan sleepily.

"Tim is clearing the snow with a snow blower."

"Good. I was beginning to think we were going to be living in an igloo before long."

Shirleen chuckled then replied, "I was beginning to think the same thing."

Juliana, who had been watching her mother suspiciously, asked, "Momma, are you feeling all right?"

"I just didn't sleep very well."

"Why not?" Juliana watched her mother anxiously.

Sighing, Shirleen replied, "For the past several nights I've been having the same nightmare and it keeps waking me up."

"Nightmare?" interrupted Juliana.

"Yes. I keep dreaming about Gordon. First, I see him murdered. I can't see the murderer's face, but I feel like I know him. Suddenly, Gordon is standing in front of me. He tells me he's sorry for all he put me through."

"I'd say it's a little too late for that," snapped Juliana.

Shirleen didn't respond, but continued with the dream. "Then, he tells me Bruce was the one who killed him."

"Daddy?" cried Meagan in fear.

"Yes," continued Shirleen. "Gordon says Bruce is more wicked than he ever was." Growing week in the knees, Shirleen took a seat at the kitchen table. "After telling me this, he goes on to say Bruce has two men looking for us. After apologizing again, he tells me to watch my back because it is only a matter of time before they find us."

"Oh no," cried Meagan jumping to her feet. "Just when I felt like we were finally safe."

Juliana wrapped her arms around her distraught daughter in an attempt to comfort her. "Don't worry, sweetheart. Grandma is just telling us about her nightmare. It could be just that … a nightmare."

Seeing the horror on her granddaughter's face, Shirleen added, "I think it's just that, Meagan. Gordon would never apologize to me, let alone warn me. I think it's just wishful thinking on my part."

"I sure hope so," Meagan said, still not convinced. "My dream turned out to be true, maybe this one is, too."

"Maybe," responded Shirleen, "but I don't think we should dwell on this. If we did , we'd never be able to really live our lives. We'd be ruled by fear."

"Momma's right, honey. We just have to take things one day at a time. Even if they figure out where we are, they'd have to wait until spring to do anything about it. We still have time to get away if we have to."

These words seemed to comfort Meagan, who sat back down and said, "I sure hope you're right."

Shirleen patted Meagan's hand to comfort her. "Let's not borrow trouble. Would you please set the table while I make breakfast? Set an extra place for Tim because he needs to eat after working so hard."

"Okay," Meagan said quietly.

"When it's ready, I'll go let him know to come in to eat," volunteered Juliana. Shirleen nodded as she continued to cook.

Before long, breakfast was ready, so Juliana donned her coat and went to get the sergeant. When they entered, Tim sniffed the air appreciatively. "It smells wonderful in here."

"It's almost ready."

Tossing his heavy coat over the edge of the couch, he asked, "Where can I wash up?"

"I'll show you," declared Meagan, leading him to the bathroom.

When Tim entered the kitchen, Meagan showed him where to sit. "You can sit next to me and Momma."

As soon as they were all seated, Juliana offered a prayer over the food. After taking the edge off of their hunger, they began to chat amiably about nothing in particular.

When the meal was over, Tim rose to go back to work. "Thank you for the wonderful food. I was right about one thing," he added. "Jeff Borton is in for a real treat when he eats here. This food was fabulous!"

"Thank you," responded Shirleen. "I'm glad you liked it."

Tim went back out to finish up, while the women started their daily routine. An hour later, they heard him shoveling off the porch steps. Leaning the shovel against the wall of the porch, he opened the door and called out, "I'm finally done, so I'll get out of your hair. I just need to know where to put the snow blower."

"There's an outbuilding next to the woodshed," explained Shirleen. "You can put it in there."

"Do I need a key?"

"Oh, yeah. We haven't been in there since we moved in. Let me get it for you." Shirleen got the key, and gave it to him.

When he'd put snow blower away, he returned the key. "Thank you for doing an excellent job, Tim," Shirleen said

"Thank *you* for the wonderful belly timber."

Shirleen laughed outright. "I've never heard food called that before."

"My grandfather used to say it. I guess it stuck." Waving as he turned to leave, he added, "I'll be around after work to see everything has been taken care of." Not waiting for a reply he hurried back to get into his truck. Shirleen watched him go, then went back inside so she and Juliana could start cleaning the house.

Juliana had just finished mopping the kitchen floor when a truck with a huge flatbed trailer hitched to the back pulled up outside. Juliana was amazed to see the trailer and truck were all full of wood. "Good morning," Juliana said to the driver. "Let me show you where you can put the wood." She led the way to a spot a little way from the woodshed. "Here will be just fine."

"Thank you ma'am." Before he could say more, another truck and flatbed trailer filled to the brim with more wood pulled up next to the first truck. The men pulled on heavy-duty work gloves and started unloading the wood. Juliana left them to their work and went back to the house to continue doing the rest of the housework.

Before lunch was ready, the men had the first truck and trailer unloaded, and moved the second truck into position to be unloaded. By the time lunch was over, they'd finished unloading and left.

As Meagan, with Juliana's help, finished up the lunch dishes, Juliana turned to speak to her, "Honey, you have worked hard enough this week. You can skip the science lesson to do whatever you want."

Meagan beamed as she studied her parent then asked, "Really?"

"Yes, really," laughed Juliana. I'm not always a slave driver, you know."

Meagan kissed her mother's check then hurriedly washed the table while Juliana let the water out. When they were finished, Meagan went to work sketching while Juliana went to her art studio. A couple of hours later, the trucks and trailers were back, filled with more wood. When they were done unloading, they went back for the last load.

An hour later, Jeff arrived with a truck loaded with lumber and supplies to complete the motorhome shelter.

Shirleen went out to see if he needed anything. "You did great with your timing, Mr. Borton."

"Well, there weren't a lot of people at the depot today, so I was able to get help with everything."

"Did it cost a lot?"

Handing her the invoice, Jeff said, "Let me get this stuff unloaded, and then we'll talk turkey." Looking at the stack of lumber and other supplies, he asked, "Do you have a place where I can store my tools so I don't have to drag them with me every day?"

"Sure, you can put them in the outbuilding where we're storing the snow blower. I'll get the key and be right back."

When she came back, she said, "Let me show you where the shed is then I'll write you a check."

"I'll let you know when I have everything unloaded."

Nodding, Shirleen went back to the house to write a check. A while later, he knocked on the door and Meagan answered it. "Please come in, Mr. Borton."

"Thank you, Miss."

"Oh, mercy! Just call me Meagan."

Smiling Jeff bowed slightly as he said, "Meagan it is."

Rising, Shirleen handed him the check.

"Thank you, Mrs. Webb," he replied taking the check and stuffing it into his billfold. "I'll get started in the morning, if it doesn't snow. It won't be the most stylish lean to, but at least it will protect the motorhome." He went on to describe what had to be done, then asked, "Will be okay with you?"

"Of course," declared Shirleen. "It's certainly better than anything we could do."

"With the A-frame roof, the snow won't cause it to cave in."

"That is the most important thing."

"Then I guess all that's left to do is get the job done. I'll be here at eight in the morning to get started. Do you have enough wood in the woodshed to last you until I can get some more cut?"

"I don't know. It is getting pretty low. Maybe you could look at the pile in the morning then let us know."

"I'll do that the very first thing. I'll see you ladies in the morning." He had just gotten into his truck when the final loads of wood arrived. He yelled out the window to the driver. "Give me a minute and I'll get out of your way."

After Jeff left, Jason Stewart backed in and started unloading the last of the wood.

Shirleen was starting to prepare their evening meal when Juliana stopped her. "I'll get supper tonight. You have your hands full with this wood."

"Thank you, dear. I have to get a check written to give these men when they're done."

"Take you time. Meagan can help me, can't you Meagan?"

"Sure. I need a break."

Smiling, Shirleen went to her room to write the check. She returned just as the men knocked on the door. Meagan invited them in and said, "Grandma will be right with you."

"Thank you, young lady," said Jason Stewart.

Shirleen walked down the hallway toward the men. They rose to wait for her to come into the room. "I see you brought us a lot of wood."

"Yes, ma'am, we did."

Handing Jason the check, she asked, "Do I have the right price on there?"

Jason scanned the check then nodded before replying, "Yes, that will do it."

"Thank you for getting it here so quickly."

"Let me know if you need anything else."

"We will," Shirleen assured them. "Thanks again."

After the evening meal was over, Shirleen turned to her two companions to say, "You know, I have been thinking."

"Oh dear," giggled Meagan, "Grandma is thinking again, Momma. We're in trouble."

Grinning, Shirleen said, "Just for that, I think I'll leave you to just stew in your own juices."

Juliana was thankful Meagan could tease her grandmother. However, she said, "Meagan, we'd better behave ourselves. She may just come up with some awful job for us to do that will keep us up all night."

Meagan pretended to protest. "Oh, dear me, I hadn't thought of that." Sighing resignedly, she curtsied gracefully. Smiling sweetly, she pleaded, "Please forgive me, oh mighty Grandmother, for my impudent behavior."

Shirleen burst out laughing at the two of them. Finally gaining control, she said, "Me thinks I'll wait 'til after dark then send the two of you out to get the wood … alone! Perhaps the cougar will have you both for supper."

"Never happen, Grandma," declared Meagan nonchalantly. "One bite of this bitter body would cause him to spit me out and run for the hills."

"Speak for yourself, daughter. I'm so plump now he'd have a feast to last him a month."

Grabbing her side in a fit of laughter, Shirleen cried, "Enough already! I can see I've lost before I even begin."

A few minutes later, Juliana said seriously, "What did you have in mind, Momma?"

"I was just thinking we should get the wood in before it gets dark in case our friendly kitty cat comes back."

"I agree," stated Meagan. "I, for one, don't want to be out after dark again. Last night was hard on my nerves."

"Mine, too, sweetheart. I'm all for going out right now."

When all of the wood boxes were filled, they made sure the house was locked up tight for the night. They were about to close the drapes when Tim pulled up.

Meagan greeted him happily, "Hello, Tim. Did you have a good day?"

"Not really, little lady." Removing his hat, he asked, "Did you have a good day?"

"I sure did. There's been a lot of activity around here today. For a while, felt like Grand Central Station."

"Well, tell me what went on."

"I guess you'd better come in first. I don't want Grandma yelling at me to close the door because I'm letting in the cold."

Grinning as he came in, he said, "Oh, no; we don't want that to happen."

Shirleen pretended to grow stern as she asked, "What is this, pick on Shirleen day or something?"

"Something is more like it, Grandma," teased Meagan.

"Then tomorrow will be pick on Meagan day," quipped Shirleen.

"Maybe," Meagan uttered, grinning. "Then again, maybe not."

"You sure are being a tease tonight," Shirleen said, secretly pleased Meagan felt secure enough to do so.

"I don't know what's wrong with me. It just makes me feel good to see things getting done around here."

"I feel the same way," said Shirleen.

"Then I take it the wood arrived, and Jeff Borton got here with the construction supplies?"

"Yep, the wood is ready to be split and Mr. Borton got here just before dinnertime. He said he'll be back at eight o'clock in the morning to start working."

"Wonderful," exclaimed Tim. "Then I can assume the three of you will be all right for a while."

"We should be, thanks to you," Shirleen assured him.

"Well, I only have one more question for you, and then I'm off. Do you have any idea when you'll be in town on Thursday?"

"As close to nine as possible. We have a lot to do."

Reaching into his back pants pocket he took out his wallet and pulled out a card. Handing it to Shirleen, he said, "This is my business card with my office address and phone. The office is in the courthouse. Meet me there as soon as you get to town and we'll go to the gun shop. I'll keep the rifles and ammunition you buy at the office while you do the rest of your shopping. You can pick them up on your way home."

"We'll do that," replied Shirleen.

Looking at the piano, he asked, "Which one of you plays?"

"Grandma," replied Meagan proudly.

"Would you mind playing something for me, Shirleen. I have had one awful day. Maybe hearing you play will calm my nerves."

"I'd be happy to." She found a soothing piece by Mendelssohn and played while Tim sat on the couch and closed his eyes. Shirleen played for an hour. When she finished, Tim opened his eyes and said, "I could listen to you play forever, Shirleen. Thanks for that, I really needed it. I'd better get going. I have to go back to the office for at least another hour before going home."

"I'm sorry you have to do that," sympathized Juliana.

"Well," replied Tim, "it's just part of the job. I'll see the three of you in town Thursday," he said as he headed out the door.

After he had pulled out, Shirleen closed the drapes and said, "Day after tomorrow is Sunday. We've been saying prayers for help and thanks, but we haven't been studying the scriptures. How would the two of you feel about taking turns conducting a little service meeting each Sunday? Since it was my idea, I'll create a sermon and pick out the hymns this Sunday if. What do you think?"

After a surprised pause, Juliana said, "I think it would be a good way to stay in tune with the Lord and show Him we're grateful for his help."

"I agree," commented Meagan. "How can we think only of praying without showing our respect for His word?"

"Does that mean you'll do it?"

"Yes," said Juliana emphatically as Megan nodded.

"Good, then I'll set everything up for Sunday."

"Momma," began Juliana, "would you mind playing some hymns before we do our nightly prayers? That would set the mood."

"I'll play, if the two of you will sing."

Going to the piano, Shirleen got out a hymnbook. The other two gathered around the piano to look over Shirleen's shoulder. For the next hour and a half they sang those hymns with all of their heart. When they were tired from singing, Meagan was the spokesperson to give the prayer. When she was finished, they were all crying. Gratitude coursed through their hearts, while a peace filled their very beings.

Juliana walked with Meagan to her room, where she hugged and kissed her goodnight. "Never, ever doubt I love you, Meagan. You are more important to me than life itself."

Meagan took a deep breath before hugging her mother close. "Thank you for those wonderful words. I feel the same way, Momma. I'm so grateful God let you be my mother."

After watching Meagan go to her room, Juliana went to her studio. Turning on the light, she got out the new painting she'd been working on. She studied it critically for a few moments. Finally, picking up a brush, she went to work. As she painted, love filled her heart, because the portrait was of her mother. She worked for several hours then cleaned her brushes and got ready for bed. Before going to sleep, Juliana knelt by her bed and offered up her prayers.

"Dear Lord, I'm so worried about Momma; she looks so tired lately. She works hard to take care of us and make sure we're happy. Being a mother, I know this is what we do — worry about our children. Yet there's something bothering her. Are those dreams she's having only dreams or are they warnings? Something tells me we can't let our guard down, but being constantly on alert isn't good for us, either.

"I'd like to pursue a teaching career, yet there's so much to do here it might be too much to take on. It's hard, not giving into fears that constantly plague me. Please keep us safe from the wrath of Bruce. He's so evil and sick. I'm afraid of what he'll do to Momma and me, but I'm even more worried about what he'll do to Megan. If he forced her to marry Jethro, it would destroy her. Please, don't let that happen.

"Finally, give us a calm reassurance that we're indeed safe here in Cardston. I don't just mean from Bruce and Gordon, but from the mountain lions, bears and any other thing that might harm us."

When Juliana was finished with her prayer, she felt a sweet peace flow into her. She knew, that at least for the time being, they were safe. Rising, she got into bed, turned out the light and was soon fast asleep.

Meanwhile, Shirleen consulted with the Lord about her upcoming Sunday service. The only thing that kept coming to her mind was gratitude. She looked in the index at the back of the Bible for scriptures to read on the subject. At midnight, she put down her pen then went to bed.

A few hours later, Shirleen sat up in bed, fear clutching at her heart. Something didn't feel right, but she didn't know what. Then she heard something bump against the house. Before she could do anything, a scream pieced the night air. The sound was right outside her window. When she looked outside, the moon lit up the surrounding landscape and she saw something move. There, bathed in the moonlight, was the most beautiful cat she'd ever seen close up. It swished its tail back and forth like it was angry.

Shirleen could only stare in awe at the magnificence of the creature. *It's not only massive but it is sleek and streamlined,* she thought. *Look at that tail.* Suddenly, it crouched down on the snow to survey its surroundings. Looking around to see what the lion was looking at, she saw a herd of Elk on the frozen snow. *It's going to attack the elk,* thought Shirleen. Her first instinct was to scare the mountain lion away, but knowing it had a right to eat, Shirleen watched and waited.

The elk, sensing the big cat's presence, began to grow restless. One old bull snorted angrily, trying to scare the cat off. Unconcerned, the cat stayed where it was. Not sure where the cat was, the herd moved ever closer. *The air must not be in the cougars favor or they wouldn't be getting so close,* she told herself.

As the elk got closer to the cat's position, Shirleen watched with baited breath. The mountain lion slowly stood up and stretched lazily. As the herd neared the cat's position, a lone female, limping badly from some unseen injury, moved from the protection of the group.

In the blink of an eye, the mountain lion pounced. Panicking, the cow tried to run, but the injury wouldn't let her. In just seconds it was over. The big cat would eat tonight. Watching in horrified fascination, Shirleen saw the cat drag the elk off into the woods. A few minutes later it was business as usual for the rest of the herd.

Shirleen pondered what she'd seen. *Now, that I've seen it all close up the stuff they show on TV doesn't really compare,* thought Shirleen. She went to the kitchen for a drink of water, then went to sit in the chair by the fire. An hour later, she went back to bed but sleep eluded her. Finally, in desperation, she knelt beside her bed to pour out her heart to the Lord. When she got back into bed, she rolled onto her right side, and immediately went to sleep.

Shirleen slept so hard she didn't hear the pack of wolves come into the yard near dawn. Had she known, perhaps she wouldn't have felt so safe living in the middle of nowhere. The wolves explored the yard and when they knew they were safe, they took a rest near the woodshed.

The alpha wolf had gotten his foot caught in a trap, but after several hours of torturous struggle he'd gotten free. The resulting wound bothered him greatly. One of the younger males, seeing his golden opportunity, had started pestering the old male. Snarling in warning, the old male rose to face the young upstart. The younger male sized up his opponent. Something inside of him knew the old male was stronger than he looked. The young male backed away to leave the leader alone.

The alpha male licked at his leg in an attempt to get the blood to stop, however the wound was serious. The gash ran the full length of his leg. Sensing he was going to die soon, he lead his pack further into the woods to make sure they were safe. They hadn't gone far when the younger male, sensing the leadser's weakness, attacked the alpha. The alpha was too weak to put up a real fight.

It was over quickly and the young upstart was now the alpha male. Marking his territory, he defied any of the other males in the pack to challenge him.

Those inside the house slept on, oblivious. Yet, the next morning when Jeff started his chores, he noticed the blood and suspected there'd been a life and death struggle.

Chapter 7

Riding home in his limo, Bruce Murdock was pleased with himself. He'd annihilated all of Gordon Spielberg's men. *What did it matter if a woman or two was taken in the process?* Bruce didn't feel any remorse, even for the orphaned children left behind. With the exception of his daughter, Bruce hated children. There weren't a lot of feelings for his daughter either, since he was disappointed she wasn't a boy. He could've taught a son the ways of the organization. *What can a man do with a sissy-acting girl?*

When Bruce thought about Leslie, his wife came to mind. *Oh, it will feel good to see the life drain out of her. I won't kill her outright. That would be too easy. I'm gonna torture her 'til she begs me to kill her and then I'll torture her some more.* As far as his mother-in-law was concerned he'd do for her like he'd done Gordon. A smile tugged at the corner of his lips as he contemplated the dastardly deeds.

His thoughts turned again to business. He knew some of Gordon's men hadn't been at the gala, so the carnage wasn't over. They'd strike back as soon as they knew who was responsible. He also knew he had to work fast to enlist more men. Men who loved to wreck havoc just as much as he did. He had several in mind, but knew he had to go slow for a while. *No use starting a war until I'm ready.*

Bruce reached into his pocket and got out his cell phone. He dialed Henry Borden and waited while it rang.

Finally, a sleepy Henry answered. "Yes?"

"It's Bruce. I'm on my way back to Syracuse. We did for many of Spielberg's men tonight."

"You did?"

"We did. Can you get to your office and call me back? We need to talk right away," he said, realizing Matilda, Henry's wife, was in bed beside him. "Call me on my cell as soon as possible."

"Yes, sir."

Bruce ended the call, then told his driver, "Paul, the next time you see an all night dinner, pull in. I'm hungry."

"Yes, sir. There should be one coming up in about an hour."

"Fine," replied Bruce. "I can hang on that long." Closing the privacy window, Bruce leaned back in his seat and closed his eyes. Ten minutes later, Henry called back.

"I'm in my office. We can talk freely."

"Good. I have some things to tell you. First of all, we found out Spielberg had a lot more men than we thought."

"That doesn't surprise me. He was in this racket a long time. He was bound to have a good following."

"Well, we've already picked off the ones we could get to without arousing suspicion."

"How many?"

"We sent nearly fifty to watery graves, another twenty we left for the police to find, and about ten more are buried at the Parson's and Sons construction site."

"Whew, that's eighty men."

"Yeah, approximately." Getting more comfortable, Bruce continued, "We sent out invitations for the rest to come to an event this evening."

"Tonight?"

"That's right."

"What happened?"

Bruce told him everything, then said, "We tallied up the names of those who registered when they came in. All of them had dates or wives with them. We let them take a few bites of dessert, then took them out. There were probably 100 of them total."

"Good grief, man. You've really opened up a can of worms."

"Well, at least we've left our calling card," chuckled Bruce. "I know the rest will retaliate. Let 'em bring it on. We're evenly matched now."

"That may be true, but don't be surprised if they're quick. Probably with something worse than what you did."

"Yeah, that's my thought too. I've decided to do something before they can get organized. I just have to have a few days to get my ducks in a row."

"Let me know how I can help."

"Thanks, I will."

"I almost forgot. Have you heard anymore about the family?"

"Yes, I have." Bruce was instantly angry. "Gordon tracked them as far as some small town in Ohio, but he botched the job."

"I knew that much. What happened after that?"

"I had Nate White take him out. Gordon Spielberg is no more."

There was silence for a moment, then Henry said, "Well, I can't say I'm sorry to hear that. He was just too slow on the uptake."

Bruce snapped back, "I know he was!

"What became of Ruth, Leslie and Gordon's wife?"

"They disappeared off of the face of the earth. I've got a good bloodhound sniffing out their trail. I know he'll find them."

"Let me know when it's going down. I'm disappointed Jethro won't be marrying Leslie right away so our companies could merge."

"Well, don't give up hope. It *will* happen — just as soon as I can find them." He hesitated a moment before adding, "Leslie will find out just what happens when she crosses me. When I'm done with her, she'll never cross us again."

"Good deal!"

"I've got to go, but I'll keep you posted."

"Thanks, Bruce. I'd appreciate that."

When the call ended, Henry shivered. *I thought I was ruthless, but Bruce makes me look like a pansy.* Shaking himself, he poured a stiff drink to calm his jangled nerves. "I'll have to watch myself around that maniac!" He slugged the drink and went to take a walk around his grounds.

He found a bench under a weeping willow tree, and sat down to try to sort out his feelings about what Bruce had just told him. *What have I gotten myself into?* He didn't have any problems with being a criminal, but murder was not something he wanted anything to do with. *I can't run because Matilda's too sick to travel. Besides, Bruce would hunt us down and kill us.*

As he sat there he tried to remember when all of this started. He'd been caught embezzling from the company he was working for. The court had assigned Bruce to represent him, and he'd assured him he would get him off. Like a fool, he allowed the man to do whatever he thought best, never realizing Bruce had his own agenda.

When the trial was over, Bruce had told him it was time to pay up. Because he didn't want his family to know what he'd done, he accepted the terms. *Now, I'm in way over my head with no way out.* Resigned, he went back to his office to get some work done, because sleep was out of the question now.

Three hours later, Jethro passed his door on the way to breakfast. "Morning, son," he called.

Jethro came in and took a seat across from his father. "What are you up to this early in the morning, Dad?"

"Just getting caught up on the mountain of paperwork I neglected when the Murdocks were here." Looking at Jethro intently, he asked, "Why are you up so early. You usually don't get up until noon."

"I don't know. Something woke me up. I tried to go back to sleep, but I had this feeling like something bad was about to happen. Isn't that stupid?"

"No," replied Henry. "Maybe it's a warning you should listen to. I've had some of them in my life. When I listened, I was safe. When I didn't, I suffered the consequences. Don't take feelings like that lightly."

"Thanks for the advice, Dad." Standing up, he added. "I'm hungry enough to eat a bear. I think I'll go see what cook has for breakfast, then I'm gonna go back to bed and try to figure out why I'm having this bad feeling. You coming to breakfast?"

"No, I ate a while ago. I'm just going to wade through this paperwork until I find the end."

"See you later then."

Three hours later, when he still hadn't seen Matilda, Henry went up to check on her. He had the strangest feeling as he approached the bed; he knew instinctively she was dead. He touched her cold body just to be sure, as tears began coursing down his cheeks. When he'd gained some semblance of control, he called 911 and went to tell Jethro what had happened.

Finding him back in bed asleep, Henry shook him gently, "Son, wake up."

Jethro turned to look at Henry and saw the pain in his eyes. "What's wrong, Dad?"

"When you mother didn't come down to breakfast, I got worried about her. I just found her still in bed. Son, she's passed away."

"No!" Kicking the covers back, he hurriedly got out of bed. Before Henry could stop him, he rushed to where his mother lay. When Henry entered, Jethro was kneeling by her side, weeping like his heart would break. "Momma, don't go," he cried. "Please, stay here with us."

Henry went to stand beside his son and put his hand comfortingly on his shoulder. Not long after, they could hear wailing sirens. Soon, Officer Robert Rhodes was at the door.

When Henry let him in, he asked "What's going on here?"

"I was up early, working on some paperwork in my office. When Matilda didn't come down at her usual time, I got worried and came up here to check on her. I found her this way." Henry broke down and went to stand in the hall while Rhodes did his job.

Soon, the ambulance arrived, and Henry stood transfixed as the paramedics rushed up the stairs and into the bedroom. Not being able to take anymore, he walked slowly down the stairs to wait until it was all over.

He sat there until they brought her body downstairs, completely wrapped in a white sheet. He lunged forward to stop them from taking her, and Rhodes allowed him to take all the time he needed. Overcome with grief, Henry crumpled to the floor. Rhodes put a hand on his shoulder and stood there silently until the grief-stricken man regained control.

Jethro, who was just as broken up, hugged his father and they watched the ambulance drove away. "I know this is a tough time for you, but which mortuary do you want to take care of the details?" Rhodes asked.

Henry looked up at Rhodes and said, "I just can't think straight. Please, make the decision for us then let me know."

"I'll do that. "I'm so very sorry for your loss, Henry."

Henry could only nod.

"I'll get in touch with you later about the arrangements."

"Thank you," was all Henry could get out.

Several hours later, Bruce phoned to speak to Henry. "Henry, I have an assignment for you."

"I don't care," snapped Henry. "I just lost my Tilly."

"What do you mean lost?" barked Bruce.

"She's dead!"

"Forget the assignment. I'll be there tomorrow to help with whatever you need."

"Thanks," mumbled Henry, and quickly hung up the phone.

Not long after that, officer Rhodes called. "Henry, Matilda's at Braden Mortuary. Mr. Braden asked that you call him and make an appointment to work out the arrangements."

"Thank you, Officer Rhodes. "I'll take care of it right away." Henry hung up the phone and sat with his face in his hands for a few minutes to gain control of his emotions. Finally, taking a deep breath, he looked up the number for the Braden Mortuary.

When Braden answered, Henry, said, "This is Henry Borden. Do I need to make an appointment or something?"

"Yes, sir."

"When is a good time to come in?"

"I have an opening at ten o'clock in the morning."

"Fine, my son and I'll be there."

Hanging up the phone, he realized he needed to notify family members and got busy contacting them. When that emotionally draining task was finished, he got up and wandered around his property. He had to clear his head so he could function.

A while later, Jethro found him sitting on the bench where he'd been earlier that morning. "Are you doing okay?"

"Under the circumstances, yes, son."

He took a seat next to his father, and they sat in companionable silence for a while. "I knew Mother was fragile, but I thought she'd be around for a long time. I just can't seem to wrap my head around the fact that she's really gone."

"I'm having the same problem. It's all I can not to just fall apart."

"What will we do now that she's gone?"

"Stick together! I need you now more than ever." He paused then continued, "Son, I know I don't tell you this often enough, but I love you. I'm proud of the man you've become. I want you to know I'm proud of you for sticking it out and graduating from college."

Jethro watched his father intently to see if he was serious. "Thank you, Dad. Knowing this makes me happy. I always want to make you proud of me."

"Well, you have."

"Thanks, Dad."

"I got ahold of all of the family on both sides. They'll all be here within three days. I think we'll have the funeral on Friday."

"Whenever. I just want to get it over with as soon as possible."

"We have to go to Braden's Mortuary in the morning to make the necessary arrangements."

"Where will the funeral be?"

"I don't know. Your mother was a member of the Presbyterian Church. I guess we should honor her by having it there."

"In a church? You know I don't do that religious stuff. I'll do it for Mom, but I won't be happy about it. After that, I don't ever want to set foot in a church again."

"That's your choice. I'll never stand in your way when it comes to religion. That's a personal decision."

"Thanks for understanding. I'm suddenly so exhausted. I think I'll go inside and get some rest. Now I know why I had those feelings of doom."

When Bruce got home, Crowley came to see what he wanted. "Let's go inside where we can talk without interruption." They went to his office and took a seat.

"From now on things are going to get wild around here," Bruce said. "I know the rest of Spielberg's organization will figure out what we did in New York. When they do, it won't be long before we have a gang war on our hands."

"I say bring it on," Crowley said, cracking his knuckles. A sardonic smile played around his lips. "I love a good fight. The nastier the better as far as I'm concerned."

Hearing Crowley's comments thrilled Bruce because he knew he could count on him to get the job done. Turning to face Crowley, he continued, "Right now, a lot needs to be done. I want you to keep your eyes and ears open. Infiltrate their organization. Suck up to them and let them think you're on their side. When you find out what they're up to, let me know immediately. I have to go to Ohio to pick up the man that killed Spielberg. You can reach me on my cell."

"Right, boss. Don't worry about things, boss. I'll get them done."

Later that afternoon, Bruce packed fresh clothes, took a shower, and then called Nate White. "Nate, I won't be able to come get you for a few days because the wife of a friend of mine died this morning. I have to go up there to help him out. I'll call you to let you know when I'll be there. For now, stay low."

"I understand. By the way, the police found Spielberg's body today. They have their dogs, so to speak, out trying to pick up any clues. I made sure to get rid of my clothes, shoes ... everything. I brought new clothes with me, so there's no way they can trace the job back to me.

"Wonderful!" After a moment, Bruce asked, "Do you have enough money to hold out 'til I get there? If not I'll wire you some."

"I got enough. I took Gordon's pocket money."

"You more than earned it. Consider that a bonus."

"Thanks."

"I'll let you know when I'll be there. Meanwhile, call Spielberg's pilot. Tell him Spielberg was arrested for disturbing the peace then tell him someone from the organization will be coming to pick up the plane."

"I'll do that right away."

"I'll see you as soon as I can."

After hanging up the phone, he went to tell Hazel he wanted something to eat before going to Henry's. He hadn't told Hazel about Ruth running away with Leslie. He was saving that for just the right moment.

After eating a hearty meal, he called Paul to take him. "Henry's wife died today, so I need to be there for him. Find me a motel nearby and then stay near the limo in case I need you."

"Yes, sir. I'll be there in about a minute."

He hung up the phone, got his suitcase and met Paul Thomas as he pulled up. Soon they were on the way to Henry's. Bruce never considered he might be in the way during this sad time. He was going for purely selfish reasons — so he could keep an eye on Henry.

The next few days were a blur for Henry Borden. He was polite to Bruce when he showed up, but secretly wished the man would shrivel up and die. That didn't happen, so he introduced him to his family as a concerned friend.

The day of the funeral was rainy. It was as if the heavens were crying. Still, moving mechanically, Henry prepared for the ordeal that lay ahead. As he sat on his bed before getting dressed, he thought back to the day after Matilda died. It was bad when he and Jethro met with at Braden's Funeral home, picked out her casket and flowers, and then spoke to Matilda's minister.

When the family started arriving, that was worse. He didn't want to speak to anyone, but did his best to do what was right. Now, here he sat on the bed they'd shared and he'd never be able to hold her close again. He felt like he was choking to death.

Finally, after several attempts to get ready, he managed the task. When he got downstairs, the family car was waiting to take them to the church. Seeing Matilda's twin sister, Melinda Jacobs, struggling to remain calm, he went over to talk to her. "I know this is hard, Melinda, but we'll muddle through somehow."

"It's just hard to know we'll never talk again. She was a big part of my life, Henry."

Hugging her close, he replied, "I know. We'll miss her, but somehow we must find a way to go on."

"You're right, and I truly will try."

With his arm still around her, they walked out to get into the car. When it was filled with the immediate family, everyone else got into their individual cars and headed to the church.

After the funeral, Henry was relieved when everyone finally left — especially Bruce. Henry suddenly hated the man with a passion he never thought possible. He never wanted to see him again, yet he knew it was unavoidable.

Three days later, Henry was trying to get back to his life, when Officer Rhodes knocked on the door. The maid showed him to Henry's office and he asked, "What can I do for you today, Officer Rhodes?"

"Sometimes, I hate being a police officer."

"Why do you say that?" asked Henry, growing concerned.

"Because I have to bring you more bad news."

Henry felt panic rise up in him. "What bad news?"

"Your son, Jethro, was in a terrible car accident. A drunk struck him head-on. He was killed instantly."

"No!" bellowed Henry at the top of his lungs. "This can't be true!"

"I'm afraid it is, Henry."

Henry lost it, pulling his hair, striking the wall with his fists, kicking chairs and yelling like a crazy man. Rhodes wisely stood back to let him get it out of his system.

Suddenly unable to deal with the shock, Henry grabbed his left arm with one hand and slumped to the ground in a dead faint.

Rhodes moved over to feel for his pulse. Finding a faint one, he called an ambulance. While he waited, he administered CPR. Henry still hadn't regained consciousness when the ambulance arrived so the paramedic took over. They hooked Henry to an IV, and not long after, transported him to the hospital.

When he was stable, they transported him to the intensive care unit where they could monitor his vitals. Three hours later, he started to come around. It was two more days before he was strong enough to move from ICU.

Unable to walk on his own, he was transported to his son's funeral. It was a closed casket service. When the service was over, Henry was moved to a recovery center for three months. He received physical therapy to regain the use of his left arm, had speech therapy, and learned to walk again.

One day, Bruce came to speak to him. "I'm so sorry for the incredible losses you're facing, Henry."

"Thank you, Bruce."

"How are you doing?"

"I'm doing better every day, but my mental health is not so great. I've decided when I get out of here, I'm going away — as far away from here as I can possibly go. My sister-in-law, Melinda, is going to help me sell the house. She's also going to help me decide what stuff to keep and what to give away. I just can't live there anymore."

"Where will you go?"

"I don't know." He fell silent as he considered what to do. Finally, looking at Bruce, he continued. "All I know is I have to get away. I've got to go someplace new so I can heal."

"Well, I'll miss you. If you ever want your old job back, just know it's yours."

Henry moaned then replied, "I don't want to do anything but concentrate on getting completely well."

"My question is still the same. Where will you go?"

"When the house is sold, I'll load everything into a U-Haul, point it down the road and then go wherever it takes me." He sighed before adding. "That's all I know for sure right now. As far as the organization goes, I want nothing more to do with it. If you want to kill me for getting out, then all I have to say is do it!"

"You'll come around in time."

Henry grew impatient with Bruce. "I don't think so. I can't think of anything past the death of my family. I don't even care if I live or die. All I want to do is go somewhere where I can forget. If you're worried about me telling what I know about you, you can relax. I can't remember anything. Literally nothing! I've only been able to remember a few things and most of them are centered around my family. I remember being a banker, but good grief man, I don't even know anything about that business anymore. I'll have to hire someone to do my bills and cook for me because I have no idea how to do it myself. I'm no threat to you, Bruce. I don't think I'll ever fully remember my previous life. Does that scare you?"

After thinking things over for a moment, Bruce shook his head. Finally, he replied, "No, that doesn't scare me. I can see you aren't the same person you were. If you ever remember things, then I might get scared. For now, I feel safe.

"I'll tell you this, I remember you're part of the mafia, but I don't even know what the mafia is."

"Thanks for being honest. I won't forget your honesty or your friendship, Henry. Good luck wherever you go."

"Thanks, Bruce. Good luck to you, too."

As Bruce left, a part of him wanted to take Henry out, but a bigger part knew it would wasting a good bullet. *Let him live what he has left of his life in peace."*

Henry was released to go home two months later. He still couldn't walk, but did regain limited use of his left arm. Melinda also graciously agreed to help him put his life back together.

When Melinda arrived, Henry was sitting in the living room waiting for her. He was looking forward to something for the first time since Jethro's death.

After hugging him, Melinda looked at him anxiously as he stared at her.

She's a carbon copy of her sister. Henry noticed that although she had come a great distance, not a hair was out of place. *Even her makeup looks fresh*, he thought.

Melinda had never married. She had been engaged once, but just before the marriage was to take place, her fiancé was killed in a terrible collision with a freight train. She'd never been able to put her loss behind her.

Henry put her in the room the Murdock's had shared while they were there. She also gladly accepted Matilda's things when Henry offered them. "I'll treasure these. Thank you for thinking of me."

"You were her twin, " said Henry. "It's only right that you have them."

It took them over two months to decide what Henry would take with him and what he would sell. Melinda took some of the paintings, along with a few knick-knacks. With the help of the maid and cook, they were able to pack up Henry's belongings and gather Jethro's clothes to donate. The rest was divided amongst the family.

Henry also found a new caretaker to share his new adventure. Theodore Brooks was a tall, strong man of about thirty-two. He had large, gentle hands and light-brown, wavy hair. His piercing hazel eyes sparkled with life and he always seemed to be smiling.

The day they loaded the van was especially difficult for Henry. Although he needed to get away, he was torn because he knew this would become part of his past. When the van was loaded, they loaded Theodore's car onto the carrier so it could be towed behind. Looking at Theodore, he said, "Well, are you ready to take on this new adventure?"

"As ready as I'll ever be, sir," replied Theodore.

Theodore was wearing a pair of blue jeans that hugged his well-shaped hips, and Henry noticed Melinda was checking him out. Suddenly, Henry had an idea. "Melinda, what have you got to keep you here in New York?"

"My job." She looked at him suspiciously. "Why?"

"Having you around is like having a small part of Matilda with me. Why don't you quit your job and travel with us? No strings attached, dear one. I'll always treat you like the sister I never had."

Melinda dropped into the chair closest to her. Finally, finding her voice, she said, "I's an interesting offer, Henry."

"Seriously, if all you have holding you here is your job, then you don't really have a valid reason for staying."

Melinda thought over for a moment then asked, "You won't treat me any different than you have up to now?"

"No," responded Henry. "Let me make one thing very clear between us. I'll never love anyone else like I loved your sister. She was the love of my life."

"I have to admit I'm tempted. I'll have to give notice at my job. Where will I find you in two weeks?"

"Call to quit your job right now. All you have to do is pick up the phone and do it."

Smiling, Melinda replied, "I guess I can call and quit my job, but what about my things? I can't just leave them behind; I need them."

"How long will it take you to get packed?"

"I don't have all that much. About a week, maybe less if I have help."

"There are a lot of boxes left from packing my things. Theodore, do you know of anyone who could help her pack?"

"My sister, Joyce, could probably help."

"Call her," demanded Henry. "See if she'll help us out." Turning back to Melinda, he continued. "We'll get a motel close by and wait for you to be ready to leave."

"What about the U-Haul you have loaded outside."

Henry looked at her questioningly, "What about it?

"You can't rent it until I'm ready. That would be expensive."

"Oh drats, I forgot about the truck."

"I thought you had." Melinda smiled. "Listen, it was a wonderful pipe dream, but it just wouldn't work."

"My sister will help you," Theodore said. "She said to tell you she has several friends who will pitch in, too. She thought we could get it all done in one day with their help."

Sighing resignedly, Melinda replied, "Well, since I have a lot of help, I guess I'll go with the two of you."

"Wonderful!" exclaimed Henry. "Instead of riding in the U-Haul, I'll ride with you to your apartment."

"Well," grinned Melinda, "you can ride with me to our new destination too." Pausing to look at Henry for a moment, she asked, "By the way, have you decided where we're going?"

"Yes. Last night I dreamed I was living in Cardston, Alberta, Canada."

"Burr, it's cold there this time of year."

"We'll get used to it."

"I hope so!" Finally, shaking her head resignedly, she said, "Well, let's get to it."

Soon they were pulling out of the driveway for the very last time. Henry, relieved to be going, never looked back once.

Chapter 8

Shirleen was pleased their little worship service had gone so well, and was so at peace she was humming the tunes that had been chosen for the little service as she made dinner.

"You sound so happy, Momma," said Juliana.

"I feel happy," Shirleen said, as she paused to kiss her daughter's cheek. "Somehow, I feel freer than I have since we left Syracuse."

"I'm glad, because you've lost a lot of weight since we took off and I've been worried about you."

Grinning at Juliana, she replied, "Have you noticed you've lost weight, too. We all have. We've all been so terrified I think we forgot to eat." When Juliana started to speak, Shirleen continued, "Oh, don't get me wrong, I still feel a lot of fear, but since we held our little worship meeting this morning, a feeling of peace has enveloped me."

"I enjoyed it, too, and Meagan told me she also found peace during the service."

"I've decided I'm going to find more ways of showing gratitude, not only for the things the Lord does for me, but also for the things the two of you do for me."

She paused thoughtfully before continuing. "I was taught about God as a little girl. My mother used to say God was the only one we could ever trust to keep our secrets, and protect us. When I was forced to marry Gordon, I gave up on God. I wouldn't go to Him with anything. I felt like it was His fault I was stuck in a marriage to a man I loathed."

"What changed your mind, Momma?"

"Meagan. When she first suggested we pray for protection, I didn't want to. I thought it was useless to even try because God wouldn't listen to us. I only went along with it to calm her down. Then the night I met that strange man, I knew it wasn't God who made me marry Gordon; it was my father's fault for not believing me. Momma tried to make me see this, but all I saw was that no one helped me when I needed it."

As Juliana set the table she said, "When you never took me to church I thought my school friends were crazy for going. One time, when I was quite young, I asked

Gordon a question about God. It made him furious. He said, 'There's no such thing as God. If there ever was one, he's long since ceased to be. Don't ever mention God to me again. If you do, you'll suffer the consequences.' Believe me, I never said anything about God or religion to him again, but I never stopped wondering if there really was a God."

"I'm so sorry I never taught you about this wonderful, loving being." Sighing thoughtfully Shirleen added, "Until recently, I didn't believe He existed either."

Just then, Meagan came into the kitchen to see what was going on. "What are you wonderful ladies talking about? Is it some dark secret I shouldn't know about?"

Juliana replied, "There's no secret here. We were discussing how we didn't believe there was a God. Your grandma and I had lost our faith in until just recently." Looking at Meagan she asked, "What made you think to have us pray? We never taught you about God."

"A friend of mine went to church every Sunday. I didn't know this at the time, but I noticed she was always happy and always seemed at peace. One day while we were walking home from school I asked why she was this way. That was when I learned there really is a God. I learned for myself He is real and he loves me. I also learned I could go to him whenever I needed Him.

"There were many times when I was afraid of Daddy's wrath, but I took it to God in prayer. It always helped calm Daddy down enough to listen to what I had to say. My friend, Georgia, took me to church with her whenever I stayed at her house. I loved going because I learned a lot."

"Well," said Shirleen hugging her close, "I'm glad you learned this wonderful lesson. Your suggestion to pray saved us the night Gordon found us. It also saved us when we didn't know where to go. Thank you for this wonderful gift."

"Thank you, Grandma. I must admit I was praying nonstop as we left home. It was the only thing that kept me from screaming my head off from fear."

Nothing more was said as they said grace then began to eat. The rest of the evening was taken up with relaxing projects. Meagan sighed as she gazed into the fire. "Oh, what I wouldn't give for a few good books to read. That is the one thing I miss the most. At home, I could go into the library to find a good book to curl up with."

Juliana readily agreed. "I loved to read a good book once in a while. There's something about reading that soothes the troubled soul."

Shirleen made a mental note to do something about this lack of reading material on Thursday. She listened to them talk about the different books they had read as she worked on a new dresser scarf. *Yes,* she thought, *I'm at peace here.* She didn't kid herself about always being safe. She knew Bruce and Gordon would never give up looking for them. Despite all of this, she felt a sweet inner peace, and for now that was enough.

Just before dark, they filled the wood boxes with wood. None of them relished the idea of getting the wood after dark, especially when they could hear the wolves in the woods, so they made sure they got everything taken care of while it was still light outside.

Shirleen woke just before daylight. She'd been having those repeating dreams again. Gordon kept warning her to watch her back. Not once did the dreams vary, which made her think they really were warnings.

She sat up to hang her legs over the edge of the bed. "What are you trying to tell me, Lord?" Putting on her robe and slippers, she went to sit in the stuffed chair by the fireplace in the living room. "Lord," she prayed, "I know these dreams are some kind of warning, but what should I do?" She rose to pace the room, trying to understand the message she was supposed to receive. No matter how she tried, nothing came to her. Finally, she sank back into the chair.

Suddenly, she no longer felt alone. Although fear gripped her, she felt compelled to look toward the front door. A man stood there watching. Shirleen nearly screamed.

"Do not be afraid, Sarah. I mean you no harm."

"Who are you?" demanded Shirleen.

"A friend. It was I who spoke to you on the road that night when you were deciding where to go." Unable to speak, Shirleen waited for him to continue. Stepping toward her he said, "The dreams you're having are a warning. When Gordon couldn't get through to you, I was sent to deliver the message. He was murdered by your son-in-law so he could take over as mob boss. You also need to know Bruce is more evil than your husband. When he was ten, Gordon's father started to groom him to take over when he died. Of course, he didn't know that. When Gordon turned sixteen, his father started to take him out on hits. At first it made him sick, but eventually his conscious was scared.

"One day, just before his seventeenth birthday, his father gave him orders to kill a man just to test him. Gordon did it without a second thought. His father was so proud of him that he made him his top hand.

From that time on, Gordon became ruthless. Taking a life meant nothing to him; it was just a job that had to be done. Theodore Spielberg was on the lookout for a wife for his son. When your father went to work for him, he decided you were the one. It didn't matter that you wanted nothing to do with Gordon. In his mind, you were just a way for him to get a grandchild. It was Gordon's father who concocted the lie."

"It's always hurt me to think my father believed I'd do such a thing. I had never done anything like that."

"Your father did anything Theodore wanted him to do. He never questioned his decisions. Your father was always sorry you weren't a boy. He wanted a boy to carry on his name. When you were eight, your mother gave birth to a boy, they named Neil Maxwell."

"I remember him," replied Shirleen. "Oh, how I loved him. I never understood why he died. They never talked about it. One day he was just gone. We were told never to mention his name around my father. What happened to him?"

"Your brother was born with a birth defect that bothered your father. He wouldn't believe it when your mother told him the doctor had told her in the delivery room that the birth defect could be repaired. He was so ashamed to have him as a son that he vowed to get rid of him."

"Oh, no! Father killed him?"

"No, he didn't do it, he paid someone."

"What happened?" Shirleen was crying as she asked the question.

"One day your father got a sitter for the two of you. When you were put down for your nap, the sitter, who also worked for your father, drowned Neil in the bathtub, then wiped him off, redressed him and put him in his crib."

"That's awful!" cried Shirleen.

"Yes, it was. It was ruled a crib death."

"Oh, I wish my father had been the one to die, not my brother."

"Sarah, if your brother had lived, he would've become just like your father or worse, like Bruce. He was saved from that kind of life."

Shirleen thought that over for a moment then nodded affirmatively, "I can see that now."

"When you die, you'll see him again. Your mother is with him now."

"Oh, that fills me with peace."

"That is as it should be. Now let's discuss your son-in-law. Bruce is downright ruthless. He delights in taking lives. Each time he kills, it thrills him.

"That's horrible! I can't imagine anyone feeling that way. I don't want to know more about him."

The messenger replied, "You don't have that luxury. When you get the newspaper tomorrow, you'll read about just how ruthless Bruce is. Sarah, Bruce ordered his men to murder one hundred people. Half of them were women."

Sarah visibly paled.

"This is an example of just how cold blooded and calculating he is. He wants to be leader of the pack, so he eliminated everyone who stood in his way. In the end, those who were loyal to Gordon will join up with Bruce, or he'll take them out."

Pausing a moment, he added, "You need to know you aren't completely safe here. Bruce has a man looking for you and when he finds you he has orders to kill you and Ruth and bring Megan back to him. He won't stop until he finds you. You need to tell Sergeant York and Jeff Borton the truth. They're in danger because they've helped you. They have the right to know so they can protect themselves."

"Is it really safe to tell them?"

"They're good, honest men. You can trust them completely. You have some time before they find you, but you need to stay alert. Remember to call on the Lord when you need help and He will be there for you."

"What do I do in the meantime?" Shirleen asked.

"Learn to shoot the rifle you buy on Thursday. Juliana needs to buy a handgun, as well. You may never have to use the guns, but it will still be good to know how to work with them. Train both of the dogs you're getting as guard dogs. Let Meagan be the one who commands them. This will give her a sense of accomplishment, as well as calm her fears. She doesn't say much, but she, too, lives in constant fear of being found. "

"I suspected that, but since I didn't know how to help myself through those feelings, I couldn't really help her."

"This is where telling York and Borton will help. There's something else you should know. Henry Borden is in Cardston right now, but you no longer have to fear him. His wife died a few months ago and his son was killed in a terrible car wreck not long after. The shock of both deaths so close together caused Henry to have a massive stroke. He can't remember much of his past and was also disabled by the stroke. Bruce didn't want to waist a bullet on him, so he let him live.

"As Henry regains his health, he'll remember everything. This happened to him so he'd have the chance to change his life for the better. He'll understand your feeling of freedom, as he realizes that he, too, was released from the evil clutches of Bruce Murdock. In time, he will come to treasure you as a friend, and ultimately cause Bruce's downfall."

"I'm so sorry to hear about Matilda. I always liked her. She was another victim of Bruce Murdock. Ruth told me there were times when she didn't like Matilda. Then when we were able to escape, she wished Matilda could also be free. I guess in a sense, she is now."

"They both are. Jethro's death was the catalyst that kept him from becoming like Bruce. Henry will come to understand this eventually and be glad."

"I hope he uses his second chance wisely."

"Your daughter's housekeeper, Hazel Lockwood, is also in Cardston."

"Why is she here?"

"While cleaning one day, she accidentally knocked over a list of people Bruce wanted killed."

"Oh, that must have been a shock."

"It was. It confirmed her worst fears. She knew if she wanted to live she had to get away. She'd been quite ill and had to have gallbladder surgery, so she told Bruce she had cancer and was going to live with her sister in Saint Louis."

"Did she have her surgery here in Cardston?"

"No, she had it in Spokane. When she was well enough to travel, she came to Cardston. She's living with her sister, Helen Jorgenson."

"Why are you telling me this?"

"Because you'll need her help to teach Meagan. She has many skills you'll need."

"How do I contact her without arousing suspicion?"

"You'll run into her on Thursday. Don't be afraid to speak to her. Ask her if she'll meet you somewhere so the four of you can talk. Hazel will be a great help to all of you. She won't give you away because to do so would also be putting her life in danger. She'll be safer with the three of you than with her sister's family. Being with you will also protect her family from those men Bruce sends to find you."

"I'll gladly talk to her. How do I tell the girls about Hazel?"

"You'll think of something. Just convince Hazel to stay here with you. For now, keep my visit from the others. There's no need to worry them. Let Meagan have time to recover from the fear. Fear is a terrible thing, as you know. The pups you're getting her for Christmas will teach her how to love something besides the two of you. Having them will also give her something to be responsible for, which in turn will give her the extra love she needs right now. The two of you are giving this love to her, but she also needs the companionship of the two dogs."

"Thank you for helping me to see this. Not having had a dog I didn't understand this bond."

"You'll also be helped by the love these dogs will bring you. Your worship services will also bring you a little peace, as well as bringing you closer to the one being who can give you the help you so desperately need.

"Again, don't be afraid to speak to Jeff and Tim. They'll be your best allies."

Suddenly something attracted Shirleen's attention. Turning to see what it was, she was surprised to see there was nothing there. When she turned back, the man was gone.

She realized she felt relieved of all the stress she'd been feeling. She was completely relaxed and immediately fell asleep.

Shirleen woke to the sounds of hammering, as well as a mixture of different smells. Turning to look at the clock, she was horrified to find she'd slept until nearly lunchtime. Jumping out of bed, she hurried to the bathroom to grab a quick shower. After getting dress, she went out to the living room where she saw Meagan and Juliana. "I'm sorry I slept so late."

"You haven't been sleeping well. You needed it."

"Are you all right, Grandma?" asked Meagan, watching her warily.

"I haven't slept so soundly in I don't know how long."

"Wonderful," replied Meagan. "You look rested."

"Thank you." Looking down to see they had started school, she sighed before saying, "Sorry I interrupted your lessons. Go back to work. I'll eat something then do a little house cleaning."

"We're a little late getting started on our lessons because we wanted to get as much housework done as we could before you got up," grinned Juliana. "We haven't vacuumed, but we'll do that after lunch."

"I can do that much," declared Shirleen.

"No, Grandma. This is our gift to you. You take the day off and rest up some more. That's not a suggestion, it's an order."

Meagan rose to kiss her cheek.

Tears glistened in Shirleen's eyes at their kindness. "Thank you both so much."

"I made a chocolate cake before breakfast," Juliana said. "I also made a batch of dough for hot rolls. It's rising in a bowl on the table, and there's a roast in the oven for lunch. After I have given Meagan her assignments, I'll add the vegetables to the roast to finish it up. When the vegetables are done, I'll bake the rolls, while I make the gravy. Then, we can have lunch."

"Wow! I'm so impressed, guess I'll just be lazy until lunch is ready."

Shirleen went to the window to see how Jeff was doing on the motorhome shelter. She was surprised to see he had all of the poles in the ground already. She watched in fascination as he worked. *He's a hard worker.* She reflected on the message given her last night. She decided she'd talk to Jeff and Tim on Wednesday night. With the decision made, Shirleen went to work on her embroidery project.

That night after Jeff went home, Tim came to check on them. After they had been visiting for a while Shirleen grew so weak she couldn't sit at the piano any longer. She stood to go to bed, but crumpled in a heap on the floor. Tim rushed over to see what was happening. She was unconscious. "I'll get her to bed; call the doctor. He doesn't like to make house calls, but he'll come."

Lifting Shirleen effortlessly, he carried her to her room. Juliana had the covers pulled back when he got there. He laid her gently onto the bed, and Shirleen began to regain consciousness. She tired to push them away, but Juliana wouldn't allow it. She sat beside her while Meagan hovered on the other side. "How did I get here?"

"Tim carried you in here," said Meagan.

"I felt so weak all of a sudden. I thought if I went to lie down it would pass."

Juliana said, "You got to your feet then crumpled to the floor. Tim is calling the doctor."

Shirleen tried to getup, but slumped back onto the bed instead. "I don't understand what's happening."

"The doctor will be here soon. He'll tell you what's wrong. Meanwhile, just rest."

Forty-five minutes later they heard a car pull up. Juliana went to open the door for the doctor and Tim. The doctor wasn't pleased at all being dragged out on a cold night, but he didn't hesitate to follow them to Shirleen's room.

Kicking everyone out, he went to examine Shirleen.

"I feel fine now, doctor. I'm sorry they made you come out here for nothing."

"Hush," said the doctor. "Let me examine you, then I'll know if it was a wild goose chase or not."

Shirleen let him examine her, and when he was done, he patted her hand. You had good reason to call me," grinned the doctor. "You have a good case of exhaustion. What have you been doing?"

"I've been having terrible recurring nightmares. I've been having them for days now."

"Well, I'm going to give you a shot to knock you out. You'll sleep for quite a while. When the shot wears off, I want you to stay in bed. You're only allowed to get up to use the bathroom. I want you to do this until Wednesday. On Wednesday you may get up long enough to shower and have breakfast at the table with your family, then it's back to bed for more rest."

"But I have too much to do to just lay around," protested Shirleen.

"Listen, you do this or I'll put you in the hospital so fast your head will spin. Which will it be?"

Thinking the alternatives over Shirleen replied. "I'll do what you say."

"Good." Grinning, he added, "By the way, my name's Gerald Stillman."

"I wish we could've met under better circumstances."

Dr. Stillman gave her the shot then rose to go. Turning back he asked, "When will you be coming to town?"

"We'd planned on going to town on Thursday."

"Fine, come to my office at two o'clock. I'll let my receptionist know you'll be coming in."

"I'll be there." Shirleen hesitated a moment then decided to come clean. "Dr. Stillman there's something you should know. We're on the run from some evil men who want us dead."

"Is that why you're having the nightmares?"

"Yes."

Dr. Stillman sat down on the edge of the bed and said, "Tell me everything. Don't leave out any of the details."

Shirleen told him everything and Dr. Stillman didn't even flinch. Finally, he asked, "Is that everything?"

"Yes."

"You can trust me to keep your secret. I'll make sure my nurse and receptionist let you in through the back door. You'll be shown to room where you can wait for me and no one else will see you."

"I'll be on time."

Patting her hand, Dr. Stillman said, "You're going to be all right, you just need lots of rest." With that, he left the room.

Everyone was waiting as the doctor came into the living room. "Well," asked Juliana, "what's wrong with her?"

"You must be Juliana," Dr. Stillman said.

"I am. What's wrong with her?"

"Exhaustion."

Juliana waited for him to say more. When he didn't she continued. "She hasn't been sleeping well. We wouldn't let her do anything today, but as you can see, it didn't help."

"I gave her a shot to knock her out so she can rest. She's only allowed out of bed long enough to go to the bathroom for the next 24 hours. You'll need to take her meals to her. Make sure she doesn't do anything but rest."

"I'll see to it."

"Good. On Wednesday, she can take a shower then go back to bed for the rest of the morning. She can have lunch with you, but then it's back to bed. She can stay up for an hour after dinner, then it's lights out.

"She told me you'll be coming to town on Thursday, and I want to see her at my office at two o'clock."

Juliana turned pale, as he continued. "She filled me in on your situation. She'll explain everything after I leave."

"I'll come and check on her before I go to work in the morning," promised Tim as they left.

Hearing them drive away, they locked up the house before going to bed. Juliana was so relieved Jeff Borton had carried in enough wood to fill the wood boxes for the night. That was one less thing they had to be concerned about.

When Shirleen woke an hour later, she still felt groggy. She tried to sit up in bed, but she didn't have the strength. Realizing she wasn't alone, she turned and saw Juliana sitting on a chair beside the bed. When Shirleen touched her hand, Juliana woke up.

Shirleen noticed how worried she looked. "You don't have to sit with me, dear. I'll be fine with a little more rest."

"I know, I just couldn't stay away," replied Juliana as she began to cry. "When you collapsed, I was so afraid I'd lost you. That made me realize just how important you are to me." Dabbing at her eyes, she continued, "I guess I always thought you'd be around. Last night, I realized how vulnerable we all are in this mortal life."

"I confess, I was a little concerned too, but Dr. Stillman assured me it's only a case of exhaustion." Seeing Juliana was still concerned, Shirleen smiled as she squeezed her hand. "You need to get some sleep or there will two of us on bed rest!"

"If you're sure you're okay."

Chuckling, Shirleen replied, "There's just one thing I need before you go. Could you help me to the bathroom?"

"Sure," declared Juliana. She helped Shirleen to her feet, steadying her so she could get to the bathroom.

Finally, Shirleen got back into bed and Juliana leaned down to kiss her cheek. "I love you so very much, mother mine."

"I love you, too, sweetheart."

"Go back to sleep so Dr. Stillman doesn't yell at me."

"Yes, ma'am!" Shirleen saluted Juliana smartly, then smiled to take the edge off of her words. "Frankly, that wont' be difficult."

"Good. I won't wake you up until I bring you breakfast in the morning."

Shirleen took Juliana's hand to detain her a moment then said, "Listen, honey. We need to talk for just a moment longer. There are some things I need to say."

"Okay," replied Juliana taking the chair again.

"We need to have some people on our side ... people we can trust. I think Tim and Jeff, along with Dr. Stillman are those people."

"But is that safe?"

"Yes. I can't tell you how I know, but I know it is. I already told the doctor, and I plan to tell the others when we're together on Wednesday night."

"I guess you know what's best, Mother."

"Thank you for trusting me; it helps me have the confidence to do what has to be done. I think we should also go to the newspaper office Thursday and pay to have the paper delivered. We need to know what's happening around us. We also need to have a landline phone installed so we can reach someone if we don't have cell reception. If we'd been alone tonight, there's no telling what would've happened."

"Momma, something else we might consider buying is a television. We could watch the news each night. We don't need it during the day, but it sure would be a good thing when it comes to the news."

"I agree." Growing thoughtful, Shirleen asked, "How do you feel about getting a tower put on the top of the hill above our house so we can use our cell phones again. We could check with Tim to see how to go about that."

"I think that's an excellent idea. That way we could call each other whenever we need to."

"I'll add those things to our growing list."

"Good deal. I'll leave you to it. I'm suddenly really sleepy. Must be that shot." Trying to stifle a yawn, but failing, she was suddenly sound asleep. Since her visit with the angel, the nightmares had ceased.

Juliana quietly left the room. She stoked the fires in all of the fireplaces, then satis fied all was well, she went to bed and immediately fell asleep.

Tuesday flew by in a blur for all of them. Other than eating in bed or going to the bathroom, Shirleen slept most of the day away. Meagan tried to keep her mind on her studies, but was so worried about her grandmother that Juliana decided to get her mind directed someplace else. "Lesson time is over for today. You just can't concentrate, so what's the use of fighting it? Let's go figure something out for a nice lunch."

Together, they worked hard to make lunch wonderful. When Jeff came in to eat, he was truly impressed. Taking a bite, he moaned appreciatively, "Oh, this is absolutely wonderful!" He winked at Meagan and added, "It's a good thing I have a lot of hard work to do, or I might get so fat that I'd just plum waddle through any door I went through."

This caused Meagan to burst out laughing. "Oh," she cried holding her side, "that would be the funniest thing ever." Puffing out her cheeks she tried to imitate how he would look.

Pretending to be insulted, Jeff declared. "Now you're just plain makin' fun of me."

Meagan, sobered instantly, and touched his hand. "Oh, I'd never do such a thing to anyone as nice as you, Mr. Borton. Please forgive me for even suggesting such a thing."

"Well," drawled Jeff, who continued to play the role of an insulted person, "I'll let ya off this time if you'll start callin' me Jeff. This Mr. Borton stuff is for the birds."

Beaming, Meagan replied, "Thank you, I will, as long as you call me Meagan."

Grinning, Jeff readily agreed. Turning to Juliana, he said, "The same goes for you. Makes me feel like I belong somehow."

Nodding, Juliana agreed. "I'll do just that if you'll call me Juliana."

"I'd like that." He took a few more bites then said, "I almost have three sides finished on the cover. I should have the last side up and the roof on before quittin' time today."

"Oh, Momma will be pleased to hear that," Juliana said. "I'll tell her when I take her lunch in to her."

"Will she be all right, Juliana?" he asked with concern.

"Yes, the doctor said it was a mild case of exhaustion. She should be up, at least for her meals, tomorrow."

"Oh, I sure am relieved to hear that's all it was. I feared she'd had a stroke or something."

"So did we," said Meagan. "I sure have been worried about her today."

"We all are," said Jeff. Finishing his dessert, he wiped his mouth on the napkin then stood to go back to work. "I'm so stuffed; I'd better get in gear before I have to find a shady spot to take a nap."

That remark struck both of his companions as funny, because it was cloudy outside. Grabbing his hat, he went back to work.

Taking a tray of food to her mother, Juliana set it on the nightstand beside the bed. Touching her mother's shoulder gently, she called softy, "Momma?"

Shirleen slowly opened her eyes. Seeing Juliana leaning over her, she asked, "Is something wrong?"

"No, Momma. I just brought you something to eat."

"Oh, wonderful!"

Helping her to sit up comfortably on the bed, Juliana set the tray in front of her.

"This food smells so delicious, dear. Suddenly, I'm ravenous."

As she ate, Juliana pulled a chair over to sit down. "I have some good news for you, Momma. Jeff said he'd probably have the cover over the motorhome finished before he goes home today."

"Oh, that *is* good news. How's the wood supply holding out?"

"I think it'll be gone after he fills the boxes tonight."

"I was afraid of that," remarked Shirleen. "It's good the cover will be finished tonight so he can get started on the wood again."

"Meagan made everything you're eating. I helped with instructions, but she was the one who made it all."

"It's absolutely delicious!" Growing curious, she asked, "How are her lessons going?"

"We tried to work, but her mind just wasn't on them. It was on you. I decided the lessons could wait a day. To get her mind off you, we had cooking lessons instead."

"That's just as important," stated Shirleen. "She'll be a better homemaker than either of us."

"I hope so." Juliana sat thoughtfully watching her mother eat. Taking a deep breath she asked, "Momma, how do you feel about us teaching her how to sew, cook and do some other things necessary for being a good wife?"

"I think that's a good idea. Perhaps we can get a good instructor to come teach her this summer. I'd like to learn to sew our clothes as well as learn how to quilt."

"Then let's plan that for the summer."

"I've also been thinking," said Shirleen between bites, "if Mr. Borton would help us till it, we could plant a garden. We even could find a woman versatile in all of these areas to help us cook, sew, can, or do different types of crafts. These things would make us reach out more, not to mention keep our minds off our problems."

"Oh, I think that's a marvelous idea. When you're back onto your feet, we'll have a family council to discuss all of this."

"That's a good idea." Tossing the covers back, she sat up on the edge of the bed. "Right now, I need to go to the bathroom."

"Let me take these things to the kitchen so Meagan can get them washed. I'll be back as quick as I can to help you."

"I feel a lot stronger," Shirleen assured her.

"That may be so, but I want to be around in case you aren't."

"Okay, I promised Dr. Stillman I'd be good, so I'll wait until you get back. I suggest you hurry, though, or you'll have an even bigger problem to deal with."

"I'll hurry." Juliana quickly left the room. Soon she was back to help. Shirleen did feel stronger, but it was evident she wasn't ready to tackle walking by herself. When she was back in bed, Juliana tucked her in and kissed her cheek. "I'll check on you often to see how you're doing."

"Thank you, dear. It's amazing how tired I am just from walking to the bathroom and back."

"Rest and I'll bring you some food at suppertime."

"Oh, I won't argue. I don't have the strength."

Shortly after Juliana left the room, Shirleen fell sleep. She woke up long enough to eat dinner, then fell asleep again and didn't wake up until the next morning when she heard the others getting ready for the day. Flinging the covers back, she rose to sit on the edge of the bed before stretching and walking to the bathroom on her own.

A hot shower made her feel a little better, even though it sapped some of her strength. Coming out of the bathroom, she saw Juliana looking concerned. "What do you think you're doing, Momma?"

"Taking a shower so I can start my day. Dr. Stillman said it would be all right. He also said I could eat my meals with you. I'm just not supposed to do anything too strenuous I'll take a nap after lunch so I can be rested enough to talk to Tim and Jeff. When Jeff gets here, could you send him in so I can speak to him for a few minutes." Seeing Juliana's look of fear, Shirleen, quickly hugged her and said, "I won't tell him anything until tonight at the meeting. I just want to ask him to be there."

Brightening, Juliana said, "I'll have him come inside immediately after he arrives."

"Thank you, dear." Together they went to breakfast.

Chapter 9

After Bruce left Henry Borden's room at the recovery center, he went back to where his driver, Paul Thomas, was waiting by the limo. "Home, Paul! There's nothing here I care about."

"Yes, sir," he said as he held the door open for Bruce to get inside.

As Bruce rode along, he remembered he'd made up some trumped up excuse for leaving his office downtown. He had more pressing matters to take care of. He needed to get a plane ticket. He needed to go to Ohio to get Nate White, as well as deal with Gordon Spielberg's plane at the airport.

When he got home, Bruce went to the kitchen to grab a snack before going to his office. He found a note on the kitchen counter from his maid, Hazel Lockwood, that read read,

> Mr. Murdock,
>
> I have a doctor's appointment at three o'clock. After that, I'll get the groceries for the week. I should be back in time to prepare your evening meal.
>
> Hazel.

Flinging the note in the trash, Bruce raided the refrigerator for the last piece of apple pie. He buried it with cool whip, and grabbed the jug of milk and a fork. He took everything to the table and flopped down in a chair. He made short work of the pie, downed the last of the milk and left the dirty dishes on the table, before heading to his office.

As Bruce was putting the finishing touches on a brief, he heard someone in the kitchen. He went to see who it was and found Hazel lugging in several bags of groceries. He watched her struggling with the bags as he leaned lazily against the doorframe.

Hazel was a short, thin woman. Her once light brown hair was streaked with gray. She wasn't beautiful, but she wasn't ugly either. She set the bags on the floor, and went back out to get some more. Bruce still didn't lift a finger to help her. Groceries and anything to do with the kitchen — that was women's work in his opinion.

"I stopped at the deli and got something easy for supper," she said as she came in with the rest of the groceries. "When I have these put away, I'll get it ready for you."

"Just let me know when it's ready," he said as he left the room.

When Bruce was gone, Hazel doubled over with pain. It took a while for it to dissipate so she could put the rest of the groceries away. When that job was over, she warmed up the deli chicken in the microwave while she set the table and then prepared some side dishes.

She started to go tell Bruce it was ready, but was hit with more pain. Gripping the back of the chair until the pain eased, she struggled to hang in there. She was just straightening up when Bruce came in. "What's holding up supper, Hazel?"

"I was just about to come and get you, sir."

"It's about time," snapped Bruce. "You've never been late with supper before."

"I'm sorry, sir."

Bruce sat down to eat, and Hazel poured coffee into his cup. While Bruce wolfed the food down, Hazel cut him a piece of cherry pie and added a generous amount of cool whip to the top, then set it before him. "I'd like to speak to you for a few minutes after you have finished your supper. It is important, sir."

"Okay, I'll be done here in half an hour. I have some instructions for you as well." Ignoring her, Bruce went back to his dinner.

Hazel went to her room to wait. It was an ironclad rule that she was to eat after the master of the house had left the table. Hazel had only stayed on with the family because of Ruth. She hated this job. Many times she'd wondered why Ruth and Leslie hadn't come home, but dared not ask.

She'd always loathed everything about Bruce Murdock. After she'd accidentally knocked a file to the floor that exposed his mafia connections and a list of people he planned to murder, she not only hated him, she also feared for her life. She knew she had to get out of this house before she ended up dead. She'd made sure she put the file back on top of the other files on his desk, exactly where it had been before it fell.

She'd called her sister, Helen, after her doctor's appointment and told her she'd be coming to see her as soon as she could get away. She'd added that she'd explain everything when she saw her.

Glancing at the clock, Hazel was surprised to see thirty minutes had passed. She got to the kitchen as Bruce leaned back in his chair. Looking up at her, he asked, "What's so important it can't wait?"

"As you know, I went to the doctor this afternoon. I had some tests a few days ago and today the doctor gave me the results." She paused to calm her jangled nerves and then continued, "I have stage four breast cancer. It seems I waited too long get tested. I only have about six months to live. So, as of today, I'm going to have to terminate my job with you."

"When do you plan to leave?"

As he watched her, another bout of pain washed over her, causing her to double over. Bruce waited until she'd gained control. Finally, after taking a deep breath, she replied. "Since today is Thursday, I'll finish out the week and leave tomorrow.

"Where do you plan to go?"

"My sister's place in Saint Louis. I have to get my affairs in order. I have to purchase a plot, make arrangements for my funeral, and pay off all my bills. I should be able to take care of that with my last check."

"I'm sorry to hear you've been given such a death sentence, and I won't try to stop you from going. I'll write you a check before I leave in the morning. I need you to have my breakfast ready at 4 a.m. I have a plane to catch. I've to go out of town on business that just can't wait. I'll say goodbye to you in the morning."

"Thank you, sir." She started to rise then asked, "Do you want me to try to find someone to take my place?"

"No, I'll take care of it."

"Thank you. I'll see that the house is in order before I leave."

"That would be most helpful. Good luck."

"Thank you, sir. Good luck on your trip. I hope all goes well." Rising, she started to clean off the table as Bruce left the room.

Hazel decided not to bother with dinner so she could get right to packing her things. She went to her car, got some boxes and took them to her room where she started packing as fast as she could.

It was late when she went to bed. Unable to sleep, she just lay there, praying she could safely get away before he found out she knew his secrets. Finally, at three o'clock, she got up to prepare for her day.

She quickly prepared a meal for Bruce and set the food onto the table. She was about to go to her room, when Bruce entered the kitchen. He handed her a check and said, "This should help with all of your expenses. You've been a loyal worker, so I want to reward you."

Glancing at the check, Hazel nearly dropped it. It was made out for seven hundred thousand dollars. "Oh my, sir. This is most generous of you."

"You deserve it"

"Thank you very much. This will help me immensely." Folding the check she placed it in the pocket of her apron. I'll leave you to have your breakfast in peace, sir."

Hazel wanted to run to her room, but wisely walked away calmly. When she was back in her room, she packed the last of her clothes and made sure everything was ready to carry to the car. Two hours later, she heard Bruce leave the house.

Returning to the kitchen, she worked hard to put the kitchen to rights. She cleaned the house thoroughly, then made some toast to eat with a glass of milk. When she was finished, she brought her car around to the front door and started carrying her belongings out of the house. It took her several trips to get everything into the car, and the pain kept forcing her to stop and rest.

When she finally had everything in the car, she came back inside to make one final check before leaving this house of horrors forever. She picked up her purse, took out her house key and left it on the table near the door. She closed the door, got into her car, and drove away from there for the last time.

She stopped at the bank and deposited her final paycheck, then asked to speak to the manager. A teller took her over to his desk.

Rising, the manager greeted her and indicating a chair, asked, "Won't you please be seated?"

"Thank you, sir." Sitting down, Hazel said, "Mr. Holmes, I'm going to be leaving town. I need to empty my account, because I won't be coming back. I don't want to carry all of that money with me in cash. Could I get a cashier's check so I can deposit it when I arrive at my destination?"

"Sure, there's no problem with doing that. How much is in your account?"

"Seven hundred and forty thousand dollars. I need to have ten thousand in cash to pay bills and other expenses along the way."

"That's a lot of money to carry on your person, Miss Lockwood."

"Oh, by the time I've paid all of my bills and bought my plane ticket, there will only be about a thousand dollars left."

"Oh, then that won't be so bad."

He went to get the cashier's check and came back quickly with her cash and check. Hazel quickly put everything into her purse and prepared to leave. "Thank you so much for your help, Mr. Holmes."

"My pleasure, Miss Lockwood. Good luck where you're going."

Nodding, Hazel walked out of the bank. Once she was in the car, she went straight to the UPS to have her boxes shipped to Canada. Her sister didn't live in Saint Louis, as she'd told Bruce Murdock, she actually lived in Cardston.

One of the UPS employees helped her bring everything into the building. As soon as it was all labeled, she paid them and left to pay her bill at the doctor's office. That took two thousand dollars of her money.

When she left the doctor's office, she went to pay off her dental bill. That took another two thousand. Feeling as light as a feather, she went back to her car. She sat there for a few minutes, feeling elated. *So far, so good!*

Starting the car, she pulled out into traffic and headed for the airport. When she got there, she saw Bruce walking through the terminal to get to his plane. She nearly panicked, but he didn't even look back. She waited until she saw him get on the plane, then walked over to the ticket counter and purchased a ticket for Spokane.

Since she shipped her car, which cost her another three thousand dollars, she would be driving to Canada. She watched from the airport's window as they loaded her car onto the plane. Relieved to see it was safely inside, she took a seat in the lobby to wait for her flight.

As she waited she smiled, thinking about the con job she'd pulled on Bruce Murdock. She didn't have cancer at all, just a bad case of gallstones. She'd be staying in Spokane for about six weeks with her sister, Carol, so she could see a doctor who'd remove her gallbladder.

Soon they called her flight and she went to get in line to board the plane. Taking a seat near a window, she strapped herself in and waited for the plane to take off. She grew impatient for everyone to get boarded so they could be on their way. Finally, the last person had boarded, and Hazel watched as the door closed and her new life began. She was finally free!

Bruce arrived in Ohio a little before five p.m. and went straight to the car rental office. He was soon on the road to the motel where White had been waiting for him. As he drove, he thought with disgust about his housekeeper's cancer. Finding a replacement was just one more thing he had to deal with. "Well, good riddance to bad rubbish."

He was hungry, so he stopped at a café on the way. He found a booth, in the smoking section and placed his order and ate his food in record time.

As he left, he called Nate White. "Nate, this is Bruce. I'm in town. Where are you and what's your room number?"

"Motel Six on D Street, room 214."

"Give me the directions." When Nate had complied, Bruce ended the call and followed Nathan's directions perfectly. He stopped in front of room 214 and shut off the car.

Nathan quickly opened the door when he knocked. When he was inside, Nathan closed and locked the door while Bruce took a seat. "Are you ready to go?"

"Almost. I just have to grab my shaving kit."

"Good. The sooner we get back to the airport and get Spielberg's plane, the sooner we can get back to Syracuse. We'll rest up at my place tonight, then we'll start for New York in the morning."

"That suits me just fine."

Riding to the airport, Bruce filled Nate in on everything.

"Whew," said White. "Sounds like you've been busy."

"We have and it isn't over yet. Spielberg's men will retaliate. There's no doubt at all about that. We need to be one jump ahead of them." White was prevented from replying when Bruce's phone rang. He pulled off to answer it.

"Crowley here, boss. I have some information you'll be interested in hearing. Where can we meet?"

"I'm on my way to the airport in Cleveland to pick up Spielberg's plane. We should be back in Syracuse in three hours. Meet me at my home."

"Good enough. See you when you get there."

Putting his cell phone back into his shirt pocket, he turned to White and said, "Looks like we'll have company tonight."

"What's up?"

"Crowley has some important information to give me. He should be there not long after we get there."

"Sounds ominous," replied White, grinning snidely.

Before long, they reached the airport. Knowing the cell number for Gordon's pilot, Luther Jones, he quickly dialed it. When the pilot answered, Bruce said, "Jones? This is Bruce Murdock."

"Hello, Mr. Murdock," replied Jones. *"What can I do for you?"*

"I've been sent to pick up Spielberg's plane and fly it to New York. I'd appreciate you getting to the airport to fly us there. I have to make a short stop at Syracuse then we'll fly out in the morning."

"Fine, I'll be ready."

"We should be there within twenty minutes."

Parking the car in the rental section, they got their gear and went inside and turned the key over to the attendant before heading to the waiting plane. Once they were inside, Bruce gave the pilot some last minute instructions before takeoff and soon they were in the air.

Bruce was outwardly calm, but inside he was gloating about his incredible luck. *Spielberg's plane's mine and soon I'll be taking his place as boss.*

Several hours later, the three men were back at Bruce's home office. Vincent Crowley and Nathan White sat across from their boss as he demanded, "Okay, spill it. What's this important information?"

"Well," began Crowley, "I went to New York like you asked. It was easier than we thought to get on the good side of those Spielberg men that didn't get bumped off. I told them I sympathized with their loss and what happened to their friends was a horrible thing. I did a few jobs for them to show my good will, too.

"One of the men, Dexter Ritter, started talking once he trusted me. He asked if I would help kill those who did their friends, and I told him I would. That's when he said they knew you were responsible."

"They figured that out already?"

"Yeah. Seems one of the men we tried to pick off lived and let the cat out of the bag."

Cursing, Bruce said, "I never miss! How come he lived?"

"I guess he was tougher than we thought, that or he was wearing a bulletproof vest. They do that sometimes, you know."

"What's his name?"

"Frank Muldoon."

"Where is he now?"

"Some house in the ritzy part of town," Crowley said and gave Bruce the address.

"Well, Nathan, that's your new assignment. Since we didn't kill him with a bullet, rig up a car bomb. That should take care of things."

"I'll get right on it."

"Wait 'til we've left for New York. Rent a car and see that Muldoon is taken care of for good this time."

Turning to Crowley he asked, "What are Spielberg's men planning?"

"They plan to take all of us down on the third of September, right here in Syracuse."

"That's only a few days away."

"Ten days to be exact."

"Then we'll be ready for 'em," declared Bruce. "When we're through, any who are left standing will get an ultimatum — either join up or be eliminated."

Crowley cracked his knuckles and smirked. "I can hardly wait to start breaking bones."

"Well, Vinnie, you'll just have to be patient. We need them all together in one place." Drumming his finger angrily on the table, he thought, *If they're gonna attack us on the third, we'll hit 'em on the second!*

For the next few hours, the men worked on their plan.

The next morning after breakfast, Nathan rented a car and was on his way to New York. Murdock and Crowley continued to contact the rest of their men.

Hazel Lockwood left the plane and went to find her car. She'd just found it when she heard someone calling her name. Turning, she saw her sister, Carol Lemming, walking toward her.

Carol and Hazel were carbon copies, even to the gray hair. The only differences was Hazel had dark blue eyes while Carol's were brown, and Carol was also a foot taller.

Carol's husband, Floyd, hung back to give them time to greet each other. He was much taller than Carol and his hair was completely white.

When he joined them, he asked, "How was your flight, Sis?"

"Uneventful." replied Hazel. Sighing she added, "It's so good to be here. I've been having a lot of pain, so I'm more than ready to get this gallbladder out."

"Well," said Carol, "let's get you home where we can take care of you."

"I'd really appreciate that." Suddenly the pain returned, doubling her over. Floyd grabbed her to keep her from hitting the ground. When the pain had finally let up, they put her into their car. Floyd would be drive Hazel's car.

When they got to the Lemming's home, Floyd carried Hazel's luggage inside and Carol took her immediately to the guest bedroom. "Rest for an hour then we'll get something to eat."

"A bowl of soup would be great. Anything else just makes the pain flare up."

"Sure," replied Carol, kissing her cheek before leaving the room.

Hazel was grateful for the chance to rest. She laid down and immediately fell into a deep sleep.

An hour later, Carol woke her to tell her the soup was ready. It took all of Hazel's willpower to get out of bed. She washed her face and combed her hair. Satisfied she could do no more, she went down to eat.

"You have an appointment with Dr. Stone tomorrow at three o'clock. He'll decide when it's best to do the surgery."

"Good. The sooner the better." She started eating the soup when she sat back and added, "It is so good to see you guys again."

"We're happy to see you too, Sis."

"I promised to fill you in on everything that's been going on. I'm so grateful to get out of Syracuse because I just learned my boss works for the mafia."

"No!" exclaimed Floyd. "Are you sure?"

"Yeah, unfortunately I am. One day when I was cleaning his office, I knocked over a file on his desk. As I was putting it back in the folder, I saw the names of some men he wanted murdered. That scared me so badly I knew I had to get away from there as fast as possible."

"No kidding," responded, Carol.

"Sis, Floyd, I lied to him so I could get off his radar. I told him I had stage-four breast cancer. When he asked me where I was going, I said I was going to stay with my sister in Saint Louis."

"Smart thinking," said Floyd proudly. "He'll never think to look for you in Canada."

"That's what I thought, too," Hazel said.

"Well, the first thing you're going to do is get well. You'll have the surgery and recover fully before you leave for Canada."

"I can't wait to be free of this pain."

"I know," sympathized Carol. "We'll know more after you see the doctor."

"I was so terrified last night I didn't sleep a wink. Suddenly I'm so bone tired I think I could sleep for a week. Would you mind if we put off catching up until I've slept some more?"

"Not at all. Rest is exactly what you need right now." Carol walked Hazel back to her room, and made sure she went straight to bed. "If you get hungry, the rest of the soup will be in the frig. Feel free to help yourself."

"Thanks, Sis. You're so good to me."

"Isn't that what sisters do?"

"I suppose it is." Hazel snuggled further under the covers. "Thanks for everything, Sis."

"You're welcome."

Hazel slept until noon the next day. When she woke up, she showered quickly and went downstairs to visit with her sister. After eating another bowl of soup, she felt much better. They spent the next two hours visiting.

At two o'clock they started across town to see Dr. Stone. When they were shown into a room, Hazel grew nervous. It was all right to say she would be glad to be free of the pain and quite another thing to know she'd have to have more pain before it would finally be over.

A few minutes later, Dr. Stone came in the room. While he was getting ready to examine her, Hazel studied him carefully. He was tall and thin. When he looked over at Hazel, she saw his eyes were the most beautiful crystal blue she'd ever seen. They reminded her of a mountain lake. With his curly coal black hair, he was easy on the eyes.

Hazel pulled her thoughts back to the present when Dr. Stone started to speak, "As you can see, I got the x-rays from your doctor. After studying them carefully, I think we should do the surgery as soon as possible. There are three stones inside the gallbladder, and one very large one is starting to come out. If that happens, you could be in serious trouble. I want to admit you to the hospital today, then operate early in the morning. We just can't wait."

"I'm ready to do whatever's best."

Before Hazel could fully catch her breath, she'd been admitted to the hospital. The next morning the surgery went off without a hitch, and two days later she was resting comfortably in Carol's guest bedroom.

Several days passed before she felt like doing much except sleep. When she was feeling stronger, she and her sister talked about their childhood and all sorts of memories. Eventually, Hazel told Carol about Ruth and Leslie. "Ruth always treated me with respect," said Hazel. "Leslie was the sweetest young thing you'd ever want to meet. She was so intelligent. I use to love talking to her when she got home from school. She'd always come into the kitchen for a couple of cookies and a glass of milk."

"They sound like nice people," mused Carol.

"I think Ruth was afraid to open up because of her husband. I understood her feelings, so kept my distance. I like to think if circumstances had been different we could've been good friends."

"Perhaps someday that will happen," suggested Carol.

"I don't think so. When I came back from vacation this year, they were both gone. It was like they'd dropped off the face of the earth. I'm afraid something terrible happened to them. I wouldn't put any thing past Bruce Murdock. He is one warped individual."

"That's scary. I'm glad you got away from that situation," replied Carol.

Time passed quickly for Hazel, and soon she was well enough to travel. It was getting late in the season, so she decided to leave before the winter snows trapped her in Spokane. On the fifteenth of October, she pulled out of her sister's driveway and headed toward Canada. She tired easily after the surgery and ended up stopping in Sandpoint for two nights to rest up. Two days later, she arrived in Cardston, Alberta.

She stopped at a café when she got there, and called her sister, Helen, while she waited for her food. When she told her where she was, her sister dropped everything and came to join her.

She hadn't eaten much of her meal before her sister burst into the restaurant and excitedly rushed over to hug her. "You're a sight for sore eyes, Sis!"

Hazel studied her baby sister as she chattered away. She was shorter, but other than that, she looked exactly like Hazel. The only difference was Helen's hair was the same light brown it had always been. She was glowing and her pregnancy was evident. Helen had married Neil Jorgenson 10 years ago, but already had seven children. This one would give them an even eight.

"Wow, Sis. You look wonderful," exclaimed Hazel.

While Hazel ate, Helen chatted amiably. "Thanks, hon. I'm as big as a house! By the way, your boxes arrived safe and sound and I have them hidden away in the room where you'll be staying. The kids have been going crazy because you took so long to get here."

Soon after Hazel had finished eating, Helen led the way back to her house. Hazel was happy to be done traveling. That night as she fell asleep, she finally felt free of the strain she'd experienced since she'd found out Bruce's secret.

Living in Cardston took some adjustment. Her sister's children, were driving her to distraction. They were rowdy and noisy and sometimes she wanted to leave and never come back. It wasn't that she didn't love them; she just wasn't used to the chaos they brought with them everywhere they went.

After one particularly harrowing day, Hazel started looking for her own place. To stay hidden, she changed her name to Gertrude North, and started going by Trudy. No matter how hard she looked, she just couldn't find a place she liked. *Maybe I'm just too picky,* she thought. *I guess I'll look for a job and let the apartment thing sort itself out in time. At least that will get me out of the house more.*

The next morning, Trudy went to the employment office. It was just nine o'clock when she finally found the building. She went inside, got the required forms and filled them out. When she had them completed, she took them back to the receptionist who told her someone would speak with her as soon as they were available.

Trudy took a seat, and a few minutes a later woman approached her. "My name's Stella Holbrook," she said tersely. "I'll contact you when we have an opening for a cook or housekeeper."

"Thank you," replied Trudy politely. "I'll check-in with you often."

"Whatever," replied Stella.

As she walked to her car, Trudy didn't hold out much hope of getting a job this way. She decided to take the initiative and visited the restaurants in town. None of them were hiring. Discouraged, she went back to Helen's.

When Trudy got there, the children were being particularly rambunctious, which only made her more frustrated and on edge. *I have to get out of here before I lose my patience with these kids!* Sighing, she went in to help Helen make supper.

When the meal was over and the dishes done, she excused herself and went to her room. Sitting near the window, she looked out at the town and saw a few snowflakes. As she watched the flakes, they became thicker. Half an hour later, she couldn't see anything but swirling white. *What have I gotten myself into? I went from fearing for my life to being trapped here with my sister's noisy brood.* Feeling overwhelmed, she started to cry.

Falling on her knees beside her bed, Trudy started to pray — something she hadn't done in years. For a long time she unloaded her burdens. When she was done, she felt a lot better.

She got ready for bed, but couldn't sleep. Lying there in the dark, she tried to plan her next steps. *I never had problems getting a job before, so why am I having trouble now?* No matter how hard she tried to execute a plan of action, nothing happened. Finally, she gave up and burrowed deeper under the covers. As she lay there, peace began to steel over her and the thought came into her mind, *Be of good cheer, my child. Something will turn up soon.*

The next few days were difficult, but Trudy doggedly refused to give up. One day she went to the store to get some things she needed. She wasn't paying attention to where she was going and suddenly heard someone calling her real name. Panicking, she looked around to see who knew her here. A woman, standing near her car called her name again.

The woman seemed familiar, but she couldn't place her. All of the sudden, she realized it was Ruth. She nearly fainted from shock. She ducked into the cafeteria in the mall and pretended she hadn't heard.

It didn't work and Ruth, along with Leslie and Sarah followed her inside and sat down at her table. After they talked for a while, Trudy had found a job and a place to live. She was going to work for them again.

As she left the cafeteria, her head was held high and there was a spring to her steps. Trudy knew this was where she belonged, and she thanked God for this happy meeting.

Chapter 10

After breakfast on Wednesday morning, Shirleen had laid back down and fell into a deep sleep. Suddenly, she awoke with a start and saw Juliana bending over her. "Momma, Jeff's here. He's waiting in the living room. You said you wanted to speak him."

"Oh," cried Shirleen rising to lower her legs over the bed. "I'll be right there."

Jeff turned his attention away from the window when he heard her footsteps coming down the hallway. Seeing he was still dressed for the outdoors, Shirleen hurried toward him. "Good morning, Mr. Borton."

"Good morning, ma'am. You wanted to see me?"

"Yes, I did," said Shirleen taking the stuffed chair by the fireplace. "Before I get down to business, you've got to start calling me Shirleen. This ma'am business makes me old and snobby, and I'm not either of those things."

"I'd be happy to, as long as you call me Jeff." Twisting his hat in his hands, he added, "I had enough of that formal stuff to last well past two lifetimes when I was in the army."

Grinning, Shirleen replied, "I can call you Jeff. I'm certainly no general!"

Squirming, Jeff turned beat red, "Ah, now you're making fun of me."

"Absolutely not. I was just joking."

"Ha! Well, you don't look like any general I've ever met. What can I do for you, ma— I mean Shirleen?"

"Sergeant York will be coming by to check on us tonight. Would you please be here then too?" When Jeff looked a little undecided, Shirleen continued, "I ... that is ... *we* need to talk to both of you at the same time. What we have to say is extremely important."

"Oh, then I'll be here. I'll just keep working 'til he gets here."

"Thank you, I really appreciate it. That's all I wanted. I'll let you get back to work." As Jeff started to leave, Shirleen added, "Jeff, the cover for the motorhome looks really good."

"Thanks. It wasn't hard at all. It isn't perfect, but it'll protect it for now. When spring comes, I'll pretty it up so it matches the rest of the buildings."

"Thank you."

"I'll see you at lunch time, Shirleen."

"That you will."

Jeff went back to work, while Shirleen went back to rest until lunchtime.

The rest of the day was uneventful. When the supper meal was done, Jeff brought in enough wood to fill the wood boxes. Satisfied, he went back to splitting the wood. An hour after dark, Tim arrived.

Meagan met him at the door and invited him in.

"Good evening, Meagan," Tim said, tweaking her cheek. "How's your grandmother feeling tonight?"

Grinning, Meagan said, "Come see for yourself, Mr. Mountie!"

"I'll show you Mountie," declared, Tim, grabbing his handcuffs, but Meagan, laughing happily, ducked out of his way. "Well, little lady, you're not out of the woods yet!" Shaking the cuffs at her, he added, "I've arrested men for saying less to me."

"I can just imagine," giggled Meagan.

That was too much for Tim, who started laughing. Finally, he looked over at Juliana to wink, then cried, "Uncle! To think I, Sergeant Timothy Titus Obadiah York have been bested by a girl." Plopping onto the couch Tim pretended to cry. Swiping at his imaginary tears, he continued, "All this time I thought I was so tough, and then you go and knock me down to size."

Unable to contain herself, Meagan put her hand on his shoulder and said, "It's all right, Mr. Mountie, better men than you have been felled by me."

This hit Tim's funny bone causing him to roar loudly. His laughter was so contagious the others joined in. Gaining control, he hugged Meagan and said, "If I didn't know better, I'd think you were one of my ornery little sisters."

Punching him lightly, Meagan stepped back. "I'm *not* ornery!"

Bowing slightly, Tim replied, "I most humbly beg your pardon for being so truthful."

That remark made Meagan start laughing again.

Sinking back onto the couch, he looked around the room and noticed Jeff was still there. "I didn't expect to see you here, Jeff. How'd you get in the good graces of these lovely ladies?"

"I was asked to stay for a meeting they want to have with us."

"A meeting?" Tim looked first at Shirleen then over to Juliana.

Taking a deep breath, Shirleen said, "Yes, the three of us have something important to talk to you about."

"That sounds ominous," replied Tim. Getting more comfortable, he waited to see what they had to say.

"It is," Shirleen said solemnly.

Seeing their suddenly serious faces, Tim knit his eyebrows together in concern.

"After you hear what we have to say, we'll understand if you don't want anything to do with us."

"Are you running from the law?" asked Tim.

"No," Shirleen said hesitantly. "We're not running from the law, we're running from something much worse."

"Now you've really peaked my curiosity," said Tim.

Jeff remained silent, deciding to keep his opinions to himself.

Looking from Meagan, who suddenly looked like she'd seen a ghost, over to Juliana's pale face, Shirleen took another deep breath before plunging in. "First of all, Shirleen, Juliana and Meagan are not our real names. My name is Sarah Spielberg. I chose the name of Shirleen Webb because my mother used that name on an account she left to me before her death. She did that so my husband, Gordon Spielberg and father couldn't get ahold of it."

"My real name is Ruth Murdock," Juliana said, as she took over the conversation. "The reason we ran is because my husband, Bruce Murdock, told me he was going to force our daughter, Leslie, whom you know as Meagan, to marry a young man she loathed.

"Things came to a head when Meagan, I mean Leslie, was almost raped by this man, Jethro. She kneed him in the privates and told him she'd have none of that. When she told me what happened, we decided it was time to get out. We pretended to go shopping for her wedding dress in New York so we could get away and have a few day's head start before anyone realized we were gone."

"Couldn't you have reasoned with your husband?" asked Jeff.

"You don't know my husband. It's his way or you suffer the consequences, which can be severe," said Ruth. "I had no intentions of allowing him to force my daughter into marrying that beast of a man."

Looking at her mother, who nodded for her to continue, Juliana said, "Both my mother and I had been forced to marry men we didn't love. Plus, I had suspicions that my husband and Momma's husband were part of the mafia."

Jeff jumped as if slapped, then said, "Are you sure about the mafia thing?"

Shirleen replied, "I had proof. One day, a man came to see my husband. I was walking past his office and heard this man tell my husband one of his men was going to turn informant. My husband told him bluntly to take him out. I wanted to run away from there that very day, but as you probably know the only way out of the mafia is death." She fell silent.

"Please, go on," encouraged Tim.

Shirleen took a deep breath before she could continue. "Knowing I couldn't escape right then, I waited for my chance. When Juliana, I mean Ruth, called me, I knew it was time to go."

"That's right," replied Juliana. "After telling Bruce I'd go along with his plan, I went to tell Meagan what he'd said." She looked from Jeff then back to Tim. "I suspected Bruce's connections too, but unlike Momma, I couldn't prove it. I only knew I had to get my daughter as far away from there as possible."

"You did the right thing," stated Tim.

Juliana continued as if Tim hadn't spoken, "After I talked to Meagan, I mean Leslie, she suggested we ask Momma if she wanted to go with us when we left. When I called her and told her our plan, her exact words were 'You bet your sweet Aunt Petunia, I do.'"

Shirleen again took over the conversation, "I bought a new van, registered it in my new name, and my gardener, Stanley Harris, put on the new plates for me. We hid it so we could pick it up when we left."

Leaning forward, Tim asked, "What did you do with your car?"

"I followed Stanley out to a place called Dead Man's Bluff. He poured gasoline all over it and pushed it over the cliff. As it started rolling, he tossed a lighted torch into the car and it caught fire. When it hit the bottom of the cliff, it exploded. We waited until it had burned itself out, then I took Stanley to the bus station where I saw him get on the bus."

"Ingenious!" declared Jeff.

Nodding Tim replied, "I agree."

"Knowing what my mother had left for me, I went to the bank and took out one million dollars of the money. I was afraid to keep going back to the bank, so I withdrew a lot."

"I understand that," said Tim. "I'm surprised you didn't get robbed, carrying that much cash around."

"I didn't think about that," said Shirleen. "All I thought about was keeping my family safe."

"Did you know about the money, Juliana?" asked Tim.

"No," replied Juliana, "I didn't find out until we were in our motel room that night. We all dyed our hair and bought clothes that were different from anything we'd ever worn before. Just before we went to bed, Momma showed us what was in the huge suitcase I'd lugged out of the car."

"It must have been a real shock to see that much money," grinned Tim.

"That's an understatement! We decided to each carry three thousand dollars with us to pay for things on our way here, and get the rest into a bank as soon as possible."

"We thought we had it all planned out so well," Shirleen continued. "We didn't take anything from our old lives, except the clothes in our suitcases. Our biggest mistake was not phoning home each night. We were so intent on getting away that none of us even gave that a thought.

"We thought things were going well, then one night in Ohio, Gordon, my husband, found us."

Jeff was on the edge of his seat as he asked, "What did you do?"

"I called the police," replied Shirleen. "We didn't do anything other than put a chair under the doorknob so he couldn't get in."

"Well," declared Jeff when Shirleen paused, "Don't leave us hanging. What happened next?"

"Gordon made such a scene that he was arrested. As soon as they hauled him away, we packed, loaded the van and got out of there. We didn't stop until we got to Cleveland, where we bought the motorhome."

"The owner must've been shocked when you paid him in cash," grinned Tim.

"We didn't pay him in cash," Shirleen said with a sly smile. "After we got the total price, we told him we'd decide by morning and left. That night, Juliana and I split the money we needed, so we could carry it easier. The next morning, we found a little out of the way bank. I told the manage we needed a cashiers check to pay for a motorhome. I gave him the paper with the price written on it. He asked if we had the money to cover the check. When we put it all on his desk, I thought he was going to have a heart attack. When he recovered from the shock, he counted it and got us a cashier's check."

"Oh, how I would've loved to have been a mouse in the corner to witness that transaction," responded Tim.

Ignoring Tim's remark, Shirleen continued. "When he gave us the cashier's check, we asked him never to tell anyone we'd been there because it would not only put our lives in danger, but also endanger those at the bank. After we left, we went back to the dealer and purchased the motorhome."

Meagan took over the conversation again. "The dealer knew we were running from someone, so Grandma told him the truth. He kindly got rid of any evidence we'd ever been there and helped us get rid of the van. It went the same way as the car."

Tim shook his head then replied, "You three think of everything." Scratching his head he added, "But ditching those vehicles without getting caught was plumb lucky."

"We didn't know what else to do," Shirleen said. "We couldn't just leave them hanging around as a way to track us."

"No, you couldn't," he replied. "I think you did the wise thing under the circumstances."

Barton asked, "What made you come to Canada?"

Juliana took over the conversation. "Let me tell you what happened before Gordon tracked us down, since that will answer your question."

Looking at her mother then over at Meagan, she began. "I had been taking my turn with the driving when we crossed the New York state line into Pennsylvania. Not knowing what direction to take, I pulled over to ask Momma what to do. After going over the Atlas, she didn't have an answer either. Meagan suggested we pray about it, so we did. What we asked was if we should stop in Canada or go on to Alaska. None of us really wanted to go to either place, but we thought Gordon and Bruce would never think of looking for us in either place. Anyway, we all felt like we were supposed to go to Canada.

Meagan piped up, "Next, we had to decide where to go once we got to Canada. We decided it would be between Cardston and Calgary. We prayed about that too, and Momma and I felt Cardston was the right place. Grandma said she didn't know, so she took a walk to pray by herself to pray for a clear answer. While she was doing this, a man came to speak to her. He called her by her real name, and told her she knew Cardston was best. After that, we headed here."

The three went on to fill in the details about the rest of their journey that led them to this conversation.

"Well," stated Tim, "you're finally safe here. I'll see to that."

"Correction, there will be two of us looking out for your safety," Jeff added.

"That's not why we told you," exclaimed Shirleen, "You're the ones who aren't safe. These men will think nothing of killing you if they find you with us." She rose to pace the floor anxiously.

Jeff stopped her and put a hand on her shoulder. "Shirleen, you don't have to worry about me. My wife died just a while back, and we lost our daughter to cancer two years before that. Working for the three of you has given me something to look forward to again. I have three new friends that mean everything to me and I'm not about to stand by and do nothing."

"I feel the same way," agreed Tim. "I've come to think a lot of the three of you. Life wouldn't be worth living if we all sat back and did nothing to help our friends. I think you're stuck with us for the long hall."

"Oh," cried Meagan. "thank you for sticking with us. It means a lot."

Placing a hand on Meagan's shaking shoulders, Tim lifted her chin so he could look her straight in the eyes. "Listen, you've touched my life more than you know. You can call me anytime you need to talk." That was too much for Meagan, who burst into tears. He held her close, and let her cry herself out.

Stepping back, Meagan tried to brush the tears from his jacket. "Oh, now I've ruined your nice uniform."

Tim grinned good-naturedly then replied, "Forget about it. Helping a damsel in distress just made this old suit more valuable."

"You're just saying that to make me feel better," declared Meagan.

"No, I'm not!" Saluting her he said, "On the honor of her Majesty's Royal Mounted Army."

A sparkle glistened in Meagan's eyes then she replied sweetly. "Don't you mean the oath of this Mountie?"

"Oh," sulked Tim. "Now you've done it! You've hurt my feelings."

"That'll be the day," teased Meagan.

Turning to Juliana, he asked, "Is she always this nasty to friends?"

"Sometimes, especially when they deserve it."

"Why I never!" Flopping back onto the couch, he pouted for a moment before saying, "I don't think I'll come back anymore if you're going to abuse me like this."

Meagan giggled as she replied. "Yes, you will. You can't stand to miss out on Grandma's cookies."

"Drats," replied Tim, snapping his fingers. "I'd forgot about them." Growing thoughtful, he sighed resignedly. "Since I can't get them without coming here, I guess I'm doomed to be your friend after all."

Meagan turned to her grandmother and said, "See Grandma, you definitely know the way to a man's heart."

Tim laughed as hard as the others. "Yes, sir. You remind me of one of my ornery sisters. Rising, he ruffled her hair as he replied, "That's what I do when they act up."

"Oh, Momma, he's ruined my hair!"

"You started this, so don't come crying to me with your problems."

Growing serious, Tim turned to speak to Shirleen, "I think we'll start those shooting lessons on Friday. You need to get to where you can defend yourself if the need arises."

"I want Juliana to get a pistol so she can learn too."

"Anything I can do to help?" asked Jeff.

"Shirleen, how many bedrooms do you have?"

"There are five on the main floor, with two more upstairs." She looked at him curiously. "Why do you ask?"

"How would you feel about Jeff taking one of the rooms on the upper level?"

"Do you think that's wise?" asked Jeff.

"Yes," declared Tim. "Having you here all the time will make me feel better. If one comes calling, you'll be here to help them out."

"That makes perfect sense," replied Shirleen.

"I don't know about this," mumbled Jeff. "Can I have a couple of days to think it over?"

"Sure," replied Shirleen. "We're going to town tomorrow, so we'll get some furniture for your room and well get some for the other bedroom too. That way there will be room for both of you to stay if it's necessary."

"Thank you for your kind generosity," Jeff said.

"Thank you for even considering this deal, especially since it will probably put you in danger."

"It's not that," replied Jeff. "I just don't want to be a burden."

"Burden?" exclaimed Shirleen. "We don't feel that way at all. We'd be in your debt forever."

"I'll let you know what I decide on Friday or Saturday."

"That will be fine."

Tim, who'd been mulling things over said, "I think you should keep your real names secret from everyone else. At least until this problem has been solved."

Juliana looked over to her mother and replied, "I agree with Tim. No one else needs to know we aren't who we say we are."

Tim added, "One good thing, no one can really look for you until spring. So we have time to get to the bottom of this problem."

"There's something else we need your help with, Tim. We were wondering if there was a way to boost our cell signal so we can use cell phones again. If there is, we'll buy new cell phones tomorrow."

"I'll look into that and let you know when I see you on Friday for your shooting lessons."

"Thank you. Do you think we could boost the TV reception too?"

"Let me take a look around to see if there was ever cable at this house," said Jeff. "If there was, we'll be able to get it turned back on pretty easily."

"Oh, good," sighed Shirleen. "We'll buy a TV then, too. We need to know what's going on in the world."

"That's a good idea," agreed Tim.

"Where's the newspaper office?" asked Juliana.

"After we get the guns and ammunition, I'll take you there."

"Good! We'll start a subscription so we know what's going on locally too," replied Shirleen. "I'd like to have the New York Times too, but I'm afraid someone would figure out who we are if I got a subscription."

Jeff replied, "That's not a problem, I'll have it sent in my name."

"That would solve the problem all right," agreed Tim.

"I'll get it set up before you leave tonight. Thanks for doing that. I'll give you the money for the subscription before you leave."

"My pleasure, Shirleen. No one will ever be the wiser."

"Oh," said Juliana, "I was so nervous about telling you our secret, I forgot to offer you something to eat. Meagan made two cherry pies for her school assignment. Would you like a piece with ice cream?"

Tim looked at Meagan, as he asked, "You made the pies?"

"Yes, this is my third attempt."

"Wow!" It was obvious Tim was impressed.

Looking at Meagan with pride, Jeff said, "I had a piece at supper, and it was absolutely delicious!"

"Then I'd be delighted to have a piece with ice cream."

"What would you like to drink with it?" asked Juliana.

"May I have a glass of milk?" asked Tim.

"Certainly," grinned Juliana. Turning to Jeff, she asked, "Would you like another piece of pie, Jeff?"

"I'll have a small one. I'm still full from supper, but that dad-blame pie was so good I can't pass it up."

"Your wish is my command," grinned Juliana. "What would you like to drink with yours?"

"I'd like a glass of milk too."

"Two pies and two milks coming right up."

"I'll help you serve, Momma."

"Thank you, honey. That would really be a big help." They disappeared into the kitchen.

Turning to Shirleen, Tim asked, "Shirleen, would you mind playing a few pieces on the piano. The music soothes me, which is nice after a long day at work."

"Sure, I can do that." Going over to the piano, Shirleen began going through her sheet music. Before she could start playing, Juliana and Meagan brought the men their pie and milk.

Looking at Meagan, Shirleen asked, "Meagan, would you please sing for us tonight? Tim said he's had a tough day."

Looking panicked, Meagan looked from Tim over to Jeff. Sighing, she replied, "I don't know if they'll like my caterwauling."

Shirleen said, "The other night, Meagan sang for us. She has the most beautiful soprano voice. I promise you it's worth listening to."

"But Grandma, I'm really not that good."

Tim, setting his pie on the coffee table, rose to face Meagan. "Meagan Webb, I'd be honored if you'd sing for us."

"So would I," agreed Jeff.

Taking a deep breath, Meagan replied, "All right, but please don't lie and tell me it's good when it's not. Be honest with me no matter what."

"I will," declared Tim.

"So will I," agree Jeff.

Going over to the piano, she asked her grandmother to play a love song. Finding the sheet music, Shirleen played the introduction, smiling when Meagan came in on perfect pitch. Setting his empty pie plate back onto the coffee table, Tim leaned back against the couch and closed his eyes as he listened. When the song ended, Meagan held her breath waiting for their verdict.

Tim's eyes were shinning, as were Jeff's. "That was the most beautiful song I've ever heard, and that's the gospel truth."

Jeff swallowed twice to clear his throat. "Meagan, I can't believe how beautiful your voice is. Did you take voice lessons?"

"No," sighed Meagan. "I just sang along with the radio."

"Well, the way you sing, no one would ever believe you haven't had lessons," retorted Tim. "Please, sing another one."

Shirleen spoke up, "The other night, she sang my favorite song. The two of you should hear it."

She picked out the sheet music for "Danny Boy," and began to play. Meagan came in and sang it with all of her heart. When she effortlessly climbed to the high notes, the men exchanged impressed looks. When the song ended, they begged for more. So, for over an hour Meagan entertained them.

Looking at Meagan with great respect, Tim said, "I'll tell you in all honesty I've never been so moved. I love to hear your grandmother play the piano, but the two of you together soar to new heights." He had to swallow past the lump in his throat before he could continue. "Thank you. That was a special treat." Jeff could only nod in agreement, as he had been so greatly touched that he was rendered speechless.

"Thank you for the wonderful compliment, Tim." She tried to say more but for a moment she couldn't. Swallowing a couple of times, she tried again. "I haven't let anyone hear me sing because I was too self-conscious. My dad told me I was horrible."

"That's horrible," Tim said, "and totally not true."

Walking over to pick up the sketchpad Meagan kept near the fireplace, Shirleen took it over to show the men. "Meagan's also an artist."

"Doodler, is more like it," confessed Meagan.

Taking the sketchpad from Shirleen, Tim looked through what she'd drawn. "Doodling, my eye," declared Tim. "These are fantastic!"

He handed the sketch pad to Borton who exclaimed,

Wow!" cried Jeff. "I agree with you, Tim, these are breathtakingly beautiful! Do you paint too?"

"No, but Momma does."

"I'd be interested in seeing what you do, Juliana," Tim said eagerly.

"I'd love to show you what I'm working on, but it's not quite ready for public viewing yet," Juliana said.

"I can hardly wait." Rising, he added, "I have to get home to take care of my dogs." Hugging Meagan to him quickly, he said, "The pie was delicious, these drawings are wonderful, but your voice is the most amazing thing about you." Putting on his coat, he picked up his hat and gloves and headed toward the door. "Don't worry, your secret is safe with me, so get a good night's sleep."

"I'd better be going, too," Jeff said, and followed Tim out the door.

After they left, Shirleen asked, "How do you feel about telling them our secrets?"

"Surprisingly more at peace," replied Juliana. "We don't have to pretend to be someone else when they're around. It will be a relief."

"I agree with Momma," said Meagan. "It's nice to know I don't have to worry about slipplng up."

"Good. Now on to other pressing matters," Shirleen said.

"What's that?" asked Meagan.

"We have to go over the list of things we want to get when we go to town."

"Oh," grinned Meagan. "I was afraid it was going to be something terrible."

"Not this time, sweetie," Shirleen said. "Have you made your lists?"

"I sure have," declared Meagan."

"I have too."

"Great. Then all that's left is to go through all of them and make sure we haven't left anything off."

"There's one thing we've forgotten to add," said Juliana.

"What's that?" Shirleen asked.

"We have the menu planned for our Christmas meal, but we haven't decided on what we want to have for Thanksgiving."

"Oh, good grief!" Shirleen slapped her forehead with the heel of her hand. "How could I have forgotten that when it's only a week away?"

"We just got caught up with what we wanted to do for Christmas, so it stands to reason that all else was forgotten."

Sinking into a chair at the dining room table, Shirleen said enthusiastically, "Then we'd better get to planning."

For the next two hours they went over their lists and planned both Thanksgiving and Christmas dinner. Satisfied their lists were complete, they split things up between them so the shopping would go faster.

"We have something else we need to talk to you about, Meagan," Shirleen said.

"What's that?" asked Meagan, curiously.

"We feel like we've neglected teaching you anything about home economics, so we plan to get an instructor this summer to teach you everything you need to know about how to run a home. While you're learning , we're going to take classes in sewing, gardening, quilting and canning."

"When do I start?" asked Meagan.

"We'll finish up with your regular classes in May, so probably right after . I think we'll even have Jeff create a garden plot for us and maybe help us decide what to plant."

"Well, if nothing else it should be interesting," Megan said.

With all their lists and family meeting business taken care of, the three went their separate ways to get ready for bed.

Chapter 11

Jeff arrived at eight o'clock the next day to start work. Shirleen came out to tell him she'd made his lunch and put it I the refrigerator so he could eat whenever he got hungry. "There are some cookies for dessert sitting on the counter"

"Thanks, Shirleen. sounds great. I started the *New York Times* subscription this morning and also asked them to send back issues from August up to today, thatway you can see what's been happening."

"Oh, that's wonderful," cried Shirleen. "Was there an extra charge for the old newspapers?"

"Yes, but it wasn't much, so we'll charge it to the dust and let the rain settle it."

" isn't right," protested Shirleen.

"Nonsense. Sometimes one has to do a little service for others."

"Well, thank you."

"The sales representative I spoke with said the papers should be arriving within two or three weeks. The current editions would be sent out by air mail every day."

"Excellent."

"She also said you could go online and download it everyday, but I told her I wanted the physical paper."

"Thank you. I don't know how to work a computer."

"It isn't hard, it just takes someone to show you how."

Juliana spoke up to say, "I'll gladly show you how to work a computer, Momma. It really isn't hard to learn at all."

"Well, let me think about it."

"You know," said Jeff, "if you have me download the paper there won't be any paper trail and no one will know about it around here."

"I hadn't thought of that," replied Shirleen. "Guess I need to learn the computer."

"I'd better get to work, ladies." Jeff left them to get ready while he went outside.

An hour later, they were on their way. As they traveled down the road, with Shirleen driving, Meagan and Juliana enjoyed the beautiful scenery.

When they finally got to town, Juliana directed them to the courthouse and Sergeant Tim's office. When they got there, Tim was sitting behind a desk working on a pile of paperwork. "Good morning, ladies," he said when they came into his office. "Are you ready to buy out the town?"

"You bet," replied Meagan quickly.

"Well then, let's get going," chuckled Tim. Getting his hat, he led the way to the door. "I'll lead the way to the gun shop."

A while later, Tim had helped them purchase a couple of rifles, a pistol, and a good supply of ammunition. After Shirleen had paid for everything, he took everything out to his vehicle.

"I'm glad you got them put away," murmured Juliana. "I just don't like even being around guns."

"I know it's hard for you, but sometimes guns are a necessity," replied Tim.

Juliana shuddered then deliberately dismissed them from her mind.

"Just drop by when you're ready to go home," Tim said. "I should be in the office all day, unless someone decides to rob the bank or something."

"I'll make sure Momma and Grandma behave themselves," Meagan said, grinning.

Chuckling, Shirleen linked her arm through Meagan's, as she said, "Come on, let's go see if we can fill our lists before you get into trouble … again!"

"Oh," interrupted Tim, "I promised to take you over to the newspaper office so you could get a subscription. I'd better do that before I leave you."

"Okay. Lead away, kind sir."

They drove over to the newspaper office, and finished their business quickly before heading out to shop. As they drove away, Tim smiled. "The day I met those ladies was one of the best days of my life." Realizing he had spoken aloud, Tim chastised himself. "Come on, old man, before someone turns you in to a mental hospital."

The girls went to the bank before hitting the mall. Once there, they separated so they could shop for Christmas gifts. They decided to meet at the mall food court at noon, then tackle their lists together.

Shirleen had just put some of her purchases in the van when she saw Meagan staggering toward her carrying a heavy load. Rushing over to her with the empty cart, she helped her place the items inside. "My goodness, did you buy out the store?"

"I tried to," laughed Meagan.

"From the packages in the van already, I have a feeling that's what we've all been doing!"

"I wonder what Momma's doing?"

Suddenly, they saw Juliana pushing a cart filled with packages. "I'd say my suspicions were correct. We're indeed buying out the store."

They helped Juliana deposit her bags in the back of the van, which was already stuffed full, before heading back inside to finish up their shopping. They realized they weren't going to have any room left for the groceries they still had to buy, so Shirleen suggested they rent a van so they'd be able to get everything in one trip.

They looked up a Hertz rental company and got a van for the day. The company sent someone right over with the necessary paperwork, and Shirleen waited for them while the others continued shopping. When she'd filled out the paperwork and got the keys, she parked it near their van. She was just getting out of the van when Juliana and Meagan emerged with two more carts full to the top.

Shirleen helped them unload the contents of both carts and as they were headed back inside, Juliana froze in place. Looking over to see what she was looking at, Shirleen turned and saw Hazel Lockwood coming toward them. "Don't be afraid, dear. It's all right. She is running from Bruce, too." Still Juliana remained frozen in place.

Shirleen called out, Hazel. Turning chalky white, Hazel started looking around to see who had called her name. Seeing Shirleen waving at her, she didn't know what to do. Shirleen smiled as she replied, "Don't be afraid, Hazel."

"You look familiar, ma'am," began Hazel. "Do I know you?"

"Yes, Hazel. You know all of us. We look a little different, but you've known us for years."

Hazel studied her closely then asked, "Are you sure I know you?"

"You were my daughter's cook and housekeeper in Syracuse."

Hazel looked puzzled, then said, "I only worked for one family, the Murdocks."

"That's right," said Shirleen. "You worked for my daughter, Ruth Murdock."

"Oh, my!" Hazel nearly fainted. When she'd recovered from the shock, she said, "When you weren't there when I got back from vacation, I didn't know what happened to you, and I didn't dare ask Mr. Murdock."

"We have a lot to talk about, Hazel. We were about to go have a little lunch. Would you like to join us?"

"Sure," grinned Hazel. "Let my put my things in the car. I'll be right back."

Hazel hurried off to her car, which was parked three vehicles away. She quickly put her packages inside, then went back to join the girls. They went directly to the food court, and each chose a different restaurant for lunch. When they had their food, they chose the table furthest away from people and took a seat. They said a little prayer over their food, then ate in silence. No one seemed to know how to start the conversation.

Finally, Shirleen said, "I know I scared you back there in the parking lot. I'm sorry."

"I thought I was safe here until you called my name."

"How did you end up here?" asked Juliana.

Sighing, Hazel laid her fork on her plate. "As I said, I had suspicions something terrible had happened to you. I have to confess I never liked or trusted Mr. Murdock. There was something about him that always made me nervous." She shuddered then continued. "One day when I was dusting the office, I saw something I wasn't supposed to. It was a hit list and some of the people on it were already dead."

Juliana gasped, but remained silent.

"I made sure he couldn't tell I'd been in the room and decided right then I needed to leave — soon."

"I'm surprised he let you leave. How did you do it without him trying to stop you?" asked Meagan.

"I'd been having a lot of pain in my side so I went to see a doctor. He told me I had gallstones and needed surgery. I decided to have the surgery in Spokane so my sister could take care of me while I recovered.

"Once that was set up, I called my sister Helen, who lives here in Cardston. I told her I needed someplace safe to get away. She told me I was more than welcome to come.

"I was trying to come up with a way to explain leaving to Mr. Murdock when he caught me during one of my extreme bouts of pain; it doubled me over. I told him I'd seen my doctor and I had stage four breast cancer. I also told him I only had six months to live. When he asked what I was going to do, I told him I was going to go to my sister's in Saint Louis so she could take care of me while I made my final arrangements. The next morning, he gave me a check for seven hundred thousand dollars."

"Wow," said Meagan. "That must have shocked you."

"It did. When I told him it was too generous, he said I'd been a loyal servant and he wanted to reward me by giving me the money."

"I'm glad he was good to you, Hazel." Juliana said, starting to warm up to the woman who'd served her family for so many years.

"Thank you, Ruth."

Juliana held up her hand to silence her. "That isn't my name anymore. We changed our names to protect ourselves. My mother's name is now Shirleen Webb. My name is Juliana Webb, and my daughter is Meagan Webb. Please call us that from now on."

"I will. My new name is Gertrude North. You can call me Trudy."

"I'm glad you understand the need for secrecy," said Shirleen. "What are you doing now that you're in Cardston?"

"I've been staying with my sister, Helen Jorgenson and her family. I love them to death, but their screaming children are rough on my nerves. I've been trying to find a place of my own, as well as a job, but haven't been successful yet."

"What else can you do, other than housekeeping or being a cook?" Shirleen asked.

"I'm a pretty good seamstress. I love to quilt, garden, and I even like to can what comes out of the garden."

Juliana nearly choked on her food. Clearing her throat, she turned to address her mother, "She would be a great addition to our household!"

Smiling, Shirleen replied, "I agree. Hazel would you be willing to come and work for us. You can live with us, too. Our hired man, Jeff Borton, knows about our situation so you don't have to be afraid of him, and there's also a Mountie who's in on the secret. They've both said they will protect us from any threat that comes our way."

"Oh, are you sure? You're not just being nice because you feel sorry for me, are you?"

Patting her hand, Shirleen said, "Look, Hazel — I mean Trudy — you'd be doing us a great service by coming to live with us. We need your expertise desperately. Juliana and I had decided Meagan needs to learn some things we can't teach her. Things like sewing, quilting, gardening and canning would be great additions to her education. Knowing all of that on top of her regular school work will make her prepared to take care of herself in any situation."

Hazel suddenly grinned. "I would love to come work for you."

"We still have a lot of shopping to do, so why don't you get your things then meet us at the supermarket. We won't be leaving town for a while because we have shopping and errands to run before we head home."

Hazel grinned, "All of my stuff is still packed, except the things I use every day. Give me an hour to get that packed and I'll be ready." Suddenly she added, "Say, give me the grocery list I'll work on that while you do your other shopping and errands."

"Oh," said Juliana, "That would really help. We're still trying to get our Christmas shopping done."

Shirleen gave Hazel the shopping list as they prepared to go their separate ways.

Hazel asked what had been on her mind since meeting them. "I just have to ask you one more thing. How in the world did you get away from Syracuse?"

"It's a long story. We'll explain it all to you when we get home."

After Hazel left, the girls agreed to meet at the food court in an hour after they'd finished their remaining shopping.

Shirleen was pleased with herself, because she'd found everything on her list, even something for Hazel. As she was heading to the food court, she realized she'd left two important people off her gift list — Jeff and Tim. Hurrying off to another store, she quickly found some great gifts for the men in their lives. Buy this time, she had so many packages that she could hardly carry them all. When she got to the food court, she saw that the others were in the same shape.

"Let's go put this stuff in the van," suggested Shirleen. "I have go to my doctor's appointment. When I get back we'll get the rest of the items on the family list."

While Shirleen was at her appointment, Juliana and Meagan decided to start working on the little items on their list while they waited for her to get done.

Driving to the clinic didn't take long, and Shirleen parked in the back. She knocked on the back door, and a nice looking nurse opened it immediately and ushered her inside. She was led to an empty room where she waited for the doctor. Looking at her watch, Shirleen was relieved to see she was five minutes early. A few minutes later, Dr. Stillman came in to examine her.

Shirleen studied him, noting, *Gerald Stillman is a handsome man. It looks like he works out all of the time.* Brown hair, graying at the temples, made him appear more distinguished, and his hazel eyes, sparkled with life.

A moment later he asked, "Did you do exactly as I told you, young lady?"

"Yes, I did. My daughter made sure of it."

He looked her straight in the eye and asked, "Are you telling me the truth?"

"I most certainly am," she replied testily.

"Well you look just as exhausted as you did the other night."

"That might be because I've been shopping all day."

"As soon as you get home, eat a light supper and go back to bed. You are to stay there for at least two more days. I'll be out to check on you then. If I'm not satisfied you're better, I'll slap you into the hospital where you'll get 'round the clock care."

"Fine. I'll do what you say," snapped Shirleen. She was still smarting from his accusation that she'd lied to him.

"Good. We'll have you back in fighting shape in no time. Now, I need a sample of your blood. I think you might be anemic. I also want to check for a few other things. I'll know more after I get the results of the blood work."

"Thank you, Dr. Stillman."

His only answer was a curt nod. Closing her file, he left the room. A moment later the nurse came in to take her blood. After that, she left by the back door.

When she got back to the mall, Juliana told her, "We now have three cell phones." Shirleen was impressed with what they'd accomplished.

Taking the list, Shirleen asked them, "Do we want an artificial tree or do we want to have Jeff cut one down?"

"A real tree is a huge mess," replied Juliana "Plus we can use an artificial one year after year."

"I tend to agree with you," replied, Shirleen."

"I like a real tree," said Meagan, "but I don't like the mess either. I guess I vote for the artificial one, too."

"Okay, let's get a big one. Okay?" Shirleen asked.

"Yes," they both chorused.

"Well then, we need to find a big artificial tree and lots of decorations." They headed off to Target to see what they could find.

When they'd done that, Shirleen told them, "We need to get furniture for the two upstairs bedrooms." They headed to a nearby furniture store and selected everything there. After paying, they gave the deliveryman their address. Relieved that was accomplished, they realized they only had enough room left in the second van for their groceries.

Shirleen was elected to drive the rented van, while Juliana drove the family van and they set out to meet Hazel at the grocery store. When they got there, she was dragging two carts toward the checkout. Shirleen paid for the food, and they all helped to load it into the van.

Their caravan stopped at Tim's office to pick up the weapons. When Tim saw Hazel, he was concerned. Seeing the look on his face, Shirleen introduced Hazel. "Sergeant Tim, this is Hazel Lockwood, alias Gertrude North. We'll explain everything in detail the next time you come to visit."

Turning to Hazel she said, "This is Sergeant Timothy Titus Obadiah York."

Hazel winced then replied, "Oh, you poor, dear soul! How'd you get stuck with so many names?"

"My mother wanted to name me Timothy Obadiah York, but my father wanted to name me Obadiah Titus Tim, so they compromised by calling me Timothy Titus Obadiah York."

"Well, I feel sorry for you just the same," said Hazel. "I can't imagine what it's like for you when you have to sign your name."

"I'm so glad to find someone who understands my challenges," said Tim.

"Oh," replied Meagan sweetly, "it isn't that we don't understand your challenges, Sergeant York. We just like to give you a hard time."

"Very funny, Meagan." He reached out to mess up her hair, but she slipped behind her mother.

Juliana stepped away from Meagan and said, "You got yourself into this pickle. Don't come to me for protection."

Meagan was saved when a someone entered the building. "I'll take care of you later," grinned Tim as he turned to retrieve their purchases.

A few minutes later, Tim returned carrying the weapons. "If you're ready to go, I'll carry these out for you." He whistled softly when he saw the three vehicles so heavily loaded with shopping bags. "Did you buy something in every store in the mall?," he asked with awe.

"It feels like it," grinned Shirleen. "It wore me out."

"Did you see Dr. Stillman today?" asked Tim."

"Yeah. He told me to eat a light supper and go back to bed and stay there for two more days."

"Then that's what you're going to do," declared Juliana.

"Oh, dear," groaned Shirleen. "I was afraid you'd be that way."

"Well, we love you and want you to be around for many more years," replied Juliana.

"Fine. I can't be stubborn when you're being so nice. Anyway, Dr. Stillman said he'd be out to see me in two days. If I'm not better he's going to put me in the hospital. He thinks I might be anemic, so he took some blood. He said he'd tell me the results when he sees me."

"Then you'd better get on home," said Tim as he put the weapons in the van. "I checked around to see about putting a tower on the hill above your house. I think it'll cost about $200 to get one installed up there."

"Well," said Shirleen, "we'll just have to pay the price."

"Here's the number for the guy you need to call. He can get it done for you," he said, handing her a business card with a number on it. "I'll be out tomorrow to check up on you, Shirleen." Turning to Hazel, he added, "I want to hear your story, too."

Soon after that, they arrived home, tired and hungry. Jeff had brought in the wood for the wood boxes, and there was a warm fire going in all of the fireplaces. They hadn't been home long when two delivery trucks pulled up. Shirleen let them in, while Hazel and Meagan put the groceries away and brought in their loot from the vans.

Seeing the mass of stuff in the living room, Shirleen wasn't sure where to start.

"Why don't we take the Christmas decorations out to the garage," suggested Juliana when she saw the look on Shirleen's face. "We'll go through them after Thanksgiving."

"That's a start," agreed Shirleen. They separated the bags and took them to the garage just as Meagan called them in to eat.

After they were done eating, they pitched in to get Hazel's room ready. "Let's just set up the bed tonight," Shirleen said. "We can deal with the rest tomorrow."

"Hang on a minute," Juliana said and went to the kitchen. When she returned, she said, "Meagan and I have a better idea. We'll share a bed tonight, and we'll deal with both of the bedrooms in the morning."

"That does sound better," agreed Shirleen. "Why don't you put fresh linens on Meagan's bed for Hazel? I mean Trudy. You'll have to be patient with me until get used to your new name. It took us a while to get used to ours too."

"No problem. I have trouble remembering, too," replied Trudy.

Running her fingers through her hair, Shirleen mumbled. "I wish I'd had time to get my hair cut while we were in town."

"Me too," said Meagan.

"Listen," said Juliana, "why don't I try cutting our hair? It won't be great, but nobody's going to see us anyway."

"I don't know," mused Shirleen.

"If it's a haircut you want," said Trudy, "I used to cut my sister's hair when we were younger. We were too poor to go to a beauty salon, so I learned how to do it. I never got a license or anything, but her hair usually looked pretty good."

Meagan laughed, "I'm game, if you and Grandma are, Momma."

Shirleen nodded, "I am."

"So am I," agreed Juliana. "We should probably color our hair again too. We've got extra bottles of die."

"After you've done your two days of bed rest, Shirleen," remarked Trudy, "I'll give you the full treatment — a cut and dye job."

"Thanks. I'm looking forward to it."

"Who's going to do your hair, Trudy?" asked Meagan.

"I've cut my own hair for years," replied Trudy.

"Wow," said Meagan, truly amazed because Trudy's hair looked great. "I thought you had it done in a beauty shop."

"Nope. It's a do-it-yourself job."

"Well, if you can make my hair look as good as yours, then you're hired!" The others nodded in agreement.

Juliana turned to speak to her mother, but seeing her look of exhaustion, she said, "It's off to bed with you, Momma."

Sighing resignedly, Shirleen replied, "I won't argue because I'm just to tired to make the effort."

"Come on. I'll help you to bed."

After seeing Shirleen was prepared for bed, Juliana tucked her in. Bending to kiss her cheek, Juliana whispered, "Good night, Momma. Get some sleep." Pausing at the door, she added, "Don't worry about your shopping. I'll have Trudy go through the bags with each of our lists so she can put them away until after Thanksgiving."

"But I have some gifts for Trudy in there. I don't want her to see them," protested Shirleen.

"So do we, but she won't know they're for her."

"That's true. Good thinking."

Blowing Shirleen a kiss, Juliana went to help where needed. Shirleen immediately fell asleep. Meanwhile, Juliana went through the house to make sure everything was locked up for the night. Satisfied all was well, she turned out all of the lights and went to bed, too.

Chapter 12

Bruce was sitting in his living room after spending all day in court defending an accused murderer. He smiled when he realized he'd reeled in a new fish. That's how he always thought of his organization's new recruits. With the addition of this latest fish, he now had the power he needed to fight the remaining Gordon loyalists.

He'd hired a new cook and another housekeeper the week before. Having two people on his domestic staff made him feel like he was moving up in the world. *Things are definitely looking up for Bruce Murdock,* he thought smugly.

As he finished off his drink, a bullet struck the window beside him, sending shards of glass flying all around him. He dropped to the floor just as more bullets struck the house.

Hearing a car race away from the house, Bruce stood to assess the damage. A painting across the room was riddled with bullet holes, and the window was completely gone. His fear was quickly replaced with furry. "Kathy, get in here at once!" he yelled. When a woman, unmoved by the incident, approached him from another room in the house, he yelled, "Clean this mess up!"

"Yes, sir," replied the housekeeper. Kathy Neilson was a short, thin woman from Scandinavia with light blue eyes that were hard as nails. She resembled a small bird of prey. Bruce had found her working nights in the office complex he shared with three other attorneys. She was always barking orders at the other housekeepers.

After he hired her, Bruce had her trained to also be his personal protection when he was in the house. She'd turned out to be a loyal asset to his business. She worked as hard as a man and she never flinched when someone was killed in front of her. Kathy had even murdered one or two men that had tried to attack her.

While Kathy cleaned up, Bruce called a repairman for the window. When that was finished, he made a mental note to start looking for another home. *Somewhere in a gated community might be good. When I'm boss of this organization, that's just what I'm gonna do.*

Going into his office, he dialed Vincent Crowley's number. "Vinnie, this is Bruce Murdock. Contact Wilson then get over here on the double."

"Yes, sir," snapped Crowley.

He ended the call abruptly and went to the kitchen to get something to drink. As he walked down the hall to the kitchen, he remembered his conversation with Wilson a few days earlier. Wilson said he'd searched all over Ohio and Pennsylvania without a bit of evidence linked to his traitorous family, so Bruce brought him back home. *They're out there somewhere. It's only a matter of time before they make a mistake and we find them.*

Bruce's attention was drawn back to the present as he entered the kitchen. The new cook, Myrtle Lawson, was busy preparing his evening meal. She never even glanced at Bruce as he got a glass from the cupboard and filled it with milk. Sitting down at the table to drink his milk, he watched Myrtle work.

She went efficiently about her work, not stopping to even look in Bruce's direction. Bruce had plans for her as well; Myrtle was stunningly beautiful. Dark chestnut colored hair complimented her delicately shaped features. *I'd never get tired of her in my bed,* he thought. Feeling suddenly aroused, he slugged down the last of his milk, and left the empty glass on the table, then quickly left the room.

Ten minutes later, Vincent Crowley and Tom Wilson knocked on the door and Kathy let them in. "Sit down," barked Bruce. "A little while ago, someone shot up my house and very nearly shot me."

"We wondered why the statues were all broken," Crowley said.

"I'm not worried about that right now. We need to have a conference. Go find Kathy and get her in here too."

When everyone was assembled, Bruce said, "From now on, you're all gonna be here to guard me from whoever is trying to off me."

"Gotcha, boss," quipped Wilson.

Turning to Kathy, Bruce said, "Set up rooms for them on the east wing."

"Yes, sir."

"It looks like the other side is striking out ahead of time," remarked Crowley."

"That's my thought, too, boss," said Wilson.

"If this was intended to make me back off, it's not gonna work. I'm more determined than ever to strike back and strike back soon." Rising, he paced the room angrily. Suddenly he stopped pacing and said, "It's time this mess ends. Either they come over to my way of thinking or they'll be done in."

Crowley asked, "What are you planning, boss?"

"I'll be right back." He disappeared into his office and quickly returned waving a book. "I have Gordon's little black book right here." The others looked at him with concern, but kept quiet. "This book contains a complete list of Gordon's employees… so to speak."

"How'd you get that?" asked Crowley.

"When we were flying back to Syracuse, I went through the stuff in the plane. Beside the bed was a built-in dresser with a bunch of clothes in it. I found this little jewel taped under one of the drawers."

"What are you gonna do with these names, boss?" asked Wilson.

"First of all, I'm gonna go through and mark out all the ones we've already taken out. For the rest, I'll make a list detailing what their options are and send them a letter."

"What are they?" asked Kathy.

"They can either join me or they'll suffer the same fate as their dead friends. I'll give them a week to decide."

"Smart thinking, boss," replied Wilson, smiling wickedly.

Crowley thought this over for a moment before saying, "I sure hope it works. Some of those guys were really loyal to Spielberg. I hope they don't just agree so they can wait 'til they can find a way to take you out."

"I have to agree with Vinnie," replied Kathy.

Thinking over what they'd said, Bruce grew angry. Finally, he hissed through clenched teeth, "Just let 'em try. It'll be the last thing they do."

"Kathy, take these men and get them something to eat. Myrtle should have it ready by now. I'm gonna work on that letter."

When they'd all gone to the kitchen, Bruce went to his office and got to work. It took him nearly an hour to accomplish the task.

While the letters printed, he went in search of Kathy. He found her sitting on the couch talking to the other men and barked out, "Kathy, I need your help immediately. Come with me."

Kathy followed him back into the office where he said, "I want you to address the envelopes. I'll put the letters in and seal them."

"I'll get started right away.

Kathy and Bruce worked hard to get the letters ready to send. When the job was done, Bruce put them all into a box ready for the post office in the morning. Smiling, he turned to face Kathy. "Now, we wait to see what they decide." They went to join the others who were waiting in the living room.

Bruce had a difficult time waiting for the responses. As each day passed, he became more and more agitated and volatile. After an especially difficult day of dealing with him, Kathy told Wilson, White and Crowley, "Bruce reminds me of a bear with a sore paw. I wouldn't be surprised if he loses it today. He's so wound up we'll be lucky to get off with just a temper tantrum."

"I've been waiting for the blow up," Crowley said.

Wilson, sitting there with a sullen expression on his face, replied, "I almost wish he'd throw the fit and get it over with."

White shook his head in disgust. "Bruce is nothing like Gordon. Gordon would wait calmly, then strike. Bruce's always been a loose cannon when something doesn't go his way. Like this thing with Spielberg's men."

The doorbell interrupted the conversation. White, who beat them to the door, was greeted by the mailman who had a bag over his shoulder. Dropping it onto the top step, he said, "This huge bag of letters is for you."

"Thanks, I'll take it."

"It's pretty heavy." the mailman warned as he turned to go.

White grabbed the bag and dragged it inside, then shut the door. "Boss, you'd better get down here," he shouted, "I think you'll want to see this."

"What are you yelling about?"

"The mailman just dropped off this huge bag of mail. I thought you'd want to be the one to open it."

Seeing Bruce's face grow sullen, White wisely got out of the way. He opened the bag, looked through its contents, and then said, "Start organizing these letters into piles while I go get the black book."

They had the letters sorted into four piles when Bruce returned. Plopping onto a chair, he opened the black book and said, "Don't just sit there looking at me like a bunch of idiots, start opening them. When you pick up a letter, tell me who it is from so I can check off the name. When you've read the letter, tell me for or against."

Without a word, they got right to it, taking turns opening letters. When all the letters had been opened, there were only three in which the recipient said he'd rather die than be connected to Bruce. As each of these was read, Bruce looked like he would choke.

When he got himself under control after the last negative letter, he said, "Nate, I'm gonna give you the addresses for the ones who need eliminated. Let's do it with car bombs. Stay close to see the job is done. I want them dead."

"Yes, sir."

As White was about to leave the room, Bruce grinned and said, "Well, it's official. I'm the new mob boss."

"What do you plan to do first, boss?" asked Wilson.

"I'm gonna take control of all of the drug cartels, set up an escort service, smuggle in diamonds and pretty much anything else I can think of."

Nathan White left the room, and the others in the room kept their doubts to themselves.

When nobody said anything, Bruce continued, "Kathy, when I have the escort service set up I want you to head that part of the organization. Crowley, I want you to do a special job for me. It'll take you a while to get this job done, but it's necessary."

"What job's that, boss?"

"I want you to be my bodyguard. I don't want to go anywhere without you by my side. I have a feeling they're going to try to hit me again."

"You got it, boss," replied Crowley.

"That's it. Get out of here. I need some time to think." When they'd left the room, Bruce sat back and grinned. *When I'm through, I'll have so much power that no one will ever threaten me again.*

◄ • ►

Henry Borden had a rough time recovering from the stroke, and traveling had taken a terrible toll on him. He made it to Erie, Pennsylvania, but had to get a motel room so he could get some uninterrupted sleep while his nurse, Theodore Brooks, went to help Henry's sister-in-law, Melinda pack up her apartment.

When everything was boxed up, they loaded it into the back of Melinda's van. Three hours later, Melinda thanked him for helping on such short notice. She locked the door for the last time and turned the key over to the office manager before following Theodore to the motel. Henry was still asleep when they go there, so Melinda stayed with him while Theodore went out to get them all something to eat.

When he returned they woke Henry up and Theodore moved him from the bed to his wheelchair. When the meal was over, Theodore walked Melinda over to her room next door. Satisfied all was well, he went back to prepare Henry for bed.

Early the next morning, they were on the road again. Henry did well until they reached Cleveland, but then he went down hill. They were forced to remain in a hotel for two nights before he could travel again. After that he did relatively well until they got to a small town in Kansas, where he was hospitalized for exhaustion.

Theodore and Melinda were starting to worry about whether they'd get to Canada before snow made travel impossible. They were careful to keep these worries from Henry until he was feeling better.

Three days later, they were able to continue their journey. It was nearing the end of October when they arrived in a small town in Nebraska. That night in their motel room, Melinda broached the subject that was uppermost on her mind. "Henry, we're still a long way from our destination in Canada and the snows aren't far away. How do you feel about renting something here until spring? Once everything thaws, we can resume our trek into Canada."

Henry thought things over then replied, "I can feel myself going down hill. I'm afraid if we stop now, I won't be able to hang on. If it's all right with you, I'd like to continue on for as long as I'm able. What do you think, Theodore?"

"Well, I'm concerned about your health." He fell silent as he thought things through. Sighing, he continued. "I think we should keep moving until we get there or we're forced to stop because of the snow."

Melinda, sighing resignedly, replied, "Okay, I guess we'll keep going."

"Thank you, Sis," replied Henry gratefully.

Henry did pretty well as they traveled through Nebraska. When they were finally in Cheyenne, Wyoming, though, he began to show signs of stress again. He insisted they continue driving, and as they rode into Idaho Falls, he collapsed when they stopped for gas.

"We're going to have to take him to the hospital," Melinda said. They looked up hospitals in the area on their phones and found Eastern Idaho Regional Medical Center. As they headed for the hospital, Theodore worried their luck had run out and the snow would keep them stranded in Idaho Falls.

Getting to the hospital took a little bit of time. After the doctors examined him, they told Henry's companions it wasn't serious, just exhaustion. He was released a while later. They spent the night in a motel by the Falls, which seemed to soothe Henry somewhat.

The next morning, he begged them to continue the trip. "Please, we have to go on so we don't get caught in the winter snows. When they got to Sandpoint, Idaho, they decided to layover for a few days to give Henry time to rest up before they continued on.

Three days later, they were on the road again, and two days later they arrived in Cardston, Alberta, Canada. Henry Borden was truly exhausted at this point, so while he rested in their motel room, Melinda and Theodore looked for an apartment. They found one with three bedrooms near the shopping center. Theodore paid for the first month, the last month, and the $550 security deposit and they were official residents.

They unloaded the U-Haul and Melinda's van, and then returned the U-Haul before going to check on Henry. He was still sleeping, so they went back to the new apartment to set up Henry's bed. When that was done, they went back to get Henry.

When they got there, Henry was lying there wide-awake. Melinda went over to check on him, while Theodore got the wheelchair ready. "I'm glad to see you're finally awake. We checked on you a while ago, but since you were sleeping so peacefully, we didn't wake you."

"Did you find an apartment?"

"We sure did," grinned Theodore. "We've even unloaded the U-Haul and Melinda's car, and we even got your bed set up. Do you feel like going to our new home?"

"Yes," replied Henry. "The sooner I'm settled the better."

"Then let's get the show on the road," said Theodore.

"What do we do about the motel," asked Henry.

"While I get you settled in the car, Melinda will go pay the bill."

"I should be doing that," protested Henry.

"Nonsense," replied Melinda. "We're family. Family helps family."

"I'll make things right as soon as I get rested up." Theodore put him into the wheelchair, covering his legs with a lap robe. "Truthfully, I'm so tired I just can't think straight right now."

When they got to the apartment, Theodore transported Henry from the car into the house and wheeled him from room to room so he could see the whole thing. "Wow, this is one really nice apartment," Henry said when the tour was complete.

"I also spoke to the manager about having a covered ramp made so it will be easier to get from here to the car. He said he'd have someone start on it tomorrow."

"Wonderful!" Looking around for a calendar and finding none, he asked, "What's the date today?"

"It's November 20th."

"Wow, I guess we cut it close and were lucky there weren't early snows."

"Yep," agreed Theodore. "Let's hope the covered ramp is finished before you need to go anywhere."

"I think the first thing we should do is get some food in so we don't get stranded and starve, Melinda said.

"That's a good idea, Sis," agreed Henry.

"How about I go out and get enough groceries to make supper tonight, then tomorrow we'll go out and get enough to keep us in food for weeks?"

"Sounds good," said Henry.

Picking up her purse and car keys, Melinda left. Theodore helped Henry get a good shower then prepared him for bed. After getting Henry's bathrobe on, Theodore took him out to sit at the table. They had only gotten him settled when Melinda got back. Theodore helped her bring in the groceries.

"I got paper plates and plastic utensils, since we haven't unpacked the kitchen boxes yet. Is deli chicken and potato salad okay for dinner?"

"Sounds great," they both said at the same time.

"I got cereal, milk, and doughnuts for breakfast in the morning. When we get back from shopping, I'll start unpacking everything. It will take a few days to get organized, so you'll have to be patient."

"Take as long as you like. I'm just sorry I don't feel like helping you. I'm so tired I feel like I could sleep for a week."

The next morning, Melinda rose early to start her day. She searched for the cereal bowls and finally found them. After setting the table, she was about to call the men, but came into the kitchen on their own. "Good morning, you two sleepy heads," she said cheerfully.

"Look whose calling who sleepy heads," grinned Henry.

"We got up a long time ago," Theodore said. "After I got Henry ready for the day we sat and talked about everything for a while."

"Guess I'm guilty of sleeping in! I got breakfast ready, though."

"I'm so hungry I could eat a horse," Theodore said.

After breakfast was over, Henry went back to bed. As Theodore covered him up, he told Henry, "I'm going to make a doctor's appointment for you. After that grueling trip, I think you should be checked out."

"I just need some rest. I'll be all right."

"Maybe so, but I still think you should see a doctor. You have to find one here anyway, so why not now?"

Grinning, Henry replied, "Thanks for looking out for me. I appreciate it."

"You're welcome, now get some sleep while I see what I can do to help Melinda get the furniture arranged." He hesitated a moment, before saying, "I think we brought more furniture than we need. We might need to rent a storage building."

"If that's the case, go ahead and do it."

"You bet. Now, go to sleep." Theodore grinned to take the edge off of his words. "I'll check on you later." Henry nodded then closed his eyes. He was relieved to see his charge was soon fast asleep.

He went looking for Melinda and found her in the kitchen. She was sitting at the table writing something. "You writing a novel?"

She had three sheets of paper in front of her. Looking at the papers she smiled and said, "It looks that way, doesn't it? This," began Melinda, holding up a sheet of paper, "is the grocery list." Picking up another sheet she said, "This is the list of other errands I need to run while I'm out." Holding up the last sheet she remarked, "And this is the list of things I need to do when I get back."

Looking at each sheet, Theodore whistled softly and replied, "You've got your work cut out for you. Those are some long lists. What are you planning to do today?"

"I'm going to rent a storage unit for anything we don't use when we get everything situated here."

"That's a good idea. I think we brought enough stuff to fill three apartments."

"You might be exaggerating just a bit," teased Theodore.

Smiling, Melinda replied, "Well, maybe just a bit." Changing the subject, she asked, "Other than finding the storage units, what else is on your agenda?"

"I thought it would be a good idea to find a doctor for Henry. I think he needs to be checked over thoroughly. I'm really concerned with how thin he's become."

"Now that you mention it, I am too. He hasn't been eating much."

"I noticed that, too," he said as he sank into a chair. He paused for a second, then asked," When do you plan on starting on those lists?"

"As soon as I finish them," replied Melinda. "I still have a lot to add. Why don't you go ahead and do what you need to do while I finish up. When you get back, I'll go do what I have to do."

"Sounds like a plan." Rising, he started to leave then paused to say, "Do you want to call the phone company or do you want me to do that while I'm out?"

"If you could do it, that would be one less thing for me to do."

"Consider it done. I'll be back as quickly as possible."

"Take your time," replied Melinda. "As soon as I get done with these lists, I'm going to unpack the kitchen boxes and get things put away."

"Don't over do it. I'd hate to have two patients in the house."

"I'll be fine," promised Melinda.

When Theodore left, Melinda went back to making out her lists. She finished an hour later, then filled the sink with soap and water and started cleaning out the cupboards before unpacking the boxes and filling them with their things. She'd finished that chore and was washing off the counters when Theodore returned. "I didn't get the stove or the refrigerator scrubbed, but I'll do that as soon as I get back."

"I'll do that." Pointing to the lists in her hands, he grinned as he added, "You've got a lot to get done if you want to cross off all the items on your lists."

Melinda laughed. "You're right."

"Be careful. It's snowed just enough to make it really slick out there."

"I'll drive slowly." Putting the lists into her purse, she looked up at Theodore. "There are leftovers from last night for lunch. When I get back I'll make something good for supper."

As she drove, Melinda enjoyed the view of the town and reflected on their move to Cardston. Truthfully, she was glad to get out of the east. She loved teaching the kindergarteners but she wasn't happy with her life there.

It had been years since Andrew Taylor's tragic death. She'd never found anyone else she felt comfortable with. She went out, but none of the men interested her and they were all so self-centered. That wasn't the case with Theodore Brooks. He was selfless, caring, and concerned about the Henry's welfare. She had to admit she was attracted to him.

All of these weeks of traveling together had stirred some feelings that were foreign to her. Shaking herself, she concentrated on doing what she had to do.

Parking close to the entrance, she got out and went inside the store. Christmas music was playing, setting the mood of the season. Taking out her list, she began to get the items she needed. Two hours later, she had gotten everything on the list.

When she got into the car, she really didn't want to go back to the apartment yet, so she sat there trying to figure out what to do with her life. *I'd like to go back to teaching, but with Henry being so ill, I feel like I should help Theodore care for him. What's to become of me now?* she wondered. *Can I handle not having a job or a true purpose to my life? Jacobs, that attitude is downright selfish. You care about Henry so knock it off right now. Besides, you embarked on this little adventure with your eyes wide open.*

Aloud she declared, "I'm *not* going to think these thoughts again. There's no shame in being a housekeeper or a cook. Someone has to do it for Henry, so why not Theodore and me?"

Finally, starting the car, she eased out of the parking lot and headed toward home. The closer to home she got, the more at peace she felt. Seeing a church close to the road, she pulled into the parking lot and went inside. Walking to the front of the chapel, she sank onto a pew to meditate. There she made a solemn promise to do all in her power to help Theodore take good care of Henry. After all, that was what her sister, Matilda, would want her to do.

The thought of her sister caused her heart to ache until tears started streaming down her cheeks. Brushing at them impatiently, she tried to push the sad thoughts of her sister out of her mind. Try as hard as she might, Matilda still invaded her mind and filled her with feelings of loss and sadness. Leaning her head on the pew in front of her, tears long held in check coursed down her cheeks. When she'd cried herself out, she pulled a tissue from her purse and blotted her face. She felt better now and decided to head home.

Chapter 13

The next morning found everyone except Shirleen hard at work. Breakfast was over when Jeff arrived to start working on the woodpile. Juliana told Meagan, "You can take today off from school if you promise to work extra hard tomorrow."

"I'll gladly do that, Momma."

"Would you like to go with Trudy and me when we take the van back to the rental company?"

"Will we be able to go back to the mall before we come home?"

"Let's ask Trudy if she has some time for us to stop."

"Okay."

They found Trudy finishing up the breakfast dishes, and Juliana asked, "Would you follow me to town when we take the rental van back to the rental place?"

"Sure, I can do that."

"Meagan and I wanted to stop at the mall for some last minute shopping. Would that be okay?"

Trudy grinned and said, "I was thinking of going back to town when I got more settled in so I could do my Christmas shopping before it snows again, so that would suit me just fine."

"Good," said Juliana. "Can you be ready to go in an hour? I want to check on Momma and tell her where we're going before we leave."

"I'll go get ready right now.

Kissing Trudy's cheek, Meagan said, "It's good to have you back with us."

Shirleen was awake when Juliana got to her room. "How are you feeling, Momma?"

"I don't feel as tired as I did yesterday, but I'm still tired."

"Well, just rest. Trudy, Meagan and I are going back to town to return the rental van. While we're there we're going to stop at the mall to get some last minute shopping done. It's barely eight-thirty, so we should be back in time to get lunch made for you and Jeff though it might be a bit later than usual."

"Don't forget that Sergeant York will be here today to teach us how to shoot."

"Oh, I had forgotten about that. I'll stop in at his office and see if he can come later this afternoon."

"I know I'm supposed to stay in bed, but I'd like to practice for an hour or so. I can go back to bed until supper, so I should be all right."

"It is important for you to learn, just don't over do it."

"I'll stay in bed until you get back. I promise."

"Good." Turning to leave she said, "I'll be back as soon as I can."

As they rode down the mountain, Meagan turned to address her mother, "Momma, I was wondering what to do for Jeff and Tim for Christmas. Is it all right to buy them Christmas presents?"

"I don't see why not." Glancing over to look at Meagan, she asked, "Why do you ask?"

"They have both been so good to us, even after they found out about who we really are. I think I should do something nice for them."

"That's really sweet, honey." They rode in silence, until Juliana said, "They really have been nice and understanding of our situation. It's a good idea to do something nice for them."

Meagan grinned and didn't say anything else until they drew near town. "I'll wait in the van while you go in to talk to Tim."

Looking at Meagan in surprise, Juliana asked, "Don't you want to go inside and talk to Tim?"

"No." Meagan fell silent for a few minutes then replied, "Last time we were here, I didn't like going in his office. I made light of it, but it bothered me more than I can say."

Parking the van, Juliana turned to ask, "Why's that, honey?"

Meagan took a deep breath before replying. "Momma, when I went inside, I thought of Dad and what a criminal he must be. I couldn't help thinking how cold-blooded he was with me sometimes. I also couldn't help but wonder how devious and calculating he was. Something had to make him like that."

Juliana sighed, as she thought of the man she had been forced to marry. Finally, she replied, "I never knew what made him turn out the way he is."

"That's why I don't want to go inside."

"I shouldn't be gone very long anyway."

"Thanks for understanding, Momma. You're the best!"

Juliana walked over to tell, Trudy, "I have to speak to Tim for a minute before we can be on our way."

"Okay. I'll talk to Meagan while we wait." When Juliana went inside, Trudy walked over to wait with Meagan. "Do you mind if I wait with you?"

"Not at all," Meagan said. "I'd be grateful for the company. I don't like being here."

"Why's that?" she asked as she got in the van. Meagan told her what she'd told her mother. "I think I can understand a little bit of why you'd feel this way," Trudy said. Taking a deep breath, she continued, "When I was about your age, my father felt overwhelmed because he had so many people he was responsible for and he couldn't hang onto a job. The day before my birthday, I went to ask him if I could have a new dress. He flew into the worst rage I'd ever seen and told me I positively couldn't have a new dress. I was so crushed by how he treated me, I ran to my room and cried for a long time."

"That's awful," declared Meagan. "Did you at least get something nice for your birthday, Trudy?"

"No, Meagan, I didn't." Tears glistened in Trudy's eyes as she replied, "An hour after speaking to my father, I heard my mother screaming hysterically. I ran in to see what was going on and I found my father hanging from one of the rafters in the basement. He was dead."

Putting her hands to her face, Meagan exclaimed, "Oh, no!"

"I remember a policeman came to the house to get him down. The shock of finding Daddy hanging from that rafter caused my mother to have a stroke, which she died from a short time later. Both of my parents were dead, and for many years I blamed myself. After all, I'd asked for the new dress. My older sister, Carol, went to work cleaning homes for the wealthy so she could keep the three of us together. When I turned seventeen, I went to work too, and that's how I ended up working for your parents."

"How did you learn to forgive yourself, Trudy?"

"My sisters, Carol and Helen, finally helped me see it was Daddy who was to blame. It was his decision. He'd never been good at dealing with the hard times life dealt him. When I turned twenty, Carol told me my father had a gambling problem. She said that after he lost a job, he would go to the casinos and gamble away what little money he had. Mother always thought he could do no wrong so she always made excuses for him. That memory of the policeman has haunted me to this day. It was a long time before I could even look at a cop without shaking all over. Eventually I overcame it and so will you."

"Thank you for telling me your story, Trudy," Meagan said, "I'm so sorry you had to go through that."

"That's life, sweetie."

A moment later, Juliana joined them. When Trudy went back to her car, Meagan told her mother what Trudy had revealed.

It didn't take long to return the van. When that had been accomplished, they got into Trudy's car to drove over to the mall.

Gazing at the other two, Juliann said, "It's nine-thirty. How about we meet back here at eleven-thirty? That should give us plenty of time."

"That sounds good to me," replied Trudy.

"I don't have a lot to get, so I'll definitely be done by then," Meagan added.

"Good," replied Juliana. "I'll see you at the food court at exactly eleven-thirty."

They arrived home at twelve-thirty, and Jeff was still cutting wood. They carried their loot inside and quickly prepared lunch.

A short time later, Trudy said, "If you want to let Jeff know it's ready then we can eat."

"You bet," replied Juliana. Going out to the woodpile, she told Jeff, "Lunch is ready."

"Oh good." Setting the axe aside, he rubbed his back as they started toward the house. "I was afraid I wasn't going to get lunch today."

"We got back later than we'd planned, but we'd never let you go hungry."

"That's all right." Patting his stomach, he added, "I could stand to lose a meal or two now and then."

Juliana laughed and said, "I don't think you have anything to worry about."

Looking up at the sky in concern, Jeff said, "I've been watching the sky today and I don't like the look of it."

Juliana looked up to see what he was talking about. She grew alarmed when she saw the heavy clouds rolling in. "Does that mean what I think it means?" asked Juliana.

"What do you think it means" Jeff asked, watching her suspiciously.

"Whenever we saw those type of clouds in the east, we knew a storm was brewing."

"That's correct," replied Jeff. "I think we're in for a nasty storm."

"Today?"

"Yep, probably before nightfall."

"Oh, dear," said Juliana. "Should we bring in extra wood?"

"Before I leave today, I'll put a good stack of wood in the garage so you can get to it and it's out of the weather. I'll also cover the woodpile with tarps so it doesn't get wet."

"I'll get Meagan to help bring the wood inside as soon as we're done with lunch."

"That's a good idea. I could usc all thc hclp I can gct."

Juliana told Meagan, "Jeff thinks we're in for a terrible storm by nightfall."

"That doesn't sound good," said Trudy.

"It isn't," said Juliana. "Get into your outdoor gear, Meagan. I promised Jeff we'd help him bring in enough wood to last us for several days."

"I'm right on it, Momma," Meagan said.

Turning to Trudy, Juliana asked, "Would you watch out for Momma for me while I help get in the wood?"

"Of course," replied Trudy.

Meagan came back into the kitchen, dressed for the outdoors and she and Juliana were soon outside gathering wood. With all of them working hard for three hours, they got the job done.

"Thanks for your help ladies, I can handle things from here," Jeff said.

"Nonsense," Juliana said. "We need to help you get as much wood as possible into the woodshed too. Many hands make light work, you know. If the storms hits, you won't be here for several days, so we're going to help you."

"Thanks," said Jeff, touched at their generosity. "It's much appreciated."

At four o'clock, Sergeant York pulled up. "Oh drats," said Juliana. "I forgot about our shooting lesson."

"You go ahead. I'll finish up here," Jeff said.

Tim joined them and said, "We're in for a storm," he said. "I've come to help you get ready for it."

Jeff, looking relieved, said, "We're getting in as much of the split wood as we possibly can."

"That's a good idea," admitted Tim. "Why don't we keep splitting the wood while the ladies get it inside the woodshed?"

"We can do that," said Juliana. Meagan nodded.

"Then lets not stand around gabbing," Tim said. "Get to work!"

Jeff paused near dark to go turn on the porch light, so they'd have enough light to finish up. "I didn't even know we had that light," said Juliana in surprise.

"I found it when you went to town today," Jeff said, grinning. "I was carrying some wood into the house and bumped the switch with my arm."

"This means we can work a lot longer," said Meagan.

"That it does," replied Jeff.

They'd got all of the split wood into the woodshed just before the first snowflakes began to fall. The two women took in the last of the wood while the men put tarps over the woodpile.

Inside, Trudy was holding supper for them. As she began putting the food onto the table, she told Juliana. "Your mother had her supper earlier. I also gave her your message, Mr. York."

"Then she knows we couldn't practice our shooting today?" asked Tim.

"When I saw you head out to help them take care of the wood, I guessed the shooting lesson had been postponed."

"Oh, Trudy, you're a real jewel."

When the meal was over, the two men left quickly so they wouldn't be caught in the worst part of the storm. An hour later, the winds picked up and the women were grateful to be inside and out of the storm.

The packages from their shopping trip were still sitting in their bags, so they decided to put them in the two upstairs bedrooms to prepare the rooms for occupancy. By ten o'clock Trudy's room was nearly finished. There were still a lot of things to do to make the rooms more comfortable, yet they felt satisfied. They'd also fixed up the connecting bathroom so Trudy would be able to use it in the morning.

Since things weren't quite finished, they decided it was best for her to remain in Meagan's room for the night. She'd be able to move into hers the next day.

Exhausted, they all went to bed early. The only sounds in the house were the snapping fire in the fireplace, and the howling wind outside.

It snowed so hard for the next tree days. When it was done, it was impossible to see past the window and the wind continued to howl mournfully. Jeff's quick thinking kept them in wood, and they worked to finish Trudy's accommodations and then moved on to dealing with wrapping their Christmas gifts.

On the third snowbound morning, they'd moved the entertainment center t where they wanted it and put the TV and other items where they belonged. This helped to make the house seem less cluttered and more organized.

Once that was done, they settled into working with Meagan on her schoolwork. Trudy took over the cooking, as well as the household chores so it freed up the others for teaching duties.

Finally, on the fifth day they heard a commotion outside. They couldn't see what was happening because of the snow, so they made sure all of the doors were locked and waited. There was a loud thud just outside the front door, followed by a scraping sound. Fear gripped them as the scrapping sound continued. Something bumped the door then moved away.

A moment later, the scraping sounds grew even louder. Shirleen looked over to see tears running down Meagan's pale face and Juliana looked like she was going to faint, as did Trudy. Shirleen's heart was pounding so hard she could hardly breathe. With their nerves stretched taunt, they continued to wait.

Suddenly, someone knocked on the door. "Who's there?" Shirleen asked when she got to the door.

"Tim. Jeff is with me."

Relief flooded through her as she unlocked the door to let the men in. Seeing how pale the women were, Tim apologized. "We didn't mean to scare you, but we didn't have any way to let you know we were here."

"You are both a good sight for sore eyes!" Shirleen said.

"We thought this storm would never let up. There are a lot of people in dire straits due to this storm," said Tim. "The snowplow couldn't get through to your place until early this morning. The driver reported your yard was piled high with snow. He couldn't plow you out because he had so many other roads left to do."

"How did he know to contact you?" asked Meagan, still visibly shaken.

"Our officers are trained to rescue people. I drove my sled dogs up here. Jeff drove his truck, but it got stuck just below your house."

"Can you get him out?" asked Juliana.

"We got him out before we started shoveling our way to your door," replied Tim.

"Good," replied Shirleen, plainly relieved. "Before you do anything else, why don't you come in for a warm drink?"

"Thank you," said Tim, "but we want to get you completely plowed out before we stop."

"When you're done," said Trudy, "I'll fix you both a cup of hot chocolate and give you some of my freshly baked chocolate cake."

"Oh, that not only sounds wonderful," said Jeff, "but it's a good incentive for us get back to work."

When they'd gone back outside, the women began to relax. Not long afterward, they heard the snow blower start up. Meagan began to work on her science class with the help of Juliana, and Shirleen listened to them as she worked on a needlepoint pattern.

Trudy watched her stitch for a while then asked, "Could you teach me how to do that, Shirleen?"

Shirleen patiently showed Trudy how to choose her colors then showed her how to make the stitches. She was surprised by how quickly Trudy picked up the techniques. "Wow, Trudy, you're a natural with this kind of work."

"Thanks. I really like doing this."

"Then this is now your project."

"No," cried Trudy, "this is *your* project. I wouldn't dream of taking it over."

"Nonsense," declared Shirleen. "I have several of these kits. I'll go get another one. You finish this one." Without letting Trudy argue the point, Shirleen went to get another needlepoint project.

Two hours later, the men let them know they'd finished their work and were ready for their treats. Everyone decided to stop and have some hot chocolate and cake. Tim set his plate down on the coffee table and picked up his hot chocolate to take a drink. "Wow, coming here is a real treat. Getting goodies like this is nice payment for the work."

"I agree, Sergeant. Since I've been working here, I think I've gained 10 pounds."

Changing the subject, Tim asked Trudy to tell the story of how she came to join them. When she'd finished, Tim said, "That sure is one very evil man."

"I feel a lot safer here now that I'm with these lovely women."

"Well," stated Tim, "you *are* safe now. I'll do my best to make sure you all stay that way."

Jeff put his empty cup on the coffee table and said, "I've been giving a lot of thought to your offer to have me move in here. I realize you'd be more protected if I'm here all the time. So, if the offer still stands I'll move in tomorrow."

"That would be wonderful!" exclaimed Shirleen. "I know I'd feel a lot more at peace if you were here."

"So would I," said Juliana.

Rising, Meagan went over to plant a kiss on Jeff's cheek. "You've made this chicken feel a whole lot better. When we didn't know who was outside earlier, I was scared out of my mind."

It was obvious Meagan's gesture had pleased Jeff. "I'll pack up my things tonight and be back here at eight o'clock in the morning."

"Thank you for agreeing to stay with us," replied Shirleen.

"It's my pleasure, Shirleen. I'll see all of you all in the morning. I'm gonna head on home to pack."

"I need to get going too," Tim said. "I'll see the three of you tomorrow for your shooting lesson."

"We'll be ready," Shirleen assured him.

The next morning, Jeff drove up with the back of his truck filled with his things. "I brought some of my tools along too so I don't have to keep going back to the house to get them. I don't have a lot of personal things, so I'll put them away before I go to bed tonight, if that's okay."

"That will be fine, Jeff," replied Shirleen.

"If you'll show me my room, I'll drop everything in there and get back to working on that woodpile."

"I'll show you, Jeff," volunteered Meagan. He grabbed his two suitcases and followed her upstairs to the room adjoining Trudy's.

Sergeant York arrived at 2 p.m. to conduct the shooting lessons. "Today, I'm going to show you the mechanics of your weapons, and give you some safety tips for handling them. Shirleen, who was felling a little better, also attended the lesson. She listened intently and tried to commit everything to memory. An hour later the lesson was over.

As they walked back toward the house, they saw the huge pile of wood Jeff had chopped. "You go back into the house, Momma," said Juliana. "I think Meagan and I should help Jeff get this wood stacked inside in case we get hit with another storm."

"I'll see you back to the house," declared Tim as he took Shirleen's arm and prepared to escort her to the house. "I'll be back out to help in a bit."

"Thank you," replied Juliana. "We're going to need all the help we can get to catch up what Jeff's done today."

Jeff looked up when they reached the split wood. "What do you think you're doing, ladies?" he asked.

"We're going to put this wood in the woodshed, while you and Tim keep chopping."

"That would be a great help. According to the weather report I saw this morning, we're in for more snow."

"I was afraid of that," moaned Meagan.

"That's why we want to help you get more stacked in the woodshed and garage," replied Juliana. "Having that wood in the garage made it so much easier while we were snowed in."

"Okay, go ahead and get what you can stacked into the garage like we did before," instructed Jeff. "Remember, there will be two additional fireplaces to keep going now, so you'll need more than before."

"Come on, Meagan," ordered Juliana, "let's get to it."

"I'm already on it, Momma," replied Meagan.

They were just taking a load to the garage when Tim joined them. "Don't take such big loads," he cautioned. "You don't want to strain your backs."

"Okay, boss," Juliana joked. "I'll take it easy."

"Good," said Tim. Grinning he barked, "Get back to work, slaves!"

"Slaves?" Meagan asked indignantly. Dropping the load she was carrying, she scooped up a ball of snow and threw it at Tim. It hit him square in the chest.

"Hey!" cried Tim in surprise. "I'm gonna get you now!"

Knowing what was coming, Juliana stepped out of the way and continued on to the garage with her load of wood. She just got inside just as the snowballs began to furiously fly back and forth. Suddenly a ball struck Tim and Meagan at the same time. Turning to see what had happened, Jeff knocked the snow off of his gloves and grinned. "If you two dilly dally throwing snowballs at each other, we'll never get this wood in ahead of the storm."

"You're right, Jeff. I apologize." Tim helped Meagan pick up the wood she'd dropped and then went to help spilt wood.

The four of them worked hard, stopping only long enough to eat supper. When it grew too dark to see what they were doing, they flipped on the porch light. The snow held off, so they decided to keep working as long as they could.

Finally around midnight they decided to stop. The men covered the woodpile with the tarps and Juliana and Meagan finished stacking the wood in the woodshed.

"I'm bone tired, so I'm going home and going straight to bed," Tim said.

"Thanks for your help, Tim," said Juliana gratefully. "I think I'm going to do the same thing."

Jeff took off his coat and hung it up, then removed his boots and positioned them beneath his coat. Yawning, he said, "I'm going to bed too. I'll get unpacked the first thing in the morning." With that, he trudged upstairs to his room and closed the door.

Juliana turned to help Meagan after she'd removed her coat and boots. Meagan was so tired she couldn't seem to do anything right. "I'm so sorry you had to work so hard, sweetheart, but I'm grateful for all that you've done."

"It had to be done, Momma or we would've been in deep trouble when the snow comes. If it hasn't snowed when we get up tomorrow, I think we should spend the day helping Jeff get in more of that wood."

Pondering Meagan's remarks, Juliana replied. "I agree with you, honey. We don't want to get caught without enough wood."

"Right now," yawned Meagan, "I'm going to get ready for bed. The thought of slipping under those warm covers is all I can think about."

"I'm right behind you," replied Juliana.

It still hadn't snowed the next morning, so at breakfast they told Jeff about their plan to help him. "Thanks. I don't know how much we'll get done before it starts to snow, but every little bit helps."

The three of them worked hard until lunchtime, took a short break to eat then worked until Tim arrived to help. They took a short break for dinner, then again worked until midnight. They finished just as the snow started to fall. Tim headed home and the rest made their weary trek to their beds just as the wind started its mournful howl.

Shirleen couldn't sleep. She lay awake wondering why Dr. Stillman hadn't come up during the break in the storms. *He's probably been too busy to get away. He'll come when he comes,* she told herself. Giving up on sleep, she got up and went out to the living room to work on another needlepoint project. She smiled as she thought about the needlepoint projects she was giving to Trudy for Christmas. As she worked, she felt peace steel over her. *It may be howling like a banshee out there, but at least it keeps us safe for a while longer.*

Suddenly she realized she no longer had to fear Gordon — he was dead. *I'm not really sad about that. He got what he deserved. Good riddance to bad rubbish! Enjoy you long stay with Lucifer!*

Laying her work aside, Shirleen went over and switched on the porch light so she could look out the window. The snow was coming down so fast she couldn't see anything past the porch.

Switching off the porch light, she went to the kitchen, got a drink of water and went back to bed. When she was through, she rechecked all of the doors to see they were all locked. She snuggled down under the covers and willed sleep to come. As she lay there, she wondered how long it would take for Bruce to find them. She was sure he would sooner or later. Suddenly, hate filled her soul.

As tears fell down Shirleen's face, she began to petition her heavenly friend. *Oh, Lord, I'm so worried about what will happen to Meagan if Bruce kills Juliana and me. Please protect her and let her live a happy, productive life. I beg you to stop Bruce somehow. Help me to be prepared when the time comes. If it means I have to meet you sooner than I'd planned, then so be it. I just want Meagan to be safe.* When she was finished, she turned onto her left side and fell into a deep restful sleep.

Chapter 14

Theodore Brooks watched Melinda drive away and then went to fill the sink with soap and hot water. He planned to clean out the refrigerator. Once he'd emptied it, he scrubbed down the inside of the refrigerator until he was satisfied and then put everything back inside. Next, he washed off the stove, cleaned the oven and wiped off the counter and table. Finally, he swept the floor and then mopped it on his hands and knees. When he was finished, he dumped the mop water then went to check on Henry.

Henry was still sleeping, so he started unpacking the dishes. Not knowing how Meagan would want them, he put them on the table and counter so she could decide. He was just emptying the last box when it was time to prepare lunch.

When it was ready, he went to wake Henry. He transferred into his wheelchair, and they went to the kitchen to eat. When they were done, Theodore washed up their dishes.

He was just letting the water out when Melinda arrived. Seeing the dishes stacked so neatly, Melinda was impressed. "Wow," she said, "you've unpacked everything and washed the lunch dishes too."

Theodore saluted and replied, "Yes, ma'am, every last one of them. I also washed out the refrigerator, cleaned the stove and oven and then swept and mopped the kitchen floor."

"You have saved me a ton of work."

"That's the idea, ma'am." Still standing at attention, Theodore winked at Henry. "Is there anything else you need, ma'am?"

Grinning, Melinda replied, "Could you get the bags from the car so I can get these dishes put away?"

Saluting once more, Theodore replied, "Yes, ma'am. Right away, ma'am!" He quickly strode out the door.

Shaking her head, Melinda looked over at Henry and asked, "Has he been this way all day?"

"No," laughed Henry. "I watched him work like a mad man to get those dishes done."

"Oh," sighed Melinda, "I sure appreciate all he's done."

By the time Melinda had the cupboard organized, Theodore had brought all of the items in from the car. Setting them by the table, he took Henry back to his room for his afternoon nap.

When he came out of the bedroom, he asked Melinda, "What can I do to help?"

"As soon as these last few dishes have been put away, I'll be ready to take care of the food."

"Why don't I put the stuff that goes into the refrigerator away while you finish up?"

"Oh, thank you, that would be great."

An hour later, the kitchen had been put to rights. After putting a roast in the oven, Melinda sank onto a chair, feeling totally exhausted. "This has been a really hectic day. I had to run all over this town to get the supplies I brought home."

"Well, you did a good job. We've got a nice start on establishing our household," replied Theodore.

"The kitchen looks good, thanks to you."

"You washed out the cupboards before you left, so I'd say we both deserve credit."

"You're right, Ted — teamwork is the way to go."

"Why don't we employ some more teamwork and get the furniture to your room. By the time we get done it will probably be time for supper."

"Lead on, oh mighty task master!" Melinda chose a matching set of furniture that went with the bed they'd set up the night before. There was still a lot to do to dress it up, but at least all of the furniture looked good. Tomorrow, Melinda resolved to find the things she'd brought from her apartment. "What I need to round out this room is a large curio cabinet so I have a place for my bric-a-brac. That would really dress up this room."

"Tomorrow, while I'm preparing Henry for the day, why don't you go buy one?"

"I think I will. That way, I can pick out exactly what I want."

"While you're out, you might find some other things that will dress up the place even more."

"What I need to do now is add the vegetables to the roast and make a salad."

"How about you do the vegetables while I make the salad."

"You can cook?" asked Melinda, watching him suspiciously."

"Yep! Ma taught me so that I could take care of myself when I struck out on my own." Giving her a strange look, he added, "You might be surprised by what else I can do."

"I'll just wait to see for myself," declared Melinda.

It wasn't long until they had supper on the table. While Melinda warmed up the rolls from the bakery, Theodore went to get Henry into his wheelchair. Melinda was setting the rolls onto the table when they came into the kitchen.

Smelling the air appreciatively, Henry moaned in delight. "Sis, something smells wonderful!"

"Well," smiled Melinda, "the proof is in the tasting. By the way, Theodore made the salad, so if it isn't good you can blame him."

"Hey," Theodore yelled, "I'm a pretty mean salad maker. You won't have any complaints about my cooking."

"Well," Melinda said, "if we don't get at this food while it's hot, you'll be sorry."

While they ate, Theodore filled Henry in on what they'd done while he was sleeping. "I told Melinda she could go purchase a curio cabinet in the morning while we're getting you ready for the day."

"Listen," said Henry, as he laid his fork down, "if I'm not mistaken, there are two large curio cabinets in our furniture stash. Matilda bought them just a year ago. She had one in the dining room and the other in the living room. You're welcome to look them over and choose the one you like best."

"Really?" asked Melinda. Tears glistened in her eyes as she gazed at Henry.

"Look, Sis," replied Henry, "they belonged to Matilda and she'd want me to share them with you."

"Thank you, that would save me some money."

"That's another thing I want to discuss with both of you." Henry had to take a minute to catch his breath as talking cost him precious energy. Finally, he was able to continue. "When I sold my business and my mansion, I got a lot of money for them. I'd like to share some of it with both of you to show how much I appreciate what you've done for me."

"That isn't necessary," replied Theodore. "I've managed to save a nice little nest egg over the years. That, along with working for you, will take care of me for a very long time."

Turning to Melinda, Henry said, "Listen, Sis, I happen to know you aren't very well off." When Melinda started to protest, Henry put up his hand to silence her. "Don't argue with me; it just won't work. Matilda told me you are a proud woman. I gave you all that Matilda owned because we both loved you."

"I know that," replied Melinda. "That's why I gladly accepted them."

"Well, my precious wife was a giving person. A while before she left me, she asked me to see that you were well taken care of. I want to honor her wishes, Sis." Again he had to pause. Looking intently into her eyes, he asked, "Would you want me to ignore her wishes?"

"No, but—"

"Don't but me. Please let me to do what she wanted me to. Let me give you some of the money that was hers."

"I'll think about it," Melinda said."

Grinning, Henry declared, "I'll give you five minutes to think it over, but it won't matter if you refuse because I'll just find a lawyer who'll give it to you anyway."

It was obvious Melinda was upset. Finally, she replied, "I feel like a beggar, taking your money."

"Nonsense," snapped Henry. "I have more money than I'll ever be able to spend in three lifetimes. Besides, I have no one to give it to when I die. If I were to help all of the people in Cardston, I'd still be a wealthy man. Please stop arguing with me and accept my gift."

Seeing no way around it, Melinda finally graciously accepted the money. "Very well, I accept, but only for the sake of my sister. You, Henry Borden, owe me positively nothing. I'm here because you love and need me. I also love you as a beloved brother."

Tears glistened in Henry's eyes. Swiping at them impatiently, he replied, "Thank you for doing me the honor of accepting my gift. There are absolutely no strings attached, other than to continue being my sister."

"That's easy to do."

Turning to Theodore, Henry asked, "Tomorrow, would you please help me go to the bank so that I can set up an account here? I also have the cashier's checks I got from escrow on my estate and the closing of my business. I need to get them deposited someplace safe."

"Sure thing," replied Theodore.

"Thank you," continued Henry. "I'll be glad to get that taken care of." After eating a few more bites, Henry looked up to ask, "What else has been happening while I was sleeping my life away?"

"Well," began Theodore, "I bought two storage units to hold the furniture and other items we don't need until spring."

"Staying here until spring is fine, however I'd like to build a house somewhere we can enjoy the beauty around us," replied Henry. Looking from Theodore to Melinda he asked, "How do the two of you feel about that?"

"That's your decision," stated Theodore. "How about waiting until spring to make it? A lot can happen between now and then."

"I agree with Ted," replied Melinda. "Right now, just thinking of getting this apartment put into shape is overwhelming to me."

"Sure wish I could help somehow."

"Well," said Theodore, "I wouldn't worry about that right now You have an appointment with Dr. Stillman at one o'clock in the afternoon. That will keep you busy."

"Ugh! Do I have to see one so soon?" asked Henry.

"Yes." Watching Henry anxiously Theodore continued, "I don't like how pale you are, or how exhausted you've been. This trip really took a lot out of you."

"I know," admitted Henry resignedly.

"Well," continued Theodore, "I just want to satisfy myself that you're going to be all right. I have heard these winters can be pretty harsh. I don't want to need to get you to a hospital in the middle of a blizzard. That would be disastrous for all of us, but especially to you."

Nodding in agreement, Henry replied, "I don't want that either. Very well. I'll do as you suggest." Growing thoughtful a moment, Henry added, "I'd like to ask the doctor about resuming my therapy. We've been doing the exercises we were given by the doctor in New York, but I want more. I want to learn to walk again if it's possible. So please, help me remember to speak to this doctor about that."

"I will, because I want to see you walk again, too."

"So do I," responded Melinda. "You were always an active man. Being confined to that wheelchair must be difficult for you."

"It's been hard, I won't lie," agreed Henry. "Before, I loved to go golfing, hiking, even dancing. Now these legs of mine don't want to do anything."

"Hopefully, with therapy they will cooperate again soon," said Melinda.

After the meal, Theodore wheeled him away from the table and over to the big window in the living room so he could look out at Cardston. For the first time since his wife and son's deaths, Henry felt at peace.

He remembered Matilda when she was young, vibrant, beautiful and so full of life. He could still feel the taste of those lips upon his as she gave herself to him. He could almost hear her laughter. The joy they'd known washed over him, leaving him feeling consumed with longing to feel her arms around him once more, and hear her telling him how much she loved him.

He remembered the day his son, Jethro, was born, too. Henry smiled as he remembered how wrinkled the baby's skin was, like an old man. How he'd loved him. All the milestones of Jethro's life seemed to unfold before his eye. His first birthday, his first tooth, his first prayer, his first day at school, his first date, the day he graduated from high school and then college, and finally the day of his death.

Suddenly he was back in the present and he was crying. He swiped angrily at the tears, as he glanced around to see if anyone had noticed. They were busily cleaning up the kitchen, so he was safe. He quickly wiped at his face again and then leaned back in his wheelchair, exhausted.

Theodore noticed how tired Henry looked and said, "Melinda, can you finish up here so I can take care of Henry?" Nodding, she watched in concern as Theodore wheeled his chair to his room.

When the kitchen was in order, Melinda went to see what she could do with the living room. The task was daunting. Just as she was about to tackle the job, Theodore returned. "Now what are you thinking up, Melinda Jacobs?"

"At first this looked overwhelming to me, but I decided to imagine what I wanted to do before actually starting the physical job."

"Well, did you decide?" he asked with a grin.

"You'll see," replied Melinda. "Are you ready to help me make it a reality?"

"As ready as I'll ever be!"

Four hours later, they stepped back to survey the results. "Wow," Theodore said in amazement. "You sure know how to take clutter and turn it into something beautiful and inviting."

"Thank you," replied Melinda, happily.

"I just have one question," said Theodore.

"What's that?"

"Can you work your magic with my room too?"

"Hum…" Melinda pretended to think about it a moment. Grinning she replied, "I think I can do that."

"Good because there's so much stuff crammed in there I can hardly get to the bed."

"There's so much stuff we don't need, I'm amazed any of us can get through any part of this apartment right now."

Looking at his watch, Theodore winced — it was eleven o'clock. "I know it's late, but could you help me arrange the furniture before we go to bed?"

"Sure," replied Melinda. "I must warn you, though, I might just fall asleep standing up."

Theodore laughed and said, "Well, if that happens, I'll stand you in the corner and let you sleep."

"That does *not* sound like the best solution!"

Theodore laughed all the way to his bedroom. Just before entering the room he turned to say, "If you do fall asleep where you're standing, I'll carry you to your room and toss you on your bed. Is that a better answer?"

His comment caused Melinda's eyes to widen in surprise. "*Toss* me on the bed?"

Again, Theodore laughed. "Well, I'd have to dispatch of you quickly as beautiful as you are, because I might forget myself and take advantage of you." When Melinda tossed a small pillow at him, he laughed and ducked into the safety of his room. *That*, thought Theodore, *wouldn't be such a bad idea.* Scolding himself for having such thoughts, he went to work with a vengeance.

They decided on a lighter set of bedroom furniture than what was currently in use, so they lugged it into the bedroom after removing the other set and a lot of unnecessary stuff. Finally, two hours later there was some semblance of order. It still needed a lot of work, but they decided to wait to finish until later that morning.

When Theodore went to check on Henry, Melinda staggered out of his room, exhausted. It was all she could do to get ready for bed.

The next morning, Theodore forced himself out of bed and took a cold shower to try to shock himself awake. When he was finally dressed, he went in to check on Henry and was surprised to see he was awake. "Good morning, sir."

"What's with this sir business?" asked Henry.

"I don't know," grinned Theodore. "Exhaustion talking, I guess."

"What time did you and Melinda go to bed last night?"

"We got through arranging the living room at eleven, so we decided to work on my room too. We finally stopped at one o'clock this morning."

"Good grief, man! Are the two of you trying to kill yourselves?"

"No," Theodore said. "We're just tired of stubbing our toes and living inside a maze."

"Well, I can understand that. The mess in this room is kind of getting to me too."

"Well, when we've taken care of your bank business, we'll get your room straightened out. After your doctor's appointment, I'll go get a U-Haul trailer so we can move everything we don't need to the storage units."

"That sounds like a plan."

"Good. We'll make it happen," replied Theodore.

When Theodore opened the door to Henry's room, the smell of frying bacon and brewing coffee, assailed them. "That has got to be what heaven smells like," Henry said after getting a good whiff.

"I think you're absolutely right, Henry," admitted Theodore.

After getting Henry settled at the table, he went to the kitchen to see what he could do to help. "Need some help in here?"

"Yes, please," said Melinda. "Could you pour the coffee while I set the food on the table?"

As he reached for the coffee, he asked, "Did you even go to sleep last night?"

"Yes," replied Melinda, looking at him strangely "Why?"

"Because," Theodore said grinning, "you look ravishingly beautiful and you've created a masterpiece for breakfast. Where'd you find the time?"

"Looks are deceiving. I'm still so tired that I'm barely standing."

Throwing up his hands as he laughed, Theodore replied, "Well, you certainly fooled me. After breakfast, why don't you go back to sleep for an hour or two while I take Henry to the bank?"

"That sounds like a wonderful idea!" Turning a pancake, she said, "I'll do just that as soon as we're through with breakfast."

Without another word, Theodore went to fill the cups with coffee. They enjoyed their breakfast, then Theodore helped get Henry ready to run his errands. As they prepared to leave, Henry turned to Melinda and said, "I know you want to nap, but could you come with us to the bank first? I want to transfer money into your account after I've set mine up."

"Okay. Let me get my coat," replied Melinda. Drying her hands on the kitchen towel, she tossed it onto the counter before going to get her things.

As they were finishing up at the bank, Theodore noticed that Henry was looking strange. His face was drooping, his speech was becoming slurred, and his face was ashen. Leaving Melinda with Henry, Theodore went outside to phone Dr. Stillman. "My name is Theodore Brooks. I take care of a patient named Henry Borden. We're at the bank right now and he suddenly started slurring his speech. I think he's had a stroke."

"Stay there and I'll send an ambulance. I'll also alert Dr. Stillman and he'll meet you at the hospital."

Theodore went inside to tell Melinda what was happening. When he saw her anxious face, he knew things weren't good. He moved quickly over to where Henry was sitting in his wheelchair and took his pulse. It was weak and thready, but at least his heart was still beating. "The ambulance is on the way."

"Good," whispered Melinda.

Looking up at the bank teller, Theodore asked, "Did he get everything done?"

"Yes, sir. I have everything here in my hands when you're ready." The woman quickly separated the documents and handed them to Melina, saying, "These are Mr. Henry's copies, and this other set officially opens your account with us."

Just then they heard the wailing of the ambulance as it approached the bank. Barking for the people to get out of the way, the paramedics moved toward Henry. Touching Melinda's arm, Theodore guided her away so the paramedics could take care of him.

The first thing they did was to transfer him from the wheelchair to the stretcher. Kneeling on each side of Henry, they began to work. Once the paramedics had Borden stable, they prepared to take him to the hospital.

When the ambulance pulled away, Theodore turned to the woman to ask, "How do we get to the hospital?"

Armed with directions, they rushed out to the car and drove quickly to the hospital. While Theodore parked the car, Melinda went inside to talk to the receptionist at the front desk. "The ambulance just brought in a man from the bank."

"Yes, ma'am. Are you a relative?"

"I'm his sister-in-law."

"Where's his wife?"

Growing testy, Melinda snapped, "My sister is dead, so his nurse and I are taking care of him. How is he?" Melinda was so anxious that she felt panicky.

"The doctor is in with him now. Take a seat here in the waiting room and he'll come out to talk to you when he's done."

"Thank you." She was about to sit down when Theodore entered the lobby.

"How is he?" asked Theodore.

"I don't know," replied Melinda "The doctor is with him now." Taking a deep breath, Melinda continued, "The receptionist said he'd come out to talk to us when he's done."

"Then I suggest that we take a seat to wait."

Melinda took a seat beside Theodore, but it was difficult for her to relax. All she could think to do was pray, even though she hadn't prayed since she was a little girl. She stood and went over to the window to look at the snow that was being blown around the parking lot. Silently, the words of a prayer formed in her mind. Giving in to the feelings, she prayed for Henry's recovery. When she was done, she sat back down.

They'd been waiting for an hour, but to Melinda it seemed like a lot longer. When she noticed Theodore calmly reading a magazine, she grew angry. "How can you sit there and calmly read that magazine?"

He let the magazine drop to his lap and calmly replied, "Just because I'm reading a magazine doesn't mean I'm calm. Just the opposite. If I wasn't looking at this magazine, I'd be pulling my hair out."

Feeling ashamed, Melinda said, "I'm sorry for snapping at you, Theodore."

"Oh, Mel," he replied in sympathy, "I didn't mean to give you the impression that I don't care. The truth is, I can hardly sit here because I really want to yell at everyone to do something. It's taking that doctor way too long to come out to talk to us."

"I know," meekly replied Melinda.

"I don't like this feeling. My father died of a massive heart attack when I was nineteen and became the breadwinner of my family. There were four children beside myself to feed, clothe, and educate. When my younger brothers and sister went off to school, I was left at home to care for my mother, who was ill by that time. One day, my mother didn't wake up for breakfast. I thought I was being nice to let her sleep in, and just went on to work. When I got home from work, she still wasn't awake. I went in to wake her—" Theodore paused to gain control of his emotions. "When I touched her cold, stiff hand, I knew she was gone."

"Oh, how awful!" Melinda said as she touched his hand in an effort to comfort him.

Squeezing her hand in return, Theodore continued, "When my family came home for the funeral, I thought I'd suffocate from the pain of loss. After the funeral, my brothers and sisters told me that they had a proposition for me. They said that since I didn't get to finish college, they wanted to pay for me to go to school."

"Was nursing your chosen profession?"

"No," said Theodore, "I wanted to be a doctor but that was too expensive, so I went into nursing instead."

"You gave up your life's dream." Melinda fell silent a moment. Finally, she said, "Why didn't you accept Henry's offer to help you so that you could go back to school?"

"I wanted to accept, but I was too proud and too old. I'm now thirty-nine years old. That's too old to go back to school."

"No it's not! You could still practice for many years."

"It's fine. I do okay as a nurse."

Melinda didn't say more, but she promised herself to speak to Henry when he got better.

An hour later, the doctor came into the waiting room to speak to them. "Hello, I'm Dr. Stillman."

"How is Henry?" asked Melinda.

"How are you related to him, young lady?"

"I'm his sister-in-law. My name's Melinda Jacobs. My sister died a few months ago, so I came to live with Henry so I could help care for him."

Stillman raised his eyebrow in surprise and looked at Theodore. "There's no hanky-panky going on, doctor. Mr. Brooks is his live in nurse."

"Well, he's stable for the moment," Dr. Stillman said, "but he isn't out of the woods yet. He won't be for quite a while." Looking from Theodore to Melinda, he asked, "Why isn't he ambulatory?"

"He had a massive stroke this past fall. At the end of August, his wife died, and then two weeks later a drunk driver killed his son. The shock of both deaths so close together brought on the stroke. He had rehab at a nursing home facility and then I went to work for him when he was released," Theodore said. "Not long after that we left Syracuse to come here."

"What in the world possessed him to move all the way to Canada?"

Melinda took over the conversation, adding, "He wanted to get as far away from his old life and those bad memories as he possibly could."

"Didn't the two of you think to override his decision?" Dr. Stillman asked.

"Yes, but he was so persistent that in the end neither of us had the heart to say no."

"If you knew how much pain Henry was in, you'd understand his need to get away, even if it meant his death in the process," Theodore said.

"Well, it nearly did cost him his life." Dr. Stillman softened his tone and continued, "We're going to keep him in ICU for a while. Give the nurses time to get him settled and then one of you at a time can go in and see him. He won't be able to talk, but I believe he understands what's said to him. Encourage him to fight. Give him the will to live."

"We will," promised Melinda.

"If you follow me, I'll show you the waiting room for the ICU unit."

An hour later, Melinda went to sit with Henry and then gave Theodore a chance to go in for a few minutes. When he came out of the room ten minutes later, they were loath to leave. Theodore suggested that they go to the cafeteria for something to eat. "After we eat, we'll come back and see him again."

When Theodore took his second turn to go in and see Henry, Melinda was alone in the waiting room. She opened her purse and took out her new bankbook. When she saw what Henry had deposited for her, she nearly dropped it. He'd given her two million dollars. Tears, long held in check spilled down her face. No one had ever been that generous to her. Now, this man she'd once loathed, had given so liberally … so freely. Gratitude and shame vied for attention as she tried to take it all in.

Suddenly she smiled. Henry knew her better than she thought he did. If he'd told her what he planned ahead of time, she'd never have allowed it. Her heart swelled with gratitude for this kindhearted man. "Someday, when I get the chance, I'll do something just as wonderful for you, Henry!" whispered Melinda.

When Theodore came out of Henry's room, Melinda could see he was worried, but he didn't say anything. Hours later, they went back to the cafeteria for dinner. Thirty minutes after they got back, a light went on over the door to Henry's room.

Suddenly they heard, *"Code blue, code blue in the ICU Unit."* People came rushing toward them with all kinds of equipment and Melinda watched in horror as they disappeared inside Henry's room.

Turning to Theodore, Melinda asked, "What's happening, Theodore? What does code blue mean?"

"It means that Henry has either stopped breathing or he's dying."

Suddenly, Melinda collapsed into Theodore arms.

Chapter 15

Two days later

Shirleen stood at the window and watched the snow falling. She was still feeling tired in spite of obeying Dr. Stillman's orders. "I just don't understand why I'm so tired," she said aloud.

"Dr. Stillman hasn't been able to get out here with all of this snow stopping him. I'm sure he'll get it figured out," said Juliana.

"I know he will," replied Shirleen. "I just have so much to do before Christmas. Problem is, I just can't seem to concentrate."

She went over to the easy chair near the fire and sat down. She'd had been gazing into the fire for a quite a while when she heard dogs barking outside.

"I'll get it, Momma," said Juliana making her way to the door. Just as she was about to open it, she heard male voices. For a moment the old feelings of panic washed over her.

There was a knock at the door, and when she finally got up the nerve to answer it, Sergeant Timothy York stood there smiling at her.

"Hi, Juliana," he said and then stepped back. "Look who I found out in the snow." Juliana saw Dr. Stillman standing there waiting to be asked inside.

"Dr. Stillman, what a pleasant surprise," Shirleen said. "When you didn't make it up here before the storm, I wondered if you were all right."

"We've been pretty busy at the hospital, so I wasn't able to get away until now."

"What brings you out here on such a messy day?"

"You," Stillman said, and smiled. "I haven't seen you in a while because of the bad weather, so I wanted to check you over while I had the chance."

"This way then." Shirleen led the way to her bedroom. She sat down on the bed, and Dr. Stillman checked her over thoroughly. When he was done, she asked, "Why am I so tired?"

Dr. Stillman pulled a chair near the bed and sat down. "For some reason you're completely stressed out and it's wearing you down. Stress is a silent killer, you know."

Taking her file out of his coat pocket, he consulted it. "I have the results from your lab work here. Let's review it together."

Shirleen waited for him to scan the file, then he said, "For the most part everything came back normal. The only thing out of the ordinary is you're extremely anemic."

"What's that mean?" asked Shirleen.

"The anemia coupled with the stress means you're going to feel exhausted all the time. You need to take these every day," he said, taking two bottles out of the right hand pocket of his coat. "This first one is an antidepressant. Don't worry, it's not habit forming."

When Shirleen started to protest, Stillman held up his hand to silence her. "I know, you don't think you need it, but you do."

"Fine.

"Good. Now this other bottle is something for the anemia. It won't happen over night, but by the time you've used these up, you should be feeling a lot better. I'll want to see you for another checkup in a month. At that point we'll see if you need to continue taking both prescriptions."

"I'll be good, doctor."

Stillman explained when to take the medications and added, "I want you to continue to take a nap every afternoon. That should help too."

"I'll do exactly as you say. This being tired is definitely for the birds."

"Now that that's done, I need to apologize."

Blinking in surprise Shirleen asked, "You do."

"Yes, I do. When I saw you in my office, I didn't believe you when you said you were following my orders. You were so run down that I thought you'd totally ignored everything I said and I was irritated."

"Yeah, I got that you were irritated. I'm not usually one to lie, so when you didn't believe me I snapped at you."

"Well, let's start over. Okay? From now on, when you tell me something I'll believe you."

"Thank you, Dr. Stillman."

"Let's go tell your family that you're too ornery to be kept down for long." He smiled to take the edge off of his words.

Grinning good-naturedly, Shirleen headed out the door.

When they were back in the living room with the others, Dr. Stillman filled them all in on Shirleen's condition. "You can all relax now. Shirleen is going to be just fine."

Jeff, who'd come in the house while Dr. Stillman was examining Shirleen, said, "I'm sure glad to hear that!"

"Thanks Jeff."

"How do you fit into this situation?" asked Dr. Stillman

"Jeff is their hired hand," Sgt. York said. "After we couldn't get here during the last storm, I suggested that Jeff stay with them in case of an emergency."

"That's good thinking, Sergeant."

"Jeff has been a Godsend," said Juliana. "He's been doing all the things we couldn't do."

"Keep up the good work, Mr. Borton." Turning to Tim, Dr. Stillman said, "I have to get back soon." Turning back to Shirleen, he said, "Make sure to follow doctor's orders."

Nodding, Shirleen replied, "I will, doctor."

"Good. I'll be back to see you in a month. Don't over do." Turning to Tim he asked, "Are you ready to go?"

"Whenever you are, Doc."

After they left, Jeff said, "Gerald Stillman has been a grouch ever since I've known him, but he is one heck of a doctor."

"I'm sure glad he was around when I needed help," replied Shirleen. "My husband was a terrible grouch. The difference between him and Dr. Stillman is like night and day. I'll take Dr. Stillman's brand of grouchy any day."

"There were several newspapers from New York in my mail today," said Jeff and handed them to her.

"Thanks," Shirleen said excitedly. She opened one of them to scan the front page and what she saw made her sick. Plastered on the front page were pictures of a car that had been blown up. The caption read:

Family of Six Killed by Car Bomb

A car bomb took the lives of a family of six early this morning as they prepared to leave on a trip to spend Thanksgiving with family.

Police report that this latest bomb is the seventh in an apparently connected string of car bombs in upper New York Sate since early September. The police suspect that these incidents are related to the mass murder of one hundred people at the Patellae restaurant last August. It is not yet apparent whether this is the work of a serial killer.

After Shirleen finished reading the article, Juliana grew increasingly angry. She paced the room trying to calm down, then said, "They're right about it being a serial killer. His name's Bruce Murdock!"

"If you don't calm down you're going to have a heart attack," cautioned Shirleen.

"I can't help it!" Finally, she stopped pacing to ask, "How can one man be so evil?"

"I think he's deranged. He has to be to be. No sane person does things like that. I just thank God we were able to get away from him when we did."

After crying to vent her frustration, Juliana asked, "Shouldn't we tell the police about Bruce?"

"If we did that, we'd just be letting Bruce know where we are."

"Shirleen's right, Juliana," said Jeff. "You have to wait until there's a way to make sure he gets caught red-handed."

"How many more have to die before he's stopped?"

"I don't honestly know," replied Jeff. "People who do this kind of evil eventually get caught because they get to cocky. They think they're invincible, and that's their downfall." He paused a moment to collect his thoughts, then said, "Sometime, they get so evil that their own kind won't put up with their behavior and snuff them out."

"Well," cried Juliana, "it can't happen soon enough for me!"

"I'm so ashamed of Daddy. I wish he wasn't my father."

"I wish you didn't have to claim him as your father either, honey. Here in Canada, that doesn't have to happen. As far as I'm concerned, he's dead!"

"But, Juliana, he isn't," Shirleen calmly replied. "We can't just wish him dead and dismiss him from our minds. Thinking like that would be letting our guard down. We can't take that chance."

"I know," sighed Juliana, "but I can still wish it."

"Let things take their course and before you know it, everything will be behind you," advised Jeff.

Sighing, Juliana replied, "You're right."

Seeing her grandmother tearing open the other newspapers, Meagan asked, "What are you doing, Grandma?'

Without stopping what she was doing, Shirleen replied, "I'm looking for the dates so I can put them in order and create a timeline."

When she had accomplished her desired goal, Shirleen picked up the first one and began to scan it.

"Well," demanded Meagan impatiently, "read it aloud."

Shirleen looked over at Juliana with concern. "She has every right to know what's happening," responded Juliana. "Even if it's upsetting."

"Fine," replied Shirleen, "but I'm not going to read these to you until after Thanksgiving. Tomorrow should be a happy, thankful day. We don't need to think about Bruce's evil."

Thinking things over for a moment, Meagan replied, "I agree, Grandma. We don't need to get upset and spoil a wonderful day."

"I'm glad you agree. I'm going to put these papers away and we'll go over them later."

They had asked Tim to come up for Thanksgiving dinner, but he declined, telling them he was going to his family's home for the day. Before leaving, he told them he would be there the next afternoon to help with the wood.

The next morning dawned bright and beautiful. Meagan seemed drawn to the window to peer out at the beauty before her. A herd of elk meandered casually through the yard toward the west field. Suddenly, feeling peace steal over her, and Meagan felt safe. Sighing, she turned from the window to look at her mother, Juliana. "Momma, Grandma, Jeff would you all please come here a moment?"

"What is it?" asked Shirleen.

"I just want to share the peace and beauty of this day," replied Meagan.

The others crowded around her in an attempt to see what she was looking at.

"Oh," cried Shirleen, moved beyond words. "I have loved the winters in Syracuse, but there's something so picturesque about the scenery here in this out of the way place. It's almost like we're being given a small glimpse into heaven."

"That's a good way to put it, Grandma. I'm so grateful we're here where we're safe from the cares of the world, as least for now."

Grinning, Jeff said, "This is my favorite time of the day. There's something to be said about the feelings one experiences when they awake to such beauty."

After breakfast, Meagan and her mother opted not to hold school so that they could help with the wood. While Trudy got the bird stuffed, Shirleen made cranberry sauce. They worked in companionable silence, content to be where they were.

At two o'clock, Shirleen called everyone in to eat. After saying grace, Shirleen looked around at those she loved more than life itself. "I think it would be only fitting if we go around the table to express the things that we're grateful for. Jeff, we'll start with you."

Jeff, thoughtfully mulled things over in his mind, and smiled as he began, "I'm so thankful for feeling useful again. Losing my daughter tore me apart for a long time. Then when my wife died a few months ago, I withdrew almost completely. When Tim came to tell me you needed help, I wasn't too keen on coming to work for you. It was only after Tim told me the three of you were in some kind of trouble, that I decided to take on the job. Then when I met the three of you, I was glad I'd agreed. I have come to love and admire the spunk, tenacity, as well at the courage you all display in the face of adversity. You've made me feel welcome, even needed, which I haven't felt for a very long time. Thank you all so much for giving me a reason to live."

Meagan, sitting on Jeff's left side, looked at those around her for a moment. Sighing, she said, "I was so angry at Jethro Borden when he tried to take advantage of me. Then when you came to my room to tell me I had to marry him, I felt so desperate I thought taking my life was the only answer if you didn't help me." Shuddering at the thought, she added, "The awful truth is that I would've gone through with it rather than face that wedding."

Juliana and Shirleen could only stare at her. Juliana said, "I didn't know you were that desperate."

"Nor did I," replied Shirleen."

"I was," continued Meagan, hanging her head in shame. A few seconds later she looked and said, "I'm so grateful that you both loved me enough to get me away from a man who never understood how to love me. I'm also glad that I can finally feel relatively safe. I'm also thankful that I've had this time alone with the two of you. Momma, Grandma, I love you both dearly and I'm grateful for the things that you've both been teaching me."

Looking at Jeff, she continued, "Jeff, when I met you, I immediately saw your kind heart. I'm grateful that you reached out to care about us. Thank you for all that you're doing to help us and keep us safe." Jeff nodded, yet remained silent.

Turning to smile at Trudy, Meagan said, "Trudy, when we ran away, I missed my visits in the kitchen with you. We didn't know that we could trust you because you were working for Daddy. Now that you're with us again, I feel complete."

When she didn't say anything else, Juliana, who was sitting beside Meagan, began to speak. "Jeff, working with you has given me the chance to get to know you better. Tim was wise to send you to us. It was one of the best things to happen in our lives recently.

"Meagan Leslie Louise Murdock, the day I learned you were coming into my life, I was the happiest woman alive. You are the most important person in my life, other than you, Momma. Loving you like I do, my darling daughter, I would lay down my life for you so that you can have the life you deserve. I tried to run away once before, when I found I was pregnant with you, but Bruce found me. He told me that if I ever tried that stunt again he would take you so far away that I would never find you. That terrified me and I never tried to leave again. I endured the treatment that he gave me because I just couldn't bear to lose you."

"Oh, Momma," cried Meagan, throwing her arms around her mother. "I had no idea that was why you never left your horrible marriage. Learning this only makes me love you more."

"Thank you, sweetheart." Juliana held Meagan in a warm embrace for a moment. When Meagan took her seat, Juliana continued. "I am and always will be grateful for you being in my life."

Turning to look at Trudy, she continued, "I always wanted to be friends with you, Trudy, yet I was told that I wasn't to fraternize with the servants. Since you've come back into our lives I'm grateful to finally get to see the wonderful jewel that you are."

Trudy gasped then dabbed at the tears in her eyes. Finally, she managed to say, "Thank you, Juliana, for that wonderful compliment."

"You're welcome," grinned Juliana. "Thank you for all of the wonderful things you're doing to help us. I know you must be scared too, but you don't let that get to you. You have so much faith and courage. I wish I could've got to know you sooner."

Looking at Shirleen, Juliana was rendered speechless. It took her several attempts to get the words to come out. Taking a deep breath, she said, "Momma, if I were to search this whole world over, I could never have found a more wonderful mother. I love you with everything in me."

Shirleen's eyes moistened and tears began to course down her cheeks. She managed to say, "Thank you, dear."

"You're welcome."

Trudy took a deep breath then plunged in. "When I returned from my vacation to find the two of you gone, I didn't know what to think. I was afraid to ask Mr. Murdock because I was afraid he'd done something to you. I was so grateful when I found out you were all safe. Coming here to work for you is the best thing I've ever done. I'm grateful that I don't have to be on my own. Thank you for everything."

Shirleen, finally gained her composure and looked around the table. Turning to Jeff, who was on her left, she said, "I agree, you coming into our lives was one of the best things that's happened to our family. You have been a Godsend. There's no way to adequately express the gratitude I feel. All I can say is thank you from the bottom of my heart."

Looking over at Meagan, Shirleen could only say, "Meagan, I'm so glad that you didn't do what you planned. I would've been the most miserable person in this world without you in my life. You and your mother are what makes my life worth living. It would be difficult to face life without either of you in it. I love the two of you with every fiber of my being. Thank you for trusting me enough to let me come with you."

Turning to look at Trudy, Shirleen continued, "Trudy, I'm very grateful for who you are. You are not only a real treasure, but you are also an example of faith, courage, hope, and determination. You're helping us to keep going forward. Thank you for all that you do for us. You're awesome!"

Juliana smiled as she said, "Now that the food is good and cold, I guess we can eat."

Jeff piped up to say, "This food may be cold, but with all of the love that surrounds this table, I for one don't care. I'm just happy to be a part of the celebration."

They fell to with hearty appetites. When the meal was over they went into the living room to bemoan their misery after overindulging.

Sitting down on the couch, Jeff moaned and said, "Why is it that we never learn not to get carried away at holiday meals? Each year I tell myself that I won't do it again, and each year I'm right there stuffing myself."

"I can't answer that," replied Juliana. "I do the same thing."

"Well," moaned Trudy. "I can't talk about why others do it, but I think that it's because everything tastes so good that we just can't get enough. It might also be that we only get a dinner like this two or three times a year, so we overindulge in case we never get another meal like it."

"You know, Trudy," said Jeff. "I do believe that you have hit the nail on the head."

"Thank you, Mr. B—"

"Oh, please call me Jeff. Can't stand for this Mr. stuff!" Trudy blinked in surprise, not sure what to say.

Finally, she replied, "Well, thank you for the compliment, Jeff."

"That sounds much better."

Grinning Meagan said, "One would think that from the way that you gripe about someone calling you sir or mister, you'd been in the military or something."

"I was," replied Jeff. "I was a General in her Majesty's army."

Meagan sat up to look at him in surprise, as she asked, "You were?"

"Yep," smiled Jeff. "I retired from the service when my daughter, Julie, got sick."

"Wow! That's really amazing." Studying him for a moment, she said, "I bet you were some looker in your uniform."

Laughing good-naturedly, Jeff replied, "I don't think so. I was never comfortable in the darn thing."

"Still, I sure wish I could see what you looked like," persisted Meagan.

"Next time I go down to check on my place, I'll dig up an old photo of myself in uniform."

"Wonderful," Meagan said.

Struggling out of her chair, Trudy muttered, "Perhaps if I clean up that kitchen I can work off some of this food."

"I was just thinking I might chop some wood to do the same thing," mumbled Jeff.

"This is a day for a body to rest," protested Shirleen.

"That may be the case," said Jeff, "but I have got to move around so I don't feel so uncomfortably full."

"I think Jeff's right," Juliana acquiesced. Looking over at Meagan, she asked, "Do you feel like you could help stack more wood?"

Struggling to her feet, Meagan replied, "Just let me get dressed for the great outdoors and I'm ready to at least try." Growing melodramatic she added, "If I burst from the effort, just remember that I love you."

Grinning, they got into their outdoor gear and started outside. All at once Juliana thought of something and asked, "Do you need our help to clean up the kitchen before we go help Jeff, Trudy?"

"I'll help her," said Shirleen. "I've got to work off this scrumptious meal too."

"But won't that tire you out, Momma?" Juliana watched her parent anxiously.

"I'll stop when I get tired," promised Shirleen.

Standing beside Shirleen, Trudy declared, "I won't let her get to tired."

"Okay," replied Juliana. "We're off to see if we can move enough to get some work done."

Early the next morning, Shirleen awoke feeling a little apprehensive. She showered, got dressed and went to the living room to stoke the fire. She sat down, then remembered the newspapers. She went to her room to get them then set them down on the floor beside her chair. She picked up the first one and started reading. She sat horrified by what she was reading.

Mass Restaurant Murders Under Investigation

One hundred people lost their lives last night to unknown assailants at, Patellae, a prominent restaurant in New York City. Police responded to a call from the owner of the restaurant, Alphonso Patellae. He told police he'd been on vacation for a couple of weeks and his manager, Antonio Higgins, had been in charge of things while he was gone.

The owner said he became concerned when he couldn't reach his manager so he returned from vacation earlier than expected. Upon entering the restaurant through the kitchen, he was surprised to see it in shambles. When he went into the main dining room, he was greeted by an entire room filled with corpses. He then promptly called the police.

After dealing with the massacre at the restaurant, police dispatched officers to the Higgins' residence. They found that the entire Higgins family had been murdered."

Shirleen shivered in spite of the warmth from the fireplace. "There's only one man capable of doing something like this and that's Bruce Murdock," she whispered. "How long will the Lord allow him to get away with such hideous crimes?" She continued to read the story.

"The Mafia is rumored to be involved, but police aren't commenting due to the ongoing investigation. However, they assure the public that no stone will go unturned in the hunt for the responsible party.

Names of the deceased have been withheld until the next of kin are notified."

Shirleen scanned the rest of the paper and saw nothing else of importance. She dropped the paper on the floor and picked up the next issue. There were stories about two car bomb incidents on the front page. Curious to see if they might be linked to Bruce Murdock, she began to read the first article.

Car Bombing in East Manhattan Kills Man

"Early this morning, James Kildare, 29, was killed when his car exploded at his home in eastern Manhattan. This is the third car bomb in the area this week.

Kildare worked at Manhattan Bank. He was survived by his wife, Jeanette, and their three young children, Mathew, 7; Thomas, 4; and Melissa, 8 months.

Police have hinted that the series of car bomb deaths recently might be the work of a serial killer. Currently, they have no leads or suspects.

Contributions for the Kildare family can be taken at the Manhattan Bank."

Shirleen laid the newspaper on her lap as she digested the information she had just read. "What are you trying to do, Bruce?" whispered Shirleen. "I wish someone would put a stop to your evil." Shirleen's mind went to the young widow with three children. She knew Jeanette Kildare well. She'd been involved with many of the same charities as Shirleen. Shirleen knew that Jeanette's mother and father weren't well, and she wondered what she would do now.

I'm going to ask Tim how I can send her some money anonymously. I'll bet he knows how to do that." With that decision made, Shirleen began to read about the next car bomb.

Car Bomb Foiled

A strange man, lurking around the neighborhood, caused a man to become so suspicious that he called police yesterday. The suspicious man had attempted to speak to one of the man's children. The child told the man to leave or she would scream and then ran into the house to tell her father what had happened.

When police arrived they questioned the girl, 11, and she said she had seen the man working on the neighbor's car. When he approached her, she said he asked questions about her father.

Because of all the recent car bombing incidents, the police called in the bomb squad to check out the neighbor's car. A bomb had been attached to the vehicle, but it had not been activated.

The family has been put into protective custody until the suspect is apprehended.

"Well, that's one family that you won't hurt, Bruce Murdock!" Not finding anything else of importance, Shirleen folded the paper and put it with the first. She went through several more papers, but found nothing out of the ordinary. When she got to an issue dated two weeks after Gordon Spielberg had found them at the hotel, she was shocked.

Mob Boss Found Murdered Just in Small Ohio Town

A New York man was found shot just outside a small Ohio town two weeks ago. Police suspect this was a mob hit.

After searching missing persons files, they identified the man as Gordon Spielberg, a resident of Syracuse, New York.

Shirleen finished the article and said, "I'm so glad I left and sadly, I'm glad he's dead." The relief that washed over her was quickly replaced by fear of Bruce Murdock. She picked up the next paper in line and continued reading.

Car Bomb Kills Family of Six

Michael Belmont, of New York City, his wife, Charlotte, and their four children were killed when a bomb exploded in their car on Wednesday. Neighbors of the family told police the family was going to visit family in Ithaca, New York.

One neighbor reported seeing a strange man wandering around the Belmont home the day before. The man's description matched that of a suspect in an attempted bombing earlier this week."

Shirleen gasped. Charlotte had been her best friend for many years. Tears began to slide down her cheeks as she continued to read the article. "Bruce Murdock, you will rot in Hell for this!"

Disgusted, she picked up the next paper in the pile. An article seemed to jump out at her.

Escort Service to Open Just in Time For Christmas

Happy Time Escort Service will open in New York City in time for Christmas Eve. Owner Bruce Murdock says this new business will boost the city's economy greatly. Citizens boycotted allowing this business in their community, but were out voted nine months ago. Many of those who opposed the service have since changed their minds.

"Boy am I ever glad to be out of that awful situation," declared Shirleen aloud. "I would've hated being associated with that business in any way."

She skimmed several more issues before finding another article that caught her attention.

3 Drug-Related Murders in Upper New York

The latest in a string of drug related murders happened in Upper New York yesterday. Three active drug lords, who were under police investigation, were found murdered execution style in a vacant apartment. These murders seem to be connected to the death of Gordon Spielberg, the suspected godfather of New York.

"They're definitely connected," mumbled, Shirleen in disgust. Folding this last newspaper in the stack, she gathered the others and took them back to her bedroom.

Chapter 16

When Melinda fainted from the shock of learning her brother-in-law Henry Borden's medical assessment, Theodore Brooks did his best to help bring her back around.

"What happened," she asked.

"You fainted," replied Theodore gently.

Suddenly, she remembered there was something wrong with Henry, "What's happening with Henry, Theodore?"

"They're working on him now." Just as he finished speaking, a nurse hurried out of the ICU. Melinda noticed that the light was still blinking over the door.

"I'll be all right now," she assured Theodore.

Together they waited to see what was going on. About five minutes later, Dr. Stillman came out to speak to them. "Mr. Borden is finally stable. It was touch and go there for a while. His heart stopped but he's stable now. We won't know the extent of the damage for a while so we'll have to keep an eye on him. With this being his third stroke, it's likely there'll be quite a bit of damage, but like I said, we don't know how much.

"Once he comes out of the medically induced coma, we'll be able to tell you more. Right now, the best thing you two can do is go home and get some rest. If you're exhausted, you won't be any use to him at all."

When they looked undecided, he added, "You can come back in the morning to visit as much as you like. Tonight, he just needs to rest."

"Okay," replied Theodore. "We'll be back in the morning. I'll leave my cell phone number at the front desk. If there are any changes, good or bad, please call us."

"Will do." Waving them away, he added, "For now, go get some rest." Seeing their hesitation, Stillman's demeanor softened. Placing a hand on Melinda's shoulder, he lightly squeezed it. "He'll have 'round the clock care, Miss Jacobs. Don't worry."

"Thank you, doctor," sighed Melinda.

"Good night you two. I'll see you both tomorrow when I do my rounds."

Theodore put his arm around Melinda's shoulders as they made their way to the lobby. He left her there and went to bring the car around.

When he returned, Melinda was asleep in her seat. He got her into the car then got in and headed to their apartment. Melinda was still asleep when they got there, so he unlocked the apartment door, then carried her in and put her on her bed.

"Melinda," called Theodore gently. Melinda opened her eyes for a moment then went back to sleep. "You poor thing," he whispered compassionately, "you are just plum worn out." He got out some quilts and covered her before leaving the room.

As he prepared for bed, Melinda's image played across Theodore's mind. "Knock it off, old man" he said aloud. "You have no business having those kind of thoughts." When he was finally in bed, he lay there wide-awake, while he assessed the foreign feelings that stirred each time he thought of Melinda.

Far into the night, he wrested to clear his mind of those images, yet they continued to plague his mind. Finally, toward morning, he fell into a troubled sleep. He awoke to the smell of coffee, mingling with the smell of frying bacon. Feeling groggy, he struggled out of bed and took a cold shower in an attempt to wake up more fully.

As he came out of his room a while later, Melinda told him, "It's ready to eat whenever you are."

Sniffing the air appreciatively, he replied, "I'll be right there."

As they ate, Theodore asked, "Are you feeling any better today, Mel?"

"A little," she absently replied. "I'm a little confused though."

"Why?"

"How did I get from the lobby of the hospital to my bed? I remember getting to the lobby, but I don't remember anything else.

"I helped you to the car, but when we got home, I couldn't wake you up so I just carried you inside and put you on your bed."

"You needed the sleep and I figured it wouldn't hurt you to sleep in your clothes, so I just put the quilt over you and tucked you in."

"Thank you. It is kind of embarrassing, though."

"You're welcome," grinned Theodore. He was having a hard time concentrating on his food because his thoughts continued to center around Melinda. The feelings he had wrestled with the night before were more intense this morning. No matter how hard he tried to push them away, they refused to go.

Giving breakfast up as a hopeless cause, he carried his plate to the kitchen and then went to his room and tidied things there. To kill more time, he organized everything the way that he wanted. He just couldn't get Melinda out of his mind. He realized that he'd been having these feelings pretty much since he met her. Finally, knowing he couldn't avoid Melinda any longer, he went out to see what she was doing.

They worked on making Henry's bedroom more homey, moving furniture and adding personal touches. Then they went through the rest of the boxes that hadn't been unpacked to decide what they needed to keep at the apartment.

By lunchtime they had emptied more than half of the boxes and decided to arrange some more furniture throughout the apartment before stopping to eat. Theodore made a salad, while Melinda put together some sandwiches.

After lunch, they headed to the hospital. As he was driving, Theodore sifted through memories of his love before she died. Brenda was beautiful with thick, rich auburn hair, flowing down her back and the most bewitching green eyes he'd ever seen. He had loved her with every fiber of his being, but a drunk driver took her from him just three days before they were to be married. She'd died instantly. Coming back to the present, he realized that Melinda had been talking to him. "I'm sorry. What did you say?"

"I just asked if you were all right."

"Yeah. I was just thinking."

"Must've been some deep thoughts."

"Yeah. Sorry about that."

At the hospital, they went directly to the intensive care unit to check on Henry. They learned he was stable but still unconscious. His vital signs were better than last night and that encouraged them.

Theodore went in first, and Melinda tried to thumb through a magazine while she waited, but couldn't concentrate. She couldn't stop thinking about Theodore putting her into bed.

After several minutes, she tossed the magazine back onto the table. "It's no use," she muttered aloud.

Just then, Theodore stepped out of the intensive care unit. Relieved not to be forced to deal with her thoughts, she went over to meet him. "How is Henry this afternoon?"

"He hasn't regained consciousness, but the nurse told me his numbers look good."

"That's great news."

"Yes, it is." Theodore continued, "I talked to him like he was awake. For a split second, I thought I saw his eyes start to open but nothing else happened."

"When I was in there last night, I talked to him in the same way. He moaned a little then settled down again."

"I don't know if it was a sign that he was trying to respond to us, but I would like to think so."

"That's how I feel, too," admitted Melinda.

"Well," he said, "It's your turn to go in." He opened the door then moved aside for her to enter. Closing the door, he sat down and grabbed a magazine.

Melinda walked over to stand beside Henry's bed and took his hand. "Hello, Henry. We were late getting here today, because we spent some time unpacking and getting the apartment whipped into shape. You'll be pleased to know that we've fixed up your room so that it is neat and cozy and ready for you to come home.

"We even managed to get through half of the boxes out in the living room. There's going to be a lot of stuff going to the storage unit.

"By the way, I chose the lighter, smaller curio cabinet for my room. I haven't had time to put anything in it, but at least it is in place. We put the other curio cabinet in the dining room, along with the China closet and the sideboard. They still have to be filled too, but we can do that later."

Melinda paused a moment to take a deep breath before continuing, "Henry, you have got to fight so that you can come back to us. We miss you. The apartment just isn't the same without you."

"Your time is up, dear," said a nurse as she came into the room. Melinda saw Henry stir and turned to ask the nurse, "Did you see him move?"

Without replying, the nurse checked him over. Again, he stirred, but didn't open his eyes. "This is a good sign," whispered the nurse. "Keep talking to him like you were. I'll let you stay a few more minutes."

"Henry, if you can hear me, please try to let me know." Nothing happened for a moment then he tried to open his eyes. "Oh, don't give up, dear. We need you to come back to us."

Henry tried, but was to weak to respond. Melinda leaned down to kiss his cheek. "I love you so much. Just rest as much as you can so you can come home. I'll be just outside the door. I'll come back when they let me." Squeezing his hand, she went out to share her news with Theodore.

Seeing the joy on her face, he got up meet her. "What has you smiling like the cat that ate the canary?"

"Oh, Teddy," exclaimed Melinda excitedly, "Henry tried to open his eyes!"

"He did?" asked Theodore in amazement.

"He did it twice. The second time I asked him to let me know if he could hear me, and he tried to open his eyes. The nurse said it was a good sign."

"Oh, saint's be praised!" he cried. Grabbing her, he spun her around then gave her a big kiss on the lips. Suddenly, he stopped dead in his tracks. "Oh, I'm so sorry. I was just so excited that I forgot myself."

"I understand." Moving quickly away, Melinda struggled to gain control of her emotions. She berated herself for nearly responding to the kiss. Walking over to the window, she peered outside. The more she thought about how close she'd come to returning the kiss, the more she silently scolded herself. Turning to address Theodore, Melinda replied, "I'm going to the cafeteria to get a hot chocolate. Can I get you anything?"

"Yes, a black coffee would be great."

"I'll be back as soon as I can."

"Take your time. We can't see Henry again for a couple of hours."

Melinda headed toward the cafeteria. She was so preoccupied that she didn't even look at anyone. Once there, she ordered the drinks and used the walk back to calm her jangled nerves.

Two hours later they took turns visiting with Henry. Melinda talked to Henry as if he could hear every word she said. Finally, the nurse told her that she had to go so that Henry could rest. "I'm going to go now, but we'll return tomorrow. We have a lot of unpacking to do before we can go to bed tonight, so guess we'd better get at it. Work hard to get better so that we can take you home soon." Leaning down, she lightly kissed his cheek.

When they got home, they ate a light supper, and then Melinda started to put more of their things in their proper places. When she was finished, the room looked fantastic. Theodore whistled softly when he surveyed what she'd accomplished. "I must confess that you have impeccable taste, Melinda Jacobs."

After he'd collected all the empty boxes and set them near the door, Theodore said, "Before we go see Henry tomorrow, I'll rent a U-Haul and take all this unused stuff and the empty boxes to the storage units."

Melinda, sighing from sheet exhaustion, said, "That will be wonderful. I'm tired of tripping over all of this extra stuff."

"Right now, I need to run out to the store for some things I forgot to pick up. Do you need anything?"

"No, I don't think so."

"Then I'll see you when I get back."

While Theodore was gone, Melinda made a batch of cookies to keep herself busy.

"I got a carton of ice cream," Theodore said when he got back. "Would you like some?"

"Sure."

"What smells so good?"

"I baked a batch of chocolate chip cookies."

"Would it be all right to have some of them with the ice cream?"

"Well, I don't know," replied Melinda, pretending to think about it. Sighing melodramatically, she replied, "I guess that would be all right."

"Wonderful!" he set the ice cream on the counter before adding, "I have a terrible sweet tooth for some reason."

"Well, I don't want to see a grown man suffer. So, I guess we'd better get you some sweets."

"Absolutely!"

"While I get the ice cream and cookies dished up, why don't you go sort out your clothes from Henry's."

"I can do that," replied Theodore. "From now on though, you don't have to wash my clothes."

"Nonsense," said Melinda. "It doesn't take any more effort to do yours than it does to do Henry's.

"Thank you," responded Theodore.

"Hurry up, now. You don't want your ice cream to be completely melted before you get done."

"Yes, ma'am!" Theodore said and saluted.

After he'd accomplished his task, Theodore took a seat at the table, grabbed a cookie from the plate and took a bite. "Mel, these are delicious!"

"Thank you. I'm glad that you like them."

"Like them? I love them!" declared Theodore. "They taste just like the ones my mom used to make."

"Now that's a compliment!"

They ate in silence for a few minutes, then Theodore said, "I rented a U-Haul for tomorrow morning while I was out. I can pick it up at eight in the morning. I even found someone to help me load and unload it."

"You did?" Studying him closely, Melinda asked, "What did you do, pull some innocent bystander off the street and demand he help?"

Grinning, Theodore replied, "It wasn't as drastic as that. Our landlord stopped me before I came in and asked how things were going. I told him about Henry and he asked if there was anything he could do to help. So, I asked him to help me tomorrow and he said he'd be glad to."

"That's good because all this furniture is too heavy for me to lift."

They cleaned up the mess from the ice cream and went their separate ways to bed. Neither was able to sleep very well due to the feelings they were forced to sort through.

The next morning, Melinda had severe bed head and her eyelids were puffy. Theodore asked, "Did you sleep at all?"

"I feel like I haven't slept for at least a week."

"Pardon me for saying this, but you look like you've been on a weekend drunk."

Bristling, Melinda snapped, "You're one to talk. Have you looked in the mirror lately? You're looking pretty rough, Mr. Brooks."

Reaching up to touch his face, Theodore smiled at the sight he must make. "Well, to be totally honest, I haven't slept much either."

"Sorry. You want to shower first?"

"No, you go ahead."

Theodore ducked back into his room to grab his things. He was worried about Melinda. "Well," he said aloud, "after I get everything moved to the storage units, there won't be so much work to get done. Maybe she'll rest then." He thought of how hard he had struggled to get her out of his mind all night, but had failed. Sighing, he thought, *Wish there was such an easy solution for my problem.* Again, images of Melinda filled his mind; bringing with them the same tumultuous feelings.

Plopping onto the bed, he began to analyze his feelings. As he did so, he couldn't help comparing them to what he'd felt for Brenda. His feelings for Brenda had been intense, and the feelings he had for Melinda were just as strong. As he continued to explore those feelings, he realized that he also felt a tenderness that hadn't been there with Brenda. He'd been possessive, even selfish in his actions, with her. With Melinda, he found that he was more concerned for her than he was for himself. The feelings that he felt for Melinda were pure, genuine, and honest, which made them seem sweeter, richer, and deeper.

He realized that the love that he'd felt for Brenda hadn't been a healthy one. The way he felt about Melinda, though, seemed to be. He slumped over and held his face in his hands as the enormity of just how much he loved Melinda struck him. *When did this happen?* he asked himself. *What am I going to do about it?*

I could woo her, he thought. *Sure, she'd probably laugh at me and I don't know if I could deal with that. Still, what have I got to lose, other than my dignity? Just do it!* came the unbidden thought. *You might just be surprised what happens.*

"Fine," he announced out loud. "I think I'll start with something traditional like flowers and candy."

Looking at his watch, he realized he'd better get a move on. Melinda was waiting for her turn in the bathroom.

He walked over to where Melinda was getting ready to make breakfast and said, "Don't make anything for me. I'm running late and barely have time to shower."

"You should eat something."

"I'll find something when we get back. Right now, I have to get cracking, or I won't be ready when the landlord gets here."

"In that case, I'll just have a bowl of cold cereal and finish up the laundry. That should keep me busy while you're gone."

"Thanks, Mel." Without thinking, he reached out to hug her close. As he released her, he gazed into her surprised eyes. He wanted so badly to kiss her again. Seeing the look of longing in her eyes, his heart leaped with hope.

Unable to resist the temptation, he lowered his head and gently touched her lips with a quick kiss. Passion coursed through him like a raging forest fire. Moaning, he wrapped his arms around her, and hungrily claimed her lips in a more passionate kiss. She responded, and the kiss grew even deeper.

When the kiss ended, Melinda sighed and put her head on his chest to calm herself. Raising her head she looked into his love filled eyes. When he saw the look of love shining back in hers, he dared to ask, "Oh, Mel, are you feeling the same thing I am?"

A teasing smile crossed her lips. "It depends on just how you feel."

"I didn't realize until this morning that what I'm feeling for you is a love purer, sweeter, more glorious than I could ever have imagined."

Sighing contentedly, Melinda hid her face in his massive chest. "Oh, Teddy," she moaned, "I've loved you for so long, but I was afraid you wouldn't return my feelings."

Lifting her face so that he could see if she really meant what she was saying, he gazed into her eyes. Her love was there for him to see. "When did you know you loved me, Mel?"

Smiling, she replied, "I don't know for sure, but each time you cared for Henry, or did sweet things for me, I admired you for them. Then those emotions turned into a wondrous friendship like I've never had with a man. Gradually, those feelings of friendship deepened into something more beautiful.

"For a long time, I wasn't ready to admit that they even existed. It wasn't until the night you carried me to my bed and tucked me in without taking advantage of me that I had to face those feelings head on. It wasn't until dawn this morning that I finally faced the truth. Then when you kissed me the way you did, I couldn't contain my feelings for you any longer." Gazing earnestly into his eyes, she asked, "Do you truly love me?"

"Oh yes, my darling. I love you with all my heart and soul. I loved another woman once, but it was nothing like the way I love you. We were to be married, but a drunk driver killed her. That's when I promised myself that I would never let anther woman into my heart, because it hurt too much to lose her.

"Somehow, you cracked the shell that protected my heart and now you've taken up permanent residency there. I want the world to know how truly special you are."

"Oh," signed Melinda, "What a wonderful thing to say."

His answer was a kiss filled with such tenderness, hunger and passion. When he felt her respond in kind, he thought for sure that he'd died and gone to heaven.

Bending down on one knee, he took her hand in his and asked, "Melinda Jacobs, would you do me the honor of being my wife?'

Tears glistened in Melinda's eyes as she responded, "Yes. I'd be proud to be your wife."

Getting to his feet, he sealed their promise with a kiss. "Oh, saints be praised, she said yes!" he cried to the ceiling. Grabbing her, he twirled her around a couple of times, set her down and then stole two quick kisses. "If I don't get with it, I'll never get this job done."

When he disappeared into the bathroom, Melinda had to sit down. She felt like she was in shock. As she sat there, she felt the sweetest feeling of joy, hope, love and wonder steal over her. She was still sitting there, lost in thought, when he came back into the kitchen. Leaning down, he quickly kissed her a couple of times on the lips then said, "I'll be back for more of these. Kissing her once more a little more tenderly, he rushed out the door to go get the U-Haul.

It took the rest of the morning to get things moved to the storage unit. When Theodore returned, the first thing he did was wrap his arms around Melinda and kiss her like he hadn't seen her for a very long time. Then, he reached into his shirt pocket and pulled out a small jewelry box. He opened it and showed it to Melinda, who gasped.

He took out the ring and tossed the box to the side, then took Melinda's left hand and slipped the ring onto her finger. "Now, it's official. This is a seal of my love and fidelity to you for the rest of my life."

He kissed her again, then said, "I'm as hungry as a grizzly bear coming out of hibernation."

"Oh, that's bad. Since, I'm the only victim here, guess I'd better find you something to eat."

Laughing huskily, Theodore wrapped her in a warm embrace, and kissed her again. "I'm more hungry for you right now than I am for food."

Pecking his lips lightly, Melinda whispered, "I know the feeling."

They kissed each other several times, then Theodore said, "We'd better eat and get this show on the road or we'll never get to the hospital today."

Chapter 17

Shirleen awoke feeling more rested than she had in a long time. Turning to look at the clock on her nightstand, she was surprised to see that it was nine-thirty in the morning. She didn't hear anyone up and about, so she slipped on her robe and slippers and went to find out where everyone was.

As she moved down the hall, she heard Juliana and Meagan working on schoolwork. Feeling a little calmer, she walked into the living room and found Meagan bent over her studies as Juliana explained a math problem.

She left them to their work and headed to the kitchen where Trudy greeted her and asked, "How did you sleep?"

"Great! I feel better than I have in a long time."

"That's wonderful," stated Trudy. "It's about time things turned around for you." Studying Shirleen critically she added, "You look better this morning, too. Would you like some breakfast?"

"If it isn't any trouble. I'm really hungry this morning."

"That's good to hear."

They continued to chat as Trudy quickly made bacon, scrambled eggs and a piece of buttered toast. When it was done, she set the plate in front of Shirleen and went back to what she'd been doing. Shirleen ate in silence, grateful for how good she felt.

"Thanks for the great food, I think I'll go get a shower before I start my day."

Once she'd showered and dressed, she went around to each of their bedrooms and collected the dirty laundry. She started a load of clothes and then went to her bedroom to make the bed and then sweep the floor. With that done, she moved on to do the same in Meagan's room. She'd just finished vacuuming, when Meagan came in. "I planned to do that after lunch, Grandma."

"Nonsense," retorted Shirleen. "I have to do my part. You need to work on your studies and then maybe do something fun for a while."

"Well, Momma told me that while the weather was holding, we're going to help Jeff with the wood."

"You two sure have been working hard at that lately."

"We have, but at least we know that it's almost done. Jeff needs to concentrate on things that need fixed in the house."

"That's true enough." Growing thoughtful, Shirleen added, "We have got to get the Christmas tree put up and decorated soon too."

"Jeff told us he'd do that as soon he's finished with the wood." Grinning, she added, "That old woodshed is fairly groaning with all the wood that's already inside. Jeff said we might have to leave some of it outside and cover it with a tarp if it doesn't all fit."

"Winter isn't even half over and already we've been trapped up inside too much. It's comforting to know the wood supply is close to the house."

Meagan started to leave then turned back to say, "Jeff said that Tim was supposed to be here after work. He got in touch with the man who knows about the tower for our cell phones. He's going to bring him when he comes, so that they can check it out. He said there's an existing tower and he's going to check it to see if it still works."

Clapping her hands, Shirleen replied, "That's marvelous news. Now if we can only get the cable hooked up."

"Oh," replied Meagan, striking her head with the heel of her hand, "I almost forgot to tell you. Jeff checked and there was cable installed here previously. All we have to do is get the cable guy to come install it for us."

"When did all of this happen?" asked Shirleen anxiously.

"This morning while you were sleeping."

"Well, it will be good to be able to see the news."

"I don't want to see the news; it depresses me. I would like to see a good movie before going to bed sometimes, though."

"That would be nice."

"I'd better get back before Momma comes looking for me. If she sees me dilly-dallying, she might just load me down with more work."

She'd barley got the words out of her mouth when Juliana came in and asked, "What's going on in here? I thought you were going to your room to get some paper."

"It's my fault," said Shirleen. "She was telling me everything you all have accomplished while I was sleeping the morning away."

"Oh, okay. Don't do too much, Momma. You don't want to relapse."

"Nonsense! The last time Dr. Stillman was out here, he told me I could start doing things again when I felt like it."

"But he also told you not to over do it for a while."

"Honey, I am so bored that if I don't do something, I'm going to go stark raving mad."

"Just be careful. That's all I'm asking."

"I will be. Just let me do a little bit around here."

"Fine," agreed Juliana, understanding how much her mother needed to feel occupied, as well as needed. "I'd better get back to Meagan before she thinks I really was mad."

Shirleen finished with Meagan's room and went on to clean Juliana's. When that was done she finished the laundry. She was feeling a little tired by this time, so she decided to wait until after lunch to vacuum the living room and went to her room to rest for a while.

Shirleen feel asleep for an hour. When she woke up, it was time for lunch. After lunch, Shirleen rested for half an hour before cleaning up the bathroom. With that done, she went to find Trudy. Sinking onto a chair at the kitchen table, she asked, "Trudy, when you have a moment, could you please help me with something?"

Trudy finished sliding two pies into the oven and asked, "What do you need?"

"I have the clothes washed, folded, and put into separate baskets, but I need help delivering them."

"I can do that while these pies are baking." Tossing the towel onto the counter, she headed to the laundry room. Shirleen rose to follow her.

When she saw all of the filled baskets, with the towels, dishtowels and other items that went in the bathrooms, Trudy scowled and said, "I could have helped with these, Shirleen."

"Nonsense! You were busy."

"Be that as it may, you should've asked for help."

"Please don't scold me," pleaded Shirleen. "I didn't do it all at once. I rested twice."

"You still need to slow down. You're making me look lazy."

"Lazy?" Shirleen's just stared at her. "There isn't a lazy bone in your body, Trudy North." Scowling at Trudy a moment, she softened. "Just the cooking can be a full time job around here"

"True," admitted Trudy.

"Besides, I saw you sweep and mop the kitchen and dining room floors. If I'm not mistaken, you also made sure there isn't a speck of dust in either room."

"That's part of my job," replied Trudy.

That's true, dear friend, but you aren't our slave. We're responsible for some of the chores too."

"Well," grinned Trudy, "I love doing my part around here because you all make me feel so wanted."

"That's because you are," replied Shirleen.

Trudy carried the baskets and Shirleen helped her put the clothes away. When they were finished, she told Shirleen, "You've done more than enough today. I'll take care of the living room as soon as the pie are done. You go rest."

"Fine," sighed Shirleen. "I'm a little tired so I won't argue with you."

"Good!" Grinning she left Shirleen to stare after her.

Shirleen went to her room and laid down. Tears of frustration glistened in her eyes as she thought of the exhaustion that continued to plague her. "Will I ever get back to normal?" she asked aloud. Turning onto her right side, she began to cry into her pillow. Finally, totally exhausted, she fell into a deep sleep. When she awoke, the evening's shadows had gathered in her room.

She felt better and went to see what she could do to help Trudy. As she neared the kitchen, all sorts of wonderful smells assaulted her nose. When she stepped into the kitchen, she saw several different types of pies cooking on racks. "My goodness, Trudy! Are you expecting to feed an army or something?"

Laughing, Trudy replied, "No. I just thought I'd get ahead with my baking so that when it gets nearer to Christmas, I won't be swamped. I still plan to make candies, cookies, and a fruitcake. I even found a recipe for Scripture cake."

"I wonder what that will be like?"

"I don't know, but I'll have to go to town to get more supplies to make everything. If it doesn't snow tomorrow, I'm going shopping. I'm anxious to get started on it. We only have three and a half weeks until Christmas."

"Would you mind a little company when you go to town?" asked Shirleen. "I have such a bad case of cabin fever. Besides I want to get some other Christmas gifts."

"I'd love your company," declared Trudy.

"Then it's a date," replied Shirleen. "Do you need help with supper?"

"Did you get some rest?"

"Yes," replied Shirleen. "I even took a little nap."

"Then if you'd like to set the table, supper will be ready soon."

"I would be happy to."

As she finished setting the table, Shirleen said, "If I get to take a nap in the afternoon, then so should you. You've just had surgery after all. Also, why don't we work together to do the housework?"

Trudy nodded. "That sounds like a good idea. That way we'll both be completely recovered."

With that settled, Shirleen went to let the others know dinner was ready. Shirleen opened the dinner conversation with, "Trudy told me she needs to go to town to get some more baking supplies tomorrow. I'm so bored from being cooped up in this house, so I'm going with her."

Juliana said, "Momma, I think we could all use a break in our routine. Meagan and I have been working so hard on her schoolwork and helping Jeff. We're both tired and need something different." Turning to look at Jeff, she asked, "What do you think about our getting a way for a while?"

"I think it's a good idea. I haven't been down to check on my place for quite a while. This would give me a good excuse to go do that."

"Would it be all right if we went in separate cars, Momma?" She grinned as she added, "Every time we go, we end up bringing back a lot of stuff."

Shirleen replied, "That's true."

Meagan said, "I thought of some things you all need, so I could do that while you're doing your shopping."

"See," chuckled Juliana, "we all have things we need to do in town. We could also have lunch out, and give Trudy a day off from cooking."

Trudy turned to smile at Shirleen. "Well, Shirleen, I think our day has been planned out for us."

Laughing good-naturedly, Shirleen replied, "I think you're right, Trudy."

"We'll help Jeff get as much wood taken care of as possible today," stated Juliana.

"Thanks to you two wonderful ladies, we probably only have one or two more days of hard work left before the wood is completely taken care of."

"Oh," cried Meagan, "that's the best news I've heard in a long time! It'll be nice to settle back into our old routine."

Shirleen added "I was just telling Trudy that it will take all of us working together to ensure our safety during this horrible challenge."

"I agree with that, Momma," replied Juliana.

"Me, too," chimed in Meagan.

After the meal, the others went back out to work on the wood, and Shirleen helped Trudy clean up the kitchen. They were just finishing up when they heard a vehicle pull up. "That must be Tim," Shirleen said, crossing over to open the door. She stepped back to let him in and realized he was with another Mountie.

When Shirleen caught sight of the second man, she gasped then fainted. Tim caught her as she fell to the ground. He laid her on the couch where he began trying to revive her.

Everyone rushed to the house to see what news Tim brought. When they saw Shirleen lying there unconscious, they grew concerned. "What happened, Tim?" asked Juliana going to her mother's side.

"When she looked at my boss, she fainted."

Trudy came back into the room with a cold washcloth, which she handed to Tim. "This should help to bring her around."

"Thank you, Trudy," replied Tim. The other man was momentarily forgotten, as those who loved Shirleen stood close to her.

"What was it that made her faint?" asked Juliana.

"She fainted when she saw me," replied the other Mountie.

Looking up into the face of the stranger, Juliana gasped, and turned visibly pale. For a moment she too appeared about to faint. Gathering all of the strength she could muster, she asked, "How did you find us?"

"I've never seen any of you before."

Meagan, who was crying softly in Trudy's arms, kept muttering, "Don't let Grandpa take me away."

Turning his attention to Tim, the Mountie asked, "What is wrong with these women, Sergeant?"

Turning to look at his superior, Tim replied, "I think I know. Just give me a moment, please."

Juliana, realized this man wasn't who she thought he was once she heard his voice. "I think we owe you a huge apology." The older Mountie softened a little, but remained silent. Juliana continued, "Please, have a seat until we can get my mother taken care of. When she's all right, we'll explain everything."

"Okay," replied the Mountie taking the proffered chair.

Going over to her daughter, Juliana gathered her in her arms. "It's all right, sweetheart. It isn't Gordon. He only looks like him."

Suddenly the man jumped as if he he'd been physically slapped. Before he could reply, Shirleen started to stir. Opening her eyes, she gazed around the room. Seeing the Mountie sitting quietly nearby, she studied his face for a moment then sat up on the couch. "Please forgive me," she sighed in relief. "For a minute there, I thought I saw a ghost."

"I assure you," grinned the Mountie, "I'm very much alive."

"I can see that," replied Shirleen."

"Will someone please tell me what this is all about?"

Shirleen sighed as Tim came to sit between them. Tim absently took each one's hand. "Sir, do you remember me telling you that I wanted you to meet four really special ladies?" The older Mountie nodded, but wisely waited for Tim to continue. "Shirleen was married to a mob boss who lived in Syracuse, but operated out of New York City. Her—"

The other Mountie interrupted, "This man wouldn't happen to be Gordon Spielberg by any chance?"

"The one and only," replied Shirleen, shivering as if cold.

"Well, now I can see why you fainted."

"You can?" asked Juliana.

Nodding the Mountie replied, "Yes, I can." Hesitating a moment, he replied, "I'm Gordon's brother. My birth name was Frances Kildare Spielberg." Seeing the strange looks on the faces of those around him, he sighed and continued. "What I have to tell you is nothing short of a long story, so please bear with me.

"When Gordon was born, his mother died an hour after giving birth due to unforeseen complications. When Gordon was six weeks old, my father met my mother. Shortly after their marriage, my father, Gordon Frances, started leaving my mother alone with baby Gordon for long periods at a time, and Mother learned to love him like her own child.

"Three years after they were married, my father came home in a drunken rage. When my mother tried to refuse his advances, he raped her. She found out later she was pregnant. Nine months later, my sister was born. She died three months later. My father never once mourned her loss.

"When Mother was stronger, about a year later, he raped her again. This time, she became pregnant with me. When I was born, he started treating her better.

"The first fifteen years of my life were wonderful, but I knew from an early age that Gordon was his favorite. When I turned sixteen, I was introduced to my father's world. For me that was the day my world shattered into a billion pieces. That day, my life as I knew it ended!"

When the man stopped speaking, Meagan asked, "Did you go into business with your father?"

"I most definitely did not," he snapped. Seeing the relief on Meagan's face, he continued. "My father wanted me to, though. When I told him I wanted no part of what he did, he was furious. I told him in no uncertain terms what he could do with his offer."

"Oh," said Meagan, "that probably didn't go over well."

"No, ma'am, it sure didn't." He grew thoughtful for a moment then went on with his story. "He hit me in the face so hard that it knocked me down. When I jumped to my feet, I told him he could count me out. I loathed everything he stood for. I even went so far as to tell him that if he dropped dead I wouldn't care a lick. He hit me again for saying that.

"I looked him straight in the eye and told him, "'You've hit me twice now, and I haven't returned the favor. If you so much as lift your hand to strike me again, I *will* kill you right where you stand. I'm leaving this house and I'm taking my mother with me.'"

"What happened then?" gasped Meagan. The others were speechless.

"He clenched then unclenched his fists several times. I thought he was going to hit me again, but something in my eyes must've told him my threat was serious. He walked over to his desk, sat down and got out his checkbook. He held the check out to me and told me it was the only inheritance I'd ever get. He then told me that as far as he was concerned, I never existed. He added that I could take my mother with me, because she meant nothing to him."

Juliana found her voice to say, "Your own father disowned you?"

"Yes, ma'am, he did!"

"That's awful!" Juliana looked over to where Meagan was sitting with Trudy and said, "I could never disown my daughter, no matter what she said or did."

"That's because you're a decent person, ma'am." Hesitating a moment, he added, "Besides that, you love her. My father only saw me as a way of furthering his rotten business."

"I'm so sorry," replied Shirleen.

Shrugging, Frances continued, "He told me that he was taking Gordon on a business trip for a month. If we weren't gone when he got back, he'd kill both of us. After he left the room, I looked down at the check he'd written me. I nearly dropped it when I saw it was for five million dollars."

Meagan rose to place a hand on his shoulder and said, "I don't like Grandpa Gordon, so I know that I wouldn't have liked your father either. I'd say we're lucky to be rid of both of them."

Frances looked at the young woman before him with new eyes and replied, "Yes, little lady, we are!"

"I have a question," said Meagan.

"Fire away."

"If Gordon is your brother, then how are you related to me?"

"I'm your Uncle."

"Oh," was all that Meagan could say.

As Meagan took her seat beside Trudy, Frances continued, "With all of the staff helping, we were packed inside of a week. We loaded everything into U-Haul and left. Mother wasn't well, so I did all the driving."

"Had you ever driven one of those big trucks before?" asked Shirleen.

"No." he sighed, "but I was forced to learn quickly. It took me an hour of struggling with the gears to get the hang of it. I nearly gave my mother whiplash before I got the hang of it.

"Mother and I had chosen to go to Coeur d' Alene, Idaho. We hoped it would suit our needs. When we got there, I checked in the yellow pages for a storage unit and put most of our belongings there before going to a motel. I left Mother at the motel to rest, called a cab and went looking for a place to rent. I ended up finding a nice out of the way place that had three bedrooms.

"I had the cab take me to the bank so I could transfer the money from the bank back home into a new account. I set it up so both of us could write checks. I got enough cash to pay for the new rental place, and we were ready to start living our new lives."

"Wow, that's a lot of responsibility for a young man," said Shirleen.

"It was rough at first, but Glenda, our cook and housekeeper, became a great asset to both of us. She taught me how to budget, how to shop for the best items, even how to cook some of the things we liked the best. She even taught me how to take care of all the bills."

Growing thoughtful for a while, he added, "Glenda was a godsend. She took over Mother's complete care, sparing us both a lot of embarrassment. She also freed up my time in the fall so that I could go back to school. Thanks to her, I was able to finish my last year of school and graduate."

Sighing, he was forced to take a moment to control his emotions. Finally, he continued, "In August of that year, Mother got worse. The doctor said that it was liver cancer. She had surgery and then chemotherapy. Eventually she was well enough that

I was able to go to college and become a CPA. She had to attend my graduation in a wheelchair, but she was there to support me.

"Sadly, before I could get my first job, the cancer metastasized into her brain. There was nothing more the doctors could do. Mother died one month after my graduation."

"Oh, how awful!" cried Juliana. "I'm so sorry for your loss."

"That's all water under the bridge," replied Frances. "Glenda stayed on until her death one year later. She taught me to believe in God again. She helped me to see that it wasn't God who made my Mother ill. She said death was part of life and that some of us were called home sooner than others.

"One day, she was on her way to see her doctor and a drunk driver struck her car head on. She didn't die right away though and her family got to say their goodbyes. After her funeral, her family came to collect her things and I felt like I had nothing to keep me there anymore."

"Was that what made you come to Canada?" asked Trudy.

"Yes," replied Frances. "When Mother died, I sent a letter to Gordon, telling him about her death. He sent a letter back telling me he was sorry for my loss, but he couldn't come to the funeral because he was just too busy. I had just turned twenty-three, and I was about to turn twenty-four when I made the decision to come to Cardston."

"What made you choose Cardston?" asked Jeff.'

"I served a mission for my church here in Cardston. I knew the people." He paused a moment before continuing. Looking from one to the other, he said, "When Mother and I left New York, we decided to change our names before we did anything else, so we found a lawyer. Mother changed her name from Helen Irene Spielberg to Judith Marie Graham and I changed mine from Frances Kildare Spielberg to Josiah Davis Graham. I've gone by that name ever since."

"I like the name you chose for yourself, Uncle Josiah." Meagan grew anxious then asked, "Is it all right to call you Uncle Josiah?"

"I'd like that a lot. What's your name?"

Meagan looked nervously over to her grandmother, unsure of what she should answer. Shirleen came to her rescue. "Before we tell you, you should know that we're running for our lives. If my daughter's husband learns where we are, he'll kill us and force my granddaughter to marry a man she loathes."

"Let's get something straight right here and now. Your secret is safe with me. I don't want to be associated with my brother in any way!" Looking over at Tim, he continued, "When I moved to Cardston, I decided to join her Majesty's Royal Mounted Police. I felt that perhaps I could right some wrongs and maybe make up for the evils done by others in my family."

"How did you get around your past?" asked Jeff.

"When I went to speak to the man in charge of the Mountie, I told him everything. He said he was impressed that I would come clean. He told me he would recommend me highly. I've been a Mountie for 35 years now … with a clean record."

"I'll add here," said Tim, "that Major Graham has been responsible for apprehending at least a hundred criminals. He won't take guff from anyone."

"Oh, that changes things," sighed Shirleen. She told Josiah how she was forced to marry Gordon, then how he forced Juliana into marrying Bruce Murdock. "When my daughter learned that her husband was going to force her daughter to marry someone she didn't love, the two of us decided we wouldn't stand for that and we ran away. While traveling, we decided that the best thing we could do would be to change our looks and our names."

"That was great thinking,"

"Well," continued Shirleen, "my real name is Sarah Jane Spielberg." She went on to tell him how she came up with her name.

Meagan took over. "My real name is Leslie Erleen Spielberg. I liked the name Meagan, so I told Momma and Grandma that's what I wanted to be called."

Juliana added, "Momma and Meagan gave me the name Juliana."

Trudy told how she'd worked for Juliana and her husband. She ended with how and why she changed her name to Gertrude North. "You can call me Trudy."

"I'm glad that I finally have some family around me." Looking at each one of them, he said, "I have something to tell you, now that I know who you are. A while back, I received a letter from a lawyer who said his name was Gregory Jones. In the letter he told me that he had represented Gordon Spielberg for many years."

"That's correct," interrupted Shirleen.

"Well, he told me Gordon had been murdered. He went on to say that he needed me to get in touch with him so he could get Gordon's affairs in order. Not knowing you existed, I wrote back to see what he wanted me to do. I'm flying to New York in a few days to settle his affairs." Gazing at Shirleen he waited for her to speak.

Shirleen sat so still that everyone worried she wouldn't speak what was on her mind. Taking a deep breath, she began. "I'm afraid that if we come forward, Bruce will figure out we're in Cardston. There are some things I'd like to have that belonged to my mother." She again fell silent as she looked at Josiah questioningly. Finally, she asked, "What do you think I should do?"

"I tend to agree with you concerning Bruce finding you. In all my years as a Mountie, there have been many times when I've found that the lawyer was in cahoots with the bad guys. There's every possibility that you could be drawn into a terrible snare. Let me go see what the lawyer wants, then I'll report back to you."

"That makes me feel better," replied Shirleen.

"I should be back with my report before Christmas."

"Thanks for your advice."

"You're welcome, Shirleen. Now that I know you're my sister-in-law, I'd like to stay in touch. I'd also like to help make sure you're protected at all times."

"I'd appreciate that," replied Shirleen.

The men prepared to leave a short time later. As they were leaving, Tim told them he had more news for them. He asked if they'd stop by his office when they came to town the next day.

Chapter 18

When Melinda and Theodore got to the hospital to see Henry, it was starting to snow.

"Teddy, I have the strangest feeling that we shouldn't stay long with Henry today. I don't like how fast this snow is coming down."

"I was just thinking the same thing," admitted Theodore. "I think we should only stay an hour, and then go get as many groceries as we can to hold us over in case this turns into another blizzard."

"That's a great idea.."

"Let's get inside and visit with Henry as long as possible." Joining hands they hurried toward the hospital entrance. When they got to intensive care, Theodore squeezed Melinda's hand as he said, "You go first this time. While you're in there, you can tell him our good news."

"Thanks for letting me tell him."

"No problem." As he quickly kissed her on the lips, they heard a gruff voice say, "There will be no hanky-panky going on in this hospital!" Both of them jumped, and turned to stare into the stern face of Dr. Stillman. "What's going on here?"

Grinning sheepishly, Theodore replied, "I was just stealing a kiss after telling Mel she should be the first to break our news."

"What news is that?"

Raising Melinda's left hand, he showed Dr. Stillman the ring on Melinda's finger. "We got engaged this morning."

Stillman stared down at the beautiful ring. There was one large sapphire in the middle with a diamond on each side. "Wow, what a gorgeous ring," said Stillman. Looking into Melinda's happy face, he added, "This feller must love you a lot to give you a ring like that."

"I do," declared Theodore.

Placing a hand on Theodore's shoulder Dr. Stillman admonished, "You have to wait to say I do until you're in front of the minister, son."

Laughing, Theodore replied. "I'll remember that, doctor."

"Seriously, I'm really happy for you both." Growing serious, he said, "Let me go check on Henry, and then you can go in to see him."

Nodding, they watched the doctor disappear behind the door. Melinda went to study the snow outside, while Theodore read a magazine. A minute or so later, Melinda turned to tell Theodore, "The snow is falling so hard I'm afraid we'll be snowed in here if we wait much longer. The wind is picking up, too. I don't like the looks of things, Teddy."

Rising, Theodore came to stand at her side. "I can't believe it's accumulating this fast."

"It will come even faster, because the weather man said we were in for blizzard conditions," Dr. Stillman said as he crossed the room. "I didn't mean to eaves drop, but I figured you'd like to know."

"It's coming down so hard," Melinda commented.

"An hour from now, you probably won't be able to see your hand in front of your face. We'd better have our talk so you can see Henry and hurry home."

"We're ready when you are, doctor," replied Theodore.

When they were all seated, Dr. Stillman said, "Henry is slowly regaining his strength, but he's not out of the woods by a long shot. Perhaps your news will be what pulls him back from wherever he is. All we can do is hope ."

Melinda asked, "Has he tried to open his eyes again?"

"Yes," replied Stillman. "Once more last night and again this morning. He's resting more comfortably, too."

"Oh," sighed Melinda, "that's good news."

"Yes, it is," agreed Theodore. "I was worried about him."

"Well, I'm hoping that your news will bring him back to us. You can go in together to tell him, but you can only stay for five minutes."

"Thank you, doctor," Theodore said.

"Be prepared. Henry won't be able to go home for a long time after he regains consciousness. Once he's stable, we'll move him out of ICU. Then when I feel he's ready, he'll have to have a lot of physical therapy. That will take a while. You can come to therapy with him if you want to."

"We want to," declared Theodore. Melinda nodded affirmatively but remained silent.

Nodding his approval, Dr. Stillman said, "Good! Since you're trained in physical therapy, Mr. Brooks, you can help with his treatment."

"I'll be his cheering section," volunteered Melinda.

"With both of you working with him from the beginning, I think he'll work harder. There will also be a speech therapist to teach him how to talk again."

"Could I work with that person?" asked Melinda.

"Yes," agreed Stillman. "The nurse told me that when both of you come into the room, she notices a slight change in him. Being part of his speech and physical therapy will play a huge part in his recovery."

"Thank you for letting us be part of his recovery," replied Melinda.

"Henry must really be special to have both of you so concerned about his welfare," replied Stillman.

"He is," said Melinda. "I'm proud to be his sister-in-law."

"As I am to be his friend and nurse," added Theodore.

"You'll find that this stroke won't hold Henry Borden down, Dr. Stillman, continued Melinda. "One thing I've learned about Henry is he doesn't have the word quit in his vocabulary."

Rising Dr. Stillman said, "You'd better get in there before the storm gets worse. I'll be around for a while if you need me."

"Thank you, Dr. Stillman," Melinda said.

Reaching for Melinda's hand, Theodore replied, "Come on, beautiful, let's go tell Henry our good news."

Hand in hand, they went into Henry's room. The nurse acknowledged them then continued to work. Going to Henry's other side they placed their hands on his and Theodore said, "Hello, Henry. How are you doing today, old man?" Henry's eyes fluttered then grew still.

Melinda squeezed his hand as she greeted him, "Hello, Henry. We have some wonderful news for you." Melinda looked at Theodore who nodded for her to continue. "First of all, we've finished sorting through all of the boxes, and this morning, with the help of our landlord, all the stuff we don't need has been moved to the storage units. You'll be happy with how lovely the apartment looks."

Pausing to figure out her next words, she said, "Theodore proposed to me today, Henry, and I said yes. What do you think about that?"

All at once, Henry's eyes began to flutter. A few seconds later, Henry opened his eyes to gaze around. At first his eyes had a blank look, but gradually he began to focus on them. "Teddy, he's coming around!" exclaimed Melinda.

Looking at the nurse, who was taking his vitals, Melinda asked, "Does this mean he's back with us."

Removing the stethoscope from her ears she turned to them with a wide grin on her face, and replied, "It sure does! Let me tell the doctor what's happening." She stepped into the hallway and told a nurse to get Dr. Stillman on the double. She hurried back to again check Henry's vitals. "Wait outside for a moment, please."

As they started to leave, Henry grew restless. "It's all right, Henry," soothed Melinda. "We won't be far away. Let them examine you and we'll be right back." When this seemed to calm Henry a little, Melinda kissed his cheek.

They had just gotten out into the waiting area when they saw Dr. Stillman racing toward intensive care. A while later, Dr. Stillman came toward them. He was wearing a wide grin on his face. "Well, you must've told him your good news, because he's back."

"We did," replied Melinda

"Well, he's trying to speak, but as I suspected, he can't form many words. He'll have to learn to speak all over again. The stroke affected his right side, but with lots of therapy, he should regain use of it."

Clapping her hands together gleefully, Melinda cried, "Oh, that's the best news we could've had today!"

"Like I said, Henry is back. However, he has a long road ahead of him before he's fully recovered."

"But this is a start," Melinda said, still undaunted.

"It is. Theodore, you go in and see if you can calm Henry down before Melinda goes in. She should be the last one to see him before he goes back to sleep. You only have about five minutes apiece, so I'll leave you to it." With that he strode off down the hall.

When Theodore had gone in to be with Henry, Melinda went to look out the window and all she could see was a blanket of white. The wind had increased, too. It was so eerie out that Melinda shivered despite of the heat in the room.

Turning from the window, she saw Dr. Stillman hurrying toward her. "I just heard the weather report. They've declared it a blizzard and everyone is encouraged to stay inside. That means that you'll have to stay in the hospital until it's over, which could be a couple of days.

"I'll tell Theodore."

"Good," replied Stillman. Suddenly a voice came over the intercom, *Dr. Stillman, you're wanted in emergency, Dr. Stillman, come to emergency!* "Like I said, things will be heating up."

Watching him bound away, Melinda sat down and picked up a magazine. A minute later Theodore came out of Henry's room. "Before I go inside," said Melinda, "Dr. Stillman said they've declared this a blizzard and we need to stay put."

"Okay."

Melinda saw the concern on his face as she prepared to go visit with Henry. Suddenly, sirens began to blare outside, announcing an arriving ambulance.

About a minute after Melinda had gone to visit Henry, a nurse approached Theodore to say, "Dr. Stillman needs you in the ER. There was a massive pile up on the interstate. We don't know how many injured to expect, but by the sound of the report, we need all the help we can get. Can you lend us a hand?"

"I'll be right there, just let me tell my fiancé where I'm going so she doesn't worry about me."

"I'll wait for you here, but make it fast."

He hurried into Henry's room and whispered, "There's been a huge pileup on the interstate and they want me to help in the ER. Is that okay with you? I feel bad about leaving you alone."

"Go! I'll be just fine."

"I love you so much, Melinda," replied Theodore. He kissed her passionately then rushed away.

The sirens continued to blare for over an hour, while nurses rushed around helter-skelter. Melinda stood at the window, looking out at the swirling snow. Soon the intensive care unit began to fill up with the critically wounded.

Melinda decided that the best thing she could do was go get something warm to drink. She had no idea how long Theodore would be. She walked wearily down the hall to the cafeteria and got a hot chocolate. She found a table and sat to enjoy her drink. She grew wearier as she sat there sipping her hot chocolate. Looking up at the clock on the wall, she realized that she had been sitting there for two hours.

As she drew closer to intensive care she saw a young mother collapse under the strain of loss as she tried to care for her baby. Melinda knew that she had to do something for them. She walked over and took the baby while its mother sobbed brokenly. The baby began to fuss, so Melinda walked it up and down the hall.

The baby needed to be changed, she asked the mother if she could change it. The grieving woman took out what she needed to change the baby, and tried to care for her child. Seeing how hard she was struggling, Melinda asked, "Would it be all right if I changed the baby for you?"

Looking up at Melinda gratefully, she began to cry uncontrollably. "Oh, would you please?" Melinda began to take care of the infants needs and when she was finished, she covered her up and held her close. The little girl began sucking on her fist. "Do you have a bottle for her?"

"Yes," replied the grieving mother. Digging into the diaper bag, she brought out a bottle. She handed the bottle over to Melinda and the little girl latched on hungrily. The baby's family members took turns going in to see a member who was in intensive care. An hour later, the nurse brought out a patient who had expired, while another nurse went to the grieving family. "I'm so sorry, but you husband didn't make it."

The mother collapsed onto the floor. The nurse immediately went to work on her, while another nurse went to get a doctor. When the doctor arrived, the woman still hadn't regained consciousness. "Get her to a room so that I can check her out."

There were two members of the family left to wait the outcome. The baby in Melinda's arms was forgotten as the family grieved over those who had left this world too soon.

About twenty minutes later, the door to the intensive care unit opened. On the bed was the body of a lifeless child. Melinda thought her heart would break for this family experiencing so much loss.

Suddenly the sirens began to blare again, as another group of people were brought to the hospital. Melinda looked down at the sleeping infant, feeling sorry for her. Two hours later, a nurse approached the family to inform them that the mother of the sleeping child in Melinda's arms was in a coma. She had internal injuries and they were amazed that she'd even able to walk. She had just finished speaking, when another nurse came up to call her away.

When she whispered in a low tone to the first nurse, Melinda saw her turn pale. She struggled to gain control of her emotions. Finally, the nurse returned to tell the old couple who were anxiously waiting, that the young mother was also gone. The older woman grabbed her chest and keeled over.

The nurse immediately went to work on her, but it was evident even to Melinda, that she was already gone. A doctor rushed forward to check her over. He did all in his power to help her, but it was no use ... she was gone. The old gentleman grew so pale that they rushed him away to a room to be checked out. Melinda was left alone with the baby.

Looking up at the clock, she noticed that it was now ten o'clock at night. They'd been busy for over nine hours. She was just deciding what should be done with the baby when a nurse approached her. "How's the old gentleman, nurse?" questioned Melinda.

"We finally have him stabilized. I'm here because he wants you to bring the baby to him."

"Okay," replied Melinda. "Let me get the baby's things and I'll follow you." Seeing all of their things still where they had left them, the nurse asked another nurse to help her transport the family's belongings to the only surviving member of the family.

When they had gathered everything together, Melinda carried the baby, along with the diaper bag. They put the family's things on a chair then left to get something to pack them in.

Melinda approached the bed to see what the man wanted her to do. As she reached the man's side, he opened his eyes to look intently at her. "How is little Katarina?"

"Is that this little darling's name?"

Smiling proudly, he nodded that it was.

"She's been as good a gold. After she finished her bottle she's been sleeping peacefully. Would you like to take her?"

"I would," replied the man. Placing the baby into his arms, she stood back to give him some private time. While she waited, she studied his features. He had the thickest white hair, which was slightly curly. *He has the most beautiful blue eyes*, she thought. *They remind me of a clear summer sky.* A slightly hooked Roman nose complimented his wrinkled cheeks. As he gazed at the little one in his arms, his eyes softened with love.

Melinda was about to leave when the old man stopped her. "Thank you for taking care of my granddaughter when everything came crashing down."

"You're more than welcome. I just saw a need and addressed it."

"None of the others in the room even lifted a finger. Do you have someone in intensive care?"

"Yes," replied Melinda. "My brother-in-law had a stroke recently and was in a coma. He just came out of the coma his afternoon."

"I'm sorry for your challenges."

"Thank you, but he'll be fine. He has a long recovery ahead, but there's every possibility that he will be up and around in no time."

"I'm so glad," replied the man, absently stroking the baby's fingers. "Katarina and I are all that's left of my family."

"I'm so sorry," replied Melinda gently. "What had them out on a night like this in the first place?"

"They were on their way here from Spokane to celebrate Thanksgiving with us."

"Oh," was all that Melinda could say.

Growing thoughtful, the man fell silent. All at once he looked up at Melinda and asked, "Do you have a husband, ma'am?"

"No, I just got engaged this morning."

"Where's your young man now?"

"He's in the ER helping those who were involved in this awful wreck."

"Is he a nurse?"

"Yes, sir."

Again the man grew thoughtful. Finally he said what was on his mind. "I have no other family left and I'm eighty-four years old. I'm also terminally ill and don't know how much time I have left. I want someone who can care for my little Katarina. Do you think you could speak to your young man and then both of you come back to speak to me?"

"Of course, sir."

"Good. Have a nurse come in here for a moment, please."

Melinda went to the door to see if she could find a nurse. A nurse was approaching the door on her way to another room. "Nurse," called Melinda.

"Yes," replied the nurse.

"The gentleman inside would like to speak to you until I can come back."

Holding the door open, Melinda moved aside to let the nurse enter. "I'll see you soon," called the man. "Nurse, would you hold the baby for me until this young woman returns?"

"Of course," replied the nurse taking the little girl into her arms. Not waiting for more, Melinda went in search of Theodore. She saw him putting a sheet over another patient. When he saw her, he reached for her. She ran into his arms to comfort him. A moment later, she asked, "Do you have a little time to come with me to see someone?"

"I guess so. Why?"

"This man just lost his whole family except for his infant granddaughter. He asked me to find you because he wants to speak to us."

"Lead the way."

Taking his hand, Melinda led him back to the room. As the nurse handed the baby to Melinda, the old man asked, "Nurse, would you remain as a witness to what I want to say?"

Looking from Melinda to Theodore and back to the old gentleman, she replied, "Sure, I can do that?"

When he saw Melinda with the baby in her arms, Theodore couldn't help thinking of her holding one of their children. He was weak in the knees with the joy of it. He turned to look at the man lying in the hospital bed and saw he was being watched.

A smile spread across the man's face and he said, "As I told you a few minutes ago, I'm eighty-four years old and terminally ill. I have stage four liver cancer."

"I'm so sorry to hear that," Melinda said.

Theodore wondered was coming next.

"As I also told you, there's no one else in my family who can help me care for little Katarina. When you helped us in the waiting room outside, I watched how you cared for my grandbaby. I don't want her to go to an orphanage or foster care. I want her to grow up in a loving family."

Looking at Theodore he continued, "I see how much you love this woman standing next to you. Do you like children?"

"I love children," Theodore responded.

"Could you love a child that wasn't your own?" Theodore took the baby from Melinda and gazed at the sleeping little girl. His heart swelled at the thought of her losing her entire family. Tears formed in his eyes as he gently touched her cheek. Unable to resist the temptation, he kissed her little fingers. That's when he knew he would love and protect her with his very life if need be. Looking up at the baby's grandfather, tears ran down his cheeks as he replied, "If you're asking me if I could love *this* baby like my own, the answer is yes. Something inside of me knows that I'd not only love her, but I'd protect her with my very life if the need arises."

The old man swallowed past the lump in his throat and asked Melinda, "Could you love this baby like she was your own?"

Gazing down at the sleeping child, Melinda replied, "I think I fell in love with her the moment I changed her diaper."

"I know you've just become engaged, but how long have you known each other?"

Theodore smiled at Melinda then replied, "We met in August, when we started taking care of her brother-in-law after his stroke. He just had another one and is in intensive care."

"How do you feel about getting married immediately so you can be my grand-daughters new parents?"

Theodore looked lovingly into Melinda's eyes and asked, "Melinda, do you love me and trust me enough to marry me tonight?"

"I love you with everything in me. I was hoping to wait until Henry was well enough to walk me down the isle, though."

The older gentleman interrupted to say, "You said your brother-in-law has a long road to recovery. What if you were to marry your young man now, so you could take Katarina, then when your brother-in-law is well enough to walk you down the isle you could have a big official wedding?"

Melinda held the baby protectively as she mulled over the man's suggestion. Her heart was beating rapidly as she asked, "How do you feel about this, Teddy?"

"Darling, I'd walk through the fires of hell to have both of you in my life."

Tears of happiness started coursing down her cheeks. She looked at the nurse standing in the corner and saw that she was crying too. Looking up at Theodore, she said, "Yes, my darling. Let's do it as soon as we can find a minister."

Theodore wrapped his arms around her and the baby and yelled "Yahoo!"

Suddenly the baby's grandfather began to writhe in pain. Grabbing the diaper bag, Melinda leaned down to kiss the gentleman's cheek. "Don't worry about little Katarina, as I'll take good care of her. She left the room as Theodore and the nurse saw to him.

The nurse hurried out after Melinda and directed her to the waiting area on her way to find a doctor. As she walked away, the nurse called, "Congratulations ma'am."

"Thank you!"

An hour later, Theodore found Melinda changing the baby's diaper. He stood there watching the two of them. Suddenly, he knew that their decision to adopt this little girl was right. When the diaper was changed, Melinda picked up the baby and kissed her little face. "You aren't mine yet, but oh how I love you!"

That was more than his heart could take. Swallowing several times to get past the lump in his throat, he strode over to kiss the baby tenderly, then kissed Melinda passionately. Forgetting where they were, she returned the kiss.

Lifting the baby from her arms, he held her up to kiss her several times on the cheek. "Mel is right, my beauty. You're already ours without the paperwork." He kissed her a couple of more times then gave her back to Melinda.

"Are the two of you still smooching in public?" Theodore turned as Dr. Stillman approached.

"Yes, sir. Guilty as charged. But when you learn why, you may want to kiss this wonderful lady, too."

His eyes twinkling mischievously, Dr. Stillman raised his eyebrows. "Well, this sounds promising. Do tell."

Theodore filled him in and when he was finished, Dr. Stillman brushed a tear from his eye and surprised them both by bending down to kiss Melinda's cheek. "What you've done deserves a kiss," replied Stillman.

"Now we just have to figure out what to do next," Theodore said.

"Well," said Stillman, with a smile, "I think I can help you find what you need. Wait here and I'll be back in a bit."

"Thank you," replied Theodore.

"I'll see you both in a few." Before they could say anything more, he was gone.

The baby began to fuss, so Melinda handed her to Theodore so that she could rummage through the diaper bag for a bottle. Finding only empty bottles and a can of formula, she asked a nurse if there was somewhere she could prepare the formula and heat it up."

"Let me see what I can do. I think I can get you a warmed and filled bottle. I'll be right back."

When the woman rushed away, Melinda went back to help Teddy. He was calmly rocking the baby. "You're a natural with children."

"Well, I have ten nieces and nephews so I've had a lot of practice."

"That's something I didn't know about you." She hesitated a moment then said, "Teddy, we really don't know much about each other."

"That's true," Theodore admitted. "As soon as we're married, we'll have a lifetime to learn all about each other."

"But what if I've done something that would make you hate me?"

"Have you killed anyone?"

"No, of course not."

"Do you have a husband I don't know about?"

"No."

"Are you a thief? Have you robbed a bank?"

"No!'

"Do you beat men, helpless animals or yell like a raving lunatic?"

"No, no, and no."

"When were you born and where?

"I was born on June 15, 1980 in Syracuse, New York. My father's name was Walter Montgomery Jacobs. My mother's name is Heleena Joyce Burtenshaw. I have a sister named Joyce Caroline, as well as two brothers. The oldest is Macdonald Radcliff Jacobs. The youngest is Sterling Montgomery Jacobs. Matilda and I were the youngest of all my siblings."

The nurse brought two large bottles of warm formula, interrupting her info session. "Thank you, nurse."

"My name's Julia Robinson."

"I'm Melinda Jacobs."

"Pleased to meet you." Handing Melinda the bottles she rushed off to go back to work. Taking the fussing baby, Melinda snuggled her close and gave her one of the bottles. Katarina hungrily latched onto the bottle.

"Continue with what you were saying," urged Teddy.

"I'm the only one of my siblings who isn't married—"

"Yet," interjected Teddy.

"Yet," corrected Melinda. "Joyce is living in North Carolina, where her husband Franklin Richards is a professor of religion at one of the colleges there. They have five boys and five girls, ranging from six down to nineteen months."

"Whew!" Theodore exclaimed. "That a good quiver full."

"Yes, it is," agreed Melinda. "My brother Macdonald, we call him Mac, lives in Anchorage, Alaska, and owns a grocery store. He and his wife, Emma Gene, have two girls, one is sixteen and the other is twenty. Ruth Ann, who is twenty, got married three months ago. Cynthia will be graduating from high school this year."

"Sterling lives in Saginaw, Michigan. He and his wife, Karen, have six boys. When the sixth one was born, they decide that since they weren't going to have any girls, they'd stop with trying. I got a letter from her just before leaving home saying she was pregnant again. She's due in March, and the sonogram showed that it's twin girls."

"It just goes to show that we never know what the good Lord has in store for us."

"It sure does. In her letter she told me she was going to call the oldest one Heleena Joyce and the other will be called Helen Joy."

"Nice names," declared Theodore

Shifting the baby to her shoulder, she proceeded to burp her. "Now, tell me your side of the story."

They were interrupted when Dr. Stillman came in, with two men following him. "Melinda Jacobs, Theodore Brooks, this gentleman on my right is Reverend Howard Bates of the Lutheran Church. The storm has stranded him here too. This other gentleman, Joel Cline, Esq., was also stranded. He's the district attorney. He came to visit his fiancé, Judge Candace Smith, who had gall bladder surgery three days ago. Joel is engaged to marry Candace Smith.

"I filled him and Judge Smith in on your situation. Cline, who says he's always making mistakes, carries extra marriages licenses forms with him at all times. He can also notarize any documents that need it. He just needs your information. Unbelievably, he also has some adoption forms with him.

"Reverend Bates said that he'd be glad to perform your wedding ceremony, and Candace has already asked to be one of the witnesses."

"Who can we get to be the other witness?" asked Theodore.

"How about the nurse who was in the room when Mr. Stokes spoke to you about adopting this little doll?" asked Stillman.

Melinda said, "She told me her name is Julia Robinson."

"I'll have her paged immediately."

He was about to leave when Melinda asked, "Dr. Stillman, would you give me away?"

Stillman, looking at her in surprise, replied, "I'd be honored."

"Thank you, doctor."

"If I'm giving you away, you must call me Gerald."

"I'd be proud to."

"Where will we have the ceremony?"

Dr. Stillman supplied the answer, "I'll put Candace in a wheelchair and bring her to Mr. Stokes' room."

Stillman looked at Cline and asked, "How long will it take to fill out the paperwork?"

"About ten minutes," replied Cline. "How about we go to the grandfather's room to get that done? I'll need to record his statements on this matter, too. Do you have a recorder I can borrow?"

"Yes," replied Stillman.

"Good," replied Cline. "Let's get busy."

Half an hour later, the marriage license was filled out and notarized. The statement from James Stokes was recorded and typed into a laptop. Meanwhile, Dr. Stillman went to get Candace and brought her to the room just as everything was finished. Candace signed as the first witness, leaving Julia Robinson to sign as the second. "As soon as the wedding's over we'll discuss the adoption of Katarina Stokes," stated Cline officially.

Reverend Bates stood before Melinda and Theodore and took out his bible. He flipped to the page he wanted and read the appropriate passages. Candace held Katarina while Theodore and Melinda were married.

The ceremony went by quickly and before she knew it, Melinda was hearing the words, "By the power invested in me by all mighty God, I pronounce you husband and wife. What God hath joined together, let no man turn asunder." Closing the book he smiled at the couple to say, "You may kiss your bride."

Wrapping his arms around Melinda, Theodore pulled Melinda close and kissed her with all the passion and love he felt inside.

"Now," said Cline, "let's talk about the adoption of Katarina Stokes. Before we proceed, what is Katarina full name, Mr. Stokes?"

"Her full name is Katarina Stokes," replied her grandfather.

Melinda hesitantly asked, "Would it be all right if we gave her my middle name, Joy?"

"That would make her more yours," replied Stokes breaking into a wide grin, "so that's more than all right with me," he added.

Gently taking the sleeping baby from Candace, Cline placed her in Melinda's arms. "Candace, you're the judge, will you do the honors?"

"I don't usually do it like this, but under the circumstances I'll make an exception." Looking over at James Stokes, she asked, "Are you absolutely sure you want to do this?"

"It's not a matter of wanting to, it's necessary. I want her to be brought up in a loving home with two parents that love each other."

Melinda Joy Brooks, do you solemnly promise before this court of law, held here in the hospital, that you will love, protect and raise this child, Katarina Joy Stokes, to the best of your ability, giving up your life if the need should arise?"

"Yes, I solemnly promise."

"Theodore Rodney Brooks, do you solemnly promise before this court of law, held here in the hospital, that you will love, protect and raise this child, Katarina Joy Stokes to the best of your ability, giving up your life if the need should arise?"

"Yes, I do."

"Very good," stated Judge Smith. "I hereby pronounce you the legal parents of Katarina Joy Brooks. From this day forward, she will be known officially as Katarina Joy Brooks."

"Mr. Stokes, as Katarina's biological grandfather, we want you to be a part of her life until you're called home to your God," Teddy said.

Tears began to course down the old man's face, and he was speechless.

Melinda added, "I have more than enough money to help you bury your loved ones. Would you give me the honor of doing this for you?"

Stokes opened his mouth to speak, but nothing came out. After two more tries, he managed to say, "Thank you so much for letting me have some time with my granddaughter." Looking over to Melinda, he continued, "My wife and I had already planned our funerals. Everything is arranged and paid for."

Again he had to take a moment to compose himself. "We weren't expecting to lose our son's family, so we weren't prepared for that." Choking up he had to take another moment. "You realize I won't be able to pay you back. I think it's probably too much to ask."

Judge Smith spoke up, "Sometimes, we need to realize that the good Lord moves someone into our path when he knows we'll need them. Let this woman do what she was put in place to do."

Melinda spoke up to say, "I've been blessed and could never spend everything I have. There will be more than enough to see that Katarina has a good education and bright future. So, don't worry about that."

Theodore spoke up to say, "As Katarina's parents, we're responsible for her family, too. When we took on the job, we took her family on as ours."

That was more than Stokes could handle. Finally, he nodded affirmatively. "Thank you. I don't know what I would've done without you."

Looking at the lawyer, he asked, "Could I have a minute of your time in private? I have some things I need to talk over with you."

"I have to go back to work. There are still a lot of patients trickling in," Dr. Stillman interjected."

"As soon as I've taken care of my new family, I'll be back to help out in the emergency room," Theodore said.

"As soon as I see to the Judge back to her room, I'll come back and talk to you," Cine said to Stokes.

"Thank you."

When they were out in the lobby, Teddy said, "I'll see how much more help they need. When I'm free, I'll come take you some place where you can rest a little." Kissing her soundly on the lips, he added, "Until later, Mrs. Brooks."

"I like the sound of that," grinned Melinda. "You'd better get busy before I forget myself and kiss you."

Kissing her once more, he rushed off to do what he could to help.

Melinda was so tired that she ached. A nurse approached her and said, "Dr. Stillman wants me to take you to the doctor's lounge so you can get some rest. I've already set a crib up in there for the baby."

"Oh, thank you! I'm so tired."

Chapter 19

Shirleen awoke to the smell of coffee and frying bacon. Looking at the clock, she saw it was just seven o'clock. She showered and dressed, then made her bed and headed to the kitchen to see if she could help Trudy with breakfast.

"Good morning," replied Trudy as Shirleen came in. "Did you sleep well?"

"Like a baby."

"Breakfast will be ready as soon as I set the table."

"I'll do that," volunteered Shirleen. By the time the table was set, Trudy was dishing up the food.

Shirleen was about to go call the others when they entered the room.

Meagan sniffed the air appreciatively. "Oh, Trudy," she groaned, "you've outdone yourself as usual."

"I agree," replied Jeff.

"She always does," bragged Juliana. "Trudy could cook rings around the best chefs in the world."

Trudy beamed at the high praise, as she poured the coffee. Soon they were all seated at the table, saying grace. Finally, taking the last swallow of coffee, Jeff set his cup back onto the saucer, and said, "I have a couple of things to do and then I'll be on my way. If I get back before you, I'll bring in the wood for the night."

"Hopefully, we'll get back before dark," replied Shirleen. "I'll leave the key under the mat just in case."

After Jeff left, the women cleaned up the kitchen and were on their way by eight o'clock. They had to go slow, as the roads were very icy. Shirleen and Juliana went in their car and Meagan went with Trudy to keep her company. The roads were clear when they got to town.

The first thing on their agenda was to visit Tim at his office. "Good morning, ladies," he said as they came in.

Josiah came out of his office to greet them too.

Meagan surprised him by giving him a hug. "I hope that you don't mind me doing that, but I've never had an uncle before."

"Listen, Meagan," said Josiah, touched deeply by the gesture, "You can hug this old uncle of yours as often as you like. I've missed having a family to care about me."

"Thank you, Uncle Josiah."

Shirleen asked, "When did you say you were going to go to New York?"

"I'm going to leave in the morning. I have some paperwork to get finished first." Growing thoughtful a moment, he asked, "If I'm allowed to take some things from the house, what would you like me to get for you?"

"There were several pieces of jewelry my mother gave me. If you could bring those back with you, I'd appreciate it."

"Listen," said Josiah, "If I can, I'll ship everything except the furniture. Things like photo albums, pictures, and knick-knacks, etcetera. Would that be all right?"

"Oh, that would be wonderful," agreed Shirleen. "Leave our clothes so no one gets suspicious."

"Anything from your kitchen or library?

"I really would like to have everything in the kitchen, as well as all of the books in the library."

"I'll have them boxed up and shipped to my address."

"Wonderful!'

"Can you think of anything else that you might want?"

After pondering what else she might need, she replied, "What about everything in Gordon's office? There might be some incriminating evidence that could crack the case with Bruce Murdock wide open."

"Great thinking!" Josiah smiled. "I never even thought of that. Here I am a Mountie and you're the one to come up with a great solution."

"It just came to me when I was thinking about what else I wanted out of the house. Could you also get the contents of the file cabinets in my room?"

"Sure."

"Use your own discretion on what you think we could have without raising suspicion."

"I'll hire a couple of people to help me pack everything up. If they ask me why I want the furniture, I'll tell them I want to surprise my wife."

"That should cover everything."

"When I get there, I'll give Tim a call so I can tell him what's happening and relay it to you. If you have any other ideas, have him tell me when I call."

"How will you be able to talk without tipping someone off?" asked Juliana.

"I'll go to a public place to call, since the house may be bugged."

"Will you let us know when you've finished and are on your way home?" asked Meagan.

"You bet. Now that I have a niece, I'm not going to miss out on getting to know her." Meagan beamed, but fell silent. "I promise I'll keep in touch with you through Tim.

Right now, I've got to get back to that paperwork so I can get out of here tomorrow." As he started back into his office, he added. "See all of you real soon."

"Good luck, Uncle Josiah."

"Thanks, Pet."

When he closed his door, Tim took them over to his desk to give them the news he'd promised. "I called the man who checks out the towers for the cell phones. He got back to me yesterday and said your tower has a few problems but he'll take care of them and get back to me. It should be working in a day or two."

"Good," replied Shirleen. "It'll be so good to use our cell phones again."

"I also got a hold of the cable company and they'll be out to hook up your cable tomorrow afternoon at two-thirty."

"We'll be able to watch the news tomorrow night," exclaimed, Shirleen. "Good deal!"

"I also called the telephone company to come out at one-thirty to set up your landline."

"Wow," said Juliana, "we're going to move from the dark ages into the present."

"That we will," grinned Shirleen. "I don't plan to use it for anything but the doctor or calling you, Tim when we're in trouble. At least we won't be without a way to call for help like we have been."

"That's all the news I have for you, so I'll let you get on with your day." As they rose to leave, Tim asked, "How's the target practice coming along?"

Meagan looked at her mother proudly to say, "Momma finally got the hang of it. She gets bullseyes all the time now."

"A regular Calamity Jane, huh?" Juliana blushed, but remained silent. Turning to Shirleen, he asked, "How about you, Shirleen?"

Meagan interrupted again to say, "I'm so proud of Grandma, Tim. She does as well as Momma. I feel safer all ready."

"Flatterer," teased Shirleen. Turning to Tim she added, "I'm getting used to it. Guns aren't as intimidating as they once were."

"Good," replied Tim. "With the wild animals around your place, it's good to be able to protect yourselves."

"Well, if we want to get home before dark, then we'd better get a move on," declared Shirleen. Turning back to Tim, she added, "When you get the chance, come out to visit with us. We enjoy your company."

"Thanks, I will."

After leaving Tim's office, they drove straight to the mall and quickly found a parking spaces next to each other. They went inside and made plans for where to meet a few hours later before they all went their separate ways.

Shirleen went to a video store to buy some clean wholesome videos. When she was satisfied that she had a good selection, she checked out and went to the furniture shop to see if she could get a cabinet to store the videos in. She also found three bookcases she liked and arranged for everything to be delivered by the end of the day.

Next, Shirleen went to the electronics store and bought a DVD player. She asked the clerk to wrap the box so no one would know what was inside. The next thing on her list was to find something for her brother-in-law for Christmas. Not knowing his likes and dislikes, she had a tough time deciding what to do. Finally, she settled on some videos, a couple of good books, a warm hat and glove set, and a sturdy wallet.

Checking that off of her list, she was relieved to find that she was nearly finished. Then she remembered she wanted to get some things for the new dogs, so she went to the pet store and asked the clerk what kinds of chew toys were good for Collies or Huskies. The clerk helped her pick out several cute ones, and she was off to choose some last minute Christmas tree ornaments. That completed her list, and she knew that she was finally ready for Christmas. All she had to do was get everything wrapped.

She saw the others waiting for her as she approached the mall entrance. When they saw how much she'd bought, they couldn't help teasing her a little. "What did you do, Grandma, buy out the stores?" asked Meagan.

"How do you expect us to get all of that stuff into the car, Momma?"

"All I have to say," replied Trudy, "is that it's a good thing I drove too!"

"You'll be glad I did what I did come Christmas morning," she chided. "I told you I was going to go all out for Christmas and I did!"

When everything was packed into the car, there was barely enough room left for the groceries. They headed to the store and it took two carts to get everything on Trudy's list. "Talk about Grandma buying out the stores," teased Meagan. "I think you're running a close second, Trudy."

"You'll be happy that I got all of this stuff Christmas day," laughed Trudy good-naturedly. "In fact, when you moan and groan about how full you are, I'll remind you of how much I bought."

Shirleen added, "Don't let them give you any guff, Trudy. I for one am looking forward to all of the goodies you're planning to make."

They checked out and wheeled the heavy carts to Trudy's car. They were barely able to get everything inside. It was lunchtime, so they decided to have lunch out before heading home. They found a small café and sat near a window. They chatted amiably while they waited for their meals to arrive. They enjoyed their lunch and were finally ready to head home.

Soon the four very tired ladies were heading home. As they drove past the jail where the Mounties worked, they saw Josiah putting suitcases in the back of his car and waved to him. Juliana made her mother go to bed to rest for a while and the others unloaded the cars. They were nearly finished, when Jeff pulled up.

Jeff helped them with the last of their purchases, then went to get some items out of the back of his truck. Meagan helped him carry his things inside. When everyone was back inside, Jeff, with Meagan's help, went to fill all of the wood boxes with wood for the night. Meanwhile, Juliana helped Trudy put the food and other purchases away.

By the time Shirleen had put her purchases away, she had to lie down. Juliana, who was worried about her, found her lying there, exhausted. "That does it. You're going to get ready for bed and have your supper right there."

"But there's a delivery truck due before dark. I need to direct them where to put everything."

"That's this evening. I'm sure Jeff help move things if they're not where you want them."

"Fine, I'll lay down as soon as I talk to Jeff."

"I'll go get him, but you stay put."

"Yes, boss," Shirleen joked.

Hurrying off, she returned with Jeff. Juliana left them alone. Jeff waited for Shirleen's instructions, but he was moved by the loveliness that she presented sitting there on the bed. "Juliana said that you wanted to speak to me, Shirleen."

"Yes, I did. A delivery truck will be delivering some furniture tonight. I don't want Juliana and Meagan to see what it is because it's for their Christmas."

"I see."

"Can you find a place to put them until Christmas Eve, then come back and set it up?"

"How about I put it behind the car then cover it with tarps?"

"That would be great."

"Your wish is my command, ma'am," he replied with a wink before bowing slightly. Shirleen laughed as she watched him leave the room.

A moment later, Juliana came in. "You're confined to your bed for the rest of the day, missy!"

"Fine," sighed Shirleen. I know you're right, but I don't have to like it."

Juliana left her mother's room and went to the kitchen. Trudy was struggling to mop the floor because they'd tracked in the snow after their shopping trip. Seeing how exhausted Trudy looked, Juliana said, "I'll take care of the floor while you go take a nap. We'll just make some soup and sandwiches for dinner."

When Trudy started to protest, Juliana waved her away, "Scram!"

After she had left the room, Juliana finished mopping the floor. When that task was finished, Juliana went out to help Jeff and Meagan work on the wood.

Later that afternoon, the delivery truck arrived and Jeff told the ladies that he was going to take care of things. "You just go on putting the wood into the woodshed while I do what your mother asked."

"I don't think Shirleen wants us to see what's in that truck," Meagan said as he walked away.

An hour later, Tim pulled into the driveway. Getting out of the truck, he came toward them. "Hello, you busy beavers."

"Hello, yourself," greeted Juliana. "What brings you up here today?"

"Just as I was leaving the office, Major Graham called to tell me he'd had a call from the lawyer asking when he's going to take care of Gordon's estate. He said Bruce Murdock wanted to go through the house, but he got a writ from a judge that prevented him from doing so. He told Josiah to get there as soon as he possibly could."

"That sounds like Bruce, the arrogant, pompous jerk!" Juliana said. Taking several deep breaths, she managed to calm down enough to ask, "What did Josiah say?"

"He told the lawyer he was leaving in the morning. He'll drive to Spokane then catch a plane two days later."

"Did that satisfy the lawyer?" asked Juliana.

"He said the lawyer seemed relieved."

"Good, let's hope he can get there before Bruce finds a way around that writ. It would be awful if he gets in before Josiah gets there."

"I agree," said Tim thoughtfully. "The more I hear about Bruce Murdock, the more I'm surprised he hasn't been killed by now."

"Bruce is very good at self preservation."

"Well, Josiah told me he was leaving as soon as we hung up.."

"I hope he takes it easy," replied Jeff.

"When I mentioned that, he promised to be careful."

"Good," replied Juliana. "We don't want anything to happen to him."

"Josiah won't do anything stupid. I've seen him take his time when hunting down a fugitive. While the fugitive is running without rest, Josiah takes his time and plans his moves. Before the fugitive knows it, he's been arrested."

Juliana asked, "What happens now?"

"We wait until we hear from him."

"In other words, be patient."

"That's right," grinned Tim.

The next afternoon was hectic. First the man who was working on the cell phone tower was at the door. He let them know the tower was working again. Then, the man from the telephone company came to install the landline. When that was done, Shirleen called Tim to give him their new number. While she was on the phone with him, Tim said that Josiah had made it to Spokane and would be boarding a plane in an hour. When Shirleen had hung up the phone, she went to tell the others the news.

At 2:30, the cable man arrived. He wasn't there long, and when he left they finally had television reception again. It would be nice for them to know what was going on in the world. They also tested their cell phones to make sure they all worked.

After supper, Tim pulled into the driveway.

When she saw who it was, Shirleen said, "Must mean he has news."

They invited him inside and got caught up with his news. Josiah arrived safely in Syracuse and met with the lawyer. He told him that Bruce had tried to get around the writ but he'd stopped him.

After learning the trip had been a success, Juliana asked, "What about the papers?"

"What about them?"

"Will they just ship the papers here, or will the police help him sort through them for evidence of Bruce's activities with the mafia?"

"Josiah said the police would go through the papers with him. If they find any incriminating evidence, they'll hand it over to the authorities."

"If they find any evidence, I hope they're smart enough to give Josiah time to get out of New York before they try to arrest Bruce," Shirleen said.

"I agree with you, Shirleen," declared Tim. "You should all pray that Josiah can get out of there safely."

"We will," replied Shirleen. "Starting tonight we'll have constant prayer on his behalf. Tomorrow is Sunday, so we'll have a special fast to petition the Lord for his safety."

"Good," sighed Tim. "I'll pray for him, too."

"What else did this lawyer tell him?" asked Shirleen.

"He told Josiah that he thought all of you had been murdered. He feared they would never find your bodies. The judge he spoke to about the matter said that Josiah was the only living heir, so he was entitled to the contents of the house."

"It's odd to know that people think we're dead," Juliana said, shivering.

"Josiah told the lawyer he was going to ship everything back here, and then in the spring he'd return for the furniture. The attorney told him that was a good idea."

"Tim," began Shirleen, "there's a lot of stuff in that house. How in the world can he get it all packed, let alone get it shipped here, in only a few days?"

"With the help of the three policewomen, he should be able to get it done. If they work around the clock it should only take them about a week or a week and a half to get it done What they can't get shipped in that time will have to wait until later."

"I shouldn't' have asked him to bring so much stuff back."

"Nonsense," scolded Tim. "Major Graham has been in worse conditions than these and come out unscathed. We have to trust in providence to come to his rescue."

"All right," sighed Shirleen resignedly.

"Josiah also said that the lawyer is worried his life is in jeopardy. He and Bruce have bunted heads in court many times. He said that Bruce hates him with a passion, and he's surprised he hasn't been taken him out of the picture."

"The attorney told Josiah he'd sent his family away to keep them out of this whole business. He also told Josiah that he planned to disappear after he was safely on his way back here."

"Good, that means that he isn't corrupt."

"It looks that way," mused Tim. "I guess we have to wait to see what happens."

Chapter 20

Theodore Brooks entered the doctor's lounge to check on Melinda. She was sleeping so peacefully that he didn't disturb her. He checked on Katarina, and was pleased to see she was also sleeping soundly. He was exhausted, and he wasn't surprised to see that it was four o'clock in the morning. The last of the people from the massive wreck had been finally been taken care of and he felt like he'd been in a war zone.

Theodore went to the restroom to wash his face and try to wake up. When he came back, he pulled a chair over and sat down to look at the sleeping child. Suddenly he saw a light appear in the corner of the room. As he watched it, the light grew larger until it filled the room. A beautiful woman dressed, in white appeared inside it. At first, he wondered what he was seeing, and was about to call out when the woman raised her hand to silence him.

"It's all right, Theodore. You have nothing to fear."

"What do you want from me?"

"My name is Elaine Stokes. That little one there is my youngest child."

"You're this baby's mother?"

"That's right. I have to talk to you. It's important. My Katarina wasn't the only child who was affected by this accident."

"She wasn't?"

Suddenly another woman came forward, also dressed in white. "No, she wasn't. My name is Arleen Bowmen and I lost my husband, as was well as five of my children. I was alive when they brought me to this hospital. I was eight months pregnant. There were just so many things wrong with me that they decided to save the twins and let me go. They had barely taken the twins by cesarean section when I was called home."

"What can I do for you?"

"We're coming to that in a moment," she answered.

Another woman came toward him, also dressed in white. "My name is Ramona Stout. My children, Effie Pearl and Ephraim Phillip are the only survivors in our family. I have one surviving family member, my sister, Elizabeth Starskie. She's not well enough to take care of my children. I don't want them to go to a foster home and I don't want them to be separated."

"I don't understand," Theodore said. "What has all of this got to do with me?"

"We've come to ask you and Melinda to raise our children," said Elaine Stokes."

"We rushed our marriage so we could adopt your baby. I don't know if we can handle more children." Spreading his hands out pleadingly, he added, "I don't want to lose her before we even get the chance to be a family. If I tell her about you all appearing to me, she'll send me packing!" The poor man felt as if he would bolt. The only reason he didn't was for his family's sake. Finally, he asked, "How can I even broach the subject?"

"As we're talking to you, there are others visiting Melinda in her sleep," replied Elaine. "She will be open to the idea when you talk to her about it. Melinda has always loved children. That's why she became a kindergarten teacher. That was her job when you two met. Children adore her too."

"That's something I didn't know about her."

"We know that you helped to raise all of your brothers and sisters when you father died."

"I did."

"We also know that you gave up your dream of becoming a doctor because you didn't want your siblings to be affected by your student debt. Because of that, you chose to become a nurse, branching off into therapy. You will be given another chance to go back to school to become a doctor. Don't refuse it; this is your mission in life."

"I'm getting to the age where I don't know if I have time to become a doctor."

"Age doesn't matter."

"All right, I won't refuse the opportunity when it comes."

"Good."

Looking at Arleen Bowman he asked, "Had you named your twins?"

"Yes, Michael Jonas and Michelle JaNae. However, the two of you have my permission to name them differently if you so choose."

"Thank you. If we take on this monumental task, we'll keep the names you chose for them. Doing that will honor you and let them feel connected to you."

"Thank you, Theodore."

"How do you know my name?"

"We were shown your past, present and future," replied Elaine. "That's why we asked if we could speak to you."

"I see," replied Theodore, who still doubted his sanity. Turning to Ramona Stout, he asked, "How old are your children, ma'am?"

"Effie Pearl and Ephraim Phillip, are twins and will be two on March 1."

Doing the mental math, Theodore exclaimed, "They're all babies!"

"Yes," replied Elaine, "but neither of you will be alone as you raise these children. You'll be able to hire help to tend to their needs."

"Good, because taking care of five children under the age of two is mind boggling!"

The women smiled, but it was Elaine who replied, "We understand that. Living in your tiny apartment with all of these children will also be a problem. As you know, my father-in-law is terminally ill. He will be gone soon, which means there will be seven funerals instead of six.

"My father-in-law has a huge eight-bedroom home a few miles outside of town. He plans to leave this house to you in his will. There's only one house near it and the people who live there know Henry Borden. Let me explain how they know each other."

Theodore listened intently as Elaine talked. When she was finished, she added, "These are four of the most honest, sweetest women you will ever meet. If you need help, don't be afraid to ask them; they will gladly help."

"If they know that Henry is living close to them, won't they panic?"

Elaine replied, "The oldest of the women, Shirleen, had an angel visit her. She knows that Henry is somewhere in Cardston, but she just doesn't know where. She has also been told that Henry is no longer a threat. Henry lost his family so that he would could start over. He isn't a bad man, but the man who trapped him is evil through and through. Henry will remember everything from the past, but instead of going to his old buddy, he will turn state's evidence."

"Knowing him as I do," said Theodore, "I believe that's exactly what he'll do. The other question I have is how will he feel about us taking in five children?"

"Overwhelmed at first, but the children will heal the hole in his heart. As you do physical therapy with him, talk to him about what happened. He'll understand in time."

"I know you doubt this is real, Theodore." Theodore snapped to attention, wondering how she could read his mind. "You'll know what we've told you is true when Dr. Stillman talks about our children when you meet him in the hospital today. You only have a small window of time before they're taken to foster care, so don't put off speaking to Melinda. The snow won't stop for two more days, so you have until then to make your decision."

"Are you absolutely sure Melinda won't send me packing when I tell her about the three of you?"

The women could see the fear on Theodore's face, so hastened to reassure him. Again, it was Elaine who spoke for them all. "She won't send you away, Theodore. She will be too busy thinking you'll think she's insane when she tells you about her dreams. Be patient with each other. It will all come out right in the end."

Looking down at her sleeping daughter she added, "Thank you both for agreeing to raise my daughter. I'm grateful to both of you. Tell Melinda thank you for coming to our rescue in the waiting room. Should the two of you decide to take on this task, your lives will be blessed accordingly. You'll have the means, resources, as well as the physical labor to help you provide for these children. In fact, you'll be surprised by how quickly this community will come to your aid once they learn what you did."

"Thank you for telling me."

"You'll be provided for throughout the years. One of your greatest supporters will be Henry Borden. He'll become their greatest ally and the children will call him grandpa."

"I can't speak for Melinda, but I want to promise that if she's willing, we'll raise these five children as our own. I'll provide for them, protect them and most of all, I'll love them."

Elaine continued, "You'll have two children of your own, and they'll never think of the others as outsiders."

Arleen Bowman spoke up, "Theodore, you will have our deepest gratitude for taking care of our children. If you decide to do this, we'll all become one family in the next life. The two of you will be as much a part of our family as you and the children will be a family in this life."

"How will you know what we decide?"

"We'll remain close by until everything is worked out. Once they're your children, we'll be able to go forward in our new life."

"If we adopt them, will you be there to see it happen?"

"Yes," replied Ramona."

"That's good to know." Taking a deep breath to gain control of his emotions, he continued, "Thank you for your vote of confidence."

"We're the ones who want to thank you."

Suddenly, Melinda moaned in her sleep. Theodore looked over at her, and when he looked back, the women were gone.

He sat there, lost in thought, thinking over everything the women said. Suddenly the door to the doctor's lounge opened and Dr. Stillman came in. "Are you still up, Ted? "I thought I was the only fool still awake. I thought you'd be dead to the world by now."

"I was just admiring my new family," replied Theodore. He decided to keep the previous incident to himself. "What are you doing up?"

"Just checking on the last of the patients. Most of them are resting, but a couple of them aren't doing well. They're stable for now, but I don't know how long that will last."

Grinning at some private thought, Theodore replied, "Gerald, when I first met you I thought you were the most cantankerous old coot I'd ever had the misfortune of meeting. That isn't the case at all. Your grouchy demeanor is nothing but a façade. Underneath you've got a heart big enough to take on the world. You're nothing but an old faker, Gerald Stillman!"

"Shush! Don't say that too loud or my secret will be out," replied Stillman with mock sternness.

Theodore laughed softly so as not to wake Melinda or the baby and replied, "That's just what I thought. Growing serious he continued, "Last night, I got to see you in action. What I saw was a doctor who fought a hard fight to save as many people as possible. When you lost a patient, I saw the look on your face, but instead of folding up and running away, you moved on to the next patient to see if you could save them. I was proud to be part of your team."

"Thank you, Ted. It was a tough fight. I think the hardest part was losing so many children. Most of the adults had lived a long life, but the children had only gotten started.

"Dr. Stillman, out of all those that died, how many of them were children?"

"Twenty-four," muttered Stillman.

"Then our Katarina was a miracle."

"In more ways than one. When Sergeant York came in with the last set of ambulances, he told me about a family who'd slammed into a wrecked semi. As they slid under the semi, the top of their car was peeled back and they didn't have a ghost of a chance of making it. The baby was asleep in its car seat. Tim said that he would never forget the horror he experienced when saw that car. How they lived to get to the hospital is still the mystery."

"How awful."

"That's not the half of it," continued Stillman. "When the oldest daughter's seat belt broke, it pinned her half in and half out of the car window. She was barely clinging to life. The two boys in the back seats never regained consciousness. Like the father and daughter, they died in intensive care. The doctor, who examined the woman, did a terrible job. If he had done a more thorough job, he would've discovered that she had massive internal injuries. How she ever lasted as long as she did is beyond me.

"When her husband died, she collapsed. When they got her back into emergency, I was the one who examined her. I knew that she didn't have a chance, but I continued to fight for her life. Her injuries were just too bad, and she died. The shock was too much for her mother-in-law and she died from a heart attack immediately after hearing about her daughter-in-law's death."

"You're talking about Katarina's family, aren't you?"

"Yes, I am."

"How is Mr. Stokes doing?"

"He's finally resting, but he isn't doing well at all. I don't think he really has much longer." As Theodore listened to Dr. Stillman, he remembered Elaine Stokes mentioning these very things. "There are also two sets of twins who were orphaned."

"One set of them is nearly two," replied Theodore.

Blinking in surprise, Stillman asked, "Were you part of the team that helped the mother?"

"No, let's just say I know about it."

Not convinced, Stillman pressed him. "How do you know?"

"Before I answer, I have a question for you."

"Fire away."

"Do you believe in ghosts?" Theodore watched Stillman anxiously.

Stillman thought about it for a moment and asked, "Did you see a ghost?"

"Before I answer that question, would you please answer my question?"

"On the chance of being called crazy, the answer is yes. I believe that people come back to deliver messages to the living."

As he watched Theodore anxiously, he asked, "Why did you ask that?"

Theodore replied, "I saw Katarina's mother, Elaine, and the mothers of the Bowman and Stout twins."

Scooting to the edge of his chair, Stillman asked, "Tell me what happened."

Sighing Theodore filled him in on the vision. When he finished, Stillman whistled softly before replying, "Boy, when it rains on you, it pours!"

"It sure does," replied Theodore. "Elaine told me that Melinda had been given the same message in her dreams. I don't even know how to approach the subject with Mel, Dr. Stillman. Katarina's mother told me she would be too busy worrying about me thinking she's the crazy one."

"Perhaps. One thing you can be sure of , if you don't ask what she thinks about adopting these children, you'll never know that answer."

"I know you're right, I'm stumped about how to bring it up."

"You'll find a way. When she needed you, you came to her rescue, just as you did for Katarina and her grandfather."

Theodore thought that over a moment then said, "I'll talk to her when she wakes up."

"About what?" asked Melinda, stretching.

"I'll leave the two of you alone to talk. I'll ask a nurse to prepare a bottle for Katarina." With that he left the two of them alone.

Just then, Katarina began to fuss because she needed changed. "Oh, dear, we're nearly out of diapers. This one should hold her for a while. Then, what are we going to do?"

"I'm sure they have some in the maternity ward," replied Theodore.

"What were you and Dr. Stillman discussing?"

Theodore squirmed in his seat as he tried to figure out how to broach the subject. Seeing no other way around it, he decided to just blurt it out. "Mel, I learned there are four other orphaned children here in the hospital."

"So did I," replied Melinda, surprised.

They took turns telling each other their experiences and then Theodore said, "Even though I was told we'd have hired help, I'm worried about how we'll handle two newborns, with three others under two years old."

"My main worry is that if I say I want to do this, you'll think I'm crazy."

Kissing her passionately, Theodore asked, "Does that prove that I don't think you're crazy? Melinda Brooks, I love you with everything in me." Stealing another kiss, he confessed, "To be totally honest, I was afraid that you'd send me packing if I told about the visitations and that I wanted to do this."

"Let me set your mind at ease. When I was younger, I use to be clairvoyant." Looking intently into Brook's eyes, she asked, "Does that scare you?"

"If you'd told me before this, I think perhaps I might have wondered about you. Now, I think it's not a bad thing, and it certainly doesn't make you crazy."

"I saw the newborns in my dream. They're so tiny and beautiful. They'll be in the hospital for a while since they were premature. The other set of twins have two nurses watching over them."

"Did you learn their names?"

"Yes. The newborns are Michael Jonas and Michelle JaNae, and the others are Effie Pearl and Ephraim Phillip. I want to keep their name to honor their parents."

"That's how I feel too."

"Does that mean you're in?"

When Theodore saw how hopeful she looked, he smiled. "Yes, I'm in."

She smiled at his answer, then said, "Teddy, I was told a lot of things about Henry. Some that I didn't like, but when I learned he'd been trapped by Bruce Murdock, I felt sorry for him." She went on to tell him that she knew about Shirleen, Juliana, Trudy and Meagan. "I was told that they would be a great help to us. I was also told that Henry would become our greatest supporter, and these children would fill the empty hole in his heart."

"I was told that too."

"So, we're going to become an instant large family?"

Taking Katarina from Melinda, Theodore kissed her cheek a couple of times. Setting her on his lap, he replied, "Yes, I am."

"Oh," cried Melinda, flinging her arms around his neck. "You're the most wonderful man in the world!" Then, she kissed him passionately.

Katarina began to protest that she was hungry, and the kiss ended abruptly. "Well, my little one, you sure know how to throw cold water on a feller." Melinda laughed.

The door opened as a nurse entered carrying a couple of bottles. "These should keep you through the morning hours. We'll get some more for you after lunch time."

"Thank you. You're just in time; she's hungry. Also, is there any way we could get some more diapers?"

"Sure thing," replied the nurse. "I'll go get you a whole box."

While waiting for the nurse to return, they fed Katarina and discussed how to tell Henry what they'd decided to do. It was going to be a shock to him; he didn't even know they were married!

When the nurse returned armed with a box of diapers and wipes, Theodore asked, "Is there someone here who could take care of Katarina for us for a little while so we can get some breakfast and take care of some things?"

"I'm sure the nursery can do it, but I'll need to check."

"Thank you," replied Melinda. "I haven't eaten since lunchtime yesterday."

"I'll get right back to you. Can't have you starving to death."

After she left, Theodore said, "If we're going to adopt the other children, we need to talk to Mr. Cline and Judge Smith so we can get the ball rolling. When we're done with that, we'll have to get cribs, bassinets, bedding, clothes. It's all a little overwhelming."

"After we visit Henry and Mr. Stokes, we can sit down and make a list. That will help us to feel organized and give us a game plan."

Katarina had fallen asleep, so Melinda laid her back in the crib.

Dr. Stillman came in and said, "I finally have an empty room for you two. It's a poor place to honeymoon, but it's all we've got." Plopping on a chair across from them, he continued. "I'll take care of the little princess while the two of you have breakfast and do what you need to do. When you get back, we'll get you settled in that room."

"Thank you, Dr. Stillman," replied Melinda.

The couple headed to the cafeteria for some much-needed food. When the meal was over, they carried their trays to the dishwasher and went to visit Henry. When they gave him all of their news, he seemed a little upset. "Remember, Henry," said Melinda, "you'll always be a part of our lives."

That seemed to calm him a little. "Henry, we know the truth about you, but it doesn't matter. We know why you did what you did," Theodore said. "We also know how Bruce Murdock forced you to be part of his evil plans. I have confidence that you'll eventually make everything right. Never doubt that we love, no matter what you've done."

Tears rolled down Henry's cheeks. "No matter what happens, we'll stick by you," Theodore continued. "We can't stay long this morning because we have so much to do, but we'll be back soon."

Kissing Henry's cheek, Melinda said. "I ditto everything Theodore just said. We love you so much. We'll be back soon."

After leaving Henry's room they took the elevator down to see Mr. Stokes. When they walked into his room, he looked pale but was happy to see them. "I see you two survived the night. How's little Katarina?"

"Dr. Stillman is staying with her so we could get some breakfast and take care of some other things.."

After they'd talked for a while, Melinda noticed Stokes was getting tired, so she said, "We'll drop in later to visit with you again."

In answer he nodded his head and promptly fell asleep.

When they got back to the doctor's lounge, they found Dr. Stillman carrying Katarina toward a door down the hall. Melinda called out to him and he turned around and came back toward them.

"I was just carrying Katarina to her new room."

"Sorry we were gone so long," Theodore said. "We stopped to fill Henry in and then went to speak to Mr. Stokes. He isn't doing very well today."

"I'll show you to your room then go check him out."

When Melinda and Katarina were settled, Theodore said, "I wish I could stay, but times a-ticking so I'd best get busy."

"You're right. Besides, I have lots to do, too."

Kissing her once more he hurried off.

After he left, Melinda gave Katarina a bath, fed her a bottle and played with her for a little while. When she fell asleep, Melinda started working on the list. When she finished, she decided she needed some expert advice so she went to find one of the nurses from the maternity ward.

She found a young nurse and asked her if she could come back to her room and answer some questions.

When they'd gotten comfortable, Melinda said, "I need help equipping a nursery for five babies." When the nurse gasped, Melinda went on to say, "My husband and I are also adopting the two sets of orphaned twins. I've made a list, but I'm not sure if it's complete."

"Let me see it." She scanned it and looked up with a smile. "This is really impressive. I only have a few more suggestions and you'll be set." Together they worked through the list until they were both satisfied it was complete.

The nurse had only been gone a few minutes when Theodore returned. "I have good news. I talked to Mr. Cline, and he took me in to talk with Judge Smith. She said she has all the required forms here at the hospital, so that won't be a problem. The only thing she mentioned was wondering where we were going to live. I don't think our apartment will work for so many children."

"Oh, I hadn't thought of that," replied Melinda. "I guess we need to show we can provide a healthy, happy home so the adoptions will go through without a hitch."

"Judge Smith gave us her blessing. She even went so far as to see if the adoption couldn't be taken care of this afternoon, as soon as Joel can get the paperwork ready."

"That's wonderful!" cried Melinda. "That means by the end of the day, we'll be the proud parents of five little ones."

"That's right. Now come here, Mrs. Brooks. I need a little sugar." Lowering his head, he took possession of her lips. The kiss deepened, and he lowered her onto the bed. "I thought we'd never get here." Removing her blouse, he began to explore her body. Their passion was interrupted by a sudden knock on the door.

Rising, they adjusted their clothes and went to open the door. "Sorry to interrupt," apologized the nurse, "but Dr. Stillman told me Mr. Stokes has taken a turn for the worse. He thought you should get down there with Katarina so he could see her one last time."

"We'll be right there," replied Theodore.

They quickly composed themselves, grabbed the baby and hurried to the room. When they arrived, they were surprised to see how his condition had deteriorated. He rallied long enough to hold Katarina for a few minutes, but grew even weaker after he handed her back to Melinda.

Taking a deep breath, Mr. Stokes reached for Melinda's hand. "Come closer, my dear." Handing the baby to the nurse, she stepped closer to the bed. "I know you and your young man didn't have much time to be engaged before you got married, but I want to thank you for what you're doing for my precious granddaughter."

"Thank you, for choosing us for her."

The old man nodded and motioned for Theodore to come closer. "This morning, Dr. Stillman told me you were going to adopt four more orphaned children."

"That's right," replied Theodore.

"He told me that you live in a three bedroom apartment." Theodore nodded. "Well," continued Stokes, "I've made arrangements for you to have something larger where you can raise those precious children." He paused to gain the strength to continue. "When I'm gone, you'll find out the details. Thank you, again, for everything you've done for my family."

"You're welcome, Mr. Stokes."

Nodding his approval, Stokes gasped one more time then was gone.

Chapter 21

Tim gasped at the words he heard on TV. Fear for his friend consumed him.

> *"Several men tried to break into the Spielberg mansion early this morning. Their plan was foiled by gunshots from the mansion grounds. Two of the would-be burglars were killed while trying to scale the fence in the back. Three others were killed at the front entrance.*
> *We'll bring you more details as we get more information."*

"I wish you could call me, Major," muttered Tim. Suddenly the phone rang.

"Tim, this is Shirleen. Have you heard about that break in at my former house? Was the Major involved?"

"I haven't heard from him, but I expect to hear soon."

"We're all so worried."

"Me too. I hope no news is good news in this case. We have to hang in there until we hear from him."

"We'll try."

"As soon as I hear anything, I'll come see you."

Nearly as soon as he ended the call, Tim's phone rang again.

"Tim, this is Josiah."

"Are all right?"

"Yes. It was a little rough there for a while. Gregory Jones had a feeling something was going to happen, so he called Judge Harris and asked for more back up. He called the police department and they sent out several more men. That was the only thing that saved us."

"This Jones feller sounds like a good guy to have on your team."

"He sure is!" Josiah paused to collect his thoughts and then continued. "We have what we were looking for, but they haven't done anything with it yet. I asked them to give me time to ship what I wanted. After I board the plane, they'll do what they need to do. With the help of the extra officers, we got just about everything packed up."

"That's a good thing, as it will ensure your getting out of there faster."

"That's my feeling exactly! I can't wait to get back where there isn't so much violence."

Chucking, Tim said, "We have our own brand of violence in this neck of the woods."

"I know," replied Josiah, "but it's nowhere near as bad as this place!"

"When do you think you'll be coming home?"

"I can't say for sure. The moving van should be here in two days, if we're ready for it. I'll let you know the night before I leave. Tell our friends not to worry about me. I'll be fine."

"I will."

"Well, I'll talk to you later."

Tim felt much better after talking to the Major. He grabbed something to eat and then got ready to visit the girls. He went out to check on the dogs before he left, and took his rifle with him to prevent surprises from furry creatures. He brought in the puppies that would soon become Christmas presents and prepared a box for them to sleep in. From this time forward, their training would begin. They curled up together and promptly went to sleep.

That accomplished, he went out and started his truck and let the engine warm up a little before taking off. As he drove up the mountain, his mind went to Juliana. He'd had feelings for her for some time now. He knew that she wasn't free, but it didn't stop him thinking romantic thoughts about her. The more he was around her, the more intense his feelings grew. No matter how hard he tried, they just wouldn't go away.

Shaking his head, he tried to concentrate on the road. Soon, however, he was thinking about her again. *Why does she torture me so?* he asked himself for the millionth time. A mile from their house, the realization hit him. *I'm in love with her. Well, you dunderhead, what have you gotten yourself into? Well, you'll just have got to suffer in silence until you can figure out what you're going to do.*

Shirleen greeted him when he knocked on the door, and invited him inside."

"Have a seat," she said after he'd removed his coat and gloves.

Taking the proffered chair, he held his hands out toward the fire and said, "Josiah called to tell me that he was all right not long after I talked to you. He said that Gordon's lawyer, Mr. Jones, had a bad feeling and called in reinforcements. That was what saved their bacon."

"When can he get out of there?" asked Juliana.

"He said at least two more days. They have to get things packed up and wait for the moving van."

"Two more days," replied Meagan. "Anything can happen in that time."

"Yes, it could," agreed Tim, "but we can't do anything about it, so we must pray and be patient."

"That's true," agreed Jeff.

"By the way, I went to check your mail at the post office, Jeff, and there was a huge package waiting for you. I picked it up, but forgot to bring it inside."

"Thanks," said Jeff. "I go out with you. It's probably the back-ordered newspapers for Shirleen."

"Oh, I hope you're right," Shirleen said. "I'll go through them after everyone has gone to bed, then we can go through them tomorrow to see what Bruce has been up to."

The two went out to get the package, and it was indeed the aforementioned newspapers. Once the package was inside, Tim said his good-byes and left.

Shirleen awoke early, and got up to face her day. She showered and dressed quickly, then went to the living room. After stoking the fire, she sank down into the overstuffed chair, and stared lazily into the fire. Suddenly a movement caught her attention. Turning to see what it was, she was surprised to see the angel who'd visited her before. This time though, she wasn't frightened.

"Hello, Shirleen. I've come to deliver a message. Last time I was here, I told you that Henry was living in Cardston."

"Yes, I remember."

"Well, just before Thanksgiving, he had two more strokes and he's still in the hospital. He's regained consciousness and will have to have a lot of therapy. He doesn't remember much of his past. He's living with his wife's sister, Melinda Jacobs. She married his nurse, Theodore Brooks, a few days before Thanksgiving. Remember the awful storm just before Thanksgiving?"

"Yes, I remember it well."

"A drunk driver plowed into a family who were headed to the hospital. He wife was in labor with twins. This accident caused several others. By the time the highway patrols could get the road closed there were over one hundred vehicles involved. Many lost their lives that night, leaving five babies motherless. Melinda Jacobs and Theodore Brooks were at the hospital visiting Henry that day, and were stranded there by the storm. Theodore helped the hospital staff with the crash victims and Melinda helped the mother of a tiny baby, who lost every member of her family, except for this baby and her grandfather."

"That's awful," Shirleen said, shivering as if cold.

"The grandfather, who was terminally ill, asked Melinda and Theodore if they would consider getting married and adopting his granddaughter. They agreed."

Swiping at a tear, Shirleen replied, "That's beautiful!"

"Seeing this action, the other two mothers who lost their lives in the accidents, visited Theodore in spirit form at the hospital to ask if they would also adopt their babies. They readily agreed. Both of them love children dearly.

"They will be coming to live in the huge house just down the road from you. Do not fear being near Henry. He won't remember you for quite some time. By the time he does remember, he'll understand why everything has happened. I want you to befriend this young couple. They will have their hands full caring for five children under the age of two, as well as Henry. They'll need all of the help you can give them."

"We'll gladly help them. I only have one question."

"I'm listening."

"What do I tell, Ruth — I mean Juliana — and Meagan?"

"The truth. Juliana will have to think it over for a while, but Meagan will have no problem because she trusts you completely.

"Now, for the last reason I'm here. It concerns your newly found brother-in-law, Josiah Graham. He's about to be in grave danger. Call your friend Tim. Tell him he has to tell Josiah that the new police officer coming to help him is one of Bruce's men. He is wicked to the core of his being. He will tell Bruce every move that's made in that house. Have Gregory Jones call his boss and tell him not to send Leonard Mandello."

"Have Tim tell Josiah not to leave today. If he does, he and his driver will be killed. Tell him to wait until tomorrow morning to leave. He is to leave at precisely 2 a.m. and take Gregory Jones with him as far as Cleveland, Ohio. He can board his plane there and go to join his family in Billings, Montana. Tell him to get his affairs in order at his office and have two of the police officers at your house go with him for protection.

"Also let him know there's a door behind the wall near Gordon's desk. There, he will find more information that will help crack the case. This room also contains other important papers, jewelry, guns, and other surprises. Tell them to make sure they have locked the door, and padlocked the double gates.

"Again, it is absolutely imperative that they leave at 2 a.m. They'll ask why, but just tell them it doesn't matter, they just have to do it. If they do as they're told, they will get safely out of there. Five minutes either way could cost them their lives."

"I'll be sure to tell Tim everything," promised Shirleen.

"Good. Now there's something else that you should know. Bruce will get his just desserts soon, however you must remain on alert. There will be someone snooping around as soon as the weather changes. Buy a set of binoculars for each of you and keep them with you at all times. You wIll be glad you did."

"I'll get them next time I go to town."

"That's good. You won't need them until the weather changes."

Pausing to collect his thoughts a moment, he added, "The Lord is pleased with how you've taken Hazel under your wing. She would've been targeted if she'd stayed with her family. Bruce Murdock is an evil individual. He has a lot of enemies One or more of them will come for him. It is only a matter of time. Until then, stay alert to all that's happening around you."

"I'll make sure we all do as you've said."

"Do you have any questions?"

"Yes, just one." Shirleen hesitated, not sure if she should ask.

Reading her mind, he replied, "It's Joseph." When Shirleen blinked in surprise, he replied, "My name is Joseph."

"Oh," replied Shirleen. "How did you know that was my question?"

"Because I can read your mind."

"Thank you for telling me. I've wondered every time we've talked."

When the log shifted in the fireplace Shirleen jumped and turned to look at the fire. When she turned back, Joseph was gone. Shirleen went back to staring into the fire while she digested the information. Sighing, she got up to go call Tim so he could contact Josiah.

She apologized for waking him, then she told him everything the angel had said. She was surprised that he had little trouble believing where the information came from. After she'd told him everything, she encouraged him to make the call immediately.

Before they ended the call, Tim said, "Let me tell you something before you go. We've been tracking a serial killer for weeks. He's continued his murderous trek all over the area. Every time we thought we were close, he got away.

"One night, Josiah and I decided we needed the help of the Lord on our side so we could apprehend this monster, so we had a prayer. Afterward, we separated to see if we could find any tracks. There weren't any signs the way I had gone, but Josiah hadn't gone far when an angel visited him. He told Josiah how far away the killer was and that he was backtracking. He even told Josiah how to apprehend him.

"Just as the angel said he would do, the man came back around to where we'd been camped. Josiah did as the angel said and the man was apprehended without incident. That has happened to him on several occasions.

"I even saw once after I arrested a particularly nasty gentleman who vowed to kill me when he got out of prison. I was out on patrol, and an angel appeared to warn me that this man was tracking me. He told me to make camp as I'd planned, then slip out of sight. I did as I was told, and when the guy came into my camp, he sat down to eat my food. I came out of my hiding place and arrested him without incident.

"That's why I'd never make fun you saying you'd seen an angel."

"Oh, that makes me feel better."

"Good. I'll let you go so that I can call Josiah."

Tim immediately called Josiah, then called Shirleen back to let her know how it went. "When I related what you had told me, Jones went into Spielberg's office," Tim told Shirleen. "Sure enough, there was a secret door and the room it belonged to was chocked full of weapons, jewelry, legal papers, and more. They were so happy you told them about the door and promised to do exactly as you told them to do. Josiah said he would call me from his cell phone as soon as they're out of Syracuse."

"Good! Keep me posted."

When the phone was back in the cradle, Shirleen turned to see Juliana waiting for an update. "Could you wake Meagan up while I go call Trudy and Jeff? That way I can update everyone all at the same time."

"Okay," replied Juliana resignedly.

A few minutes later everyone was gathered in the living room. Shirleen paced the floor trying to figure out how to break the news to them. Finally, she just went for it. "Juliana, you and Meagan know about the angel that came to tell me that we should come here to Cardston. Well, he's appeared to me twice now." Shirleen told them what happened both times.

When she'd finished, Trudy said, "That's how you knew that it was me in the parking lot?"

"Yes, he told me it was safe to help you because you were also running from Bruce."

"Henry is here in Cardston?" asked Juliana. It was plain for all to see that she was terrified.

"Yes, but he's had several strokes and doesn't remember much of his past."

"Oh," sighed Meagan. "Daddy's still alive, isn't he?"

"Yes, honey, he is," replied Shirleen gently. "He's still causing his brand of trouble all over New York. I know you miss your friends, but we still can't go home."

"I know, Grandma. I was just hoping that they'd arrested him."

"I don't know how long it will be, but rest assured Bruce Murdock will get his just desserts in the end. For now, we still must be on our guard. That doesn't mean that we can't help Henry's family with all of these children, as well as Henry."

"Let me digest all of this for a while," mumbled Juliana fearfully.

"I understand, honey. It's a lot to take in."

"I don't know if I believe in angels, Momma. I'm just now coming around to believing in God. Give me a little time to deal with angels appearing to you."

"I believe in angels," Jeff said. "When my wife died, I was inconsolable. One day, she came to tell me that she and our daughter were fine. She told me that I still had a life to live and I still had lots to do."

Juliana remained thoughtfully silent. Shirleen changed the subject by asking, "Jeff, do you think we could put up the tree today? Christmas will be here soon and we need to decorate."

"Sure, we can, " he grinned. "How about after breakfast?"

Shirleen laughed. "Just like a man to think of his stomach first."

"I'll have breakfast ready in a jiffy," Trudy said, heading toward the kitchen.

"You can skip lessons this morning," Juliana said, "if you promise to work hard this afternoon."

"I promise. I don't want to miss decorating the tree."

After breakfast, they set the tree up and decorated it, while Jeff strung lights around the outer edges of the roof and decorated the yard. After they finished, each went off to wrap Christmas presents so the others couldn't see.

After they were finished, Shirleen asked, "Jeff, do you think you could go with me to the neighbor's house so I can find out what they need?"

"Sure, I'd be happy to."

When Shirleen and Jeff left, Juliana and Meagan went to help Trudy bake cookies. For a while they were good about not snitching a cookie, but it was plain for all to see that Meagan was having a tough time refraining. Finally, she asked Trudy, "May I have a glass of milk and three of these yummy cookies?"

"Of course." Turning to Juliana, she asked, "You want a few too?"

"Definitely! They smell amazing."

After they finished their treats, the went back to the job of baking and had finished by the time Jeff and Shirleen got back. "The Brooks family isn't settled in yet. They're still packing up their old place, but they happened to be there today so we got to meet them," Shirleen said. "Their newborns are still at the hospital and won't be coming home for a while. I liked Melinda Brooks immediately, and Theodore seems nice and helpful. They said that once they get settled, they'll be hiring nurses, a housekeeper and a cook. I told them we'd help them move, if you're okay with that."

Juliana inquired, "What about Henry?"

"He's doing well and is receiving physical therapy. They said he's doing well with the physical side of things, but his long-term memory is gone. Theodore, who is a therapist, works with him every day at the hospital and Melinda has been working with him so he can regain his speech. Will you help get them settled?"

Juliana was silent a moment. Finally, she replied, "Sure."

"I'll be glad to help where I can, too" Jeff said.

"Me too," agreed Meagan.

"I'm in, too," Trudy said.

"Thank you for being so generous with your time," grinned Shirleen, pleased with all of them.

After dinner, Tim called and told Shirleen that Josiah wanted to know what she wanted to do with the house she and Gordon owned in upstate New York.

"What does Josiah suggest?" she asked.

"Well, Josiah thought you might want it. If you don't, he said he can arrange to have it sold. Someone has already expressed an interest in buying it."

"How much did he offer?"

"Four million, cash on the barrel head. He also wants to buy the contents for an additional two million."

"Did you say he would pay *cash?*"

"Yes."

"Have the police gone through everything?"

"Yes. They found some more incriminating evidence in the office, and a secret room that contained the same things as the room at the mansion in Syracuse."

"I'm not surprised."

"They've collected all of your personal items and have shipped them to Josiah's address. They're just waiting to find out what you want to do about the property."

"Sell it. I'll never live in New York again. There's nothing for me there."

"I'll let him know."

"How long will it take to get settled?"

"I don't know. However, Josiah did sign the agreement; he anticipated you'd want to sell. It will probably take a while to get things finalized."

"Thank you for letting me know."

"Shirleen, Josiah said when this is all said and done, you'll be one wealthy lady."

"No," corrected Shirleen, "we'll be *three* wealthy ladies. Thanks for calling."

After ending the call, Shirleen told the others what she'd just learned. They continued to talk about the conversation with Tim for a while longer. Finally, while the rest of the family went to their separate beds, Jeff secured the house.

Chapter 22

Melinda Brooks stood transfixed as she watched the nurse pull the sheet over Katarina's grandfather's face. He hadn't been doing well when they saw him earlier, and he slipped quietly out of this world a few minutes later.

Looking over at his wife, Theodore slipped an arm across her shoulders and said, "Come on, sweetheart. We can't do anything more for him now."

She allowed her husband to lead her from the room and when they were outside she asked, "Can we go to the prenatal unit? Maybe seeing our babies will help to cheer me up a little."

"Sure. We can go see Effie and Ephraim, too."

They went to the maternity ward and as they neared the nursery window, a nurse came out of a room. "Are you looking for someone?" she asked.

"Yes. We're Melinda and Theodore Brooks. We'd like to see the Bowmen twins."

"Why?" asked the nurse.

"We're in the process of adopting them but we haven't seen them yet. We also want to see the Stout twins."

"Are you going to adopt them, too?" asked the nurse, gazing at them both as if they had suddenly lost their minds.

"Yes," Melinda said proudly.

"Come this way, please," the nurse said.

They followed the nurse to a room where the two infants lay sleeping. The little girl had curly dark brown hair and soft creamy cheeks. Her chin quivered in her sleep, and her tiny lips made a sucking motion.

The little boy was a carbon copy of his sister, except that his hair was a little less curly and he was a little more chubby.

Melinda's heart went out immediately to them. "Oh, Teddy, they're so sweet!"

Theodore agreed with her and said, "I can't believe I have the most beautiful wife in the world *and* five children!"

"I was just thinking the same thing. I can hardly believe that we'll be a family so fast, but it seems right somehow."

They followed the nurse out to the prenatal unit. "They're so tiny, Teddy."

"They're doing really well for being so premature," the nurse said.

"When can we take them home?"

"They're doing well, but are still having a little problem breathing. That will take a while to correct. I'll get Dr. Stillman so he can explain it more thoroughly."

After the nurse left, Melinda said, "I can hardly wait 'til these little ones are ours."

"I know."

The nurse returned shortly and said, "Dr. Stillman couldn't come right now, but he said it would be a great idea for you to bond with the babies. He'll talk to you more about the specifics later."

After leaving the twins, they went up to visit with Henry for a while. They told him about the children and how much they wanted to care for them. Henry couldn't respond by voice, but his eyes showed his approval of their decision. Kissing his cheek, Melinda told him, "I can't wait until we can bring you home."

Squeezing his hand, Theodore added, "Keep fighting so you can come home. We miss you."

Henry just listened as they encouraged him to keep fighting. He silently vowed to do just that.

After leaving Henry, they started to return to their room but were met by the Joel Cline, the lawyer. "Do you have a few minutes to spare?"

Theodore looked at Melinda who nodded. "Sure."

"Good." Smiling, he said, "Judge Smith wanted us to go to her room so she can hear our conversation. We were both surprised to learn you want to adopt both sets of twins."

"We've been to see the children and have fallen in love with them all."

"As big hearted as the two of you are, I don't doubt that one bit." They continued on to Judge Smith's room, and once they were inside with the door closed, they settled down to business. "Judge Smith, as you know, Mr. and Mrs. Brooks adopted Katarina Stokes last night. Now they want to adopt the two sets of twins that were orphaned as well."

Studying them critically, Judge Smith replied, "I must admit this is a surprise. You just got married last night, now you want to add to your family again?" She paused to study them closely. Shaking her head, she asked, "How do you think you can make this marriage work, when you're suddenly blessed with five babies?"

Looking at Theodore, who smiled and nodded, Melinda said, "We've been to see the little ones and we fell in love with all of them. We'll make it work. We're financially stable and will be able to hire all the help we need to make things run smoothly.

Suddenly the lawyer and judge both smiled. Joel said, "We just wanted to be sure you knew what you're getting yourselves into."

"We know exactly what we want," said Theodore. "We want to adopt those four other children."

"Okay," replied Cline. "Then be seated." Theodore looked at Melinda as they both found a seat and sat down. When they were comfortable, Cline continued, "I have here, in front of me, a new will that Mr. Stokes made out before his death. I of course haven't had time to get it filed with the court, but Candace, Judge Smith has consented under the circumstances to forgo this formality."

"Thank you, ma'am."

"Nonsense," she snapped. Smiling to take the edge off of her words. "We don't need to stand on formalities here, so please call me Candace. After our adventure last night, I feel like we're old friends." Getting more comfortable on the bed, she continued, "Now, go ahead, Joel."

Nodding, Joel began. "As I said, Mr. Stokes had me make out his last will and testament." Lifting the papers, he scanned them a moment. Finally he began to read the document, "I James Earl Stokes, on this day of our Lord November20, 2029, being of sound mind do hereby make out a new will and testament. Therefore, the old will is null and void as of now. Having lost all of my family in a terrible car pileup, I only have a granddaughter, who is under two years of age that survived. I witnessed the marriage of Theodore Brooks to Melinda Jacobs at my bedside tonight. After their marriage, this couple adopted my granddaughter, Katarina Joy Stokes. As far as I'm concerned, they have now become my son and daughter through the adoption of this little angel." Tears sprang into Melinda's eyes and spilled over. Cline gave her time to gain her composure and then continued, "Therefore, I James Stokes, do hereby leave my home on 483 W. Magnolia Drive to Theodore and Melinda Brooks. It has eight bedrooms and four bathrooms. I feel that it will be more than adequate to raise my granddaughter in.

I also want them to have all of the items that are inside, as well as the money that is in both my savings and personal account to go to them to help with my granddaughter, Katarina Joy Stokes Brooks. The car, which is parked in the parking lot of the hospital, goes to Melinda Brooks to do as she pleases. The key to this vehicle is in possession of Joel Cline, my lawyer.

There are one hundred and fifty acres of land that is nestled a mile from the house, of which I bequeath ten acres of it to my manager, Lance Ramey for the long years of service that he has given me. I would also like one milk cow, a dozen chickens, two beef cows and the horse that he loves to ride to go to him to start his own spread.

This rest of this land goes to Theodore and Melinda Brooks. It will help them if it is sold. However, it is their decision as to what they want to do with it. There's a huge barn, a large bunkhouse, as well as several out buildings to work this farm. There are twenty head of horses, thirty milk cows, three thousand head of beef cattle, as well as approximately one hundred laying chickens.

Lance Ramey, manages the farm, as well as supervises thirty hired hands. If he agrees you may keep him on. The hired men can make up their own minds on what they want to do. Lance would keep records of the men's activities and we'd meet together at the end of the day to go over any problems that may have arisen." Joel Cline paused to say, "I have called Lance Ramey to let him know what is happening. He said to tell you that he would be happy to work with you, if that is your desire."

"It most definitely is my desire," stated Theodore. "I don't have the foggiest idea of how to run a ranch. Perhaps he could take everything over, as well as what needs to be done, until I get settled in with my new family."

"I'll contact him as soon as I can and get back to you on this matter."

"Thank you. I'll leave everything in your capable hands."

"Okay. Let's get back to the rest of the will. Okay?" When the others nodded for him to continue, Joel began to read the rest of the will. "There are several pieces of machinery to run the place, for which you will need to oversee the repairs. Thank you with all of my heart for taking in my granddaughter. Also for accepting the terms of this will." As he folded the will, Joel added, he signed it as James Earl Stokes."

No one spoke for a moment. Finally, sighing deeply, Melinda stated, "This is an awful lot to take in all at once."

"I concur with Mel," admitted Theodore. "This will take some getting my head wrapped around. One thing is for sure, we now have a way to take care of those children."

"Well, think it over for a while and get back to me as soon as possible."

Melinda asked, "Will, you be here with Candace so that we can give you our decision?"

"Yes, I will, unless I go down to the cafeteria to have something to eat."

"Good, we'll get back to you just as soon as we can," replied Theodore.

"Okay, we'll be here."

Taking Melinda's hand they left the room. They walked in silence for sometime before either one of them spoke. Finally, Theodore pulled her over to a seat near the intensive care unit. When they were seated he began to speak. "Mel, there's so much information in the will of Mr. Stokes that we have to consider."

"You can sure say that again."

They discussed the pros and cons of the situation for some time. Seeing that there were more positive reasons for accepting the ranch and home, they decided to accept the gifts offered them. Having made a decision, they went back to Candace Smith's room and knocked on the door.

"Hello," answered Joel Cline as he opened the door. "Come on in and spill the beans."

When all were settled comfortably, they began to discuss the will. A moment later, Theodore replied, "We have decided to accept the conditions of the will as soon as possible. We'll also need to get settled as soon as we can so that we can bring the children home."

"We can get the adoptions taken care of today. Once we're freed from this awful storm we can record it in the courthouse. We'll also take care of the will."

"Wonderful!" Melinda turned to smile at Theodore, who squeezed her hand. "What do we do with the children while we get settled?"

Candace spoke up to say, "The newborns won't be released from the hospital very soon and the other children can be taken care of with the help of those in the community. Of course the state will pay the expenses. You will have enough to do to get moved in without having to deal with the children."

"Oh, thank you," sighed Melinda, "that would really be most helpful."

"You're welcome. Just concentrate on what you have to do and not worry about a thing."

"I will." It was plain to see the relief on Melinda's face.

Joel, shifting on the chair beside Candace, said, "Let me have a few minutes to get the paperwork ready for you to sign. That way we can get right to the adoption process."

"When do you want us to return," asked Theodore.

"Give me at least an hour."

"Okay, we'll be back in an hour," replied Theodore. Rising, Melinda squeezed Candace's hand and preceded Theodore out of the room.

They went back to the nursery to see the premature twins. They did all in their power to let the little ones know that they were loved. The nurse who had given them so much guff entered the room. This time, she was polite, even courteous. "Hello," she greeted. "I see that you are bonding with these precious little ones."

"Yes," replied Melinda. "They really are beautiful, aren't they? I can hardly wait until they have become ours."

"Is that a possibility," asked the nurse.

"Yes," replied Theodore. "It is going to happen very soon. In fact in an hour or so."

"That's really wonderful," replied the nurse.

"Thank you," replied Melinda. "We're really excited about it."

"I heard one of the nurses say that you also adopted a little girl that is also under two years old."

"That's correct," replied Theodore.

"She also said that you were going to adopt another set of twins. Isn't that taking on an awful lot?"

"Yes, but then we won't be doing it all by ourselves," replied Theodore. "We'll be hiring people to help us."

"Oh, that makes a great deal of difference. I wish you both the best of everything. There aren't a lot of people who would do what you are doing. They wouldn't do it even if someone were to pay them enough."

"Well," replied Melinda, "in this case we're doing it for the love of it. We love those children very much!"

"I can tell that by the way you are with these little tykes." She paused a moment then added, "I don't mean to be a wet blanket, but we need to take the vitals on these two and see to their physical needs. You are welcome to come back later though."

"Thank you," replied Theodore. "We will."

Leaving the nursery, they went to visit the other twins who were crying when they entered their rooms. Melinda, whose heart ached for them, went over to pick up the little boy. "Come here, Little Man." Cuddling him close, she gently kissed his cheek. Sinking into a chair, she began to check him over. "Wow, sweetheart, you're soaked up to your armpits. I'd be fussing too if I were in this mess." Putting him back into the crib, she went in search of help. Finding a nurse approaching them, she called to her, "Excuse me nurse, but are you the nurse on duty here."

"I am."

"Couldn't you hear these children crying?"

"Yes, but I was with another patient who was in worse need than these two were."

"The only way that patient could be worse was if it was on its deathbed."

Bristling, the nurse calmly replied, "It was! I just lost her to the results of that mass pile up."

"I'm sorry, I had no call to snap at you. I'm just concerned about these children."

"I know. We all are. Then to top everything off, we're so exhausted that we can hardly function. I want to help you, but there are two other patients that aren't doing well."

"Perhaps my husband, who is a nurse, may be of service to you. Let me ask him."

"Thank you. We're so shorthanded, that any help will do."

Melinda slipped back into the room, where Theodore Brooks was trying to deal with both children. "The nurse outside is strapped for help, because they're so shorthanded. She said that she just lost one patient and there are two patients who aren't doing very well. I told her that I would speak to you about helping. I know that you are so exhausted so it is your choice on what you want to do."

"Let me speak to her and I'll decide, replied Theodore. Theodore walked out to speak to the nurse, who's name was Robin Weaver. She quickly filled Theodore in on the situation. "Let me tell, Melinda what is up then I'll go with you to help." He started to go into the room then paused to ask, "Where can we get the items needed to help care for these two little ones in here?"

"Let me quickly show you." Going inside she quickly showed Melinda where to find everything. While Melinda set to work taking care of the baby's needs, Theodore went to help where needed. Melinda took care of the little boy who was in much worse condition than his sister. While she worked, she talked to him in a calm and soothing voice. "Well, Little Man, you really did a good one this time. I'd be screaming my head off too if I were as messy as you are."

When she had the little fellow cleaned up and redressed she cleaned up the mess and washed her hands. She changed the little girl after which, she also cleaned up her mess. She had just washed her hands and was coming back into the room when a nurse entered to see what was going on. She had two bottles in her hands. Giving Melinda a bottle she picked up the little girl. "I'll feed her if you will feed the little boy," said the nurse.

Smiling gratefully, as she took the bottle, Melinda picked up Ephraim. "Thank you for the help, ma'am."

Smiling, the nurse picked up little Effie. When they were both settled, they began to feed the hungry children, stopping every so often to burp them. As they fed the children, the two women talked about the events of the night before. They were just putting the children back into their clean beds, when Theodore Brooks entered the room. "Are you about ready to meet with Joel and Candace?"

"Yes," replied Melinda. "Just as soon as I tuck Ephraim in."

"Good, we'll have to hurry to get there in time. We don't want him to think that we have changed our minds."

Straightening, Melinda turned to address the nurse. "Thank you for all of your help. I was getting pretty desperate when you came to my rescue."

"My pleasure, Mrs. Brooks."

Once outside of the children's room, Theodore took Melinda's hand and they hurried toward the elevator. As they entered Judge Smith's room Joel got to his feet to greet them. "I was about to give up on the two of you."

"Melinda took care of the Stout twins," responded Theodore, "while I was asked to help with an emergency in the nursery. There were two little girls who weren't doing very well. It was nip and tuck for awhile, but they're both going to be just fine."

"That's great," exclaimed Candace Smith. "There have been enough tragedies around here to last everyone a life time."

"Well," declared Cline in an attempt to change the subject, "let's get to it."

After the forms had been signed, Candace Smith took care of the adoptions. "I'll keep these documents and get them filed with the court," replied Judge Smith. "I'll let you know when to come in to get them.

"Thank you," Melinda said through her tears.

"No," responded Smith. "It is the two of us who are grateful. You have prevented five children from being forced into adoption. This is one case that I won't soon forget."

By the time the Theodore left Judge Smith's room they were now the proud parents of five infants under the age of two. By now, poor Theodore was so exhausted that it was all that he could do to function coherently. Melinda grew greatly concerned when she saw how drawn his features were. Glancing up at the clock over the nurse's station, Melinda turned to ask. "Teddy, What do you think about getting something to eat before we go back to our room for some much needed sleep?"

"I'd say, lead on!"

Smiling, Melinda linked her arm through Theodore as she replied, "Let's just walk side by side. I'd like that much better."

Covering her hand with his free hand, he chuckled lightly, "I'd like that too."

An hour later, they were back in their room. A nurse had taken Katarina back to the nursery so that the Theodore could rest without the baby waking them up. Emerging from the bathroom, Theodore staggered toward the bed, where he plopped down. "I'm so exhausted, Mel that I feel as if I haven't slept in over a month."

"You have only been awake thirty-two hours," teased Melinda. "I don't see why you couldn't go at least another eight hours. That way you will only have been awake for forty-eight hours."

"Oh, have mercy, you slave driver!" Reaching out to take Melinda into his arms, Theodore muttered into her hair. "You've had it now, lady mine!"

"Promises, promises, promises," giggled Melinda. As Theodore's lips found hers, all else was forgotten as they sought to pleasure the other. Sometime later, sleep claimed them both.

Theodore woke up at nine o'clock the next morning. Melinda was sitting near the window, watching the snow swirling outside. "Good morning, beautiful. Did, you sleep well?"

"Like a log," grinned Melinda.

"How long have you been up?" Theodore asked.

"About an hour. I've been watching the snow falling and thinking about how fast we got engaged then found ourselves with a family."

Rising, Theodore went to take Melinda's hand. Gently pulling her to her feet, he wrapped his arms around her then kissed her passionately. Drawing back, he gazed down into her love filled eyes. "I know this all happened quick, but I'm not sorry about any of it. I know what we've decided to do won't be easy, but I'm sure it'll be worth it."

"I don't have any doubts about that, it's just a little overwhelming. Sometimes, I'm so scared and other times everything feels so right." Sighing, she leaned her head on his shoulder as she continued, "The biggest question I ask myself is can I do it? I love those children, Teddy, but we didn't even get a chance to enjoy our engagement before we were married with children. What if you get tired of this whole situation and head for the hills?"

Theodore hugged her close, then spoke with conviction. "Melinda Brooks, I promise you right here and now there will never be a chance of that happening. You're stuck with me forever." When Melinda looked into her husband's eyes, she knew it was going to be all right. "Besides," he continued, "I love those little ones with all my heart. I know that sounds strange, but from the moment I first held them I felt something stir in my heart."

"I know," sighed Melinda. "I felt it, too."

A teasing light came into his eyes. "I learned something wonderful about you, darling, when I was visited by the mothers of our children."

Melinda looked at him suspiciously for a moment and asked, "What was that?"

"You love children. So much that you went to school to become a kindergarten teacher."

"That's true," grinned Melinda, greatly relieved. "I was afraid you'd learned my deepest, darkest secret."

"Oh?" Theodore pretended to be scared. "Is there something terrible in your past I should know about?"

"Well ... I've got two other husbands."

Seeing she was teasing him, Theodore's heart swelled with love. Scooping her up in his arms, he carried her to the bed, where he laid her down and began covering her face in kisses. He claimed her lips with a kiss that sent fire coursing through her. Raising his head, he looked at her sternly and said, "Well, Melinda Jacobs Brooks, if you've stashed those extra husbands somewhere, they'll just have to wait. You're mine now and I won't share you with anyone! Before she could reply, he kissed her again.

They gave in to their passion, and quite a while later, they fell asleep in each other's arms. An hour later the sound of someone tapping lightly on the door woke them.

When Theodore answered the door, Dr. Stillman stood on the other side, looking sheepish. "Good morning, Theodore. I thought I'd better check on you. You've been in here a long time."

"No, we woke up a while ago and talked. We ended up going back to sleep. Sorry."

"Yeah, I bet you were just talking."

"That's my story and I'm sticking to it," grinned Theodore.

"If you two can manage to get out of bed and get dressed, I'll meet you in the cafeteria so we can talk about how your little brood's doing."

"We'll be right there," called Melinda.

A few minutes later, the three of them were seated in the cafeteria. "I see the snow's still coming down," Melinda noted. "Sure hope it stops soon."

"The weather report said we were in for heavier snow by tonight," reported Dr. Stillman. "I think they said that there would be another six to ten inches by tomorrow."

"Oh," groaned Melinda. "I'm tired of snow."

"Even if it stops snowing, we'll have to wait for the plows to dig us out. That will take some time."

"I remember the first bad storm after we arrived," Melinda said and shuttered, as the memory overwhelmed her."

"When did you get here?" Stillman asked.

"Near the end of October," said Theodore. "We were stuck in a motel across town for several days."

"That must have been difficult, with Henry so ill."

"He slept a lot, which helped."

"Even going from room to room was difficult," said Melinda. "The snow was falling so hard we could hardly see in front of us."

"That must've been boring." Dr. Stillman said.

"Not really. While Henry slept, we talked and got to know each other or we played game or read books."

"At least being stuck here has a lot more advantages than being in a small motel room," Dr. Stillman said.

"There hasn't been a dull moment for these past few days, that's for sure," Theodore said in agreement. "I must admit that it would be nice to have a little of that monotony."

"I tend to agree with Teddy," sighed Melinda.

"We don't have too many of these bad nights, but when we do they're real dillies." Having finished his meal, Dr. Stillman abruptly changed the subject. "Now, let's get down to business. Katarina is doing really well, as are the Stout twins. This morning, the Bowman's boy had trouble breathing but he's more stable than he was. I have a nurse with him now.

"The little girl was jaundiced, so we're working on that. She'll be all right in a few days. I'm worried about the boy though. We had trouble getting him to breathe when he was born. I think his lungs just need to develop more. Only time will tell. Until they're out of danger, continue to do as the nurse suggests. If you do that, things should be all right."

"We'll follow instructions to the letter," promised Melinda. "We want them healthy so we can take them home and spoil them rotten."

"You can go see them as often as you'd like, just don't get yourself spread so thin between the five children that you get run down."

Theodore spoke up to say, "We'll make sure we don't overdo. It's important to keep our health up so we can take care of them properly."

"How's Henry doing this morning?" Melinda asked.

Dr. Stillman smiled and replied, "Henry is coming along nicely. In fact, he's trying to talk, though he hasn't been too successful so far. As I'm examining him, he tries so hard to speak to me."

"That's a good sign, isn't it?" asked Melinda.

"Yes, it is," replied Dr. Stillman. "Keep talking to him and encouraging him and he'll continue to improve. I think he's trying so hard because he knows you want him to get better. I have rounds, so I'll leave the two of you to do what you need to do."

After Dr. Stillman left, Melinda and Theodore began to discuss James Stokes' will. "Teddy, I can hardly believe how our lives have changed so drastically.

"I've been thinking about that too," confessed Theodore.

"I'm having trouble coming to grips with realizing he willed us his huge ranch."

"I know," Theodore said. "Our lives are like the snow storm outside, a whirlwind of change"

"If someone had told me this was going to happen to me, I wouldn't have believed them."

"Me either."

"The most mind boggling of all is that this has happened within 48 hours. To think, I was feeling overwhelmed with getting our apartment organized, worrying about Henry and hoping you'd notice me."

Sighing, she continued, "Somehow, that all seems so distant and trivial now. Don't get me wrong, I'm happy, it's just that everything happened so fast."

Suddenly, Melinda began to cry. Looking confused, she said, "I feel so strange. I'm overwhelmed and I'm so cold."

Theodore slipped an arm around her and led her out of the cafeteria. They hadn't gone far when Melinda collapsed. Scooping her up his arms, he rushed her to the emergency room.

Dr. Stillman saw them and helped get Melinda to a chair so he could examine her. As he looked her over, Melinda began to come around. She opened her eyes and tried to stand, but Dr. Stillman said, "Stay still a moment, Melinda. I want to make sure you're all right."

"What happened?" she asked.

"You fainted on me as we came out of the cafeteria."

"You're mentally exhausted, Melinda," Dr. Stillman said. "Both of you need to get some more sleep. I'm going to prescribe a sleeping pill so your sleep will be undisturbed."

"Is that really necessary, Dr. Stillman?"

"Yes, it is. With everything you've gone through in the past two days, your mind and body both need rest. I want you both to get some more sleep. That's an order."

"We'll do that right now," replied Theodore. "Thank you, Dr. Stillman."

Chapter 23

Josiah put down his cell phone and turned to Gregory Jones. "That was Sgt. York from Cardston. We need to call Judge Harris and tell him Leonard Mandello's connected to Murdock.

"We'll leave here precisely at 2 a.m. I'll take you as far as Cleveland, then you can fly out to join your family in Billings. Get things in order at your office and take two officers you trust with you for protection. Be sure to take only your personal affects with you when you leave."

Jones, thought for a moment, then asked, "Why don't you go with us? The four of us could get things done faster."

"Okay, that makes sense."

Jones started to leave, but Josiah stopped him. "Wait, there's more. There's a hidden door in the wall behind Gordon's desk. The room it leads to contains some information that will help crack the case wide open. There should also be some jewelry, guns, and other surprises in there, too."

"Why is it so important to leave at precisely 2 a.m.?" asked Jones.

"If we do as we're told, we'll get out of here safely. If we leave five minutes before or after, we won't get out here alive."

"How do you know this?"

"You've had hunches, right? Well, this is a hunch and I trust it."

"Then I won't question you." He picked up his hat and valise and leaned out the door. "Fred Holmes and Frank Kessler, could you come in here?"

Two buff men entered the room and waited to see what Jones wanted. "I need the two of you to act as my body guards for a while. I'm going to my office to get my things and to speak to Judge Harris."

"Sure thing," said Kessler.

"We'll take the Bentley, since it's faster," Jones said. "They won't recognize us in that car. It hasn't been out for a while.."

"Great idea," said Holmes.

They went to the garage and got into the silver Bentley. Holmes was the designated driver. Soon they were speeding toward Jones' office complex.

As they drove, Josiah had the chance to study Jones more closely. He was solidly built and neatly dressed. The only flaw in his features was a slightly hooked nose, which made him look like a bird of prey.

When they arrived at the office, the four men went inside. Jones's secretary watched them as they approached the reception desk. Josiah was amazed by how beautiful she was. Her honey colored hair was done up in a simple style, which enhanced her delicate features, and her light blue eyes reminded him of a crisp azure sky. *What a knockout,* thought Josiah.

As they reached the secretary, she asked, "Is there anything you need me to do, sir?"

"Yes, Carol," he replied. "You and Fred go to the basement and bring up as many boxes as you can. I'm going to pack up my personal items."

Carol could only stare at Jones in disbelief as she asked, "Are you leaving?"

"I am. When I've got everything packed, I want you to call in the staff for a quick meeting."

"Yes, sir."

"Don't say anything to anyone until I've finished in my office."

"I won't say a thing," she said as she turn to go to the basement with Fred Holmes following her.

When they returned with several boxes, Josiah and Frank helped Jones gather his things. They had the boxes filled by the time Carol and Fred returned with more. With all of them working, it didn't take them long to get done.

When they were finished, Jones asked the janitor to bring two dollies so they could pile the boxes on to them and roll them out the car. Holmes, Kessler and Graham took everything out and put it in the Bentley.

When they returned, Jones was writing out several checks. The three men moved to the back of the room and kept watch. A few minutes later, people began filing in.

When he was done writing checks, Jones looked up and scanned the faces of his employees. "What I have to say will surprise you, but must be said. I'm leaving the firm as of today and I'm closing down the office. Carol will oversee getting everything packed up and put into storage. I'm sorry to do this to you, but my life is in danger. I've slowly been sending my clients to other trusted attorneys, so there shouldn't be a problem with that."

Turning to Carol he said, "Carol, don't come to the office unescorted. Fred, will you and Frank see that she's protected at all times until the office is officially closed?"

The men looked at each other then back to Jones. "We will," promised Frank.

'Good. Carol, when you've finished here, I want you and your family to leave town if you can."

"Why?" Carol said in surprise.

"Because the people who are after me may try to hunt you down and interrogate you to get to me. He's a violent man and will think nothing of killing you and your family to get what he wants. I want you to be safe."

"But we have family here," protested Carol.

"Then I suggest you tell them of what's happening and ask them to leave too."

"Okay, I guess."

"Be ready to leave as soon as you've taken care of the office."

"Okay, I'll tell my husband what's going on. I'll leave the decision to leave up to him."

"Please tell him how serious the situation is." Carol could only nod in the affirmative. Jones turned to the other employees. "I feel bad about this, but there's no other way. I have to leave."

One man asked the question on everyone's mind. "What about your family?"

"I've already moved them and they're safe."

"That's good," replied the man. "We understand the gravity of the situation. We'll get by somehow. Take good care of yourself."

"Thank you, Walt." Picking up the checks, Jones continued, "I've written checks for severance pay for all of you. When I call your name, come get your check." When all of the checks had been handed out, Jones ended the meeting.

The room slowly emptied until only Carol, and those who had come with Jones remained. Adding some papers to his valise, Jones stood to leave. "Take good care of yourself, Carol. You've been an exceptional secretary."

"Thank you, sir. You take care of yourself and be safe."

Nodding, Jones left the offices for the last time. When they were back in the car, they headed for Jones's home. When they got there, Jones went to the basement and grabbed his luggage. He packed his things while the men cleaned out the refrigerator and took out the trash. It didn't take Jones long to gather everything.

Looking at the men, Jones asked, "Do you think we could stop at the bank? I need to close out my account. I'm going to wire most of the money to my wife's account. That way I won't be carrying a lot of cash with me."

"That's a good idea," Josiah said.

After Fred and Frank checked to see that they weren't being watched, the men left for the bank. It didn't take long to take care of the transactions there so they were soon on their way to the courthouse to speak to Judge Harris.

The Judge's secretary announced them and showed them into the judge's chambers. Judge Harris greeted them and Josiah noted his white hair and penetrating hazel eyes.

The men introduced themselves and got down to business. "As you know, I've come from Cardston to settle Gordon Spielberg's estate. He was my brother," Josiah said.

"I'm sorry for your great loss, Josiah," the Judge said. "Nasty business with your brother and his family."

"Yes, it was."

Just then, the secretary rushed into the room, her eyes large with fright. Harris asked, "What's wrong, Millicent?"

"Sir, your wife called to say that your son, Jeffrey, saw a man doing something to your wife's car. Wendy said she watched from a window after Jeffrey told her what he'd seen. She said he was acting nervous and he put something under the hood—"

"A bomb!" Josiah turned to see who had spoken. Frank Kessler was leaning forward in his chair.

Judge Harris was visibly shaken. "I was afraid of this!" he exclaimed. "I took Bruce Murdock to task about three days ago for trying to do something dirty in a court case. He was furious. Something warned me he would try to get even." Pausing a moment, he continued, "I guess I was right."

"How do you know it was Murdock?" Jones asked.

"Because I've been suspicious of him for a while. It always seemed odd that he was able to get most of his obviously guilty clients off so easily."

"That's the reason I've come to speak to you," Jones said. "Since I was assigned the task of getting Gordon Spielberg's estate taken care of, I've had several run-ins with Bruce Murdock."

Leaning forward in his chair, Harris asked, "What kind of run-ins?"

"When he wanted to take some of Gordon's things from the house, I told him he had to wait until the estate was settled. He stormed out of my office yelling, 'You shouldn't mess with me, Gregory Jones!' I didn't think much about it until we started having little skirmishes.

"At one point I heard a man say, 'Bruce Murdock isn't going to be happy with this situation.' Then, they saw me and it was only by the grace of God that Fred Holmes rescued me." Jones went on to tell about the attempted raids on the estate, and he finished by telling Harris that he'd sent his family away and was leaving town with Josiah. When he finished, a deep silence filled the room.

Harris paced the room, then stopped to stare at Josiah. "Mr. Graham, would you mind taking my family with you when you leave?"

"I don't mind but you'll have to be ready to go by 2 a.m."

"We'll just pack up what we absolutely need and leave the rest behind. I'll call and give my notice effective immediately. After that, I'll call my wife and get her packing while I go to the bank and close out our accounts.

Going to the phone, he dialed his boss, and promptly resigned. With the help of his secretary and Josiah's crew he packed his personal items and prepared to leave. They were just taking everything to the car, when the phone rang.

The secretary answered, listened a moment then handed the phone to Judge Harris. He listened to the person on the other end, then said, "Good. Thank you for taking care of things so promptly. Are my wife and children all right?" Again he listened and responded. "Is Wendy where I can talk to her?" A moment later those in the room heard him say, "Hello, my dear. Are you sure you're all right? Good. I've resigned, effective immediately. I'm going to the bank to close the accounts.

"Meanwhile you should pack up what we'll need until we get settled somewhere. Throw sheets over the furniture, make some food to take with us. As soon as I've finished at the bank, I'll come straight home.

"Do not go anywhere. Just pack as fast as you can. I'll take care of the stuff in my den. See you in a bit."

He placed the phone back onto the cradle; turning to addressed everyone in the room. "Millicent, I'll have your severance pay mailed to you before I leave town today. If anyone asks why you can't reach me, tell them I'm ill and can't be disturbed."

"Yes, sir." Taking a deep breath, she added, "Please be safe, sir."

"Thank you, we will."

Kessler and Holmes went with the Judge when he went to the bank. When he'd finished, they saw him back to his car. He agreed to meet them at the exit to the freeway at 2:15 a.m. the next morning.

As Josiah and his crew neared the Spielberg's house they saw a car driving slowly past. Jones pulled over and called the house. A woman officer answered the call and Jones said, "We're only a block away. Open the gate."

"I'll do it right now," she replied.

They pulled back onto the street and got to the gate just as it began to open. Relieved to have arrived safely, they all began to relax.

Josiah and Jones went straight to the office. There was a huge floor to ceiling bookcase that ran the full length of the wall. On a hunch, Josiah tried to move a section, but nothing happened. Jones did the same at the other end. Finally they looked at the middle section and Josiah saw a strange devise on one of the shelves. He touched it several times and there was a clicking noise. Soon after, the section of wall moved inward.

Josiah felt along the wall in the room and his hand touched a light switch. Flipping it on, he was amazed to see a huge room.

As Jones stepped inside, he whistled softly. "I've never seen anything like it."

"Neither have I," muttered Josiah in awe.

They each took a side and explored the room. What they saw filled them with terror. There were enough weapons and corresponding ammunition to launch a full-scale war. There were also cases filled with all kinds of jewels and several filing cabinets filled with documents. They didn't look at anything closely yet, and continued toward the back of the room. There, they saw an entryway to another room. "I'll be right back," said Jones. "I think we need some help. I'll go get Holmes and Kessler."

"I think that's a good idea," admitted Josiah. "I don't have a good feeling about this."

"I don't either," sighed Jones.

After Jones left, Josiah continued exploring. He was going through one of the files when Jones and the other two joined him. "What in the world did your brother want with all these guns?" Holmes asked.

"I don't know," sighed Josiah. "When our father tried to get me to join the organization, he was fighting with another cartel that was trying to take over in the city. Maybe this is part of the arsenal he used. I wanted nothing to do with any part of that, so I didn't pay attention to details."

Reaching into the entryway, Jones felt for another light switch and flipped it on. There was a long tunnel, and they couldn't see where it ended. "What we need to do first," said Jones, "is explore this tunnel. We need to know where it leads."

"I'll go first," Holmes said, and took off.

As Kessler stepped back a step, he replied, "I'll take the rear."

Josiah followed Holmes into the tunnel, and they walked for a long time before they came to a door. Holmes listened to see if he could hear anything on the other side, and then cautiously opened the door. It was pitch black on the other side, so he took out his lighter and lit it.

It looked like an empty room, but there was a ladder on the left. Holmes went over and began to climb. At the top, he called for Kessler to hold the lighter higher. When he did, Holmes began feeling around until he felt a handle. He pushed on it and it opened. He climbed another step and saw an alley that led to the street. He decided this had been Gordon's escape route.

Pushing the cover to the side, he climbed out of the hole. Walking cautiously toward the street, he felt the hairs along his neck stand on end. Once he reached the street, he looked for a street sign, then went back and climbed down into the tunnel.

Turning to the anxious men, he said, "It was his escape route. This opens into an alley near the corner of Glover and Main."

Jones wrote the information down on a scrap of paper and put it in his shirt pocket. "Let's get back to that secret room and get busy. What we need to do is get all of this stuff cataloged so we can let the chief of police know what's in here. Frank, you take care of the wall to the right, and Fred you take the wall on this side of the office. Josiah and I will work on the wall to the left."

Josiah attacked a filing cabinet near the entryway, and wrote down the names on each of the files in drawers. When he was finished with that, he began to catalog the weapons. Between the four of them, they had the job done quickly.

Suddenly, Holmes whistled softly. "I think you should all take a look at what I have just found." He handed a book to Jones, who took it over to where Josiah was standing so they could both examine the contents.

When they opened the book, Jones blinked in surprise. Groaning, Josiah exclaimed, "This is a list of all the jobs these men did. Are there any other books like this one?"

Holmes went back, searched in the same place and pulled out another book similar to the first one. Handing the book to Josiah, he went back to searching. Eventually he pulled out several more books, and with each one they grew more excited by what was revealed.

"Some of these date back to when your father was running things," Jones said. "These entries have names of everyone involved and each job they did."

"I'm so glad that I got away from here," Josiah said in disgust. "Seeing these books fills me with more repulsion than I can express."

"I don't know about the rest of you," said Jones quickly changing the subject, "but I'm starved. We'll finish up after we get something to eat. By that time, the U-hauls should be here."

When lunch was over, the four men went back to finish cataloging the contents of the secret room. When they were finished, Jones put the books in a huge bag then labeled it and got out his laptop and typed out a complete list of what they'd found. He also made a diagram of the tunnel and instructions for how to open the room's door. After putting both documents into a manila envelope, along with the extra set of keys, he sealed it and said, "I'll leave this envelope at a drop point once we're safely out of town."

A few minutes later, the phone rang, signaling the two U-hauls were at the gate. Once they were inside, the four men began to load them while the rest of the officers continued to patrol the grounds.

Once the items from the secret room were taken care of, they started loading the furniture. They finished everything with a few minutes to spare and made one last sweep of the house to make sure they hadn't forgotten anything. That done, they left the grounds and locked the gates so no one would know they'd been there until they went inside the house.

Five minutes after they pulled out, several cars came up to the gate. Men got out carrying machine guns, and one of them climbed over the wall to investigate. It wasn't long before he returned looking perplexed. He went up to Bruce and said, "They're gone! No one's there, boss."

Cursing, Bruce began to pace. "Who was the man on watch?"

"Joseph Haroldsen," came the reply.

"Where is he now?"

"Over there near the gate."

Bruce went to speak to Haroldsen and demanded, "Why didn't alert us, Joe?"

"Three police cars came roaring down the street after some teenagers who'd just robbed the house two doors down. I thought it best to get out of here 'til the police left."

"How long did that take?"

"Fifteen or twenty minutes. I got back about a minute before you got here."

Bruce began to pace in frustration. Suddenly, whirling around, he shot Haroldsen in the heart, then walked away without looking back. "Take care of the body," he ordered. Two men came forward and carried the body to the car and put it in the trunk. "No use waiting around here. What we need to do is find out where they went. Marks, you and Reed dump Haroldsen's body someplace outside town where it won't be found for a few days." After that, they all got back into their cars to go search for the route that Josiah's group had taken.

Meanwhile, the police were escorting Josiah's vehicle and the two U-hauls to the Cleveland exit. When they got there, Judge Harris was waiting for them. Josiah was surprised they were in two cars, but quickly realized it would take two cars to haul all they had to take with them.

The five men stepped out of the vehicles to talk. Josiah started to speak first, "The driver and I have been discussing our feelings and it turns out that neither one of us feels safe stopping here for long."

Jones, looking at the driver of the truck that he was riding in, said, "We feel the same way. If Bruce and his men tried something after we left, they'll know we're gone. We need to get back on the road right now. When we get to Erie we can find a place to stop so we can figure out what we're going to do."

Judge Harris listened intently, then said, "My wife has been feeling nervous since we arrived. I learned to pay attention to her intuition a long time ago."

"I'm glad we all agree," Josiah said. "I think the judge's family should be positioned between the two U-hauls. That way we can keep track of them and form a caravan of sorts."

"That's an excellent idea," grinned Jones.

"As soon as we're loaded we'd better be on our way," responded Josiah. "We have a long way to go."

Josiah's vehicle drove out first, followed by the judge's two vehicles. Not long after that Jones moved followed. Once they were on the freeway, they pushed it hard. Fear rode in the hearts of everyone involved.

They hadn't been gone long when Bruce and his men arrived. When he saw no one was there, Bruce began cursing. He got out of the limo to pace and think. There were still two other options he could try. *I'll go to the next exit,* he told himself.

"Get out of the car!" he bellowed angrily. "Every last one of you — out!" They all knew not to cross him when he was angry, so they got out quickly. They went to stand near him beside the limo and waited for his orders. As soon as he issued them, they quickly complied.

Several hours later, Josiah's small caravan pulled up to an all night truck stop in Erie, Pennsylvania. Once they were all seated inside, they ordered breakfast. While they waited for the drinks, introductions were made. The man sitting near the outside of the table started first. "My name's Harvey Metcalf, and I'll be helping Josiah Graham, who's sitting beside me, drive the lead truck."

"My name's William Barnes, but I go by Bill," the next man said. "I'll be driving the second U-Haul along with Mr. Jones."

"This is my wife, Wendy," Judge Harris said, "and I'm Judge Eugene Bernard Harris. My friends call me Gene." Placing a hand on the young man next to him he continued, "This is my oldest son, Michael; his wife, Judith; and their three year old son, Timothy; and two month old daughter, Gwendolyn. Next to him is my sixteen-year old son, Jeffrey; my fifteen-year old daughter, Ruth; my daughter, Candace, who will turn thirteen in two weeks; and my daughter, Pauline, who just turned eleven."

Turning to Pauline, Josiah asked, "May I call you Polly? I had an Aunt Pauline and we always called her Aunt Polly."

"I guess that would be all right." She didn't seem thrilled about the new nickname.

"Good, then Polly it is."

Just then the waitress brought them their meals. When she left Josiah asked, "Judge Harris, have you and your family decided where you want to go?"

"Yes. We think it's best to go to Coeur d' Alene, Idaho. My wife has family there, so we could start over with their help, and possibly commute to Spokane."

"Then you plan to go with us?"

"If that's all right with you."

"That's more than all right with me."

"Good then it's settled."

While they ate, Josiah listened as the others talked. He was impressed by Harvey Metcalf's appearance. He had the brownest eyes Josiah had ever seen; yet they twinkled merrily as he laughed. Black, curly hair and a heavy beard complimented his dark features. He wore a black and red plaid shirt with blue jeans, which made his huge frame look buff.

Turning to look at William, he smiled to himself when he saw that William was the exact opposite of Metcalf. He was short, thin, as well as wiry. His hair was medium brown, which seemed out of place on his dark features. It was obvious that he needed a shave, but then most of the men did. His eyes were a crisp, light blue that seemed to see right through a person that he was looking at.

Looking over at Judge Harris, Josiah wondered how he could look so calm at a time like this. He was reminded of a snowshoe rabbit when he looked at Harris' thick, wavy white hair, with a lock of it falling across his forehead. He noticed that Harris' wife, Wendy, was a stunning blond with light blue eyes and porcelain skin.

Josiah was drawn back to the conversation when Jones asked, "What do you think we should do, Josiah?"

"I've been thinking things over and I think we should change drivers after we drop you off at the Cleveland Airport. We can drive until lunchtime, then stop and eat. We'll change drivers there and keep driving until dinnertime. After that, we can find an out of the way motel for the night. What do you think?"

"That's a great plan," declared Judge Harris. After they ate, they headed out to set the plan in motion. As they came out of the diner, they were surprised to see that it had started to snow.

When they got to the airport in Cleveland, they went inside to wait for Gregory Jones to get his one-way ticket and check his luggage. When he was finished, they went to wait for his plane to leave.

◀ • ▶

Bruce drove to the next exit, becoming more and more angry when they didn't find them. As they started to pull out, they heard sirens and it started to snow. He sent two different cars to the other exits, with the same results — nothing.

As he sat there in the limo, Bruce thought back to the night he discovered his wife and mother-in-law had taken his daughter and made a run for it. It was hard enough for him to deal with that situation, but to have Josiah and his group flat out disappear made him furious. Killing Joseph Haroldsen hadn't given him enough satisfaction. He wanted someone else to die, so he decided the next person to botch a job would lose his life.

When the drivers of the two cars reported there was still no sign of them, he made up his mind to take out his anger on one of them. He told them he'd be joining them, then sent the others back to his house, then told his driver to go to the exit where he'd sent Gary Trout.

Soon they were on their way. When Bruce saw Trout waiting beside his car, smoking a cigarette, he took out his gun and attached the silencer. As the limo pulled up beside him, Bruce got out and walked calmly over to Trout and shot him between the eyes. When Trout hit the ground, Bruce pumped five more rounds into his body. Trout never knew what had happened.

Bruce got back into the limo and instructed the driver to go to Bloom's location. When they got there, Bloom suffered the same fate. When it was done, Bruce threw his head back and laughed fiendishly. Killing these two men satisfied his bloodlust for the moment.

His driver dropped him off at the front door of his house, then took the car around to the garage. Before getting out of the car, the driver, Thompson, thought about what he'd just witnessed. He'd wanted out of the organization for the past 10 years, but realized that would only happen when he was dead. The thought made him feel ill.

Chapter 24

Once Bruce Murdock came in, the men noticed the crazed look on his face and knew they needed to tread lightly. Bruce was livid. He paced back and forth in his living room, all the while cussing a blue streak. No one said a word; they just waited for him to calm down.

Finally he flopped into a stuffed chair and sulked. This worried the men more than the pacing. When he was sulking it usually meant he was plotting something sinister. They didn't have long to wait to learn what it was.

"I'm going to get into that house, even if I have to shoot my way in!"

"When do you plan to do that, boss?" asked Wilson.

"I have a court case to take care of today, so we'll get in there tomorrow night."

"We'll be ready," replied Crowley.

For the next two hours they made plans for breaking and entering. What none of them knew was that at that very minute the police had converged on the house and were removing everything from the hidden room.

After Josiah and his group left the mansion, Fred Holmes and Frank Kessler had gone to the police captain with the evidence Gregory Jones had typed up, including a map of the secret room. They waited at their desks while Captain Charles Abram went through everything. A while later, he called them to his office and said, "This is the evidence we've been hoping for. Since Bruce Murdock is involved, I want to keep things locked down until we can get enough info to bring him down."

Holmes looked from Kessler to Abrams to ask, "What are we going to do with the evidence until then, sir?"

"We'll take it to a warehouse and post 'round the clock guards. I want the best men we have doing the guarding."

"Leonard Montello can't be one of them. He's is one of Murdock's men."

Abrams looked from Holmes to Kessler, who nodded in agreement. "We have a dirty cop in our ranks?"

"Yes, sir," declared Kessler. "If my suspicions are correct, there are others, too."

Jumping up, he angrily paced the room. "Do you know who these men are?"

"No, sir," admitted Holmes. "We've noticed Montello has a lot of friends, though. There are a couple, Josh Hamlin and Jethro Sparks that seem particularly close to him. Perhaps they're innocent, but where you find one dirty cop you'll find the others."

"Well then, we'll just have to keep everything under wraps until we have all of the pieces to the puzzle put together," snapped Abram. Do you have a suggestion for the best men to put on guard duty?"

"Yes, sir," responded Kessler. He began to name off the men who were on the detail to help Josiah and Jones get the mansion cleaned out.

"Okay, we'll put them on guard duty." He paused a moment before adding, "We'll split them up and have them work morning, afternoon and graveyard shifts."

"We're also willing to help where needed, sir," replied Holmes. "We promised Gregory Jones and Josiah that we'd have someone watch out for Jones executive secretary until she has left town.

"That can be arranged," agreed Abrams. "Meanwhile I want the two of you to work as foremen of this operation."

"I'll take the graveyard shift, sir," volunteered Kessler. "I'm a night owl."

"Good," responded Abram. "Then that leaves you the dayshift to cover, Fred."

"I'm fine with that," grinned Holmes. "How about getting Jason Anderson to take on the afternoon shift?"

"I'll call in several men I can trust and we'll get over to the mansion and get busy."

"What if we use those same female officers that helped pack the mansion? Kessler asked. "They were fast. I know Janis Willard keeps good records too. Maybe she and Joyce Toleson could categorize the items once we can get everything into the warehouse. We have the list we made when we were in the secret room."

"Make it so," ordered Abram.

Abram called in several officers, both those who were in the office, as well as those who were soon to come on duty. When they were all assembled, he told them what he wanted. Soon thereafter, they went to the mansion. The two women, Janice Willard and Joyce Toleson were assigned to match the lists of items against the list that Jones had typed up.

Josiah Graham was exhausted from riding in the U-Haul. It had been days since they had left Syracuse. They'd seen Gregory Jones off at the airport in Cleveland, then got a motel for the night. They'd been through some pretty rough weather that had forced them to stay in a motel for days at a time.

Judge Harris and his family, had been doing well through it all. His son, Michael, and his wife had wisely brought along things to keep them entertained.

Shaking himself out of his musings, Josiah consulted his watch. He was relieved to see that it was almost noon. They were approaching Idaho Falls, so he decided they should find a place to stop for lunch. After parking, Josiah got out and stretched lazily. He was relieved that Spokane was only a few days away.

After lunch, Josiah took over driving. By the time they'd gone 30 miles, the show was coming down hard. When they finally arrived in Butte, Montana, Josiah's arms ached from gripping the steering wheel to navigate the snowy roads. They ate a good meal then found a motel for the night.

When he got into his motel, Josiah phoned Timothy York to report in. They discussed the weather, then Josiah gave him the details of the trip thus far. Tim let him know his family missed him and wanted him home in time for Christmas.

Josiah also told Tim about the call from Frank Kessler and giving him the list of Gordon Spielberg's men, the map and the list of items in the secret room, as well as telling him Bruce Murdock was part of the mafia and giving him the name of the dirty cops. He finished by telling Tim that a few select honest cops went back to the mansion and collected all the evidence and moved it to a secret location.

Tim was happy to hear that Josiah had retrieved everything from the house and said he would relay the information to the girls. He was also shocked to find out that Josiah sold the mansion to Bruce Murdock for $4 million, and that Spielberg's estate totaled $4 billion dollars. They agreed to break this news to the women gradually. Josiah told Tim he'd had the money wired to his account so it couldn't be traced, and then he would disperse it however the ladies wanted.

Their final topic of discussion was Shirleen's New York home. Josiah told him that the sale was complete as well and that money had been wired to his account too.

Early the next morning, Tim got into his truck and drove over to report what Josiah had told him to the Webbs.

Meagan met him at the door and greeted him warmly. "Well, look what the storm blew in," teased Meagan.

Pretending to be offended, Tim scowled at her and turned to leave. "I had some good news to share, but after that rude comment, I'm going home."

"If you leave, I won't share the cookies that just came out of the oven," quipped Meagan.

Tim turned back, licking his lips in anticipation. "Warm cookies?"

Laughing, Meagan pulled him inside and replied, "Yes. You're really pitiful, Tim."

Gazing at Meagan sternly, Tim said, "I am not. I just love cookies!"

"Stop teasing, Tim. I'll gladly trade him cookies for news," Juliana said.

"At least there's one soft heart in this house after all!" Sticking his nose in the air, he walked past Shirleen and Meagan and took Juliana's hand as he headed to the kitchen for cookies.

"Oh, dear," cried Juliana, "give this man some cookies quick." Juliana said.

Going over to Meagan, Tim tweaked her on the nose. "That's what you get for being so rude, Miss Webb. Can't have no young upstart messing around with the law. Next time you insult this Mountie, I'll arrest you and throw you in a jail cell!"

They all laughed and got the poor man some cookies. Once he'd eaten one, Meagan asked, "So, what's the news?"

"Ain't agona say nary a word 'til I get another cookie," Tim joked.

"Then I'd best get you one," laughed Meagan. "Would you like a glass of milk, or a cup of coffee to go with that?"

"I'd love a glass of milk, please." Finishing his cookie, Tim told them the news Josiah shared with him. He left out the information about the money, feeling it would be wiser to wait until Josiah got back to discuss that.

Later, after Josiah had left Syracuse, Bruce sent his men to the mansion to ransack it. Half an hour later, they returned to report everything that had been in the secret room was gone. Roaring like a mad bull and cursing, Bruce finally said, "Those men must've taken everything with them when they left. I know the police don't have it. No one knew about that room but us."

Vincent Crowley asked, "You don't think the police knew about it?"

"No, or we'd all be in jail by now." Pacing the floor, Bruce said, "That idiot Spielberg kept a list of everyone who worked for him. I have one list, but I know for sure he had another, larger list in that file cabinet in the secret room. I told the fool he should put it somewhere safer. He wouldn't hear of it. Said it was safer there than anywhere else."

"Since everything's gone, you can be sure someone has it," declared Crowley.

"No kidding," snapped Bruce. "Why would they want all of that stuff if they didn't know what they were getting?"

"Who knows," replied, Thomas Wilson. "One thing's for sure, we've got to find out who has it."

Murdock, who was thoughtfully smoking a cigarette, listened to what his men had to say. Taking one last drag, he crushed the cigarette out in the ashtray and said, "You're right Wilson. Let's find out if Montello knows anything. He's on duty tonight."

Murdock got out his wallet, thumbed through it for Montello's private number, then made the call. As he waited for Montello to pick up, he tapped his fingers on the arm of his chair. When Montello answered, Murdock said, "We have a problem and we're hoping you can solve it for us."

"What's going on?"

"Some of my guys went over to Spielberg's place to retrieve some stuff from a secret room, but when they got there it was empty. You know what's going on?"

"Nothing's been happening here, other than the usual murders and thefts." Pausing a moment, he added, "I'll snoop around and see what's goin' on."

Good. Get back ASAP."

"Will do."

Murdock ended the call and thought, *If Montello doesn't find anything, I'll off him. He's outlasted his usefulness.* Aloud, he said, "We have to wait until Montello can get back to us, so what say I have the cook whip something up?"

They headed to the kitchen and Murdock told the cook to prepare a meal for everyone. She was still preparing the meal when Murdock's cell phone began ringing. Murdock picked it up and it was Len saying he hadn't found anything yet, even though he'd talked to the people who helped to move Spielberg's brother. No one thought anything was going on and they said the papers in Spielberg's office were nothing important. He said he'd asked someone who was there, and he said there was nothing out of the ordinary. The two speculated that Spielberg had arranged for someone to remove the items in the event of his death.

Bruce decided that might be what happened. *There were a few men who never took to my being boss and we never found out what happened to them. Maybe they took the stuff so they could break out on their own.*

Bruce filled in Crowley on his suspicions and went to his office. He returned with a list of names. Plopping into a chair, he said, "There were three men we couldn't find. They just vanished into thin air." Turning to look at White and Crowley, he asked, "Did you do everything you could to find them?"

Nathan White spoke up first. "We checked their businesses, their favorite haunts, their hometowns, their relatives, pretty much everywhere we could think of."

I even checked to see if they'd skipped the country," Crowley said, "but they hadn't. I also checked the bus stations, car dealers, every place, but no luck."

"If they were the ones who got the files, we can relax," said Bruce. "They aren't about to come forward yet. You need to keep looking for them before they get a chance to do something with that information." Both men agreed.

They heard the tinkle of a bell, signaling dinner was ready. They headed to the dining room, but Bruce stopped Nathan White, letting the others go ahead. "Nate, I have a big job for you."

"Okay."

"I want you to do Leonard Montello and his three friends. They know too much about our operation. I want to take care of it tonight. Got it?"

Nodding his head, Nate said, "Yeah, boss. You want it any certain way?"

"Do 'em at home. Make it look like a robbery."

"Two of 'em have wives and children. Do you want me to do them too?"

Bruce thought about it, then asked, "Which two have wives?"

"Josh Hamlin and Jethro Sparks."

"Wait 'til they get home then do them before they go inside."

"Good enough. I'll get it done tonight."

Smiling, Bruce patted him on the back as he said, "Good deal! Report to me once it's done."

Later that night, while Bruce entertained his men, Nathan White went to carry out the hits. He shot Josh Hamlin in his driveway. Next, he shot Leonard Montello in the face as he walked in his yard. Jethro Sparks was shot as he got out of his car. Unfortunately his wife witnessed the shooting, so White short her as well and quickly drove away.

After he was finished, White went home, showered and changed his clothes. He threw his bloody clothes into the washer, the Montello hit had been a little too up close and personal. That done, he went back to Murdock's house to report to his boss.

When he got there, Murdock led him to his office and poured two whiskeys. When he'd settled on the couch, he handed White his drink and asked, "Well, how'd it go down?"

"It's done. I had to kill Jethro's wife. She came outside right as it was going down and she saw me. Couldn't be helped."

"Don't worry about it. Good job, Nate."

"Thanks, boss," replied White in relief.

"I can always count on you to get a job done."

Setting his glass on the coffee table, Nate asked, "Did anything else happen while I was gone?"

"No, we're still trying to figure out who got the stuff from the Spielberg mansion."

"Where'd Spielberg's brother come from?"

"Somewhere in Montana. I never could remember where. The only men who knew where it was for sure are dead."

"That's too bad. I think he and Jones took it."

"I've never doubted your hunches, Nate. I'll keep it in mind."

"I don't like not knowing. We could find ourselves in real trouble."

"We can't worry about that now. We have to keep ahead of what's left of Spielberg's men, plus I still don't feel too comfortable about some of the ones that joined us."

"Neither do I," agreed White. "I don't like the way the drug lords are acting either. Something's not right, but I can't put my finger on it."

"What do you mean?"

"When they don't know I'm watching, I see the looks they give you. They ain't nice."

"Don't worry about it, Nate. They can't do anything because I have Wilson and Crowley with me all the time."

"Just the same, I'd be careful if I were you."

"I will," Bruce assured him. "Did you read about Judge Harris retiring?"

"He did?"

"Yeah. Guess your bomb threat worked. Too bad you didn't get the chance to make good on it. Let him stew for a few days then try it again."

"Sure."

"I owe you for all those jobs. I'll be right back." Bruce went into his office and came back with a fat envelope filled with cash. "I'm sure I'll have other jobs for you soon."

"Thanks, boss. You gonna stick it to the drug lords?"

"Yeah, but not for three or four months. I need 'em to get used to things first."

"Smart thinking. Don't wanna start a war."

"My thoughts exactly."

"How's the escort service comin' along?"

"Kathy Neilson's a natural. She's raking in the dough." Smiling at some private joke, Bruce continued, "That woman is as hard as nails. She don't take guff from anybody. She shot a guy a couple of weeks ago, just for givin' her flack. She followed him to his house and he slapped her. That was his mistake. She pulled out her gun, and shot him in the heart."

"Wow! Remind me never to cross that broad!"

"You got that right."

"When will you get Spielberg's house?"

"Sale's done. I paid him cash."

"Good deal."

"I'm moving in right after Christmas."

White stood up to leave. "Well, I'd better get going so you can get some rest before court tomorrow."

"This is turning out to be a difficult case. The man is guilty as sin, and I can't seem to find any loopholes to get him off." Shrugging, he continued. "He's a real lug nut. I really don't care if I get him off or not, but I gotta play the part."

"How do you get away with living so high on the hog when you don't charge your clients much?"

"My father had some oil fields in Texas and he left me a lot of money. I use that to fund my other business and I've made a mint. Spielberg paid me well, too."

Murdock walked Nate to the door and was glad to be rid of him. *If Nate knew how much I hate him, I'd probably have a bomb in my car,* Bruce thought and chuckled as he shut the door.

Chapter 25

Two days after adopting the two sets of twins, Melinda was having a late breakfast with her husband, Theodore in the hospital's cafeteria. She had nearly finished eating when she glanced up to look out the window. "Oh, darling, it's stopped snowing at last."

"It's about time!"

"I thought it was going to snow for days," Melinda said. "I'm so glad it's finally stopped."

"Me too, I'm more than ready to go home."

"It's been a trying few days," admitted Melinda. "However, if Henry hadn't had the stroke, we never would've adopted those precious babies." Grinning, she added, "I also wouldn't be married to the most wonderful man in the world already, either."

"That's the best part of it all for me!"

Dr. Stillman entered the cafeteria and came over to speak to them. "Good morning you two."

"Good morning," grinned Melinda. "Did you have a better night last night?"

"Sure did. I haven't caught up on my sleep yet, but I feel much better this morning than I have for days. How did you two sleep?"

"Good," replied Theodore. "We feel better too. How are all of the accident victims doing?"

"We had a young patient in ICU who was touch and go for a while, but he's doing much better this morning. One of the children in the nursery, a little girl, didn't make it. We all fought a hard fight, but there were just to many things wrong with her."

"That's awful," cried Melinda. "I was hoping we wouldn't lose any more children."

"I think we all were," said Dr. Stillman. "At least the rest of the patients are doing better."

"What will happen to the man who caused the accident?" asked Theodore.

"Tim assigned a Mountie to stay with him. He's resting comfortably right now. The officer told me that the man is going to jail as soon as he's well enough to leave."

"Then he has to stand trial?" asked Melinda.

"Yes," replied Dr. Stillman. "He's responsible for several deaths, so he has to pay for what he did."

"I've always hated alcohol," declared Melinda. "It's not only addicting, but it destroys minds and ruins lives."

"Alcoholism is a terrible disease," agreed Dr. Stillman. "My oldest brother died from sclerosis of the liver. Let me tell you, it was a terrible death. My younger brother, who was especially close to Jack, committed suicide because of it." Pausing reflectively, he added. "Alcohol is a curse on the human race. Not only have I seen the effect of alcohol in my own family, but I've seen many others die because of it, too."

"I'm so sorry for your loss, doctor," responded Melinda. "My Uncle Gary was an alcoholic. He finally died from the same disease as your brother. It took his wife and children a long time to get back on their feet after that. Aunt Jena remarried a wonderful man, who adopted her children, so it all worked out. Sometimes though, it doesn't."

Changing the subject, Dr. Stillman said, "By this afternoon the roads should be cleared enough for you newlyweds to go home."

Theodore, who'd been listening to the conversation, said, "I can hardly wait to get home."

Dr. Stillman looked at Theodore with a teasing expression on his face. "Are you saying that our motel isn't accommodating enough for you?"

"No offence intended, but it sure isn't!"

Laughing, Dr. Stillman said, "I agree with you completely. There's no way a person gets the full rest they need in a hospital."

"I'm glad that you agree," grinned Theodore.

After talking a while longer they went their separate ways. Melinda and Theodore went to check on their five new charges before going to check on Henry.

"How is Henry?" Melinda asked the nurse when she entered the room.

"He is doing really well," said the nurse. "In fact he's doing so well we're going to move him to a private room later this afternoon."

Squeezing Henry's hand, Melinda grinned excitedly. "That's good news, Henry. That means you're making great progress. Wait until Theodore hears, he'll be so excited." Squeezing his hand again, she continued. "You'll be glad to know that it's stopped snowing. As soon as the roads have been cleared, we're going home. We'll be in to see you every day, but we have lots to do to get ready for you and the children to come home."

Melinda went on to tell him about how well the little ones were doing. A few minutes later, she left so Theodore could have some time with him.

As Theodore went in, Melinda saw Dr. Stillman walking toward her. "Good news about Henry, isn't it?"

"It's wonderful!"

"I think his progress is partly because the two of you keep encouraging him. When he's moved to his new room, keep on encouraging him and he'll be home in no time."

"We'll definitely keep it up."

"He's one strong individual, Melinda. He'll survive this setback, and his recovery will be faster with a lot of support from you. I'm going to check on him before I start my rounds."

"See you later, Dr. Stillman."

As Melinda waited for Theodore, she began to make plans. *The first thing we have to do is go see the home we inherited from Mr. Stokes to see how big it is. Will it be big enough for all of us? What will the ranch manager be like? Will the crew work out?*

Suddenly, she had a more distressing thought. *"Will Theodore and I be able to get this accomplished? There's so much to do. The list is so enormous. Plus, we have to hire the help to take care of the children.*

Melinda mentally chided herself. *Just take a deep breath. Everything will work out.* Moving away from the window, she took a seat and began to read a magazine. She'd only turned a few pages when Theodore came out of Henry's room.

He walked over and kissed her lightly on the mouth, then sat down beside her. "Isn't it wonderful how well Henry's doing?"

Tossing the magazine back onto the rest of the stack, Melinda squeezed Theodore's hand. "Yes, it is. That means his therapy can start soon. Before we know it, he'll back home with us."

"That's true."

Growing thoughtful, Melinda gazed at Theodore to say, "I've been doing some thinking."

"Oh dear," teased Theodore. "What do I have to do now?"

Punching his arm lightly, Melinda pretended to pout. "I'm not a task master yet, Theodore Brooks, but if you keep it up I may just become one."

Rubbing his arm in pretended pain, he said, "Then I'll think twice before opening my mouth."

Melinda laughed. "You don't have to do anything just this minute. I've had a lot on my mind is all and I wanted to talk to you about it."

"Fire away then." Pulling on his ears, he said, "I'm all ears."

Snuggling closer, Melinda giggled happily. "Seriously, I was thinking while you were visiting with Henry. Don't you think the first thing we need to do, after we've rested up, is go see the ranch Mr. Stokes gave us? We need to talk to the ranch manager and work crew, and we need to see what has to be done to make the house function for all of us.

"We also have to buy things like clothes, diapers, and formula for the children, and hire the help we need to care for them. I'm not complaining, but there's so much to do to get ready to take care of them. I'm feeling overwhelmed."

"I've been thinking those same thoughts," admitted Theodore. "I agree that we need to go out to the ranch first. We also have to pack up the apartment so we can get moved. Truthfully, I'm glad we won't have the children with us until we get settled because we wouldn't get a lot accomplished if we did."

"I'm also worried we won't have much time alone to get to know each other better."

"I've thought about that too." Touching her cheek he added, "We'll just have to make time for each other."

Melinda sighed in relief. "I'm so glad you understand."

"I do. This is going to be a rough transition for both of us, darling. We just have to be patient with each other."

"You're right."

"You'll find I'm always right," teased Theodore.

"Then we're already in trouble," declared Melinda, "because *I* know all there is to know about everything!"

Kissing her soundly, he said, "Then I'll just have to keep these in ready demand." He pulled her to her feet, and they went back to the nursery for a few more minutes with the children.

When Melinda and Theodore Brooks arrived home several hours later, they made some tea and sat talking about their future. Since Henry had a king size bed, and their beds were twins, they went to sleep in Henry's room.

The next morning, they got up early. As soon as the apartment was clean they made a list of what needed to be done. When they were finished, it was nearing nine o'clock. They quickly got ready and went over to Joel Cline's office so they could follow him out to the ranch they'd inherited from James Stokes. Melinda kept looking at the passing scenery as they drove. "It so beautiful out here, Teddy."

"I agree," responded Theodore.

"The only problem I see is when it snows like it just did, there's no way to get out in an emergency."

"I've been wondering about that, too. Maybe after we see the house and surrounding area, we'll figure that out."

Theodore was speechless as he looked out the car window. Huge snowcapped crags surrounded them on both sides. A mountain goat was standing on top of one of the high peaks, looking down at them. Seeing that Cline was getting further ahead of them, Theodore began driving a little faster. A few minutes later they saw a break in the rocks.

Coming through the clearing, they both gasped. A huge area of what they guessed were fields, met their gaze first. Then nestled against a backdrop of mountains was a huge house surrounded by many outbuildings, one of which was a huge barn. As they neared the house, the beauty that stretched out ahead of them was impressive. Beyond the house and surrounding buildings lay more fields.

Cline was waiting for them when they drove up. "I thought you'd gotten lost. You weren't behind me when I got here."

Theodore grinned as he said, "We stopped to look at a mountain goat standing on one of those high crags."

"Let me introduce you to Lance Ramey," Cline said. "He's the ranch manager." Pointing to Theodore and Melinda, he continued, "Lance this is Theodore and Melinda Brooks. They're the two who adopted Katarina. Can we go inside so we can talk without freezing to death?"

"Sure thing," replied Ramey. "I forgot my manners." Motioning toward the house he added, "Please come inside. When you called and said you were bringing Melinda and Theodore Brooks out to see the house, I built fires in the fireplaces and turned the heat up a little."

"Thank you," replied Melinda. "Suddenly, I'm feeling really cold."

Once inside, Cline led them to the dining room where he invited them to sit. "It will be easier to talk in here so I can spread out all of the papers." As he talked he did just that. When he was ready, he picked up a large document and began, "This is James's last will and testament, so let's get this part over with so we can move on to other things."

"Maybe I should leave so you can do that," Lance said, rising to leave.

"No, Lance," said Cline, "this applies to you too."

From the blank expression on his face it was clear that he was surprised.

Looking up at Lance, Cline began to read. "There are 150 acres of land nestled starting a mile from the house; I bequeath 10 acres of it to my manager, Lance Ramey, for the long years of service he gave me. I would also like a milk cow, a dozen chickens, two beef cows and the horse he loves to ride to go to him so he can start his own spread.

"Surely that can't be right," declared Lance jumping to his feet.

"It's true Lance," grinned Cline.

"I never thought he would do something like that for me." Scratching his head, he swallowed a couple of times to hold the emotions in. It was no use because tears began coursing down his cheeks. He rushed from the room and disappeared outside. A few minutes later, Lance came back into the dining room and said, "I apologize. My emotions got to me."

"It's understandable," responded Cline. "Let's get back to the will."

When the will had been read, Cline set it aside and asked, "Have you told the men about the Stokes's accident yet?"

"Yes," stammered Ramey. "I broke the news to them last night. I told them you were bringing some people out to the ranch today that these people would speak to them about what would happen."

"Very good." Putting the papers back into his briefcase, Cline continued, "I suggest we show the Brookses around the house first, then we'll talk to the crew."

"That's a good idea," replied Ramey.

As they went to explore the house, Melinda got a good look at Lance Ramey. He was an older man with snow-white hair and a long beard. Bushy eyebrows partially hid his deep-set blue eyes, which were kind and gentle. He was short and bowlegged. Melinda liked him immediately.

They started with the living room, which was massive. As one entered and turned to the right there was a huge alcove that held the coats, which could be closed off. Against the connecting wall was a picture window that took up most of the wall. Melinda went to look out and saw a house nestled a good distance away. "Three women live in the house you're looking at," Cline said as he walked up beside her. "They're about five miles up the road."

"Are they friendly?" Melinda asked.

"Brad Johnson, the realtor who showed them the place, is a great friend of mine. He speaks highly of them."

"Then once we've settled in, and before we bring the children home, I'll drive over and introduce myself."

"That's a great idea."

As she looked around, Melinda was already deciding which furniture to keep and which she'd like to give away. She also made a mental note to pack up all the family pictures and store them for Katarina when she was older.

There was a large fireplace against the outer wall with a wide mantle, and next to it was a baby grand piano that took up the rest of the room. A wide double door separated the wall to the left of the room. As they went through, the massive kitchen impressed Melanie. There were wall-to-wall cupboards everywhere, except over the stove, which had a hooded fan. There was a window over the sink, and a breakfast nook that ran down the middle of the room.

A door to the left led into a large pantry that had two freezers, as well as floor to ceiling shelving. She was pleased to see all of the shelves were fully stocked. *That's one thing we don't have to do right off,* she told herself.

From the kitchen, they went to the dining room, which was also huge. There was enough room to put up two long tables with chairs around them. There was a hutch, as well as a sideboard sitting along the one wall. The floor was covered with green and white tile.

As they started down the long, wide hallway, Melinda wasn't surprised to see family photos on the walls. The first room they entered was a large laundry room. There were three washers lined up against the right wall and Melinda noticed there was another outlet available for another washer. On the opposite wall, nestled under a window that ran the length of the wall, were three dryers. This pleased Melinda, due to the heavy volume of clothes they would need to wash. There were cupboards over all of the washers, which again pleased Melinda. The cabinets in here were also fully stocked. There was also a folding table, an ironing board and a long drying rack.

Next they saw the master suite. The room had been decorated in soft lavenders and purples. The carpet was white with flecks of lavender running through it. There was a king sized bed under the window, and long ornate dressers were against each wall. A matching vanity was near the door. There was also a colossal walk in closet and bathroom. The rooms were stunningly beautiful.

There was three more bedrooms on this level, each one decorated nicely. One room had a light blue theme running through it, another a pink theme and the third was done with aqua tones.

The room with the blue theme had a country feel to it. It was simply decorated in a masculine style that immediately appealed to Theodore. "Let's put Henry this room. Okay?"

"I think he'd love it," agreed Melinda.

They walked back to the winding staircase between the living room and kitchen. The staircase twisted to the next level. There were four bedrooms on this floor with a bathroom at each end of the hall. Melinda wasn't surprised to see that each of these rooms also had a theme.

All of the rooms contained perfectly matched furniture. Each room in the house also had its own fireplace. Wide windows, with matching drapes made the rooms light and airy. As they walked back downstairs, Melinda's mind was full of ideas for how to make the home's decor their own.

Next, they went outside to look around. The wind had picked up since their arrival, and Melinda felt like she was freezing. Tucking her hands into the pockets of her coat, she tried to ignore how cold she was.

They visited the barn, which was well built and massive. There was a room designated for storing milk and eggs. On the wall to the right was a huge cooler filled with jars of milk and cream. A refrigerator on the opposite wall was filled with cartons of eggs. It was immaculately clean. A door led into a room where a large milk tank sat waiting to be filled with milk. It too was scrubbed immaculately clean.

In where the cows were milked, there were several rows of stanchions on one side of the room. Each stall had been washed down and sprayed with disinfectant. The floors were also scrubbed and sprayed with more disinfectant. At the end of the rows of stalls there was a door that led to the holding pens.

They left through the door that they had come through and went to another building that housed several sows and a large boar. Here again, everything was neat and clean. The floors had been layered with fresh straw. A large pen was located to the right of the building, which connected to the door at the side of the building.

Next to the pigpen was a large chicken coup. It was well insulated and the lights were on. There were two doors on the side of the building that led to two long chicken runs. Ramey explained that they used one run until it got too messy to use. They would turn the chickens into the other run so they could clean up the first one.

The horse barn had several stalls. At the end of it was a good-sized tack room that held saddles, bridles, and other items used for taking care of the horses.

Next to the house there was a gigantic woodshed that was filled to the rafters with wood. Ramey explained that the hired hands brought in wood every night so the fireplaces could be fed. "We get the wood in through the summer months so that we're prepared for the horrible winters."

Finally, they went to a long, wide building Ramey said housed him and the hired hands. As they entered, a cook stepped back from the bread he was kneading. A pot of beans was cooking for the evening meal. Melinda loved the smell. There was also the smell of coffee in the air.

They moved on to the bunkhouse. There were bunk beds lined up along both walls. A bathroom was located to the left of the room. Melinda was surprised to see that every bed was neatly made up.

When they came back through the kitchen, the cook, Adam Morgan, asked, "Would y'all be interested in a cup of coffee?"

"I don't know about the men," declared Melinda, "but I'm so cold I could really use a cup."

"It's as good as done," grinned Morgan.

They had just started to drink their coffee, when several men came in. After introducing all of them, Lance said, "Would you ask the rest of the men to come inside for a few minutes? Chores can wait."

"You bet, boss." The man quickly disappeared outside returning a few minutes later with the rest of the men.

"Men," began Ramey, "this couple is our new boss. I'd like you all to meet Theodore and Melinda Brooks. Mr. Stokes willed the place to them just before he died. As you know, his entire family was killed in that terrible accident a few days ago. The only surviving member of his family is his granddaughter, Katarina. Mr. Stokes asked the Brookses to adopt Katarina."

Cline took over the conversation. "Mr. Brooks helped the doctors with the victims of that crash as they came into the emergency room. Two sets of twins survived the wreck but their families didn't. These wonderful people adopted them as well, which means they are now parents to five infants."

The men looked at them in awe as Lance continued, "Since Mr. Brooks will be busy helping with the children and therapy for his brother-in-law, who will also be living with them, he won't be able to help out much with ranch work.

"They've asked me to stay on as the manager, and I agreed. They'd like you all to stay on, too. How many of you want to stay?" Every man quickly agreed to stay.

"Thank you all," replied Theodore in relief. "I really don't know anything about running a ranch, so I'll leave pretty much everything up to you. If you don't mind, there's one thing we'll need help with right away, and that's moving in. There will be two U-hauls full of stuff coming. Would any of you be willing to help unload them?"

"You bet," said one man. "Tell us when, and we'll come a-runnin'."

"Thank you. We probably won't be finished packing for about two weeks. There's still a lot to do, and we're visiting the children and my brother-in-law, Henry Borden, at the hospital every day too."

Lance smiled as he said, "I'd say you have your work cut out for you. I have a suggestion, if you don't mind."

"I don't mind one little bit," said Theodore emphatically.

"How about the men and I collect things as you get them packed. We'll put everything in the living room and then you can put it all away. That way you won't have a bunch of boxes stacked around all the time. We've got several trucks between us, so you won't even have to get a U-Haul."

"That's an excellent idea!" cried Melinda.

"Give us a week to get started, then you can start coming by to pick up boxes," Theodore said. Turning to Cline, he asked, "Joel, do you know anyone who could take care of Katarina for a few days?"

"Sure do," he declared. "My mother loves children. She's always taking care of her grandchildren, so what's one more? Let me ask her when we get back and I'll let you know."

"Thank you. That will let us concentrate on packing."

Not long after that, the Brookses and Cline headed back to town. They stopped at the hospital and went to see Henry first. They told him about the house and the moving plans, then Melinda said, "When you're strong enough, we'll let you tell us what you want to take with you. Would that be all right?"

Henry, nodded yes.

"Wonderful! That means you have to work hard so you can come home." Henry surprised Melinda by squeezing her hand slightly. "You squeezed my hand! Now I know you're getting better."

A few minutes later she left and gave Theodore time to visit. When he was finished, they went to see Katarina. Her eyes lit up when she saw them and she began to coo.

Melinda picked her up and began dotting kisses all over her face.

"May I hold her when you're done?" Theodore asked.

"You can hold her right now," laughed Melinda. As she watched the interaction between them, Melinda's heart swelled with love. When the nurse came in with a bottle, Melinda fed and burped her. Afterward, Theodore rocked her gently until she fell asleep.

They handed her back to the nurse and waited until she was tucked in before going to see the preemies. They were sleeping, so they took turns touching each one for several minutes. Finally they went to see the other set of twins. They were being prepared for bed, so they helped the nurses get that done, then gave each of them a bottle. Soon they were fast asleep. Kissing each one, they tucked them in and left them for the night.

Once they got home, Theodore helped Melinda make a light supper. When the kitchen was cleaned up, they went to bed.

The next morning, Theodore went to the storage units to retrieve the boxes that Melinda thought they should keep. As he loaded the car, he was grateful she'd had the foresight to keep them. When the backseat and trunk were full, he went back to the apartment.

Melinda came out to help him unload the boxes, then they started packing up Henry's room. Melinda sank onto the bed and said, "I think I've been here before."

"I know I have," declared Theodore, "and I didn't like it then, either!"

"Moving is terrible," said Melinda. "What's worse is we have to unpack it all and put it away again."

"Ugh!"

He went over and kissed her lightly on the lips. Things soon progressed to the point that packing was forgotten.

Sometime later, they began to pack in earnest. By lunchtime, Henry's room was finished. They ate a light lunch in silence, content to be in each other's company. When they were done, they started to pack the living room. They finished that room in time to have some dinner before going to the hospital. When they got home, they started to pack Theodore's room. By midnight, they had it nearly packed up. They decided to wait until morning to complete the job.

Three days later, Cline called to tell them his mother would take care of Katarina for them while they got moved into the new house. He told them she had a crib already set up and would be happy to watch her as early as that afternoon. He said she also had some baby clothes they could have if they wanted them. In the end, the only thing they needed to provide was diapers, bottles, and formula.

Theodore told Melinda the news, and they decided to let the packing go so they could go shopping for the items Katarina would need. "One thing we need for sure is a car seat," declared Melinda.

"Why don't we get that first?"

"Good idea. We should get a heavy blanket and a receiving blanket, too."

"I hadn't thought of that," confessed Theodore.

"It's really cold outside. I don't want her to get a chill."

They headed to the mall and had their items purchased in no time, other than Katarina's clothing. Finally, Melinda let Theodore pick it out because she couldn't

266 • *Mabel Ebner*

decide. He chose a beautiful lacy pink dress with a matching hat. They also got her a pair of white shoes, and a couple of packages of socks.

They paid for assembly on the car seat, and when it was assembled, they put it and the other items in the back seat and headed to the hospital. They looked for Dr. Stillman when they got there, and found out he wasn't there. Theodore explained what they wanted to do to a nurse and asked if she would call the doctor to see if they had the okay to take her out of the hospital.

The nurse called Stillman's office, and when she had hung up she was grinning. "He agreed to let her go home, so we'll start processing her this minute."

While the paperwork was being taken care of, they went to Katarina's room to get her ready. When she was dressed in her new outfit, she was gorgeous. Tears came to their eyes as they looked at her.

Melinda had just picked her up when a nurse came in with the discharge papers. Not long after that they had Katarina secured in her car seat and were headed to Cline's mother's house.

Melinda read off the directions, while Theodore watched the street signs. When they got there, the met Mrs. Cline, who was a short and slightly plump woman. Her merry hazel eyes and soft features made her look like the perfect grandmother. She immediately made them feel welcome.

After Theodore and Melinda promised to return before going to the hospital each night, they kissed Katarina goodbye and left.

Chapter 26

Shirleen woke feeling better than she had in days. As she lay there, she suddenly realized it was only twelve days until Christmas. There was still so much to do. She felt overwhelmed. She'd wrapped a lot of presents, but wasn't finished yet. She got up and got ready for the day. When she was satisfied that she was presentable, she put her dirty clothes in the hamper in the laundry room and started for the kitchen.

As Shirleen neared the living room, she heard excited voices. Suddenly, Meagan rushed toward her yelling, "Don't come in, Grandma."

"Okay. I'll be in my room. Let me know when it's safe to come out."

"We're almost done," replied Meagan. "Just give us a few more minutes."

She chuckled as she went down the hall to her room. Once inside, she got started wrapping presents. As she worked, she began to hum a Christmas carol. She lost track of time as she worked, and only had three small ones left when she heard footsteps coming down the hall. She threw a towel over the unwrapped gifts, and answered Meagan's knock on her door.

Seeing the huge pile of wrapped packages near her grandmother's closet, Meagan's eyes grew large. "Wow, Grandma! You weren't kidding when you said you were going shopping."

Seeing the expression on Meagan's face, Shirleen laughed and said, "I sure wasn't! I've had more fun this Christmas than in all of the years leading up to it."

Hugging her grandmother, Meagan said, "I'm so happy you're having a good time. I love Christmas, it's the best time of the year."

"That it is, honey. It's not only a time for giving and getting presents, but it's a time for showing more love. It's also a time to reflect on the true meaning of Christmas."

"Our Savior's birth," grinned Meagan.

"Yes. His gift to us was the greatest gift of all … his life for us so that we have a chance to return to be with him."

Meagan stood there letting her grandmother's words sink in. "You're right. I guess I forgot to consider anything but giving you and Momma a wonderful Christmas. Thank you for reminding me."

"You're welcome, honey." Linking her arm with Meagan's she added, "We'd better get back to the living room before they send out a search party."

Once in the living room, Shirleen said, "Wow, the tree looks fantastic with all those presents under it!"

"When you put your presents under the tree," affirmed Meagan, "there won't be any room left."

"I still have a few more to wrap," moaned Shirleen. "That reminds me. I need to speak to Jeff this morning before he goes back out to work."

"What about?" asked Juliana.

"Christmas," stated Shirleen in a matter of fact way.

The phone rang. Juliana answered it. It was Tim, calling to tell them that he'd spoken to Josiah and they were in Spokane. They spent a few days with Judge Harris's family so they could rest before making the trek into Canada. He also wanted to let them know he'd be coming out later to give them some more sensitive information he didn't feel comfortable about discussing on the phone. Juliana suggested he join them for lunch and fill them in then.

Juliana hung up the phone and let everyone know they'd be having a guest at lunch.

"I'm glad that the long trip is almost over with for Josiah," sighed Shirleen. "I've been really worried about him lately."

"So have I," said Meagan.

"Well, we'll learn more at lunch."

They went into to eat breakfast, and a minute later, Jeff joined them. When grace was given they all dug in. When they had taken the edge off of their hunger, Juliana told Jeff about the conversation with Tim.

Wiping her mouth with her napkin, Shirleen looked up to ask, "Jeff, could I have a word with you after you're finished eating? I have some things that I need help with."

"Sure," agreed Jeff.

Juliana helped clear the table then went to her room. Jeff and Shirleen went to the living room, and Shirleen began, "As you know, I've had several huge items delivered. They were pieces of furniture that need to be put together. Could you help me with that? Then after everyone's gone to bed on Christmas Eve, will you help me move them to the living room?"

"Sure."

"Thank you so much. Most of the boxes are in the garage."

"I have something to finish for Meagan. When that's done, I'll start on your furniture."

"Great." Growing curious, Shirleen asked, "If it isn't being too nosey, what you are doing for Meagan?"

"I'm making a vanity for her. I asked her mother and she said she didn't have anything like that for her makeup and perfume."

Clapping her hands together gleefully, Shirleen cried, "That's wonderful! I can't believe I didn't think of that. Oh, Jeff, she'll love it. What a kind thing to do."

"Thank you." Looking around to see if Juliana was within hearing, he continued, "I also made something for Juliana. Since she loves to paint, I bought a bunch of canvas and cut it into different sizes, then put them in wood frames. I also made her some shelves so she can store the canvases, and her paints and brushes."

"Oh, she'll love that!"

"Good. I almost have your gift done, too. I learned that Trudy loves to read, so I made some bookcases for her room as well."

"When did you have time to do all of that?"

"Mostly at night," Jeff said and grinned. "I'd wait until everyone went to bed and sneak out to the workshop. I enjoy working with my hands."

"We're all going to love what you've done for us."

"I hope so." Rising, he started for the door, calling over his shoulder, "I should be done with the project I'm working on by lunch."

"There isn't any hurry. I just need it done before Christmas Eve."

"No problem," assured Jeff. Donning his outdoor gear, he went out to do his chores and work in the workshop.

Going back into the kitchen, Shirleen wasn't surprised to see Trudy making more Christmas goodies. "Can I do anything to help you, Trudy?"

"No, I have everything under control."

"I'm going to finish wrapping the last of my presents so I can get them all under the tree." Nodding, Trudy continued working. For days the house had smelled like a bakery. *Somehow it smells like home,* thought Shirleen. As she left the kitchen, she was in time to see Meagan put some more items under the tree. Surprised, she asked, "Haven't you finished yet?"

"This is the last of them," Meagan said and smiled.

Working as hard as she could, due to the bulkiness of the packages, Shirleen was finished wrapping at ten o'clock. It took her several trips to get the gifts placed under the tree. Feeling exhausted, she went to rest for a little while and was still sleeping when Meagan came to tell her that Tim had just arrived. "Oh dear. I didn't mean to go to sleep. I just wanted to rest for a few minutes.

"It's okay, Grandma. You did a lot this morning."

"Well, let me get freshened up then I'll join you at the table." Stooping to kiss her check Meagan left her to get ready.

When she got to the kitchen, Tim was teasing Meagan. Not long after that they said grace and started to eat. When the meal was over, they went into the living room to talk.

When they were seated, Shirleen began the conversation, "Tell us your news, Tim."

"While he was in Coeur d' Alene, Kessler called Josiah to give him an update on what was happening."

"Oh," was the only response from Juliana.

"Have they found anything more?" Shirleen asked.

"Nothing has been happening, other than the investigation. It seems that they have uncovered a drug ring, whose drug lord is being coerced into paying Bruce a hefty commission right off of the top. From the information their informant gave them, these drug lords aren't very happy."

"I don't imagine they are," retorted Juliana

"Well," continued Tim, "They're biding their time until they can strike out at him. The biggest drug lord, who is from deep in the heart of Mexico, has been talking to other drug lords to see what they can do about it. Rumor has it that Bruce is upping the fees on them sometime in January or February. I fear that if that happens, Bruce Murdock will have tightened the noose around his neck."

"Good," exclaimed Juliana. "He needs to see that he isn't infallible."

"I agree," replied Shirleen.

Taking a deep breath, Tim continued, "There's still more to share."

"More? Shirleen was plainly disgusted, as was Juliana.

"Yes. It seems that Bruce has started an escort service."

Meagan, who was scowling in confusion, asked, "What is an escort service?"

Silence filled the room as Shirleen looked at Juliana, who was looking at her in panic. Sighing, Shirleen looked at Meagan to say, "An escort service is where bad girls, or women take care of men's sexual needs."

"Oh, sick!" retorted Megan. "Why would someone do that?"

"For many reasons, replied Shirleen, but the biggest reason is for the high pay they get."

As Meagan fell silent, it was obvious to the others that she was having a tough time dealing with this information.

Finally, Tim continued. "He has a woman, Kathy Neilson, who is the manager of it. Kessler said that she has a wrap sheet as long as both of his arms put together. They suspect her of several murders. One of which happened quite recently. Kessler told Josiah that they're about to arrest her for these murders. They're trying to decide if they should wait until they can get Bruce at the same time. It's been decided to give Bruce a little more rope to see if he will hang himself. Kessler said that he is getting blatantly cocky all of the time."

"Well," sighed Shirleen, "Let him hang himself and see if I care what he gets. It's my opinion that the sooner they get him and euphemize him the better!"

"My sentiments exactly," shuddered Juliana. "I never thought I could hate anyone worse than I did Gordon Spielberg, but I hate Bruce just as much, if not more."

"I'll never call him Daddy again," stated Meagan emphatically. "I'm ashamed that I have his blood running through me!"

"I don't blame you," softly replied Tim. "Anyway, in the course of their investigation, they also believe that he is into smuggling jewels of all kinds into the country, putting them into all kinds of trinkets, you know, necklaces, earrings, rings, broaches etcetera, which he sells for an exorbitant price."

"Isn't there anything he won't do?" snapped Meagan.

"Apparently not," replied Tim in disgust.

Suddenly, Meagan began to sob hysterically. Shirleen moved over to wrap her arms around her, while Tim knelt at her feet to take her hands. Juliana, guessing at the reason for her pain moved over to whisper, "It's hard when those we know are this bad, but you're not like him, honey. You are one of the most wonderful young ladies there ever was."

Wiping impatiently at her eyes, Megan began to stammer, "I'm … so … glad … that we changed our names."

"As are we," affirmed Shirleen.

"You're mother and grandmother are right, Meagan. There isn't a wicked bone in your body." Reaching up to tweak her nose to distract her, he teased, "Except when you sass me with that mouth of yours. Who would ever believe that someone so young and beautiful could be so sassy?" When Meagan's bottom lip began to quiver, he added. "Personally, I'm glad that you feel that you can give me heck like that. It makes me feel as if I'm part of this family."

"Thank you for saying that," muttered Meagan. "I feel that you are a part of this family."

Kissing her on the cheek, Tim blinked back his tears and said, "Thank you for those generous words." Rising, he made ready to leave. Stopping as he thought of something, he continued "I almost forgot to tell you that Josiah will be leaving Spokane tomorrow so should get to Cardston by late tomorrow night."

"Oh, that's wonderful," cried Meagan, still trying to wipe the tears from her eyes. "I was afraid he wouldn't get here before Christmas."

"Well, he will be," laughed Tim. "I have it from the horse's mouth that he is looking forward to seeing all of you just as soon as he can."

"I can hardly wait, confessed Meagan.

"I'll let you know what else is happening, just as soon as I know." Waving, he went out the door. As he started to step down from the porch, he called back," Goodbye for now."

As he drove away, Trudy, with Juliana's help, went to put the kitchen in order, while Shirleen started Meagan's class. Because they had gotten so far behind because of Shirleen's illness, they were spending longer times with each subject. Finally, at five o'clock, they stopped for the day.

◀ • ▶

Josiah Graham hired Judge Harris' son, Michael, to ride with the other driver and trade off driving until they got to Cardston. He would ride back with the other drivers. That night when they stopped for dinner, Josiah told Michael and the other men they needed to keep their destination a secret. They all agreed, and were soon back at the motel so they could get some sleep.

Early the next morning they were on their way again. Josiah, who was driving the U-Haul with William Barnes, was relieved that the roads were clear. He knew it could get bad before they reached the Canadian border, but thought it best to keep that information to himself.

They were following the van Harvey Metcalf was driving. Michael and he had hit it off immediately — they were about the same age — while, William Barns was just a couple of years younger than Josiah.

They stopped to have lunch in Sandpoint, then decided to drive until they found an out of the way motel for the night. When they'd eaten dinner, they all went back to Josiah and Michael's room to visit for a while. William said, "I've had a lot of time to do some heavy thinking. I don't have a family to hold me down, so I'd like to live in Spokane. It's big enough I can get lost and remain safe."

Harvey said "I have a wife and eight children. I called her last night to ask her how she felt about moving to Coeur d' Alene or Post Falls." Chuckling, he continued. "I could tell I'd completely bowled her over. I explained it would be better for our children to get out of the city. It's been hard, but with the high pay that I got, plus what my wife makes from working in the bank, we have quite a bit saved. We can easily start over with that. I told her she could get another bank job and I could go to school to learn another trade."

"What kind of trade?" asked Michael.

"I have always wanted to be a physical therapist."

"They're paid well," agreed Michael.

"I say, go for it," encouraged Josiah. "What have you got to lose but some time?"

"That's what I told Julia. We talked for a while longer, then she surprised me when she said that she thought getting out of New York was a good idea."

"Wonderful," stated William.

Michael, who heartily agreed, asked, "So when are you coming back to our neck of the woods?"

"Julia's going to pack up the house in the evenings. She thought, with the four older children's help, she could be ready to go as soon I get back. I told her I'd call my boss and resign immediately. After I rest up for a day or two, we'll leave."

"That's great," chorused the men.

"I've already told the boss my plans," said William. "He didn't like it, but he wished me well." Finally, William looked at Metcalf and said, "Hey, how about we stick together until we get back here. I can help drive one of the U-hauls."

"That's a great idea. I'd feel safer with you around while we get ready to leave."

By the end of the next day, they were just outside of Cardston. They stopped to eat before going on to Josiah's home on the outskirts of town. After helping them make up the two beds, he called Tim.

"Tim, we got in a little while ago, and we're beat so we're going to hit the hay. I wondered if you could get some men to help us unload the vans. There's so much stuff I think it's going to take up two or three storage units."

"Sure, I'll call them right now. I'll let you know what's up in the morning."

"Thanks, I owe you one."

"I'll collect later. Get some rest and I'll see you in the morning."

The next morning, his cell phone woke Josiah. It was Tim calling to tell him he'd lined up several men to help. He also volunteered his services and extended an invitation from Shirleen for all of them to come for dinner at 7 p.m. After he ended the call, Josiah was surprised to see it was 9:40 a.m. *I can't believe I slept this late!*

Two hours later, the men joined Tim at the office just as Josiah called. "We're late because we stopped for lunch," explained Josiah when Tim answered.

"That's fine," Tim assured him.

"Tell your men to meet us at the storage unit. We want to get this job over with.

"We'll be there in 10 or 15 minutes," Tim said.

They all met at the storage units and after working hard for two hours, everything was unloaded. Josiah was relieved to hear the doors come down on the final unit. After driving the vans over to the drop-off point, they joined Tim at the office and he gave them a tour of the facilities, while Josiah went back to get a little more rest before it was time to go to dinner.

Shirleen had invited Josiah and the men with him to dinner without thinking. Suddenly she had a panicked thought, *What if they blow our cover! What was I thinking?* Finally, she calmed down and called Tim. "Tim, this is Shirleen."

"Hello, Shirleen. What's up?"

"Ever since I invited Josiah and the men to dinner, I've been feeling panicky."

"To be honest with you, so was I. It got so bad I called Josiah a few minutes ago."

"You did? What did he say?"

"He assured he had it under control. He's going to introduce you as his mother's sister. I was just about to call you to tell you."

"Oh," sighed Shirleen, relieved. "That's smart thinking! I'll let everybody know so they don't blow our cover. Thanks, Tim. I feel a lot better."

All at once she thought of something else, "Tim, you do know I was inviting you, too, don't you?"

"Oh," replied Tim in surprise. "Thank you, I'll be there after I feed the dogs, shower and change."

"We'll be eating at seven-thirty or eight o'clock."

"I get off at six, so that'll give me plenty of time."

"Good! I'll see you when you get here. Good-bye, Tim."

Feeling more at peace, Shirleen went to tell everyone what was going on. They were all relieved Josiah had come up with such a simple solution. They all went about getting ready and preparing the meal. They were just finishing up when they heard someone pull up.

Meagan answered the door and let Josiah, William Barnes, Harvey Metcalf and Tim in.

"Hello, Pumpkin," he said. "How's business?"

"Still business," replied Meagan. "I have five months before I'll be through with school."

"Do you plan to go to college?" asked William.

"I've been thinking about it, but don't know if I'll do that or start a business." Growing thoughtful, she added, "I'd like to go to veterinary school, as I've always liked animals."

Looking at her curiously, Tim asked, "You do?"

"Yes, I've just never had any animals of my own."

Catching on to Meagan's playacting, Shirleen sniffed her nose disgustedly. "I've never liked dogs, so I won't have them in my house."

"That's a shame," Harvey said. "We have a huge great Dane that thinks it's one of the kids. He's getting pretty old and my wife and I are afraid we may have to put him down before too long."

"I hope not," groaned Meagan. "Maybe there's some kind of medicine that would help him live longer. You should ask your vet."

"I'll look into that."

Trudy called them in to eat and they all found their places at the table. When they were finished, Harvey said, "Thank you for the great meal, Mrs. Webb."

"Don't thank me," exclaimed Shirleen. "Trudy did all the work."

"You've outdone yourself, Trudy," Josiah said. "This meal was fit for a king!"

"Just wait until you taste the desert," Meagan said.

William moaned, but didn't refuse.

Trudy brought out the pies and said, "There's pumpkin, apple, banana cream and cherry."

As everyone made their selections, Trudy put the pie on plates and topped each piece with a huge dollop of whipped cream. By the time dessert was finished, everyone was stuffed.

The men all went to the living room while Shirleen and Trudy cleaned up. When they came out of the kitchen, the men were boasting about sports. "I was wondering if you'd play for us, Shirleen," Tim asked when he saw her.

"Are you sure?" she asked in surprise.

"You can play this beautiful instrument?" asked William.

"Can she play?" bragged Tim. "Just wait until you hear her!"

Shirleen chose a song and began to play. An hour and a half later, she turned and asked Meagan if she'd sing. Meagan nearly panicked, but when everyone encouraged her, she agreed. She sang one song after another, until finally Tim asked her to sing "Danny Boy." Shirleen played the introduction, and Meagan came in perfectly. When the song ended, there was total silence. As Shirleen and Meagan sat down, the men swallowed several times to gain control of their emotions.

Sighing, Harvey was the first to speak, "I think I must've died and gone to heaven."

"If you did then I went with you," stated William.

"I never tire of hearing Shirleen and Meagan. Doesn't Meagan have the most beautiful voice ever?" asked Tim proudly.

"Aunt Shirleen is one gifted lady," Josiah said. "It hurts to know I'm the only one in the family that never got one ounce of musical talent." Turning to look at Meagan, Josiah said, "I've been so busy I haven't had the chance to hear Meagan sing before. I agree with you, Tim, she has an incredible voice."

"We have to catch the bus tomorrow, so guess we'd best get some shut eye," William said. Turning to take Shirleen's hand he said, "Thank you, dear lady, for an absolutely fantastic evening."

Laughing, Shirleen replied, "You're more than welcome, William."

Rising to go, Metcalf turned to each lady, and bowed gallantly. "Thank you all for a perfectly wonderful evening."

After the men started for home. Jeff told Shirleen, "I'm going out to the shop to work for a while before I go to bed."

"Okay. Don't work too hard."

"I won't," he promised. Donning his outdoor wear, he slipped out into the cold night. The rest of the family prepared for bed. Meeting in the living room the four of them had their nightly prayers. When that was over, they retired to bed.

Chapter 27

For the next two weeks, Melinda and Theodore divided their time between the hospital, packing up their apartment and getting the new house move in ready.

They had lunch with Henry, Katarina and the two sets of twins at the hospital on Thanksgiving Day. The older twins were doing so well they had been released to go home. When they talked to Dr. Stillman, he suggested Muriel Cline would be willing to help with the twins. Not wanting to burden her, yet needing help, they decided to ask her when they went to visit Katarina later that day. They planned to ask her if she knew of someone who could help them take care of the children.

When they'd spoken to Muriel she said, "Maybe I could get my oldest granddaughter to come and help. She's between jobs right now. She might just be interested."

"We'll pay her the same as we're paying you," Melinda said.

"That would be more than fair. Let me call her right now."

"Thank you, that would be great."

Melinda and Theodore played with Katarina while they waited. They couldn't hear what was being said, but it was plain Muriel wasn't happy. All at once, they heard her say, "Margaret Irene, you are downright lazy. You can't keep a job because you don't want to work. This would be good for you and it would help me out." After a long pause they heard, "Fine! Goodbye!" They were afraid that they'd caused a family dispute and felt bad about it.

A few minutes later, Muriel returned. "I must apologize, but my granddaughter exasperates me."

"We didn't mean to cause any problems," apologized Melinda.

"You didn't. The family is frustrated with Margaret. She doesn't want to do anything to help herself. She just wants to have everything handed to her on a silver platter. When that doesn't happen, she gets nasty."

"I have a brother like that," Theodore said. "Eventually everyone got tired of his behavior and no one will help him. He's also an alcoholic."

"We're afraid Margaret will end up the same way." Sighing, Muriel changed the subject by saying, "I called my other granddaughter, Heather. She's also out of work but is looking for a job. When I told her she would get the same pay I earn, she was more than happy to help. She said to let her know when you need her and she'll be there immediately."

"They wanted to release them today, but because we hadn't made arrangements they changed it to tomorrow at noon."

"I'll let Heather know." Muriel left to call Heather, and a few minutes later returned to say Heather was on her way.

Growing excited, Melinda asked, "So, we really can bring them home tomorrow?"

"You bet!"

That means we have to buy two more car seats, more diapers, bottles, formula, jars of baby food — Oh," cried Melinda, "the list is huge!"

Patting Melinda hand reassuringly, Muriel said, "Don't worry about the baby clothes because I've found donations of baby clothes and cribs, so you'll just need to get diapers, bottles, formula, and that kind of stuff. You also might want to get them a set of clothes to bring them home in."

"We can do that," Theodore said with relief. "Well, honey, we'd better get going and get that shopping done."

They bought everything they could think of and had a lot of it delivered to Mrs. Cline's, then went back to the hospital. They stopped in and visited with Henry, then went to see Effie Pearl and Ephraim Phillip. They could hear them crying all the way down the hall. When they went in the room, a nurse was trying to take care of the baby girl, but apparently Effie didn't think she was doing the job fast enough. Ephraim was crying, too. Melinda, immediately picked him up. "Hello, little man. Are you hungry?"

As soon as she was changed, Effie began to whimper hungrily, too. A nurse carrying two bottles filled with formula came in just before the real wailing started. The new parents happily fed the babies.

The little ones were almost asleep when Dr. Stillman came in. "Have you got everything ready for these little guys to come home tomorrow?"

"Yes, we've been shopping most of the day," grinned Theodore.

"Good. They'll be ready to leave at 9 a.m. I'll give them one last check before I let you take them home."

"How are Michael and Michelle doing?" asked Melinda.

"I just came from there and Michael is doing a little better, but he still has a long way to go. Michelle is doing great. I think she'll be coming home soon."

"I can't wait until both of them are strong enough to be with us," Melinda said.

"Well, I have other patients to see, so I'd best get a move on." As he got to the door he paused to ask, "Have you been in to see Henry?"

"Yes," replied Theodore. "He seemed a lot more chipper than he did this morning."

"He started therapy this morning. He's coming along nicely. I've also called in a speech therapist to work on his speech and motor skills."

"That's' wonderful," cried Melinda excitedly.

"When do you want me to start working with him?" asked Theodore.

"You have enough to do right now, so let the therapy department handle things for a while. When you're settled, we'll get you working with him.

"That would be good. We still have a lot to do."

"How's the packing coming along?"

"We're nearly ready for Mr. Ramey, Mr. Stokes' ranch manager, to come and get a few loads. By the end of next week we should be moved in."

"That's good news. Good luck with everything," he said as he left.

They watched him leave then went in to see Michael and Michelle. They spent half an hour with them talking and touching them. Beaming his excitement, he turned to Melinda. "He just latched onto my finger. Before whenever I touched him or spoke to him, he was as limp as a dishrag. This has to be a good sign."

The nurse walked over to observe and said, "I'll let Dr. Stillman know about this while he's still in the hospital."

Melinda left Michelle's incubator to come over and touch Michael's hand. He latched onto her finger as well. Suddenly Melinda started to cry. "It's all right, honey … I'm not crying because I'm sad. I'm crying because I know he'll be all right."

Slipping an arm around her, Theodore hugged and said, "It is wonderful, isn't it?"

"Oh, yes," sobbed Melinda, smiling through her tears. "I'd better go back to Michelle so she doesn't get lonesome."

A few minutes later they started for home. "I'm hungry," said Theodore. "Let's stop somewhere and eat before go home. We have enough to do without trying to cook too."

"I was secretly hoping you'd say that."

"Good, let's go to the Burger King drive-thru."

"That sounds fine."

Reaching for Melinda's hand he said, "I should take you to a nice restaurant, but I'm so hungry that I don't want to wait."

"I understand. To be honest, I just want to eat so I can get busy with the packing. The only rooms left are the bathrooms and the kitchen. I'll be so glad when we've moved and gotten settled. This moving business is for the birds!"

"My sentiments exactly," Theodore said.

Soon they were on the way home with their fast food. Once they were back in the apartment, Theodore made a couple of calls while Melinda got the food ready.

His first call was to Muriel Cline. He wanted to let her know they would be picking up the twins at 9 a.m. She agreed to take care of the twins along with Katarina. He also told her they'd like her to be the children's honorary grandmother.

His next call was to Lance Ramey. He wanted to let him know they'd be ready to start moving right after they picked up and delivered the twins in the morning. Lance guaranteed he'd have plenty of men and trucks ready to go.

When he was done with the calls, Theodore joined Melinda in the kitchen, where they quickly ate their meal. When they finished, they packed up the kitchen, leaving enough dishes out for breakfast. They continued to pack throughout the night. Just as it grew light, they stopped and ate breakfast. Both of them were so exhausted, but they didn't have time to sleep.

They showered, got dressed and headed to the hospital to pick up the twins.

The next three days passed in a blur for Melinda and Theodore Brooks. Each day, Shirleen's family, Jeff and Trudy, came to help where needed. It was ten o'clock the morning of the third day, when Melinda saw a car followed by several huge trucks coming down their drive. Surprised, she turned to Shirleen and asked, "What do you think's going on?"

Shirleen moved over to look out the window. "I don't know."

Meagan came to stand beside the two women, but remained silent. Suddenly, Theodore came in and asked, "Did you order something, honey?"

"No, we were all just wondering what's going on."

"Well, I guess we'll know in a few minutes."

Everyone congregated to the living room waiting for the vehicles to pull up to the house. Meagan began to read the logos on each truck, "Gerber's baby food, Wal-Mart, J. C. Penny—" Gasping, she turned and said, "I think you're about to be showered with many blessings."

Theodore moved over to open the door. Cline was the driver of the first car. Smiling, he greeted the Brookses and said, "Boy, oh boy, do I ever have a surprise for the two of you!"

Cline waited as the drivers got out and came up to the house. "This man is Frederick Walker, Vice President of Gerber baby foods."

Walker stepped forward and said, "The president of the company and I would like to furnish you with a year's supply of baby formula and baby food."

Gasping, Melinda could only look at the man in stunned disbelief. "Oh," she cried, "thank you so much!"

"My pleasure, ma'am."

Stepping back, Cline introduced the next man. "This is Jared Maxwell, from J. C. Penney Company." He motioned Maxwell forward.

"As the representative of J. C. Penney, we want to furnish you with a year's supply of infant clothes, shoes, blankets, and receiving blankets. We also want to give you five dressers, five lamps, and five rocking chairs, as well as all the towels, washcloths, bath towels, hand towels, bibs, booties, and burping cloths that you will need. "

"Oh, thank you," replied Melinda gratefully."

"You are more than welcome. It isn't every day that we witness such generosity as yours." Bowing slightly, he stepped back to let Cline continue.

"This here is Adam Kendall, who manages our Wal-Mart store at the mall."

Stepping forward, Kendall said, "We know you were in the store last night to buy two car seats, and more diapers and bottles. We have also learned from Mr. Cline here that there are two more children waiting to come home. Therefore, we'll furnish the four cribs, five playpens, two more car seats, and all of the bottles you'll need until they've been weaned. Also a two-year supply of diapers, baby wipes, baby power, shampoo, and baby oil."

"This is not only wonderful, but takes the stress off of us to get all of this bought and brought home," exclaimed Melinda. "Thank you all so much."

"Where would you like us to put all this wonderful stuff?" asked Cline.

"Let's put it in one of the bedrooms down the hall," suggested Theodore "We can get it organized later."

As the women stood there rooted to the spot, the men started unloading the trucks. When all of the trucks had been unloaded, they went to see what had to be done. Melinda nearly fainted at what she saw. "Oh, heaven help me, how will we ever get this all sorted out?"

"One thing at a time," replied Shirleen."

"You're right," sighed Melinda.

Slipping an arm around her, Shirleen said, "It's going to be all right, honey. We'll be here to help you."

"Thank you!"

Meagan helped Trudy put the kitchen together, while Juliana helped Melinda organize the master bedroom and Shirleen vacuumed all of the floors. By that time they were ready to go home. "Tomorrow," said Shirleen, we'll help you clean up your apartment so that you can return the key to the owner."

"That will be one less thing to do," sighed Melinda.

"See," piped up Meagan, "with all of us helping, we got three rooms put together in just one afternoon. We'll get the rest of the house put in order in no time."

"That we will," declared Shirleen.

Soon thereafter the women and Jeff went back to their own home.

For the next week and a half the weather held nicely. The sun even came out from behind the gray clouds, as if it didn't want to miss anything that was going on. By the end of that time, the house was ready to receive the three children. The premature twins were showing great signs of improvement, as was Henry, who was slated to come home in time for Christmas. "You're sticking by Henry has helped him to work hard so that he can go home. If he keeps this kind of work up, he may be able to go home for Christmas."

With the good news that their new family would soon be complete and living under one roof, Melinda and Theodore set about finding enough hired help to let their household run efficiently.

Melinda was at the hospital to visit Henry, and found him sitting up in a chair when she entered his room. Henry reached out to take her hand when she approached, something he hadn't been able to do before. Melinda took his hand and squeezed it gently. "Now this is the Henry I remember."

She got a chair from the corner of the room and carried it over so she could sit next to him. "I'm by myself this morning. Teddy said he had some errands to run."

Henry tried to say something, but nothing came out. "It's all right," Melinda said. "When I asked him what he had to do, he just told me to mind my P's and Q's. He said I'd find out when the time was right."

Henry grinned and again tried to speak, but only managed a grunt. Melinda could tell it was frustrating for him.

She spent half an hour with him, chatting about nothing in particular, then excused herself and went to see Michael and Michelle.

She talked to Michael first, touching first his head, his hand and then rubbed his back gently. He responded by sighing contentedly. Melinda noticed that he was starting to gain a little weight and that he wasn't fighting to breathe. "I love you sweetheart!" He latched onto her finger, and she said, "I'll see you tomorrow. For now, just get all of the rest you can and keep fighting."

Gently extracting her finger, she went over to spend some time with Michelle. When Melinda started talking to her, Michelle began to squirm. "I love you, sweetheart. Keep fighting so the two of you can come home real soon."

A few minutes later, Melinda went down to the lobby and saw Theodore coming in the door. Smiling, Melinda watched him come toward her. "Well, did you get your errands finished?"

"Sure did," grinned Theodore as he bent to kiss her lightly on the lips. "Are you ready to go home?"

"I sure am," replied Melinda. Rising, she walked with him toward the lobby's exit.

When they got into the car, Theodore said, "I got the address for the employment agency from Joel Cline, so let's go there first."

"I can't wait to get someone in to help us so we can start bringing our children home."

"That's how I feel, too," Theodore said.

They went inside the employment agency when they got there and were shown to Stella Holbrook's desk.

"What can I do for you?" she asked after offering them seats.

"We have five infants, all under two years old, and need to hire several people to help us care for them."

Blinking in surprise, Mrs. Holbrook asked, "Did you say *five* infants?"

"Yes, ma'am," replied Theodore, smiling at the woman's shocked expression.

"Why didn't you hire someone when you first had these quintuplets?"

Melinda smiled as she nodded for Theodore to continue, "These are our adopted children." Theodore saw that she needed more information, so he told her the whole story from the beginning.

"Okay," she said. "Tell me what you need, and I'll get started on this right away."

Melinda said, "First, we need a cook and two housekeepers so that I can spend all of my free time with the children." Pausing a moment to think, she continued, "I also think we need to hire three nurses and six aides who can help with the children. That should be enough."

Quickly writing everything down, Stella said, "I'll need your address so I can send them out for interviews." When Melinda gave it to her, she said, "I don't think you'll find anyone who wants to make that drive each day. These roads are a real bear in the wintertime."

"We plan to have them live-in. We need someone there 24 hours a day. We were thinking of running three shifts. We have plenty of room to house them."

"That might work, then."

"We'd need them to start immediately."

"Okay, I'll get right on this."

Trudy opened the door and came out, just as they reached their front door. She said, "I'm leaving, Mr. Brooks."

"What did I say about calling me Mr. Brooks?" grinned Theodore.

"Oh, sorry. I'm so used to being formal when I work for someon that I forgot."

"Well," he teased, "I'll forgive you this time, but don't let it happen again."

"No, sir. I won't forget."

As she started past him, Theodore said, "Thanks for helping me today."

"You're welcome, Theodore."

Melinda was curious about Theodore's comment, but remained silent. When she started to go inside, Theodore said, "Don't go in just yet, Mel." She watched as he walked Trudy to her car. As she started to back out, Theodore returned to Melinda's side. Before she knew his intentions, he scooped her up and carried her over the threshold. Once inside, he kissed her passionately before putting her down. "Welcome to your new home, Mrs. Brooks."

"Thank you, darling."

"Now, close your eyes and let me lead you." Giggling, Melinda complied. Stopping, he said, "Open your eyes."

Melinda squealed in delight, "Oh, Teddy, the room is absolutely beautiful!"

A dozen long stemmed red roses had been placed on the decorative table set for two, and something smelled delicious.

"You like it?" he asked.

"Like it? I love it!"

Helping to seat her, he kissed the top of her head, then walked over and grabbed two heavy mitts. He reached into the oven and pulled out a casserole and set it on top of the stove. He then went about getting the side dishes from the refrigerator and brought everything to the table. After grace, they ate with hearty appetites. "This is delicious," Melinda said. "Did you make this?"

"No, Trudy made it for us as a welcome home present."

"Well, it's scrumptious. If she weren't already taken, I'd say we should hire her to be our cook."

"I agree.

"Perhaps our new cook will be just as good as Trudy."

"I sure hope so."

When they were finished with the main course, Theodore went back to the refrigerator and brought out two pies. "Would you like apple, cherry or a slice of each?"

"The apple sounds wonderful."

"One slice of apple pie coming right up." He cut the pie and put a generous dollop of whipped cream on top. She waited until he had his piece before tasting the pie. "Oh, heaven help me, this is amazing!"

"I agree completely!"

It didn't take them long to make short work of the pie. When they were finished, Theodore cleared the table. Melinda started to help but was told this was her night off. She felt so much love for him as she watched him work.

"Please close you eyes again, sweetheart," he said when he was finished. Melinda complied, and suddenly she heard something being placed on the table. A moment later, something cold was placed around her neck. "Now, you can open your eyes."

When Melinda opened her eyes, Theodore was grinning like the cat that ate the canary. Reaching up to touch the necklace, she gasped. "It feels so beautiful, but I wish I could see it."

"Let's get you to a mirror then," Theodore said.

They went into the bathroom off of their bedroom and Melinda gasped with joy when she saw the seven different colored semiprecious stones and diamonds. "They're for the children, and the one in the very center is my birthstone, a ruby. The emerald stone next to mine is your birthstone. Katarina was also born in May, so the emerald on the left represents her as our first adopted daughter. Effie and Ephraim were born on the tenth of March, so they get aquamarines. Michel and Michelle were born in November so we have a citron for each of them. Because each of us is like a diamond in the rough, I put diamonds on either side of each stone."

Throwing her arms around Theodore's neck, she kissed him so passionately it took his breath away. "You're so thoughtful. This is the perfect gift to represent our new family."

Soon they were wrapped in each other's arms. Then, Theodore picked her up and carried her to the bed, where he laid her down gently. After kissing the hollow of her neck, then her face, he passionately kissed her lips as he began to unbutton the buttons on her blouse. Moaning in pleasure, she responded to his touch by hungrily exploring his body. Soon they were lost in each other's embrace as they sought to pleasure the other.

A long time later, lying in each others arms they talked about their hopes and dreams for the children, then fell asleep, still wrapped in each other's arms.

The next morning, Melinda lay in bed wondering what her day would be like. Finally, she got up, showered and went to start breakfast. She had nearly gotten the bacon fried, when Theodore came in looking dapper. "Good morning, Teddy. Did you sleep well?"

"Like a log. How about yourself?"

"The same."

"What have you got planned for the day?"

"Going to the hospital to see Henry and the twins, then over to see the other children, then I thought I would take some time out to read. To be honest, I'm feeling a little tired today."

"We've been going non-stop," admitted Theodore. "Maybe taking some time to read would help to relax you a little bit."

"Thanks for understanding, darling."

Theodore continued to set the table while Melinda started on the pancakes. Soon they were having their breakfast. Not long after they'd finished eating, there was a knock at the door.

"I'm here to apply for the cook's position," the woman said when Theodore answered the door.

"Come on in."

Smiling sweetly, she said, "Thanks. It's a little brisk out here."

"This way," Theodore said as he led her toward the kitchen. "Mel, we have our first applicant for the cook's position."

"Hi. My name's Annabelle Croft."

"Nice to meet you, Annabelle. Have a seat." When she was settled, Melinda asked, "Do you have references?"

"Yes," she said as she reached into her large handbag and pulled out a file folder. "As you can see, I've been working for a Mr. Robison for the last eight years, but he passed away last week."

Looking up from the file, Melinda said, "It says here that you've cooked for large groups, as well as for families and individuals. May I ask why you're not working in a restaurant?"

"I worked in a restaurant here in Cardston for about fifteen years. It's really stressful and that eventually impacted my health. I decided to work for families exclusively after that." Nodding toward the file, she continued. "As you can see, I've only worked for two other families and Mr. Robison."

"Yes, I see that."

"The first family I worked for wasn't honest. They'd promise to pay me but didn't. After a while, they told me they'd already paid me. I quit after that."

"I don't blame you." Looking at Annabell, Melinda asked, "What about the other family?"

"They were really nice people and a pleasure to work for. The husband was killed in a head on collision, but I continued to work for the family until they were all killed when their car hit a moose.

"After that, I went to work for Mr. Robison. He'd just turned 80 when I started. He was good to me. When he was 88, he had a fatal heart attack while I was away shopping. I found him when I got home. I've been out of a job since."

"I see." Placing the folder onto the table, Melinda gave her some details about their life, "My husband and I have just adopted five children and they're all less than two years old."

Gasping in shock, Annabelle exclaimed, "No way!"

"It's true, but it's a long story. We'll also have another person in the household once my brother-in-law, who had a massive stoke, is released from the hospital. We need a cook who can deal with cooking for twelve or thirteen people. We don't need anything fancy, and we'd all eat our meals together, other than three of the women who will be working for us who will need to have their meals during the night shift. Will that be a problem for you?"

"No, I can work with that."

"Would you be willing to cook something for us today?"

Smiling, Annabelle reached into her bag to extract a couple of items. "I thought you might want to know what my cooking was like, so I made these rolls early this morning." She handed the container to Melinda.

Melinda broke off a piece and the moment she put it into her mouth she was surprised to find that it soft, light in texture, and delicious. "This is excellent, Annabelle."

"Thank you, ma'am."

Annabelle got out the other container and said, "This is a sample of my desert baking."

"This cookie is moist and delectable, Annabelle. You *are* a good cook."

"Thank you, ma'am."

Theodore sampled the roll and said, "Melinda's right. These rolls are fantastic! I agree with my wife you are a good cook."

"Thank you, sir."

"This sir stuff has to go," declared Theodore emphatically, smiling to take the edge off of his words. "Just call me Theodore."

"Okay."

While Melinda spoke to Annabelle about her duties, Theodore got a chance to look at her closely. She was tall and very willowy. She wasn't beautiful to gaze upon, but her demeanor was flawless. *Perhaps she wouldn't be so bad to look at if she didn't have such a hooked nose,* thought Theodore. She had such a high protruding forehead, with large cheekbones. Her dark blue eyes were spaced wide apart, with well-defined eyebrows. Her mouth seemed to be no more than a thin line. The simple cut blue dress that she had on was clean and crisp. Her boots were so ugly that it caused her drab appearance to appear even worse. Suddenly, he was brought back to the present, when Melinda asked, "What do you think, Teddy?"

"I'm sorry, I was lost in thought."

"Do you think Annabelle will work out for what we need?"

"If she can cook other dishes as well as she did these," said Theodore. Then I think we should hire her."

"Then you are hired, Annabelle."

"When do you want me to start?"

"Could you move in this afternoon then start cooking in the morning?"

"I sure can. I'll go get my things and be back by four o'clock so I can cook dinner."

"Oh, that would be great!"

"Just so you know, we plan to hire a couple of housekeepers as soon as we can."

"Do you want me to do the housework until then?"

"That would be great and we'll make sure your pay reflects the extra work."

"Then, that's what I'll do."

Nodding affirmatively, Annabelle rose to leave. "I'll see you both around four. Thanks for hiring me. You won't be sorry."

Chapter 28

Shirleen and her family had been helping Theodore and Melinda Brooks with their large family. During this time, they grew close. Shirleen was impressed with how selfless the two young people were in adopting all the orphaned children.

As they prepared the house for the children's arrival, Melinda told them how happy she was to bring the children into her life, and how scared she was that she'd fail them. Shirleen assured them they would be fine.

One day, Shirleen found Melinda in tears. She was frustrated because she couldn't find anyone suitable to help care for the children, even after numerous interviews. She'd helped her get through the crisis then and now, five days before Christmas, she had a strong feeling she was needed again. This time, Shirleen took Trudy with her.

Theodore, answering their knock, told them, "Mel's having a tough time right now. I don't know if she's up to having visitors."

"I had a feeling I needed to come see her. Maybe I can help."

"Then please, come in. I've been trying to console her, but I've failed pretty miserably."

Smiling, Shirleen replied, "Show us where she is and we'll see what we can do."

Theodore led the way to the kitchen, where Annabelle Croft was working at the kitchen sink. Seeing it was Shirleen and Trudy, Melinda began mopping at her face to get rid of the tears. Failing, she began to cry harder.

Shirleen walked over to wrap her arms around Melinda, wisely letting her cry it out. When she finally calmed down, Shirleen said, "Can you tell me what has you so upset?"

"I've interviewed so many people, but none of them can start work immediately."

"Do you have a list of them?"

"Yes," replied Melinda indicating the file before her on the table.

"Let us take a look." Shirleen said as she and Trudy moved around to sit next to Melinda. "Sometimes a new sets of eyes can see something you missed."

"I think maybe the problem is your remote location," Shirleen said after reviewing the application information.

Trudy added, "It's obvious they don't really want the job. They wouldn't have made up such absurd excuses if they did. In my opinion, you don't need them. The right people are out there for you, you just haven't found them yet."

"I agree wholeheartedly with Trudy," Shirleen said. "Do you have more applicants to interview?"

"Yes," replied Melinda. "The next one is due in 30 minutes."

"Well, go freshen up and we'll tackle this together."

"Oh, thank you," declared Melinda gratefully. "I'm truly out of my league here!"

"I've dealt with a large household staff before. We'll get it figured out."

A short time later, a middle-aged woman applying for the nurse's aid position was at the door.

Melinda thought she looked pleasant and confident. Her blue eyes sparkled with life and there was a ready smile on her lips.

"What is you name?" Shirleen asked after the woman was seated.

"Harriet Beal."

"Have you taken care of infants before?"

"Yes. I've taken care of children all of my life. For the past five years, I've been working in Calgary at a day care center. I recently moved to Cardston so I could be close to my mother, so I need a new job."

"Then you have worked with infants?"

"Off and on. Mostly I worked with the older children though."

"Did you like working with the infants?"

"Oh, yes."

She gave them her resume and Shirleen studied it carefully, impressed with what she read, as was Melinda when she read it. "How soon could you start to work, should you be hired?"

"Immediately,"

"You'd need to move in here so that you don't have to travel the roads every day. The weather can get pretty bad at times."

"Staying here would suit me fine. However, I would like to go see my mother once a week, when the weather permits."

"That's no problem," responded Melinda.

Looking Harriet in the eyes, Shirleen asked, "Since there are only eight rooms, you'll need to share a room with another person. Will that bother you?"

"Not at all." Ginning she added, "But the other person might not like bunking with me, because I snore."

"We'll get some ear plugs," teased Shirleen. They laughed and then Shirleen said, "First of all let me tell you a little bit about who you'll be working for and what you'll be doing. Melinda and Theodore, you met him at the door, have just adopted five infants. There are two set of twins and an additional baby."

"Excuse me?" interrupted Harriet, "Did you say *five* infants?"

"Yes, I did."

"Oh, honey, you sure have your work cut out for you. No wonder you're hiring help." It was obvious that Harriet was impressed.

Shirleen continued, "One set of twins was premature and they're still in the hospital. The little girl can come hone in a couple of days, but the little boy will need to stay there for a while longer."

"They'll need special care then?" questioned Harriet.

"Yes, there'll be a nurse here to show you what you need to know," replied Melinda.

"Good enough," sighed Harriet. "I feel better about that."

Shirleen motioned for Melinda to take over the interview. Taking a deep breath, Melinda began to give Harriet her instructions. "You'll be working the dayshift, from 7 a.m. to 4 p.m." Nodding, Harriet waited for Melinda to continue, "We'll provide your meals here and you will be paid $9 an hour. You'll also have two days off each week." Melinda paused to give Harriet time to assimilate the information before asking, "Could you start working in the morning?"

"Yes, ma'am, I can."

"Good, then I'll see you at 7 a.m."

"Could I come this afternoon to get settled in?"

"Yes, that would be fine."

"Good, then I'll be here around 3:30."

"Fantastic!"

Rising, Harriet shook Melinda's hand, and said, "I'm anxious to learn why you chose to adopt five little ones."

"We'll tell you tonight when you come back," replied Melinda.

As she left, Shirleen said, "That's one down at least."

"You handled that beautifully," sighed Melinda.

Before she could say more the doorbell rang again. A woman, clad in a heavy fur coat smiled at him from the other side of the door. She was thin with graying hair and Theodore guessed she was in her late thirties or early forties. Her brown eyes seemed to stare into his very soul.

"May I help you?"

"I'm here about the nurse's position."

Theodore showed her in and led her to the kitchen. "This lady's here about the nurse's position." Winking at Melinda he went back into the living room.

Indicating a chair near Trudy, Shirleen said, "Please have a seat and tell me your name and qualifications."

Handing Shirleen a folder, she said, "My name is Susan Thomas, and I've lived and worked here my whole life."

"Your resume says you're a pediatrics nurse and you've been working at the hospital for most of your career. Why do you want to take on this job?"

"I've worked with Dr. Stillman for years. He suggested I take a break from the hospital and work here. When I asked him if I was being sacked, he told me he knew you needed the best nurse available and that was me."

Looking at Melinda for approval, Shirleen nodded for her to take over. Melinda smiled as she said. "If Dr. Stillman recommended you, then that's good enough for me."

"Thank you." Looking at Melinda intently, she said, "When Dr. Stillman told me how you came to adopt five infants, I must admit to being impressed by your story."

"Were you at the hospital that terrible night?"

"No, I was in Spokane visiting my parents. I was stranded there for a week."

"No wonder I haven't met you." Melinda paused to collect her thoughts and continued. "If you take the job, you'll need to live here. You'll be sharing a room with the other two nurses, we hired yesterday. They're the only two women who could start immediately."

"If I were to get the job, when do I start?"

"You probably need some more information before you decide. First of all, my brother-in-law, who is in the hospital recovering from two massive strokes, will be living with us as well. Part of your job will be caring for him. If you take the job and can start immediately, you'd be working the graveyard shift from 3 p.m. to 7 a.m. We'll provide all of your meals and $15 per hour. You'll also have two days off each week."

"That's more than fair."

"Does that mean that you'll take the job?" Melinda asked hopefully.

"Yes," replied Susan. "I'll be here at ten o'clock in the morning to get settled in and get a little rest before I go to work tomorrow night."

"Great! We'll see you then."

After she left, the women had some coffee and cookies and Theodore joined them. "Juliana, Meagan, Trudy, Jeff and I have been talking," Shirleen said. "We wondered if you'd spend Christmas with us."

"That would be wonderful," Theodore said. "But I don't think it would be a good idea to take the children out in this weather."

"What were we thinking?"

"What if we had Christmas dinner here?" asked Melinda.

"We don't want to put you out," said Shirleen.

Looking at Annabelle, Melinda asked, "Would you be willing to help cook a meal for about 16 people, Annabelle?"

"Sure," said Annabelle. "We'd need to go shopping though."

"We have a huge turkey and all of the trimmings," said Shirleen. "We could prepare the meal, Melinda, if you and Annabelle could set the tables and provide the drinks. We can bring our dining room table over so there will be enough room for everyone. I think it would go well with yours."

"That would be wonderful," said Melinda. "Since you're making the turnkey, maybe we could bake a ham." Turning to Annabelle, she asked, "What do you think, Annabelle?"

"Sure. No problem."

"Good, then that's settled. We could manage to set the tables couldn't we, Theodore?"

"I think I could manage that," he said.

"That seems like a simple solution to our problem," grinned Shirleen, pleased to have some help. Looking at Trudy, she asked, "What kind of pies are you making, Trudy?"

"Three pumpkin, three apple and two cherry," replied Trudy.

"What if I were to bake two banana cream, two chocolate cream, two pecan and three more pumpkin pies?" asked Annabelle. "We can never have enough pies."

Theodore began to rub his tummy, as he moaned, "Yum! Is it Christmas yet?"

This made everyone laugh. "Not quite," replied Shirleen.

"Shucks."

They were interrupted when the doorbell rang. Theodore went to answer the door and was surprised to see two young ladies on his doorstep. From first glance they looked like carbon copies of each other. Their clothes, although clean and neat, had seen better days. Both of them had the same hazel colored eyes and the same brown hair. "Good morning ladies. What can I do for you?"

"We're here to apply for the nurse's aide positions," said the taller of the two.

"Please come in and I'll take you to the boss." He led them to the kitchen to meet with Trudy, Melinda and Shirleen.

After Theodore told them why the women were there, they introduced themselves. "My name is Joyce Watson and this is my sister, Clara."

Studying them a moment because they looked so young, Shirleen asked, "How old are you?"

"I'm twenty years old and my sister is eighteen."

"Have you had experience caring for infants and children?"

Smiling, Joyce replied, "We sure have. Clare and I come from a family of 14 children. The youngest one is two years old. We've helped take care of her since she was born."

"I'd say you've got experience then," grinned Shirleen. "Have you had experience with premature infants?"

"Yes. The twins that were born before Nellie, that's the two year old, were born six weeks early. Momma had complications and was bedridden for six months. It was up to Clara and me to take care of them."

Shirleen exchanged glances with Melinda, who nodded in agreement. "I'm curious," said Shirleen, "why doesn't you sister speak for herself?"

"My sister has a speech impediment. When she talks, she stutters."

"Well, Clara, if you work here, you'll need to talk. Will that bother you?"

"N-n -no." No one reacted to the stuttering, so Clara continued, "I w-w-was scared that if I cu-cu-couldn't talk right yu-yu-you wouldn't hire me."

"I understood you just fine," said Melinda.

"Th-th-thank you."

"If we were to hire both of you, would you be willing to live here? The weather, as you know, can get pretty bad and we'd need to be sure you were here to work your shift. Also, would you be able to start work immediately?"

"Sure, there's no problem with our staying here, we already share a room," replied Joyce. "We need to let our parents know where we are and pack our clothes, and then we can start." Looking at Clara to see if she agreed, which she did, Joyce added, "We could start this afternoon, by five o'clock if you'd like."

"Joyce," asked Shirleen, "why do the two of you want this job?"

"My father's ill and hasn't been able to go to work. When we heard about you hiring and we thought we could help our parents."

Melinda grinned in relief, "That's a good reason. You're both hired."

"If you still needing help, we have a 16 year old sister who would also be qualified. We could all share the same room."

Growing excited, Melinda exchanged glances with Shirleen, who motioned for her to proceed. "Wonderful! We'll provide all of your meals and pay you $9 an hour. You'll also have two days off each week. Do you want the jobs?"

"Oh, yes," said Joyce.

"We'll have a room ready for you when you get here this afternoon," said Melinda. "By the way, what is your sister's name? The one who will be coming with you?"

"Leslie."

Nodding, Melinda continued, "We'll put the three of you in the same room. One of the rooms is large enough to accommodate a set of bunk beds and a twin sized bed."

"That would be great."

"We'll see you soon."

After the girls left, Melinda said, "We have a woman taking care of three of the children, with the help of one of her granddaughters. Do you think I should ask her if she'd like to work here. Muriel's husband died six months ago, so maybe she could use the job."

"It won't hurt to ask," replied Shirleen.

"While we're waiting for another applicant to show up, I think I'll give her a call."

"Good idea."

Melinda made the call and was thrilled when Muriel said she'd like the job. She said she'd close up her house and be happy to move in. She told Melinda she'd get back to her within the hour to settle the details.

"Muriel was excited and said she'd take the job! That will give us six people so far."

By two o'clock, they'd filled all of the positions except for two housekeepers.

As Shirleen and Trudy prepared to leave, there was a knock at the door and Theodore was surprised to see Sergeant York and another Mountie standing on the other side of the door. "How may I help you two fine gentlemen?"

"We've come to speak to you and Melinda."

Blinking in surprise, Theodore asked, "Is something wrong?"

"If you'll invite us in, we can explain."

"Oh, excuse me. Please come on in." A sick feeling came over Theodore, but he tried to calm the inner turmoil as he closed the door.

When Tim saw Shirleen, he grinned. "Fancy meeting you here. How're you today?"

"Great." Seeing the anxious look on Theodore's face, Shirleen said, "We were about to go, so we'll make our exit and give you all some privacy."

"No, please stay. Your being here saves me a trip to your place."

"What's the matter?"

"Josiah got word today that there's a serial killer on the loose. He is reportedly coming from Spokane, where he's accused of killing 14 young girls."

Shirleen, whose face had grown ashen at the news, exclaimed, "That's horrible!"

"When did he leave Spokane?" asked Theodore.

"Sometime yesterday."

"That worries me," said Theodore. "We've just hired a bunch of women. They'll be arriving throughout the day."

"Who are they and we'll personally escort them out here."

Melinda handed Tim the list of people they'd just hired. Scanning the paper, Tim's face grew paler. "There are quite a few women on this list."

Explaining the situation, Melinda said, "We'll need all of these people to help us with the little ones."

"We were told he has family in this area. No one knows who, so be on the look out for someone with Washington plates."

"Do you have a name for this suspect?" Annabelle asked.

"Yes, ma'am. His name is Arthur Quigley."

Placing a hand over her mouth, Annabelle suddenly fainted. Theodore caught her before she hit the floor. Lowering her so that they could revive her, Theodore looked up at Sergeant York. "Unless I'm mistaken, I'd say you found his family."

A moment later, Annabelle regained consciousness. Looking around, she asked, "What happened?"

"You fainted," explained Tim. "Do you know Arthur Quigley?"

"Yes, sir." For a moment Annabelle couldn't speak, Finally, she looked up at Tim to say, "He's my brother."

"When did you last see him?"

"Three years ago at the funeral. When our parents were killed in a car accident, he kind of snapped. He'd always been moody, but after that he was different. There was something sinister about him that made my flesh crawl." Annabelle paused in an attempt to gain control of her emotions. "When I tried to talk to him, he glared at me and walked out of the room. I never saw him again."

"Do you think he's coming here to see you?" asked Tim.

"I'm the only family he has left," calmly replied Annabelle. "I don't want to ever see him again, though." Sighing, she asked, "Isn't there some way to stop him from coming here?"

"Why are you so afraid of him?"

"When I was 15, I saw him beat a boy senseless. When I tried to stop him, he beat me unconscious. I've been terrified of him ever since."

"Did the boy die?"

"No, but he had brain damage."

"No wonder you're afraid," replied Tim.

"My mother wouldn't do anything about it when I told her, so I ran away."

"Does he know you live here?"

"Yes, sir. I made the mistake of telling him at the funeral."

"Does he know your address?"

"No, sir. I just got hired to work here yesterday."

"Then maybe you'll be safe here."

"We'll see she's protected," declared Theodore, "even if we have to have the hired hands assist us."

"Good. The officer who called said they had an all points bulletin out on him. They've also set up roadblocks at different points along the way. Hopefully, we'll get him before he gets here." Turning back to Annabelle, Tim asked, "Is your brother older or younger than you?"

"He's two years older. One time, I got a beautiful doll for Christmas. I was quietly playing with it in the living room when suddenly he grabbed it from me. Before I could say or do anything, he ripped the head and arms off, then got a knife from the kitchen and began stabbing it. I started crying hysterically and he laughed and continued to stab the doll. Momma said not to worry about it, that she would get me a new doll."

"Did she reprimand him for what he had done."

"Not really. She just told him that he shouldn't have done that. When Momma left the room, he took the hammer from Daddy's toolbox. I watched in horror as he began hitting the doll's head until it was completely smashed to pieces."

"That's what he has been doing to his victims," stated Tim. "When you go to town, stick together. Don't get separated. Actually, don't go unless you absolutely have to. I'll let you know when it's safe."

"We haven't gone Christmas shopping yet," protested Melinda.

"Then I'd suggest you go in a pack. If possible, go out today so you can get everything done in one trip. Don't go out except to the hospital."

Just then the phone rang. Theodore answered, then said, "That's wonderful news, doctor. We can. Super! We'll be there as soon as possible. Thank you."

Theodore was beaming. "That was Dr. Stillman with the best news ever. We can bring Michelle home this afternoon!"

"Wonderful!" cried Melinda. "What about Michael?"

"He said he wanted to keep him for another three days. If he continues to do well, we can bring him home then."

"Oh," sighed Melinda. "Our little family will finally be together soon."

"Dr. Stillman also said Henry was doing so well that he will be released two days before Christmas."

"That's day after tomorrow," Arthur Quigley was momentarily forgotten.

Melinda's cell phone rang. It was Muriel calling to accept the job. She also volunteered the extra beds from her house and the bedding to go with them. She told her the good news about Michelle and welcomed her to the staff.

After ending the call, Melinda filled them all in. "Now if we can only get one or two housekeepers."

"What do they need to do?" asked Tim.

"Clean the house, and do the laundry."

"Well, I know a lady who just got out of an abusive relationship. Her children are grown and she's by herself. This job would be ideal for her."

"Can you give me her number?"

"She doesn't have a phone, but if you'll tell me all of the particulars of the job, I'll bring her over her if she's interested."

"That would be wonderful," cried Melinda.

"Also one of my parents' neighbors just lost her husband and needs a job badly. I'll speak to her too."

"Thank you, Tim."

"You're more than welcome. If I'm going to escort those you've hired back here before dark then I'd better get a move on. Remember, until further notice, no going out by yourselves. Especially you, Annabelle."

"I won't forget."

"I'll escort you home if you're ready, Shirleen."

A few minutes later the house was silent. Excusing herself for a moment, Annabelle went to her room to cry. When she came back into the kitchen, Melinda said, "Annabelle Croft, don't you worry about your brother. We'll do our best to protect you."

"I know," signed Annabelle. "It's just hard to have a member of your family be so evil. The sad part is, I hope he gets caught and they throw the book at him."

"I can't even begin to imagine your pain," replied Melinda. "If you want to talk about it sometime, I'll gladly listen."

Annabelle surprised Melinda by giving her a quick hug. "That means everything to me, Melinda." Stepping back she added, "To be honest, I was afraid you were going to fire me after you found out."

"Nonsense," replied Melinda with feeling. "It isn't your fault your brother's the way that he is." Smiling sweetly she continued, "I have my share of skeletons in my closet too, so I have no room to judge. Besides you're an exceptionally good cook and I don't want to lose you."

Beaming at the high praise, Annabelle quickly went back to work.

After making a casserole for dinner, Annabelle and Melinda went upstairs to prepare the rooms for the newly hired help. When they were satisfied that they had done all that they could, they went downstairs to get ready for the children to come home.

Theodore had put one of the new car seats into the car, along with the diaper bag that contained Michelle's coming home clothes and gone to the hospital to get her while they worked on the house. It had bothered Melinda that she couldn't go with him but she also understood the importance of getting the house ready.

Soon the doorbell rang, and Melinda greeted Susan Thomas and Harriet Beal. Seeing other cars coming up the road, she knew that the others were arriving earlier than planned. "Please come in out of the cold. When everyone gets here, I'll show you all to your rooms."

At the end of the column of cars was Tim's truck. He stopped and rolled down his window and said, "Both ladies want the job. They're packing right now. When they're ready I'll escort them back out here."

"Thank you, Tim."

"Glad to be of service." He turned around, waved and started back down the lane.

Melinda and Annabelle showed the women to their rooms. Before they'd completed the room assignments, the doorbell rang again. Melinda hurried over to answer it and saw the Watson sister's standing there, each with a suitcase in hand. An older woman was with them. "Please come inside," Melinda said.

Joyce took over the conversation. Indicating the older woman she said, "Mrs. Brooks, this is my mother, Ethel Watson."

"How do you do, Mrs. Watson?" replied Melinda.

"Great, thank you," greeted Ethel. "It's nice to meet you, Mrs. Brooks.

Laughing, Melinda said, "Oh, dear. Please, just call me Melinda."

"Melinda it is," agreed Ethel. "I wanted to meet the woman my girls would be working for."

"I'm so glad that you came with them."

"When the weather permits, we'll pick them up on their days off so they can be with the family."

"That's fine." Melinda immediately liked Ethel Watson. Ethel was an older and plumper version of her daughters. "Can I get you something to drink?" asked Melinda.

"No, thank you. I have to get back to the house and get supper started." Turning to the three girls, she hugged them and gave them some last minute instructions. A few minutes later, Melinda saw her driving down the long lane.

Two hours later, Tim arrived followed by two cars. When they all got out of their vehicles and joined Tim at the door, he made the introductions, "Mrs. Brooks, this lady to my right is Louise Rogers. She's the one who had the problem with her husband."

"Hello, Louise. Welcome aboard."

"Thank you, ma'am."

"I'm just plain Melinda. May I call you Louise?"

"Of course."

Tim continued, "This woman on my left is Dawna Twitchell."

"Hello, Mrs. Brooks."

"Hello. May I call you Dawna?" Before the woman could speak, Melinda continued. "I would also like you to call me Melinda.

"You may use my first name, ma'am."

Laughing, Melinda replied, "No ma'am stuff either, just plain Melinda will do."

Consulting his list, Tim looked around the room. "It looks like everyone's present and accounted for, so I'll get back to the office. If I learn anything new, I'll let you know. Good luck with your new jobs, ladies."

By the time Theodore got home with the children and they'd been put into their new beds, it was time to eat. After the meal was over, the beds from Muriel's place were set up and room assignments had been given. It was getting late, and Muriel and her granddaughter, Heather helped where needed.

Not having the schedule made up yet, some of the women volunteered to take the nightshift. When the house had quieted down, Melinda realized just how exhausted she really was. As she got ready for bed, her body ached from sheer exhaustion.

"Are you all right, darling?" asked Theodore.

"I'm so tired." Suddenly tears started streaming down her face. "I'm sorry for the tears. I don't know why I'm crying."

Slipping his arms around her, he held her tight until the tears stopped. "You've been such a trooper, honey. Just go to sleep. If there are any problems, I'll deal with them."

"Oh, bless you, Teddy!" Moving from the circle of his arms she got into bed and said, "I love you so much."

"I love you too, Melinda Brooks." He kissed her soundly and then tucked her in. Theodore's eyes misted as he gazed at this woman whom he loved more than life. Getting into bed, he too quickly fell asleep.

Chapter 29

Major Josiah Graham was working at his desk the next morning when Tim knocked on his door and poked his head inside. "Sergeant Dixon from the Spokane PD is on line one."

"Thanks, Tim."

Josiah picked up the phone as Tim left.

"This is Sergeant Melvin Dixon from the Spokane PD. We have confirmation Quigley's moving closer to Cardston. I got a call this morning from Justin Richards at Sandpoint PD. He said Quigley ditched his car near the bridge coming into town when it broke down. He walked into a residential area, broke into a home and held an elderly gentleman hostage for five hours before killing him. He even took some of the old man's clothes and his car. A neighbor called the police but he was gone by the time they got to the scene.

"They alerted the police on the route to Cardston, since that's where everyone seems to think he's headed. They set up roadblocks, but he got around 'em. Could you lend us some of your men for the manhunt?"

"Sure," replied Josiah. "I'm sure you're aware this guy will stop at nothing to get what he wants."

"When we talked to a criminal psychiatrist, he told us that men like Quigley explode when they're pressured too much. According to the psychiatrist, something awful must have happened in his past to make him willing to kill at the drop of a hat."

"I was just about to call you with some information."

"What have you learned?"

"Seems that some people who just moved into town hired a cook recently and it turns out she's the fugitive's sister."

"You don't say?"

"Yeah. She told Sgt. York she was afraid of her brother and that he's had these violent traits since he was a boy — nearly beat a kid to death when he was 15. When her parents ignored the incident, the sister ran away from home. Their parents were killed in a car accident later, and she went to the funeral. Quigley was there and something happened that scared her so bad she ran for her life because she's let it slip she was living in Cardston."

"Then this is who he's coming to see."

"That's correct. We've got the sister and the people she works with under constant surveillance."

"Smart. All of the news stations from Spokane to Cardston have his photo. Maybe we'll get lucky and someone will turn him in."

"As to helping you, we'll set up a roadblock when he gets closer to us."

"That would be great. We'll keep you posted. My partner and I are an hour or two behind him. We almost caught up with him twice, but he managed to give us the slip."

After they'd exchanged contact information and ended the call, Josiah went to Tim's office and filled him in on what he'd just learned. When he finished, he asked, "Is there an officer stationed out at the Brooks ranch yet?"

"Yes, sir. Mathew Higgins and Jacob Turley are both out there."

"Thanks. That's one less thing we have to deal with. Now, I have an appointment to meet with the Mayor to let him know what is going on."

"This isn't going to make him happy. He doesn't like surprises."

"That's for sure. It can't be helped, so he'll just have to deal with it."

When Josiah got back, he got a call from Melvin Dixon.

"Two hours ago, Quigley was spotted crossing into Canada. He stopped at a local restaurant and the waitress recognized him. She took his order and reported him to her boss. The police rushed over but he was gone when they got there. He left some destruction in his wake — hit a lady over the head and sole her car. The woman died. A cruiser pursued him and there was a high-speed chase, but they lost him when he played a deadly game of "chicken" and tried to hit them head-on.

"His wave of destruction continued. He took out two cars during this chase. One of the cars flipped and exploded resulting in four dead. They backed off after this because they didn't want anymore casualties."

"Smart move," stated Josiah.

"The next report we got was he'd taken a woman hostage about 50 miles from down the road. Unfortunately, she'll probably end up dead too."

Frustrated, Josiah declared, "That man is as slippery as an eel!"

"You've got that right, Josiah," sighed Dixon resignedly.

"It doesn't sound like the police are at fault for not catching him," Josiah said. "This Quigley character may be insane, but he's not stupid. Where are you now?"

"We're about two hundred miles from Crow's Nest."

"I see. Well keep me posted. We're ready on this end."

"When we get to Crows Nest, I'll be back in touch."

Sitting back in his chair, he sighed audibly. *I have a feeling it's gonna get worse before this is all over. I hope we catch this guy before anyone else dies.*

While Tim was getting the area map from the file cabinet, Josiah remained silent. As Tim put the map on the desk in front of him, Josiah sat forward to scan it. "Tim, I don't have a good feeling about this. Ever since we found out Quigley was on his way here, I've had this gnawing feeling that we're in for an awful battle."

"Me too. This is nothing like any manhunt we've ever been on."

"That's for sure. I keep praying for inspiration, but so far nothing has come to me. How do you feel about our having a prayer together?"

Nodding in agreement, Tim said, "In the past when we've had a dangerous job to do, prayer has been a good thing." Bowing their heads, Josiah prayed for safety for all of the men involved. A few minutes later, both men felt a peace steal over them.

Studying the map carefully, they finally decided on the location for their road-block. When that was done, Josiah said, "I'm hungry. Let's go get some lunch while we wait for things to heat up."

They were just finishing their pie when Josiah's cell phone rang.

"Quigley just robbed a gun shop," Dixon quickly said. "He pulled out a Magnum .45 and shot the owner six times, then took five or six automatics, ten handguns and a ton of ammunition. He's now armed to the teeth."

"Oh, no," Josiah said. "That means he plans to shoot it out!"

"That's what we thought too," replied Dixon. "We're in Crow's Nest now. We're gonna grab a bite to eat and get back on these icy roads."

"I'll have the men get ready for this shootout. Keep me posted."

When the call ended, Josiah asked Tim, "Are you ready to set up the roadblock?"

"Yes, We were just waiting to hear from Dixon."

"Quigley's got the peddle to the metal, according to Dixon, so you'd probably better get to it. Be safe"

Tim called an emergency meeting of all the officers, including the dispatcher and filled them in. "I just want to stress that you should do nothing to provoke this man. He's dangerous and wont' think twice about ending your life. We'll get the roadblock setup and wait for him to come to us."

"This man is tired and possibly desperate, so stay alert." Josiah cautioned. As his cell phone started to ring, he saw it was Dixon again.

"We just learned Quigley's holed up somewhere near Crow's Nest. He broke into a home and killed the family before stealing their car."

Groaning Josiah said, "Then we could be looking at several hours before he gets here."

"Quigley hasn't had any sleep for well over twenty-four hours. He has to sleep some time. That might give you even more time to get things set up."

"Are you sure he hasn't had any sleep?"

"Yeah," replied Dixon. "We've been pushing him so hard he hasn't had a chance to stay put for long."

"Then he'll be a ticking time bomb by the time he gets here."

"That's right."

"We'll get the roadblock set up and wait until we hear from you again."

"That shouldn't be more than another hour or two. When we're 50 miles out of Cardston, I'll call you."

Disconnecting the call, Josiah turned to face the anxious men. After quickly filling them in, he said, "Let me make one thing clear, none of you are going to play the hero today! I want everyone to come out of this alive."

When the men had gone to get things ready, Josiah turned to Tim and said, "This is going to be a long stake out, be sure everyone is prepared."

"I will," promised Tim. Josiah left him to call Shirleen to tell her wouldn't be there for dinner and warn her about what was about to go down. He also told her that Gary Baugh would be keeping an eye on the house until he could get there.

Forty-five minutes later, several cruisers filled with armed men were driving out of town. While some men were setting up roadblocks, Josiah had ten others working on digging a long, wide, deep trench. They nearly it ready when Josiah's cell phone rang. It was Dixon.

"We're nearly to Cardston," Dixon said when Josiah answered. "There's no more news on Quigley. He's probably someplace sleeping for a while. That's good for us! I also got the plate number on the latest car he stole," Dixon added, giving him the number.

"We have the roadblock set up here, as well as a good-sized trench to shoot from."

"Fantastic! When we get close enough to see the roadblock, we'll honk three times to let you know that it's us."

"Great. We'll start checking cars. We have the block set up so you have to come around a bend positioned between two long hills. You'll be right on it before you know it. You have time enough to stop, but that's it."

"Wise choice," praised Dixon. "See you soon."

Not long after Dixon's call, the men had everything ready to go. Josiah was grateful that Tim had not only gotten several thermos bottles of hot drinks, but that he had also brought a case of bottled water and several snacks for the men. *It's a good thing Mayor Cox told me not to spare the expenses for this operation,* thought Josiah. He took a deep breath and settled down to wait.

All at once they heard three loud blasts of a horn. Dixon had arrived. Rising from his cramped position in the trench, Josiah went to meet him. "You made record time, Sergeant," Josiah said as he shook Dixon's hand.

"I feel like I've been driving forever. It's good to stop and walk around." Dixon turned to motion for his partner to come forward. As he did this, Josiah studied the man he'd been speaking to over the last 24 hours. At first glance, Dixon looked pudgy, but Josiah realized that he wasn't really fat — it was all muscle.

302 • *Mabel Ebner*

When Dixon spoke, he used his hands a lot. Getting a good look at them he was surprised to see how massive they were. *My goodness his hands are like a pair of beefsteaks,* thought Josiah.

When the other man started forward, Dixon said, "This man is my partner, Dick Harris."

Josiah studied Harris and saw he was also muscularly built and had thick curly black hair.

Josiah liked both men immediately and said, "Come meet my men." When introductions had been made, Josiah turned back to address Dixon. "Have you heard anymore?"

"About ten minutes ago someone saw him at a Wal-Mart store. They reported that he looked exhausted. He has a full beard now, so his appearance is slightly different."

"That means that he hasn't been able to sleep or shower since he killed the man in Sandpoint," remarked Josiah. "That might not be good for us." Running his hand across his face, Josiah continued, "I don't like this situation one bit."

"Neither do we," replied Harris. "We're both exhausted, so I can't even imagine what Quigley's feeling."

"Well," said Josiah, "I guess we'd better start checking the oncoming cars." Turning to Dixon, he asked, "You got any suggestions, sir?"

"I think we should send one man down the line to stop cars before they get to the roadblock. That way they can check the license plates and pretend there's been an accident up ahead. That would give us and extra heads-up before he gets here."

Josiah looked hopeful as he said, "If your idea works, maybe this will go down quiet without any shooting."

"I doubt it, based on his track record, but it doesn't hurt to try," responded Dixon.

"I'll go find us a volunteer." Dixon nodded, and watched as Carl Davis quickly volunteered.

For the next hour, they checked cars, but Quigley didn't show. Three hours passed, and he still hadn't shown. It was starting to get dark. Twenty minutes into the fourth hour, Davis finally saw him and radioed the others. He approached the car cautiously as the driver rolled his window down. "Sir, there's been an accident up ahead. Be patient for a little while. We have to let cars go through one at a time."

Davis noticed he seemed calm enough, but as they talked Quigley kept tapping his fingers nervously on the steering wheel.

Leaving Quigley to stew, Davis went to the next car. "Stay where you are when the car ahead of you moves forward. Understand?"

Nodding, the gentleman replied, "Sure, officer."

Just then Quigley's car inched forward. The officer stayed where he was as Quigley's car moved out of sight. "I don't understand why you want us to wait here," the man whined. "What's so all fired important?"

Suddenly shots rang out. Looking at the man in the car, he replied, "The man in front of you is a serial killer and there's a roadblock up there meant to catch him. If you'd followed him, you would've been in the direct line of fire."

Swallowing, the man meekly said, "Oh, okay."

Soon there was a greater commotion, more gunshots and then silence.

A few minutes later he saw Josiah coming toward him and went to meet him in the middle. "Quigley's dead," Josiah said when they met.

"Was anyone else shot?"

"A stray bullet ricocheted and hit Sergeant Harris in the back."

"Did it kill him?"

"No, but he's in bad shape. We called an ambulance."

"Oh, thank goodness everyone else is okay."

"We're going to keep the road closed until we get the scene under control."

"What should I tell the people lined up waiting to get through?"

Wiping his hand across his face, Josiah replied, "Tell them to sit tight for awhile. We'll let get them through as soon as we can."

As Josiah started back toward the scene, Davis went to tell the man in the lead car that he'd be there for awhile. Once that was done, he went to help clear the scene.

A short time later, they could hear the screaming of the sirens as the ambulances rushed toward them. Tim checked on Harris and was surprised to see he was still alive. Josiah and Dixon were taking turns holding pressure on his wound. He'd obviously lost a lot of blood.

The ambulance attendants were quick and efficient and soon had Harris on his way to the ER. Two hours later, the scene was cleaned up and traffic was allowed through again.

Tim woke to the ringing of the phone. Reaching for it, he mumbled sleepily, "York here."

"Tim, this is Josiah. How soon can you get back in here?"

"Would 30 minutes be too long?"

"Just hurry."

"Yes, sir."

Tim threw the covers, stretched and took a quick shower. He went out to take care of his dogs, ate a quick breakfast and hit the road.

When he arrived, Josiah was pacing "What's up, Josiah?"

"About an hour ago, Harris took a turn for the worse. He and Dixon were partners for 20 years and Dixon is beside himself."

"That's awful!" Tim waited for Josiah to continue.

"Dixon called Harris's wife to give her the news. Two of her friends can bring her as far as Sandpoint, but we need someone to go pick her up when she gets there and bring her here. You'll need a motel for one night. There's no way you can make the round-trip in one day. The department will furnish the car, and pay for gas, food and lodging. We don't want you to go by yourself, is there anyone who could go with you?"

"My sister, Louise, probably would if she can get some time off."

"Where does she work?"

"At the bank. She's a teller."

"Let me give Harold Weeks a call. He's the manager. When I explain how important it is to get Dick's wife here, I'm sure he'll let her go."

"While you do that, I have to find someone to take care of my dogs."

"I can do that."

"If you're sure. I know you don't like dogs much."

"I don't hate dogs, I just don't like messing with them. How many times a day do you feed them?"

"Twice a day when it's cold."

"Go home and pack a few things and I'll call Weeks."

"Thanks for taking care of the dogs."

"Get out of here before I change my other mind," grumbled Josiah.

"I'm gone!" Chuckling at Josiah's disgusted expression, Tim left.

When he got home, he packed quickly and put his bag in his truck. Then he went out to check on the dogs and feed them. Satisfied they would be all right, he started back to the house. Josiah drove up before he could get there and Tim went over to talk to him. "If you're ready, I'll show you what to do with the dogs," asked Tim.

"Okay," Josiah said hesitantly.

It didn't take long to show Josiah what had to be done. "I have two pups in the house that need to be taken care of at night. I'm weaning them so they can go to Meagan for Christmas. Her grandmother and mother got them for her."

"That's wonderful!" Then realizing what was coming he asked, "Does that mean I have to take them home with me?"

"Yeah." Seeing the scowling expression on Josiah's face, Tim laughed outright. "They won't bite."

Sighing resignedly, Josiah said, "Okay, I'll take them home with me."

"Thank you, Josiah."

"If I didn't need you to do this job for me, I'd charge you for this service."

"Me thinks thou doest protest too much!'

Mumbling under his breath, Josiah followed Tim back to the house. Although he would never admit it, he was glad to have the chance to do something for Meagan. Once inside, Tim showed him what he had been doing with the pups. "I have these leashes so that they can be controlled until they learn what they're supposed to do."

"Oh, great," snarled Josiah. "I get to go walking with the puppies."

"You old bear," teased Tim. "Ill bet that by the time that I get home, both you and these pups are in love with each other."

"Humph! Not likely."

"I'll help you get their box to your car." As Tim started to lift the box, he asked, "Were you able to talk Weeks into letting Louise go with me?"

Beaming proudly, Josiah replied, "I sure did. She's gone home to pack and will meet you at the office."

"What did you have to promise him?" asked Tim. "It isn't just anyone who can get around Harold Weeks."

"I told him our department would pay for the two days she'll miss from work."

"Aha!" Grinning Tim continued. "That old skinflint would do anything to save a penny."

"Yes, but when someone's in dire straits, Harold comes to their aid. Always anonymously of course, but he does it just the same. "

Motioning for Tim to pick up the box, he declared, "Come on man. Times a-wasting." Chuckling, Tim saluted. Lifting the box, with the pups inside, he carried it out and put it into Josiah's car, while Josiah grabbed all their paraphernalia. Soon Josiah was ready to go and Tim followed him back to the office.

As they were getting out of their vehicles, Tim's sister drove into the parking lot. She grabbed her suitcase from the back seat, and she started toward the two men. "Here, Sis," Tim said, "I'll carry that for you."

"Oh brother," groaned Josiah. "Now, he is buttering you up for the kill. He's already got me to volunteer to take care of his dogs."

"Wow," cried Louise. "Wonders never cease!"

"Not you, too," protested Josiah. "Is your whole family this way?"

"Yes," laughed Louise. "With so many of us, we have to be able to tease each other or we'd be destroyed."

"I'm glad I get to go on this little trip. I needed a break. Working all the time gets so monotonous."

"I'm glad I thought of you then," laughed Tim.

Growing thoughtful, she asked, "Are we going straight there, get a room and wait, or can we get checked into a room and go shopping?"

"We can go shopping if you'd like."

"Good, I'd like that."

"Then before we leave town I need to stop at the bank and withdraw some money."

"Great! I've been saving my money, so a good shopping spree will do me a world of good."

They were interrupted when Josiah entered the room carrying a pile of papers and a manila envelope. Taking his seat, he said, "The first item in this massive pile is a picture of Dick's wife, Julie, so you'll be able to recognize her." He slipped the picture into the envelope.

Picking up the next item, he explained, "This is the lease agreement for the car we rented from Hertz Rental Company, along with the keys." After slipping the paper into the envelope, he handed the keys to Tim.

"This envelope contains the money you'll need for meals and gas. Don't worry about the expense." Picking up another slip of paper, he said, "This is the name of the hotel where you've got reservations." Putting that inside the envelope, he handed it over to Tim.

"Since Mrs. Harris won't get to Sandpoint until late tonight, I've given the police your cell phone number. When she arrives, the police will call you to let you know. It's only 8:30 now, so you should get there around 3:30 or four o'clock. Do whatever you want until she gets there."

"Good, that will give us some time to go on a shopping spree."

"I figured as much." Getting out his checkbook he, wrote out a check, which he handed to Louise. This is the pay you have coming from Mr. Weeks. I told him I'd pay if he'd let you go."

Looking at the check, Louise gasped. "This is more than I get paid for two days of work, Mr. Graham."

"The rest is for taking this trip with your brother."

"Thanks so much."

Writing out another check, he started to hand it to Tim. "This will pay for you taking this trip." As he handed the check to Tim, he added, "Although this comes out of the department's funds, it's been approved by Mayor Cox."

Taking the check, he started to put it in his pocket when his eyes caught the amount. "This is way too generous, even for Mayor Cox."

"Nonsense! It was his idea to pay you this much."

"Tell him I said thank you."

Nodding, Josiah continued, "Well that's everything, so you'd best be on your way. You have a very long drive ahead of you."

Rising, they followed Josiah to the entrance of the building. Tim picked up the suitcases before going out to where Josiah had parked the light blue Ford minivan rental. Tim stuffed the suitcases into the back and closed door. "We'll see you when we get back, Josiah."

Chapter 30

Shirleen heard the phone ringing in the living room. After four rings she heard someone pick it up. Turning on her side, she burrowed deeper under the covers. When someone knocked on her door, she sighed and called, "Come in."

Opening the door, Meagan looked in to say, "Grandma, you have a phone call."

Growing concerned, Shirleen asked, "Do you know who it is?"

"No. We almost didn't let you know you had a call for that reason."

Shirleen slipped into her slippers and robe and followed Meagan to the phone. She stared at it like it would suddenly bite her. Finally, conquering her fear, she picked it up and said hello.

"Am I speaking to Shirleen Webb?"

"You are."

"We haven't met yet, but I'm Tim York's sister, Diane Weaver. He told me you had asked for two dogs for your granddaughter's Christmas present."

"Oh," sighed Shirleen in relief. "Yes, I did."

"Tim said you'd be needing my services to train the dogs."

"That's correct."

"I take it that your granddaughter's nearby."

"You're right."

Laughing, Diane replied, "I understand. The reason why I'm calling is to see when would be a good time to come out and meet you. We're closed on Christmas day, so I thought I'd call to make an appointment."

Shirleen pondered the question then answered, "How about that same afternoon, if you get my meaning."

"Are you saying Christmas afternoon?"

"Yes, that is correct."

"I won't be in town that day. My family is going to be out at my parents for lunch. Afterward, we're going over to my husband's parent's place."

"Then how about the next day?"

"I can do that. How about ten o'clock in the morning?

"That would be perfect."

"Good. I look forward to meeting you. Tim has told us how sweet you all are."

"I'm looking forward to meeting you too."

"I'll be at your place at ten o'clock on the twenty-sixth of December."

"Thanks so much.

Hanging up the phone, Shirleen turned to smile at her family. "I have an appointment on the twenty-sixth of December for something special. Since it's almost Christmas, I refuse to answer any questions, because I would have to lie. So, don't ask me and we'll be just fine." Humming to herself, she went to get a shower before stating her day.

Looking at her mother in surprise, Meagan replied, "That was strange. I wonder what that conversation was all about."

"I don't know what to think either. Since she said it was almost Christmas, it must be some kind of surprise. We'll just have to be patient for a little while."

"I guess," replied Meagan, plainly not convinced.

"We'd best get ready for our day, too, honey. We have a lot of schoolwork to do."

"All right," sighed Meagan. Rising, she went to take a shower before breakfast.

They took turns teaching Meagan's classes and at the end of each class she got huge homework assignments. "I know this is a lot of work, but just do the best that you can. I'll give you another test at the end of the week," Juliana said.

"With all of the work that you're giving me," protested Meagan, "I won't be finished until long after next Christmas!"

"I know it seems daunting, but you'll be surprised at how quickly you'll be able to get it done."

Sighing, Meagan replied, "I sure hope so."

That evening, Melinda Brooks called to let them know that Henry was getting out of the hospital, but baby Michael had to stay a few more days. Then she passed on the good news Josiah had given them. She said officers from Spokane had caught Athur, Annabelle's brother, and he was killed in the resulting shootout. One of the officers involved was also seriously injured.

She also wanted to pass on the news that they were inviting their 12 ranch hands to join them for Christmas dinner. Shirleen saw no problem with that other than deciding they'd need to buy another large turkey and it would have to be cooked at Melinda's house. They also decided that plastic ware would be easier with that many people.

Shirleen offered to go to Melinda's house so they could figure out the rest of the shopping list and Melinda agree.

Shirleen went back to help in the kitchen. While they worked, she told everyone about the conversation with Melinda.

"I'm nearly finished up with this last batch of fudge so as soon as I've cleaned up the kitchen, I can be ready," said Trudy.

"I'll cut up this last batch of peanut brittle," volunteered Shirleen.

When everything was finished, they got ready to leave. Meagan volunteered to go tell Jeff about their plans. Slipping into her coat, hat and boots, she hurried out to the shop where Jeff was working. Knocking on the door, she called out, "Is it all right to come in, Jeff?"

"Just one minute, please," called Jeff. A minute later he opened the door and came outside. "What's wrong, Meagan?"

"Nothing's wrong," grinned Meagan. "I came out to tell you we're going down to meet with the Melinda and Theodore Brooks concerning Christmas dinner."

"Oh, for a moment there I thought something was wrong." Sighing in relief, he continued, "Take all the time you need. I have a lot to do out here before I can come inside."

"We shouldn't be gone too long."

"See you at supper then," responded Jeff.

"You bet," called Meagan as she hurried back to the house.

Five minutes later they headed out. When they got there, Theodore came out to meet them. "Hello, you beautiful ladies. Melinda and Annabelle are waiting in the kitchen."

They followed him inside. Once everyone was settled, Shirleen took out a notebook and pen to write the list. Melinda was also prepared to write down the menu. Soon everyone was talking at once. Annabelle spoke up to say, "I'll make more pies so that you don't have to do all of them, Trudy."

"That would be great. Since we're going to have so many men, we have got to make many more pies." Snickering, she added, "In fact we're going to need to make more of everything."

"I was talking to Mrs. Brooks just before you came and I thought it would be great if we did the potatoes, candied yams, Gravy and other hot foods here. That way you won't have to pack everything up to bring it here."

"Why didn't we think of that?" asked Shirleen. "That's ingenious, Annabelle."

"We won't be able to have the meal ready until late in the afternoon," Juliana mused.

"That's a fact," agreed Melinda. "What time do you want to start cooking?" asked Melinda.

"No later than 7 a.m.," Annabelle acquiesced.

"I agree," said Shirleen. "There's a lot to do."

"We'll have the children taken care of too," declared Melinda.

◀ • ▶

The next morning, Meagan was up early to do school work. She turned to greet her mother and grandmother when they entered the living room. "Wow," declared Meagan, "you both look fantastic!"

"Thank you, honey," replied Shirleen. "I feel fantastic this morning."

"So do I," pronounce Juliana. "Look out world, 'cause here I come!"

Meagan laughed. "Well," she teased, "if you aren't back by midnight, I'll know that a handsome guy nabbed you and took you off to his man cave."

"He'll have to catch me first," stated Juliana.

"I'll pull out my trusty .44 and threaten to singe his back side for him," declared Shirleen.

"Next thing you know, I'll be calling you Annie Oakley!"

"That I've got to see," declared Trudy coming from the kitchen.

When Jeff came down the stairs, he saw Shirleen and his heart nearly failed him. Suddenly, he knew he loved her. This revelation was so shocking, he almost turned around to go back upstairs. Getting control of his emotions, he whistled softly. "Wow, Meagan. You'd best hogtie these ladies before they go to town. Some men might decide to keep them and we'd never see them again. They're looking good."

"Flatterer," laughed Juliana.

"Not on your life. It's the truth and nothing but."

"Well, you'd all better get in the kitchen and eat, or I'll throw it out," ordered Trudy.

"Like that would ever happen," quipped Meagan as she followed the others to the kitchen.

After breakfast, Meagan said, "I'll do the dishes before I go back to doing my homework. That way you all can go ahead and leave."

"You don't mind?" asked Trudy.

"No," assured Meagan. "Go have a good time. You three deserve it."

"Thanks, we will," replied Shirleen.

"I made you and Jeff some sandwiches and a tossed salad for lunch. There's also some apple pie and milk."

"I'll take care of things here so don't worry about anything." Meagan assured her.

"Thank you," said Juliana, kissing Meagan's cheek. "We shouldn't be gone too long."

"Take all of the time you want. I'll be just fine."

Soon they were driving away, and Meagan wasn't surprised to see that Juliana was in the driver's seat.

When she was done with the dishes, Meagan went back to her schoolwork. She was so engrossed that she lost all track of time. The next time she looked up, it was nearly lunchtime. She went out to the shop and told Jeff, "When you can break away, come in and eat. I'll have it on the table in two shakes of a dead lamb's tail."

Jeff grinned. "See you inside in five minutes or less."

When Jeff came inside, she asked, "How's it going out there?"

"Christmas has me tied up in that shop," replied Jeff "There's still a lot to do before I'm finally finished."

"I won't bother asking what you're doing."

"Good, 'cause I couldn't tell you anyway."

"That's what I thought."

While they ate their lunch, they talked about their likes and dislikes and about Christmas traditions. When they finished eating, Jeff went back out to the shop. Meagan cleaned up and went back to her schoolwork. At four o'clock, she was finally caught up and decided to sit near the fire and read a book.

She was still reading it when she heard a car drive up. When she looked out the window, there was a strange car in the drive. When a strange man got out of the car, Meagan nearly panicked. Then she saw Jeff come out of the shop and move toward the man. Meagan couldn't hear all that was said, but she continued to watch.

A few minutes later, the stranger got back in his car and left. Meagan ran to open the door for Jeff. Seeing the fear on her face, he hurried toward her and said, "He's one of my neighbors. He came to tell me someone was messing around at my place. He called the Mounties, and they came to check things out. When my neighbor told Josiah what the man looked like, he didn't say anything. He just took the information down."

"Do you think my Dad has found us?"

"Let's not jump to conclusions."

"You're right of course, but it hard not to be scared."

"I know. But try to keep it together until we know more"

"I will." Suddenly, Meagan fainted and Jeff caught her before she fell off of the porch. He carried her inside and put her on the couch. A few minutes later she regained consciousness. "How did I get here?"

"You fainted. I guess the stress was more than you could take, so your lights went out."

"Oh," She tried to sit up, but was too weak.

"Just let your body catch up to the shock. You'll be all right in a minute."

Jeff talked about other things until the color started to come back into her face. She sat on the edge of the couch until she felt stable enough to stand. "I'm all right now."

"I'm going to call Josiah and see what he found out."

"Good," sighed Megan. "It will be nice to know what is going on."

Jeff called Josiah's office and told him what was going on. Then asked if the neighbor's account was correct."

"That's right. I was going to come out to talk to you in a little while."

"What's going on?"

"When John described the stranger, I thought it sounded like one of the men who was with Bruce Murdock when he came to the mansion to speak to me."

"That's what I was afraid of. Why was he at my place?"

"I don't know. Are Shirleen and Juliana home?"

"No, the three of them were going to meet Melinda and Theodore Brooks at the mall."

"Oh, that's not good!"

"I expect them back any time."

"Keep our conversation to yourself until I can get over there."

"I will."

"I would send Tim up there, but I sent him and his sister to Sandpoint to pick up the wife of the man who was injured in the shootout. I just hope they get here in time for her to say good-bye. He's in a comma and the doctor doesn't think he'll come out of it."

"Well, I guess that it's up to me to hold down the fort until you can get here."

"If that man comes there, don't answer the door."

"Believe me, I won't!"

"Are you by yourself?"

"No, Meagan's here."

"Is she okay?"

"She is now. She got so scared she fainted."

"Poor kid! She sure has been through a lot."

"That she has."

"That young lady has a lot of spunk and tenacity."

"I agree with you there."

"I'll be there in 30 minutes or so."

"The man in question has a dark complexion with blue eyes and jet-black hair. When John said that he had a mean disposition, I knew he was describing the guy I saw to a tee."

"I don't like this one little bit," declared Jeff.

"Nor do I. Just don't let anyone in."

"I won't!"

When the conversation ended, Jeff turned to see Meagan watching him intently. "They've found us haven't they?"

"Not necessarily. Josiah said he was coming out in about 30 minutes. He'll fill us in then. For now, we have to remain calm."

"How do I do that?" demanded Meagan.

"You told me you prayed when you ran away initially."

"Yes, that's true."

"Well, why not pray for safety, now?"

"I will."

Leaning back against the couch, Meagan closed her eyes and began to pray silently for protection. Sitting on the couch beside her, Jeff calmly let her work things out.

A few minutes later, a car pulled up and Jeff went to see who it was. Seeing Meagan's ashen face, he smiled and said, "It's all right, Meagan, it's your family."

"Oh, what a relief!"

Jeff went out to see if they needed help and they were out there so long Meagan began to worry. Then she heard the women chattering away in the garage and Jeff came in and set down some shopping bags, then went out to get more. After three more trips, the women followed Jeff in, each carrying more bags.

Jeff closed the door and joined them all in the living room. Shirleen and Juliana sat down on each sides of Meagan. Taking her hand, Juliana said, "I'm sorry you were so frightened, honey."

Sobbing quietly, Meagan replied, "I didn't know what to do! I didn't know the man so I wasn't going to answer the door."

"That was good thinking," stated Shirleen.

"I was so grateful Jeff was here."

"Me too," declared Shirleen.

"Josiah should be here before long to fill us in on what's happening," Jeff said. "I suggest that we stay calm until he gets here."

"I agree," said Shirleen. "No use getting worked up until we know more."

"Momma's right," stated Juliana.

Trudy, who had remained silent, nodded in agreement. "I'm going to start supper. We'll all feel better with full stomachs."

Shirleen, in an attempt to change the subject, asked, "Did you get all of your homework done?"

"Yes," announced Meagan, sounding happier.

"That's wonderful," praised Juliana.

"I must confess that I enjoyed my time alone, and I enjoyed giving Jeff a bad time at lunch, too."

"That she did," grumbled Jeff, pretending to be disgusted.

Suddenly a car pulled into the driveway and Jeff sighed in relief when he looked out the window. "It's Josiah."

They invited Josiah inside and when he was seated, he leaned forward to address them all. "Murdock's man's in town. I saw him at the post office. He didn't see me, but I recognized him. I looked him up and his name's Vincent Crowley. He is suspected of murder, theft and a host of other crimes."

"Then he's someone Bruce would want on his team," stated Juliana.

"How do you think he found us?" asked Meagan.

"I suspect that he is looking for me," Josiah said.

"Why do you think that?" Shirleen asked.

"Murdock paid me four million dollars for Spielberg's mansion. I think he wants it back."

"Sounds like something Bruce would do," snapped Juliana. "You have got to be careful. He'll stop at nothing to get what he wants."

"I figured that. I have two men tailing Crowley. If he so much as blows his nose wrong, he'll be arrested and shipped back to New York State."

"Good!" cried Meagan. "The sooner he leaves the better I'll like it."

"Have you got everything you need for Christmas now?" asked Josiah.

"Yes, we got the last of it today, with the help of Melinda and Theodore Brooks."

"Then I don't want you to go to town anymore until we have this situation under control."

"We're going for Christmas dinner at Theodore and Melinda's house tomorrow," said Shirleen. "We'd also planned to ask you to join us."

"Do they know you're inviting me?"

"Of course," replied Juliana. "They think it's a grand idea.'

"Then I accept. That way I can keep an eye on all of you."

"Wonderful!" cried Meagan. "It wouldn't be Christmas without you, Uncle Josiah."

"Thanks, Meagan."

"Uncle Josiah, do you think we're still safe here?"

"Yes, for now. We just have to be careful while that man's here."

"I'm worried about you," continued Meagan.

"I have two men assigned and they'll be with me at all times."

"Then they'll be with us for Christmas, too," replied Shirleen.

"I hadn't thought of that. Maybe I shouldn't join you."

"Nonsense," Shirleen said. "Let me call Melinda and let her know to set two more places."

When she ended the call she said, "Melinda said the more the merrier!"

"Then I'll be glad to join your party."

"Do you think it's safe for you to stay in at your place while Crowley's here?" asked Juliana.

"I hope so," replied Josiah.

"Why don't you stay here?" Juliana asked. "If Meagan slept with me, then there'd be an extra room for you. We could set up beds in the fourth and fifth bedrooms for your men."

"I don't want to put you out," protested Josiah.

"You're not," said Juliana. "Not only would you be safe, but we'd feel safer too. With Jeff and the three of you here, we have a much better chance if someone tries to get us."

Mulling that thought over in his mind for a minute, Josiah looked at Jeff and asked, "What do you think?"

"I think it's a great idea. No one would think to look for you here, or at the Brooks home."

"I can see the wisdom in what all of you are saying, but I have one major problem."

"What's that?" asked Shirleen.

"I'm pup-sitting for Tim. He said that he had someone who wanted two pups, but he was to housebreak them first."

Shirleen looked at Juliana who nodded in agreement. "I guess we can tolerate two pups in the house, as long as you make sure they go outside when they need to."

"That's no problem."

"Then by all means don't let two pups stop you from coming to stay here."

"Okay. I'll do it."

"We'll need to get some beds," Juliana said.

"One of the men has a truck. I'll call the furniture place in the mall to see if I can buy beds and mattresses. They can pick them up and bring them here, while I go get my things. No one will suspect they're connected to me."

"Good, that's settled," replied Shirleen.

"Wait Momma, What about pillows, and bedding?"

"Oh, right."

"They can buy some bedding when they pick up the beds. We just have to give him a list of what we need."

"I'll get that ready for him," grinned Shirleen, satisfied that everything was working out.

"When you go to get your things, may I suggest that I go with you for safety's sake?" asked Jeff.

"That's a good idea, Jeff."

Josiah called the furniture store and ordered what they needed. By that time, Shirleen had the list prepared and he gave the list to the guys guarding him and explained what needed to be done. With that done, he and Jeff headed to his house so he could get the dogs and his things.

The women prayed for their safety then went to help Trudy with supper, being sure to let her know there would be three more mouths to feed. Trudy took it all in stride.

Three hours later, the men were back with the beds and bedding. Shirleen let them in and showed them where to set up the beds. By the time they were done, Josiah made the introductions. Indicating the man to his right, he said, "This is Officer Mark Holmquist, and on the left there is Officer David Black."

When she first set eyes on Mark, Meagan thought he was absolutely knockout gorgeous. He had the blackest hair she had ever seen. It was so thick and curly that for a moment she had an irresistible urge to run her fingers through it. He was tall and well built. When she gazed into his light blue eyes, she felt something inside her come alive. As her eyes fell onto his thick full lips, she wondered how they would feel against hers.

Meagan silently chided herself. *Get a grip on yourself, you ninny. He isn't that handsome!* Looking at him again, she told herself, *Yeah, he is!*

Looking up into his eyes, Meagan decided he must have good sense of humor. A tiny smile played around his lips when he noticed her checking him out. "Well, Miss Webb, do I pass inspection?"

"The jury is still out, so we'll have to see."

Josiah, who had seen everything, chuckled. "This is one tough nut to crack," teased Josiah. "Don't be surprised that she rules foul."

"Ooh! There's a challenge here is there? Well, time will tell, my beauty. Time will tell."

"Be careful, Miss Webb, old Mark here has a huge string of girls dangling from his fingers." David said.

"You're just jealous, Black."

"Nah! Just wise. No girl will ever trap David Black into marriage."

"Party pooper!" retorted Mark.

While the men were verbally sparring, Meagan had the chance to observe David Black. Where Mark's complexion was dark, David's was fair. His blond hair was coarse and straight. A lock of it fell across his forehead. His brown eyes sparkled with life. Meagan noticed that he was a lot shorter than Mark, but was very muscular. There was a long, jagged scar across his right cheek, which made Meagan wonder what had happened to him. Although his cheekbones were well shaped, his wide, thick nose seemed to spread across his face. *Somehow it fits him*, thought Meagan.

Looking from one man to the other, she thought, *Mark Holmquist may be more handsome than David Black, but that doesn't mean a thing. What is it Grandma says? Oh, yeah. Handsome is as handsome does. Mark is right. Only time will tell.*

As she listened to them, she couldn't help comparing their personalities. Mark was open, where David was more reserved, even calm. She realized she liked them both.

Josiah put his things in his new room and went back out to his car. When Meagan saw him struggling with a huge box, she wondered what was inside. When he set it down and went back out to his car, she looked at it and realized it had two pups inside. The pups were trying to climb out of the box and began to whimper. Meagan immediately fell in love with them.

"Oh, you're precious. She reached in to pick one up, but Juliana stopped her, saying, "If you want to love on the pups, please do it after supper."

"Okay, I'll go wash up and set the table."

After the meal was finished, they got everyone situated in their rooms and Meagan finally got a chance to play with the pups. She took them out of the box and began to pet them. They got a little rambunctious and began to lick Meagan's face, which she didn't like. One even nipped her on the ear. She was hard pressed to control them.

As she roughhoused with the pups, Mark and David looked on, awestruck. After watching for a while, it was David who finally came to Meagan's rescue.

He picked up one of the pups and looked at it closely. It's markings were that of a true husky. The pup's silver colored coat was thick and shone with a rich healthy luster. As he held him by the scruff of the neck, the pup bared his fangs. "You're going to make someone a fine watch dog."

Exchanging pups with Meagan, he began to examine the female. Her tan and brown coat was just as healthy as the male's. She too, bared her fangs when he held her by the scruff of the neck. David noticed that the female had a calmer temperament than the male. "Are you selling these dogs?" he asked Josiah.

"No, I'm dog-sitting for Tim. He said he was trying to housebreak them because they were going to be someone's Christmas present."

"Darn, that's too bad. I would've bought them right off. With proper training, these would make excellent police dogs."

"Maybe we should look into getting some dogs from Tim to train," replied Josiah thoughtfully. "When he gets back, I'll speak to him about it."

"Good," replied David.

"Well, one thing's for sure. I can't go to bed until I've taken them for their nightly walk. Can't have them messing up the house, now can we?"

While he went to get their leashes, Meagan calmed them down. When Josiah returned with the leashes, Meagan asked, "Would it be all right if I walk one of them for you?"

"Sure, I don't see why not."

Mark rose from his seat on the floor to take the leash from Josiah. "I'll help Meagan walk the dogs. We can't have you meandering around outside with that goon looking for you. I'll make sure that Meagan is safe."

"Safe from whom?" queried Josiah. "Crowley or you?"

"She's safe with me, sir."

"Sure," teased Josiah.

"On my honor, sir. I wouldn't want you or these two beautiful ladies mad at me."

As they walked across the yard, Mark covertly watched Meagan. "*I've dated a lot of girls, but none of them ever affected me this way. Maybe because none of them have a sweet personality like this beauty beside me.*

Mark was jarred back from his thoughts when Meagan asked, "How long have you been a Mountie, Mr. Holmquist?"

"Please, call me Mark."

"Okay, Mark, how long have you been a Mountie?"

"Seven years. I joined the force in May of 2025."

"How do you like it?"

"It isn't always pleasant, but someone has to do it. I care about our little community, Meagan. May I call you Meagan?"

"Sure. I'm glad that there are people like you who want us all to be safe."

"What brought you to Cardston?"

Meagan froze. *"How do I answer his question?* Meagan wondered. *I can't tell him the truth about us, so what do I do?* Suddenly, a thought came into her mind. She didn't like to lie, but she didn't dare tell the truth either. Taking a deep breath to steady her nerves, she replied, "Momma was married to an abusive husband. One day she packed us up while Dad was at work. We stopped at my grandma's house on our way and she decided to join us because Grandpa had died from an accident a few months before that. We wanted to get as far away from Dad as we possibly could, so we started driving and eventually ended up here. Someone said it was a nice place to live."

"Where did you live before you came here?"

"Idaho Falls, Idaho," Meagan lied. *Well I've been there,* she thought.

"Well, welcome to Cardston. Idaho's loss is our gain."

"Thanks, replied Meagan.

Chapter 31

"Grandma, wake up!" Shirleen opened her eyes and saw that it was still dark outside. Sitting bolt up right on her bed, she looked toward the bedroom door and saw Meagan was standing there with a huge grin on her face.

"What is it, Meagan? Is something wrong?"

"No, Grandma. It's Christmas Eve!"

Flopping back onto the bed, Shirleen struggled to gain control of her pounding heart. "The way you sounded just now, I thought Crowley was here!"

Meagan hastened over to sit on the side of her grandmother's bed. "I didn't mean to scare you. I was just so excited!. I can hardly wait to see your face when you open your presents."

"Oh, honey," Shirleen said, reaching for her granddaughter, "I thought it was because you were excited to see what you were getting."

"I am, but for once in my life it's more important to see the two of you happy."

"That's sweet, honey."

Meagan continued as if she hadn't heard what her grandmother had said. "My whole life, I couldn't wait to see what was under the tree for me but somehow, since we ran away from home, I don't feel that way anymore. It's more gratifying to see you and Momma happy."

"You're growing up, sweetheart."

"It feels good."

"When we think of another's welfare over our own there's something that happens inside of us. When we're busy seeing to other's needs we lose ourselves. It's a feeling that only comes through serving others."

"I don't know about all of that, I just know this feeling is wonderful and I like it. Trudy is up already and she's preparing breakfast."

"That early?" Looking at Meagan questioningly, she asked, "Speaking of early, why are you up?"

"I was helping Uncle Josiah walk the dogs. We had some quality time together and we talked. I've come to love Uncle Josiah. He has the same background we have, yet it never made him evil like it did Grandpa and Daddy."

"I know," said Shirleen. "I admire him too. He's almost like a brother. I actually had a brother, but he died as a baby."

"Oh, Grandma," Meagan said in surprise. "You've never said anything about him before."

"I wasn't allowed to talk about him."

"Why?"

"He had a birth defect and Daddy was ashamed of him. Neil was born when I was about eight years old. Momma told me years later that she had miscarried three before him. Anyway, I fell in love with him the moment I saw him. His birth defect didn't matter to me.

"I was always fussing over him, well as much as I was allowed to anyway. The truth is, I idolized my baby brother. Suddenly one day little Neil didn't wake up from his nap; he was dead.

"Oh, how I missed him. When I asked where Neil had gone, my father got angry. That's when he forbade my mother and me to speak of him again. When Daddy was gone, I'd talk to Mother about him. We did our grieving together when he wasn't around to get angry. Momma never spoke of him around the staff or in front of Daddy again."

"How did he die, Grandma?"

"Later, I learned he was drowned by his nanny. Daddy was the one who said he died in his sleep."

"Grandma," exclaimed Meagan, "that's murder! Why wasn't she arrested and made to pay for her crime?"

"Because, Daddy covered it up."

"What a terrible man! I'm so glad I never knew your father, Grandma."

"I am, too." Shirleen sighed. "Daddy wasn't a nice man, even at the best of times. When Momma died a year after I married Gordon, Daddy got nastier toward me. Between him and Gordon, my life was not my own. They dictated what I wore, where I went and even what I ate. I learned to loath my father. When he died two years later, I didn't even grieve for him."

"I don't think I would've liked him much. I never really liked Grandpa Gordon either."

"They never deserved love or respect."

"Thank you for sharing some more aspects of your life, Grandma. It makes me feel closer to you."

"You're welcome, honey." Hugging Meagan tightly, she added, "I love you with all of my heart and soul."

"And I you, Grandma."

Releasing her, Shirleen started sat up. "If we're going to be ready for tomorrow, we'd better get a move on. Besides, everyone will have eaten all of the food if we don't get down there soon."

Rising, Meagan started for the door. "I'll see you in the kitchen. You'd better hurry!"

Laughing out loud, Shirleen declared, "You'd better leave me some breakfast, missy!" Shirleen could hear Meagan laughing all the way down the hall. Flinging the covers back, she went to prepare for the day..

Rising, Josiah held out a chair for Shirleen when she came into the kitchen. "Good morning. I trust that you slept well."

"Like a rock," grinned Shirleen, taking the chair that Josiah held out for her. "How about you?"

"Like a log! What's on the agenda today?"

"Getting ready for tomorrow," replied Juliana. "There's still a lot to do."

Turning to address Jeff, Josiah asked, "Will you need our help, Jeff?"

"Not until later tonight, then I'll need all three of you. I'll have plenty to do in the shop until then."

"I have to go back to my house; I forgot some things. I also have some last minute shopping to do, so I'm taking these two guys with me. I'm going to stop off at the office, too. We should be back before two."

"Won't it be dangerous going into town?" Meagan asked, voicing everyone's unspoken concern.

"I can't neglect business just because I'm being stalked by a crazy man. I'll have these two guys along to protect me, and the courthouse is full of cops. I'll be fine. The only problem I have is those two fur balls in the other room. They need to go out every so often and I won't be here to do it."

"I'll take care of them," promised Meagan. "I like doing it."

"Thank you," replied Josiah, plainly relieved. "Tim should be back in the office this morning."

"Tell him we said hello," Shirleen said.

Josiah noticed that Juliana became flustered every time someone mentioned Tim's name. *Is she in love with him? I know Tim loves her because he gets a strange look on his face every time I mention her. Oh, heaven help them. With Bruce Murdock stuck in the picture they don't stand a chance of happiness!!"* Aloud he said, "I will. I got a call from him at 1:30 this morning. He said they'd just dropped off Sergeant Harris's wife at the hospital. There was still no change in his condition, but he's holding his own."

"I'm glad to hear he's still fighting," replied Shirleen in concern. "I sure hope he makes it."

They said grace and everyone dug into the hearty breakfast. Shortly after the meal, the three men prepared to go to town. Shirleen caught up with Josiah as he headed toward the door. "Josiah, would do me a favor while you're shopping?"

"Sure, if I can."

"Would you take this money and get some presents for Mark and David? We haven't bought anything for them."

"Sure thing. Do you want me to get anything in particular?"

"I don't know what they'd like. Any ideas?

"Leave it to me."

"Thank you, I appreciate it."

When the men left, Juliana and Meagan went to start their classes and Shirleen helped Trudy in the kitchen. They baked pies all morning, stopping only long enough to prepare a light lunch.

They had just finished up when they heard vehicles pulling up. Cautiously, Meagan gazed out the window, and was relieved to see Josiah and his two bodyguards along with Tim York.

Meagan went back to work at her schoolwork, and one of the pups came over to tug on her pants. She bent down and picked her up to cuddle her. The male was sleeping near Shirleen, who had been rubbing him with her foot.

When the men came in, they were loaded down with wrapped packages. Josiah, handed his packages to Meagan. Grinning he replied, "We tried to buy out the store! "

The others put their packages under the tree as Shirleen quickly hugged Tim. Turning to Josiah, she asked, "Did you have trouble in town today?"

"We saw Crowley talking on his phone, but he didn't see us."

Mark snorted in contempt and said, "I was watching him the whole time, but he didn't look up once. In fact he was scowling as he listened to what the other person said."

"It was probably Bruce, chewing him out for not getting the job done," Juliana said in disgust.

"You could be right," replied Josiah thoughtfully.

"Well, at least you were safe," Shirleen said. "I worried about all of you while you were gone."

"When we left the office, I saw a strange car parked across the street from the courthouse," Tim said. "I guessed it was the person you told me about so I pulled out in front of him so he couldn't get behind you. Then, I deliberately drove really slow. I could see it was making him hopping mad. Every time he tried to go around me, I would speed up so he couldn't pass.

"When I knew the three of you had enough time to get onto the road coming here, I sped up a bit and then let him pass me. He shook his fist at me as he went by and I tipped my hat and followed him to the stop sign. Since there was no one behind me, I stopped and watched to see what he'd do next.

"He sat there for a long time, then finally turned left. I knew we were safe long enough to get here. By the time he figured out he had lost you, we'd all be long gone and he'd be one angry man."

Grinning mischievously, he added, "It was pretty funny to see him lose his prey. "

"Thanks for running interference," declared Josiah. "I must admit I saw him, but didn't know what else to do. I hoped we could lose him somewhere along the way. I'm glad that we didn't have to try to do that. I won't be going back to town for a few days, maybe he'll get tired of the hunt and go back to New York."

"We can all hope," retorted Shirleen.

Changing the subject, Josiah asked, "Is Jeff still working in the shop?"

"Yes," replied Meagan. "He only came in long enough to eat lunch. I'm curious about what has him so busy."

"He's working on some things for me," Shirleen said, "and there's enough work to keep him busy long after Christmas."

"I think I'll go see if I can lend a hand," laughed Josiah. Donning his outdoor gear, he slipped out of the house and trudged to the shop.

He called out before entering so he didn't surprise Jeff, then said, "Need some help?"

"Definitely! I have two more bookcases to go. Then, I'll be done."

The two men got busy and had finished in a couple of hours. "The hardest part is still ahead of us," Jeff said.

"What's that?" asked Josiah.

"Getting them inside someplace close to the tree."

Josiah burst out laughing. "That poor tree already has so much stuff under and around it that putting anything else near it is hopeless."

Signing in resignation, Jeff replied, "That's what I figured."

"What if we talk Shirleen into letting us leave them out here until after the other gifts are opened?"

"That's a good idea."

"I'll go get her so we can discuss it."

A few minutes later, Josiah brought Shirleen to the shed. When they were inside, Josiah and Jeff presented her with their problem, she had no issues with what they'd suggested."

Relieved, Jeff sighed. "I also wondered what we're going to do with all of it until you decide how things will be rearranged."

"I was going to set the bookcases in the spare bedroom to make a library."

"I meant to tell you, I was exploring the attic the other day," stated Jeff. "I couldn't understand why there were only two bedrooms upstairs and no other rooms. I wanted to know what they'd done with that extra space. There are windows you can see from the outside. What I found may surprise you."

"What?"

"Six more bedrooms!"

"Really?"

"Yes. Someone had walled them off."

Shocked, Shirleen asked, "Why in the world would they do that?"

"I wondered too, so I went to the newspaper morgue to see what had been written about this house. I mentioned what I was doing and the woman working there said she remembered something her grandmother had told her about this house."

Curious, Shirleen asked, "Tell me already!"

"Mr. Torrance, the owner at the time and an eccentric old man, had closed it off so he didn't have to heat the extra space. Apparently before he bought it, this old place was an orphanage."

"I wonder what he did with the doors?" Shirleen mused.

"When I learned about the history, I started snooping around the shop and found six doors in the storeroom."

"Would it be hard to open things back up and put the doors back on?"

"No," said Jeff. "If that's what you want to do I can look into what it would take to complete the job."

"Could we do that after Christmas?"

"Sure thing. That would give me something to do when I'm not plowing snow."

Growing excited, Shirleen exclaimed, "Let's do it."

"There's enough time before we go to bed that we could work on the room next to mine," Jeff said. "If we can put up the door, we could put Josiah's bed upstairs tomorrow. Then we can convert Juliana's art studio into the library. The bedroom that she has now could be her new studio, and we can put Meagan in the room next to yours, Shirleen."

"Wonderful!" replied Shirleen.

Catching the fever of the possibilities, Josiah said, "I'll help.

The three of them went back to the house and went upstairs. Jeff and Josiah began banging on the walls until they heard a hollow sound. Jeff used a pry bar he brought from the shop and started prying the boards away from the wall.

It didn't take them long and before they knew it there was a door-sized hole. While the men went to get a door, Shirleen grabbed a candle and examined the room. She was surprised that it was large and still contained furniture.

A huge painting hung over the mantle of a fireplace. When she examined it, she saw it was an original. The scene was of two elk sizing each other up, ready to do battle. The mountains in the background were majestic, with a waterfall cascading down the cliffs face. Female elk were grazing in the grassy meadow. *This room is huge.* Shirleen thought. *We can clean it the day after Christmas and Josiah will be comfortable here.*

Shirleen went to the landing and called down, "Juliana, could please bring everyone up here for a moment?"

"Sure," replied Juliana.

When everyone was assembled, Shirleen told them about Jeff's suggestion.

They were prevented from saying more when Josiah and Jeff brought in the door and got ready to hang it.

While they were doing that, the rest of them except Shirleen went back down stairs. Seeing the damage above the door, Jeff assured her it wouldn't take much to repair and said he would do in the morning.

"What I don't understand," Shirleen said, "is why the previous owner just didn't close the doors and put something on the floor to block the cold air."

"Who knows what he was thinking," Jeff said. "The woman I talked to said he was a recluse and only came to town to get supplies. A relative put the house up for sale after the old man died. I talked to the realtor and he said the relative had to do a lot of work before they could sell it. My guess is no one knew about the hidden rooms."

"When I looked in there, I was surprised by the size and the antiques. I suspect that the other rooms will be the same."

"Well," said Josiah, "when Christmas is over we'll see what's in there."

They went back to the living room and Shirleen asked, "How did your trip go, Tim?"

"Really well, until we got checked into the motel. My sister, Louise, proceeded to buy out all of the stores. When she was done, I could hardly get everything in the van. I was proud when I got it all stuffed in there, and then she asked if we could shop some more after lunch. She was killing me!"

"I'll bet you were just as bad as your sister," teased Juliana."

"Oh, drats! You've got me," groaned Tim. "You're right. To be honest, I was having just as much fun as she was. We shopped 'til we dropped and didn't leave until the stores closed."

Josiah, pretending to be stern, said, "It's a wonder that poor Mrs. Harris had room to get into the car, let alone a place to put her luggage,"

"Oh," grinned Tim mischievously, "I forced her to put it on top of the van."

"No way!" protested Meagan. "You couldn't be that mean."

"You're right, Meagan. I had plenty of room. Louise rode in the back and Mrs. Harris rode in the front."

"That's what I thought," grinned Meagan. "You're just an old softie."

"That he is," agreed Josiah.

Rising to stretch, Tim declared, "Well, this old softie is going to go home and get some sleep. There's a lot happening tomorrow." Picking up the pup's box, he prepared to leave. "Thanks for dog-sitting for me, boss."

"I'll think twice before I volunteer again. They're nothing but a huge nuisance to. Your other dogs are probably hungry by now, too."

"Well, I'll see you day after tomorrow."

"Wait," yelled Meagan, rising to face Tim. "You have to come here tomorrow before you go home."

"I do?" Tim asked.

"You do! We have presents for you, too."

"Oh," grinned Tim. "Why don't I just take them home now? That way I won't intrude on family time."

"Not on your life, Mountie York!"

"What happens if I forget to come?"

Meagan knew Tim was teasing so she said, "Then I'll just take them back and get a refund!"

"Ah, you wouldn't do that now, would you?"

"You bet your sweet Aunt Petunia, I would!"

"All right, you win. I'll be here at noon."

"We'll expect you no later than nine o'clock in the morning, Timothy York."

"Okay. Can't have you pouting on Christmas day." As he started to duck out the door, he called back. "See you in the morning."

When Tim didn't come to the house at nine o'clock, Josiah started to worry. "If Tim isn't here by nine-thirty, I'm going to go check on him. Crowley may've nabbed him."

"It's not like Tim to be late for anything," said David. "I say we go now."

"Before we go, I'm going to call some of the troops to meet us out there."

"That's a good idea," Mark said.

While they were getting ready to leave, Josiah made the call and asked a detail of six men meet them at Tim's home. They decided to take Mark's vehicle, since it was closer to the road. They put the pedal to the metal in an attempt to get there as soon as they could. As they pulled up to Tim's place, they heard gunfire.

They left the car on the side of the road and got out to assess the situation. They drew their guns and started making their way around to the kennels where the dogs were barking wildly.

It took them some time, but they managed to get into a position where they could see Tim. He was pinned down in one of the kennels, a dead dog at his feet. The six officers were near their cars, shooting it out with a man in the house.

All at once a man ran from the house into the woods. Josiah managed to get a shot off at him before he disappeared into the trees. "He's gone," shouted, Josiah. "Cease fire."

When Josiah got to the kennel, Tim held the dead dog close to him and sobbed brokenly. "Are you all right, Tim?"

Nodding, he continued to rock the dog gently. "Molly gave her life for me, Josiah."

"I'm sorry, Tim."

"She's the mother of the pups I was taking to Meagan this morning."

"Are they all right?"

"I don't know. I had them shut up in the truck while I was taking care of the other dogs." Laying the dog gently on the ground, Tim looked up and said, "That man kept me pinned down in here all night. When he tried to get to me, Molly kept herself between the him and me. He shot her then went back in the house. Good thing the kennel's heated or I would've froze to death out here."

"I'll check on the pups. You stay here."

Josiah saw that the pups were fine. When he got back to the kennel, he told Tim, "Other than a terrible mess in the truck, the pups are just fine."

As Tim stood up, Josiah saw blood coming from a wound in his left shoulder. "You're hurt, Tim."

"I am?"

"There's a nasty wound on your shoulder. Let's get you to the house." Suddenly, Tim grew weak from blood loss and Mark came running from the house to help Josiah bring him the rest of the way. Between them, they got Tim inside. After that, Josiah went to the truck and came back with the pups. "I'll go take care of the rest of the animals, then we'll get you to the hospital."

"Thank you, Josiah. We need to do something with Molly's body."

"Don't worry about that. We'll take care of her."

"Thanks." Suddenly, Tim slumped over. "Mark," barked Josiah, "get your car over here so we can get him to the hospital. I'll meet you as soon as we take care of things here." Going to the door, Josiah hollered, "Pierson, get in here on the double." A large burly man entered, and Josiah said, "Help Mark get Tim to the hospital."

The two men got Tim seated in the front seat of Mark's car and sped off to the hospital. They used the emergency entrance and the two of them carried Tim inside. A few minutes later he'd seen a doctor and was on his way to surgery to get the bullet removed from his shoulder. Josiah joined them before Tim got out of surgery.

An hour later, Dr. Stillman came to speak to them. "We've removed the bullet and he'll be out of recovery soon. Does he live by himself?"

"Yes," Josiah said, wondering why he asked, "except for his dogs."

"Has someone contacted his family?"

"I did just before I got here."

"So, they're on their way here?"

"Yes, sir. They were leaving immediately."

"I want to keep him here for a little while longer to make sure he is okay. Since it's Christmas, if he checks out, I'll let him go home with his family."

Just then several people, looking pale and scared came into the waiting room. Josiah said, "There's Tim's family now."

Turning to address them, Dr. Stillman told them he was fine and would probably be coming home with them in an hour or two. "I want to see him in my office in three days to check the wound and change the dressing."

"All right, doctor," replied Mrs. York. "He'll behave himself, I'll make sure of it."

Grinning, Dr. Stillman said, "For the next couple of days, he'll be as mellow as a new born kitten so you don't have to worry."

"Thanks for taking care of our son," the older York said gratefully.

After Dr. Stillman left the room, Josiah said, "We'll stay with you until he is released."

"What happened?" asked Mrs. York. Josiah filled them in on the situation, ending with the loss of his dog Molly. "Oh, no. Molly was his favorite. He must be heartbroken."

"When the shooting was over, he fell to pieces," Josiah said. "He told me she gave her life to save his."

"There are two of her pups left. Maybe he'll keep one for himself instead of giving them away."

"Who was he giving them to?" asked Mrs. York.

"A young lady who needs them for protection. Tim told me your daughter, Diane, is going to start training them for her tomorrow."

"That will be good."

"Tim befriended this family when they moved here and they've all gotten pretty close."

Beaming, Mrs. York asked, "Are you talking about the Webb family?"

"Yes."

"Tim told us they had a rough time of it. He really likes them. I'm glad that's where the pups are headed."

"I need to ask Tim what he wants me to do with them, then we'll be on our way."

They all settled down to wait for news of Tim. Finally, a nurse told them he could have visitors. Tim's parents suggested Josiah speak to him first. "Thanks, I won't be long." Rising, he followed the nurse to Tim's room.

Tim was a little groggy, but he smiled when Josiah came in the room. "Howdy, boss."

"Howdy, yourself." Looking at Tim's arm he mumbled, "Sure is a nasty way to get out of coming to work."

Grinning slightly, Tim replied. "Yeah, I didn't get enough of a vacation going to Sandpoint, so I opted for the next best thing."

"Did you get a good look at the shooter, Tim?"

"Yes, I did."

Taking a picture out of his pocket, Josiah asked, "This him?"

Looking at the picture closely, Tim replied, "Yes, sir. It is."

"That's Vincent Crowley, Bruce Murdock's hit man."

"He's one mean dude," declared Tim.

"I have one thing to talk to you about, then I'll turn you over to your parents."

"What's that?" asked Tim.

"I'll take care of the dogs for you until you can do it yourself."

"You don't like dogs. Are you sure you want to do this?"

"Yes, I do." Smiling, Josiah continued, "Meagan showed me what it's like to take care of an animal. Yesterday, she told me we have a responsibility to take care of God's creatures. I've thought about that a lot and I have decided I want a dog of my own."

"Wow!" cried Tim. "Wonders never cease."

"I've decided I want a female Collie."

"I have a dog that's about to whelp any day now. I'd be happy to give one of them to you."

"That would be great."

"It's a deal then, the best of the litter will be yours."

"Thanks. Now what about the two pups that go to Meagan? What do you want me to do with them?"

"Could you take them to her today?"

"Not a problem," Josiah assured him. "Oh, I almost forgot to tell you. The guys cleaned up your truck for you."

"Tell them thank you. I wasn't looking forward that."

"Take care and I'll see you soon."

"Thanks for taking care of my dogs, Josiah."

Josiah met the other two officers in the waiting room. Together, they went back to the office to pick up David Black and let Pierson go home to his family. "I have to stop at Tim's to take care of his dogs and feed them. We can go home after that."

Just before leaving the office, Josiah called the Webb's to let them know what had happened to Tim. Shirleen was relieved to know Tim was going to be all right. She also told him they would wait to open gifts until they got there.

When they got to Tim's place they all worked together quickly to take care of the animals. When they were finished, they hurried back to the Webb's.

When they arrived, Meagan asked, "How is Tim?"

"He is going to be fine. It will be a few days before he'll be able to go back to work though. He'll be staying at his folks' place for the next few days." Looking at his men, Josiah winked and asked, "Shirleen is it all right to bring the pups in the house? We left them in the car."

"Well, I don't know..." She looked at Meagan, who was looking at her hopefully, and pretended to think about it. Sighing dramatically, she replied, "You might as well bring them in. It's too cold to leave them in the car.."

"Let me help you bring them in," pleaded Meagan.

"Come on. We don't want to hold up the show."

A few minutes later, the two of them brought the pups inside. The women were in the living room waiting for them. Josiah questioningly glanced first at Shirleen and then at Juliana, who nodded. "Meagan, since we're opening our gifts now, let me be the first to give you a present from your mother and your grandmother."

Picking up both puppies, Josiah handed them to Meagan and said, "Tim has been working with these pups so they could be ready to be your Christmas presents."

"Really?" Meagan squealed.

"They're both yours, honey." Juliana assured her.

Meagan took the pups from Josiah and buried her face in their fur as tears coursed down her cheeks. Turning with both pups still in her arms, she ran into the other room to try to get her emotions under control.

Chapter 32

When Meagan calmed down, she came back into the other room, and the pups tagged along. She picked them up and went to sit between her mother and grandmother. Kissing her mother's cheek, she leaned closer and said, "Thank you, Momma."

"You're welcome, honey, but it was Grandma that talked me into letting you have them."

Kissing Shirleen's cheek, Meagan said, "Thank you Grandma."

"It's my pleasure. To tell you the truth, I'm kind of fond of them, too."

"Really?"

Shirleen took the male pup and began to absently stoke him. "Jeff, would you ask Trudy to come in here?" asked Shirleen. We need to open presents." Turning to Josiah, she asked, "Would you like to play Santa Claus?"

"I'd like that very much." Rising, he started toward the tree. "Mark, you and David be the elves and hand out the gifts for me."

It took Josiah quite awhile to get all of the presents passed around to everyone. Once that was done, everyone started ripping their packages open.

When Juliana saw the computer, she gasped in delight. "Oh, Momma! Now I can take my teaching courses!"

Opening her box, Meagan found it filled with all types of books.

Shirleen's first box was filled with different colors of embroidery floss, and the next box contained more of the same. Opening another box, Shirleen was surprised to see a stack of pre-stamped embroidery projects. "It will take me the rest of my life to get all of these done," declared Shirleen happily.

All at once, Meagan squealed in delight. "I don't believe it," she cried. "My very own computer!"

Trudy opened one of her boxes to find the same selections of pre-stamped pillowcases, dresser scarves, and tablecloths that Shirleen had received.

Josiah's gift from Meagan contained a pair of heavy gloves, a scarf and a warm hat."

Megan opened the gift from Mark and it was a beautiful pink pearl necklace and matching earrings.

When Jeff opened his gift from Shirleen, he was thrilled. "Oh, these outdoor things are just what I needed. Mine have seen better days." Looking up to smile at Shirleen, he said, "Thank you, Shirleen."

Meagan opened her gift from Josiah and gasped in stunned disbelief. Nestled in a jewelry case was a antique necklace and matching earrings. "Oh, Uncle Josiah—" That was as far as she got, for tears began to stream down her face.

"They were my mother's favorite set. Her father gave them to her when she graduated from college. They were the only gift my father allowed her to keep."

"Shouldn't these go to your wife or daughter someday?"

"I don't plan to marry. Besides, who would want a crusty old geezer like me anyway?"

"You're not crusty," ginned Meagan.

"Just old!" laughed Josiah.

"You're not old either, you're just well seasoned."

Josiah started laughing uproariously and everyone soon joined in. Finally, holding his side, he said, "I'm so proud you're my niece, Meagan Webb!"

"Thank you, Uncle Josiah."

Shirleen started to unwrap one of her large gifts. It was heavy and a little awkward and she was having difficulty opening it. Seeing her dilemma, Josiah asked, "Would you like a little help with that, Shirleen?"

"Please!" Bending down in front of her, Josiah helped her get the wrapping off. It was a large handmade jewelry box. "Oh," cried Shirleen in joy, "Jeff this is absolutely beautiful! I can't believe you made this for me, it's so ornate"

Jeff watched as the others opened their presents. Meagan noticed that Jeff wasn't opening his presents and asked why.

"I was enjoying watching you all so much that I forgot I had presents of my own to unwrap."

"Well, we want to watch your joy, so get to unwrapping." She grinned to take the sting out of her words.

"Yes, ma'am," Jeff said and saluted.

Meagan picked up a present from David Black. She unwrapped it and saw it was a jewelry case. When she opened it she was surprised to see a butterfly necklace and matching earrings. "This is so elegant, Mr. Black.

"Please, call me David. We're friends."

"Well, David this is absolutely beautiful."

"I'm glad you like it."

When Trudy opened a gift from Shirleen, she saw it contained several needlepoint kits. Juliana next gift from Shirleen contained several programs for her computer. Shirleen burst into tears when she opened her gift from Juliana. It was a portrait of Meagan. When Meagan opened a present from her mother, she too burst into tears. It was a portrait of Shirleen.

When Jeff opened his present from Juliana, he could only stare at it. It was a large 30x40 scene of the field where the elk liked to congregate. Finally, he said, "I love this. Sometimes, when I'm working outside, I watch these very elk grazing in the field. Thank you so much."

When Trudy opened her gift and saw it was a portrait of her painted on a 24x26 canvas, she said, "Oh, I'll treasure this forever, Juliana. No one has ever done anything so wonderful for me. Thank you."

Josiah's painting was a 30x40 nature scene. In the distance were mountains with a small stream running through it, that turned into a frothy waterfall. "Wow, Juliana! I had no idea you could paint like this. I'll treasure this always."

"I'm glad you like it, Uncle Josiah."

"Oh, Kitten, I don't just like it, I *love* it!"

When most of the presents were opened there were still two large ones left, with Meagan's name on them. When she opened them she was surprised to see the pet carriers. Inside each one were two bowls, chew toys and grooming tools. One of the pet taxis was from her mother, and the other was from her grandmother. "Those are the things you'll need to take care of your dogs," explained Shirleen. "By the way, have you decided on names for them?"

"Yes," replied Meagan. "Prince and Lady."

"Those are great names," praised Josiah. "They fit them somehow. I am so fond of these pups that I had to ordered a pup for myself because I'd miss them so much. Tim said one of the Collies is about to whelp, so I'm getting the best female in the litter."

"Uncle Josiah, that's wonderful!"

"You might want to talk to Tim's sister, Diane Weaver," Shirleen said. "She's a veterinarian who also trains dogs. We have an appointment with her at ten o'clock tomorrow morning."

"That's not a bad idea," declared Josiah brightening. "Can you give me her number?"

"You'll be here in the morning, won't you? Why don't you just talk to her then?"

"I don't know about the rest of you," Shirleen said in frustration, "but I'm all in favor of leaving this mess right where it is for the time being."

"I agree," stated Juliana.

Shirleen pulled Juliana and Meagan off to the side and said, "There are more presents for you out in the shop, Jeff assembled them for me. They'll help us organize things tomorrow."

Meagan grinned. "I had Jeff assemble some things for you and Momma, too, Grandma."

"So did I," Juliana said and laughed. "No wonder the poor man was always out in the shop."

"Well if we're to get our part of the dinner down to the Brooks' we'd better snap to it."

Trudy had already gone to the kitchen and was checking on the turkey. The ham was already cooling on the counter. The side dishes were ready as well. Soon the rolls that Trudy had made earlier were in the pans to rise. They'd bake them there.

When it was all ready, Jeff and Josiah helped box everything up and take it to the cars. Not long after that they were on their way.

Melinda Brooks awoke to the sounds of crying infants. Moaning, Melinda struggled into a sitting position. "How can you possibly sleep with all of that noise," Melinda asked Theodore as she shook him awake.

"Who says I'm sleeping? There's no way a body can get any shut eye in this house when all of them are crying at once."

"I miss waking up to quiet," sighed Melinda.

"You came into this with your eyes wide open."

"Can I start over?"

"Is that what you want to do?"

"Truthfully, no. I'm not sorry I agreed to do this. I'm just tired from helping Annabelle bake all those pies yesterday."

When Melinda had gotten her shower, she dressed quickly, kissed Teddy and went to help the nurses. One nurse, as well as the aides that worked graveyard shift, where eating breakfast when Melinda came into the kitchen. "Good morning every-one. I hear our little darlings declaring war already this morning."

"Two of them have colic," Heather Cline said, "and the rest are pitching a fit because they haven't been fed and changed yet. They're in the process of doing both. Chuckling, she added, "I feel sorry for the ones with colic."

"Which ones have it?"

"Michelle and Effie. The nurse is trying to help them right now. Hopefully, she can get them feeling better soon."

"I'll go see if I can help" Melinda walked into the nursery, where she found the nurse working on Michelle. "Could you use some help?" asked Melinda.

"Yes, I could." Looking toward Effie, she said, "If you could rock Effie and her close, I can get Michelle taken care of."

Melinda went to pick Effie up, holding her close as she patted her back. The heat from Melinda's body soothed her, and few minutes later she had quieted down.

Once they had these two under control, the other three children, who had also been fed and changed, went back to sleep. Sighing in relief, as the dayshift took over, Melinda went to the kitchen to have breakfast.

When she was finished, she helped Annabelle get the turkey in the oven and work on the rest of the dinner. Theodore, with the help of the crew, brought in several chairs and the two housekeepers, Dawna and Louise, began to set the tables.

The men had just put the chairs in place, when Shirleen's group arrived. The women went to help Trudy with the last minute things, and a few minutes later, Adam Morgan, the Bunkhouse cook, knocked on the door. He and several men entered, carrying boxes of food he had prepared. The kitchen fairly groaned with the amount of food.

Theodore went to wheel Henry out so he could visit with everyone. Henry was self-conscious about his condition, but with everyone encouraging him, be began to relax and listen to the conversations going on around him.

Two hours later, the meal was ready to serve, and the kitchen tables, as well as all of the counters were filled with food. They formed a line and started filling their plates, buffet style. While they ate, they got to know each other. Soon, everyone was so full, and conversation lagged. Some of the crew said they had chores to do, but many suspected they went back to the bunkhouse to sleep off the feast.

Everyone had opted to wait for dessert, since they were all too full to enjoy it. Seeing that Henry was exhausted, Theodore took him back to his room so he could take a nap.

When clean up was over with, the women went to sit in the living room to relax while they talked amongst themselves. Some, who brought needlework, began working on it, while the others just relaxed.

Meagan looked over to where Melinda was sitting and asked, "Melinda, what did you do for a living before you moved here?"

"I was a kindergarten teacher."

"What inspired you to do that kind of work?"

"I've always loved children," replied Melinda. "In fact, I've always been the most comfortable around children." Shrugging she added, "It was the most rewarding decision I've ever made. Have you given any thought to what you want to do with the rest of your life?"

"Not until recently," sighed Meagan. "I was too busy being a social butterfly to think about my future. I knew I wanted to graduate from high school, but I never went farther than that. When I met Tim's dog team, saw the elk feeding in the meadow between our properties, and watched the birds feeding in the snow, I seriously started considering going to veterinary school so I could care for the animals."

"That's a worthy goal," replied Melinda, plainly impressed.

"It is, but I don't know if I have the courage or the brains needed to get through all the schooling I'd need."

"If you set your mind to it," replied Shirleen, "you can do anything. You're a hard worker and you're intelligent. If you want to go to veterinary school, I say go for it!"

"Momma's right, honey," Juliana said. "I've seen how hard you've worked this year."

"Thank you for the vote of confidence," responded Meagan. "That makes me feel better about pursuing my dream."

"Good," Melinda said. "Don't let anyone discouraged you."

"Tell us a little more about yourself, Annabelle," prompted Melinda.

Annabelle sat so quietly that everyone thought she hadn't heard Melinda's question. Sighing, she finally began to speak, "I haven't had anything easy in my life, but somehow I've managed to go on." Smoothing out a wrinkles in her apron, she continued. "I've fought to forgive my parents for how they treated me, especially how they allowed Arthur to treat me when I was growing up."

"You said you were afraid for your life, the day Tim came out to tell us he was on his way here," said Melinda. "Why were you so afraid of him?"

Annabelle looked as if she was about to bolt from the room, but she didn't. Finally, she sighed and answered Melinda's question. "When I was fifteen, I was on my way home from school when my brother Arthur started bullying Abner Jones. Abner was about three years younger than me so he was no real threat to Arthur. My brother loved to bully people every chance he got. "

"Was Arthur older or younger than you?" asked Trudy.

"Arthur was two years older than me."

"Sounds like he was jealous of you," Shirleen said. "He hated having to share your parents."

Thinking Shirleen's comment over for a moment, Annabelle replied, "I never thought of it that way. Maybe you're right."

"Please, continue with your story," encouraged Meagan.

"As I said, Arthur loved to bully people. Abner Jones wasn't doing anything to Arthur, but that didn't matter, he began to slap him around anyway. When the other kids and I begged him to leave Abner alone, Arthur laughed and slapped him again.

"Poor little Abner began to cry, but he never hit Arthur. He just let Arthur slap him around. Arthur was furious that he wouldn't fight back, so he punched Abner in the stomach. When Abner doubled over, Arthur just grinned and taunted him.

Suddenly, Annabelle began to sob quietly. "I got between Abner and my brother, which just made Arthur more furious. The rest of the children ran home because they got scared when Arthur flew into a rage. He called me some vile names, then backhanded me across the face and knocked me down.

"That's when my brother seemed to go insane. He started to beat Abner, who still refused to fight him. I was afraid he was going to kill him, so I jumped onto my brother's back and started hitting him. He shook me off and went back to beating little Abner.

"Seeing I couldn't stop him, I began to scream hysterically and Arthur turned his rage from Abner to me. He had me on the ground, beating me when he heard a police siren. He got scared and ran away, leaving me there, bruised and battered.

"When the police tried to help us, I told them it was my brother, Arthur, who had done it. After that, they took Abner and me to the hospital. I wasn't in bad shape, but Abner was.

"When I got home, I told my mother what happened and she told me it wasn't my business to interfere when a fight was going on. I told her that Abner hadn't done a thing to Arthur, but she didn't believe me.

"Later that night, when the police came to question Arthur, I was told to stay in my room if I knew what was good for me. Since I couldn't do anything more for poor Abner and fearing the repercussions from my brother, I packed my things and left. I didn't know where I was going to go, I just knew I had to leave."

"I'm so sorry," replied Shirleen sympathetically. "That sounds awful."

"It was," calmly replied Annabelle.

Meagan, who was thinking of how horrible her father was, asked, "Where did you go, Annabelle?"

"First, I went to see Abner's parents to tell them I was sorry for how mean my brother was and to see if he was all right. Seeing my battered face, they asked what happened. I told them my brother had done it when I tried to stop him from hurting Abner. They told me I probably saved Abner's life and thanked me.

"When they saw my suitcase, they asked me where I was going. I told them what had happened at home and that I felt like I had to leave. I just wanted to go where I was safe. They told me that because I tried to defend their son, they'd take care of me."

"Good," Dawna Twitchell, one of the housekeepers, said. "At least you were safe."

"How long did you stay with this family?" Louise Rogers asked.

"I stayed until I turned eighteen. When they brought Abner home from the hospital, he was never able to speak properly and he never walked again. The doctors said all the blows to his head caused brain damage. I did all that I could for Abner ... as much as his mother would let me. Two months before I left, Abner became gravely ill and died."

Gasping, Juliana exclaimed, "Oh, no!"

"I was overcome with grief. Finally, I realized I couldn't stay there any longer. It was too painful to be there without him. I told his family I needed to be on my own. They said they understood and that they planned to move soon.

"Maude taught me all I know about cooking. That was what kept me sane, besides taking care of Abner. When I told her I wanted to go as far away as possible, she said she had some friends in Cardston who could use my help.

"A couple of weeks later, I was on my way here to work for the Wiggins family. They were the ones who didn't pay me. I found work with another family, and stayed with them until they were killed. Then, when I met my husband, Gerald Croft, I worked for a while in a fast food place."

"So, you finally found happiness?" asked Dawna.

"For fifteen years, I did. Then a drunk driver killed Gerald. We weren't blessed with children, and didn't have much money, so I've been forced to work ever since."

The men came back into the room at that point, interrupting the women's emotional discussion. "Well," Theodore said, "that walk was refreshing and our appetites are back. What say we all have some of those pies we've been smelling for the past two days?"

"That sounds like a plan," Melinda said.

"I'll go get Henry," Theodore said."

"I guess we'd better start cutting pies," Annabelle said.

Laughing, the women went to the kitchen to get everything ready.

When they were all together Josiah asked, "Will you play some Christmas carols for us when we've finished eating, Shirleen?"

"I didn't bring any music."

"I did," Meagan said. "I remembered seeing a piano when I was helping to organize the house.

"Will you play for us?" asked Theodore.

"Sure."

"You haven't lived until you've heard this woman tickle the ivories," bragged Josiah.

They all enjoyed Shirleen's impromptu concert, then everyone got ready to go home. Everyone was well fed and tired, so they all retired to their respective beds.

The group wouldn't have been so happy if they knew Crowley had followed them to where they took the road up to the house. When the lights were turned out in the house, he turned around and went back to town.

Later that evening, he called Murdock to report in. "Hello, boss."

"What's up, Vinnie?"

"I tracked the men to the hospital, where that man I shot was being patched up. When they left, I followed them, then found a place where I had a good view of the house. I waited until I saw Josiah come out of the house. Boy was I surprised to see your daughter, Leslie come out of the house with him. They were out walking some pups. I heard him call her Meagan, but I knew it was Leslie. Her hair's short now, but I'd recognize her voice anywhere."

"So they're in Canada." Bruce said, considering his options. "Well, we'll let them enjoy the winter. It's too risky to try to do something and chance getting stuck there.

I hear the snowstorms are murder this time of the year." Laughing at his own joke, he added, "Get it, murder up there?"

"I get it, boss," Crowley said, rolling his eyes.

"Anyway, when spring comes, I want you and Wilson to do them. Got it?"

"You bet, boss."

"For now, get back here. Things are heating up here. I want to be prepared for the backlash when I up the percentage on the drug business."

"I'll leave the first thing in the morning, boss."

Early, the next morning, Crowley ate breakfast at the local café and then headed home. He was relieved to be going back to the states. As he drove along, he fantasized about what he'd do to Ruth Murdock and smiled sardonically as he pictured the tortures that he would perform. The smile was soon gone as his thoughts turned to his boss. *Murdock thinks I don't know how he feels about me, but I do. What do I care? I hate him near as much as he does me. That man's a greedy mental case. If it weren't for Wilson and me, he'd be shark bait already. Ya never know, I may just do him after I do his old lady.*

Late that afternoon, he pulled into Sandpoint and got a motel room before going to get something to eat. After he ate, he went back to his room and went right to sleep.

The next day, he got to the Spokane airport, returned his rental car, and went to the terminal to wait for his flight to be called.

Chapter 33

Six o'clock the next morning found everyone in the Webb household up and busy. As soon as Shirleen got ready for the day, she went to the kitchen to help Trudy with breakfast. It was snowing, but it didn't look too bad yet.

When breakfast was ready, they called everyone in to eat. Jeff, Josiah and Mark were busy discussing their remodeling plans as they came to the table in the dining room. They had outgrown the kitchen when Josiah's group had come to stay.

When they were all assembled and had said grace, Jeff looked over at Shirleen and said, "Once we've eaten, we're going start tearing up the walls. Once we're done with that, will you and Juliana come and help us decide what goes in what room?"

"Sure," replied Shirleen, growing excited at the prospect of what might be hidden in the rooms.

"Good deal. We're going to wait to hang the doors until we've moved in the furniture."

"It will be wonderful to have some order in the house again," sighed Shirleen.

"We'd better eat so we can get busy," Josiah said and chuckled.

After breakfast Trudy and Meagan cleaned up the kitchen, while Juliana and Shirleen took care of some other housework.

A few hours later, Josiah found Shirleen and said, "We're ready for you and Juliana."

Growing excited, Shirleen cried, "Wonderful! I'll get all the girls and we'll be right up. You guys did that job in record time!"

They found many surprises waiting for them when they got upstairs. Two of the rooms had leaks in their ceilings and water had come down on the beds and ruined the mattresses and there were some water spots on the carpet in places. The rest of the furniture, however, was in excellent condition.

"We'll move the furniture into one of the rooms t you won't be using until we can take care of the leak in the roof," Jeff said. "We may have to put on a new roof, which can't be done 'til spring. We'll try to patch things up for the time being, and put down something to catch the drips where we can't make repairs."

"I'm so glad the furniture wasn't ruined," Shirleen said. "We can always get new mattresses and carpeting. I'll leave everything in your capable hands, Jeff."

The three men put the furniture in the last bedroom and then started ripping up the ruined carpets. When they were done, they loaded the carpet and mattresses into Jeff's truck and went to the city dump.

When he got back, Jeff assessed the condition of the floors and saw they were starting to mold. The men took the floorboards up and were relieved to see the mold hadn't reached very far. They applied chemicals to kill the mold and decided to leave things open for the time being.

The doorbell rang a short time later and Shirleen went to see who was there. There was a woman standing on their doorstep. When Shirleen opened the door the woman introduced herself as Diane Weaver.

"Please come in," Shirleen said. "Let me get my family and we'll be ready to start. Please, take your coat off and make yourself comfortable."

Shirleen studied Diane closely when she came back from letting everyone know they had a guest. She was tall and slender with beautiful brown eyes that sparkled with life. She was dressed in blue jeans, with a green, long sleeved shirt that buttoned down the front. Her shiny brown hair was styled in a pageboy with the bangs pulled to the side *She looks just like Tim,* Shirleen thought.

Everyone came in and met their guest and Megan brought in the pups, prepared to learn how to train her dogs.

The lesson began, and Diane was firm but gentle as she worked with the dogs. "When they've done well, remember to give them a treat. This gives them an incentive to work hard and do well. Always praise them when you give them their treat."

Taking the treats, Josiah tried to get the pups to do as he asked, but they wanted nothing to do with him or the treats.

"You have to be firm with them, but not mean," Diane explained.

Josiah tried again and the female did as he asked and got a treat. When the male saw this, he grew impatient with the whole thing and tried to take it away from her. Diane gently but firmly pushed him back. After several tries, the people and dogs had come to an understanding and both were getting what they wanted. By the time the lesson was over, both dogs had learned to sit, come and stay.

"Good job, Meagan and Josiah. Continue working with them on this this week. These little guys are really smart. My brother, Tim, picked two winners for you, Meagan."

"Thank you for helping us train them," replied Meagan.

Trudy came from the kitchen and said, "I just baked a batch of your brother's favorite cookies. Would you like to have some with either coffee or milk?"

"I've tasted those cookies of yours, Miss North and I'd be delighted to have some along with a glass of milk."

Trudy brought in milk and cookies for everyone. Meagan went to ask the men if they'd like some, but they wanted to finish their work, so Josiah went to help them.

Meagan asked what the others were thinking, but was too polite to ask, "How is Tim doing, Mrs. Weaver?"

"Call me Diane, please. We're going to be seeing a lot of each other over the next few weeks, so we should be on a first name basis."

"I agree," Meagan affirmed.

"Tim's doing great, he is anxious to get back to work though. He says he feels fine." Diane imitated her brother's actions, which caused the other to laugh. "Seriously though, he was pretty lucky. As crazy as that man was, he would've killed him in a few more minutes if Josiah and his men hadn't shown up."

"It was sad to hear that Tim lost the mother to my pups," said Meagan.

"Tim and Molly were really close, so it was no surprise when she jumped in to save him and lost her life in the process."

"I tease Tim a lot, but I really like him," Meagan admitted. "He's been so good to us."

Diane smiled and said, "That's my brother all right. Always looking out for the community. I'm proud of him for doing that. He was that way even when we were in school. He always protected me from the bullies. One time in particular, Howard Nelson, was a nasty character. He was three years older than me, which made him a year older than Tim.

"Anyway, he would wait to catch me alone so he could be mean to me. One day, he tore my dress. I screamed at the top of my lungs, and Howard hit me in the face and knocked me down.

"Suddenly, from out of nowhere, Tim showed up and he was mad. I'll never forget how awful Tim looked when he said, 'So you like to pick on little girls? Well, let me show you how it feels,' and he hit Howard in the nose.

"Well, Howard cried like a baby. Tim told him to leave me alone, or next time he'd get a lot worse. Then, he wrapped his arm around me and walked me to the bus stop."

"I like him more for that," declared Juliana. "I never had a brother to protect me. It would've been nice."

"I had my share, of bullies pick on me," said Meagan quietly. "There was this tall, mean tempered boy who was two years older than me who picked on all the girls. One day he caught me after school and told me he was going to show me what boys did best.

"He grabbed me and dragged me into the bushes, then grabbed my dress and yanked down. I think I was 12 at the time and had just started to develop. Then he threw me to the ground and got on top of me.

"Before he could do anything, I scratched his face all the way from his eye to his chin. When he moved to grab his face, I kicked him where it hurts the most. While he was rolling around moaning, I ran as hard as I could toward home.

"After that, I didn't want to go to school any more, but I had to. I didn't see him around and learned he was home sick. I went to the principal and told him what had happened and the boy was expelled. After that, his family suddenly moved away."

"Why didn't you ever tell me this, Meagan?" Juliana asked.

"Because, I couldn't talk about it." Tears began to course down Meagan's cheeks.

Juliana moved over to comfort her. "Don't you ever feel you have to keep secrets from me, Meagan. I'll always believe you and help you any way I can."

"I know that now, but I didn't know it then. I was afraid you'd think I had caused it somehow."

"Never!"

"We had it bad then, but children today have it even worse," Diane said. "I hired a private teacher to teach my six children because I didn't want them exposed to drug abuse and violence in the public schools. This way, I can go to work every day knowing that my children are safe."

Sighing wistfully, Meagan said, "I wish I could've been homeschooled the whole time. I think I would've been better off academically."

"Well," said Diane, "we can't cry over spilled milk."

You're right," agreed Shirleen.

Setting her glass on the table, Diane stood to go. "I have got to get back to the clinic. I have a surgery scheduled this afternoon. I'll see you next week."

After Diane left, everyone went back to what they'd been doing. By later that afternoon, all the housework was done and the men got Josiah's bed and furniture arranged in his room. After that, they moved Juliana's art studio to the room across from Trudy's. By the time that was done, it was time for dinner.

Three days later, Tim came out to visit with Shirleen's family. They gave him all of their gifts and he was delighted with the hat, scarf and gloves Meagan gave him. His heart skipped a beat when he opened Juliana's gift. It was his portrait painted on a huge 24x28 canvas. "Where did you ever get a picture of me so you could paint this?"

"Out of here," replied Juliana, touching her head. "I studied you when you weren't looking, then after you went home, I'd work on the painting."

"It's so realistic. Thank you!."

When he opened Shirleen's gift he was thrilled to see it contained several movies and mystery books. "I'm going to enjoy these."

When he opened Trudy's huge gift box he chuckled appreciatively. Inside were different candies and cookies, as well as several pieces of fruitcake and scripture cake. "Well, there goes my new pants! By the time I eat all of these goodies I'll be waddling through the door!"

Laughing, Megan said, "We'd love you anyway."

Not long after he finished opening his gifts, Tim decided it was time to go home and rest.

A week later, they had the rest of the rooms changed around. When Meagan and Juliana saw the shelving destined for the library they were ecstatic. They also set up the computers in the library so that they could work in peace, moved Juliana's room to where Meagan had been and put Meagan in the room Mark no longer needed.

After Diane's visit, the men learned that Crowley was no longer in town so they went their separate ways, but not before helping Jeff set up Megan's room and rearrange living room. Everyone was happy with the new arrangements.

January and February were uneventful, except for training Prince and Lady, who were turning out to be good guard dogs. Jeff made them a pen just outside the garage where they could do their business without so much snow.

Jeff was kept busy keeping the snow plowed and wood boxes full, as well as doing small repairs around the house.

Shirleen and Juliana continued with Meagan's schooling, and Trudy added cooking and sewing lessons to the curriculum.

Tim and Josiah came up to visit regularly, which kept Shirleen and Meagan busy entertaining them.

Shirleen had regained her health and was finally back to doing what she wanted. She had also learned to relaxed more, and enjoy family life — even playing with the two dogs. Prince was her favorite.

Shirleen and Trudy often went to visit Melinda and Theodore, and helped out with all their children when needed.

Henry had slowly been regaining his strength and ability to speak. Trudy was able to care for Henry much of the time, freeing up Theodore so he could help Melinda with the children. There was a special bond growing between Henry and Trudy that everyone could see but them. As Trudy worked with Henry, they would talk for hours.

Juliana's feelings for Tim kept growing, even though she tried to push them away. She felt guilty about what she was feeling because she was still married. On the other hand, Tim was struggling to hide how much he loved her. Despite their best efforts, each time they were together, they grew closer.

Those who loved them, struggled silently right along with them. Shirleen wanted happiness for Juliana more than anything, yet she knew things had to happen in their own way and time and kept her opinions to herself.

Meagan wasn't exempt from the love bug either. Mark and David vied for her attention every chance they got. She was hard put to decide which one she wanted as the two young men grew fonder of her every time they saw her. Shirleen knew there would come a time when at least one of these special young men would lose out. This made her a little sad, because both men were kind, generous and compassionate.

As Shirleen and Jeff got to know each other better, the love bug bit them, too. When Jeff didn't think anyone was looking, he lovingly watched Shirleen's every move. Shirleen, who loved Jeff desperately, did the same. It took Meagan to finally move things along.

One night, Meagan went to her mother's room to speak to her. "Momma, have you noticed Grandma and Jeff?"

"What about them?" asked Juliana in surprise.

"They're in love with each other, but neither will admit it. We've got to find a way to get them together."

"You need to let them do things in their own time."

"Well, I think they need a little push in the right directions. I'm going to find a way to make them notice they're in love."

"Are you saying that you'd be happy if Jeff married your grandmother?"

"Oh, Mom, having Jeff for a grandfather would be the most wonderful thing in the world. He's kind, gentle, and loving. Who wouldn't want him in the family? Besides, Grandma loves him. That's the most important reason of all. She'd finally know true love."

A smile slowly began to spread across Juliana's face and spread into a full-blown smile. "You're right, Meagan, Momma would have true love and happiness for the first time in her life. Let's wait for an opportunity to get them together."

"It's a deal," Meagan said, reaching out to hug her mother close.

As the dogs followed Meagan out of the room, Juliana was surprised to realize how glad she was they'd given them to Meagan. *The responsibilities of caring for and training those dogs is causing Meagan to blossom. There's even a spring to her step because she feels freer to be herself because she knows the dogs will alert her to danger and protect her.*

It's rough on all of us knowing that Spring is coming and Bruce and his goons are out there somewhere just trying to find us. She realized she was crying as she thought about what Bruce wanted to do to her and her family. *It isn't fair. I have just as much right to live my life as he does. I have a right to happiness, too. Oh please, dear God, stop him from hurting us!* .

March came in like a lion bringing another blizzard that socked them in for four days. As the wind howled, they were grateful for the roaring fires in the fireplaces. When it was over, there was so much snow Jeff had to shovel a path to the shed to get the snow blower.

By the time Jeff had paths cleared through the snow, Trudy had breakfast ready. Once he ate, Jeff headed to the workshop to get to work on more things for the rooms he was repairing. A couple of hours later he returned and started removing the sheetrock that was damaged by the leak.

When that task was finished, he hauled the sheetrock out to put it in the back of his truck. When he'd finished loading, he came in and told Shirleen he was going to take it to the dump and then head to the store to get supplies.

Shirleen watched him leave, then went to her room to dig out the newspapers she'd been collecting. She hadn't been able to read any of them since before Christmas because she'd been so busy. She stacked them by date and picked up the first one. Plastered across the front page was a picture of her house in Syracuse with a moving van parked in front. The caption read:

Spielberg Mansion Has a New Owner

Bruce Murdock is officially the new owner of the Spielberg Mansion and has made it his principal residence. Rumor had it he inherited if from his father-in-law, Gordon Spielberg but no one knows for sure. He sold his former residence to Nathan White, a family friend.

"He killed the owner, that's how he got it!" snapped Shirleen aloud.

Disgusted, Shirleen folded the paper and picked up the next. There was nothing of interest in the next five papers, but when she picked up the sixth, she gasped, There was a photo of several bodies on the front page. She read the caption and knew Bruce had to be involved somehow. She went on to read the accompanying article:

Drug Sting Results in Mass Murder

Police responded to a call reporting a disturbance and were greeted by a grizzly scene. Someone had massacred a local drug lord and his minions. This is the third such mass killing in a matter of weeks. Police suspect a mafia connection but would not comment further.

Police have information indicating all players in the drug game have been forced to hand over a bigger percentage of their take to an unknown mafia boss. They said the three mass killings were the result of refusing to pay. They suspect the murder of drug cartel leader Jon Montello, who was found murdered in his home on Sunday, is connected.

Police have said they have several leads, but refused to comment further.

Oh, Bruce, Shirleen thought, *how can you be so greedy and brutal?" What drives you?" There has to be something because you certainly weren't born this way. I'm so glad we got away from you.*

Shirleen continued to scan papers, and found another that caught her attention.

Police Captain Charles Abram Shot

Police Captain Charles Abram was shot Monday evening while trying to make a drug-related arrest here in Syracuse. The bullet just missed his heart and punctured his right lung. Surgeons were able to remove the bullet and he is in stable condition.

Police said there are no definite leads in the case.

Well, Bruce, at least you aren't part of this heinous crime, thought Shirleen. *At least I hope you're not.*

She picked up the last paper and found a follow-up on the shooting story.

Captain Abrams Out of Coma

Syracuse Police Captain Charles Abram, victim of a shooting earlier this week, is conscious and in stable condition. Doctors said he is improving rapidly.

Police apprehended the shooter, George Stern, earlier today at his home and transported him to the county jail. As Stern was being escorted from the squad car to the jail, he was shot multiple times by an unknown assailant.

Officer Jack Carson, who was escorting Stern, was also shot and killed. He leaves behind a wife and six children.

Knowing Bruce as she did, she figured he'd had Stern killed so he wouldn't rat him out. She kept the three papers that had interested her and threw the others away.

"Your classes are about to start Momma," Juliana said as Shirleen came into the room.

"Before we do that, I have something to show you both." She showed them the papers and Juliana was disgusted at the thought of Bruce living in her mother's house. Meagan just stared at the picture of her grandmother's house. Suddenly, she burst into tears. "Oh, Momma, why doesn't God do something to make Daddy stop doing these awful things?"

"I don't know, honey. I've been asking the same thing."

"The good Lord knows what's best," Shirleen said, "so we have to wait on His timing. As I've studied the scriptures, I've noticed that when God has had enough, he allows the wicked to punish the wicked. We can be sure that God isn't pleased with

Bruce Murdock. My feeling is, that Bruce's reign of blood and terror will end soon. We just have to be patient."

"Okay," replied Meagan meekly.

"After reading this, it looks like Bruce has grown cocky and brazen. He's sure to slip up soon because he thinks he's invincible. Someone will take him down. It is only a matter of time before it happens."

The phone rang and Shirleen answered it. It was Josiah. "Hello, Shirleen Have you heard the news?"

"What news?"

"I just got a call from Frank Kessler. He told me his police captain, Charles Abrams, was shot a few weeks back, but is doing much better."

"I just read that in the paper. I'm glad he'll be all right."

"Me too. Anyway, Bruce Murdock has been snooping around trying to find out what happened to the stuff from Spielberg's secret room. Frank told me Bruce thinks I took it. He has no idea that it was the police. That's why Crowley was snooping around. He wanted to know if I had the stolen loot."

Growing concerned, Shirleen said, "That means that your life is in danger, Josiah."

"I know it is, but I also know our buddy, Bruce is worried. He wouldn't have sent Crowley if he wasn't"

What should we do?"

"Keep watch for Crowley's return. With spring just around the corner, we've got to stay on the alert."

"Okay."

"Now, on to more positive news. I got my new pup a few days ago and she's a real beauty and so smart. Tim house-trained her for me, and I've been teaching her to stay, sit and come. Can I bring her over to show Meagan."

"That would be wonderful."

"I'll be out around seven."

"We'll be looking for you."

Shirleen told the family what Josiah had to say about Bruce and Crowley, and then let them know he would be bringing his new pup to visit.

This news immediately lifted Meagan spirits. "Did he tell you her name?"

"No, but I'm sure we'll find out soon."

Two hours later, Jeff returned with new sheetrock and carried it upstairs.

When he came down, Trudy asked, "Have you had lunch, Jeff?"

"No. I was so busy I didn't even think about it."

"Then when you've finished hauling in the sheetrock, I'll make you something."

"I won't be long," he called as he headed back upstairs.

Chapter 34

It was the last of April and the snow was slowly disappearing. The spring birds were back, filling the air with their songs. Shirleen was sitting in the stuffed chair in front of the cold fireplace working on a set of pillowcases. "What are your plans for this bright beautiful morning?" she asked Trudy when she came in the room.

"Would it be all right if I went down to help Theodore work with Henry?"

"I don't see why not. You don't have to stay here all the time. Besides, a little time away will give you the chance to relax."

"I baked two cakes this morning. I thought I'd take one with me when I go. I'll pay you back for the ingredients."

"Trudy North," scolded Shirleen, "this is just as much your house as it is ours. You have every right to make goodies and take them to whoever you want."

"Thanks, Shirleen."

"Trudy, it is always good to serve others. I want you to feel free to do that."

Trudy sank onto the couch to stare at Shirleen in amazement. "I've never been allowed to care for others this way. I especially didn't dare do that around Mr. Murdock. He would've sacked me on the spot."

"Well, this is your home, too, Trudy. I'm glad you want to do something for that sweet family."

Rising, Trudy surprised Shirleen by kissing her cheek. "Thank you for making me feel so special."

Tears sprang into Shirleen's eyes as she looked at this woman that she had come to treasure as a friend. "Have a great time helping Henry."

"I will. I'll be back in time to make lunch." Trudy bounded up the stairs to get ready to go, and left a few minutes later.

Shirleen thought about the Brooks family as she worked on the pillowcases. The twins born in late November were doing really well. It was obvious that Michelle was the leader of the pack, maturing faster than Michael. Katarina was the same sweet baby she'd always been. Effie and Ephraim were two little peas in a pod. When she saw them three days ago, she'd noticed they'd been growing in leaps and bounds. Soon they'd outgrow their clothes and bottles. Melinda was the best little mother a child could ask for and Theodore loved his time with the children.

When she thought of Henry, she smiled. Trudy seemed to be blossoming more each time she was with him. He was improving daily, and Shirleen suspected it was due in part to his long conversations with Trudy.

Suddenly, Meagan came in grinning from ear to ear. "Grandma, you'll never guess what Prince did."

"Probably not."

"As I threw a stick out of the garden, Prince took off like a shot to retrieve it. He brought it back and dropped it at my feet. Then he waited for me to throw it again. For the last half hour we've been playing fetch."

"That's great, honey. Those two never cease to amaze me."

"Me either." Growing thoughtful Meagan replied, "Do you remember when Tim was going to ruffle my hair, like he sometimes does, and Prince came at him, his teeth bared and the hairs on his body stiff?"

"Boy, do I ever," declared Shirleen. "I thought for a moment he was going to rip Tim's leg with those razor-sharp fangs of his."

"I thought so too. That was the last time Tim did that. I was going to reprimand Prince, but Tim told me he was only trying to protect me." Shirleen nodded, but remained thoughtful. "What about the day Lady thought Momma was going to hit me when we were play fighting. She immediately let Momma know she needed to stop it."

"I'm so glad we let you to have the dogs. They make me feel safer."

"Me, too," admitted Meagan.

"If Crowley, Bruce, or any other of Bruce's goons come around, those two dogs of ours will make short work of them."

Leaning down, Meagan kissed Shirleen's cheek. "Thank you for giving me the best Christmas present ever."

"You're more than welcome, sweetheart."

"Well, I promised Momma I'd help her plant more flowers, so I'd better get to it before she sends the dogs after me." Laughing happily, Meagan rushed back outside.

Shirleen heard a vehicle drive into the driveway and felt vulnerable all of a sudden. Laying her embroidery work to the side, she went to see who it was.

It was Jeff, with his truck loaded to the brim with shingles, and another larger truck pulled in behind him. Jeff began barking orders to the other two men that got out of the truck. When everything was unloaded, the men in the larger truck left.

"How much did all of this come to?" Shirleen asked.

Jeff handed the invoice to Shirleen, who scanned it and went inside to write Jeff a check.

"Thanks, Shirleen. As soon as I get things sorted out, I'm going to start on the roof."

"Great. That means we can start work on those two rooms upstairs."

"Yup! I'll be busy for a while."

"I'm sorry that you have so much work to do," sighed Shirleen. "It *will* be great to have the house back in working order."

"It sure will. Guess I'll get to work."

Before long, Shirleen heard ripping sounds coming from the roof.

At eleven, Trudy came home carrying a covered dish.

"What have you got, Trudy?"

"Hot rolls Annabelle just made. They smell so good, don't they?"

Sniffing the air, Shirleen nodded as she replied, "They sure do!"

"I'm going to make a pork chop dinner to go with them."

"I'll help."

Later that afternoon, Shirleen and Juliana had some target practice. Juliana hit the bulls-eye dead center every time. Shirleen missed the first two shots then she too hit the bulls-eye. Meagan, who stood watching behind them, grinned. "I'm going to start calling you Annie Oakley, Grandma, and Momma I'm gonna call you Calamity Jane … the two fastest shots in all of Cardston."

Julian blew on her gun, as she puffed out her chest and lifted her head in a haughty manner. "Don't forget it neither."

As they started back to the house, they heard a vehicle approaching their place. Turning to look at the others, Shirleen wasn't surprised to see fear in their eyes. It was replaced with joy when they saw Josiah Graham approaching the driveway.

When he got out of the car, his Collie, Princess, bounded after him and ran to Meagan. Her tan and white fur was brushed to perfection, and she wagged her tail happily as Meagan stroked her. Prince and Lady, not to be left out, came over to get their share of attention.

Soon they heard another vehicle coming toward the house, but Josiah didn't seem concerned so the others relaxed. Soon they saw Tim's truck come into sight and turn into the driveway. He had Dr. Stillman with him. Looking at Josiah, Shirleen said, "Let us get these weapons put away and we'll be right back."

When the women were seated, Shirleen asked, "To what do we owe the pleasure of your company, gentlemen?"

Josiah started the conversation by saying, "We have some things to discuss with you and because of the nature of them Dr. Stillman came along."

Fear gripped Shirleen, rendering her speechless. Finally, finding her voice, Shirleen asked, "What's going on? Have they found us? Do we need to flee again?"

Throwing up his hands, Josiah cried, "We'll explain it all to you in just a minute. First of all, we don't think they've found you. Don't worry."

Sighing from sheer relief, Shirleen relaxed a little. Taking a deep breath, she waited for Josiah to continue.

"As you know, I went to Syracuse to take care of Gordon's estate. Well, I had to wait until the right time so that Dr. Stillman could come out with us. You see, when Gordon's estate was taken care of, there was a huge amount of money I hadn't told you about."

"Why not?" asked Juliana, in surprise.

"Because it was massive! Coupled with the fact that you were ill, Shirleen, we thought it best to have the doctor with us when we told you about it."

"Oh," Shirleen said. "Since I'm much better, I think I can handle the news now."

First of all there were several items that didn't go with the sale of the estate. There was a lot of garden equipment, lawn furniture and fountains. Inside there were many gorgeous paintings, as well as knick-knacks, including many other miscellaneous items. Those, we have packed up and they're in the storage units here in town. A few days after I got home, the boxes filled with the items from your mansion in upstate New York arrived. Purchasing two more units, I managed to get everything inside. When you feel like it, you can go down to the storage units and go through everything."

"How much did the five units cost?"

"Forty dollars a piece, times four months, which brings the total to eight hundred dollars."

"Before you leave, I'll reimburse you and get the address so that I can take care of the bill myself."

"I have it, as well as the other items that I need to speak to you about."

"Very, well." Shirleen grew quiet to let him speak.

"I sold Gordon's Bentley and Rolls Royce for forty thousand a piece, which made the total eighty thousand dollars."

"I didn't think it would go for that much," Shirleen said in surprise. That's good."

"The mansion that you and Gordon had in upstate New York, brought in four million dollars. With the lawn equipment, lawn furniture, and garden items, there was another forty thousand dollars from that. That gives you another four million and forty thousand dollars." Shirleen looked at her daughter and granddaughter then turned back to hear Josiah say, "Bruce bought the mansion in Syracuse for four million dollars." Looking first at Dr. Stillman then over to Tim, he continued, "Gordon amassed a huge amount of money."

Seeing his look of concern, Shirleen leaned forward to ask, "How large was the sum of money that was still in his account?"

Taking a deep breath, Josiah replied, "Four billion dollars."

"Oh," cried Shirleen, who promptly fainted.

Dr. Stillman jumped to his feet to start working on Shirleen. Juliana, who had suddenly grown pale, also fainted. Meagan, sitting where she was, started crying in concern for her Grandmother and Mother. Josiah went to put his arms around her to comfort her as the doctor and Tim worked over the two women.

Trudy, hearing the commotion in the living room, rushed from the kitchen to see what was happening. Seeing both women lying there unconscious, she began to wring her hands, as tears ran unheeded down her cheeks. Finally, Juliana began to come around. Opening her eyes she saw Tim bending over her. "What happened," she asked.

"You fainted," grinned Tim.

"Oh," She murmured. "Hearing how much Gordon had was an awful shock"

"I know," said Tim.

Just then Shirleen came around. Opening her eyes, she looked around to get focused again. "What just happened?"

"You fainted," Stillman said briskly.

Rising to sit up straighter, Shirleen blushed in shame. "I guess I wasn't as tough as I thought I was," she replied.

Ginning sheepishly, Josiah confessed, "When I heard Gordon's lawyer, Gregory Jones tell me how much Gordon had amassed, I fainted too."

"I don't want it," stated Shirleen, emphatically.

"Wait a minute, Shirleen," stated Josiah, you aren't thinking clearly."

"Josiah, that is blood money!"

"That may be so, but you can use this money to do good to others. When Meagan gets through Veterinary school, set her up with a new office and clinic. When this mess that you are in is all over, you can start an orphanage, start up a culinary school ... oh the list is endless."

"I hadn't thought of that," admitted Shirleen.

"Take some time to think about it, before you toss this money aside."

Sighing resignedly, Shirleen replied, "All right, I will."

"Good," smiled Josiah. It was plain for all to see that he was greatly relieved. "I thought that when this mess is over, you could go through the items in the storage units and have a huge sale to get rid of what you don't want."

"That's a good idea," Shirleen said thoughtfully.

"Anyway, the amount that you have from the sale of both mansions, the two cars, and the money that Gordon garnered, is four billion, eight million, one hundred and twenty thousand dollars."

"Whew! Whistled Shirleen, that's a humongous amount of money to have."

"Yes, it is," replied Josiah, However, instead of thinking about how much it is, think about what you can do with it."

"I will," sighed Shirleen.

In an attempt to change the subject, she asked, "What ever happened to Mr. Harris? We haven't heard anything since before Christmas."

Grinning, Tim took over the conversation. He lived! It was nip and tuck for a while, but he made it. He is back in Spokane again, where he is still working with Melvin Dixon."

"Oh, that's the best news ever," Shirleen said. "I've thought of him often and have meant to ask you when you come out, but I forget to ask."

"I'm sorry that I didn't tell you. I guess I thought that I had."

"Well," smiled Shirleen thoughtfully, "you were shot yourself by that rascal, Vincent Crowley, so it just slipped your mind.

Trudy came out of the kitchen to announce, "Lunch is ready when you are."

"You'll stay for lunch," offered Shirleen.

"I don't know," muttered Josiah thoughtfully.

"Well, you had better," declared Trudy. "I have made enough for all of you."

Chuckling, Josiah replied, "Well, since you put it like that, we'll stay for lunch."

As Meagan went to get Jeff, Tim addressed Dr. Stillman, "You haven't lived until you've eaten Trudy's meals."

"That's for sure," agreed Josiah.

"We'll see," declared Stillman. "To me, food is just that … food!"

"Just wait and see if we aren't right," predicted Tim.

When Meagan and Jeff joined them at the table in the dining room, Stillman was surprised to see all that was on the table. After Grace, they fell to with hearty appetites. When the meal was over, Stillman rose, complaining of his full stomach. "I've got to go back to the office, but heaven help me, what I really want to do is find a shady place and take a long nap."

"That sounds like a good idea," agreed Jeff.

Turning to Trudy, he grinned, as he said, "That meal was truly delicious, ma'am. It's been a long time since I've had a good home cooked meal."

"Please, call me Trudy and thank you for the compliment."

"Trudy it is. Thank you for a wonderful meal." Trudy only nodded.

"Well," said Stillman, turning back to Tim, "I've got to go back to the office to take care of all of my patients so do you think we could leave now?"

"Sure thing," quipped Tim.

"I forgot to ask the name of the bank that you want me to deposit the money into, Shirleen, so I'll be back after work to take care of everything."

"That will be good. See you then." A short time later they left.

An hour after the evening meal was over, Josiah returned to take care of business. Letting him in, Meagan offered him a seat at the kitchen table. "I have to get home early, as I'm going to go on a manhunt. A man escaped from prison and he is somewhere out there in the woods. I don't know how long I'll be gone, but a few days at least."

"Is Tim going with you?" asked Meagan.

"Not this time. I need him here to hold down the fort, so to speak. Holmquist and Black are going with me. They're good men, as well as great trackers.

"That's good. At least you won't be alone out there. We wouldn't want anything to happen to you, Uncle Josiah."

"Thank you Pumpkin." Looking first at Shirleen and then over to Juliana, Josiah said, "I have a huge dilemma that I need to ask your help with."

"What would that be?" asked Shirleen.

"I can't take Princess with me, as she would alert the fugitive that we were there. I was wondering, if Meagan could dog sit for me?"

"I'd be happy to do that for you, Uncle Josiah." Looking at her mother and grand-mother, Meagan pleaded, "Please say that I can do this. Uncle Josiah has done so much for us, for me that I want to grab this opportunity to do something for him."

Shirleen looked at Juliana to see how she felt about Meagan doing this task for Josiah. When Juliana grinned and nodded her head yes, Shirleen sighed in relief. "Of course you may."

"Thank you," cried Meagan, hugging her mother and grandmother.

"Thank you," replied Josiah, It was plain for all to see that he was greatly relieved.

"Do you have to go get her?" asked Meagan.

A huge grin spread across Josiah's face, as he replied. "She is asleep in the car. I take her everywhere I go, except to important meetings. I let her have a run before I got here. I was so hopeful that Meagan could do the job that I brought her food, bowls, leash, grooming tools and her pet taxi."

Both women burst out laughing. Gaining control, Juliana replied. "What would you do if we'd said no?"

"Begged Tim to take her," Josiah calmly replied. "However, knowing Meagan's way with her dogs, I knew that she was the one that I wanted to take care of my Princess."

"Thank you for the vote of confidence, Uncle Josiah. That means a lot to me."

Nodding, Josiah turn to Shirleen to asked, "What bank do you want me to deposit the money from Gordon's estate?" Shirleen gave him the name of the bank, which he wrote down on a piece of paper.

Josiah gave her the address and name of the manager of the Storage Units. Taking the paper, Shirleen asked, "How much was the total for those five storage units again?"

Giving her the information, Josiah waited for Shirleen to make him out a check for eight hundred dollars, which paid for the four months that they had been using the units. Writing out the check, Shirleen handed it to him. Josiah gave her all of the receipts that he had gotten from the manager. Rising to go, he smiled down on them all. "Congratulations on the money you received from the estate. I'll take care of the transaction as soon as I return with the prisoner."

"Whenever you get time, would be just great by me," stated Shirleen. "I'm in no hurry."

"Goodnight, ladies. I'll see you when I can."

Hugging him, Meagan told him, "Stay safe, Uncle Josiah."

"I will." Walking over to the door, he disappeared in the night.

◄ • ►

Several days later, Shirleen had worked hard to help Trudy with the housework so she could visit her sister, who was having a baby. She was excited to learn they'd named the baby Hazel Irene.

Shirleen went to her room to rest for a while. Since she'd been taking the medication Dr. Stillman gave her, she'd been improving nicely. Some days she was even able to go without a nap. But today, she'd taken on more than she should have.

An hour later, Juliana woke her to tell her it was her turn to teach Meagan. It was time for finals. While Meagan was taking her English final, Shirleen worked on an embroidery project. An hour later, Meagan was finished and went to take the dogs out for their run. When she came back in, it was time for the next test and Shirleen had the first test corrected and the results entered into her notebook.

The final test was reading comprehension. An hour later, the tests were finally over and Meagan, who was feeling brain dead, went out to sit in the flower garden to recuperate. She didn't come in until it was time for supper.

Seeing how tired she was, Trudy asked, "Are you all right, Meagan?"

"I've had finals all day and I'm tired. I have a humongous science test in the morning, then hopefully, I'll be finished with school."

"You'll be done just in time to do the gardening, sewing, quilting, and canning classes."

"I know," sighed Meagan. "Right now though, I could sleep for a week."

"Why don't you plan to go to bed early tonight?"

"That sounds like a plan."

"You'll be happy to know you passed all your tests today with flying colors," Shirleen said as she came in the room.

"What was the score for all of my classes?"

"All As."

"That's great, Meagan!" cried Trudy.

"I should say it is," grinned Juliana as she entered the room. "I have the rest of your final scores, except for science: algebra A+, calculus A, geometry B+ and trigonometry B."

"I'm totally impressed!" Trudy said. "I would've flunked all of those different math courses."

"They were truly hard, so to get these scores is amazing," declared Meagan, humbly.

Three hours after they'd all gone to bed, Shirleen woke with a start. Something didn't feel right, but she couldn't put a finger on what it was. Suddenly the dogs started barking, so she put on her robe and slippers and grabbed the rife. She also put some shells into her robe pocket. When she got to the living room, Juliana and Meagan were already there and shaking visibly.

Jeff came bounding down the stairs with a pistol gripped tightly in his hand, while Trudy remained at the head of the stairs with a death grip on the railing.

Suddenly, they heard something rolling across the yard. It came to an abrupt halt when it connected with something. Every hair on Shirleen's body seemed to rise. Knowing that she had to remain calm, she loaded the rifle, then moved toward the door.

"You don't want to go out there, Shirleen," whispered Jeff. "Let's wait and see what else happens."

Just then there was a deafening sound just outside the door. Shirleen froze. Turning, she whispered, "Jeff, when I say go, open the door and step back out of the way."

"Are you sure about this?" It was plain for all to see that she wasn't. When she nodded, he moved over to the door and waited.

Before she could speak, something bumped against the door so hard it threatened to break the door down. Raising the rifle, Shirleen looked down the barrel, and waited as Jeff unlocked the door. "Now!" yelled Shirleen.

Jerking the door open, he quickly got out of the way. There on the front porch, bloody and enraged, stood a huge male grizzly. Shirleen nearly panicked, but managed to remain calm. Getting the bear clearly in her sights, she gently squeezed the trigger. The sound the rifle made was deafening. The bear jumped back, and fell off the porch.

Seeing he wasn't dead, Shirleen moved another shell into the chamber and aimed again. Suddenly the bear rose to his full height and pawed the air. His claws were long and curled. Roaring in rage, he started forward again. Aiming at his mouth, Shirleen squeezed the trigger.

Again, the bear was knocked to the ground. This time, it lay still. When it hadn't moved for five minutes, Shirleen cautiously approached it. She jabbed it with the rifle, but the bear was dead. Jeff pulled Shirleen inside and closed the door.

When she leaned the rifle against the couch, Jeff sighed in relief. Then he grabbed her and kissed her with such passion that it left her weak in the knees. Before she realized what she was doing, Shirleen reciprocated. Realizing what he'd done, Jeff released her.

They looked into each other's eyes, and saw only love and admiration shining back. "Well," declared Jeff, "now you know what I couldn't tell you. I love you. I won't stay any longer, as I don't want to embarrass you."

"Embarrass me?" For a moment Shirleen could only stare at him. Moving closer to him, she asked, "Didn't you notice that I returned your kiss?"

"I did, but didn't want to assume too much."

"Well, Jeff Borton, I love you too!" She slid her arms around his neck and gazed lovingly into his eyes.

Jeff claimed her lips hungrily. The kiss was so filled with promises, that everyone and everything was forgotten, but their love for each other. Lifting his head, he gazed down into Shirleen's loved filled eyes. "I thought I could never love anyone else like I loved my wife, but somehow you found your way into my heart."

Giggling contentedly, Shirleen rested her head against his chest, and said, "Good!"

Jeff suddenly realized they were being watched. When he saw the smiles Juliana and Meagan were wearing, he blushed. "Oh," he stammered, "I forgot that we weren't alone."

Turning to look at her family, Shirleen giggled again. "Well, Jeff, I think we've been caught with our hands in the cookie jar."

"I have to agree," grinned Jeff.

"Well," declared Juliana, "It's about time you both admitted how you feel. The rest of us have known for a long time.

"You have?" asked Shirleen.

"It was *so* obvious," laughed Trudy, coming down the stairs. "Like Juliana said, I've been trying to come up with a way to help you both figure it out but I guess I don't have to now."

Meagan walked over to take both of their hands. "This is the greatest! I'm so happy you've both found happiness." She stood on tiptoe to kiss first Jeff's cheek and then Shirleen's. "Don't wait too long before you take her to the alter, Grandpa Jeff."

"You know, Shirleen," grinned Jeff, "I think this granddaughter of yours has a point. I've waited all these months to let you know how I feel, and I don't really want to wait much longer to start our lives together."

Turning to Juliana, she asked, "What do you think, Juliana?"

"Why wait for happiness when it is standing right in front of you?"

Looking over at Meagan, who was grinning from ear to ear, she asked, "Are you really happy about me marrying Jeff?"

"I wouldn't have suggested that you grab this happiness if I didn't mean it. Grandma, you've had to suffer all those years with a man you didn't love, so latch onto this happiness with both hands!"

Turning back to Jeff, she kissed him lightly on the lips and said, "If you really want me then I'll marry you right away."

"Oh, saints be praised!" shouted Jeff. Scooping her up into his arms, he kissed her soundly. Then, he turned to everyone else and said, "Thank you for giving us your blessings. I'll love this wonderful lady until the day that I die." After kissing her again, they went to sit beside each other on the couch.

Suddenly, Meagan said, "I can't believe you shot a real live bear, Grandma! That thing was huge!"

"I have a tape measure upstairs," declared Jeff. "Let's go find out just how big he was."

By the time that he got back downstairs, the women were outside examining the bear. When the bear had been measured, Jeff whistled. "This thing must weight fifteen hundred pounds. Look at those paws!" Lifting one of the paws to examine it, he shivered. "Look at the size of those claws!"

"That thing could have done a lot of damage," exclaimed Juliana. "Momma, you saved the day with your rifle."

"For the first time, I'm glad I have it."

"Well, one thing is for sure," said Jeff, "We can't leave it here."

"What can we do with it?" asked Shirleen.

"I saw some tow rope in the shop. I'll go get it, then use my truck to drag it away from the house."

"Oh, that's a good idea," Juliana said.

Jeff went out to the workshop to get the towrope and dragged the carcass a good distance from the house. When he was done he returned to the house and helped Meagan take the pups for a run, while Trudy made them all a cup of hot chocolate.

When they were all settled comfortably in the living room sipping their hot chocolate, Meagan said, "We neglected to include Tim and Uncle Josiah in the plans."

"Meagan's right, honey," Shirleen said. "They've played an integral part in both our lives for months now."

"You're right. We definitely can't leave them out of our plans; we'll hurt their feelings."

"When Josiah gets back, we'll talk to him about what we want to do, and you can call Tim in the morning," suggested Meagan. "Ask him to come out here." When the others hesitated, Meagan continued, "Well, we have to tell him about the bear anyway. When you've done that, you could casually mention that the two of you are getting married."

"Sounds like a plan, Meagan," grinned Jeff."

The first thing the next morning, Juliana called Tim at his office and asked him to stop by as soon as possible. Juliana chuckled as she turned to face the others. "He hung up the phone without saying good-bye. He's on his way."

Twenty minutes later, they heard Tim drive into the driveway. Meagan met him at the door, looking serious. "Hello, Meagan. Is everyone all right?"

"Yes, but you should come inside for a minute." Moving aside to let Tim enter, Meagan hid the smile that played around her lips. "Everyone, Tim's here."

Everyone came in and said hello. Tim noticed that Shirleen looked happier than he'd ever seen her.

"It was so good of you to come on such short notice," Shirleen said, "but it's really important."

"What is going on, Shirleen?"

"Follow us outside. The evidence speaks for itself."

Intrigued, he followed them outside. When Tim saw the massive body of the bear, he asked, "What happened here?"

Jeff, taking Shirleen's hand explained, "Late last night, we heard something going on outside. Shirleen came out of the bedroom with her trusty rifle, thinking Bruce had found them. Instead, it was Mr. Bear trying to knock down the door." He went on to explain how Shirleen had calmly shot the bear.

Looking at Shirleen blankly, Tim asked, "You shot the bear?"

"Yes, I did, twice."

"You say that you only shot him twice, but there are four other bullets in him. Was the bear wounded before you shot it?"

"I noticed he was bleeding before I shot him," confirmed Shirleen.

"Shirleen, when a bear is badly wounded they go on the rampage. It's a wonder he didn't attack you."

"I think the reason he didn't was the lights temporarily blinded him," explained Jeff.

"That's probably right," replied Tim. Looking at Shirleen in awe, he said, "You've bagged a real prize, Shirleen."

"The only thing I was grateful for at the time, was that I had that rifle. Thank you for making me get it and learn to use it."

Meagan took over the conversation, after winking at Jeff and Shirleen. "Well, Tim, Jeff here was so relieved that Grandma was all right, he grabbed her and planted a big kiss right on her lips."

"Good for you, Jeff," praised Tim. "I'm glad you finally got up enough courage to make your feelings known. Did Shirleen deck you?"

"No," said Jeff. "She let me know she's been feeling the same way for a while. I probably wouldn't have ever gotten the courage to do anything else if not for Meagan. She told her grandmother to latch onto happiness with both hands and run with it. We wanted you to know that we're getting married as soon as possible."

Grabbing Shirleen, Tim spun her around, then set her onto the ground and exclaimed enthusiastically, "Congratulations! I couldn't be happier if I tried. I'm tickled pink."

Suddenly, he started to laugh. "Who would ever believe that it would take a big old bear to get the two of you together!" Shaking Jeff's hand, he continued, "Well, I for one, am glad that the bear showed the two of you just what needed to happen."

Turning to Meagan, he asked, "How do you feel about this?"

"I love it!" cried Meagan, proudly. "If he'll let me, I'm gonna call him Grandpa Jeff."

"I'd be honored, Meagan Webb."

"Then Grandpa Jeff it is."

Juliana, smiling happily, said, "Jeff, I'd be the proudest woman alive if you'd allow me to call you Dad."

Tears glistened in Jeff's eyes, and he was speechless. Finally, finding his voice, he replied, "It is I who would be proud to call you daughter."

"Thank you," replied Juliana through her tears.

"Will you help us find a preacher to perform the ceremony?" asked Jeff.

"Sure, I know just the man."

"When we've got the marriage license we'll let you know so you can help us set everything up."

"Sounds good," declared Tim. Looking at his watch, he told them, "I've got to get back to the office; got paperwork to catch up on. If I don't get it all done before Josiah gets home, I may get sacked."

"Never happen," laughed Meagan. "Uncle Josiah's an old softy!"

"Well," chuckled Tim. "I don't think it's a good idea to press my luck. See you all later."

Chapter 35

Bruce Murdock woke up feeling testy. Itching for a fight, he encountered Crowley, who was sitting on the couch with a cup of coffee and the morning paper. "Good morning, boss," Crowley said. Murdock just grunted, and Crowley went back to reading the paper.

Still irritable, Murdock clenched and unclenched his hands and growled, "Where's White?"

"Shower," Crowley calmly replied.

"When?"

Looking his watch, he said, "Fifteen minutes ago."

"Send him to my office when he gets down here."

Without another word, Bruce went to his office and slammed the door. He sat down to write and smiled fiendishly, *It's time to take Ruth and her mother out of the picture permanently like I should've done three months ago. White will do my dirty work.*

There was a knock at the door. "Come in," Bruce bellowed.

"You wanted to see me?" White asked.

"Get in here and shut the door. I've got a special job for you."

"Okay," replied White, taking a chair across from Bruce.

"You remember when Crowley went to Cardston?" White nodded. "Well, he found Josiah Graham, Ruth, Leslie *and* Sarah Spielberg. They're all living there, just outside town."

"That's good news, boss," interrupted White.

"My thoughts exactly. I want you to catch the next plane to Spokane, then drive into Cardston. When you get there, get a motel room and wait 'til I contact you with further details. Crowley will give you directions to their place. Get packed and get out of here right away."

"Yes, sir."

"Make sure that you don't botch this job up," Murdock said as he handed him some cash. "You do and it'll cost you your life!"

"I'm your man. It'll get done."

"I want you to bring Leslie back here and kill those other two hags. When I'm through with her, she'll know she'd better do what I tell her. Now, get going!"

Without a word, White went to pack. When he was ready, he carried his suitcase to the living room just as Bruce came out of his office. "You ready to go?" asked Bruce.

"I'm gonna grab some food and get going."

A few minutes later, White left and Crowley, wondered what was up, but wisely remained silent. "Well, Vinnie," began Bruce, "I've decided to increase the druggies pay from ten to fifteen percent … effective immediately. They don't pay, they don't play if you get my drift."

Crowley's heart sank. Bruce Murdock was signing their death warrants. "I'm letting them know today."

"What do you want me to do, boss?"

"Stay close. They may come after me."

There's no doubt about it — they definitely will, thought Crowley. Aloud he replied, "Yes, sir."

Since moving into Spielberg's mansion, Bruce had become even more demanding. The first thing he did when he moved in was hire more servants. The move and staff additions earned him interest from the authorities, who were building a case against him, and police Captain Charles Abram had been combing through every piece of paper that was taken from the Spielberg mansion. It was only a matter of time before he was arrested. Had he known this, he might've proceeded more cautiously.

Murdock was operating in ignorant bliss, working as an attorney and struggling to get more men on his side of the faction. He'd been losing a lot of his cases, which was due to the new judge who took Judge Harris's place when he resigned. The losses infuriated Bruce; he was used to winning no matter what his client had done. The new judge, Arthur Petersen, watched for every opportunity to catch him in his schemes, and he'd already decided to take care of that problem as soon as White got back from Cardston.

When White was gone and he'd finished with breakfast, Murdock headed to his office. He was in such a foul mood that even his secretary avoided him. His day went from bad to worse when Judge Petersen overruled his objection to the prosecution's motion. At the end of the day, the prosecutor had sewn up the case against Bruce's client so well, that Bruce had to use every trick he knew to get his client off.

When it was time for Bruce to present his closing arguments, he gave it his best shot. When he'd finished and taken his seat, Bruce knew the jurors weren't convinced by the looks on their faces. When the jury left to deliberate, Bruce went back to his office to await the verdict. Only thirty minutes later his phone rang and he was told the verdict was in.

Bruce headed back to the courthouse, knowing his client was in deep trouble, but not really caring what happened to the man."

When the judge asked for the verdict, the jury foreman said, "We find the defendant guilty of murder in the first degree."

Hearing this, the judge decided to pass sentence immediately. "You are hereby sentenced to fifty-nine years in the state penitentiary, without possibility of parole, effective immediately."

Bruce's client hissed, "You'll pay for this, if it's the last thing I ever do!"

"I've heard that before," Bruce calmly replied. "You'll find it hard to get to me from behind bars."

"I know men in high places, so you'd better watch yourself."

Instead of going back to his office, Bruce went to a local bar and got rip-roaring drunk. Later, he was lonely, so he grabbed a taxi and went to see Kathy Neilson, his favorite escort.

Kathy had been loyal to him from the start, so he used her as often as he could. Looking up, she smiled and said, "Hello, Bruce. What brings you here at this time of day?"

"I just got out of court and I need a place to cool off."

"It didn't go too well, I take it?"

"No." Walking over to see what she was working on, he asked, "How's business?"

"It is booming."

"At least that's one good piece of news."

Suddenly, the door burst open and several police officers came in. The one in front, Frank Kessler, walked past Bruce and said, "Kathy Neilson?"

"Yes?"

"You're under arrest for the murder of Torrance Hanks." Turning her away from him, he placed her hands behind her back so that he could handcuff her. As he did this, he mirandized her. When he was done he asked, "Do you understand these rights as they have been given to you?"

"Yes," she snapped. As they started to lead her away, she yelled. "Will you represent me, Mr. Murdock?"

"I'll follow you to booking."

He waited until they'd taken her away, then called Crowley. "Get over to the escort service building on the double!"

"Yes, sir."

While Bruce waited for Crowley, he began to pace the room. A few minutes later, Crowley came to find him. Seeing the state his boss was in, Crowley tried to calm things down. "Howdy, boss. What's up?"

"The police just arrested Kathy Neilson for murder."

"Oh, that's bad."

Bruce, finally lost control and yelled, "Bad isn't the half of it! If she cracks under the pressure, we'll all be in trouble. You've got to find a way to snuff her before she can talk."

"We've got a guy at the precinct. He can slip something into her coffee."

"Than don't just stand there jawing, do it!"

"Right away, boss." Crowley made the call and told the man to let them know when it was done. He ended the call and waited to see what Murdock was going to do.

An hour later, Crowley's phone rang. He answered it, listened and ended the call. "It's done. Kathy Neilson's dead. They ruled it a heart attack."

"That's one less thing for me to worry about," sighed Bruce.

I'll just bet it is, thought Crowley. *If there was anybody else even close to taking over, I'd go work with them. I'll just bide my time and off you myself when I get the chance.*

As they came out of the escort service, Crowley saw something flash to the side of him. His immediate thought was *Gun!,* and he knocked Bruce to the ground just as bullets started flying all around them. Pulling his gun, he started returning fire. He heard someone grunt just as the shooting stopped.

Quickly pulling Bruce to his feet, he dragged him to his car and stuffed him in the passenger side before coming around to the driver's side. As soon as he was inside, he started the car and sped away. When they had gotten safely into the traffic, Crowley asked, "Are you all right?"

"Yeah. How'd you know?"

"I saw a flash and just reacted."

"Quick thinking. Thanks."

A few days later, Bruce started getting reactions to the percentage increase. They'd agreed and Bruce was elated. What he didn't know was that these same drug lords were planning a little party for him and his men.

Crowley could read between the lines and knew Bruce had just tightened his own noose.

Trudy North, knocked on the Brooks residence's door. "Good morning, Trudy," Theodore said when he answered. "What brings you out on this beautiful day?"

"I came to see how I could help with Henry."

"Wonderful! I'm about to start his therapy; you can help me. I think he has a great surprise for you, too."

"Really?" asked Trudy.

"Yup! Let's go see what he can do," Theodore said and led the way to Henry's room. He knocked and peaked in to see if Henry was decent. Henry, smiled when Theodore asked, "Are you ready to have company and work on you exercises?"

"I am," replied Henry, motioning Theodore forward.

"Trudy's here to help us with your speech exercises."

Soon they were working with Henry. When they were finished, Trudy stayed to help him with his speech therapy.

Henry's memory had come back to him gradually, until it was complete. He recognized Ruth and Leslie right away, and when Trudy started to help him with his speech he remembered she'd been Bruce's cook and housekeeper. He'd been angry when his memory first returned and refused to have anything to do with any of them. This bothered Melinda, who'd never seen Henry act this way before.

One day, while the children were asleep and Theodore was busy helping the men with a project, she'd gone in to talked to Henry about it and found out he didn't know why Shirleen, Meagan and Juliana were in Canada. He also didn't know that she'd figured out he'd embezzled money from the company he worked for to help his late wife. In the end she finally got him to admit that Bruce Murdock had been forcing him to work for him since he got Henry acquitted of the embezzling charges.

She convinced him that the best way to get his vengeance, make everything right with the women, and stay out of prison was to turn state's evidence against Bruce Murdock. Henry agreed and his efforts to regain what he'd lost to the strokes were increased.

That's when he finally allowed Trudy to help him with his speech therapy. During the course of their work together their friendship blossomed. He loved her spontaneity and her generosity. Before he realized it, Henry had fallen in love with her.

At first he felt that he was cheating on Matilda, but then he knew she'd want him to be happy. Before he could express his love for Trudy, though, he had to make a clean breast of everything.

When Trudy arrived that morning, he knew it was time to make a new start. They'd been visiting for quite a while when Henry said, "Trudy, I know your real name's Hazel Lockwood."

She froze and looked him in the eye. Fear was written all over her face and she seemed ready to bold, so he took her hand and said, "It's all right, Hazel. Your secret's safe with me. I guess in a way, I'm running away from my past, too."

"How do you know my real name?"

"I met you right after I was acquitted of embezzlement, even though I was guilty. My wife, Matilda was very ill, and I took the money to pay her humongous medical expenses. I'm not proud of what I've done, but I just couldn't lose my Tilly either."

"I might've done the same if I was in your shoes," replied Trudy.

"Somehow, I doubt that."

"Listen, Henry, I have nothing but the deepest respect for you. I'm the last person to ever judge you. I told Bruce Murdock a blatant lie to get away from him."

"Why'd you do that?"

Trudy told him about finding the folder with Bruce's murder list. "Henry, your name was on it."

Blinking several times, Henry asked, "It was?"

"Yes."

"Oh, then it looks like I was lucky to get away from him too."

"Yes, it does."

Absently stroking her fingers, Henry asked, "Then you don't hate me?"

"No, we'll always be friends."

Looking at her intently, Henry asked, "What if I said I wanted you to be more than my friend?"

"What're you asking me, Henry Borden?" She could only stare at him in confusion.

"When I get out of prison, would you marry me?"

Tears glistened in Trudy's eyes and for a moment she was speechless. Taking a deep breath to calm her jangled nerves, she nodded. "Yes, I'll wait for you, no matter how long it takes."

"Wonderful!" Pulling her close, he kissed her passionately. Trudy was lost in the bliss of it.

When the kiss ended, Trudy confessed. "I've never been kissed before, so forgive me if I did it wrong."

Chuckling happily, Henry replied. "You did fine. Besides, when we're married we'll have plenty of time to practice."

"I like that thought," Trudy said, grinning.

"I guess the next step is finding out who to go to report my crime. The sooner I serve my time the sooner we can be married.

"There's Josiah Graham, he's a Mountie we know. If you want, I can contact him for you."

"Go ahead."

Trudy called Josiah and asked him to come the Brooks' home. When that was done she said, "Let me go tell Melinda to show Josiah in when he gets here, then we can talk."

"Ask Theodore and Melinda to come in so that we can give them our good news."

"I'll be right back."

"Hurry," declared Henry, "because there's lots that I have to say to you."

A few minutes later, they were all gathered in Henry's room. Taking Trudy's hand, Henry looked from Melinda to Theodore and asked, "What would the two of you think if I told you I'd asked this wonderful lady to marry me?"

Melinda was elated. "You proposed marriage, Henry Borden?" Not giving him a chance to reply, she hastened to add, "I'd say it's about time you asked her to marry you. I would also say that you should both go for it."

"I told her everything and she doesn't hate me. I can't believe she agreed to marry me."

Pumping Henry's hand up and down, Theodore declared, "That's wonderful!"

Reaching for Melinda's hand, Henry said, "Melinda, I want you to know there will always be a special place in my heart for your sister, Tilly, but now there's a new place that is just for Hazel — I mean Trudy."

"I know," replied Melinda.

"I'll always think of the two of you as my brother and sister. That will never change."

"That's how we feel too," Melinda said.

There was a knock on the door, and Theodore went to answer it, coming back with Josiah Graham.

"Hello, Trudy," greeted Josiah.

"Hello, Josiah. Henry needs to talk to you for a while."

"What can I do for you, Henry?"

"We'll leave so the two of you have some privacy," said Melinda.

"No!" cried Henry in panic. "I need your support so I have the courage to do this."

"Okay," replied Theodore.

Henry took a deep breath to clear his mind, then said, "What I'm about to tell you isn't something I'm proud of. But I had my reasons for doing what I did. I won't give any excuses, but please don't interrupt me until I've finished, or I might not be able to."

"Okay," replied Josiah.

"About two years ago my wife, Matilda, Melinda's sister, got liver cancer, and it nearly took her life. The doctors operated and removed two thirds of her liver, while she was in the hospital she got a staff infection that took a long time to treat and cure.

"I had a good job, but there was no way I could cover the medical bills. After a while, we found ourselves so deep in debt we were sinking. The bank was about to foreclose on the house and the car and I couldn't even keep us fed. I didn't want to take our son, Jethro, out of college so that was the only thing I kept current."

"At first, I only took a little money from the company payroll. Then as the bills poured in, I had to take more just to put food on the table and keep the bill collectors at bay. I did this for several months with no one the wiser, then the company got audited and they discovered the missing money.

"My boss didn't want to have me arrested but the higher-ups came down on me hard, and the court appointed Bruce Murdock to represent me. I didn't like him, but I was forced to keep him as my lawyer because I couldn't pay anyone else.

"I'd managed to hang in there long enough for Jethro to graduate from college, but we lost our house, car, and everything else we'd worked for. If it hadn't been for my boss, Matilda and Jethro would've been out on the street. He made sure that they had a house and food to eat, while I went to trial."

"Murdock managed to get me off on some technicalities and then he told me he owned me. I was forced to do some deals for him, and I hated it. My boss, Mr. Sanders, rehired me and trained me to be a manager. When I asked him why, he told me he knew I did it for my wife and was basically an honest person. Between us, and good hard work, we built up the company until Sanders was able to buy the company from the others. They told him, right in front of me, that he was stupid if he thought I would amount to much.

"Because of his belief in me, I worked hard to prove them wrong. Six months later, we reached over two billion dollars in profits. Mr. Sanders congratulated me and promised to take me on as his partner. That night, he had a massive heart attack and died. I was devastated. I had no partnership and nowhere to work. I didn't want to work for Murdock, but I didn't think anyone else would hire me.

"Three days later, the Sanders' will was to be read and his lawyer contacted me and said I needed to be there. I was surprised. I didn't figure that I'd be included."

Sighing, Henry fell silent for a moment. Taking a deep breath, he continued, "Well, you can imagine my surprise when he read the part about giving me the business. Sanders' wife and son were furious and threatened to contest the will. However, when the lawyer continued to read, we learned that if his family tried to contest the will they'd forfeit everything."

"I can see how that would've been a great shock," stated Josiah.

"That wasn't the half of it. Mr. Sanders willed the house in New Hampshire to his wife and left his son only two thousand dollars. He told him to go get a job and learn to be a man. The lawyer finished up by saying the house in Syracuse and its contents had been left to Matilda and me. I took Matilda to live in that house, and that's where she died. By the end of that year, I had amassed another two billion dollars worth in the company and it had been done legally."

"You do know you'll go to jail, don't you?" asked Josiah.

"Yes."

"Since you aren't well enough to go to jail, I'm putting you under house arrest. Let me talk to Judge Smith and I'll let you know what'll happen next."

"I want to pay my debt to society so I can marry Hazel — I mean, Trudy."

After Josiah left, Henry was so exhausted he took a nap while Trudy left the room to call Shirleen..

"Shirleen, Henry has confessed everything."

"He knows who we are?" Shirleen asked, plainly worried.

"Yes, he knows." Taking a deep breath Trudy continued, "Shirleen, Henry was charged with embezzling and the court appointed Bruce as his lawyer. He got him off, and blackmailed him into doing his dirty work."

"That Bruce Murdock is an evil man."

"That he is. Shirleen, Matilda had liver cancer, and he took the money so he could cover her medical bills and keep a roof over their heads."

"So he's not evil?"

"No, he was desperate to take care of his family, and Bruce took advantage of that."

"Bruce Murdock has ruined so many lives."

"He sure has. We're all waiting for Josiah to get back to us about what will happen to Henry now." She omitted telling her about Henry's proposal. She wanted to tell them when Henry could be there too. "I'll be home as soon as I find out."

"Don't worry about things here; we're fine. Tell Henry we send out best and wish him luck. Tell him we'll talk to him later."

"Thanks, Shirleen."

Three hours later, Judge Smith with Josiah came back to talk to Henry.

Trudy was nervous as she waited to see what they'd say. Soon Theodore wheeled Henry into the living room and everyone prepared to leave so they'd have some privacy.

"Don't go, please," Henry said. "I want you all to be here. I'm ready to hear what my future holds."

Turning to Judge Smith, Josiah said, "Henry, this is Judge Candace Smith."

"Are you going to pass sentence on me?" Henry asked.

"First, I want to hear your side of the story, then we'll decide the best course of action." Judge Smith listened intently as Henry told his story. When he was finished, the judge asked, "When you said that you had to do some jobs for Bruce Murdock, what kind of jobs were they?"

"I only did two jobs for him. One was stealing some files from a lawyer's filing cabinet and the other was detaining someone so he could snoop through some files."

"I see, please go on."

"The day that Tilly died, he called to tell me he had another job for me. I told him I didn't care what he wanted me to do because I'd just lost my Tilly."

"Did he threaten you?"

"No, but he stuck his nose in where it wasn't wanted."

"What do you mean?" asked Judge Smith.

"He came to the funeral and made a complete fool of himself."

Melinda spoke up to say, "To be exact, Bruce Murdock arrived in a limo and acted like a pompous you know what!"

Smiling, Judge Smith asked, "Would you be willing to go under cover to expose this man, Mr. Borden?"

"Yes, ma'am. I sure would!" declared Henry. "In fact it would give me great pleasure to bring him down so no one else will be hurt."

"That's good." Smith grew silent a moment then looked at Henry with compassion. "Mr. Borden, it's my, opinion that you've suffered because of what you've done. The fact that even though you were acquitted of the embezzlement charges, you came clean on your own recognizance — that says a lot about your integrity. It is my opinion that your punishment has been dealt to you by a higher power. Therefore, you're exonerated from any further punishment. I'll contact the New York police and let them know you're willing to help them. They'll send someone to interview you and when you testify, we'll transport you to New York.."

"Thank you, Judge Smith. I'm so grateful that I can finally put my past to rest!"

"Thank you for helping to put an evil man away for a very long time."

"There's something else that you should know, Judge Smith. It was Bruce Murdock and his men who murdered all of those people in that restaurant in New York. The dead men were part of Gordon Spielberg's organization."

"How many were killed?"

"One hundred."

Judge Smith looked ill when she heard that number. "Then you're definitely doing a good thing by helping the authorities catch this man."

"Yeah, Bruce Murdock is one very evil man," replied Henry. "If you cross him, you pay for it with your life."

"Well, after that revelation, I'm positive the New York police will be extremely interested in what you have to say."

Standing to go, the judge said, "If that's all for now, I'm have to get going. Tomorrow is my wedding day! Also, I won't be in the office for a couple of weeks because I'll be on my honeymoon." Picking up her purse, she began to rummage through it. "That reminds me, Theodore, I have an invitation for you and Melinda to attend my big day. After all, I got to witness your wedding, so I'd be thrilled if you attend mine."

"We'd be honored," replied Theodore.

"Henry, I'll be in touch with you just as soon as I have spoken to the New York Police."

After Josiah and Judge Smith left, Melinda went into the kitchen to help Annabelle. Suddenly, she fainted. Theodore bent over Melinda and then yelled for the nurse on duty who rushed from the nursery. As the nurse checked her out, Melinda regained consciousness. "Lie still, honey, until we see what's wrong."

"I feel fine. How did I end up on the floor?"

"You fainted," replied Theodore in concern.

"Oh," was all that Melinda could say.

"I want you to make an appointment with Dr. Stillman as soon as you can. You don't just faint for no reason."

"Okay, I'll do it right away."

Helping her to her feet, Theodore asked her to rest for a while. Trudy looked at Henry, concerned. "Maybe I should go home. It looks like you've got your hands full."

"Please stay for a little while longer," Henry said. "I want just a little more time with you." She sat back down and he put his arm around her and kissed her passionately. "I can't believe I've found happiness again."

"I never thought I'd love someone enough marry them. Oh, Henry, I love you so much it scares me."

"When I lost my Tilly, I never wanted to look at another woman. Then you walked into my life and cracked that shell I'd placed around my heart. Wham … just like that I was a goner!" Kissing her again, he continued. "I can hardly wait until we're married so that I can show you just how much I love you."

"It can't happen soon enough for me either," sighed Trudy. Suddenly, Trudy looked up at Henry to ask, "Henry, how do you think Melinda would feel if I asked her to be my matron of honor?"

"I think she'd be ecstatic! Are you going to?"

"Yes, I think it would bond the two of you even closer."

Kissing her soundly, Henry said, "Your thoughtfulness is one of the reasons I love you so much."

A few minutes later, Melinda emerged from the bedroom with Theodore. They sat down across from Trudy and Henry. "Are you feeling better?" asked Henry.

"Yes," grinned Melinda. "I don't know what happened. Perhaps I got up too fast."

"I'm glad you're better, Melinda," said Trudy. "I have to go home soon, but I wanted to ask you something before I leave."

"What's that?" asked Melinda.

"Would you be my matron of honor?"

Elated, Melinda replied, "I'd be honored!."

"Good, then that's one less thing to worry about."

Henry looked over at Theodore and asked, "Would you be my best man, Ted?"

"You bet." Looking at Melinda, who nodded for him to continue, Theodore said, "As you know, we got engaged in the morning and married that evening."

"I remember that," said Henry.

Melinda hastened to add, "We wanted you to be at the wedding, but it was impossible, so Mr. Stokes suggested we have another wedding when you were better and could give me away.

"I don't remember you saying anything about that," responded Henry.

"Well," said Theodore, "we were just talking it over while Melinda was resting and we've decided that after your wedding, we'll get married again."

Theodore nodded for Melinda to continue, "Henry, would you give me away?"

"I'd love to."

"Where will you be married?" asked Trudy.

"Right here," replied Melinda. "The men have been working to beautify the yard and the rose garden and flowerbeds look lovely. I was thinking the preacher could stand under the trellis with the bride and groom facing the preacher." Pausing to see what they thought, she asked, "What do you think?"

"I love it," responded Trudy.

A few days later, Henry called to ask Trudy, "Can all of you come down here for a few minutes?"

"Let me ask everyone," replied Trudy.

Chuckling, Henry replied, "Go ahead, this old man isn't getting any younger. Besides, I think you need to hurry; I want to ask them if I can have your hand in marriage."

"Oh!" Henry waited until her return. "We'll be right down."

A few minutes later, Theodore heard a car pull up and went to open the door for Shirleen, Juliana, Meagan and Jeff. "Welcome to our mad house."

Trudy's glowing cheeks and the smile on Henry's face told them everything. Teasingly, Shirleen asked, "What's so important? Why, you'd think you were getting married or something."

Henry nodded for Trudy to give them the news. "That's just it," Trudy said, grinning. "We are!"

"Oh," cried Shirleen excitedly, "that's the best news ever!"

Juliana reached out to hug Trudy and said, "I couldn't be happier for you. No one deserves to be happier than you. Well, except maybe my mother."

"Leslie—" Henry started.

Meagan jumped and nearly fainted at the use of her real first name. "It's all right, honey. Your secret's safe with me. I just wanted you to know that I realized running was the only thing you could do."

"Oh," was all that Meagan could say. Dropping onto the couch, she started sobbing hysterically. Going to her, he took her hands and said, "Crying is okay; it heals a wounded heart. I can see it all clearly now. If Jethro hadn't died, Bruce would've ruined him and that would've ruined me. Tilly's death opened my eyes and gave me a way to break away from Bruce. We've all been his victims in one way or another, you know."

"Thanks for understanding, Mr. Borden."

"Please, call me Henry. I want to be your friend, Leslie."

"If that's the case, please call me Meagan. It's too dangerous to call me Leslie."

"You're right. Meagan it is." Kissing her hands, he asked, "Can we be friends?"

"I'd be honored Mr.— I mean Henry."

Turning the chair so that he could look at Juliana, he said, "You did the only thing you could do under the circumstances. Bruce would've forced all of our hands otherwise. Our children would've been two of the most miserable people on the face of this earth."

Juliana surprised Henry by kissing his cheek. "I'm so grateful you don't bear any grudges."

"I did at first, then I had time to think about it and I'm relieved you had enough courage to break away and save us all a lot of heartache. I was actually proud of you. I didn't want to see you right after my memory came back. I was ashamed that I didn't have the backbone to stand up to that black-hearted snake in the grass husband of yours."

"Henry, my father forced me to marry Bruce. I wasn't about to force Meagan to endure what I'd gone through. That's why we ran."

"I never knew that," Henry said compassionately.

"Momma's father did the same to her, too. That's why neither of us wanted to see Meagan suffer. It wasn't fair to Jethro, either."

"You're right."

"So, can we start over and just be good friends?"

"I'd like that!"

Changing the subject, Henry continued, "I saw Judge Candace Smith and Josiah Graham today and I may be going back to New York to testify against Murdock, White, Wilson and Crowley."

"Your testimony would put Bruce and his henchmen away forever!" Juliana said excitedly.

"That's my hope," Henry said. "Someone has to stop him. It might as well be me."

Juliana kissed his cheek again, and grew teary eyed. "Thank you. When it's all over we'll finally be safe to live our lives without looking over our shoulders all the time."

Walking over to take Jeff's hand, Shirleen nodded for him to give their news. "No, you go ahead, honey," Jeff said.

"We wanted you all to know that Jeff and I are also getting married."

"That's wonderful!" cried Melinda.

"When?" Henry asked.

"In one week," Jeff said and grinned.

Smiling, Henry asked, "How about we make it a double wedding?"

Shirleen and Jeff looked at each other, as Henry asked Trudy, "What do you think, darling?"

"I'd love it," declared Trudy.

"What do you think," Shirleen asked Jeff.

"All I want is for you to be my wife. It doesn't matter how it's done. I'll let you decide."

Pausing to think about it a moment, Shirleen grinned and said, "I say let's do it!"

"Shirleen," asked Trudy, "will you be wearing white?"

"When I married Gordon, I was forced to wear a black dress. Father said I had disgraced him so I didn't deserve anything better. I most certainly *am* going to wear white! I'm marrying the love of my life. I want to celebrate it to the max."

"Never having been married, I'd also like to be married in white."

"Then the two of you should go shopping tomorrow and get the most gorgeous gowns you can find," ordered Henry. "We grooms will find a preacher to perform the ceremony."

"It's a deal," cried the women together.

"We have to wait for a few days because I want to stand when I say I do." Winking at Theodore, he motioned him forward. "I told you I had a surprise for you, Trudy. Well, I do."

"Wait a minute, Henry," Theodore said. "It isn't time to say I do yet. You have to wait until the preacher asks the question first." That made everyone laugh, which in turn eased the tension.

Theodore locked the brakes on the wheelchair, made sure the footrests were out of the way and stepped back to let Henry do what he needed to. Slowly, yet deliberately, Henry stood on his own and started to walk across the room. Trudy's eyes lit up with pleasure, as did Melinda's. Walking over to Trudy, he wrapped his arms around her and kissed her with all of the love that he had in his heart.

"Oh, Henry, I'm so proud of you," Trudy whispered in his ear. That earned her another kiss.

Realizing Henry's legs were shaking, Theodore pushed the chair over to him and said,. "That's enough for now, Henry. You'd better take a seat." He smiled to take the edge off of his words.

"Okay, I guess I'm a little wobbly. It's all the excitement from this wonderful lady saying she'll marry me."

"We have something important to share with all of you, too," Melinda said, grinning.

Looking at Theodore, she waited for him to speak, but he replied, "I think you should be the one to tell them, sweetheart."

"When I fainted the other day, there was a good reason for it." Smiling she continued, "We're expecting! I'm almost six months along. That seems strange, I know, but things have been so hectic around here that I didn't pay any attention to my cycles."

"That's wonderful!" cried Shirleen.

"I got a sonogram yesterday. We're having twin girls!"

"Oh, my," Meagan said in shock. "That will mean you have *seven* children."

"It sure will," laughed Theodore, "and they're all less than two years old."

Chapter 36

After arriving at the Spokane airport, Nathan White rented a car, then went to have something to eat. Once he was done eating, he found a cheap motel and went to sleep. It had been a long, drawn out ordeal for him. A dream woke him some time later and he lay there reliving it.

White didn't usually remember his dreams. That this one was vivid and it surprised him. He shook it off and went back to sleep.

Near morning, he sat straight up in bed. Fear held him in its grip so tightly that for a moment he couldn't focus. He was sweating, and his heart was beating so quickly it was difficult to breathe. Giving, sleep up for the time being, he went to sit in a chair near the window. He pulled the curtain back a little, and looked out into the parking lot as the dream replayed in his mind.

What's wrong with you, White? You never dream. You've never felt remorse for what you've done. Why start now? It's just a job . Why is it so different now?

An unbidden thought came into his mind. *You thought you could play God and never get caught. You will be caught and this dream is just a sample of what's coming.*

"Stop it!" he cried aloud. "You've just got the jitters."

White had never killed a woman in all the time he'd been a hit man. His father taught him that a woman was to be respected and cared for. Now he'd been ordered to kill two women. It went against everything he knew. *But if I don't do the job, Murdock will put a hit out on me.*

Again, he heard more audibly in his mind, *Who're you trying to kid? Your parents taught you it's wrong to take the life of another human being. Why are you lying to yourself? You've silenced your conscience for so long that you've convinced yourself it's just a job. Be honest for once in your life and admit the truth. You know that it's wrong, wrong, WRONG!"*

"All right!" cried White aloud. "So it's wrong. I'm not sorry I did it, and I don't give a dang about how some lousy man feels about it."

Realizing he'd spoken aloud, he thought, *You're going dotty, White! Now, isn't the time to start getting religion! You've made your bed, now lie in it!"*

Feeling better, he went back to bed, and fell asleep instantly. Just before daylight, he woke again. This dream, like the two earlier dreams, was even more vivid. This time, he saw what was going to happen to him and he didn't like it one little bit. Giving up on sleep for the night, he went to shower and prepare for the day.

When he was done, White sat by the window and thought about the dreams. He was dead and traveling some place foreign ... a place he'd never seen before. After traveling for a while, he came to a beautiful place where the people were happy and singing beautiful songs.

Suddenly a man appeared before him and everything he'd ever done, good or bad, went through his mind and he began to quake at the enormity of what he'd done. He knew in an instant that he didn't belong in this beautiful place. The man looked at him with such disdain that he wanted to flee.

The dream changed abruptly and he found himself in a place that literally had no happiness. There was a feeling of abject misery and extreme discontent. Then, those whose lives he'd stolen stood before him. One of them was Gordon Spielberg, a man he'd once looked up to. For the first time in his life, White felt agony. Then the dream ended.

Pushing these thoughts away, he left and drove around with the window of his car rolled down, trying to ease the distress he felt, while the dream continued to play over and over in his mind. He found an all night diner and went inside.

He placed an order and waited for his food. He pushed thoughts of the dream further from his mind by concentrating on finding Murdock's family. When his meal arrived, he ate it without tasting it. He left the waitress a hundred dollar tip and went out into the fresh air. He felt better.

He didn't want to go back to the motel, so he drove around to investigate the area. He found a little park, near the river, and stopped the car. He leaned back against the headrest and fell asleep. He woke with a start, and a police officer was standing next to him. "Are you having trouble, sir?"

"No," replied White. "I was enjoying the cool breeze and the sound of flowing water. I must've fallen asleep."

Smiling, the officer replied, "This setting has that affect on people. Have a good day, sir."

"Thank you, officer. I will."

White watched the policeman stroll back to his car, get inside and slowly drive away. Looking at the watch, White was surprised to see it was 8 a.m. He got out of the car and decided to let Murdock know he'd arrived. "Bruce, it's Nate. I'm in Spokane and I'll be on my way in a little while."

"Well, get going soon. I need you to get done and get back here. There's trouble brewing."

"Yes, sir."

"When you get to Cardston, call me and I'll give you further instructions."

White put his phone away and went back to his car. He drove to the motel, packed and turned in his motel key.

He stopped and got a large cup of coffee at a roadside restaurant and decided to get some pie with whipped cream while he was there. When he'd finished his pie, White left a generous tip, paid his bill and left. He was soon speeding out of town, intent on getting to his destination.

As he drove, he suddenly thought of his mother, who'd been dead for ten years. Somehow, he knew that she wouldn't be happy with the way that he'd lived his life. She was a great mother — an example of kindness, love and compassion. She'd always been the first one on the scene when something bad happened to someone or when someone just needed a friend. He'd always thought that made her seem small and insignificant and had wished was more domineering, like some of his friend's mothers.

Disgusted by his thoughts, he pulled over to get more coffee. Soon he was back on the road, speeding toward Cardston.

Shirleen woke with a start. Looking around the room, she was surprised to see it was still dark outside. They were going to get hers and Trudy's wedding dresses today. She loved Jeff and couldn't figure out why she wasn't happier about the whole thing.

Slipping into her robe and slippers, she went to the bathroom, she started feeling almost panicky. She sat down on the edge of the bed, and tears started to come unbidden. Suddenly, there was a small light near the doorway. Fascinated, she watched it grow brighter until it filled the room. Stepping out of the light was Joseph, her special angel. "You're wondering why you feel so negative, when you should be soaring among the clouds with happiness."

Shirleen nodded.

"There's a valid reason for your feelings, Shirleen."

"Bruce has found us, hasn't he?" She started to tremble uncontrollably."

"Yes, they've known where you are since just before Christmas. Vincent Crowley followed Josiah and his men back here. When Meagan and Josiah were walking the dogs, Crowley recognized her voice."

"Do we have to go on the run again, just when we're finally starting to feel secure?"

"No, but you have to be constantly aware of all that's going on around you. Bruce sent one of his hit men to kill you, but his plans will be foiled before he can accomplish the deed.

"Tell Meagan to keep her binoculars and the two dogs close to her at all times — even when she's working in the garden."

Looking at Joseph intently, Shirleen asked, "Is he on his way here, even as we speak?"

"That's correct."

"Should we cancel our trip to town?"

"No, the trip to town will help to alleviate the tension you're all feeling. He won't be here for another day or two. When you get done shopping, you can tell the others this message. You should also keep your cell phones with you at all times — all of you."

"It's hard to stay calm, when someone's on their way to kill you."

"It is difficult, but if you remain calm you will be more prepared. Alert Timothy York and Josiah Graham to the situation; they will help protect you."

"I'll do that."

"Stop at their office on your way home from shopping. That will be a good time to alert everyone to the situation. The man who's coming for you is Nathan White. He's been to your daughter's home and yours on many occasions."

"Nathan White? I didn't know he was a hit man."

"He's the one who killed Gordon and is responsible for sending many men to their deaths."

"Thank you for the warning."

"You're welcome. If you obey my instructions, you'll be safe. Your ordeal will soon be over, and then you can return to a normal life. One final thing, make sure someone is with Leslie at all times. Nathan will try to kidnap her. If he gets her, Bruce will send her as far away as he can so that you'll never see her again. Do not let her out of your sight."

"We'll follow your instructions to the letter."

"Good!" Joseph was swallowed by the light, which slowly dissipated until the room was back to normal.

Shirleen pondered everything the angel told her. Deciding to stay up, she chose her clothes for the day and went to take a shower. Everything the angel had told her was indelibly imprinted on her mind. She was suddenly tired, so she laid down and immediately fell into a deep sleep.

"Grandma?"

Shirleen tried to focus on the voice.

"Grandma?" came the voice again. She recognized it as Meagan's voice and opened her eyes. "Oh, you're all right," sighed Meagan, watching Shirleen anxiously.

"I'm fine, honey. Why do you look so worried?"

"I called your name four times before you woke up."

"I'm sorry. I must have been sleeping pretty soundly."

"I'm glad you were able to sleep, Grandma. Momma sent me to get you up so we can have breakfast before we go to town."

"Let me freshen up and I'll be right there."

Noticing that Shirleen was dressed, Meagan asked, "Have you even been to bed Grandma?"

"Yes. I woke early and get ready for the day, then I went back to sleep." Looking at her clothes, she added, "I'm all wrinkled, guess I'll change before I come down."

"Okay, I'll see you at the breakfast table."

"Good morning, Momma," Juliana said as Shirleen entered the kitchen.

Jeff stood to kiss her and said, "Good morning, beautiful!"

"Good morning yourself, handsome." Kissing him, she took her place at the table. Shirleen noticed that Trudy was positively glowing. "I'm so glad to see you so happy, Trudy."

"Thank you. I feel like I'm soaring."

"That's as it should be when you have found the love of your life."

Jeff, who had been watching Shirleen intently, asked, "Are you sure you're feeling okay? You look tired."

"I had an interesting night, but I'm going to be just fine."

They ate quickly so that they could leave for town. As they were leaving, Shirleen turned to Jeff and asked, "Would you meet us at Tim and Josiah's office at noon?" When Jeff looked at her anxiously, Shirleen hastened to add, "It is important, Jeff. I don't want to go into things right now, but let me say this ... it's extremely important that you're there. I'll explain everything when we're all together."

"Sure, I'll be there. I have to go over to my house to check on it, so I'll meet you at noon."

As Nathan White continued to drive to Cardston, he ignored the scenery. All that was on his mind was the job he had to do for Murdock. Around two o'clock, he stopped in Sandpoint to have something to eat. He went to a restaurant on Main Street and noticed his waitress was beautiful.

She handed him a menu and filled his coffee cup. "What'll you have?"

Scanning the menu, White replied, "A bacon burger and fries." Holding out his thermos toward her, he asked, "Can I also get this filled with coffee when I'm ready to leave?"

Taking the thermos, she replied, "Sure thing. Need anything else?"

"What kind of pie do you have?"

"Blueberry, rhubarb, cherry, apple and banana cream."

"I'll have a slice of rhubarb."

"With whipped cream or alamode?"

"Alamode."

"Okay, it'll be a few minutes."

A few minutes later, the waitress brought him his meal and he dug right in. He was nearly finished with his meal when the waitress set his pie on the table and refilled his coffee. When he was finished, the waitress brought his thermos and left him with the bill. He left a hundred dollar tip for the waitress, then paid his bill and left.

He drove for a couple of hours before stopping again. He pulled into a rest stop and took care of business before walking around a bit to stretch his legs. A gentle breeze played with his hair, as he walked over to a picnic table and took a seat. As he sat there, he felt a sense of peace like he hadn't felt in a long time.

Finally, he got back into the car and poured himself a cup of coffee from his thermos. He left the peaceful scene, pulled back onto the highway, and sped away.

Late that night, he made it to Crow's Nest, Canada. He drove around until he found an all night diner and went inside to get something to eat. When he was done, he found a motel, checked in and promptly went to sleep.

Several times that night he was awakened by dreams. Eventually he gave up on sleep and grabbed a cigarette. When it was finished, he went back to sleep. This time, the dream found him face to face with Gordon Spielberg. He cursed him vehemently, but Gordon just stared until he ran out of curses, then Spielberg said, "Curse me all you want, but you'll soon be here with me. You're just as evil as me, and you have to pay the price same as I do."

Suddenly, White began to feel remorse for what he'd done, but it was much too late to do things over. Those he'd killed were there to haunt him. He began to run, but when he looked down he realized he was running in place. He woke up shouting, "No!"

Looking at the clock on the nightstand, he was surprised to see that it was five in the morning. He dressed quickly, he repacked his suitcase and sat on a chair near the window to smoke a cigarette. Finally, he crushed it out and said, "This is only a stupid dream. Get over it!"

He picked up his suitcase and took it out to the car. He went back inside, checked the room, then slammed the door and took his key to the front desk.

He drove over to the all night diner to eat and fill his thermos with hot coffee. When he was finished, he got in the car and drove on toward Cardston. He didn't stop for lunch and arrived in town late that afternoon. *What an ugly town*," White thought.

He was hungry, so he stopped to eat before finding an out of the way motel. Once in his room, he tossed the keys onto the table, walked over and flopped onto the bed. He was asleep almost instantly.

He awoke at seven the next morning, and called Bruce Murdock. "I arrived late last night, found a motel and crashed."

"Good! Just a minute. I'll get Vinnie to give you directions out to the house. Check around for a good hiding spot where you can watch them for a while. When you get the chance, take them out. Make sure you don't leave any witnesses."

"Will do."

"Remember, I want Leslie alive. She'll never forget the lesson she'll learn from seeing those two hags shot up. When I get her back here, she'll learn an even bigger lesson from me!"

"I'll see she gets back to you soon."

Suddenly, White saw Bruce as he really was. *He's one selfish, manipulative maniac. I should've put him down a long time ago. When I'm finished here I'm gonna do just that.* Aloud, he said, "I'll call when the job is finished."

He got ready to face his day, took the directions Crowley had given him and studied them carefully. When he was sure he'd memorized them, he headed out.

He found the house easily, and continued on up the road. When he got to the end of the road, he got out of his car to look around. He found a good place to camp in sight of the house, then he went back to his motel room in town to make a list of things he needed to set up camp.

He went shopping for what he needed, then headed back to the motel again. Once there, he quickly. packed and took the key back to the manager.

He went back to the spot in the woods and set up camp. He hadn't put up a tent before, so it took him a while. With that done, he put rocks in a ring so he could build a fire, then organized his food.

When Shirleen and her family got to town, they found parking places and went into a store that sold wedding gowns. As Shirleen looked at the gowns, she realized she really was going to marry the love of her life. She'd never have to live with a man she loathed again. Joy filled her heart. *Gordon Spielberg is finally out of my life forever!* This caused her to grin.

Juliana, seeing the smile, guessed what she was thinking, "It feels wonderful to not have to think of Gordon, doesn't it, Momma? When I saw you smile just now, I just knew that's what you were thinking."

"It gives me a bounce in my step and makes my heart soar free."

"I'm glad I don't have to call him father anymore."

Trudy, who had gone ahead to look at the wedding dresses came back and asked, "Aren't these dresses absolutely beautiful?"

"Yes, they are," sighed Shirleen. "Have you found one you like?"

"I have three picked out and ready to try on. "

Meagan was holding two of the most beautiful dresses Shirleen had ever seen. "Meagan, these are absolutely fantastic!"

"When I saw them, I thought so too. Why don't you try them on, Grandma?"

"I will!" Taking the dresses from Meagan, she turned to speak to Trudy, "Come on, let's go see how these look."

Soon, Trudy came out of the dressing room in a full-length gown with long sleeves. She was stunningly beautiful, but the dress didn't do her justice. Meagan said, "Let's see you in the next dress."

The other dress was more elegant, but again it wasn't quite right, so Meagan went with her to help pick out some other styles. Meagan found one she thought was perfect. Trudy tried it on and when came out wearing it, Juliana and Meagan gasped. Trudy was beyond stunning.

Juliana said, "That dress will make Henry gasp!"

The dress was lace with a rose design that covered the satin material of the bodice. Beautiful beadwork was sewn into patterns across the front and back. Pearl buttons held the dress closed in the back. The sleeves, covered with the same delicate rose lace, were puffed at the shoulders and tapered to the wrists. From the elbow to the wrists, the same pearl buttons added to the look. It was gathered at the waist and had the same lace and beadwork all the way to the end of the train. The veil they chose, had the same rose lace, with a crown covered with white jewels. The complete effect was spectacular.

When Shirleen came out wearing her first choicer, all vetoed it immediately. Her second choice was simple, yet elegant and made Shirleen look ethereal. It was gathered at the waist and hugged her curves. The lace on the veil reminded Juliana of a delicate cloud.

"Oh, Momma," was all Juliana could say, as tears glistened in her eyes.

"Grandma, you're dazzling!" Blinking to clear her eyes, Meagan added, "This is the perfect dress for you."

They paid for the dresses and veils, and the cashier boxed them up. Their next stop was at a shoe store, then they went on to the courthouse to see Tim and Josiah. As they were parking, Jeff pulled in and parked next to them. "Hello, you beautiful ladies," he said as they got out. "Are you done shopping?"

"Yes," replied Shirleen. "As soon as we speak to Tim and Josiah, we're going to go grab some lunch. Why don't you join us?"

"I like that idea. How about going to the Chinese buffet?"

"I love Chinese food!" declared Meagan.

When the others agreed, Jeff said, "Then I'm buying. You've made all those homemade meals for me, so it's my turn to feed you. Let's ask Tim and Josiah to join us."

"That's a great idea," agreed Shirleen.

Taking Shirleen's hand he said, "Let's shake a leg. This old man's starving to death."

Laughing, they all went inside. They were at the front desk when Tim came out of his office. "What brings you here today?"

Shirleen looked at the others, who waited for her to speak. "I need to talk to you and Josiah. It's important."

"Let me get Josiah and we'll talk in his office."

They followed him to Josiah's office, and he asked, "What's going on, guys?"

"I need to talk to all of you," said Shirleen.

When everyone was seated, Josiah said, "You've got the floor, Shirleen."

Looking at each one in the room, Shirleen sighed. She told them everything the angel had said and all of them were shocked.

When she was finished, Josiah stood and paced the room. Turning to look at Shirleen, he said, "I have to trust you when you say you've been talking to an Angel. I've had an angel come to warn me and ultimately save my life. What we've got to decide is how to protect you without tipping our hat."

"I know Nathan White well," Trudy said. "He's also one of the names I saw on Bruce's list. He's in line to be killed. Mr. Murdock hates him."

"That doesn't surprise me," Shirleen said. "I've come to realize Bruce Murdock will stop at nothing to get what he wants. When he no longer needs someone's service, he'll have them killed."

"Bruce may hate White," Juliana said, "but he has no qualms about using him to get jobs done."

Josiah, who'd been listening intently, grew thoughtful. He turned to Tim and said, "I think we should take Holmquist, Black, and Adams and camp out at Shirleen's for a while. Make sure you have plenty of rifles and ammunition." Suddenly, he grinned at Shirleen as he continued, "As good a shot as Shirleen is, I don't think we'll be needed, but better safe than sorry. I mean she did shoot a fifteen hundred pound bear without getting mauled."

Blushing, Shirleen replied, "When it comes to the safety of your loved ones, you'll do just about anything to protect them."

"All joking aside, Shirleen, I'm really proud of the way that you handled the situation. You were cool, calm and collected. It says a lot about you."

"Thank you for the compliment, Josiah."

"It'll take us the rest of the day to get prepared so we'll come sometime early tomorrow morning. Can you set us up with a place to sleep?"

"Sure. We have two extra rooms upstairs. They're not finished but they should do."

"While we're there, we'll get some of the work done if you want us to."

"Thanks," Jeff said. "I could use all the help I can get. I want to get everything done before I marry this wonderful lady."

"That reminds me," said Josiah. "When's the big day?"

"We've been thinking about a week to two weeks from now. With this business with White, we might have to be put it off for a while."

"We'll just have to take it one step at a time," advised Josiah.

"Hey, we're going to go to the Chinese restaurant for lunch. Want to come? It's my treat."

"That sounds great," replied Tim. "I was on my way to lunch when you got here."

"I'd like that too," admitted Josiah. "Suddenly I'm starving."

Rising, Jeff said, "Lt's go get some Chinese food!"

"Lead on," ordered Josiah.

Chapter 37

After their trip to town the next morning, Meagan and Trudy went to work in the garden. Watching them go out the door, Shirleen was struck by how grown up Meagan had become. She'd completed high school and was an accomplished young woman now.

She remembered how the high school principal had commended them on the good job they'd done teaching her. She not only passed each test, but she ranked higher than any of the local students. He'd even taken her results to a college professor, who said he'd recommend her to any college she wanted. *She wants to go to veterinary school. Where has the time gone?*

Shirleen was brought back from her reminiscing, when her cell phone rang. Seeing it was Meagan, she grew concerned.

"Trudy and I were working in the garden, when Prince and Lady started growling. I saw something or someone on the hill above our house. I grabbed the binoculars and I searched the hill. That's when I saw him. Grandma, Nathan White was watching us through a pair of binoculars."

"Did Trudy see him?"

"Yes, she's still watching him."

"Stay right where you are. Don't get up or come toward the house. Act normal. If he comes close to you, send the dogs after him."

"Okay," promised Meagan.

"In the meantime, I'll tell Jeff and Juliana what's going on, and try to get Josiah on the phone."

"Thank you, Grandma."

Shirleen ended the conversation and rushed upstairs to find Jeff, shouting, "Jeff! Jeff, where are you?"

Popping out of one of the damaged bedrooms, he asked, "What's got you so upset, honey?"

"Nathan's up on the hill above the house, watching with binoculars."

"Call Juliana," barked Jeff.

Going to the railing, Shirleen called, "Juliana, come upstairs quick, and bring your binoculars."

"I'm coming, Momma," yelled Juliana. A moment later she came bounding up the stairs. "What's going on?"

"Meagan and Trudy saw Nathan White. Look up on the hill. Can you see him?"

"Yes, as plain as day. You two keep an eye on him, while I try to call Josiah." Moving away from the window, Shirleen dialed Josiah's cell number.

"Josiah, it's Shirleen. Nathan White's on the hill above the house."

"We'll be there in a few minutes. We've almost finished loading the car. As soon as that's done, we'll be on our way."

"Please hurry."

"Don't go outside for anything."

"Meagan and Trudy are in the garden. They have both dogs for protection."

"Tell them to stay put."

"I did."

"I'll get there as fast as I can."

Joining Jeff and Juliana, she asked, "Is he doing anything?"

"No," replied Jeff, "he's just watching the house."

"Josiah said we shouldn't go outside and that they'd be here as soon as they finish loading the cars."

"I hope it's soon because I don't like the way Nathan's acting."

"What is he doing?" asked Shirleen.

"He stands there looking at the house with binoculars, then all of a sudden, he stomps off. It's like he's looking for some kind of reaction from us so he can strike. The longer we go without reacting to him, the more irate he seems to get. He leaves for a few minutes and just when I think I can tell Meagan and Trudy it's safe to come back to the house, he reappears. He's done that the whole time you were talking to Josiah."

"I'm going to call Trudy's cell and let them know what's happening," declared Shirleen.

"Tell them to stay calm, no matter what Nathan does," cautioned Jeff.

"I will. That's why I'm calling."

"Trudy, this is Shirleen. Whatever you do, don't come toward the house. Nathan's acting strange."

"I know," replied Trudy. "I've been watching him. He acts like he wants us to panic or something."

"That's what we think, too. I know it's hot, but you need to stay where you are. Try to get under the shade of the plants as much as you can."

"We're near the corn, which gives us a little shade. Meagan ordered the dogs to stay close to us, too."

"Good. I called Josiah and he said they'd be on their way as soon as they finished loading the cars. I expect them any minute."

"That's wonderful news."

All of a sudden, Nathan stalked off in a huff and stayed out of sight for a good five minutes. He had just gotten repositioned when cars started pulling into the yard. White suddenly disappeared. "It's all right to come in now," stated Shirleen. "White won't show up with the men around."

"We'll be right in." Turning off the phone, Trudy told Meagan. "Josiah and his men are here. It's safe to go back to the house."

"Finally!" Rising, she called the dogs as she started toward the house. They got inside just as White reappeared to watch the action going on in the house. Unable to see very well, he went back to camp to sulk. *I'll wait for my chance to attack. they'll be alone later.*

Inside the house, the group held an emergency meeting. Jeff and Juliana, who had seen most of Nathan's antics, filled Josiah and his men in on his actions. When they finished, Meagan and Trudy told how he tried to get them to show their hiding place. "I was so scared. I wanted to run to the house, but Trudy kept talking to me and kept me from doing something stupid."

"Well," said Josiah, "it's a sure bet he won't show himself anymore during the day. When it gets dark, we'll try to sneak up to his hiding place and flush him out."

"I sure wish this was over," sighed Juliana. Tim, noticing how pale she was, longed to comfort her. Yet he wisely refrained from doing so. For sometime now, his feelings for Juliana had been growing so strong that it was difficult to hide them.

For the rest of the afternoon, the men brought in their gear and unpacked. The rifles and ammunition was stored in ready use should the need arise

Nathan White sat at his campfire, flabbergasted by the fact that no one in the house showed any reaction to him at all. *P* Remembering the men who'd just arrived, White wondered why no one panicked. *Maybe this isn't the right house,* he thought. Taking his cell phone from his pocket, he dialed Murdock's number and waited for him to answer. "Murdock here."

"Bruce, Nate. I've been trying to raise some action at the address Vinnie gave me, but nothing's happened yet." Giving Bruce the directions Crowley had given him, he asked, "Are these right?"

"The directions are right."

"Then I'll try again later. They have company now. There are just too many for me to storm in on them. I'll sneak down there tonight and do them when they're alone."

"Just don't get caught," snapped Bruce, "and call me when it's done and you have Meagan."

White put the phone back into his pocket, got out a cigarette and struck a match on a rock. He took a few good deep drags and absently let the smoke curl from his mouth as he pondered his next move. He walked around the woods, looking at all avenues of escape. There weren't any good options.

He went back to his car and moved it between some trees to camouflage it. Still not satisfied he was safe, he tried and again explored everything around him. He smelled something dead, and eventually came upon the grizzly Shirleen had shot. He was surprised to see the four bullet holes in the carcass. *This is one huge bear. I wonder who shot it. It couldn't be one of the women; they don't know the first thing about shooting a gun. Someone inside that house shot it though.*

For the first time, White was worried. Examining the wounds again, he noticed two holes were from a 30-30-gauge rifle, while the other two were from a .22. *I don't like this one little bit. Something just isn't right here.*

Surprised to see it was now 3:30 p.m., he went to the creek to bring back a bucket of water. After filling the bucket, he took it back to camp and set it near the fire pit. After that, he took a short nap.

When he woke up, he was hungry, so he made a fire and cooked four hot dogs. He slipped them into buns and began wolfing them down. By the time that he was finished, it was dark. He added some wood to the fire, and sat there staring. He heard brush snapping off to the right and pulled out his pistol. As the noises got closer, every hair on his head stood on end. *Whatever's out there, it's huge.*

He threw some more wood on the fire and checked his gun to make sure it was fully loaded. Suddenly, something snorted. Turning in that direction, he was surprised to see a female grizzly and her twin cubs approaching him. Apparently she'd smelled his food. After looking at him for a long minute, the mother turned and she and the cubs disappeared into the night.

Feeling more secure, he went back to watching the fire. Eventually he called it a night and went off to sleep. Two hours later the fire had died down and the grizzly was back. Ambling toward the cooler, she slapped it hard, sending it flying. The noise woke White and he quickly put on his pants and reached for his pistol. As he moved toward the tent entrance and opened the flap, he saw the bear.

He yelled, trying to scare her away. She rose to her full height and turned toward him. Seeing how tall she was, White wished he'd kept his mouth shut. The bear dropped back to all fours and backed up, gnashing her teeth in warning. When White didn't respond, she growled and slapped the ground hard.

White was terrified and rooted to the spot. Pure adrenalin surged through him as he watched the bear. Suddenly, she charged. White began pumping shells into her. The stinging bullets infuriated her more

When he ran out of bullets, White tossed the gun to the side. Fear like he'd never known coursed through him, and he panicked and began to run. He didn't get far, before the female was on him. Screaming from the searing pain, White was forced to the ground.

The female bit into his shoulder and raked him with her claws. She grabbed him and shook him like a rag doll, then dragged him away from the campsite. White continued to scream the whole time.

Her massive paws held him down and she got a good grip on his throat, then bit down hard and ripped his flesh. Suddenly shots rang out, and several bullets struck the bear. Like a towering oak, she fell to the ground, dead.

Josiah, Tim, and the men with them got a long, heavy stick to prod the bear. When she didn't move after several rough jabs, they knew it was safe to approach. They went to where White lay, but he was beyond help.

Josiah, called for an ambulance, and motioned for the men to move away from the scene. About thirty minutes later, they could hear the wail of the siren. The ambulance came to a stop at the end of the road and the attendants brought a gurney and joined Josiah and his group.

"What happened here?" the first attendant asked. "The dispatcher said there was some kind of accident up here."

"A female grizzly mauled this guy and he's dead. Apparently he shot her several times, but the wounds weren't serious. We shot her with several high-powered rifles and killed her. There isn't much of this guy left. She really did a job on him.

"When we examined her, we saw that she had a gaping wound on her left shoulder. Don't know how she got it, but we figured she wasn't able to hunt and was starving. That would explain the attack."

"Do you know who this is, Josiah?"

"Yeah. He's name's Nathan White. He's from New York."

"What was he doing out here?"

"I can't divulge that right now."

"Well, we'd better get to it then." Three hours later the police cleared the campsite, and the bear carcass had been dealt with. When they were done, there was nothing left to show that anything had happened.

Afterward, the men slowly went back to the house to shower and change clothes. When the others saw how bloody the men were, they feared asking what had happened.

A while later, Josiah came down stairs to ask, "May I have a large garbage bag to discard our clothes in."

"Sure," replied Shirleen. "We can soak your clothes in one of the bathtubs upstairs. That should get the blood out."

"There's so much I don't think you can get it all out."

"Okay, let me get you a garbage bag." She returned from the kitchen with several bags. "If you need them you'll have them. Otherwise you can return them."

The next time Josiah came downstairs, he had all of the bags stuffed with the men's clothes. He and Jeff took the bags outside, and when they returned it was time for

Josiah to let them know what happened. "Nathan White was mauled by a wounded female grizzly tonight. He didn't make it."

No one said a word for several minutes. Finally, Juliana replied, "It's a terrible way to die."

Josiah said what Juliana couldn't say, "That's true, but at least you're safe for now."

Theodore, Melinda, and Annabelle, were watching the local news on television, when they heard the anchorman say:

> *"A New York man was mauled by a wounded female grizzly tonight just west of town. Reports say he shot her several times but the bear got the better of him. He did not survive the attack. The man's name is being withheld pending notification of his family."*

Henry grew alarmed when he heard the location. "That can only be somewhere above Trudy's place. I hope they're all right."

"Let's give them a call and put our minds at rest," encouraged Theodore. Rising from his chair, he went to phone the Webb's.

"Hello," said Shirleen.

"Shirleen, this is Theodore. We just heard on the news that there was a man that was mauled by a wounded female grizzly just west of town. Do you know anything about it?"

"Yes," replied Shirleen. "It happened just above our house. A man was camping in the meadow above us. We knew him, as he was stalking us. He had been watching the house most of the morning."

"Stalking you! Then he was connected to Bruce Murdock."

"That's correct. He was sent to take care of us, if you get my meaning."

"Oh, no! That means that the cat is out of the bag."

"Yes, it is."

"Were you alone when things came down?"

"No, Major Graham and Sergeant York were here to protect us. We heard the commotion all the way down here. It sounded so grizzly. Oh dear, I'm sorry for the sick pun."

"No problem, as your comment said it all." Theodore paused a moment then asked, "Were any of you hurt by the incident?"

"No, we were shocked and shaken up, but otherwise we're fine. Is Henry worried about Trudy?"

"Yes, he is. In fact we're worried about all of you."

"Tell Henry that we're all fine. As soon as things calm down, we'll come down to see you all."

"That would be wonderful! Sure glad to hear that you are all right. Take care and I'll talk to you later."

"Tell Henry that when he sees his bride he'll not believe how beautiful she is."

"I will."

"Goodbye, Theodore.

"Goodbye, Shirleen. Talk to you soon." Hanging up the phone, Theodore went back to report the conversation. When he was finished, everyone visibly relaxed. When Theodore gave Henry Shirleen's message, he beamed.

After talking to Theodore, Shirleen turned to tell everyone, "That was Theodore Brooks. They were watching the news just now and heard about Nathan. They were really worried about us. Especially, Henry."

"Well, there's no getting around it now. Once White doesn't call Bruce, he will suspect that something is up. Perhaps he will send Crowley back to investigate what happened."

"Oh, I hope not," cried Meagan. The incident had affected Meagan the most. She had not slept well the night before, due to the nightmares that plagued her. She had been pale most of the day and had eaten very little.

"We'll be here to take care of you," consoled Mark. "We'll see that you remain safe."

"Thank you, but you don't know how evil my father is. He will stop at nothing to get what he wants."

"Then we'll have to be on our guard at all times, won't we?"

"Yes, we will."

Rising, she called the dogs as she walked outside to get some fresh air. Juliana watching her go, felt bad that she was struggling so hard to stay focused. Juliana could understand her feelings, as she was struggling too.

Shirleen appeared calm on the outside, but everyone there knew that she was nearing her breaking point. She was trying desperately to hold her family together, yet feared that there was no way to accomplish that feat. Trudy became the rock that the others could cling too. She bustled around them like an old mother hen. Her calming effect seemed to settle the women down.

A few minutes later, Mark Holmquist went in search of Meagan. What met his gaze touched him, causing his heart to go out to her. For some time, Mark had been experiencing feelings that he couldn't understand whenever he thought of Meagan, or was around her like he was now. Meagan, with a dog on each side of her, was sobbing as if her very heart would break. Mark was about to go back inside, when suddenly Meagan crumpled to the ground. Rushing over to kneel beside her, Mark felt for a pulse. Relief flooded over him, when he got one. At first the dogs weren't going to let him touch her, but he commanded, "Stay." Whimpering, they obeyed. Somehow they sensed that he was trying to help their mistress. Scooping her up in his arms, he started for the house. "Josiah," he yelled, "Come quick."

Josiah, followed by the others, rushed out of the house toward Mark. Seeing his precious niece so limp, Josiah cried out, "Give her to me." Mark did as he was told. Rushing back to the house, Josiah laid her onto the couch, where he began to work over her in an attempt to get her to regain consciousness. When she didn't regain consciousness, Josiah ordered, "Call for an ambulance immediately."

Tim pulled out his cell phone and made the call. When the dispatcher answered, Tim told her, "We need an ambulance out here on the double!" Giving him directions on how to get there, Tim hung up. Meagan moaned, but couldn't open her eyes. "Poor kid," he replied. This has been a trying eight months for her. Fear is a terrible thing to live with."

"That it is," replied Josiah.

Mark asked, "Since we're now involved in this mess, don't you think we need to know what is totally going on so that we can be of better service to this family. If you are afraid that David, Adams, or I'll spill the beans, we won't."

"That's right, replied Adams. "I for one will protect them to the best of my ability."

"So will I," responded Black.

"Please, we'd like to know what is going on," said Mark.

"Mark is right, Josiah," stated Shirleen. "His very life, as well as these other two brave men, may depend on their knowing the truth."

"Tim," barked Josiah, "You fill them in while I work on Meagan here." Just as Tim was finishing up, they heard the blaring of the siren approaching. When he had come to the end of the story, the men remained silent as they pondered all that Tim had told them. Suddenly the ambulance had backed into the yard. Shirleen went to show them in and stood to the side of the room to give them room to work over Meagan. As the paramedics worked on her, Meagan moaned and tried to open her eyes.

A moment later she opened them to look around. It was obvious to everyone there that she was having trouble focusing. As she struggled to rise the paramedic gently pushed her back down. "Just lie still for a moment so that I can get your vitals."

Meagan complied, although tears ran down her face. "What's wrong with me?" she asked.

"You fainted," replied Mark.

"Oh," was all that Meagan could say.

Calling the hospital, the paramedic waited for the one working on Meagan to give him her vital signs. "Heart beat rapid and pupils dilated. Blood pressure one ninety over ninety-eight."

The second paramedic relayed the information over the phone. "Yes, sir. Will transport as soon as stable enough to do so." Hanging up the phone, he told the first paramedic, "Dr. Stillman wants her transported to the hospital as soon as we have her stabilized. "

"We're going to lift you onto the gurney so that we can take you out to the ambulance."

"Please, I don't want to go." Suddenly, Meagan began to shake uncontrollably. All at once, she fainted again. Getting her onto the gurney, they took her out to the ambulance. As soon as she was loaded into the back, the paramedic started to work on her some more. "May I please ride with you," asked Juliana.

"Are you her mother?"

"Yes, sir. I am."

"Come on."

"Momma, would you please bring my purse when you come?"

"Yes," replied Shirleen.

Getting into the back with the paramedic, Juliana prayed that Meagan would regain consciousness. A moment later, opening her eyes, Meagan looked around. "Momma," she cried, growing restless. "Momma, please don't let them take me to the hospital."

"It will be all right, honey. I'm right here with you. Please relax so that this paramedic can help you."

"Okay," Terrified, Meagan began to sob hysterically.

The paramedic moved so that Juliana could take Meagan's hand. "Listen, sweetheart, you're going to be all right. You are safe now. I won't let anyone near you."

Meagan, knowing that her mother would try to protect her, wasn't convinced that she could protect her. Growing more restless, she began to thrash about in an attempt to get away. "NOOO!" she yelled at the top of her lungs. "Don't let Daddy find me!"

It took the paramedic and Juliana to restrain Meagan. Panic gripped her so strongly that she couldn't be consoled. They were pulling into the emergency entrance when Meagan's fear escalated. Flaying out in a desperate attempt to get away, Meagan began to scream hysterically. Getting her out of the ambulance as fast as they could, the men wheeled her into the emergency room. Dr. Stillman was waiting for them as they took her to a room. Suddenly, Meagan fainted again.

"What happened," demanded Stillman.

Juliana filled him in as Stillman worked over her. When she was finished, Stillman replied, "No wonder she is acting out. I'm surprised that she isn't worse."

Turning to place a hand on Juliana's shoulder, he replied, "It's going to be all right, but I need you to wait in the waiting room so that I can work on her."

"I understand. Thank you for taking care of her."

Nodding, Stillman watched her leave. "Nurse, I want you to get a hold of Dr. Reese immediately. Tell her that I have a patient that is nearing a nervous breakdown. Tell her that she needs to get here just as soon as she possibly can."

"Yes, sir." Not waiting for further instruction, the nurse rushed from the room to do as instructed.

Ten minutes later a well-dressed woman entered the emergency room. "What's going on, Dr. Stillman?"

After Dr. Stillman filled Reese in on why Meagan was nearing a nervous breakdown, Dr. Reese, replied, "I'm surprised that she isn't comatose."

"Her grandmother has been struggling with depression and anemia. I've been treating her, but Meagan here was doing so well that I never suspected the turmoil that she was under."

"Don't berate yourself. After all, no one could foresee this turn of events. Now that I know what is happening, I can work her through this awful fear."

"Good. I gave her a shot, so she will sleep for a while at least. However, I want you to be close so that if she starts panicking, you can help her."

"That's a good idea. Is her mother here?"

"Yes, she is in the waiting room."

"I'll go speak to her while you take care of your patient."

"Tell her that as soon as I get her into a room, I'll meet with all of them."

Walking out to the waiting room, Dr. Reese saw several people waiting. Going to the reception desk, she asked, "Which one is Ms. Webb?"

Smiling the nurse asked, "Which one, the older one or the younger one?"

"Both."

"They're sitting there between the men. Would you believe that this little slip of a girl has that much family around her?"

"That is just what she needs right now." Walking over to the group who were waiting, she asked, "Which one of you is Meagan Webb's mother?"

Juliana, leaning forward in her seat, replied, "I'm Juliana Webb. This lady to my right is her Grandmother, Shirleen Webb."

"Let me introduce myself. My name is Dr. Clara Reese and I'm a psychiatrist."

"How do you fit in to the mix?" asked Josiah.

"Hello, Major Graham. What are you doing here?"

"Meagan is my niece."

"Oh." Getting a chair, she faced them to say, "Well, Dr. Stillman gave Meagan a shot to help her sleep. As soon as they get her settled in a room, Dr. Stillman will meet us there to explain her situation."

"You say she is asleep?" asked Josiah.

"Yes, that is correct. I'll be with all of you so that when she wakes up, I'll be there to help her."

"Oh, wonderful!" sighed Juliana in relief. "There's so much that you don't know."

"Dr. Stillman told me some of what all of you are going through. Rest assured that your secret is safe with me."

"That makes me feel better," said Juliana, plainly relieved.

A few minutes later, a nurse approached Dr. Reese to say, "They have Meagan settled in a room so I'll take you there now if you'd like." Rising, they followed the nurse to Meagan's room. Seeing Meagan lying there so quiet tore at the hearts of those who loved her. They had just gotten seated when Dr. Stillman entered. Going over to stand near Meagan, he looked into the anxious faces of those assembled., "Meagan is going to be all right, but these past eight months have played havoc with her nerves. She nearly had a nervous breakdown. She has got to have some counseling, or she will have one. I have asked Dr. Reese to come here, as she has dealt with people Meagan's age. It wasn't like it was in our day, when life seemed easier. Teenagers have a lot more to deal with than we ever did. I recommend that you get Meagan in to see her as often as Dr. Reese deems it necessary."

"We will," declared Juliana.

"With the situation that you have, I'll gladly come out to your place where Meagan will feel more comfortable, as well as safer."

"Thank you," replied Shirleen. "We'd really appreciate that very much."

"Then since Meagan won't wake up for several hours, I'll return to speak to her then."

"Thank you." replied Juliana.

"You're more than welcome. Together, we'll help Meagan deal with all of this trauma." Rising, she left the room.

Stillman listened to Meagan's heart and checked her pulse. Satisfied that she was all right, he left the family to wait until Meagan woke up.

Chapter 38

Several days later, when Bruce hadn't heard from Nathan White, he tried calling his cell phone. After letting it ring six times, he got voicemail. He left a message, but was growing suspicious. Turning to Crowley, he said, "It's not like White to disappear like this. Something's up."

"Maybe there's no cell phone service where he's camped. Or, he may be setting the trap and can't answer."

"That's possible, but if he hasn't called in after three more days, I want you to find him."

"Why don't I check the Cardston news online?"

"Good thinking," praised Bruce.

Crowley followed Bruce into his office. Pulling up a chair, he watched as Bruce typed into the search engine. He found the newspaper's website and searched through the dates since White's last contact. One article caught his attention and he read it quickly:

Man Mauled by Bear

A New York man was mauled by a wounded female grizzly last night. Reports say he shot the animal several times without killing her. The bear, who appeared to be starving, mauled him. Witnesses said that it was over by the time they could get to him. The man's name is being withheld.

"Well," Bruce said, "that's sure one nasty way to die."

Crowley was furious with Bruce's callous reaction to the loss of his employee. It took every bit of restraint he had to control his temper. Bruce didn't notice the anger that surged through his employee. Crowley thought, *Nathan was an okay guy, who was loyal to you. All you can say is, that's a nasty way to die? Nice to see how much you care about all of us who've been so loyal to you and done your dirty work over the years. If I had my piece on me, I'd do you right here!*

He was pulled out of his thoughts when Bruce said, "It looks like you'll have to go back to Cardston, Vinnie. I know you can get the job done without botching things."

"Thanks for the vote of confidence, boss. If I go back to Cardston, there might be trouble because they've seen me."

"That's true," replied Bruce, thoughtfully. "I'll send Wilson. He's just as good as you. Besides, I need you here to protect me. I'll speak to him today."

Not if I warn him first, you won't. Aloud, he replied snidely, "Whatever."

Bruce was surprised to see it was time for the dinner meal and wondered why Myrtle hadn't called them in to eat. Just as he stood to go investigate, he heard her yell, "Come on, Vinnie, let's eat. I'm starved." Without a word, Vinnie followed Bruce to the dining room.

After they ate, they went back to the living room and Bruce acted like nothing had happened to White. This angered Crowley more than he was ready to admit. He was disgusted with Bruce and it was all that he could do not to punch him in the face. Finally, Crowley said, "I have a terrible headache, boss. I can't concentrate on what you're saying."

"We've both had a busy day. What I have to say can wait 'til morning."

Crowley went up to his room and the pent up anger spewed from him as he paced, smoking one cigarette after another. Crushing out the last one, he prepared for bed.

Meanwhile, Bruce sat in his office thinking about White. "Well, you sure have botched things up for me this time, Nate. Now I'm stuck dealing with Crowley." *I hate Crowley. I'd love to off him, but I need him.* He heard Myrtle walking to her room, and decided to go pay her a visit.

Several days later, Bruce and Crowley went to his office complex. They had no more than gotten there when a man approached and asked, "Bruce Murdock?"

Bruce snarled, "You know I'm Bruce Murdock."

Handing Bruce a huge envelope, he replied, "You've been served."

"What?" Bruce could only stare at the envelope. He stomped and jerked open the door to his personal office, went in and sunk onto the chair in front of his desk. He ripped the envelope open and scanned the documents inside. He was shocked to find that he was being sued by the state of New York for misrepresentation in several legal cases.

Tossing the papers onto the desk, he stood and paced the room. *This is ludicrous! There's absolutely no way they can prove I falsified documents, let alone paid witnesses to lie on the stand.* Pounding his fist on the desk, he yelled, "There's no way they can win this case. Absolutely no way!"

He sat back down and sulked. His secretary's voice came over the intercom, "There's two policemen here to see you, Mr. Murdock."

"Send them in."

A moment later, the officers entered the office. Frank Kessler calmly approached Bruce and handed him a document. "Bruce Murdock, this document declares that from this moment forward you are legally banned from practicing law in the state of New York."

Bruce snatched the document from his hand, fuming. Unruffled, Kessler handed him another legal document, and continued, "This document is a search warrant, giving us the right to confiscate the entire contents of this building. As of this moment, this building is also off limits to you. Please leave now, or we'll be forced to arrest you."

Indignant, Bruce stood and glared at the man, as he shouted, "You can't do that!"

"We can and we are. Step away from the desk and leave."

Feeling helpless for the first time in his life, Bruce complied. He and Crowley left the office, and the police started boxing up the contents in Bruce's office. Just before he got into the car, Bruce saw several officers enter the building and suddenly he didn't feel so cocky anymore.

Crowley was secretly enjoying Bruce's predicament. He didn't stop to think that just because he was associated with Bruce, he was in trouble too.

When Bruce got home, there was a padlock on the gate and two officers were waiting for them. "What's the meaning of this?" Bruce demanded.

"Until further notice, your home and bank accounts have been seized. You need to find other accommodations until further notice."

As Bruce moved away from the gate to get into the car, an officer, told him that he had to turn the car over to them as well. Bruce called for a taxi with his cellphone.

While he was waiting, a stretch limo pulled up to the gate. Before the officers could do anything, two men gunned them down. Two other men grabbed Crowley and Bruce, and shoved them roughly into the back of the limo. Bruce was surprised to see Thomas Wilson was already inside the car. He couldn't help asking, "Are you with them, Wilson?"

"No! They nabbed me a few minutes ago as I was leaving home."

"Shut up!" barked one of the gunmen.

They drove until they were in the Adirondacks. They continued, going up a winding, twisting road until they were far from civilization. The car pulled over to the side of the road, the driver waited for the men to get out, then turned the limo around and drove to a spot that offered good cover.

◀ • ▶

At six a.m., Megan woke up. When she opened her eyes, she didn't recognize her surroundings. Turning to the left, she saw her mother sitting there, sound asleep. She was still holding Meagan's hand. Turning to the right, when saw her grandmother, who was also asleep and holding her other hand.

She heard a soft sound and looked around to see what had made the noise. A beautiful woman moved closer to the bed. At first, Meagan was terrified, but when the woman spoke, her voice was soft and soothing. "It's all right, Meagan."

"Who are you?"

"My name is Dr. Clara Reese."

"Where am I?"

"You're in the hospital. You fainted last night. Apparently you were extremely distraught."

"I fainted?"

Smiling, Dr. Reese replied, "You did, several times in fact."

Hearing voices, Shirleen and Juliana awoke. "You're finally awake," Shirleen said. "Do you feel any better?"

"A little bit, but mostly I'm confused."

"You will be for a little while," replied Dr. Reese, "but as we talk, you'll start to remember what happened."

Juliana squeezed Meagan's hand as she comforted her, "It's all right now. We're all safe, honey."

Looking confused, Meagan asked, "From whom?"

Dr. Reese replied, "Don't worry about that now. We'll explain everything later."

"Okay."

"I'll be right back," reassured Dr. Reese. "I'm going to let the nurse know you're awake."

"What time is it?" asked Meagan, looking around for a clock.

Glancing at her wristwatch, Shirleen replied. "Six o'clock."

"Oh," replied Meagan. "It seems later somehow." She started to scan the room.

"It's to your right, honey," Juliana said.

When she'd closed the door, Shirleen whispered, "I'm worried she might've blocked everything out to cope with her fear."

"That's possible," Dr. Reese said as she came back into the room, "but it could also be that the medication hasn't completely worn off."

Meagan got back in bed just as Dr. Stillman came into the room. "Well, how's my patient this morning?"

"I don't know," replied Meagan. "I can't remember much about how I got here."

"It'll all come back in time. Sometimes, when we're stressed out, our coping mechanism kicks in to shut us down. That's what your body did."

"Then I'm going to be all right?"

"Yes, you are."

Sighing, Megan snuggled further under the cover. "That's good."

"I want to listen to your heart, while the nurse take your blood pressure." Meagan grew still as Dr. Stillman worked on her. Leaning back from the bed, he smiled encouragingly, and said, "Just as I thought. You're going to be fine. If you continue to improve, I'll release you this afternoon. Your blood work shows you're anemic. I'm going to prescribe the same treatment I did for your grandmother. I want you to take the pills faithfully, and for the next three days I want you to stay in bed. That means meals in bed, too."

When Meagan began to protest, Dr. Stillman raised his hand for silence and said, "Either do as you're told and get to go home, or stay here in the hospital where we can make sure. It's your choice."

Sighing in resignation, she said, "Fine. I'll follow orders like a good little soldier." Looking at her mother, she said, "You guys will have to take care of the dogs for me."

"We'll all take turns. It's no problem," declared Juliana.

"I want to see you in three days to see how you're doing," the doctor said. "I'll even make a house call to check on you."

"I'll go batty just lying in bed!" cried Meagan."

"After the first three days, you can get up and walk around, but no strenuous activates. Along with the iron pills, I'm giving you something else to help to calm your jangled nerves."

"Meagan does charcoal sketches," replied Shirleen. "Would it be all right for her to do that while she's resting?"

"Absolutely!" declared Stillman. "Just stop when you feel tired. Rest is the best medicine."

"I see it all now," groaned Meagan. "I'll be living a life of boredom. Just what I don't need."

"Well," calmly replied Dr. Stillman, "it's being bored at home, or being stuck in here."

Shuddering at the thought of staying in the hospital, Meagan replied. "I'll take the boring at home."

Chuckling, Dr. Stillman patted Meagan's hand and said, "I knew you'd see it my way. I'll be back to see you around eleven. If things look good, I'll release you. While you're waiting, ladies, you should go get something to eat. I don't' want you ending up in here with Meagan."

"That's a good idea," replied Shirleen. "It's been a long time since we ate."

Turning to Juliana again, he said, "I want you to come and see me before you take Meagan home. You need a check up, too. That's not a suggestion, that's an order.."

"Okay. I'll be there."

"Good. I'll let my receptionist know that you're coming. See you beautiful ladies later."

When he had left the room, Dr. Reese spoke to Shirleen and Juliana. "If Meagan can stay awake a while longer, I'd like to talk to her for a few minutes. I'd also like to come out to see her every day for at least five days. After that, we'll meet once a week."

Looking at Dr. Reese, Meagan asked her bluntly, "Why do I have to see you?"

"Do you like all the stress you've been living with?"

"No," declared Meagan, as tears sprang to her eyes and slid down her cheeks. "Of course not!"

"Well, when we get together, I'll teach you how to deal with it. We'll also talk about all that is troubling you and why."

When Meagan nearly panicked, Dr. Reese, hastened to add, "Meagan, as a psychiatrist, I keep everything you tell me in the strictest confidence. The only time that doesn't apply is if you've committed a murder. I doubt you're a murderer, so your secrets are safe with me."

"But you don't understand," cried Meagan. "If you help me, then your life is in danger, too."

"Meagan, Dr. Stillman told me what's been happening to you. He told me so I could help you. Otherwise, wild horses couldn't have dragged it out of him." Leaning over to squeeze Meagan's hand, she added, "Believe me when I say your secret is safe with me. Together, we'll get you through this."

"Okay," replied Meagan meekly. "I'll work with you."

"Good girl."

"I have to get home to get a little sleep before I start seeing patients. I'll be out to see you tomorrow. I'll call you with a time once I've checked my schedule. "

"Okay." Meagan waited until the door closed before turning to look at her mother. "Will it really be okay to talk to her about everything?"

"Yes, sweetheart," declared Juliana "You've got to talk to someone before this makes you truly ill. We have to trust her to keep her word, Meagan."

"Your mother's right, Meagan. It's crunch time and we have to have those who can help us on our side. I believe Dr. Reese is here to help."

"I've been feeling so terrible lately. Fear has been my companion longer than I've had Prince or Lady."

"I know," replied Juliana. "He's been with us ever since we left Syracuse. I haven't said anything before now, but the other night, I saw my first angel. I, too, had been having nightmares for days. The angel, a beautiful woman dressed all in white, told me it was going to be all right and that we'd be safe soon. She told me that Bruce and his men wouldn't be able to hurt us anymore and his reign of blood and terror would end soon."

Smiling, Shirleen asked, "Does that mean you believe in angels, too, my dear?"

Grinning, Juliana nodded affirmatively. "Yes, I do."

"It seems there are still many miracles in this life."

"It sure does," agreed Juliana.

"Well, if we're going to have breakfast and get back here to see if Meagan can go home, we'd better shake a leg."

They kissed Meagan and left. They hadn't been gone long, when Meagan fell into a deep, restful sleep. When she awoke again, it was 10:45.

When Juliana and Shirleen returned, they took a seat on each side of her. "How are you feeling, sweetheart?"

"Tired, but a little better."

"You'll be tired for quite a while, honey. Being anemic is not pleasant!"

"Well, once I'm home, I think I'll feel even better."

They were interrupted when Dr. Stillman entered the room. "Well, I see you're looking a little better. Did you get any sleep?"

"Yes, sir, I did. I haven't been awake very long."

"That's great!" Checking her over, he grinned. "Your heart rate is much slower and your blood pressure is back to normal."

"Does that mean that I get to go home?"

"It does." Turning to Juliana, he asked, "Did you get the prescriptions filled?"

"Yes, I did. They're in my purse."

"Well, as soon as the discharge papers have been signed, you can go home."

"Dr. Stillman, since you're coming out to see me, why don't you plan to stay for supper?"

Smiling, Dr. Stillman declared, "I'd be delighted to, Meagan. I've secretly hoped that I'd get invited back for some more of Trudy's scrumptious cooking."

"Then it's a deal," grinned Meagan, feeling pleased. "I want to thank you for taking such good care of me."

"That's my job. It's no big deal."

"Well, it is to me," stated Meagan, emphatically.

"Be good and I'll see you in three days," he said and squeezed her hand before leaving the room.

Once Meagan was home and in bed, her Uncle Josiah came to check on her. "You sure scared this old man! I'm so glad you're going to be fine as hen's teeth soon. You obey that doctor, or you'll have to answer to me."

Laughing, Meagan saluted him smartly, quickly replying, "Yes, sir."

Seeing that he was being teased, he swatted her playfully. "Just see that you do, private."

Laughing happily, Meagan reached out to hug him close a moment. "Thank you for caring about me, Uncle Josiah." Kissing his cheek she added, "I love you so much."

Touched beyond words, Josiah rose and replied, "I love you too, Pet."

When he had left the room, Juliana came in to tuck her in. "When Trudy has supper ready, I'll bring in a tray. Right now, you are to take a nap."

"I won't argue, Momma. I'm so tired I think I could sleep for a week."

Kissing Meagan's cheek, she whispered tenderly, "I love you, daughter mine."

"I love you too, Momma."

"What did the doctor say about you," asked Meagan.

"I have to take things easier, but otherwise I'm doing good. He said my blood work is good, my heart rate is good and my blood pressure is normal. I'm as fit as a fiddle."

"I'm so glad," Sighed Meagan.

Grinning, Juliana said, "Get some sleep and I'll be back with lunch before you know it."

As soon as Juliana left the room, Meagan fell asleep. She didn't wake again until her mother brought in her lunch. "This smell scrumptious, Momma. Trudy outdid herself again."

"Well, enjoy it and I'll be back soon to take the tray."

Meagan, ate every bite of food on her plate, then leaned back to rest. A moment later, Juliana brought her a piece of cherry pie topped with ice cream. She waited until Meagan had eaten it all, then took the plate and helped Meagan get comfortable. "Remember, we all love you," she said as she left the room. "I'll check on you later."

With guns pointed at their backs, Bruce, Crowley and Wilson were forced to walk further into the woods. Bruce, no longer the organized crime kingpin, cried like a baby, showing himself for the coward he was.

As they trudged through the woods, Bruce began to think of his past, because there was no doubt in his mind that he was going to die. He'd hated everyone his whole life. His father, a drunken sot, had abused him and his mother, and when his father beat his mother to death, he killed him. He got off on self-defense and didn't even go to jail. This gave him a taste for blood and a lust for the rush he got when he got his way no matter what he'd done.

He'd been a hit man for Gordon Spielberg's father, who in turn paid for his law school education. To return that favor, Bruce defended all the mobsters who got caught. Gordon was always jealous of Bruce's relationship with his father.

When Gordon married Sarah Clements, he'd watched as Gordon got meaner and became ruthless, calculating, domineering. He'd kill a man for the sport of it then gloat about it. Gordon's Father praised his son highly each time he made bigger decisions, or took greater risks. It was a pleasure to work beside Gordon.

The changes came when Ruth was born. He doted on that child. He confessed to his father and Bruce that he hoped she would someday take his place as leader of the syndicate.

When Ruth became more interested in helping others, something good died in Gordon. As she grew up, it started taking longer for Gordon to make decisions. It was as if Ruth goodness was rubbing off on him. Bruce saw this as a weakness and felt that anything weak had to be eliminated.

When Gordon and his father suggested Bruce should marry Ruth, it infuriated him. He hated her with a passion. However, after a lot of consideration, he decided it was best to stay on the good side of the Spielberg men. When Bruce saw Ruth had no love for him either, he decided it would be fun to marry her and make her life miserable.

Once they were married, he treated her with contempt. When she ran away when she learned she was pregnant, Bruce lost it. It irritated him that she ran, but to know that she had ran to keep him from his child made Bruce look bad. When he got her home, he had raped her repeatedly. She nearly lost the baby because of this, and he regretted his actions.

When Ruth gave birth to a girl instead of a son, he got good and drunk and didn't come home for two days. Nathan White watched the house for him while he was gone, making sure she couldn't leave. Ruth did finally get away and she took Leslie with her.

As he returned to the present, he heard one of the men bellow. "This is far enough!" Stopping, Bruce and his two companions turned to face their assassins. Bruce had always thought he'd live to be an old man. That wasn't going to happen. Three men stood before them, holding machine guns.

Little did they know, just above them, peering down from a huge boulder was a young newlywed couple. They were camping and had been sitting beside their dead file, talking about their future. They heard someone say, "This is far enough." Curious, they looked down and watched in horror as they watched events unfold.

The man who appeared to be the leader handed his gun to the man next to him and said, "Your reign of terror is over, Bruce. You've done more than enough damage. I'm here to avenge the death of my brother's family. You put a hit out on him just because he told he wanted no part of your syndicate. You killed his whole family! You're about to pay dearly for that crime."

"I'm not sorry for taking out your family," Bruce said brazenly.

The man slugged him hard in the face and he fell to the ground with his nose broken and bleeding profusely. "You'll pay for that," Bruce barked.

Smiling, the leader replied, "Don't think so, Brucey. I'm gonna send you right where you belong — hell. But first, you're gonna watch me kill both of your men."

The young woman watching from above put her hand over her mouth to keep from crying out. Her husband put an arm around her, and whispered into her ear, "I think justice is being served here. Let's move back over to the campfire and leave them to it." They could still hear what was happening, but didn't have to watch.

The leader began to speak again, "Vincent Crowley, you're well known for cracking your victims bones before you break their necks. I think it's only fitting to do the same to you."

"No!" screamed Crowley as he turned and tried to run. One of the men shot at his feet and Crowley stopped, but didn't turn around. The leader barked angrily, "Turn around and act like a man you coward!"

Slowly, Crowley turned to face the man. Walking over to Crowley, the leader grabbed his wrist. Before Crowley could pull away, he pulled Crowley's little finger back against his hand and it made a snapping sound. Crowley screamed.

The leader did the same with each finger on that hand. Crowley was going wild, cursing the leader vehemently and trying to strike him with his free hand.

Next, the leader took Crowley's other hand and pushed it hard, backward against his wrist. The bone snapped cleanly in two. Bruce and Wilson , who were being forced to watch, grew physically ill. "Not pretty, is it?" the leader asked. Looking at Crowley, who was writhing in pain, he asked, "How does it feel to be the one on the receiving end, Vinnie boy?"

Crowley's spit into the man's face and screamed, "You can go to—"

He wasn't able to finish because the leader grabbed his other hand and began to give it the same treatment. When that was done, he stepped away and told his men, "Shoot this jerk!" His men filled Crowley full of bullet holes, and when his body stopped twitching the leader turned and asked Wilson, "Did you enjoy the show?"

"You're one sadistic lunatic!"

"Not as sick as you, Thomas Wilson. How many men have you killed? Ten, fifteen, a hundred?"

"Not enough, because you're still walking around."

The leader hit Wilson hard in the stomach, and he bent over double. Next, he connected with his chin, and he was out cold. "Drag him over to that tree and tie him up."

When the men started to obey, Bruce saw his opportunity to get away. He'd only gone one step, when bullets sent dust up around his feet. "The next time to try that, I'll shoot you in the leg so you can't run."

Knowing the man meant what he said, Bruce remained where he was. Once Wilson was tied to the tree, the men picked up their machine guns as the leader went to a nearby creek, filled his hat with water and tossed it into Wilson's face.

Gasping, Wilson regained consciousness. "Got any last words before we turn your lights out permanently?"

"Only to tell you that you can go to—" His words were cut off when the leader yelled, "Fire!" Bruce's body began to quake as he saw Wilson's body convulsing from the impact of the bullets. Then, just as suddenly as it started, it was over.

Looking at Bruce, the leader asked, "Was that thrilling enough for you, Brucey boy?" Silence was Bruce's answer. Smiling sardonically, the leader replied, "Well, guess the cat's got your tongue. Doesn't matter, 'cause now it's your turn. Before I ship you off to hell, there's something you should know. That man to my far left is Tucker O'Malley. He was a good friend of Leslie's. She told him that you beat her mother so badly she was afraid you were gonna kill her. Tuck started watching you and vowed you'd never beat your wife again. When they ran away, he was tickled pink."

Growing irate, Bruce looked at Tuck and asked, "You've been watching me?"

"Sure have," the man said and smiled. "I was the one who shot up your place and took pot shots at you when you were coming out of that escort service."

"Why didn't you just kill me?"

"I didn't want you dead, I wanted to leave a calling card. I wanted you to know we knew all about you."

"Well, if you think you scared me, you didn't. You just ticked me off."

"Then you're even more stupid than we thought," replied the leader.

"You know me too, Bruce," said the man in the middle.

Hearing the man's voice, Bruce squeaked, "You're one of the drug lords I deal with. Nelson Richards?"

"Dealt with — past tense," corrected the man. "After today, I'm free of you and your greed."

"Tie him to that tree behind him," ordered the leader. When he was tied securely, they returned to pick up their weapons and aimed them at Bruce. The leader asked, "Any last words, scumbag?"

Shaking his head no, Bruce began to whimper. Feeling nothing but loathing, the leader aimed his gun at Bruce and yelled, "Shoot him, boys!" They started firing at Bruce's head and continued all the way down his torso.

When the shooting stopped, the husband peeked over the ridge. He was just in time to see the men cutting Bruce down. He was no longer recognizable. The men, who were covered in blood by this time, removed their clothes and went to the creek to wash up. They buried their clothes under some rocks and called the limo driver to bring the car around. They had clothes in the trunk, and when they were dressed, they got into the limo and drove away.

On the hill the campers were quietly discussing what had happened. "Oh, Jason, you realize that was my Uncle Todd down there. I had no idea he was so evil."

"Neither did I" confessed Jason. "I can't go back to face him now that we know."

"Neither can I," Patricia said. "What are we going to do?"

"We're going home to my place. We'll stay there until our honeymoon's over. While we're there, we'll pack everything, then tell your mother I got another job and we're moving. Then we're gonna hightail it out of there."

"What about my mother? If I leave, there's no one to look after her except Uncle Todd."

"Let's see if she'll go with us. But if she wants to stay, we can't make her go."

Kissing Jason, Patricia replied. "Thank you, darling."

"You're welcome."

Jason and Patricia waited another hour to make sure that no one was around before packing up their camp. They made sure nothing was left behind to incriminate them, then got into the car and headed to Jason's place.

When it came time for them to leave after their honeymoon, they asked Patricia's mother to go with them and she said yes. They helped her pack her things and were ready to leave, when Patricia's mother, Hilary Monson, said, "I should call Todd and tell him what's going on."

"Don't, Mom," begged Patricia. "There's something you don't know. Uncle Todd's a bad man." They told her what had happened up in the mountains.

"Oh, that changes everything," sobbed Hilary. "As far as I'm concerned, my brother died today." Wiping her nose, she added, "He can never know where we are, Patricia."

"We know that," replied Patricia. "That's why we're leaving. We don't want anything to do with him."

Hilary began to sob brokenly, and they did their best to comfort her.

They stopped by the bank on their way out of town, and Hilary withdrew all her money and closed her account. Jason and Patricia did the same. With that done, they got into the U-Haul and headed for Colorado. They planned to find a remote home in the mountains, where they wouldn't be easily traced.

Chapter 39

Four days after Meagan's return from the hospital, she was sitting on the couch reading. She'd taken a shower and was ready for her day. Reading helped to pass the time. Looking up, she was surprised to see it was nearly noon. Bored, she put the marker in her book and walked outside. Prince and Lady got up to go with her. They'd been stuck to her like glue since she got back.

Walking out into the bright sunlight felt wonderful. Two days earlier, Jeff had gone to the nursery to get a marble bench for the porch. When the ground thawed sufficiently in the spring, they planted climbing roses along the porch. Across the road, near the bank of the hill, Jeff had made a flowerbed for perennials. They'd also bought several hanging baskets to decorate the porch. It made for a picture-perfect look.

Meagan went to sit on a bench near the flowerbed so she could enjoy nature. It was late July and the garden was coming along nicely. The cool breeze caressing her skin was comforting.

For some reason Meagan thought of the night the grizzly attacked Nathan White. Dr. Reese had gone over this with her. She'd been so sad when the two orphaned bear cubs died.

When Prince raised his head to look toward the house, Meagan looked too and saw Shirleen coming toward her. She couldn't believe how incredibly beautiful her grandmother was. "What are you doing out here in this gorgeous sunshine?"

"The same thing as you — enjoying the beauty around me." She sat down and asked, "Are you feeling better today, honey?"

"Yes, but I'm bored. Being out here, watching nature helps a little."

"Being so tired is hard, isn't it?"

"Yes, it is. Sometimes I want to get out and do things, but the exhaustion strikes me down. I can't wait till I'm back to normal."

"How long have you been having trouble sleeping?"

"A little over two months or so."

"Why didn't you tell us so? We could've helped you."

Tears began to form in Meagan's eyes, as she replied, "Because, I knew you'd worry. I also knew you and Momma were just as scared as I was. I didn't want to bother you with my problems."

"Oh, honey," Shirleen said tenderly, "don't you know by now that we're all in this mess together? We have to be there for each other."

"I know, but I couldn't tell you about the nightmares and the fear just became my constant companion. Giving me Prince and Lady was the greatest gift ever. They've been more healing than anything. Taking care of them helped to keep me from thinking about Dad finding us."

"Joseph, my angel, told me the dogs would help you. I'm so glad he told me to give them to you. He also told me the dogs would be a blessing for me too. Prince always knows when I'm feeling down. He comes over and lays his head in my lap and looks up at me with such love. That always makes my heart feel lighter."

"Momma doesn't seem to pay much attention to them," sighed Meagan.

"That's not true. When she thinks she's by herself, she starts talking to them. Once, I thought that she was talking to you, then I heard her tell Lady she was glad she was there. I peeked into the room and saw her petting Lady, and hugging her close as she sat there crying."

"Oh, I'm glad they've been helpful for her too," cried Meagan.

"I've also caught Trudy feeding them little tidbits from the table, and talking to them like they're people."

Meagan laughed at the thought of Trudy doing this.

"A few days ago, I was working in the garden, when Prince and Lady bounded over to get some attention from Jeff. He played fetch with them for a long time. I think the dogs have been the best medicine for all of us!"

Looking at her watch, she saw that it was time for lunch. "Let's go have some lunch. Don't forget, you have an appointment with Dr. Reese this afternoon."

"I know," sighed Meagan. "Sometimes, talking about what I'm feeling, makes me tired."

"That's because you're unburdening yourself."

"I sure hope so. I'm tired of carrying all of this around with me."

As they rose to go into the house, Meagan grinned and said, "It was so good to see Dr. Stillman yesterday. He seemed to like Trudy's cooking."

Smiling in return, Shirleen replied, "Yes, he did. You know, he's one really great doctor and a wonderful friend."

"I've learned something about Dr. Stillman," beamed Meagan.

"What's that?" asked Shirleen, guardedly.

"He uses that gruff voice to cover up his soft heart. He's one of the sweetest, kindest men I've ever known. I've also learned that when Jeff is silent, it isn't that he's being antisocial, he is taking it all in so that he can think about it all later. He's a wonderful man, too. I'm so excited that you're marrying him."

"You're perceptive, Meagan. I'm glad I'm marrying him, too. For the first time in my life I've found true love."

"That makes me so happy, Grandma."

They went into the kitchen where Trudy had just finished making lunch. Soon after, Josiah, Holmquist and Black came in as well. They joked around with Meagan and she appeared to be back to her old self and everyone was relieved.

When the meal was over, Meagan went to take a nap, while the men went back to work on the two damaged rooms upstairs. The women cleaned up the kitchen so that Trudy could go see Henry, while Juliana went to work on a painting.

Shirleen began working on her needlepoint project as she sat in the living room. An hour later, she'd completed the project and left it on the stand when she went outside to walk around. Lady and Princess were with Meagan, so Prince went with her.

Absently stroking the dog's head, she went to the garden to do a little weeding. Jeff was in the corn patch and didn't see her at first. Shirleen went to weed the carrots and looked up to see Jeff coming toward her. "Hi, sweetheart," he said. After kissing her passionately, he whispered into her ear. "I can hardly wait 'til we're married so that I can show you just how much I love you."

"That sounds promising."

"Let me show you a little sample of what's to come." Claiming her lips, he kissed her until she could hardly breathe. Lifting his head, he whispered huskily, "Does that meet with your approval?"

"Uh-huh," she sighed.

Chuckling at her awed response, he kissed again. Releasing her, he said, "If I don't quit, I won't be able to stop myself."

"Who says that I want you to stop?" giggled Shirleen. Kissing him quickly, she moved away.

Raising his eyebrows, Jeff laughed lightly and said, "You little minx."

"If I keep busy, perhaps I can behave myself," Shirleen said as she went back to weeding the carrots.

They worked in the garden for an hour. When Jeff finished what he was doing, he joined Shirleen at the opposite end of the carrots and worked toward her. They got the carrots done just as Meagan came out to join them.

"Hello, honey," Shirleen said, kissing her cheek. "Did you sleep well?"

"Like a log. I'm just getting a little exercise before I start reading again."

"It sure is good to see you doing so well," declared Jeff.

"While the three of us are together," said Shirleen, "I have a question to ask you, Meagan."

"You do?" It was obvious that Meagan was instantly curious.

"I do," replied Shirleen. "I wondered if you'd be my bridesmaid when I marry Jeff."

"Me?" cried Meagan.

"Yes, you. I want you to be part of my wedding. Juliana is going to help me get ready and Josiah is going to give me away. When I told Juliana that I wanted you to be my bridesmaid, she thought it would be a nice thing to do." Looking at Meagan, she asked again, "Would you be my bridesmaid?"

She grabbed her grandmother in a bear hug, and said excitedly, "Oh yes, Grandma. I'd love to do it!"

Shirleen returned the hug, as she replied, "Thank you, honey."

Jeff, who was beaming his pleasure at the decision, asked, "Can I get in on the hugs, too?"

"Of course," grinned Meagan. Wrapping her arms around Jeff's neck, she hugged him close.

"You know, kitten, soon you'll be my granddaughter. When that day comes, I'm going to be the proudest man on earth. I'll not only have the most beautiful, elegant woman as my wife, but I'll also have the best granddaughter in the world."

"Thank you, Grandpa Jeff."

Linking her arm through Meagan's, Shirleen headed toward the house. "Let's get you out of the afternoon sun, honey. It's pretty hot out here."

They were nearing the house, when Dr. Reese pulled into the drive. As she got out of the car greetings were exchanged. "Come on into the house," invited Meagan. "We can talk in the kitchen."

"Lead the way," acknowledged Reese.

For the next hour, Meagan unloaded all of her pent up emotions. She felt much better when she was done. The last thing they talked about was her fear that her father would kill her mother and grandmother. "Dr. Reese, what if he forces me to marry someone I don't love, like Momma and Grandma had to do?"

I don't think you have to worry about that. All the caring people around you would make sure that never happened.."

"Oh, I hope you're right!"

"Why don't you just take each day as it comes, and find joy and peace in everything you do."

As she came in, Trudy greeted Meagan, who was sitting on the couch reading with both dogs curled around her feet.

"How's Henry doing, Trudy?"

"He's doing great! Come sit in the kitchen with me while I prepared supper. I need some company."

As she followed Trudy to the kitchen, she said, "Grandma's upstairs overseeing the bedroom projects and Momma's working on a painting done for Dr. Reese. She told Momma she wanted to put it in her office so it would advertise her beautiful work."

"That's wonderful news," responded Trudy. "She's a talented lady."

"She sure is. Every time I look at the painting she did of Grandma, I feel just like I'm looking at her. Have you seen what she's making for Grandma's wedding present?"

"No, I didn't know that she was painting something for her."

"It's a picture of our home and property."

"Oh, she'll love that," replied Trudy.

"This house has kept us all safe from my father, and that makes it special to all of us." Growing thoughtful, she added, "Trudy, I hate Daddy and all that he stands for. Do you think I'll ever be able to fully forgive him?"

Trudy paused a moment before replying, "Your father is not just evil; I think he's mentally ill."

"He has to be mentally ill to be able to kill a man just for the pure pleasure of it."

"That's true," agreed Trudy. "You can't hate someone who's mentally ill; there's no logic in it. Hating someone like that is a waste of time and energy. I believe the time will come when he'll have to pay for his crimes. When that happens, you'll be able to move forward. Can you ever forgive him? In time, I believe you will because you're a good person."

"Thanks, Trudy. That makes me feel better."

They were interrupted when Shirleen came in. She was positively glowing. "In about an hour, the two rooms upstairs will be completely refinished. They're putting the floor down in the last room right now."

"That's good news, Grandma," Meagan said.

"Now we need to pick out drapes when we go to town. Jeff promised to put them up for us."

"We'll also have to decide what furniture to use. There's all that stuff in the storage units, and I'm sure we can use some of it. The rest we'll sell."

"That means that we'll be having another Christmas in August," cried Meagan.

"That's right."

Clapping her hands together excitedly, Meagan replied, "Oh, that is going to be so wonderful!"

After the evening meal, everyone settled down to watch the news. At first there wasn't anything of interest, then the announcer mentioned Syracuse.

"*Today, in Syracuse, New York, two police officers, Harvey Bernstein and Humphrey Taylor, were gunned down in front of the prominent Syracuse lawyer Bruce Murdock. Police had confiscated Murdock's files earlier today as part of an ongoing investigation and officers were posted at the mansion to prevent Murdock from entering.*

"*An eyewitness said a limo drove up to the estate and was stopped by the officers as they were speaking to Murdock and an associate, Vincent Crowley. The occupants of the limo shot the officers, killing them both, then forced Murdock and Crowley into the limo.*

"As an update to this story, hikers discovered three dead bodies. Todd Hobart, Nelson Richards and Tucker O'Malley were arrested for these murders. The dead men have been identified as local Syracuse residents. As soon as we receive further news, we'll let you know who these men are. "

"Do you think it's Bruce?" asked Shirleen.

"It looks hopeful," said Josiah, "but we need to wait until there's absolute proof."

"You're right," responded Shirleen.

Josiah's cell phone rang. It was Frank Kessler. "Hey, what's up? You got more information on Bruce Murdock?

"That's why I'm calling."

"I'm listening."

"Did you see the news tonight?"

"We just saw it. Know who the dead men are?"

"Sure do. None other than Bruce Murdock, Vincent Crowley and Thomas Wilson."

"Yes!"

"It seems Todd Hobart wanted vengeance for the murder of his brother and his family. Murdock put a hit out on Martin Hobart because he wouldn't join his faction. Nelson Richard was one of the drug lords Bruce was extorting and Tucker O'Malley was Martin Hobart's best friend."

"What about Myrtle Lawson? I met her when I went to close the real estate deal with Murdock. Was she part of Bruce's gang?"

"No, she was the witness who saw it all go down. She told us she hated Murdock and had been trying to figure out how to quit without ending up dead. She told us she was going to leave town as soon as the trial is over. We have her in protective custody."

"That's a good deal for her then."

"Yeah. Just before Murdock bit the big one, he paid her a month's salary. She'll have something to keep her going until she gets moved."

"I'm really glad about that," said Josiah. Pausing a moment, he asked, "Frank, what happens to Ruth Murdock's things?"

"They'll be released as soon as the investigation's over. Do you know what happened to Sarah, Ruth and Leslie?"

"Yes, I do."

"Are they all right?"

"Yes."

"Why'd they disappear?"

"Bruce was going to force Leslie to marry someone she loathed, so they ran. Knowing Gordon and Bruce would put a hit out on them, they've been hiding ever since."

"Thank God they're safe. If you know where they are, tell them to lay low for a while until this garbage with Todd Hobart is over."

"If I see them, I'll tell them."

"Take care and I'll let you know when it is all over."

When he ended the call, Josiah turned to the anxiously waiting group. "That was Frank Kessler. Bruce Murdock, Vincent Crowley and Thomas Wilson were the three dead men they found in the Adirondacks. Frank said for you to lay low until the trial's over."

Throwing her arms around her mother's neck, Meagan began to cry with relief. When she had gained control, she said, "We never have to look over our shoulders again!"

"You're right, honey," declared Shirleen. "Now we can officially start over."

Juliana, who had been silently holding Meagan as she sobbed, was rendered speechless. Her mind was on another matter. She knew that Tim loved her as much as loved him. Now that Bruce was dead, they could finally make it official. *That is if he's as serious as I am. I'll think about that later.*

They heard a car pull into the driveway, and Josiah, out of habit, went to see who it was. Seeing Tim, he smiled and asked, "You saw the news didn't you?"

"Yes, I did. I came up to see if you knew more details."

Tim came inside and Josiah filled him in on his conversation with Frank Kessler. He saw hope in Tim's eyes as he turned to look at Juliana. She was watching him cautiously with the same look in her eyes.

"Tim, Juliana, it's no secret how you feel about each other. Why don't you go for a walk and talk?"

Tim walked over and took Juliana's hand. "I think your mother has a marvelous idea. Come on, you beautiful woman. Let's go have a serious talk about our future."

Tim helped her into a light jacket and they slipped out into the warm night. They sat on a bench in the flower garden. "Juliana, I love you, but until now I never dared to hope that I could do anything official about it."

Juliana put a hand on his mouth to silence him, then kissed him lightly on the lips. With a moan, he grabbed her and gave her a kiss filled with all of the love he had in his heart.

Stepping back, yet continuing to hold her hands, he asked, "Tell me I'm not dreaming."

"You're not dreaming, Tim. I love you. I think I fell in love with you when we were taking care of the wood. Your kindness touched something in my heart and at some point friendship turned to love. "

"I have waited long enough to make you mine. I don't want a long engagement. I want to make you my wife as soon as possible."

"Before I say anything, there are three people who have to give you their permission. Once you get that, I'll give you my answer."

"Okay, I'll ask Josiah, your mother and Meagan, but if they say no I don't know what I'll do."

Laughing, Juliana replied, "You'll be fine. Go ask them already."

When they came back into the house, Tim asked, "Josiah, Shirleen, Meagan, could I see you in the kitchen, please?"

"Oh, dear," teased Meagan. "Are we going to be arrested or something?"

"Or something," grinned Tim.

"Then let's get this over with before we die of curiosity," mumbled Josiah.

Tim followed them into the kitchen and while they were getting seated, he paced the room nervously. Once they were seated, Tim looked from Shirleen, to Josiah and finally over to Meagan. Taking a deep breath, he plunged in. "Meagan, I have come to treasure you dearly. I want you to know that I love your mother with all of my heart and soul. May I have permission to marry her just as soon as it is at all possible? I promise you that I'll never treat her with anything but the deepest respect and I'll cherish her always." Tim watched Meagan closely, fearful that she would say no.

"Does she love you in return, Tim?"

"Yes, she does. I don't know what I ever did to earn her love, but I'm very grateful that she does. At first she was going to tease him, but seeing the love for her mother in his eyes, she grinned. Suddenly, she nodded her head affirmatively and replied, "Yes, I give my consent for you to marry my mother."

"Josiah may I have your permission to marry your niece, Juliana?"

"Yes, you have my blessing to do so."

Turning to look at Shirleen, he started to ask her, but she quickly said, "I most assuredly give my permission, Tim."

"Do you have any objections to my marrying her just as soon as we can make the arrangements?"

"I have a suggestion," replied Shirleen.

"You do?"

"Yes, but it is up to the two of you to decide."

"I'm listening."

"Trudy and I are going to have a double wedding. Why don't we speak to Henry and Trudy to see if they would go along with making it a triple wedding?"

"Do you think that Juliana would go along with it?"

"Let's go find out."

They went to the living room and saw Juliana sitting nervously in the chair by the fireplace. Tim walked over to take her hand, and said, "We need to talk, so please come with me." Juliana allowed herself to be led back outside.

Silently, they walked back over to the bench in the flower garden. Wrapping his arms around her, he said happily, "They've all given me their blessings." He reached into his pocket and took out a small jewelry box, then got down on one knee. He opened the box and asked, "Juliana Webb, will you do me the honor of being my wife?"

Tears ran down Juliana's face as she gazed into the eyes of the man that she loved. "Yes," she replied breathlessly. "I'll marry you."

Sliding the ring onto her finger, he rose to kiss her with passion. A few minutes later, he told her what her mother had suggested. "What do you think?"

"I love it. Getting married on the same day as my mother would be so fitting somehow."

"Then let's go tell them." Together, hand in hand, they walked back into the house and Tim said, "We want to make this a triple wedding, if Trudy and Henry agree."

"I'd love that," Trudy said, "but we'd better check with Henry."

Shirleen called Theodore's cell number, and anxiously waited for him to answer. When he answered, she said, "Theodore, this is Shirleen. Is it too late for a visit? Wee need to talk to you all and Henry.

"Come on over. We'll be waiting for you."

"See you in a few."

The eight of them piled into three cars and headed down to the Brooks residence.

Theodore met them at the door and invited them in. Henry and Melinda joined them, and Josiah told them the news that Frank Kessler had given him.

"Bruce and his two cohorts are really dead?" Henry asked. "I can't say I'm sorry about that. Actually, I'm relieved."

"Well, because he's dead," continued Josiah, "Tim and Juliana want to get married. They thought maybe instead of a double wedding, perhaps it could be a triple wedding." He looked at Henry to see how he reacted to the idea, and was relieved to see he was calm. "What do you think, Henry?"

Henry turned to Trudy and asked, "Are you okay with this?"

"I love these two women like they're my sisters. If it's all right with you, I think it's a great idea."

Smiling, Henry said, "Then I let's do it."

"We'll go to town tomorrow to get a wedding dress for Juliana," Shirleen said. Turning to face her daughter and granddaughter, she added, "I want to approach you all about something I've been thinking about for a long time."

"Okay. Shoot," Juliana said.

"When I marry Jeff, I don't want the name of Spielberg associated with me in any way. I'm sure you feel the same way about the name Murdock, Juliana. What about you, Meagan?

"No way!"

"How would the two of you feel about going to a lawyer and permanently changing our last names to Webb? That way, when we fill out the marriage certificates we can use our legal names."

"Oh, Grandma, I'd like that," agreed Meagan.

"So would I," affirmed Juliana.

"Henry, would you and Trudy be a witness to this transaction?"

"I'd be honored," replied Trudy."

"Me too," stated Henry.

"Are you going to change your first names too," asked Josiah.

Shirleen replied, "My given name was Sarah — I didn't have a middle name — so I'd like to change my name to Sarah Shirleen Webb."

"My given name was Ruth Ann, but I'd like to change my full name to Juliana Rose Webb."

"I want to change my to Meagan Rose Webb.

"Those are all beautiful names," declared Melinda.

"I say change them," said Josiah.

"So do I," grinned Henry.

"Then we'll find a lawyer tomorrow and make it happen," cried Shirleen.

"I know of a great Lawyer," said Theodore. His name's Joel Cline. He's the one who helped us with the adoptions. I'll get you his number."

Chapter 40

Shirleen awoke to the ringing of the phone. She rose to slip into her robe and slippers then went to answer it, but as she came out of her bedroom, she heard someone talking. From the sound of things, they were growing very excited. Becoming concerned, Shirleen rushed toward the living room. She was just in time to see Juliana hanging up the phone. "Momma, Melinda has gone into labor."

"She had another month to go before the twins are due," cried Shirleen.

"I know," agreed Juliana, "but she has been in hard labor for most of the night. Theodore just called to say they're at the hospital and Dr. Stillman is with her. She is hemorrhaging, so they're afraid that the twins are in some kind of danger."

"What does Theodore want us to do?" asked Shirleen in concern.

"He was wondering if we could go to their house to get Henry and take him to the hospital. He didn't have time to get Henry ready, as he was helping Melinda."

"Let me get dressed and alert Trudy."

As Meagan rushed to her room, Shirleen hurried upstairs to knock on Trudy's door. "Trudy, are you awake?"

"Yes, I'm nearly dressed. Give me another minute and I can come to the door."

"I'll wait out here, but please hurry. There's an emergency."

"I will."

"Going to knock on Jeff's door, Shirleen called, "Jeff, are you awake?"

"I sure am." Opening the door, he asked, "What's up?"

"Melinda has gone into premature labor and it's bad. She is hemorrhaging, which has put the twins into some kind of danger."

"That's not good!"

Coming out of her room, Trudy asked, "What is the emergency, Shirleen?"

Filling her in, Shirleen added, "Theodore wants us to go get Henry and take him to the hospital. He didn't have time to help Henry, as he had to help Melinda."

"How soon do you want to leave?" asked Borton.

"Just as soon as I can get change," declared Shirleen.

"All right. I'll get the van out of the garage while everyone is getting ready."

"Thank you, darling." Kissing him soundly upon the lips, Shirleen rushed back to her room to dress quickly.

Five minutes later, they were on their way to get Henry. When they arrived, Jeff went in to help the nurse get Henry ready. Soon they were speeding to town. Suddenly, they heard a siren behind them. "Oh, great," murmured, Shirleen. Just what we don't need ... a ticket for speeding."

"Well," grinned Borton, as he pulled over to the side of the road. "We were speeding."

"I know," replied Shirleen. "But it was for a good reason."

Tim came up to the van, wearing a huge grin. "This isn't good, pulling my future family over for speeding. What is going on that has you speeding down the road so fast?"

"Melinda Brooks went into premature labor and it's bad," declared Shirleen. "We're trying to get Henry there as fast as we can so that he can be with Theodore during this situation."

"I know about the situation with the Brooks'. I pulled them over too. When Theodore told me want was happening, I gave them police escort to the hospital. I'll do the same for you."

"Thank you," replied Borton in relief."

Pulling out in front of their car, Tim turned on his siren and the two cars sped toward the hospital. Pulling into the parking lot, they turned off the engine. Borton and Tim got Henry into his wheelchair. While they went into the hospital, Tim went back to work.

When they got to the waiting room, a nurse came to see what was needed. Henry told her, "I'm the brother-in-law of Melinda Brooks. Can you tell me what is happening to her and the babies?"

"They're in surgery at this time," she replied. She has lost so much blood that they're taking the twins by caesarian."

"How long ago was that," asked Henry.

"About twenty minutes ago." She was about to speak when another nurse came to speak to her. Together, they rushed to another room.

Growing anxious, Henry said, "Something must be wrong for them to rush off like that."

As the minutes ticked away, those awaiting news, grew very concerned. Finally, when they were about to give into their tears, the nurse returned to say, "Melinda is in recovery, so in about an hour she will be wheeled back to her room."

Feeling exasperated, Henry asked, "What about the twins?"

"They're holding their own, but it doesn't look good. They have been placed in an incubator until their breathing gets better. This is a precautionary measure until we know how they'll do."

Growing a little impatient, Henry leaned forward in his chair to ask, "What is the sex of these infants?"

"I'm sorry. In telling you about their condition, I guess I thought I had told you that they're both girls."

Meagan grinned as she said, "Poor Theodore! He has been out numbered by girls ... five to two."

Suddenly, Henry started to laugh. Finally, gaining control, he replied, "That's a fact, Meagan."

"The nurse continued, "When they went in to take the children, it seems that there was a tear in the uterus, so they were forced to do an immediate hysterectomy. They nearly lost her on the operating table. However, she is improving."

Looking around for Theodore, Shirleen asked, "Where is her husband?"

"In the chapel."

"Where is that?" asked Shirleen.

"I'll show you where it is." Without another word the nurse started off. They quickly fell in with her.

When they got to the chapel, Theodore was coming out. Seeing Henry and the others, he sighed in relief. "You are all a sight for sore eyes."

Placing a hand gently on his arm, Juliana asked, "How are you holding up, Ted?"

"Relieved." As they started back to the waiting room, Theodore continued, "Everything seemed to be going well with the cesarean, when all of a sudden, Melinda coded on us. They kicked me out of there. That was the last time I saw her. I was in the chapel praying for her when the nurse came in to tell me that she was in recovery and the twins were holding their own, but were in incubators because of their breathing problems. I had stayed in the chapel praying for them, when Dr. Stillman came in to tell me that Melinda's uterus had to be removed. She will never be able to have other children."

"The nurse told us that too," said Henry.

"I'm so sorry, Theodore," said Shirleen.

Trudy, whose hand was resting lightly on Henry's shoulder, replied what the others were thinking, "At least Melinda and the twins are doing okay."

"We hope the twins are going to be okay," replied Henry.

"I have to believe that they are," Theodore said in agony.

"We'll keep them in our prayers," Shirleen assured him.

An hour later, a nurse came to tell them that Melinda was back in her room. They went back to the room to be with Melinda as she woke up. Seeing Theodore, she asked, "How are the twins?"

"They're holding their own."

"What are they, boys, girls, or one of each?"

"Two beautiful girls who look just like their mother."

"Girls?" When Theodore nodded his head, Melinda grew thoughtful, as a smile slowly spread across her face. "Oh, darling, that means that you and Henry are outnumbered six to four. Can the two of you handle that?"

"You bet," declared Theodore.

"I have to think about that one," replied Henry, teasingly.

Seeing that Melinda was growing sleepy, they all left her room.

"We'll leave you to be here with Melinda. If we can be of any other service, please let us know and we'll help you any way that we can."

"Thank you," replied Theodore.

"Thank you too for coming to get me to bring me here to the hospital," replied Henry.

"You're welcome," replied Shirleen.

"Would you mind staying with us, Trudy?"

"When she turned to look at Shirleen, Shirleen told her, "Please stay. "We'll be back to get you later this afternoon."

"What about the meals," asked Trudy.

"We're big girls, Trudy North, so we can get the meals just fine."

"Thank you for your thoughtfulness," responded Trudy.

"Thank you for allowing my girl to stay with me, Shirleen. "We need her to be with us."

"Happy to oblige,"

Jeff, who had remained silent, replied, "You two just hang in there, as things have a way of working themselves out."

"Thank you, Jeff." replied Theodore.

A few minutes later the little group left to go home. As they got to the parking lot, Shirleen asked, "Since we're here in town, is there anything anyone needs to get before we go home?"

"Not that I can think of right off of the top of my head," replied Juliana.

"I don't either," replied Meagan.

"I have a good idea," said Borton.

"What's that," asked Shirleen.

"Let's get some chicken, salads, rolls and other items from the deli," suggested Borton. "That way, we can have a picnic." I don't know about the rest of you, but I'm not ready to go home just yet."

"That sounds wonderful, agreed Meagan. Ever since Uncle Josiah, Mark and David went back to their own homes, it is so boring around there."

"We'll go back to the house to get the dogs. I know a beautiful spot to have our picnic," said Jeff.

◀ • ▶

Two weeks later, Theodore and Melinda brought their twins home from the hospital. They were doing well after the scare at their birth, and Melinda was back doing what she could for all seven children.

A few days later, Shirleen called to ask if she could come for a visit.

An hour later, Shirleen's family was at their door.

"We don't want to stay too long so that we don't tire Melinda out."

"She'll be right out. She's taking care of the twins right now." Motioning to the couch and stuffed chairs, he said, "Make yourselves comfortable."

When they were all seated, he went to get Melinda and Henry.

Trudy was excited to see Henry walk into the living room. "You do that so well," she said.

"Thank you. It feels so good to walk again."

Coming out of the nursery, Melinda smiled in greeting. "I've been wanting to talk to all of you about the wedding."

"We didn't want to rush you," explained Juliana. "We wanted to make sure you had completely recovered first."

"Well, it will be October before we know it and then winter will set in again."

"To be honest," began Shirleen, "we've been pretty busy."

"Trudy told us all about that when she came to visit me at the hospital. She also told me that you went on a spur of the moment picnic."

"We did," Jeff said. "We went to a beautiful meadow on my property. There's a little stream with lots of trees surrounding it. We spent the whole day getting to know each other better."

"I'm glad that you were able to get away for a while," said Henry.

"We haven't been anywhere else other than here or to town for supplies," explained Shirleen. "It was good to go someplace new, even if it was still on the property."

"Prince and Lady had more fun than we did. They chased squirrels to their heart's content. They were so tired when we got home that they slept all night."

"Say," said Meagan, "we'd like to know what names you've decided on for the new babies."

"We named them, Linda Marie and Leslie Meagan," Melinda said.

"Oh," was all that Meagan could say.

"Linda is my grandmother's name. Marie came from Annabelle's mother. Leslie Meagan is named after you, Meagan. You've done so much to help us get settled in. This is our way of thanking you."

"I'm honored. Thank you."

Growing thoughtful, as she looked at Shirleen, Juliana and Trudy and asked, "How do you feel about having your weddings the third week of October? That should give you ample time to finish your canning projects."

"That sounds like a good idea," agreed Shirleen. "How do the rest of you feel about it?"

Trudy looked at Henry to see what he thought. "We can wait that long," agreed Henry.

"I'll need to call Tim before I commit, just in case he doesn't want to wait," replied Juliana.

"Why don't you give him a call now so we can start planning?" suggested Melinda.

Juliana grinned and got out her cell phone and went into the other room for some privacy. When she came back, she said, "Tim wasn't happy that he'd have to wait, but he agreed."

Shirleen looked at Jeff and asked, "How do you feel about waiting, darling?"

"I'm with everyone else. That sounds like a fine plan."

Kissing him lightly on the lips, Shirleen said, "Thank you for being so sweet."

"I'll have the men start working on the trellis and other decorations, while you finish up the canning," replied Melinda

"Sounds good," said Trudy.

Taking a deep breath, Jeff asked, "I don't want to be a wet blanket, but have you heard anything further about going to New York to testify?"

"Yes, I have," replied Henry. "Judge Smith, oh she's Judge Cline now, came to see me a few days ago. When Bruce Murdock was murdered it meant it was no longer necessary for me to testify.

"That's wonderful," cried Trudy in relief. "I felt like you would've been in danger if you went back."

"I know," replied Henry. "I'm relieved, too."

"Josiah came out to see us last night," Shirleen said. "He said that Frank Kessler called him to tell him what was happening with the case against the crime figures."

Shirleen continued, "It seems that Charles Abram, with the help of Frank Kessler and Fred Holmes, poured over every document in Gordon's files. They not only have the names of every man in Gordon and also Bruce's employ, but also a list of all of the crimes they committed. There's now another faction that's been fighting against Bruce and Gordon's syndicate."

"Does that mean they'll go after those men as well?"

"Yep. The crime boss of the other faction is a woman named Katherine Mortenson. They call her Momma Kathy. Captain Abram showed the information to Frank Kessler and Fred Holmes. Josiah said that Mr. Kessler described her to him. When he told me what she was like, it made me shiver. Josiah said Kathy was tall, with a huge gut. She walked around as if she owned the world. Kessler told Josiah that she was a terrible braggart, who not only manipulated those who worked for her, but she was conniving and dictatorial as well. If you cross Momma Kathy, it means sudden death. She rules her faction with an iron club."

"Oh," shivered Trudy, "she sounds downright evil."

"When I said the same thing to Josiah, he confessed to having said the same reaction. He said she made Bruce and Gordon look like children play-fighting. She's responsible for several hundred deaths over her 25-year reign."

Shirleen, pausing to get a good breath, continued. "When the police tried to arrest her, she ordered her men to open fire. When the battle was over, only three of Momma Kathy's people were left alive. Momma Kathy was among the dead, while the police lost six of their men."

"What will happen to those who were in Gordon and Bruce's faction?" asked Juliana.

"They were also rounded up and are serving long prison sentences. New York is a little calmer now."

"That won't last," predicted Henry. "Evil men find a way to do what they want, without thought of how others feel."

"You're right about that, Henry," replied Shirleen.

"What is going to happen to all of the items that were taken out of the secret room they found in Spielberg's mansion?"

"When I asked Josiah about that, he said most of it went back into the city. Some of it was put into Swiss banks so will take a while to get located. Kessler told Josiah, that what Bruce amassed would go to Juliana and Meagan. The jewels that Bruce had made up into jewelry would be auctioned off to the highest bidder, while the loose stones found in Gordon's secret room would be sold to the highest bidder. The proceeds from these jewels would go to help the city."

"That's good," responded Theodore.

"After the guns are melted down, they will be sold to the highest bidder ... a company that deals in metals. Again the proceeds would then go to the City. The files and other items will be placed in a secure place so that no one will ever find them."

"That's good news," Henry said thoughtfully.

Shirleen continued, When Frank Kessler told Charles Abram that we were alive and well, he also told Captain Abram that we were on the run from both Gordon and Bruce. Mr. Kessler told Josiah that when he told all of this to Captain Abram he had replied that he was so pleased to know that we were alive."

Juliana, sighing thoughtfully as she reached for Tim's hand, said, "All I have to say is that it is good that Bruce and Gordon's rein of blood and horror are finally over and they can never hurt us again."

"Oh," sighed Meagan, "I'm so grateful that I never have to see that evil father of mine again. That's awful about the police officers, but at least they closed down that faction as well," replied Meagan.

"Oh, I'm so grateful to be away from that awful scene," Henry said.

"So am I," chorused the others.

Henry asked, "How much did Bruce amass, if I'm not getting too personal."

"It is estimated that he amassed close to twenty million dollars from the smuggling of jewels, the huge cuts from the drug lords, along with the proceeds from the escort service and other dirty deals."

"So how much of this money will be yours?"

"About fifteen million," replied Juliana. "We didn't want to take it, but after discussing it with Josiah, we're going to put it to good use. When we see a need that needs filling, we'll address it. For instance, Meagan wants to purchase a good sized piece of land to put those animals on it that are not able to go back into the wild."

"Oh, Les … I mean, Meagan, that is one very worthy cause," declared Henry. "I'm glad that you are going to do that. You will have your hands full with this project, yet it will benefit a lot of animals."

Meagan took over the conversation to say, "I also plan to make a zoo. Through these animals, perhaps we can train the people to be more tolerant of our furry friends."

"How do you propose to run it by yourself."

"I'm not," ginned Meagan. "I have spoken to Diane Weaver and her husband, Mathew … you know … the ones that own the animal clinic in town. They're going into partnership with me. While I go to school to become a veterinarian, they will run the sanctuary and start to turn it into a zoo. It seems that they have had the same idea as have I, only they didn't have the funds to do so. I didn't have the training as a vet, so we're going to help each other make this zoo a reality."

"That's wonderful," agreed Melinda.

"Teddy and I have been thinking of adding on to this house. We were going to go out further then add a third floor, maybe even a fourth floor and turn this place into an orphanage."

"Oh," cried Meagan. "Please let us help make that a reality."

"I don't know," said Theodore. We can afford to do this."

"Helping to make your dream a reality would help me to feel better about accepting the money that Daddy got illegally."

Smiling, Henry said, "Obtaining money through greed is a terrible thing. However, helping to make others more comfortable will be putting this money to a good cause."

"Then we'll gladly accept your offer," stated Theodore.

"There's something else that I think would be beneficial to your family," stated Shirleen.

Looking at Shirleen blankly, Theodore asked, "What's that?"

"One day, when Melinda and I were talking, she told me that you gave up your dream to be a doctor, opting for a nursing career because you didn't want to put your siblings in debt."

"That's correct, I did."

"Well, Juliana, Meagan and I talked it over and we'd like to pay for you to go back to school so that you can become a doctor."

Theodore jumped as if slapped. Suddenly, he heard Elaine Stokes telling him that he would have another opportunity to go back to school to become a doctor and that was what he was to do. Looking over at Melinda, he was surprised to see her crying. He had told her about Elaine's statement. Swallowing several times to clear his throat, he was finally able to say, "I gladly accept your offer. I'll enroll just as soon as Melinda has completely gotten back upon her feet."

"Good," cried Juliana. "This will make it easier for me to accept the money that Bruce left behind."

Seeing that Melinda was growing very tired, they gave the baby gifts to Melinda. Rising, the Webbs, along with Trudy and Jeff, went home.

For the remainder of September and the first part of October they worked hard. There was canning, quilt making and sewing. At the end of each day, they all fell into bed, exhausted. The last thing they preserved were the apples from the orchard at Tim's parents' house. They made applesauce, apple butter, and many jars of pie filling. They also wrapped several boxes of fresh apples, and stored them in the insulated shed Jeff, Josiah and Tim built. They'd enjoy eating those during the winter.

Finally, Shirleen, Juliana and Trudy's wedding day arrived. They gathered at the Brooks home to dress for the ceremony. Reverend Howard Bates, from the Lutheran church, was on hand to perform the services.

The three grooms were a total wreck, worrying that they'd mess up the ceremony somehow. Reverend Bates suggested a prayer to calm them down.

The brides were also struggling to remain calm. Shirleen also suggested a prayer to calm everyone's nerves. Before they knew it, it was time to walk down the aisle. Shirleen would walk first, followed by Trudy, and then Juliana. They were visions of loveliness as they made their way to their grooms.

Mark Holmquist was Tim's best man, and Annabelle was Juliana's bridesmaid. Theodore stood with Henry, and Melinda was Trudy's bridesmaid. David Black was Jeff's best man and Meagan stood with her grandmother.

Juliana's satin dress was covered in lace at the bodice and along the sleeves, which tapered to a V at the wrists, with buttons from the elbow to the wrists. The back of the bodice also had the same buttons down the entire back. The full skirt, gathered at the waist, had a long train and the veil was the same length as the hem of the skirt. The Watson sisters, Leslie and Clara, carried the train.

Both of Tim's parents and all of Tim's siblings and their spouses were there. Louise came with her fiancé. They were planning to be married in another two weeks.

Once the brides were standing beside their men, Reverend Bates began. "Who gives this bride, Shirleen Webb, in marriage?'

"I do," beamed Josiah proudly.

He then went through the same process with Trudy and Juliana. There was a lot of giggling during this part of the ceremony.

When it grew quiet, Reverend Bates began the ceremony. A few minutes later the three couples were man and wife. When they'd made their way back down the aisle, they went inside for the reception and dance. There were piles of gifts for the happy couples, all sitting atop three long tables decorated with banners and balloons.

A band was set up near the piano, and they began playing quietly as the couples greeted their guests in a receiving line. A table filled with punch, the wedding cakes and all that went with it, was positioned near the gift tables.

An hour later, people started dancing. At seven o'clock, they stopped long enough to eat, then continued dancing until nearly midnight.

Jeff and Shirleen went to Jeff's home to live for two weeks. Tim's parents had a cabin up in the hills, outside of town, and they let Tim and Juliana have it for their two-week honeymoon. Candace Smith Cline's parents also had a cabin in the hills, and Henry and Trudy were staying there for their honeymoon.

Meagan, who was staying with the Brooks family for two weeks, helped the housekeepers clean up after the wedding. She put the gifts into separate boxes for the happy couples and put them aside until they were back from their honeymoons.

While Meagan was with the Brooks family, she was able to help with the little ones, which brought her a lot of joy. Even so, there were days when she missed her mother and grandmother. She never let anyone know how she felt, because she was glad they'd found the happiness they so richly deserved.

One day, Mark Holmquist came out to see her. They took a walk down the road, keeping in sight of the house, yet alone to talk. "Meagan, are you feeling better these days?"

"Now that my father is dead, I haven't been so afraid, which is good."

"I'm so glad to hear that. I felt so bad when you nearly had a breakdown. You see … I know just how you feel. A sexual pervert kidnapped me when I was 12. He wanted me to do things, and when I refused, he beat me. I lived that terror for six months. When I was just about to give up and commit suicide, the police rescued me."

"That's horrible. I'm sorry you had to go through that."

"The police killed him, and I had a nervous breakdown. It took me nearly a year to recover. When I turned 20 I joined the Mounties, and my job has been a source of strength."

"You're good at what you do, Mark. Thank you for all that you did to protect us from Nathan White."

"I'm just glad that you're all right." Growing thoughtful, he turned to face her, and asked, "Would you go out with me tonight? We could go to dinner and then see a movie."

"I'd like that."

"I'll pick you up at six."

"I'll be ready to go."

As they walked back to the house, they continued to talk and get to know each other. After he saw her to the door, Mark went back to his apartment to get ready for their date.

Meagan told Theodore and Melinda that she had a date with Mark. "I don't know how long the movie will last, but I should be home before midnight."

"No parking and necking, now," ordered Theodore.

Saluting him, she replied, "Yes, sir!"

By 5:30, Meagan was ready. She was a little nervous. At five minutes to six, Mark's car came up the lane. Meagan wisely waited for him to come to the house and knock on the door. Theodore answered and invited him in.

After Theodore grilled him about the plans for the evening and told him when to have her home, Mark took Megan's hand and walked her to the car.

As Theodore watched them leave, he said, "The way I feel, you'd think it was my daughter or little sister going out for the first time."

"That's because, she is like a sister to both of us."

"You're right."

When nine-thirty came and went, Theodore began to worry. At nine forty-five, there were still no headlights coming up the lane. At ten minutes to the hour, he finally saw headlights coming up the lane to the house. A few minutes later, Mark pulled up to the house. He kissed Melinda goodnight, after bringing her to the door.

"Well," scolded Theodore, "You just made it on time. Did you stop and neck awhile before coming home?"

"No," scowled Meagan. "We stopped to have a soda before we came home."

"Good."

"I'm tired. I think I'll just go to bed, that way I won't get into more trouble."

"Goodnight, Meagan." Theodore said, and surprised her by kissing her on the forehead. "Sleep tight, little sister."

Tears glistened in Meagan's eyes as she walked to her room.

Two weeks after the newlyweds got home, Melinda and Theodore were planned to be remarried. Meagan, Trudy, Shirleen and Juliana worked hard on two quilts for Melinda's wedding presents, and Trudy sewed up the binding on each of them.

The morning of the their remarriage dawned bright and clear. At nine o'clock, the family went down to help with wedding preparations. Everything was ready by 10 a.m.

They were having a garden wedding, and the guests were seated when Reverend Bates, Theodore, and Jeff, who was best man, came to stand by the trellis. As Melinda started down the aisle with Henry, Meagan sang, "Oh Promise Me." Her voice was beautiful.

Melinda's wedding dress was made of white satin and was simply cut. The bodice, which tapered down to her waist, had puffed sleeves that went straight from the elbow to the wrist. The skirt, gathered at the waist, hugged her curves and then flowed down to her ankles. The simple lace veil came a little past her shoulders. Melinda was radiantly beautiful.

Reverend Bates asked, "Who gives this woman?"

"I do," said Henry, and gently placed Melinda's hand into Theodore's.

Reverend Bates proceeded with the ceremony, and a few minutes later the ceremony was complete. Afterwards, they all returned to the house for the reception.

After the guests had said their good-byes, only the family remained and were sitting around talking. "Frank Kessler called me this afternoon," Josiah said. "He wanted to tell me that the men who murdered Bruce Murdock, Vincent Crowley and Thomas Wilson, were each sentenced to three consecutive life sentences. That means they'll die in prison for sure. The drug kingpins have also been caught and sentenced to many years in prison. "

"What about Bruce's staff?" Shirleen asked.

"As I told you before, it was Bruce's cook who witnessed the murders of the police officers and the abduction of Bruce and Vincent. The police questioned them all. They told them what they heard Bruce and Crowley talking about. After they gave their statements, they were released. Myrtle Lawson decided to come to Cardston so that she could be near all of you. She hopes that you won't judge her too harshly for working for Bruce."

"How can we possibly judge her?" cried Trudy. "After all, I worked for him, too."

"I had to live with him," declared Juliana.

"When she comes, we'll treat her fairly," Shirleen said, and smiled.

Josiah continued, "There's something else you should know."

Henry, look at Josiah suspiciously. "What's that?"

"Bruce's driver, Paul Thompson, went to the police. He told them that he wanted to quit working for Bruce, but knew that if he tried to leave Bruce would kill him. Thompson also gave a statement and details about everything illegal he'd seen Bruce do. He even gave the police a list of Bruce's employees. He said the only reason he took the job in the first place was because it paid so much and he was covering his mother's medical bills. The police checked into his background and found nothing incriminating in his past, so they only sentenced him to three years of probation.

"I'm glad to see that he was only given probation for his part of Bruce's actions," Juliana said.

"I met Myrtle when I went there to have the papers signed on the house," Josiah said. "I've been watching for her. She arrived in town today and I went to speak to her. She wants to talk to you, Shirleen. She hopes you'll hire her as a cook and housekeeper."

"I'll be happy to meet with her. I've lost my best cook, so I'd like to interview her."

"Good, I'll bring her to see you in a day or two."

"The most important thing for all of us to remember is that we don't ever have to look over our shoulders again," Shirleen said. "We're finally free to live our lives any way we see fit."

"Shirleen's right," declared Henry. "We also need to remember that if we live our lives righteously then we never have to fear being caught in the spider's web of evil. I, for one, will never be anything but honest, no matter what life throws at me."

Epilogue

Shortly after Melinda's wedding, Meagan, with the help of Dr. Diane Weaver and her husband, Dr. Mathew Weaver, searched for the perfect site to buy for their zoo. The mayor of Cardston helped them find the best location. Shirleen paid for the ten thousand acres, with the understanding that when the money arrived from Bruce's settlement, Meagan would pay her back. She wanted Meagan to just take the money, but Meagan explained that this was her dream and she wanted to pay for it herself, so Shirleen relented.

As soon as the deal closed, Meagan went to Seattle to start veterinary school. Both Mark Holmquist and David Black followed her there to pursue their own interests. All through her school years, they constantly sought her love. As Meagan got to know Mark, he became extremely possessive of her. When she told him she was there to get an education, not to be his play thing, he grew mean. She finally broke off all contact with him.

David, on the other hand, was kind and generous. He supported her schooling, and was proud of her accomplishments. He even studied with her, since he had enrolled in several courses to improve his skills as a Mountie.

When Meagan finally graduated from veterinary school, she and David went back to Cardston. When he wasn't working as a Mountie, he helped set up the zoo and sanctuary. Three months after their return to Cardston, Meagan and David were married.

The zoo was a huge success with locals and tourists alike. It had visitors from all over the world. David and Meagan had eight children, six boys and two girls. The six boys also became veterinarians, and eventually helped to run the zoo. Their two girls married and had families of their own.

Jeff and Shirleen spent lots of time with Meagan's family, as well as with the Brooks children. Every child in the orphanage, called them Grandpa and Grandma, just as they did Henry and Trudy.

Henry and Trudy built a home on 20 acres of the Brooks property so they could be close to all of the children. Henry and Meagan became close as they helped the Brookses build up the ranch and turn it into an orphanage while Theodore went to medical school.

Theodore and Melinda were the happiest when surrounded by their children. Every one of them made good lives for themselves, and made Theodore and Melinda proud. When Theodore completed his residency, he set up a practice in a suite in the hospital and helped many people throughout his career.

Tim and Juliana went to live in Jeff's house. They had two little girls who were close with their older sister, Meagan. Tim and Juliana loved Meagan's children, Theodore's children and the kids in the orphanage.

Theodore and Melinda instilled a great love for each other in each of their children and were called Momma and Daddy by all of the children at the orphanage. Only a scant few were placed into other homes, because they had all become so dear to Melinda and Theodore.

When Theodore died at the ripe old age of 89, Melinda ran the orphanage for another five years. She died of a massive stroke at the age of 83. The entire town came out to honor them at their funerals. Their great love story was told over and over again.

Candace Smith Cline, who outlived Melinda, always spoke of her with fondness. They had become best friends through their work at the orphanage. When Candace and Joel's five children were born, they spent a lot of time at the orphanage with the children. Joel's mother, Muriel, was loved by all of the children, and they called her Grandma Muriel.

Henry Borden lived to be 92. A massive stroke finally claimed his life. After that, Trudy went back to work for Shirleen and Jeff and continued to work there until her death.

Jeff continued to build beautiful furniture, which he sold to the locals and tourists at a great profit. Shirleen, became really good at making quilts, which she sold to the same people. They bought a piece of property in town, and converted the house into a hobby center. Shirleen hired Myrtle Lawson to work for them. When Jeff died at 93, Shirleen continued to run the shop. One day, a customer found her in the back; she'd died from a brain aneurysm at the age of 100, only missing her 101st birthday by eight days.

Tim and Juliana were killed in a head-on collision while traveling home from seeing their daughter and grandchildren. She was sixty-nine and he was seventy. Meagan was devastated by their deaths, as were her sisters, Annabelle Lee and Hazel Ruth. The two sisters went to live near Meagan. Annabelle married a lawyer named Samuel Jeffries. When they had their fourth child, they moved to Seattle, Washington, where Samuel became a great attorney. During her life, Juliana painted many pictures that graced the homes of many in the community. She also sold many of her paintings to tourists through her mother and stepfather's shop.

Hazel became a great surgeon in her own right. She never married, but she did adopt six children, four girls and two boys. Her best friend, Sheila Hazelton, and her husband, Todd, were killed when a crazy man stormed into their grocery store, shooting them several times before the police could get to them. Hazel took the children in, raising them to adulthood. All six of them became pillars of the community.

Josiah retired three years after Meagan's graduation from veterinary school. He went on to help Meagan run the zoo. Princess, his collie, was his constant companion. Prince remained with Shirleen, while Lady remained with Meagan.

Josiah was a prominent member of both families. He became Uncle Josiah to all of Meagan's children, Juliana's children and grandchildren, and all of Theodore's children, too.

Three years after Meagan graduated from veterinary school, Josiah married Annabelle Croft. He told his family that marrying Annabelle was the smartest thing he'd ever done. Their love story was poignant and beautiful. It took Annabelle a long time to warm up to Josiah, but when she finally did it was true love.

When she broke her leg at the grocery store, Josiah helped her heal. That's when their love began to blossom. One day, many years after their marriage, Annabelle told Shirleen, Melinda, Trudy and Juliana that Josiah made her happier that she had any right to be. She preceded Josiah in death by two years. When he died at 85, the whole town turned out for his funeral. Josiah had made a lasting impression.

When David Black died at 63, the town erected a statue of him on the town square in honor of his bravery. He was responsible for saving over one hundred people during one of the worst blizzards ever known in that area. When it was all over, the people of Cardston declared him their town hero.

Meagan worked at the zoo, with the help of Diane and Mathew Weaver, until her death at 74. She was responsible for helping to build another hospital, even larger than the first. She also built a college, helped to build an orphanage, and started several businesses that employed many people. Even with all her philanthropic endeavors, she was still a wealthy woman at the time of her death.

Most of her good works were done anonymously, but many guessed that she was the town's angel of mercy. The day of her funeral, the entire town turned out to honor her. A statue of her stands next to that of her husband, David, since she, too, left behind a great legacy.

What had started as a desperate situation for Shirleen, Juliana and Meagan, became a great blessing to them and the town of Cardston. These women not only found true happiness, but they also touched the lives of many around them. Indeed, they had made the little corner of their world a better place in which to live.

The End

www.ingramcontent.com/pod-product-compliance
Lightning Source LLC
Chambersburg PA
CBHW020243120726
47904CB00001B/79